PRAISE FOR M. L. BUCHMAN

Top 10 Romance of 2012, 2015, and 2016.

— BOOKLIST: THE NIGHT IS MINE, HOT POINT, HEART STRIKE

One of our favorite authors.

— RT BOOK REVIEWS

Buchman has catapulted his way to the top tier of my favorite authors.

— FRESH FICTION

A favorite author of mine. I'll read anything that carries his name, no questions asked. Meet your new favorite author!

— THE SASSY BOOKSTER, FLASH OF FIRE

M.L. Buchman is guaranteed to get me lost in a good story.

— THE READING CAFE, WAY OF THE WARRIOR: NSDQ

I love Buchman's writing. His vivid descriptions bring everything to life in an unforgettable way.

— PURE JONEL, HOT POINT

THE COMPLETE EAGLE COVE

A SMALL TOWN OREGON ROMANCE

M. L. BUCHMAN

Buchman Bookworks

CONTENTS

RETURN TO EAGLE COVE

CHAPTER 1

(FRIDAY MORNING)

"*A*lmost home, sweetie."

"Oh joy," Jessica Baxter tried to clamp down on her sarcasm. It was a bad habit that worked fine in her social set back in Chicago, but sounded more petty with each mile they drove toward the Oregon Coast. She slumped down in the passenger seat of her mom's baby-blue Toyota hybrid. It still had that new car smell. As much as she'd dreamed of owning a hot sports car some day, she knew that she was enough her mother's daughter that this was probably the exact sort of eminently sensible car she would buy when her VW Beetle finally gave up the ghost.

Just like her mom.

Maybe she'd get it in red to be at least a *little* different.

Jessica sighed again, keeping it to herself so that she wasn't being overly offensive. Her mother was one of the many reasons that she'd gone as far away as possible for college and did her best to rarely return—she didn't want to turn into her mother and it was too easy to imagine doing so if she'd stayed in the small town of Eagle Cove, Oregon.

They were like twins separated by twenty-two years. The two of them had been able to trade clothes since Jessica hit puberty and had shot up to match her mother's slender five-foot-ten. Other than a very brief mistake of dying her hair black as part of a tenth-grade dare, which had turned her fair complexion past goth and into bloodless vampire, they were both light blond.

The one part of twin-dom that she couldn't seem to pull off even though she wanted to was Mom's casual-chic. Monica Baxter was always dressed one step above the world around her; not fancy, just really well put together. The closest Jessica ever managed was Bohemian-chic which wasn't really the same thing, but she'd learned to make it her own. Of course, Bohemian was easier on the budget and often available in consignment stores which had only reinforced her chosen style.

Jessica did her best to not regress as they drove up into the Coast Range that separated the beach towns from the rest of Oregon…and failed miserably at that as well. She felt as if she was rapidly descending back toward being a pouty, pre-pubescent twelve from her present urban and worldly thirty-two.

Why did crossing the Oregon state line always take twenty years off her intelligence?

Maybe it was only Coast County. Because of the landscape the Oregon Coast felt incredibly far from anywhere. The Coast Range topped out at a mere four thousand feet high, but only a half dozen passes made it through the three hundred mile range of rugged hills that separated the beaches from the broad farming and industrial realm of the Willamette Valley. The interior of the state might as well be in a whole other country for how little it had in common with where she'd grown up.

"It's so strange being back here," Jessica rolled down the window and sniffed at the air. The scents were so rich and varied that they tickled. Bright with pine. Musty with undergrowth. Damp. A first hint of the sea.

"Well, it has been four years, honey. That's bound to make it seem a bit odd. But I'm so glad that you came."

"Me too, Mom." Better. She managed to say it as if she meant it, however unlikely that might be. Chicago fit her like a…but it didn't.

The city was…something she was not going to give a single thought to for the next eight days. If she didn't fit there and she didn't want to fit in Eagle Cove, Oregon, then where did she belong?

Jessica breathed in deeply this time, trying to clear her thoughts with the fresh air of the Coast Range and nearly choked herself on how green everything smelled. The harsh slap of the mountains was almost an affront. The two-lane road dove and twisted along narrow corridors sliced through towering spruce and Douglas fir trees. The babies were sixty feet high along the shoulder as the car twisted up toward the pass; the mother trees behind them were much, much bigger.

And it wasn't just the trees that were lush. As they wound deeper into the Coast Range, each branch became covered with mosses and lichens. It soothed her eyes, so used to towering concrete and glass, with a living tapestry of greens, golds, and silvers. Beneath the trees grew an impenetrable tangle of salal and scrub alder. Old barns on the roadside didn't have shingle roofs, they had moss ones; some of them were covered inches thick. Many RVs, left unattended in front yards for too long, had a sheen of green growth on their north side.

"I really want to hate this," the Coast Range had three times the rainfall of Chicago, often surpassing a hundred inches a year. She expected to feel the weight of all that biomass crashing down on her shoulders, but instead she noticed the start of a disconcerting lightness as if coming home was a good thing. Jessica did *not* like that encroachment of pending appreciation, perhaps even enjoyment, upon her *true* feelings. "But it smells so good. Like sunshine and new growth."

Her mother's laugh was amused as they twisted along the two-lane road slowly climbing up a narrow valley.

"I didn't mean to say that out loud."

"But you said it anyway."

"Not helping, Mom."

Thankfully her mother's laugh said that she had understood Jessica's response as a tease. Which it mostly was, partly.

Jessica didn't *want* to like coming back to the coast. She didn't have small-town dreams. That was the main reason she'd left Eagle Cove. She had big city dreams…which weren't exactly coming together for her despite her efforts over the last fourteen years. But scurrying home wasn't going to fix those. And the selection of men in such a tiny town was, to put it kindly, pitiful. Puffin High—

Why they hadn't called it Eagle High in Eagle Cove was a subject of heated debate by every single class.

Puffin High's problem was that she knew every male her age all too well. The only reason the town had its own high school was that it was too far away from everywhere else for busing to make sense. Her senior class had just thirty-four students. Grades seven through twelve numbered under two hundred. And she knew far too much about every single one of them.

Even more obnoxiously invasive on her sense of right and wrong, instead of dumping rain, it was a perfect day. The sun sparkled down revealing a thousand shades of green in the living walls that lined the road. The air coming through the open window was thick with pine sap and the gentle tang of rotting undergrowth. There was so much oxygen in the air that it made her feel a little giddy.

Yes, a perfect day, if she'd been alone…and still in Chicago.

"I could have rented a car and saved you the drive, Mom." Actually, her budget had been thrilled when her mother had offered to come and fetch her. Also, once in Eagle Cove there wasn't a lot of use for a car, except when the rain poured down. The whole town was only a few miles long and she could walk most places she'd want to go. As if there were any old haunts that she'd care to revisit. She'd made good her escape to Northwestern University's School of Journalism at eighteen but every now and then the town still sucked her back.

"Nonsense, honey. I'm always glad to drive up and get you. Besides, I needed a few things for the wedding."

"How many is this?" As if she didn't know. It took much of her journalistic skill to keep "that judgmental tone" out of her voice. Something her early teachers had dinged her on until she'd learned to eradicate it. But since she was regressing as they neared the coast, it was trying to make a comeback.

"Number four."

"Why, Mom?"

"Because I love the man." Her mother actually glanced away from the road to offer her a scowl. "I'd have thought that was obvious."

"It is. But you've divorced him three times."

"Because *your* father can drive a woman bat-shit crazy without even trying." They giggled together because that was an absolute truth about Ralph Baxter.

"I meant, why marry him again? You're both legal age, your daughter lives in Chicago," and wouldn't complain if she lived on another planet entirely. "Just shack up together. Then you can lock the door whenever Daddy becomes too much like himself."

Ralph Baxter was always getting caught up in monster projects. Without a word of warning he would suddenly rip out the entire kitchen, once on the morning before a dinner party, because he'd thought of a better way to design it. Or he'd start building a new boat from scratch in the middle of the driveway, rather than in the generous side yard, which blocked parking near the house for months.

"Oh, honey. I'm too old fashioned a girl to 'just shack up'."

Which was almost believable, even in the twenty-first century. To hear Aunt Gina—who despite her name was as not-Italian as a pastrami sandwich—tell it, Monica Lamont had chosen Ralph Baxter as her sweet sixteen love. She'd never even shopped around. How 1950s was that for a woman who hadn't even been born then?

Jessica had shopped plenty, or at least window-shopped. She'd found only a few men worth the cost of trying on for size. Definitely not a one worth taking home to keep. She might look like her mom, all blond, tall, and waiflike—which she kind of hated though the men seemed to like it—but inside she wanted to be like Aunt Gina.

Luigina Lamont looked nothing like her twin sister...or Grandpop...or much like Grandma for that matter. She was a statuesque redhead, in every voluptuous sense of the word and completely lived up to her name: Luigina meant "Famous Warrior." Her merry laugh slapped up against you at the most unexpected moments and constantly poked at your ticklish spot until you were curled up on the couch begging her to stop. Unlike Mom and her serial marriages to the same man, Gina brought home plenty yet had only tried to keep one.

That "unholy disaster" (as the family tales described it) had produced Natalya Daphne Lamont—Jessica's three-hour-older (and Natalya never let her forget it) first cousin and best friend. Just like Gina, Natalya didn't look like either her mom or Gina's brief husband. Maybe that was hereditary on that side of the family to balance out how much Jessica resembled her own mom and their shared grandma. Jessica had a sudden flash of her own future daughter looking just like her…and felt the world spin just a little at thinking about children at all.

"If I hadn't seen her come out between my legs myself," Aunt Gina would announce loudly, "I'd have thought I adopted the kid. Maybe I signed up to be a surrogate then forgot all about it."

Mom blushed every time Aunt Gina let that one loose in public, without understanding that if she didn't, Aunt Gina would have stopped long ago.

"Such an exotic offspring deserves an exotic name. Natalya for the Russian Bond girl in *GoldenEye* and Daphne for du Maurier the romance writer, *not* the nymph who had to turn into a tree to escape that lusty jerk Apollo." The fact that *GoldenEye* hadn't come out until Natalya had already been in grade school hadn't changed Aunt Gina's story one bit.

Maybe Jessica's own child would be lucky and take after Cousin Natalya who was slender like Jessica, but had all of the curves Jessica had prayed for throughout her teenage years but never been granted. Natya was also dusky skinned like a permanent tan and leggy like some French model. Jessica's and her mom's fairy light hair and Aunt Gina's mass of red curls had been transformed to a smooth cascade of dark chestnut on her cousin. Yet she and Jessica felt like twins from different mothers: one light, one dark, but much the same on the inside.

Jessica smiled at the sign as they cleared Maxine Pass: eight-hundred and three feet according to the sign. The "three" always made her laugh. It was like Becky, her other best friend from Eagle Cove, firmly insisting that she as five-four "and a quarter" as if it made a difference.

Maxine Pass was technically Maxwell Pass. Or it had been until the day that Aunt Gina had declared it just wasn't right for all of the passes to have male names merely because men were the ones who drew the maps back in the 1800s.

For her sixteenth birthday Jessica hadn't received her first kiss—already happened a year before—or gotten laid—two more years until that event. Instead, she'd been recruited for a "Mission!" At two in the morning on their shared birthday, Aunt Gina drove her and Natalya up to repaint the Maxwell Pass highway sign to Maxine. It had become a tradition that every time the highway department changed it back to Maxwell, the three of them would have a two a.m. gals' outing and change the sign once again. The highway department had given up years ago. A few of the more recent road maps had even changed the name.

"Girl Power!" they'd shout after each time they finished repainting the sign, usually about three a.m. Then they'd break out the thermos of hot chocolate and drink it from a shared cup while they admired their handiwork by moonlight.

One time Martin, the town cop, had shown up while they were doing it. Jessica and Natalya had ducked, but Gina hadn't slowed down a single brush stroke.

"Thought it would be you," Martin had observed through his open car window, obviously talking to Gina.

"Out of your jurisdiction, Marty," had been Aunt Gina's awesomely calm reply. She had always been Jessica's hero, but that totally clinched it. The town limits had been left far behind.

He'd joined them for the hot chocolate and had a good laugh at the "Girl Power!" chant.

Today Jessica just waved hello to the sign as they crested the pass and began their descent.

"Didn't you ever bust out, Mom?" Jessica tried to imagine her doing so, but couldn't quite conjure it up in her mind.

"Bust out? You mean cheat on your father? Never!"

"But what about between times, when you were divorced? That wouldn't be cheating."

Monica Lamont's lips thinned as she tightened her jaw and finally shook her head in a sharp little snap. "I was only living in the other end of the house."

"What about with Dad? You and Dad could just…you know?" The thought of her parents having sex was uncomfortable enough that she couldn't quite say it aloud.

"Ralph says that if I feel so strongly about things that I have to divorce him, then I shouldn't be expecting any special concessions while we are divorced."

Jessica felt she had to side with Dad on that one. He'd become used to his wife's antics, but that meant he didn't get any either in the interims. No wandering for him—it had always been clear that Ralph Baxter was absolutely crazy about Monica Lamont. Jessica felt kind of sorry for him.

"Wait. You mean you haven't had sex in two years?" This latest was their longest divorce yet.

Again that little snap that made Jessica's neck ache in sympathy. Mom moved to the right as the road added a climbing lane to reach the six-hundred and thirty-four foot (not quite so much bragging) Rogue Pass. That name at least made perfect sense by Oregon standards…because it wasn't anywhere near either of the two separate Rogue Rivers in Oregon. A half dozen cars roared past. Mom always drove exactly at the speed limit instead of the nearly mandatory ten over that prevailed throughout the state.

"So you're waiting for the wedding night?"

This time her mom's nod was a little sad.

"I'm sure tomorrow will be a great night, Mom."

At that she smiled brilliantly. "If the past three are anything to judge by, yes, it will be. It's just too bad we had to delay it."

"Delay it? Wait! What?" Jessica bolted upright in the car seat and almost throttled herself with her seatbelt. The wedding was supposed to be *tomorrow*. She'd secretly planned on staying just one day past the wedding, and then catching the Airporter Express that wandered through the small coastal towns once a day. She'd already warned Natalya to expect her in Portland for the rest of the week until her flight back to the Windy City.

"Well, we were meeting with Judge Slater about the ceremony. As he performed the first three weddings…"

Jessica resisted pointing out that he'd done all three divorces as well. Maybe her Oregon civility was coming back. Yeah, like a toothache.

"…and he had all of the old records in a file; even had the new marriage license pre-filled out, the dear man. However, it turns out that the first time we were married was on July fourteenth, not July seventh as I had remembered. You know how your father loves the cycle of things. So we moved the wedding to next weekend to coincide properly with the original. I knew you already had your plane tickets, so I didn't see any point in telling you."

Didn't see any point? She'd have moved heaven and earth to— Actually, her mother was right because she'd purchased the cheapest non-refundable, non-changeable tickets she could find.

A week! She was going to be trapped in Eagle Cove from Friday morning until Sunday morning nine days later? Oh, that was so bad.

"I can't believe that we celebrated it wrong for all of those years," her mother continued, completely oblivious to the panic she'd just created. "The seventh was the date that had always stuck in my head for our anniversaries."

Mom's dropping voice spoke volumes. She'd always been terrible at keeping a secret.

"So why *did* the seventh stick in your head?" Jessica kept it as casual as she could, rather than rubbing it in that her mom always gave up whatever she was trying to hide. It must be the journalist in her coming out: ask the question and then wait patiently for a reply. Not pushing was another change between them. Jessica didn't feel as if she was mellowing with age, but perhaps she was. Being disillusioned at thirty-two was no more newsworthy than it had been at twelve or twenty-two; but a woman shouldn't mellow until…well, maybe a hundred-and-two.

On the back side of Rogue Pass, Mom concentrated on the winding descent. Jessica waved at a massive Roosevelt elk who grazed in a small clearing beside the road. Coming back to Eagle Cove might be only one step better than a nightmare, but it was a very scenic one. The road was soon joined by a stream rushing in a deep ravine on Jessica's side of the road; the problem was that they were both racing in the wrong direction—toward, not away from, her childhood home. The stream tumbled along almost as fast as they did down toward Eagle River which would eventually define the end of town where it opened into a broad bay before it reached the sea.

No one quite knew why the bay had been named a cove, but it showed that way on even the oldest maps. It gave the town an off-kilter personality to Jessica's mind, as if it was always seeking to find its true identity. No bridge crossed the Eagle to the wilderness area on the other bank. To reach that required either a boat or an hour drive back up to Highway 101, across the river, and then a long crawl back to the Coast over marginal logging roads.

"C'mon, Mom, give." Since not pushing at her mother had failed, Jessica went with regressing and shifted to the wheedling tone she'd perfected as a child. She might hate herself in the morning for slipping back into it, but it always worked. Sure enough, her mom gave in right on cue.

"July seventh was the one time we cheated. We didn't actually wait for our first wedding night," the blush on her mother's fair skin was almost bright enough to lighten the dark corridor between the towering trees. "Your father made it amazing. But that's also the day I became pregnant, though I didn't know it until after the wedding. All those years I was celebrating the wrong date. That's why we never fool around unless we're married."

"Sounds like you were celebrating *exactly* the right date, Mom." She tried to pin down the exact date of her own first time, but it hadn't been all that memorable. Good, but "earth-shattering" was just another one of those 1950s' myths that didn't happen in the twenty-first century. Except, apparently, for her own mother. How unfair was that.

"Maybe," her mom admitted, "but we're going to get married on the fourteenth anyway."

"So, I'm a bastard?" Not that it bothered her, but she couldn't resist needling her mother about it. Maybe she hadn't matured all that much.

"Yes dear, but only by one week. I swear I didn't know." This time Jessica heard that her mom's confession was a sigh at Jessica's question rather than sounding contrite. Maybe it was time Jessica grew up a bit—even when in Eagle Cove.

"Does Aunt Gina know about all this?"

"No one does, except your father and now you. You only arrived three days early, which was actually four days late. No one gave it any thought."

Excellent! To hell with being mature. Aunt Gina would love the extra dirt for teasing her sister and Jessica couldn't wait to be the one to tickle her aunt's funny bone.

<hr>

It had been another long morning of assisting the Judge—always with a capital J. Monday through Friday, six a.m. to ten, Greg Slater helped his father. At first it had been something that Greg did to help out, but he'd come to like the simple routines and structure to his mornings.

"Ready?" he called back to the kitchen as he did every day. There was no real need to ask. The big old clock hung high on the wall said it was exactly six a.m. and the Judge was a very punctual man.

But Greg looked for the solemn nod before moving out into the diner and flicking on the fluorescents, "The Puffin Diner" sign, and the porch lights. There wasn't much need for the last, sunrise was twenty minutes ago, but the sun itself wouldn't clear the Coast Range ridge until at least six-thirty. For now, Beach Way, the town's main street, was mostly cool shadows and darkened buildings.

The bell mounted on the back of the door rang almost right away as Cal Mason Jr. came in. Greg had already set a mug of coffee on the counter for him. Cal ran the Blackbird Bakery and was hours into his day. Five days a week he was as punctual as the Judge. Cal Sr. wouldn't be in for a few hours yet.

"Your standard, Cal?"

"Double," though Greg knew that was a joke. Cal was one of the few men in town big enough that he could have eaten two of the Judge's generous portions. Six-two and as powerful as a bulldozer; his hands dwarfed the coffee mug.

Because Cal sat at the six-stool wooden counter, the Judge was less than five feet away through the broad service window that connected the dining room with the kitchen, but he waited for Greg to fill out the order slip and clip it to the spinner.

It was Greg's own damn fault. The diner's service had been a bone of contention, or rather "lengthy negotiation" just as most things were with the Judge.

"They can pick up their own damn plates at the window. Coffee pot is right there behind the counter where anyone who wants a refill can get their own."

Greg had won that round by subterfuge. He'd numbered the tables and then only put the numbers on the order slips, making it impossible for the Judge to boom out with "Veronica, your order is up." Customers had slowly adapted to not having to leave their tables for every little thing.

At least Greg thought he'd won, until a full three weeks later his father had winked at him while sliding across a short stack with bacon and hash browns for Karen Thompson, "Like I don't know who orders what on a Thursday."

Now the Judge wouldn't cook a thing without a proper ticket. Well, he'd cook it, but he wouldn't serve it no matter how busy or harried Greg was.

Cal's plate came up less than thirty seconds after Greg hung the ticket just as it did every morning: western omelet, hash browns, farm sausage, and English muffin. The last was about the only kind of bread that Cal didn't bake.

"Gotta have something that I can order out for and enjoy without baking it myself."

Greg moved the plate across to the counter and refilled Cal's half-drained mug of coffee.

There wasn't much call for a judge in a town the size of Eagle Cove. Semi-retired for the last five years, he no longer spent three days a week in Newport to sit on the bench as he had throughout Greg's childhood. Instead he'd set up a small courtroom in town. He mainly handled family matters like marriages and estates, and fines for drunk and disorderly tourists who soon learned that Judge Slater was a fierce protector of the town. There was only the occasional speeding ticket—no matter how hard Martin the cop tried to catch someone. The town was perched against the Pacific Ocean at the dead end of a winding two-lane that had left the coastal highway a dozen miles back; it had enough "Sharp Curves Ahead" signs to quell even the most lead-footed of souls.

So, "for something to keep me busy," the Judge held office hours only in the afternoons because his weekday mornings were all spent working as a short-order cook. And ever since Greg's return to Eagle Cove three years ago, he'd been his father's front-of-house man: waiter, cashier, and busboy.

The Puffin Diner had been a near derelict before his dad had bought and reopened it. It was a classic small town place built to serve the early morning fishermen, especially those returning from a long night's work on the offshore shoals; it was little changed over the last ninety years.

The clapboard building stood high enough on a heavy stone foundation that even the Christmas storm flood of 1964 had crested two steps below the front entry. It was one of the only structures on the town's main street that didn't have a street-level entry. All of the other businesses that had existed then had high-water lines drawn halfway or more up their walls. The Grouse Hardware store, the lowest spot in town close beside the docks, had a small wooden plaque of a fish screwed in just above the main door lintel. It was bright yellow with "Dec 22, 1964" painted on it in tropical blue—it was generally considered to be a little boastful, but old man Jaspar refused to tone down the color scheme that he'd painted on that fish in his youth.

The interior of the diner was so retro that it would have been ironic-modern if it wasn't quite so authentic. The steel-edged tables of blue Formica were scuffed nearly colorless by the thousands of plates and silverware settings that had been slid across their surfaces over the years. The chairs' red leather was sun-faded and the old chrome had pitted with rust from the salt air, making them uncomfortable to the touch without quite being painful. The linoleum floor had been replaced...back in the 1980s when mauve and hunter green had been trendy colors. The six round stools bolted to the floor at the counter squealed every time someone spun on or off them. The kitchen was authentic right down to the large service window, the steel spinner rack for order slips dangling in one corner, and the big grill and burners in the back. The scents of eggs, hash browns, and frying bacon filled the main street each morning enticing all passersby to come and find comfort food.

Ralph Baxter and Manny McCall came in and took their usual spot by the corner window. They'd have tourists out fishing off their boats within the hour and were both after black coffee and tall stacks.

At first Greg had resented serving the Judge's fare—it was as invariable as his father. Scrambles, omelets, pancakes—no waffles because the iron had broken the same day Mom had died and he couldn't seem to fix it and wouldn't let Greg try. The pancakes were big and fluffy. The very crispy hash browns were not an option; they were on every single plate, even with the pancakes. Farm fresh sausage or bacon was the other staple on every plate—not that it was a choice. Everyone received whichever Carl Parker had delivered the day before along with the eggs.

All of Greg's efforts to vary the oatmeal recipe, served with bacon or sausage and hash browns of course, had been in vain. The Judge served only rolled oats—not steel cut—with sliced, not diced, dried apricots and diced, not sliced, fresh apple. Whether brown sugar or maple syrup was used to sweeten it was wholly up to the customer; local honey was also available.

Omelets were the Judge's real specialty and by six-thirty there were already a dozen slips up for them. Omelets were the only dish where variations were allowed. He offered them with cheese, mushrooms, or smoked salmon fillings. Never all three of course, because there were limits to what was proper.

The Puffin Diner mostly served coffee. Greg's sole triumph at adjusting the menu had been when he managed to switch from Dad's "fresh ground" granules purchased in large plastic tubs to fresh-ground French roast. Tea or hot chocolate were the only other options, but asking for marshmallows with the latter was frowned upon unless you were a kid—the whipped cream came out of a spray can.

They'd fought royally over the Judge's inflexibility, but of course fighting over things was a tradition in the Slater household. Not that voices were ever raised, because that would never do. The few times Greg had tried that tactic he'd been ruled "Out of Order" and banished from the dinner table: the sole forum for Slater "discussions." With Ma gone to cancer three years before—Greg's original reason for returning to Eagle Cove—he didn't have the heart to "force" the Judge into driving him from the table after that first time. When he'd been remanded to the kitchen two weeks after Mom's funeral, he'd made the mistake of glancing back as he'd moved off to finish his meal. His father had looked old, sad, and impossibly alone.

Greg hadn't been able to face living in the big old house out on the beach, so he'd moved into the guest house. Once he finally understood that no number of cogent debates were going to sway the Judge, Greg had let the menu go. It had been unchanged in either content or price in the last decade—other than the wavy black line of magic marker through the "Waffles (with blueberries when in season)."

Greg had been on the verge of leaving town when the Judge sat him down at the big house's dining room table. Ma Slater had been in the ground for a month. Greg knew he didn't really have anywhere to go, he'd learned all he was going to from the banquet chef at the Sorrento Hotel in Seattle and there weren't any top positions open for an untested executive chef wanting to make his mark. He didn't have the capital to make his own splash, not in the insanely competitive restaurant markets in the big cities. But he'd find something.

"Been watching you, son. Been tasting your food," the Judge had tapped a fork on his dinner plate. Greg had roasted a pair of fresh-caught trout in hazelnut butter with a dressing of spring greens and homemade basil vinegar. Though Greg had cooked half the meals since Ma's funeral—"fair is fair" the Judge had declared—it was the first time his father had spoken of it.

"Uh-huh," Greg had gone for a neutral acknowledgement. He knew the Judge hated such prevarications, but Greg didn't know where this was heading and went for caution.

"This is good. Damn good."

Greg hadn't been able to offer even a neutral grunt over his surprise at the Judge's remark.

"Still needs some work, though."

Before Greg could snap at him about what did a man who scrambled eggs and ruled on law know about fine cuisine, the Judge continued.

"You need more seasoning," and he aimed a fork at Greg's chest, "and I'm not talking about salt. Your technique is the best I've ever seen, but I don't taste anything special. There's nothing here that isn't in any other fine restaurant. You need time to find your own voice, not some other chef's."

"My own voice?" But he didn't need to ask, he'd heard it a thousand times growing up.

The Judge looked down at the trout, one of the only times he'd ever said anything without looking at whoever he was addressing straight in the eye, "Your mother taught me that."

Ma had been a painter, a good one. Her seascapes had sold in galleries up and down the coast. Tillamook, Newport, Gold Beach, they all snapped up as much as she could produce and was willing to let go of—Grosbeak Gallery in town had always gotten first pick though. She'd often talked about finding your voice in your art so that it didn't look like everyone else's.

"So, here is the deal I'm offering you."

Greg knew that it wouldn't be open to negotiation; no one negotiated one of Judge Slater's "deals."

"The diner is mine on weekdays from six to ten every morning. I'd like you to stay as my assistant because you're good at it. That pays rent here at the house, a small salary, and we split the tips. What you do with the diner for the rest of the time, that's up to you."

And for three years, Greg had stayed in Eagle Cove and searched for his own voice. In the first year, he'd never cooked for anyone but himself and his father—who never again spoke about the food itself. Then one night Greg had invited a couple of buddies from high school who were still in town to the diner, as a test audience. Word got out about how good it was and folks had started asking when he'd do it again.

He'd eventually started "Irregular Friday Dinners at The Puffin." He only opened when he had a new meal to test. It was all *prix fixe,* fixed price—a twenty in the jar—and a set menu. After two years of those he felt almost ready to take his cooking out into the world; maybe spend a while as a pop-up restaurant—there and gone—rather than a full launch. He'd been saving his half of every morning tip and every goddamned cent for when he went back to the cities. At first he'd simply been trying to be better by the time he left Eagle Cove, but he'd become obsessed with finding and perfecting his "chef's voice." He wanted it to be so clear that it was undeniable. When he went back to Seattle, no one would label him the protégé of Charlene at Maximilien's or Angelo at The Tuscan Hearth. He'd be his own—

The old brass bell screwed into the top of the diner's front door rang like a small ship was coming into port. Morning service peaked as usual around eight and had now tapered off to just a few lingering diners.

Greg glanced at the big-face clock above the cash register—9:57— and suppressed a groan. Judge's rule was that if you were in the door by ten, you could take as long as you wanted. If it was ten sharp plus a second, you were turned away—"Fair is fair." Maybe they'd be quick; he'd had an idea for a savory roulade that he wanted to try out.

Greg turned back and had to blink, then blink again. The morning sunlight shone through the front window and silhouetted two dazzling blondes, their hair practically set afire by the sunlight streaming in from behind them.

Then his eyes adapted as they moved farther into the room.

Mrs. Baxter who was soon to be Mrs. Baxter once again.

And a woman he hadn't seen since the day she'd left for college, but he'd know anywhere.

Jessica matched his own five-ten and her hair, instead of being the waist-long waterfall he'd remembered, now floated about her shoulders in choppy wisps that framed a face of high cheekbones, full lips, and eyes that sparkled with mischief.

Halfway across the old linoleum floor, she stopped and looked at him.

"Greggie's gaping, Mom."

And he couldn't do a thing about it.

"He is, dear," her mother replied cheerily.

"Does he do that to you a lot?" It was starting to get unnerving. In very short order, it would start pissing Jessica off. He'd been three years behind her in school. She'd dated his older brother for a while—he's the one who earned her first kiss at fifteen, but not all that much more. Her prior visits home hadn't overlapped with either brother being here, though she'd eaten the Judge's breakfasts before and had been looking forward to some comfort food since they'd turned west across the Willamette Valley. Her lemon-curd brownie from Loretta's in Chicago was many hours behind and much too far away.

"I don't think he's doing it to me, Jessica."

"Well, it had better be us and not just me. We are two fairly dazzling women after all. Besides, if he does it much longer, he's likely to get a dinner plate cracked over his skull."

Greg Slater shook himself like a wet dog and replaced his gape with a cautious smile. He'd done a lot of growing up since she'd last seen him. The gangly kid—who'd spent large portions of his freshman year in the principal's office—had turned into such a decent-looking guy that she might not have recognized him if they'd passed on the street.

"Hi, Jess."

"Jessica." Her high school nickname was one of the things she'd left behind along with Eagle Cove. She and Jessie Hamilton had been in a lot of classes together and everyone had called them both Jess despite their opposing genders. "I'm not a man, so don't expect me to answer to a male nickname."

"No you're definitely not—" she could see where his eyes were going, along with his smile. She gave him a second to recover, then two. She didn't give him three.

Jessica picked up a dirty plate from a freshly vacated table. It had a pool of syrup and a large splotch of leftover ketchup on some crispy hash browns. With a quick grab, she captured both the front of Greg's apron and his belt—maybe his underwear as well but she wasn't going to think about that. She tipped the plate into the space over his flat abs and managed to shove it half down his pants for good measure.

Jessica ignored his squawk of protest, letting go as he backpedaled away and almost landed on Cal Mason Sr.'s lap right in the middle of eating his tall stack.

"Let's sit over there, Mom," she waved hello at the Judge before they sat down. He flapped a spatula back in her direction.

The Judge never whispered, so she and the half dozen other late morning diners could hear him clearly when he told Greg, "Lady's got your number but good, son."

Did she ever.

Greg had been a real slouch, the classic underachieving little brother. A decade and a half later and he was still in town working as a waiter for his dad. He'd grown up lean and dark. His neat black hair hung to his collar and the close-cropped beard accented a strong chin. He'd have looked Keanu Reeves' dangerous if it wasn't for the easy smile that still hadn't quite gone away. Greg Slater had come a long way from being fifteen…other than being another Eagle Cove failure-to-launch kid.

The last time she'd seen him, he'd been just starting his sophomore year in high school and panting after Dawn something—the hussy of the class. They probably had a trailer down at the end of Shearwater Lane that was slowly returning back into forest in a state of semi-decay, with a half dozen little Greggies bouncing about.

Maybe she should track down Greg's big brother Harry when she returned to the real world. Last she'd heard he was still single and practicing law in New Orleans…not that she was that interested in living in New Orleans, but it was a great place to visit. Maybe have some fun while she was there. She could even set up a few interviews in the jazz clubs and then write off the trip as well as selling a couple of articles to the trades. A couple of human interest stories, maybe find something unique enough to turn into a feature as well.

Though that was getting harder and harder. A few years ago she'd been able to get an article by the *Rolling Stone Magazine* editor way more than twice a year. And AAA used to give her bimonthly space in their magazines, but that had dried up as well. The collapse of print journalism was finally catching up with her.

Maybe if she'd been a straight newsie, she'd have stood a chance, but she wasn't. She'd always enjoyed the special interest story. Someone or some place that had found a way to be exceptional. A hot band, an innovative inventor, an amazing kid…those were the stories that had fascinated her. They'd shaped her career. And now they were "fringe" stories that didn't command much share in the shrinking print journalism bucket.

E-magazines were worse, paying crap. The *Huffington Post* had offered her a regular blog column, for no pay at all, which said too much about the state of that part of the industry. Maybe she should do a piece on The Puffin Diner; there was a laugh. That was probably below even *HuffPo's* standards.

"So…" she took a deep breath and decided that since she didn't have a choice about being in town for the whole week that she'd agreed to come for anyway, she might as well put a good face on it. It wasn't like the editors of the world were in a bidding war for her next story.

She and her mother settled at a clean table beneath a watercolor painting of The Puffin Diner, one of Ma Slater's last, based on the date. "Not for Sale" was in bold type on the little card taped to the wall close beside the frame.

"So, tell me about the dress, Mom."

GREG RETREATED. Hell, he didn't retreat, he ran away. The old Monty Python gag about "That's one nasty rabbit" came too easily to mind. Jessica Baxter was beautiful and looked all sweet and…fluffy.

Then she shoved a plate of cold food down his pants, ramming it right down inside his underwear in front of everyone. Cal Sr.'s howl of laughter had followed him right back through the service door into the side hall.

The one bathroom was occupied, so he detoured through the service door into the kitchen, his only other option.

Judge Baxter kept tending his omelets, "temperamental things omelets, can't look away from them for a second." But Greg also knew from experience that the Judge missed nothing of what happened in his restaurant.

With nowhere else to go, Greg moved over by the clean-up sink and shed the apron and his pants. At least his underwear had caught most of it. He shed those, wiped himself down with a couple of wet paper towels and pulled his pants back on commando. Greg wasn't really a commando sort of guy.

His shirt had taken the brunt of the attack. He stripped it off over his head and chucked it into the laundry bag along with his underwear and yesterday's service apron. He crossed to where he kept a spare shirt on one of the dry good storage shelves, but had never thought to keep underwear there as well. Greg yanked on the fresh shirt and buttoned it up.

"Not a word," he muttered at the Judge as he wound a fresh apron about his waist.

"The court will maintain a respectful silence at this time," the old man said with a tone as dry as week-old toast.

Restored to some semblance of order, Greg returned to the dining area. Cal Sr. gave him a smile he wished he hadn't seen. "Don't know what you did to piss her off, boy, but you did it good."

Greg considered telling Cal a thing or two, except he and the Judge had been friends since before Greg was born, and Greg knew that was dangerous ground.

Plastering on his best *maître d's* smile, he grabbed two menus and returned to the Baxters' table. Yes. That was a safer way to think of it. Not Jessica's; the Baxters'.

"Good morning. Welcome back to town, Jessica."

If she had any remorse for her abrupt action, she wasn't showing it in the least. "Thanks, Greg," she took the one-sheet menu and turned to study it without saying anything else. He'd swear there was a laugh lurking somewhere below the surface, but with her face turned down, he couldn't see it.

"Can I get you anything to drink?" He already knew Mrs. Baxter's preference for black teas before noon and herbals after lunch and had brought that to the table with the menus.

"Hot chocolate. No whip. With marshmallows if you have them."

"What? Are you a child?" And Greg could have shot himself. The Judge's crazy rules about what people should and shouldn't want had ruined his brain.

Jessica looked up at him with steady eyes the light blue of an ocean wave with the sunlight shining through…just before it crested and broke, smashing the unsuspecting rocks.

"No," her look was very cool, but her tone had a laugh hidden in it somewhere. "Are you?"

"Am I what?"

"A child? Still twelve maybe?" The last added with a wry smile.

Greg opened his mouth, saw Mrs. Baxter's widening eyes—

perhaps at the danger zone he'd just flown into. A quick glance to the side revealed that the Judge was watching him intently.

"Um, that would be no. I'm not still twelve. Nor thirteen."

"Fourteen then?" Jessica's smile lit her face, as if bantering with him was the best part of her morning. This wasn't Jessica Baxter of eighteen. He was now facing a formidable woman who absolutely knew that she'd totally unnerved him.

"Not fourteen either," was the best rejoinder he could come up with. Before he could lose even more ground he said, "I'll get your cocoa," and turned for the wait station. Greg did his best to ignore his father's courtroom stare—the one he used when the defense counsel was making a particularly specious argument fabricated from too many Internet searches.

"Chicken!" Jessica whispered just loud enough for him to hear. "Buck-buck-bu-caw!"

Then she and her mother broke into a flurry of giggles that he did his best to ignore.

Cal Mason, who'd been leaning over to hear the exchange, added another of his loud guffaws.

Jessica listened and made appropriate sounds in the right places about this time's wedding dress.

But she was having trouble focusing. The last time she'd seen Greg Slater he'd been a pimply underclassman. When she'd been dumping the plate's contents down his shorts, she'd found a flat stomach with no give. He was now a handsome man awesomely in shape.

That was a point that had been emphasized when he'd stripped off his shirt. She could only see him from the midriff up over the edge of the steel service shelf that separated the dining room from the kitchen, but Greg clearly worked out and, loser or not, it looked very good on him. She wasn't that shallow, not really. But she was less certain about how shallow her Coast County regression might ultimately make her.

When he delivered her hot chocolate, with the marshmallows, she kept her head down and pretended she was paying more attention to her mother than she actually was. He was nothing more than a Puffling—a baby puffin being the lamest sports mascot on the coast if you didn't count the UC Santa Cruz Banana Slugs. Greg might be a Puffling who hadn't had the skills or drive to get out of town, but he was a very attractive one. That utterly shallow part of her double-checked for the ring or a tan line as he set down the cocoa. Nothing. Didn't mean he wasn't—she'd learned the hard way—but it didn't mean he was either.

Not that she could possibly care.

Nine days and she'd be gone again, Friday through next Sunday.

A glance out the window showed that day one was almost half done already which she'd count as a good omen. The sun was almost due south, lighting the length of Beach Way brightly. She could see Cal Jr.'s beat up red pickup parked right next to Cal Sr.'s beat up blue pickup alongside the Blackbird Bakery. By the speed the people on the street were moving, they were locals running errands. They moved much slower than a Chicagoan but with purpose—like crows walking over to see if something was edible. The few tourists who were checking out the taffy and kitsch shops moved slower but with a frenetic energy—like sparrows never quite coming to roost.

Eight and a half days to go. It wasn't enough time for anything to happen, even if she was interested. Flings had stopped working for her before she got out of college. Since then it had become a slightly depressing quest for what she was starting to fear she'd never find, someone who loved her the way that her dad loved Mom.

She'd make sure to hit Cal's bakery while she was here. And see if Maybelle had any particularly good used books in Early Bird Books. At least one lunch at the Plover Bay Inn... Jessica turned away from the street with the sad realization that she could do everything she wanted to in the town in about a day and she still had eight to go.

Greg kept his fifteen-year-old thoughts to himself as he served them a pair of the fluffiest mushroom omelets available anywhere.

She turned to nod her thanks to the Judge—he didn't cook fancy fare, but it was always the very best.

She also noticed that the Judge hadn't missed a single jot of his son's shortcomings. She'd always liked Harry and Greg's dad, but she wasn't so sure that she liked the look in his eyes at the moment. Jessica had learned the day after her first kiss with Harry that she could read Judge Slater's facial expressions *far* too easily, even if everyone else in town declared him to be wholly inscrutable. It was a skill that had served her well in journalism, too. She'd always been able to tell exactly what topic the interviewee was doing their best to avoid.

However, right now the Judge was looking at her as if he was having an idea that he found both interesting and curious. The last shift in his expression surprised her, partly because it was clear enough that anyone except a dunderhead like Greg would be able to see it.

Judge Slater had just decided that whatever he was thinking was pretty damned funny and that worried Jessica.

Not much amused the Judge.

GREG KEPT to the shadows after locking the door behind the last customers. It was almost eleven; the Baxters had taken their time. Jessica and Monica Baxter walked across Beach Way. Except Jessica didn't walk. She...

He wasn't sure what she did, but it was doing strange things to his thoughts.

Her sudden reappearance had hit him as hard as any slap—and he'd earned a few before he'd learned decent manners while still a high school sophomore. Seeing her so out of the blue took him back to when he was in seventh-grade and she was already an over tall and impossibly sophisticated fifteen; even then she'd had an amazing sense of style that set her apart from all of the other girls. That was the age when he'd started thinking that girls weren't just different than boys, but that the differences were very interesting.

Today she wore light slacks and a blouse that looked loudly... Hungarian, though he had no idea what a Hungarian blouse might actually look like. Perhaps it was the blue scarf loosely knotted about one wrist that made her look a bit like a blond gypsy.

Half of the fights he and Harry had as kids, and there'd been plenty, didn't have a thing to do with being brothers. Though he'd forgotten the reasons until this moment.

He'd seen Harry kiss Jessica Baxter, and a need to pummel his brother had burned to life inside him. They'd battled often enough over the next three years before Harry went to college for Greg to completely forget the reason behind it. Even after he'd grown up enough to stop getting into fistfights with his own blood-kin—an offense the Judge had curiously left completely for them to work out —Greg had never been able to explain why he'd begun in the first place. By the time he and Harry had discovered that they actually liked each other, about the same time Greg graduated from the Culinary Institute of America, Greg hadn't remembered the Jessica-based origin.

He did now...and felt incredibly stupid. He'd have to apologize to Harry the next time they talked. Jealousy, deep and dark green as the Coast Range forest. Impressively stupid, even on his personal, deeply sad scale of stupidity.

Out the window, Jessica slid into the far side of her mother's blue Toyota hybrid. Just before her face disappeared below the roofline, she looked back toward the diner. No—she looked right at him. Without noticing, he'd moved up to the diner's front window until his nose was practically pressed against the glass between the black-and-gold "e" and "C" in "Eagle Cove."

He could feel her laugh like a blow to his chest even if he couldn't hear it through the glass. Her sparkling laugh had him retreating once more into the shadows.

When he turned, his father was watching him watch Jessica, the grill's wire brush clenched in one yellow-gloved fist and a large sponge in the other.

"What?"

The Judge offered one of his thin, unreadable smiles.

"What?" Greg was sufficiently aggravated with himself for getting caught staring that the word came out loud and sharp. He half expected to be banished from the room.

Instead his father simply raised his eyebrows in mock surprise and said softly, "You always did have a soft spot for that girl." Then he turned back to cleaning the grill.

Greg didn't have a "soft spot" for Jessica Baxter.

She'd been his first mad crush and just now he'd learned that he'd never gotten over it.

CHAPTER 2

(FRIDAY AFTERNOON)

It had been almost a decade since the previous wedding between her parents, and four years since Jessica's last visit to Eagle Cove. Her life had kept her busy and the time had slipped by too easily to notice.

To push back the guilt, she concentrated on the view out the car window as they drove through town.

It was amazing how little yet how much Eagle Cove had changed. Or rather how little it had changed and how much she noticed each detail that had. The Flicker movie theater across from the diner still had a massive chainsaw carving of a northern flicker woodpecker clutching the marquee, but it also sported a fading sign which proudly declared: "Now in Digital!" They were running *The Big Year*. She'd bet that they reran the birding film every year for the summer tourists coming to Eagle Cove for fair weather coastal birding. They'd probably bring it back in the spring too.

Grouse Hardware still had a pile of wheelbarrows stacked up out front that might be the same stack old man Jasper had rolled out there each morning since she could remember, but they also had a riding lawnmower parked in the next-to-the-door place of pride. She tried to think who in town had a big enough spread to justify a riding mower—coastal lots tended to be small and grass rarely thrived in the heavily salted wind. Then she realized that the town was growing older. The Judge's hair had mostly gone silver. Cal Mason Sr., in the diner eating his tall stack, was even rounder and balder than before. Maybe there was more demand for things like riding lawnmowers.

Jessica glanced worriedly at her mom, but she looked the same. Some lines around the eyes and mouth, but they made her look like she smiled more rather than less which Jessica knew to be true. With her good eye for clothes, and her automatic slap that dropped her cell phone into the hands-free mount every time they got in the car, Mom definitely looked in charge. However, Jessica's journalistic eye didn't miss that even in July, Eagle Cove Real Estate wasn't too busy for her to run up to Portland to fetch her errant daughter.

Mom wore her hair shorter than she had a decade ago, a neat, chin-long cut that looked good enough on her that Jessica might have to try it next time she cut her own hair. Of course Jessica also wore her own hair shorter than a decade before, so maybe that change didn't count for much.

The center of town stretched six blocks from the docks to the Rusty Pelican, the town's dive bar in both senses of the word. The Pelican looked even more disreputable than usual. Alistair Thomlinson had clearly found even more crap. An import from Cornwall, he was fascinated by "beach décor" beyond even cliché. The tired porch was curtained by a line of battered fisherman floats hanging from a beam. Old crabbing pots, a mostly deflated rubber raft, fishing poles, and chunks of driftwood added to the look. His *pièce de résistance* had always given Jessica the creeps. It was an old style dive suit with the sagging rubber body and the bulbous helmet now rusting in the coastal air.

Maybe she was okay with not being here so much.

Mom and Dad had taken to visiting her for the week between Christmas and New Years wherever she was—decreasing her need to come back. The first year in Chicago had been so bitterly cold, that they'd sworn a family pact to never make that mistake again. Washington, D.C. had been a little better the following year.

Since then they'd met in different, warmer locales until it had become their new tradition, working right across the bottom of the country: Key West, New Orleans, Austin, Phoenix, and a hilarious holiday at Disneyland and Universal Studios. The fact that Mom and Dad were divorced for that one hadn't diminished the fun in the least.

The first divorce had shocked a nine-year old girl to her very soul. Family was supposed to be forever. She knew because both her mother and her father had told her so. Mom hadn't gone far. At all. She'd moved through their home's breezeway into the mother-in-law unit that Granny Lamont had never occupied—she'd fallen for a Costa Rican millionaire and called herself his eighty-year old, bikini-clad squeeze. Her Christmas cards were invariably just that, the two of them on a gorgeous tropical beach in skimpy enough attire that the main thing they were each wearing was smiles.

Her mother, in staking her claim to the mother-in-law unit, had taped the divorce decree to the glass door that connected the two parts of the house. That first decree had been covered over with a marriage license after less than six months.

Jessica had been less shocked when the second decree covered over that in her junior year. Their shortest of the three divorces, the piece of paper that covered it was dated less than three months later. When her mother had declared she was done with him but good on Jessica's thirtieth birthday, Jessica had asked just one key question.

"Where did you put this time's divorce decree?"

"Why right over the top of that godforsaken third wedding license. I don't know what I was thinking when I remarried that man." The fact that it had lasted thirteen years this time and she hadn't moved *completely* out of the house since the day she'd moved in thirty years before was so irrelevant that Jessica didn't even bother to comment on it. Someday she'd find a man, housebreak him, and move in with him. Not a chance was she going to go to all the waste of doing paper-work to keep him.

Jessica's decision not to worry had been reinforced by the fun family vacation in southern California as well as when the three of them had made plans for Hawaii this next winter. They were already joking that Fiji would be the next stop after that, though Mom had temporized with maybe spending a Christmas at each Hawaiian island before going so far afield. It was just as well, Jessica's vacation fund wasn't likely to reach even to Hawaii.

But she wasn't going to think about that.

Past Jane's Warbler Market, her Mom turned onto LBB Lane.

"Your father has a group of tourists out on the boat fishing for the day—you might recall that it's inshore halibut season. He promised to try and be back in time for dinner. Meanwhile, I thought we'd get you settled in at Gina's." Jessica's old bedroom, with her blessing, had long since been turned into her mother's fitness room.

LBB Lane had always been one of Jessica's favorites. The town had been platted by a mother-daughter team. *The Book(let) History of Eagle Cove*—actually a double-sided tri-fold sheet of letter-sized paper run off on the Town Hall copier but bearing a grandiose title—listed them as amateur ornithologists. As if there'd been so many "professional" opportunities for women in an 1890s coastal fishing village.

What the brochure didn't say, though the local scuttlebutt definitely did, was that mother and daughter couldn't stand each other. So they'd divided the town in half. Everything toward the ocean from Beach Way had been decreed for Mother Mason to lay out, which she'd done with the names of all of her favorite land birds. In retaliation Daughter Mason had chosen seabird species for everything in her control, from Beach Way to the forest. Unwilling to risk the ire of either, who were apparently both elemental forces, store owners cautiously named their businesses for which side of the main street they were on. Land bird businesses stood on the ocean's side of Beach Way and seabird-named ones roosted on the side toward the forest.

But a dozen streets on either side of Beach Way were all that would fit between the sea and the narrowing of the river valley back up toward the pass. Mother Mason, in a fit of despair at not being able to include so many of her favorites, had made the last road LBB Lane. Little Brown Bird Lane covered finches, wrens, tits, juncos, and a whole gamut of others even if the proper name wouldn't fit on a street sign. The lane had been extended with time until it became the longest street in town. It ducked down close to the sandy beach before climbing south and up on top of the basalt cliffs. A straggling, graveled one-lane finally ended at the long-since automated and incongruously named Orca Head lighthouse.

Jessica had somehow forgotten how breathtakingly beautiful the beach and cliffs were, though they were the least changed of anything in Eagle Cove. Just a block off Beach Way, LBB Lane took a sharp left turn to the south and ran along a bank that stood a dozen feet above an amazing stretch of sand. No Florida or California beach could compare. Those were tamed, crowded with condos, or fenced away in tiny sections for rich people's personal enjoyment.

Almost the entire Oregon Coast had been grabbed for the state by Governor Oswald West back in the early 1900s. It had ruined his political career; but it had also guaranteed that the beach would remain unspoiled and accessible to all. There was a wildness to it that she'd never seen anywhere else.

"Stop! Mom, stop the car. I have to—" she didn't know quite what came over her. She was wrestling the door open even before the car was fully stopped.

In panic, Mom stomped on the brakes and the door nearly slammed forward out of Jessica's grasp.

"Sorry, I just—" Jessica tried to apologize as she jerked her seatbelt free. Out of the car, she clambered down the bank over the big rocks and a couple of driftwood giants that some massive storm had cast up high on the beach. The former were scrubbed clean by hard wave action and the latter were dark brown, stripped of their bark by the same relentless pounding of the waves that eventually had delivered them.

The beach south of the Eagle River's outlet was a stretch of feldspar buff-yellow sand with streaks of darker iron from the erosion of the basalt cliffs to the south. At low tide, like it was now, the beach was fifty yards wide and a couple of miles long. High tide would shrink it to ten yards and chop it into three or four sections—depending on the height of the tide—divided by rocky headlands that stretched out from the shore.

She shed her sandals and dug her toes down into the cool sand. Even on a sunny day, the sand was rarely hot along the coast. And a few inches down, a layer of cool dampness eased it even further. The waves were small today. Rollers of just three to five feet fell on the beach with a deep-throated sigh of relief. Having traveled across thousands of miles of ocean from Alaska, Japan, or Hawaii, they had reached their goal and arrived with a thump of joy and a sand-slapping high five of a job well done.

Jessica closed her eyes to the bright sun glinting off the white of the breaking curls and simply breathed in. The air, cleansed by a hundred storms as it crossed the wide Pacific, tickled her hair about her neck. Gulls nattered as they debated whether it was time to walk the beach as dignified as stout old men waddling off to the pub or should they fly out past the waves to ride the gentle swells up and down through the pleasant afternoon. Any sounds made by the tourists on the beach were whisked away before they reached her.

"I don't think I've ever seen you so affected by the ocean," her mother spoke from close beside her.

"I—" Jessica didn't know what to say. It wasn't that she'd missed the ocean. She'd been at a conference in St. Petersburg just two months back, but it hadn't felt like this. Her reactions were backward anyway. St. Pete's had bath-warm water and languid waves that lapped a few inches higher when it was high tide; a thoroughly enjoyable place to lounge and swim.

The Oregon beach was all about character, tough character—often as not it tried to kill you. The water driven by the Japanese current and coming down from Alaska was so bitterly cold that in mid-summer a person's life expectancy still could be counted in minutes—a dozen or so. Riptides dragged logs and tourists out to sea every year. Up in the more heavily touristed sections like Newport and Lincoln City, they lost a half dozen tourists every summer.

Surfers flocked to these beaches, and the incautious ones were battered against reefs of volcanic rock even less forgiving than coral. Tides climbed ten feet up and down the beaches marooning the incautious beachcomber in rapidly narrowing coves surrounded by harsh cliffs.

To the north of the outlet of Eagle Cove, a great sea stack of dark basalt smeared white with bird guano rose from the thrashing waves. It was home to cormorants, common murres, and, most popularly, to over sixty pairs of puffins who came to Eagle Cove each summer for the breeding season. They favored deep rocky burrows high on the big sea stack just offshore from the outlet of the Eagle River. It was July and they'd be there now, each nursing their single egg. Soon the pufflings would break out and mayhem would reign up and down the length of the cliffs.

Jessica knew every nuance of this beach, even the fact that it never stopped changing from day to day. A strong wave came up the beach, but the tide was out and it didn't quite reach her.

Why had it taken a trip to Eagle Cove to realize that her Chicago career, if not in shambles, was not doing well. The days of merely being a good journalist was no longer enough. You needed a blog and a powerful, multi-threaded social media presence. She was paid to write for a living, but now she was supposed to give her writing away for free so that she'd accumulate enough of a following for someone to pay her. Totally backwards.

Besides, it wasn't working. The new car had gone on hold. The condo of her own was still stuck in a roommate budget—that was even after her dreams had diminished to a damn small condo. Takeout was Moon's Sandwich Shop or a slice of Chicago deep-dish rather than The Cotton Duck or a table at Antico. The flight to the wedding would be a budgetary strain that would take a month or more to backfill.

"It's all screwed up, Mom." Jessica hadn't even known that was true until she said it aloud.

"I know, dear."

She turned to her mother, "You know?"

"Of course. Just because I'm fifty-five doesn't mean that I wasn't ever thirty-two. At least I wasn't single— Oh, sorry about that, Jessica. But it's true, even though that's how old I was the first time I divorced your father. You were nine and I woke up one morning and couldn't understand how I'd ended up still in Eagle Cove and married to him."

"But Dad was always a good man, wasn't he?" Jessica dug her toes deeper into the cool sand that was rapidly making her feet cold despite the warm day. Of course a warm summer's day on the coast was barely seventy degrees; Chicago had hit ninety-three by the time she'd gotten on the plane early this morning.

"He's the very best, which is why I married him." Then her mother offered one of her wry smiles. "That's why I married him every time."

Jessica looked back out to sea. She'd never met a man who was "very best" and after playing the field in a dozen different cities across America and a few in Canada, she'd become convinced that such a man didn't exist out there.

And as if she'd needed Greg Slater to remind her, such a man certainly didn't exist in Eagle Cove.

GREG SET out the ingredients for a simple roulade sponge base of flour, milk, butter, and eggs. He separated and whisked the yolks and set the whites to beat in the mixer.

The Puffin Dinner was now closed and quiet for the day. He loved the peace of cooking, only one light over the stove and another over the prep table. The dining room was shielded from the midday sun by the deep porch and let him imagine its shadowed interior just waiting for the eager crowd to come.

Once he had the roux built, he folded in the egg whites, but the oven wasn't up to temperature yet. He could afford to wait a few minutes.

For the filling he mixed together some Italian Parmesan cheese and a couple cups of the goat yogurt that Tiffany made on her farm up in the woods. Her boyfriend had dragged her to Eagle Cove a couple of years back. They'd bought a chunk of property back above Orca Head that no one in their right mind would want, including her boyfriend. He left her there in the teepee they'd erected together and driven off to parts unknown. Tiffany had stuck. She'd cleared land, planted a garden, and bought a pregnant goat and a pregnant sheep.

It always surprised him each time she showed up in town. She'd come walking in—because it was her truck the boyfriend had driven on his way out of town—wearing worn corduroys, a flannel shirt, and a big straw hat atop her waist-length soft brown hair. She'd also wear a backpack sometimes with little bottles of goat milk, sometimes with containers of huckleberries or perfect heads of lettuce.

Tiffany mostly talked to herself, but they were lively conversations. And at times when Greg had been buying some of her products which were always fresh and well made, he overheard enough to learn that she was quite funny, often laughing at her own jokes.

The one time he'd joined in on her laugh at a particularly funny observation about seagulls' mentoring habits for their young, she'd stopped and studied him with dark eyes from beneath the wide hat. Then, she'd pocketed the money, not nodding her thanks this time (which was a fifty-fifty proposition at best), and wandered down the street to the hardware or grocery store before walking the two miles to the end of LBB Lane and then a mile or more back up into the forested hills behind Orca Head Lighthouse.

Greg dug parsley and scallions out of the walk-in fridge and began to chiffonade them on the maple chopping block. The only sounds were the quick snicking sound of his knife and the occasional ping from the oven's warming metal.

There was a lot of speculation among the townsfolk about what they'd find if they went up to Tiffany's farm. The few adventurous souls who had tried quickly learned that she was a crack shot with a bow and arrow which discouraged any active interest, if not the idle speculation.

Nicky Vance had bought himself one of those high-end camera drones for himself last Christmas.

"I'll do flyovers for Mrs. Baxter's real estate listings, and adventure videos for the whale tours and fishing trips. This sucker will pay for itself in weeks," he'd patted it proudly on the head.

On his first town flyover, he flew a circle around the Orca Head lighthouse. Then he decided to see just what *was* going on up on the cleared patch in the forest beyond. They'd all been huddled around him when he flew toward Tiffany's place. There had only been two really clear images. The first was a wide open clearing with animal pens, though no sign of a teepee or other house. There had been no time to zoom in before the second clear image was captured and transmitted back to them from the small onboard camera. The last frame of video the drone ever captured was the head of an arrow the moment before it hit. That night, the remains of the three thousand dollar machine had been staked to Nicky's front door with a second arrow through its heart—and most of the way through the thick wood.

Tiffany's ability with a bow also explained the time she'd brought Greg a thirty-pound slab of fresh bear meat. When he'd later asked if she had any more bear meat she could bring down on the next trip, she'd answered "Too salty for you" and gone on her way. Six months later, after he'd forgotten the whole incident, she'd given him a single pound of bear jerky. He'd shared it with the Judge who decreed, "Girl has finally got it right." It was the only bear jerky Greg had ever had, but it had been damn good.

He'd had a fantasy or two about Tiffany. She was pretty, at least everything that wasn't hidden by that oversized sunhat and hippie-loose clothing, and she smelled of pine and fresh river water. Perhaps a little younger than his twenty-nine, perhaps a little older, it was hard to tell. But as she spoke no more to him than to anybody else in town, he didn't see any point in trying to see if that fantasy led anywhere. But she was almost as intriguing an enigma as Jessica Baxt—

After a few trial sniffs, Greg sprinkled a little coriander into the yogurt and greens mixture and then poured it into the still uncooked sponge mixture.

"Crap!" His voice echoed about the silent kitchen.

He'd utterly ruined both.

Well, the oven now had plenty of time to reach temperature.

He scraped everything into the trash and started over on his second sponge base of the morning. He had plenty of eggs, but he was running low on yogurt and Tiffany's was exceptional. It had a tang without being goaty that would make a fine match for the flavor profile he was after. He made a mental note to buy extra yogurt the next time she came down the mountain. And maybe this time he'd try chatting Jessica up.

Jessica?

He scorched the flour and butter roux that lay at the heart of the roulade past golden brown and well into molasses-brown.

How had Jessica gotten in there?

He poured in milk to try and rescue the roux and ended up scalding the milk. By the time he had dumped that out and scrubbed off the brown layer glued to the bottom of the pot, the air had come back out of the egg whites and the whole thing had to be trashed again. He'd made hundreds of roulade sponges over the years; this was Chef 101.

All he'd been doing was having a happy little never-going-to-happen fantasy about the local mystery girl, and Jessica Baxter had floated into the diner's kitchen uninvited.

Greg glanced around, but there was just him and the second ruined roulade. With a sigh he started cleaning that one up as well.

Jessica had always been a knockout. He used to hide up on the dunes just to watch her run on the beach each afternoon along with the rest of the women's high school track-and-field team—half a head taller than any others except her cousin and running as if born to it.

Out of goat yogurt, he substituted cottage cheese in the third roulade which completely ruined the balance of Parmesan and coriander. When he caught himself reaching for cumin, he knew he was losing his mind. With slow and methodical care, Greg scraped the third mess into the garbage. The smoked salmon that Ralph Baxter had sold him wouldn't spoil. The scallops, still sitting in a bag in his seawater tank to keep them fresh, would live another day.

He needed air before he suffocated.

Out the back of the diner, he just started walking. It was early afternoon and his stomach growled to remind him that he'd missed lunch. He was almost to his destination before he figured out where he was going.

Greg was less than a hundred yards from Vincent's place when he heard the shout.

"Your head is up your ass, Vin. Go on! Keep it there!"

Greg hesitated for a moment and then kept walking forward, figuring he'd better go and see what was up.

Vincent McCall was standing like a cornered bull—or maybe a cornered bulldog...a puppy—in front of the rolled up door to his two-car garage turned woodworking shop. The space was so crammed with projects and lumber that Vincent had to pull his table and chop saws out under the eaves every time he wanted to make a new piece of furniture.

What had cornered him was Dawn McCall. She'd been hot since fifth grade when her body had decided she was done with being a kid. Now at twenty-nine the view of her back had gone from attention-grabbing to awesome. Two kids showed nowhere on her hips. It was the ultimate joke that the school's soccer captain had become the stay-at-home dad and the girl that most had thought was the tramp of the school had become the most beloved science teacher at Puffin High. Of course it didn't take much imagination to understand why the boys all loved her.

Vincent glanced in Greg's direction in vain hope. No way was Greg dumb enough to take on Daw—

"And don't think I don't know you're back there thinking thoughts, Gregory Slater!" Dawn didn't even turn to glare at him.

Shit! He hadn't meant to be thinking thoughts about his best friend's wife; it was just hard not to. She was the antithesis to Jessica Baxter. Dawn's curves just reached out and grabbed a man by his balls. He'd bet that her thick brunette ponytail, sparkling blue eyes, and killer figure dumbfounded every teenage boy trying to focus on the equations behind electron orbitals or celestial spectra, or any of the rest of that stuff that she'd distracted *him* from when they shared those classes over a decade ago. Her looks were a hard slap whereas Jessica's were a soft caress.

The funny thing was that Dawn's personality was normally soft and gentle whereas Jessica's was clearly pure osprey—one of the biggest and most dangerous predators of the coastal bird community.

Not holding true at the moment. Vincent was looking at him wide-eyed and desperate. Dawn didn't have much of a temper, but when it did cook off, it could be lethal. She was way smarter than either of them separately, but sometimes when they joined forces they could get around her. Vincent had pulled his butt out of scrapes often enough, so Greg took the risk and stepped forward.

"Sorry, Dawn. Sometimes I just forget what a lucky bastard Vincent is that he married you."

"Remind *him* of that," she pointed an accusing finger at her husband. "I'm going to pick up the girls at Mom's and we're out of here." The twin girls were the perfect second-grade spitting image of their mother, who had been vivacious even before her body had developed. The town's seven-year old boys were already in twice as much trouble as he and Vincent had gone through with Dawn. *Good luck, little guys.*

Dawn stalked over to her SUV and roared off in a flurry of dirt and gravel, which was particularly messy after last night's rain storm. Greg ducked too late and was spattered with mud right along with Vincent. Her tires jumped from driveway to paved lane with a jerk and a sharp squeak of rubber that left a dark black stripe on the wet pavement and had old Mrs. Winslow checking out her window to stare at the two of them for a long moment. There was the other side of second grade, Dragon Winslow had been the terror of every seven-year old in town since before the dinosaurs had walked the earth.

Greg decided that he'd harassed Dawn and Vincent recently enough about living across the street from their old terror of a second-grade teacher to let it go this time. Besides, standing here beneath the Dragon's evil eye, it felt as if she'd somehow know if he did.

Greg brushed at his clothes. Between Jessica and her syrup and ketchup plate down his pants and Dawn's muddy departure, he'd definitely have to do a load of laundry sooner rather than later.

"What the hell, buddy?"

"Sorry, Greg. The woman works like a demon for nine months of the year and then once school lets out she expects me to take time off during *my* busy season to go to a movie and shopping up in Newport. No notice on a family outing…that she insists the girls told me all about last night. The two girls talk so fast when they get going in unison that I don't catch half of what they're saying no matter how I try. Dawn also wasn't too pleased about the Kriegson's place."

"The Kriegson's—" Greg had to do a real brain shift to navigate that turn in the conversation. "You got the contract?"

Vincent nodded sadly.

"But that's huge! Shouldn't be surprised, because you're the best custom furniture guy around. You figured it would go to that those guys out of Portland. So why the sad-dog face, Dawg?"

"The timeline. These summerfolk want everything by yesterday. It's enough money to carry me right through the winter and shove a chunk into the twin's college fund, but…" he waved a hand at the stacks of lumber in the garage.

Greg finally focused on what was crowding the shop. It wasn't local pine with a bit of oak trim. It was oak, maple, and cherry.

"The trim is all exotics and won't be here for another week. It's going to take the guts out of my summer with the girls and even worse, delivery is right when my folks are visiting and you know the Kriegsons are going to want a thousand little changes that they claim will only take a minute."

"Okay," Greg knew enough about Dawn and her mother-in-law to feel Vincent's pain; without Vincent available to act as a buffer between the two women it was going to be ugly. "I'm already dirty. Let me give you a hand."

"Oh, dude!" Vincent held up a fist in thanks.

"Dude!" Greg replied with a fist-to-fist punch hard enough that they were both shaking their hands in pain. It wouldn't be his pal Vin if it didn't hurt.

They picked up the first big board, Greg's hand still zinging a little, but it made up for not teasing Vincent about Mrs. Winslow.

Vincent maneuvered his end over toward the sawhorses. "You know, I saw Jessica Baxter driving into town with her mom this morning."

Greg dropped the board and barely managed to rescue his toe before it hit.

The end of the board bounced off a concrete block and the end of it split.

"Oh dude," Vincent said sadly, clearly not referring to the dropped board. He was the only person Greg had ever told about his teenage crush. Though of course everything Vincent knew, Dawn knew as well. "You're so goddamn pitiful."

"Tell me about it."

And like a true friend, Vincent ignored the wry tone and began to do exactly that, fully relishing every dumb detail Greg had ever admitted to.

Shit!

JESSICA COULD HAVE SPENT the entire day simply standing with her feet planted in the sand of the main beach, except she'd forgotten how cold the coast could be on a summer day.

Freshwater runoff from last night's rain was slipping to sea just below the surface of the sand, rapidly turning her feet into ice cubes. A thin fog was sneaking over the water and toward the beach. The inland Willamette Valley on the other side of the Coast Range must be heating up to drag the fog in off the water even at midday. And then the first wave of the rising tide reached her ankles and she yelped. The Pacific Ocean was damned cold.

She scooted up the beach to get clear of the next wave. Her mother was wisely back at the car, well clear of the rising tide. She'd also pulled on a light jacket the color of their eyes. Jessica might have to steal that one. It was irritating, useful but irritating, that her mom had better taste in clothes than she did. And she'd have to steal it soon, the fog wasn't put off by her Second City Improv Annual Revue t-shirt.

Even fifty feet from the beach the air was warmer, but not enough. As they got in the car, her mother spoke the old mandate, "Sand stays…"

"…outside the car. I haven't forgotten." Jessica did her best to dust off her feet but they were wet and sandy to the ankles and most of what she brushed off stuck to her hands. Soon it was like one of those oozing metallic encapsulations in science fiction movies, where the heroine barely has time to scream before becoming completely covered.

Her mother sighed when Jessica gave it up as a bad cause and pulled her feet aboard.

"Just like always, we're going to have to hose you down when we get to Gina's."

Jessica no longer felt twelve. The shift had occurred when…she was sparring with Greg Slater. Handsome men did have their uses, even when they were from Eagle Cove.

Her mother drove them up the winding lane toward the last house in town. A pair of massive Victorians dominated the south end of the beach before it was completely bookended by the rocky prominence of Orca Head. There was the Judge's place and then Aunt Gina's massive Lamont B&B.

"What's his story, anyway?"

"Whose, dear?"

When an eye roll didn't elicit any better response because of her mother's depressing habit of looking where she was driving, Jessica finally spoke his name.

"What about Greg?"

"Now you're being obtuse on purpose, Mom."

"Me?" She offered in a sweet tone that was so innocent that Jessica almost believed it. It was a tone from her childhood that Jessica had never been able to cultivate despite a fair amount of practice.

"Mo-om!" She said in her complaining teenage voice and they both had a laugh over it. "Did Greg even make it out of high school? Can't he do anything more than wait tables for his dad? How lame is that."

"Greg is—" Her cell phone rang. Her mother slipped it into the no-hands rig even though they were on a country lane moving about ten miles an hour.

"Hi, honey," Dad's voice boomed enthusiastically out of the speaker. "Is our little girl here yet?"

"Hi, Daddy," Jessica called out.

"Hey, Squirt!"

If she'd been twelve before, now she was feeling five and waiting at the dock for her father's boat to come back in.

"We're just on our way to Gina's now." Classic Mom didn't accelerate on the straightaway past the Slater spread.

Jessica stared at it as they slid by. The main house was almost as much of a monster as her family's home. When she was a little girl Judge Slater had added a mother-in-law unit that mirrored the grand house in miniature: a complete match down to small turrets and impossibly steep conical roofs. It had always struck her as so cute and cozy, even though she'd only been in it a few times during Grandma Slater's last years.

"I caught a monster halibut," her father's big voice filled the car. "Sold half to a customer who got skunked. Just got close enough to shore for the cell to work and called Greg. Must say that he sounded pretty damned relieved when I reached him. Any idea what that's about?"

"No idea at all," but her mother eyed Jessica as if she was somehow the cause.

"He took the other half," her dad announced.

"Wonderful. I'll get word out."

"Can't wait to be married to you again, honeybunch."

"Last time, I promise, Ralph."

"I'll hold you to that," her father's oversized personality shifted to a soft caress over the airwaves, making it a private joke. One so intimate that Jessica could feel herself blushing for overhearing.

"Still a couple hours to dock," his normal boom was back. "I promised the tourists I'd swing them by the puffin nesting grounds out at Chickadee Rock."

May through August they were thick with a hundred or more

foot-high birds with brilliant orange beaks. Right now the pufflings were fledging and the parents were scrambling about the sky and diving hundreds of feet into the ocean to keep them fed. It really was a grand sight.

"I'll come and fetch you both as soon as I'm ashore and cleaned up. Bye, my honeys," and he was gone.

"What does Greg Slater have to do with Dad catching a halibut?"

"He—" Then her mother actually looked away from the road even though the last curve was close ahead. She looked straight at Jessica for a long moment.

"What?"

Then her mother offered one of her radiant smiles. "You want to know what Greg does? Fine. Keep your questions until tonight and they'll all be answered."

"I don't want to know that badly."

"Oh, Jessica. Of course you do."

GREG'S LEVEL of distraction was high enough that he wasn't sure who was more relieved by Ralph Baxter's call about the halibut, him or Vincent. He hadn't dropped or damaged any more boards, but he'd knocked himself to the ground twice by catching his foot on the sawhorses. And he'd spent twenty minutes trying to round up the box of screws he'd knocked onto the garage floor. They were stainless steel, so he couldn't even use a magnet to gather them back up out of the sawdust. The sharp points pricked like blackberry thorns as he scrabbled about in search of them.

And every stupid-ass thing Greg did, his best friend had just rubbed it in more.

"Give me a break, Vincent. I don't even know who Jessica Baxter is anymore."

"Oh, like you knew so much then. But you've been pining after her pretty ass for every one of the fourteen years she's been gone."

"No, I haven't!" *Yes, I have.* "How do you know she's pretty? You said you just saw her drive by."

"Because she was awesome in a slim girl way when she was eighteen and you're *way* distracted now, dude." *Dude* had gone out of fashion when they were in middle school, so it had become their trademark greeting. Their theory had been that they were both out of the mainstream anyway, so maybe they'd become cool for being so *far* out of it. It hadn't really worked out that way. Though some part of it must have worked for Vincent, he'd married Dawn after all. By the end of high school, she wasn't just the hot chick, she was the hottest "get" as well. Beauty and brains joined together in a female Puffling. And despite all of the rumors, she'd been picky as hell—even if she had been dumb enough to pick Greg's best friend.

There'd never been heat between he and Dawn. Plenty of admiration, he had been a teenage boy after all and Dawn had been, well, daunting. But the connection had always been as friends. Vincent had fallen under her spell early and never recovered, though he had been damned slow on the uptake. He didn't figure it out until Dawn had asked him to the Senior Prom, then he'd never looked back.

Greg had taken Vicki Highland, who had the romantic soul of a razor clam. After the prom, when everyone had been headed to a beach bonfire in tuxes and gowns, she'd asked for a ride home. "I've seen a bonfire beneath the stars before," she'd kissed his cheek and gone inside leaving him dumbfounded on the porch. She'd married an accountant in Salem and worked as his assistant and business manager. About right.

By the time Ralph Baxter's call came in, he and Vincent both decided that it was a saving grace that there was now a massive piece of fish coming into dock.

Greg called around. Dawn and the twins often helped him when he did one of his "Irregular Friday Dinners at The Puffin." Even at seven years old, the girls already could do a fine job of setting tables or making sure a pot was well watched; he could trust them with most of the stirring on a risotto now, though they'd have to trade off a couple times because it was a long process. But they were out of town.

He sent Dawn a text to be sure to be back in time to eat and got back a thumb's up emoticon.

Gina would be busy with her niece. Could Jessica cook? Or was she now one of those urbanites who could "order takeout with the best of them?" He'd wager on the latter. He briefly considered Tiffany, but he had no way to reach her so it didn't matter anyway.

He called Peggy out at the small Eagle's Airfield that served a few locals and the occasional tourist with their own plane. She was rebuilding an old Stearman Model 4 biplane with the idea of offering fixed-wing flights to tourists in addition to her father's aged Bell 206 helicopter. Peggy was also a fair hand in the kitchen. Unable to reach any of his other "regulars" he finally called his dad.

"Hi, Dad. You've never helped me with my food before, but Ralph Baxter is bringing in a side of halibut for me and I can't find some of my regular folks. I was wondering if you could help out tonight? Actually starting pretty much right now. I know that it's short notice but I would really…" Greg got the impression that the Judge was just letting him ramble on until he was done. So Greg grabbed a clue off the shelf and shut up.

"All you had to do was ask, son."

"You'd have to do exactly what I tell you. This isn't an omelet or a stack of pancakes. This is—"

"Greg," the Judge cut him off this time. "Remember who taught you to cook."

"Ma did," and he felt the pain of her loss all over again. He'd learned a lot of technique since, but Ma had taught him all of the basics, especially the passion for food. She would have *loved* what he was doing which was sometimes the only thing that kept him going.

"Exactly. They didn't make me a judge for all of those years because I was stupid. You tell me what to do and I'll do my best to help."

Greg pulled the phone away to look at it, as if he could somehow see the mysterious man on the other end of the connection. It sounded like his father, it just didn't speak like him.

He reeled the phone back in.

"I'll see you there, Dad. And thanks."

"Uh-huh," neither positive nor negative, just an acknowledgement. Greg wondered if he should reprimand the Judge for "offering such a neutral sound of minimal form and a complete lack of content," but then the connection was cut off at the other end and he'd lost his opportunity to do so.

Greg was halfway down the driveway when he pulled up short and turned back to Vincent. "You bring Dawn and the girls to dinner. I'll make sure you get a table. And get her some goddamn flowers."

"Yes, sir, Mr. Chef, sir!" Vincent saluted him as if either of them had been in the Navy.

"And don't pick them from her own garden."

He could see by his somewhat abashed look, that's exactly what Vincent had been about to do. How Vincent had ended up married to Dawn was a mystery…to all three of them—well maybe not to Dawn, but he and Vincent had never figured it out. Then Vincent smiled that bad idea smile of his that had so frequently led their trio into disastrous trouble as teens.

"What?"

"I'll just slip over and pick them from Dragon Winslow's garden!"

Greg decided that scarcity was the better part of valor and made himself scarce very quickly. He just hoped that Vincent was still alive to bring his wife and the kids to The Puffin later tonight.

"Natya!" Jessica shrieked with delight. She jumped out of the car, not slowing down to close the door, and raced barefoot across the lawn. Jessica hadn't seen her cousin since she'd come through Chicago last year for a tech seminar.

"Jessica!" Natalya shrieked out their customary greeting in turn as she leapt down the front steps of the grand Lamont Victorian home.

They came together with a quick kiss and a hard hug that made Jessica feel like maybe it wasn't too weird to be home.

"I thought you were in Portland." Natalya was supposed to be there because then she'd be Jessica's secret refuge from the reality of Eagle Cove.

"I came down to help with the wedding."

"Didn't they tell you it had been delayed?"

"They did," and the way Natalya said it, Jessica knew that her friend had come down mostly to help Jessica survive the upcoming week.

"You're a true friend," Jessica whispered as she gave her another hard hug of thanks. They turned toward the house with their arms around each other's waists.

"Actually, the way I figure it, you're going to owe me big time. And don't think I won't collect." And she would. At four years old, Natalya always knew how to get someone in her debt and she never failed to make them pay. Of course, she was so damn pleasant about it that you wanted to anyway. Natalya had always been the slippery one who appeared to have the road ahead of her paved in gold, or at least a high-grade oil that eased her quickly on her way. She could lie with a straight face and no one ever seemed to care to prove her wrong.

Mom handed over Jessica's abandoned sandals then proceeded up the broad front stairs onto the verandah and headed inside.

Despite knowing better, Jessica had always fallen for every one of Natalya's traps and, worse, she'd never gotten away with anything. Just once in her life she'd like to really pull the wool over someone's eyes. She sighed. If it hadn't happened for her in the first thirty-two years, she wasn't going to bank on it in the next thirty-two.

She stopped at the bottom of the stairs and looked up at the grand old house.

It looked like...home.

The old Lamont homestead was a grand, glorious, and utterly charming place. In true Queen Anne style, it had a wrap-around verandah encircling most of the elevated first floor. The porch was safe from the heavy coastal rains beneath deep awnings which perched atop tall posts connected by ornate railings—safe except when the weather was driven sideways by the equally impressive coastal winds. Steep gables popped out of odd places with the least invitation and a great circular turret rose well clear of the second story to lord itself over the rest of the house. Small second-story balconies were tucked in odd corners. The roof and siding were black, the trim and porch rails were white, and the turret's pointy, dunce's cap roof was as bright orange as a puffin's beak in mating season—a color so bright that it didn't exist in the Crayola crayon box, not even the sixty-four set with the sharpener in the back.

Mom had moved into Dad's house thirty-five years ago and Aunt Gina had turned the home into a B&B, but much of Jessica's summers had been spent playing on the porch here—and later necking with boys here where Mom wasn't around to watch. Gina was more tolerant as long as Jessica or Natalya didn't go too far.

"So how's the grand voyager?" Natalya teased her.

"Glad to be home."

They both stumbled to a halt and looked at each other in surprise.

"Did I just say that?"

"You did," her mother swept back out of the house, deposited her knitting bag by a chair, and went back inside.

"No way did I say that."

Natalya was eyeing her closely, "Actually, Cousin, you did."

"Weird." They started up the porch steps together.

"Very weird."

"I think this calls for alcohol."

"Too early. But Mom had ice tea and lemonade made."

Glad to be home? Jessica felt depressed by the thought.

Chicago was home.

It was almost as if for the next week the rules that so tightly bound her life had come unbound. Job? Who cared? It was a disaster anyway. Car? Safely at Chicago O'Hare airport in long-term parking. Cat? Belonged to her roommate.

"Stepping out of yourself from time to time isn't necessarily a bad thing."

Jessica twisted to see a woman she didn't know sitting in one of the porch's heavy Adirondack-style chairs. She had a round face with striking brown eyes that matched her gorgeous cascade of hair.

Just as Jessica's mother had made her wish to cut her hair, this woman made her want to grow it high-school long again.

She wore corduroys the color of summer leaves and a blouse of white cotton. A gigantic straw hat rested on the next chair over. She was knitting a vest on circular needles in an intricate Fair Isle pattern. The colors were tea-dyed brown background with accents of Kool-Aid dyed natural wool—the dusky purple of Grape Berry Splash and Dark Cherry if she remembered correctly.

Jessica may not have knit much since leaving Eagle Cove, but the Lamonts had always knit. Aunt Gina would never have tolerated kin going out in the world not knowing how to make at least socks and hats, though vests and sweaters were better. Jessica recognized both the color work and the skill of the nameless knitter: better than she was, about the same as Natalya, and not as skilled as Aunt Gina or her mom.

Jessica saw a second set of knitting dropped on another chair. Natalya was making an elegant cowl in lines of alternating dark gray and jewel tones with custom-dyed fingering yarn. Jessica hadn't even thought to bring her own knitting. She was halfway through a second mitten that she'd been feeling guilty about for at least six years.

"Hi, I'm Jessica."

"Tiffany." And she didn't offer anything else. In fact, she gave the impression of never having spoken in the first place, as if her bit of advice had simply manifested itself out of thin air.

"Have you been in town long?"

Tiffany held up two fingers, barely breaking her rhythm with the needles.

"Days, weeks, months, or geologic eras?"

That stopped her knitting and had her looking up. "No other options? Centuries? Milliseconds perhaps?"

Jessica shared a smile with Tiffany and then shook her own head in the negative.

"In that case I'll take 'since the world was young.'"

Natalya gathered up her own knitting and sat back down with all the style and grace that Jessica had never been able to muster, not even on a good day when she wasn't feeling both jetlagged and age-lagged. She showed no surprise at Tiffany's presence which meant it wasn't months that the woman had lived in town, because Jessica knew that Natalya hadn't been home in that time span. So Tiffany had been in Eagle Cove for two years.

Jessica sat between Tiffany and her mother's chair and began dusting one foot against the other. The gritty sand slowly shed off her skin.

"I put you in with Natalya," Aunt Gina came out on the porch bearing a big tray of glasses and cookies. "It is the high season after all —though I did keep it empty for tonight until your mother moved her wedding date at the last minute—but tomorrow we'll be full again and I knew you girls wouldn't mind." As soon as her hands were empty, she wrapped Jessica in a bone-crushing hug. Jessica returned it for all she was worth. Though her aunt looked to be the sort of woman who reeked of scotch, fast men, and faster cars, she smelled of her kitchen and Jessica had missed her horribly by not coming home these last several years.

Mom followed close behind with massive pitchers of ice tea and lemonade.

Jessica eyed the tray, "Even I can't eat that many cookies. Especially not right after one of the Judge's breakfasts." She rested a hand on her stomach for a moment in sympathy with it for how much good food she'd eaten, leaving nothing on her plate despite her typically sparse eating habits. Then she reached out, "But I will start with *one* chocolate chip."

"You'll have some help. It's Friday afternoon knitting, dear."

Another change. Before she could remark on it, a car crunched up the gravel driveway and three women climbed out. Melanie Andriessen who owned The Flicker and knew a little too much about Jessica's use of the back row of her theater during her senior year in high school, Andrea Martins in dirt-smeared jeans and a t-shirt advertising Eagle Cove's only landscaping business, and Mrs. Winslow.

Jessica couldn't help herself, she screamed again and raced back down the steps to hug her second-grade teacher. It had been her guidance that led Jessica into journalism. She looked little changed—perhaps her hair was gray rather than salt-and-pepper, but she'd never been one for "all that hiding your age nonsense." And perhaps her face was a bit more lined—but she still stood every inch of her five-eight and looked as if she'd just come from a long hike, perhaps up Mount Rainier or maybe Everest. She had to be in her mid-sixties at least, but she still hadn't quite transitioned to the dubious honor of "she's a tough old bird."

Mrs. Winslow patted her on the back while they hugged, and was surreptitiously wiping at her eyes as she and Jessica climbed the stairs arm in arm. Jessica was feeling a little sniffly herself…and more than a little horrified. How in the world was she ever going to tell Mrs. Marjorie Winslow, a woman who had wrangled her way into being a front-line reporter in the last years of the Vietnam War, that her star pupil was on the brink of total failure? Jessica did her best to shove the question aside, but it wasn't shifting offstage nearly as easily as Jessica would like.

Soon they were all sitting together on the porch, and cookies and drink were headed around as knitting projects emerged. Her old classmate Becky Billings rolled up in her bright blue delivery van —"5B" it declared in gigantic letters, then underneath it read "Becky Billings BlueBird Brewery." They exchanged squeals and hugs as well. Becky had become "tight as bees" with Jessica and Natalya ever since the day they first met in preschool. It was like there was a small rip in the universe whenever the three of them were together and merry mayhem had always ensued. Others arrived, some of whom she knew, some not so much, until a dozen women were gathered on the B&B's spacious front porch.

Mom dug out a spare set of number six straight needles and a ball of Lamb's Pride worsted in a soft butterscotch gold and another of light woodland green.

"Why don't you make yourself a nice scarf for when you go back to Chicago, dear?" As if she couldn't manage anything more complex than a scarf. She was on the verge of taking umbrage when she looked down at the needles. Jessica had to squint at them a little to remember how to cast on. Maybe she'd keep her mouth shut for a change.

She put the first slip-knot loop over her needle and then caught a very slight headshake from Tiffany, more an unexpected ripple of hair than a headshake. Making it look casual, Tiffany took the tail of her own yarn and slid it out to arm's length.

Right.

As subtly as she could, Jessica undid the slip knot, pulled out an extra three feet of yarn and made another knot; the long tail would be absorbed during the cast on. She'd have discovered the problem herself in a dozen stitches, but she'd been saved the embarrassment of pulling it out and starting over properly. No one else seemed to notice except Natalya, who was grinning at her like a co-conspirator in an international crime. Jessica offered a nod of thanks that Tiffany returned infinitesimally before turning her attention back to her own project. Jessica stuck her tongue out at her cousin.

So, whoever Tiffany might be, she missed nothing. That had always been one of Jessica's strengths, too. Natalya was the slippery one of the team, Becky the rowdy, and Jessica the observant one. They'd often agreed that what they'd been lacking was a smart one. She'd have to wait and see about Tiffany.

Wait and see?

What in the world was she thinking?

This was Eagle Cove and she'd be gone just as fast as her mother's wedding allowed.

GREG WADED INTO "THE ZONE" on occasion as much by chance as by planning. Sometimes it was a smooth slide, other times a heart-stopping plunge as bad as when the surfboard dumped him into the ocean and the wave action didn't release him until his head ached with the cold.

Tonight there'd been too little warning for him to be anywhere else except the zone. By the time the seventy-pound slab of cleaned halibut, Airport Peggy, and the Judge all arrived at the restaurant, prep time had already been tight.

In minutes he was spewing out directions like a master chef. He was so wound up that he slid into his commercial kitchen mode. He only ground to a halt when Peggy came to stand directly in his path and wouldn't let him by to reach the fresh herbs he kept growing in the restaurant's south window.

"What?" He snapped at her.

Peggy stood still. She was half a foot shorter than he was…and could snap him over her knee if she'd felt like it. She should have been an Alaskan bush pilot. Not like Maggie O'Connell in *Northern Exposure,* delicate for all her bravado. Peggy Naron was shorter than the model who had played Maggie and not much bigger around. But Peggy gave the distinct impression that if she had to wrestle a polar bear, it was going to be a bad day for the bear. She had dark curly hair pulled back in one of those ponytails that exploded behind the rubber band making it look as if she was racing in his direction just the way a diving eagle might moments before it killed its puny prey. She was closer to the Judge's age than his own, finishing high school while he'd been starting diapers.

"What?" He managed to tone it down this time.

"I've known you since you were still inside your mama, Greg. Babysat when she needed a break from you and Harry. Now answer me one question straight and I'll let you by."

What was it with tricky women today? First Jessica, then Dawn, and now Peggy. "Okay," he said cautiously.

"Where are you right now, Greg?"

"The Puffin Diner." He tossed it out as a joke, then wondered if he was about to get another plate of greasy food down his pants for being so flippant. How else was he supposed to answer such a weird question?

"Good boy. Remember that," and, that simply, she stepped aside. She returned to her work of shelling the scallops with knife and spoon. At least he hadn't wasted the beautiful shellfish on some earlier test just for himself; they'd be perfect in tonight's dinner.

He'd been moving so fast that, having come to a halt, there was an inertia against moving again. He glanced at his father. The Judge had been shaving shallots on a mandoline, but now had stopped. He wasn't watching Greg, instead he was looking at Peggy. Inscrutable as ever, there was no way to tell what he was thinking, and Greg wasn't sure if he wanted to know.

Then the Judge looked up at Greg and offered his "my decision is final" nod in obvious agreement.

I'm in the Puffin Diner?

Which meant what?

Oh! Duh! He wasn't in a pressure cooker like the Westin or The Herb Farm before that or the…he was in Eagle Cove, Oregon. He'd never enjoyed those high pressure kitchens, so why had tried to bring that attitude here? The only place more laid back than a small town on the Oregon Coast had probably been left behind along with the 1960s.

Greg hadn't done that on Friday night before, entering the commercial kitchen frame of mind, at least he hoped he hadn't. No, if he had, Dawn wouldn't have the least compunction about reaming his ass and she wouldn't have been half as gentle as Peggy had just been.

And the time pressure wasn't *that* bad. He glanced at his watch. Okay it *was* that bad, but that didn't make his manners any more excusable. Peggy and his father were helping him out of kindness; they wouldn't be paid much more than food. The twenty dollars *prix fixe* often barely covered the ingredients he used and the beers that he paired with them.

Yes, Oregon now boasted the number two wine region in the country, gaining ground on Napa, but for some reason all that changed when you crossed the Coast Range. Out here beer ruled. The first microbreweries of the new era had been founded in Oregon. Now you couldn't drive a dozen miles down the coast—except in the long wilderness gaps—without finding another master brewer with their own set of techniques and flavors. He'd worked a lot with Becky's flavors from her 5B brews and already knew exactly which pairings he'd use tonight…except with the dessert. Blackbird Porter or Deep Bay Stout? The porter. Just a four-ounce glass with the dessert—No! He'd go with tiny servings of the Espresso stout. Crap! Except he had no dessert. He needed a dessert to complete the meals' overall flavor profile and if he couldn't think of—

Calm. Take a breath. Be calm.

Yeah, right.

He was being totally stressed, but he couldn't dump that on his crew. He was trying to arrange the most complex dinner ever of his Irregular Fridays and there were so many elements to coordinate. He wanted to blame it on his father's presence, but the Judge had taken instruction well and without comment.

Yet still Greg couldn't move from where he stood rooted in the middle of the kitchen.

It was so important that this meal was utterly perfect because…

The first question he'd asked Ralph Baxter even before how much halibut he'd be bringing ashore was whether or not his daughter would be here tonight.

Vincent, who'd been standing close by, had slapped his back hard enough that Greg had almost lost his phone into the sawdust.

Ralph promised that he was calling his wife next to make sure all three of them were there. That's when the panic had settled over him nastier than a bar rag at the end of a busy night.

Greg took one last deep breath…and didn't feel cleansed at all. He could hear the scraping of metal spoon on scallop shell and the light tick of his father once again sliding the shallots back and forth on the mandoline to make paper thin slices.

He could do this.

He could make it good.

And it was as he rushed toward his window box herb patch that he understood the second level to Peggy's question.

Where are you, Greg?

He was in The Puffin Diner, though he preferred to think of it as The Puffin when he was serving fine dining here. He was in a kitchen that he knew better than any other in his past. And he was here to serve a meal to his family and friends.

His real goal however—absolutely proving just how totally lame he'd truly become—was to impress the hell out of a beautiful woman he hadn't seen in fourteen years.

"Why is everyone being so damned mysterious about this?" Jessica whispered to Natalya as she climbed the steps to The Puffin Diner for the second time today.

"Because it's making you crazy."

That was certainly the truth. Mom had simply declared, "Greg is doing a Friday night," which was greeted with a swell of excitement from the knitters, "and Jessica doesn't know what that means." That had elicited a half dozen "You're in for such a treat, dear," comments.

And when she'd pushed, they'd all shut down. When she'd tried being subtle about it Mrs. Winslow had snorted out a laugh at her lame technique and Tiffany had merely rolled her eyes. It reached the point where she couldn't even mention it tangentially without getting shut down.

"Are you going?" she'd asked Tiffany.

Before the quiet woman could even look up, the other women were once again telling her not to pry. After everyone else had returned to their knitting, Tiffany had glanced up and offered another one of her minimal, hair-rippling headshakes. A mouthed *why* had only elicited a widening of her eyes and an uncertain shrug.

Afterward, while Jessica had been inside clearing plates and glasses, Tiffany slipped quietly away to who knew where. There one moment and then gone.

"Doesn't talk much, does she?" Jessica had asked Mrs. Winslow when they had a moment alone.

"Only when the girl has something to say."

Jessica glanced over to see if that was a remonstrance of some sort. It had been in the second grade that Mrs. Winslow had taught her the first key to good journalism: "Shut up and let them talk." It was a skill that she'd had a hard time learning as a seven-year old, but after a year in Marjorie Winslow's class—often sitting isolated in the front left desk scooted well away from the others—she'd learned it well. But Mrs. Winslow's comment didn't appear to be accusatory this time, so she didn't mind the gentle reminder of the axiom.

When asked how soon she'd be ready to go to dinner, she'd shrugged that she already was.

In response, Natalya had grabbed her arm and dragged Jessica up to the room they'd be sharing.

"What?"

"We're going out to a nice dinner. You need to put on some finer duds, girlfriend."

"I thought it was just Greg doing something."

Natalya had merely shoved her toward her suitcase.

"Since when did people in Eagle Cove play dress up?" She received no answer as she started sorting through possibilities.

Oregon evenings grew chilly early, so she'd selected a pair of white linen slacks with just a hint of a bell-bottom, sandals with knit Christmas socks because she wanted to be fancier than her battered running shoes, but didn't want to risk messing up the only nice shoes that she'd brought for the wedding. She swiped a black denim shirt from Natalya, but it was warmer than she thought so she'd ended up tying the shirt tails together high on her midriff. A little skin never hurt. A filmy scarf of spring green borrowed from Aunt Gina had completed the outfit.

"Put a flower in my hair and I'll be certifiable," she whispered to Natalya as they climbed the steps to the diner.

"No, then you'd be perfect and that wouldn't be fair to the rest of us."

They stepped through the door arm in arm, and Jessica had to glance back to make sure that she hadn't just slipped through some kind of space-warp, time-portal thingy. But she hadn't; Beach Way was still behind her and a steady trickle of townsfolk were flocking this way.

She looked back at the room. Rather than harsh fluorescents and sunlight slamming onto battered Formica tables, the space was now lit by rows of twinkle lights running around each fluorescent fixture and tiny spotlights on Ma Slater's paintings. The tables had been transformed with midnight blue tablecloths, buff-colored napkins, and the soft oranges of the sun settling into the inevitable bank of fog that was forming far offshore.

"Maybe I'm certifiable without the flower in my hair."

GREG HAD BEEN TRANSFIXED by the vision entering his restaurant. He'd been trying to find something to say, when he overheard her comment. He turned, selected a small dark-red dahlia from the vase that Vincent had dropped off to be a surprise at their family table—good man, he'd bought a nice arrangement that wouldn't miss the one bloom Greg had just liberated—and he nipped off most of the long stem with the chef's knife he kept sheathed on his hip.

"If I may?" He approached Jessica. While she'd stared at him in astonishment, he'd slid the palm-sized flower into her hair where she'd gathered it in a sidetail to flutter on one shoulder.

"There." It brightened her appearance, making her look even more exotic and other-worldly than she already did.

"Uh thanks. So, that makes me completely certifiable?" Her smile made him feel far taller than his eye-to-eye height.

"Absolutely. Certifiably lovely."

She snorted a laugh at him.

All he could do was grin in response. Even next to Natalya she was the standout in the room.

"Where do you want us, Greg?" Ralph Baxter looked the sea captain role. He stood six-two, fisherman-shouldered, and his own blond hair lightening toward white. He hovered protectively close to the women with him. He turned as Gina Lamont and Jessica's mother entered as well.

"I don't have a six-person table," Greg was looking around for which two tables to pull together, but there were only so many tables in The Puffin and he hated to turn anyone away. Next time he'd push them together in long, communal rows so that there wasn't a wasted seat.

"Oh, don't worry, dear," Gina hooked her arms around her daughter and her niece. "We'll just squeeze in all friendly-like at a four-person. Monica, you can just sit in Ralph's lap, you lovebirds."

Jessica rolled her eyes and Greg tried to smile at her in sympathy. But Gina's comment only reminded him of the unbearably sad scenes he'd witnessed as the Judge had tried to figure out how to say goodbye to his wife of thirty years—sometimes cradling her for hours in his lap though he clearly had few words to offer. Greg did his best to ignore that memory as well as Jessica's "And what the hell is your problem?" look by turning to seat the other arrivals.

Soon, The Puffin was crowded to the limit. In addition to the six stools at the counter, he had two couples standing at either end. He found a few more stools from the back and seated them behind the counter, facing their partners across too small a space. Next time he'd have to take reservations, perhaps even do two seatings. That was a first, which was absolutely incredible...and was freaking him out more than just a little. So many people, so many servings to do.

He took one last look about the room as he stood up from asking Vincent's twins about their outing to Newport. It had included a visit to the aquarium which was always a big hit: Emma was more of a shark gal, Irma preferred the otter tank. Dawn looked only moderately harried from trying to satisfy them both. Vincent was doing a good job of getting the girls to tell him every detail and giving his wife a chance to breathe.

"How about next time, I go with you?" Greg told the twins. "Then when no one is looking, your dad and I can toss you both in to swim in the otter tank."

Beneath their squeals of fearful delight, Dawn whispered to him, "Thanks for the flowers."

"They're from—" he didn't get to finish.

"I've been married to Vincent for ten years and two children; I know who to thank, Greg."

"He means well," Greg did his best to reassure her. He'd never heard her as rough as she'd been this afternoon.

"Always," she said it with a sigh, but he could also hear that she really meant it which made him feel more relaxed about what was going on with his two closest friends.

Greg stepped away before Vincent could know that their flower-ploy was blown.

He headed for the service counter, bewildered by the miracle of everything that was happening. The restaurant was packed solid with people and they'd dressed up to come—as if this was important. There was a buzz of merry anticipation in the air. Fine dining in Eagle Cove. It was enough to make him laugh, or hide in the back of the walk-in freezer and shudder with terror until they all went away.

Peggy began setting up the trays of Halibut-Scallop Ceviche appetizer and he served them out. He'd decided to use the heavy-bottomed wide Old Fashioned glasses he'd picked up cheap at a bar supply store. The thin slivers of red onion, the teasing microgreens, and the spheres of the dwarf cherry tomatoes made a nice contrast to the white halibut and pale scallops through the glass. He'd done all of the knife work on the fish himself, because first impressions were so important.

Becky came along behind him doing her brewmaster spiel and talking about the salmonberry pale ale as she poured just a few ounces into small juice glasses. She also had a soft cider that she served to Vincent's twins and those who wished it.

Greg didn't serve Jessica's table first, but he didn't serve it last either. A customer who received their meal mid-service didn't feel the guilt of being served first along with the boredom of waiting while others finished.

He was delivering one of the final trays close by Jessica's table when he heard her speak up, "When did the Judge get so fancy?"

He almost bobbled the last glass of ceviche into Dawn's lap. He managed to recover and offer her a smile.

So much for trying to impress Jessica. It felt as if his longest chef's knife had just been pounded in right between his shoulder blades. He abruptly wished she'd just go back where she came from. Why did she have to come back tonight of all nights? Gods, he sounded like a whiny Jewish Passover ceremony. *Why on this night of all nights do we... let our hearts think there's even a sliver of a chance?*

He turned for the kitchen to oversee the First Course and all he could hear was the roaring in his ears.

"Jessica, you idiot!"

"What?"

Natalya looked pissed. A glance around the table showed her parents and aunt were suddenly very focused on their glasses of ceviche. It was fantastic and by far the best food she'd ever had from the Judge. There was a lightness to all of the elements so that it didn't overwhelm the mild seafood, but rather complemented the bursts of tomato or the light zing of onion. It was bright without the usual ceviche problem of being too acidic.

"This is Greg's food, and he was standing right behind you when you said that."

Jessica hunched her shoulders as if he still was, even though she could see him back at the window.

"Greg can cook?"

"Oh my god," Natalya rolled her eyes. "Please tell me I'm not related to you."

"Since when can Greg cook?" She glanced surreptitiously to see him, but he didn't look any different. He was picking up a tray and Jessica could see the Judge right there in the kitchen. "But the Judge is the one cooking. Greg is just waiting tables."

"Odd," her father was rubbing his chin as if checking to see whether or not he'd shaved well enough. "I seem to recall selling that big halibut to Greg Baxter, not John. I'm not losing my mind, am I?" He aimed the last at his presently ex-wife, or maybe now she was his fiancé. That was her dad, always stepping in with a bit of humor to save the day. If Mom ever tried divorcing him again, Jessica was going to stage an intervention. As a matter of fact she'd make sure that the

Judge had her phone number so she could tromp on it hard if it ever came up again.

"No more than normal, dear man," she patted his cheek affectionately. "We simply didn't tell Jessica about the treat she was in for."

"This is really Greg's cooking?" Some idiot part of her brain was having a particularly hard time with the concept. Cooking took skill and patience to learn which she couldn't reconcile with how firmly she had Greg Slater pegged as another Eagle Cove failure. She could feel Mrs. Winslow berating her for "preconceived notions have no place in a journalistic view."

The ceviche was more than good. It was a fine-dining chef's work; she'd interviewed any number of them over the years and knew that for certain.

She watched Greg move about the restaurant with a practiced ease. There had to be fifty people here and he didn't appear to hurry even once. It seemed that she watched him for a long time before she thought to ask the next question of her parents.

"Since when did Greg Baxter commit to anything?" That hadn't come out right. "I mean—"

"I," Greg was standing right by her elbow, causing her to practically leap out of her chair. He expertly balanced five plates of gorgeous fish, "spent two years at the CIA, apprenticed for two years at The French Laundry, and five years working with some of the finest chefs in Seattle. And how is *your* life going?"

He served them with only the barest of courtesy. Jessica half wondered if she was going to end up with a plate of fish down her blouse just as Greg had received hash browns down the pants from her. But he resisted whatever urge he was feeling, and stalked back to the kitchen. She noted with some chagrin that they were the last ones served this course.

Jessica looked down at her plate. It was just a simple piece of fish. Except it wasn't. The white halibut had a layer of herbs crisped on it. It flaked at the tiniest nudge with her fork and when she bit into it, her mouth was flooded with powerful flavors of chive, shallot, basil, and fresh parsley. The crisping of the herbs had added a bit of crunch and had muted the flavors just enough for the fish to shine through. The fish itself rested on a double swirl on the plate of strawberry and blueberry puree—as beautiful as art and so rich that every ingredient must have been fresh that morning.

A sip of Becky's Evergreen Lager—which thankfully didn't taste like pine trees—added a freshness that brought the fish completely to life. The roasted green beans were an attractive contrast.

"That's incredible. What the hell is he doing in Eagle Cove?" And Jessica could see she'd put her foot in it again. Why couldn't she stop doing that? She'd turned into an idiot with a dash of bitch thrown in and didn't like that side of herself at all.

"Okay," she tried again. "You all have lives here, I understand that. But the chef who can cook this could go anywhere. Anywhere." The next bite just melted on her tongue and she knew full well that she'd never have been able to afford the restaurant that someone like Greg would cook in, not even in her heyday as a rapidly rising journalist.

GREG overheard that as he was clearing the tables he'd served before hers.

He could go anywhere.

Somehow he knew that now. He hadn't until this moment, but he did now. Sure, these were Eagle Cove locals, but just because they were coastal didn't say what most people thought it did. A couple decades back, all of these little communities were busted flat logging or fishing towns—and some still were. But others, like Eagle Cove, were now tourist retreats and retirement communities. He was constantly astonished at what the people here had done before coming to live here.

And now he was the one astonishing Jessica Baxter and he liked the way that felt on several fronts.

As guests finished the crispy-herbed halibut, he replaced it with a coconut gelato palate cleanser served in tall martini glasses with tiny sugar-bowl spoons. The unexpected flavor, floated on just a dribble of

Becky's hard cider, would jar their palates enough that they wouldn't be overwhelmed by three courses of seafood.

Watching their reactions, thanking them for the compliments, he knew that he *could* go and start his own restaurant, even make a go of it. If it wasn't for the money. He could solve the startup money issues with a partner, but he didn't want to be burdened by some other chef who would try messing with his recipes. And a manager-level partner would probably end up trying to manage the kitchen as well as the front of the house and that would never do. No, Greg wanted the control. He rather liked being his own master here at The Puffin.

He ducked into the kitchen to start working up the Second Course.

This was the trickiest of the lot and it took everything he, Peggy, and the Judge had to pull together the Halibut Veracruz. He left the floor to Becky's charm, which bubbled out of her as easily as the fizz in her cider, and focused on the food. The paper-thin slices of chorizo sausage had to be seared, but not burnt. The tomato-and-Spanish olive sauce had to be hot enough to finish cooking the intentionally underdone fish as it traveled to the table, yet the long curves of sliced avocado and the final dollop of sour cream must remain cool on the tongue.

"I knew you were good, son," the Judge spoke as he ladled the sauce over each piece of fish in the long line of plating that covered every available surface.

"He just had no idea how good," Peggy finished for him as she nestled in the thick slices of buttered and toasted French baguette from Cal's bakery.

Greg set the avocado and sour cream himself, checking that each plate looked perfect as he went.

"I'll give you whatever else you need," the Judge finished and began gathering up the first plates to carry out.

"What you're doing is just great, Dad."

"No, I mean whatever bankroll you need to get started, I'm your man," and he was gone from the kitchen, his arms laden with plates.

For the second time tonight Greg's mind went into full lock-up—

skidding sideways, unable to get his foot off the pedal. He knew he was headed for some kind of a crash, but he had no idea what it was or what he could do about it.

Peggy slapped his butt hard enough to jar him loose. "Damn, boy. You're almost as cute as your father when someone catches you out." And with a bark of laughter, she headed out with the next tray of food.

His own restaurant? It was finally in reach...and due to the most unlikely of sources.

SERRANO CHILI, garlic, oregano, capers...it didn't matter that there was no salt and pepper on the table; the dish had been seasoned to perfection. The cherry porter harkened back to the sweet berry puree under the First Course without adding an unwanted sweetness to the Halibut Veracruz.

Jessica wanted to wallow in the dish: like a luxurious trip to the spa. It was an adventure of flavor and texture. She'd done some restaurant reviewing—had chiseled out a brief niche among the new chefs of Chicago, though the niche had gone away when some New York reviewer had decided to move to town to make their name, imitating the huge splash Cassidy Knowles had made in Seattle. But in those first six months she'd learned a lot about innovative food. Greg didn't innovate, at least not in the way most of them did. It wasn't all molecular techniques, odd foams, and food that had been manipulated until it looked like anything other than what it was.

He'd found his challenge in simplicity, a much harder technique. When the dish was simple, when it was designed to highlight just one or two key ingredients, then perfection was required. There was no hiding a flaw when the artist's palette was something as simple as a piece of mild white fish.

"For dessert," Greg announced to the room, "I made a chocolate-strawberry roulade with a hazelnut meringue. Becky has paired it with her Deep Bay Espresso Stout." Which Jessica was charmed to see served in little espresso cups.

"You can't ruin this one," Greg whispered to her as he served dessert to their table.

She looked up at him in surprise. Something had shifted in him during the course of the meal, and she didn't think it was just in her own perceptions. There had been a nervous energy about him; of worry, thinking back to it. This meal had scared him initially and she could see why, it had been a large and complex undertaking for such a small crew. But now he carried himself with a confidence, a surety that he had lacked before. It was as if the boy had become a man over the last hour or so.

"How would I have ruined it?"

Then Greg did something wholly unexpected, he blushed. Deeply, until she could see his face was bright red despite the subdued lighting from the twinkle lights.

"How..." Jessica trailed off unsure if she wanted the answer to that question.

"I had to toss three roulades in the trash this morning..." he too trailed off.

"Because of..." there was only one thing that Jessica could think of that would explain his reaction, "...of me?"

After trying twice to speak unsuccessfully, he nodded, offered a charming shrug of, "And there it is," then moved on to serve other tables.

Nobody at the table was studying their dessert this time, instead they were all looking at her.

Choosing discretion over stark embarrassment, she focused on her own dessert.

"Always knew he was sweet on someone—" her father's voice carried far too well. Thankfully Mom shushed him. Even in what he considered to be a whisper, Dad's voice still carried. "Well, it was as obvious as a hard bite on a long leader that there was some reason he never got serious with a girl."

"We just never knew who." At least Aunt Gina's whisper didn't carry past the table with how cozily crowded together they were, but it reached Jessica well enough.

"He's certainly never made a meal as good as this one before," her father's voice carried again and people at nearby tables started agreeing, and then a round of applause broke out.

Under cover of the applause, as Greg did a fine job of bowing and looking both humble and pleased, Natalya whispered to her. "And now we know exactly why he cooked like that as well." She offered a bawdy wink and a nudge with her knee where they'd been bumping each other under the small table all night.

Jessica could feel her ears going as hot as Greg's face had been. She reached up to release her hair from its sidetail so that she could hide a bit, but her fingers caught on the flower she'd forgotten all about—the one that Greg had tucked there.

Certifiably lovely.

Oh crap!

Once the buzz at the table turned to other topics, she looked up and spotted Greg. He was squatting down between Dawn—the freshman-year hussy—and the cutest pair of twins Jessica had ever seen. By how Dawn and the girls were dressed up, maybe that old hussy assessment had been wrong as well. Vincent McCall sat with them. She vaguely remembered Dawn, Vincent, and Greg being close in school; three years behind her, she actually hadn't given them much thought. Wouldn't have given Vincent any at all if Dad's best friend and fishing-and-crabbing buddy wasn't Danny McCall.

And back in the day Jessica had only noticed Greg separately from the others because he was Harry's little brother and had always been hanging around. As a matter of fact, he'd been a real pill to shed when she and Harry had been trying to finagle some alone time for experimenting. Greg had been a seriously tenacious little shit.

As if he knew that Jessica was thinking of him, he looked up from whatever the twins were telling him; looked right at her.

For the first time she didn't see Harry's little brother. Instead she saw a darkly handsome chef who had just served one of the finest meals of both their lives.

CHAPTER 3

(FRIDAY NIGHT)

The Judge didn't cook on Saturdays or Sundays—*Don't much like damn tourists anyway*—so there was no urgent need to finish cleaning up The Puffin, but ten years of habit had Greg staying even after the others left. He liked making sure that everything was shipshape and tucked away.

He'd also enjoyed the chance to think about the night. He'd often received thanks and handshakes for his meals, but he'd never received a round of applause like that before.

He still didn't know what to make of his father's offer. His parents had set up a college fund that had seen him through the two years at CIA, plus the extra courses he'd crammed in during summers and weekends. The day he'd graduated the Judge had taken him aside and handed him a check for ten thousand dollars.

"This is your startup fund, Greg. We gave the same to your brother. You work your ass off and you make this last. It's all there is until your mother and I pass. Not because we can't afford it, but because a man has to make his own way in the world and he won't do that if there's some damn safety net bailing him out every time he goes overboard." It was one of the longest speeches of the Judge's life.

Greg still had every cent of that original ten grand in a savings account. For ten years it had been the symbol of his own restaurant and he'd built on that, never once touching it. He hadn't done it fast. That money in the bank gave him a confidence that allowed him to work for less where he could learn more.

And his father had just broken his own rule and offered to bankroll his new restaurant. Greg had thought that was still two or three years away. He didn't want to squander the opportunity, so it was going to take some thinking and planning before he took any action at all. He'd treat it as a venture capitalist's investment which he would repay with very high interest.

One last check and he could find nothing else to clean or straighten. The kitchen stood ready for whatever came next—a blank template. He liked that. Unlike so many of the restaurants he'd worked, this one wasn't all pre-stocked for some repeat performance of a fixed menu. There wasn't a dinnertime's estimated stock of a dozen racks of lamb, fifteen lobster tails, twenty pounds of beef tenderloin ready to be made into filet mignon, and all of the other culinary traps of a successful restaurant.

His favorite part of any restaurant had always been the Fresh Sheet. What was at its very best *today*. What could be done with it. His Puffin's kitchen was like that. Nothing pre-decided. A halibut had been caught a dozen hours ago, reached his hands two hours later, and had now fed fifty-three people.

He patted the thousand dollars in his pocket. Even after paying back all of the vendors—because Ralph had comped him the fish in exchange for dinner for his family, making it a very expensive meal for Ralph—he'd have over seven hundred dollars which was going straight into his restaurant fund.

Lights out, he pulled the door shut behind him and turned to face the night. It was warm and the ocean freshness was thick on the air. The Flicker's marquee was out. The late show was done; it must be later than he thought. Usually it lit this entire end of Beach Way.

Everything was shadows.

Like most coastal towns, Eagle Cove had rolled up its sidewalks and only the Bobbin' Red Robin Tavern remained open, its neon sign advertising "5B Brews On Tap" as a muted statement in the front window that barely lit the stretch of sidewalk in front of it.

"What the hell, Slater?"

He jolted. The voice, the tone, even the words themselves told him exactly who sat in one of the big wood chairs on the diner's dark porch. The three elements blended together made a nuanced statement even without the visual.

"Hi, Baxter," he wondered what Jessica was doing here. He'd bet that falling into his arms wasn't exactly likely.

His eyes had adapted enough to the dark to see her sitting in the second chair to the right of the diner's door. Greg could just make out the dark spot of the red dahlia that he'd tucked into her light hair. She still wore it. Had she been here since the patrons had left hours ago? Maybe, which was interesting.

He sat in the first chair and only in that moment could feel the familiar pounding of the blood in his feet. Restaurant work did that to you and it wouldn't be the end of a good day without that particular throb and ache. He kicked off his shoes, peeled his socks, and rested them on the cool, rough wood of the porch.

"Oh god, that feels so good."

"When did you start?"

"Today? After working for Dad from six to ten, I spent a couple hours helping Vincent with some cabinet work before your dad called with the halibut."

"Does he do that a lot? Or was it just because I was here?" He caught that the second part of the question was the important one, but answered the first.

"Some. I get fish from him. Danny McCall gets me crab when they're in. Tiffany brought me bear once, but more often sells me some elk."

"Tiffany? Quiet woman about my age with long hair? A good knitter?"

"She knits? I didn't know that. And she's definitely not quiet; she's always talking to herself—probably comes from living alone up in the woods. But the long hair fits. She's one of the best bow hunters in town. And you remember what they say about deer in this town…"

"Don't need a gun, just need a baseball bat." It came out in unison and they both laughed. He'd forgotten that Jessica Baxter had such an amazing laugh. The deer in Eagle Cove were so tame, that you could practically walk up and pet them.

"A lot of folk bring me venison whenever I need it. Beef in the fall from Mr. Greene… I get food from all sorts of folks in town."

"I actually meant how long have you been doing this?"

"Irregular Fridays at The Puffin or cooking?" *Or crazy about you?* But he wasn't going to say that one out loud. Or answer it.

"Both actually." In other words all three, but she wasn't any more willing to ask him about the unspoken part than he was to say it.

He wished he could see her more clearly than just her general location. She was facing him, in a casual posture that didn't place her hand on the chair arm next to his, but still she sat in an open way. In a… journalist's way. As a matter of fact, her questions were…

"Writing an article about me?"

"No. I just…" Jessica slipped into silence. When she spoke again, her tone had softened. "I don't know you, Greg. Everyone says that you're crazy about me, but you don't know me either."

"Making me just plain crazy." He slid down in his chair, extending out his feet until his toes were wiggling in the cool night air. "I can live with that."

Again that patented, secret sauce Jessica Baxter laugh.

He decided to go back to the first questions for safety. "Mom started teaching me to cook when I was tall enough to work on the counter while standing on a stool. I can't even remember when I didn't cook. What about you?"

"Cooking?" Jessica kept searching for some anchor in the conversation but wasn't having much luck. "I cook out of desperation, not skill. Mostly because my budget doesn't allow for a personal chef. Or even going out much for that matter." She hadn't mentioned that last bit to Natalya, never mind anyone else.

She'd been sitting here in the dark for hours trying to wrestle with that. Mrs. Wilson had seen clean through the thin facade that Jessica had been feeding her parents for a while now—along with everyone else who asked. Her mentor had been kind enough to not prod for details in front of the others, rather offering a kind "come and talk when you're ready" along with a hard hug.

Jessica had been feeding the story to herself as well. And the journalist who had been telling the story—herself—was good enough that she'd almost bought it.

It will turn around soon.

Just need a couple solid contracts.

Maybe get that big interview next week.

But she'd gotten the big interviews, as many as ever.

Jessica had landed the contracts too, more than many of her friends, but the terms had grown worse and worse with each one. The pay was going down and the draconian terms were worthy of the most heinous lawyer.

"My career is against the rails..." Worst, there were no signs of it turning around at all. "...and I don't see it turning around anytime soon. I also can't believe you're the one I'm telling this to. I haven't told this to anyone, only just figured it out while sitting here."

"I'm a little surprised myself."

"And yet I'm finding it comfortable to do so?" She hadn't meant it as a question.

"I'll take that as a good sign," his voice was lazily pleased as if of course he deserved whatever good came his way.

"Don't get cocky, Slater."

"Whatever you say, Baxter." Smug bastard.

"Never mind. Forget I said anything." She struggled out of the chair, stiff from not having moved in hours. She'd gotten cold despite the atypically warm evening. Her knees were a little wonky as she descended the steps.

"Hey! Wait a sec."

Jessica got her knees in order and turned right at the bottom of the steps because Greg was descending to her left. Wrong way. LBB Lane was at the other end of the main strip. But Greg was now between her and her escape. She kept going. She'd hit the beach and walk back that way. She could see ahead through the darkness, by how the docks floated, that the tide was down low. Good, there would be enough beach to walk on.

"Jessica?" Greg's voice came from so close that she jumped in surprise. The quarter moon that had been hidden by the deep eaves over The Puffin Diner's front porch offered enough light that she could see him clearly enough. He was barefoot and had moved very quietly.

She turned and continued toward the beach. The street was completely empty. There were a couple of cars parked down by the bar. Weekenders, because any local would have walked on such a beautiful night.

"Could you at least tell me what I said to send you running off so fast?" He was still following her. She decided that was a point in his favor, for not being scared off by the first flash of her temper—another thing she could thank Mom for. The way he'd asked it earned him another point.

"You didn't say anything wrong, you simply hit the nerve that I've been trying to ignore since the moment I crossed the goddamn Coast Range this morning." The high-water fish on the front of Grouse Hardware was way over her head as they walked Beach Way's faded yellow centerline. "Actually for a while before that too. Like you drove a spike into it."

"Ouch! I could break in here," he hooked a thumb toward the hardware store, "and grab a pair of pliers. Would that help?" He headed toward the dark and locked doors as if he really would.

She was in such a fume that for just a moment she thought he was being serious. "Okay!" She huffed out a breath. "Okay! I'm being foolish. If you're going to keep walking with me, please have the decency not to point that out again. I hate whining almost as much as I hate being ridiculous."

"Ridiculous?" Greg offered amiably and veered back across the lane to walk beside her toward the docks once more. "You want ridiculous, you should talk to my buddy Vincent. He doesn't even know to get his wife flowers when she's upset. Now that's ridiculous."

Greg, Dawn, and Vincent. And now the twins. "Does it bother you that she married Vincent rather than you?"

"Not really. Vincent was gone on her all the way back to kindergarten. I love her to death and would do anything for her, but there was never a click between us."

"Not what it looked like in high school."

"Hey, I do have a Y chromosome, you know. Dawn was a knockout way early; still is. But she was always the level-headed one out of the three of us. Always knew what she wanted. Double major in physics and chemistry and she came back to marry a carpenter and teach the high school kids. How cool is that? But it wasn't her I was crazy about." He stated the last as a blunt fact; again that supreme arrogance. No attempt to hide the fact or whisper it or keep his damn mouth shut.

Jessica closed her eyes; allowed herself the freedom of walking for a moment with her eyes closed. The gentle breeze off the ocean brushed across her eyelids and tugged lightly at her hair until it felt as if she was floating.

Floating for now, and about to drown.

She opened her eyes and there were the docks sticking out into the bay that was Eagle Cove. A half dozen fishing boats and three sailboats. Not a lot of sailors were willing to brave the reefs, sea stacks, and generally nasty weather of the Oregon Coast—a storm was just as likely to come crashing in tomorrow as a day of light winds and pleasant sun. And if she made one more goddamn metaphor about her suddenly storm-tossed life she was going to turn in her journalist's artistic license.

"Tell me something, Greg. Anything. Just get my mind out of the rut that it's in."

GREG CONSIDERED THE CHALLENGE. He'd never really imagined himself just walking along with Jessica Baxter. Of all the things he'd ever imagined with her, he'd never thought of something so simple.

He did wish he hadn't blurted out that she was the one he was crazy about, but it was truth and it was out there. He remembered Chef Manuel telling him, "Once you break the damned egg, let it go and move on." So, he'd said it. No taking it back.

The other thing he'd never expected from Jessica Baxter was the amount of distress she was showing. He'd always been attracted to her simple confidence. She'd walked down a high school hallway with an ease of passage, without tipping over into her being some kind of a queen bee. It was the same way she wrote. He had an online search alert that kicked him an e-mail of every article she published. Her written voice was as engaging as her spoken one—straight ahead, true, no evasion or softening of hard facts.

And here she was asking him to help her avoid whatever she was thinking. She looked so sad, rooted in place at the end of Beach Way and staring at the small working docks floating at the edge of Eagle Cove. Daring greatly, he rested a hand lightly on her lower back and turned her toward the beach. With just the slightest pressure he was able to get her moving again.

And from that brief contact, he could imagine how she would feel to hold. The warmth of her against palm and fingertips, the extra little pressure where her spine and the inside of his knuckles had lined up. The soft smoothness of the thin fabric of her blouse. The tip of his thumb had just brushed the lower edge of her bra's back strap.

Way too easy to imagine holding her close.

"There's a moment in cooking," he had no idea what he was going to say, but if he didn't speak soon, a sudden dryness might close this throat forever. "I'll wrestle with a dish a hundred times. I follow the recipe. I work the ingredients. I get to the point where if I eat another lobster-stuffed pork chop I'm sure that I'll die."

They moved down the concrete boat launch ramp until they reached the beach and then turned south. The town lay sleepily atop the bluff to their left. On the moonlit sand, giant driftwood logs looked ten times their size with their dark shadows. The sand was a mixture of tide-packed hard and wind-blown soft that tickled his feet.

And his shoes and socks were still on the diner's porch. Well, he wasn't leaving Jessica's side to go back and get them.

To their right, the ocean waves sparkled outward forever. The steady *whump* of waves hitting the sand then scraping up and down the beach kept them company. Seagulls slept on the sand as bright lumps, who scowled when "forced" to stand and step out of the humans' way. A few miles to the south, Orca Head lighthouse towered above the beach, casting its sweeping lights out across the water, but passing high above the beach and town—a guiding beacon that offered no illumination to their next steps.

The ocean breeze didn't draw on the infinite fresh air and sea salt to intrigue his nose. Instead, Jessica, walking just windward of him, scented the breeze like warm honey. Like...what in the hell had he been talking about?

Food. Tough guess. He was a chef after all. Pork chops. That was it.

"Then after a hundred meals of merely good," he continued, "and occasionally awful, something happens. I'll cook without looking at the recipe. After all, I've long since gleaned every scrap that the prior chef encoded in coarse-minced versus fine-diced and dash versus pinch. And maybe I'm in too much of a hurry to look at the recipe again. I just cook."

He tried to assess what Jessica was thinking, but she ambled along beside him watching the beach ahead. They were moving too slowly for it to be walking. They were like two old friends heading down the beach as somewhere to talk rather than actually heading anywhere.

"There's something that happens at that moment. I..." he tried to recapture what he'd felt while cooking tonight. "I was no longer just cooking. I was..."

Somehow they had stopped walking and were facing each other in the moonlight. The sliver of a moon was behind her and her face was cool skin and deep shadow, like a modernist painting of herself.

Well, if he was going to go down for anything, he might as well go down for the truth.

"I was cooking for you."

It wasn't something he could have said even this afternoon. But the Judge had been right; he'd never cooked like this before. After so many meals for himself, for the Judge, and for the town, he could now feel the difference. And some part of him knew now that he'd finally glimpsed how to be a chef rather than just a cook. He wouldn't be sliding backward anytime soon. Just as thoroughly as Jessica had ruined the morning's roulades, she'd *made* the dinner, but he owned that now.

Jessica watched him without blinking. No tilt of her head to show what she was thinking.

He waited, too tired to do anything else. Too certain that once again he'd utterly blown it.

"I'm going back to my original premise," her voice was as neutral as her expression.

Was it some journalist's tool? Never show your own emotions so that the interviewee must fill the void? Well, his voice was food, not words, and he'd spoken with everything there was inside him.

"My first question was, 'What the hell, Slater?' That still seems appropriate."

If she couldn't see it or couldn't let it in… Somehow he'd thought more of her. He'd given her all that he had and it hadn't been enough.

"You know what? You were right. Teenage crush, decade-long delusion, whatever. I hope you enjoyed the meal." And to hell with her and to hell with himself.

He turned to continue down the beach.

Jessica grabbed his sleeve.

He shook her off, surprising himself as much as her.

"Okay!" It came out as a shout that he couldn't seem to clamp down on. "I don't know who you are. You left this town fourteen years ago at a dead run and you think I'm a failure because I didn't. Well, I did leave. But after eight years I came back because my mother was dying and then my father needed me. And you know what happened? I discovered I liked it here."

Still that neutral damned expression.

He almost blasted her with the rest of it. That he knew it was still a stupid schoolboy crush, but it was one that even just the sight of her brought roaring back to life. He wasn't an idiot, except about Jessica Baxter. He—

Unable to face what he did and didn't know, he turned from her and headed down the beach. She didn't try to stop him this time.

He waded through one of the half-dozen little runoff streams that cut just inches deep across the sand. The chill water did nothing to slow his steps as he passed the small, sleepy hotels perched along the bluff. The cuffs of his jeans now slapped wetly at his ankles chafing the sand into his skin.

When he glanced back, Jessica was still standing there, a shimmering figure in the moonlight—as ephemeral as the waves and just as indifferent. Maybe he should go back and apologize or placate or something, but he didn't feel like it. He was only now putting together why he'd cooked the way he had. He hadn't even known it until he said it aloud and it scared the crap out of him. The food had always been his and his alone. No one should have the power to ruin roulades or create the best meal he'd ever put together.

And the worst fear—the one that had him practically sprinting down the beach—was that he was fooling himself and he'd never again be able to cook just for himself.

"WHERE HAVE YOU BEEN?" Natalya's sleepy mumble greeted Jessica as she tried to slip into the room without waking anyone.

"Hell," she whispered. "Just go back to sleep, Natya."

And for a blessed moment it appeared that's what she did. But after Jessica had washed her face, brushed her teeth, and found a nightshirt, she could see Natalya sitting up in her bed.

"Care to explain that one?"

"It's two a.m. my time," the hall clock had softly chimed midnight as she'd snuck in, again making her feel like a teen past curfew. "I had to catch an early flight. We can talk about it tomorrow."

"I thought you were maybe necking with Greg Slater."

"So not," Jessica shifted her bag and the rest of her clothes onto the floor and crawled into the other bed. Even though it was the high season, Aunt Gina had saved them one of the largest rooms which just fit a double and a single bed with a tiny nightstand between them. Natya, arriving first, had grabbed the double, of course, just as Jessica would have done.

"Then I'm guessing that you weren't having your way with his body either."

Jessica didn't bother to answer, just hugged her knees to her chest and was momentarily glad that she could see so little of the room. Aunt Gina had decorated by genre and she and Natalya were in the Sci-Fi room. The lone shaft of moonlight just now reaching in through the west facing windows lit a small side table with a foot-tall Princess Leia doll facing a pair of Lieutenant Uhuras: one classic and one reboot. The three miniature women and one life-size one watched her with shadowed gazes. Thankfully only the life-size one was expecting an answer.

"Tell me that isn't why you stayed behind after dinner."

"That isn't why I stayed behind after dinner."

"Shit!" Natalya didn't curse often, but she put some heat behind it when she did.

"Stop that. You'll shock Anne." Even though it was invisible in the darkness, Jessica knew that a poster of Anne Francis and Robby the Robot from *Forbidden Planet* hung above Natalya's bed. Linda Hamilton from *Terminator II* hung above Jessica's bed brandishing her massive machine gun and wrapped in crossed bandoliers of bullets implying a deep cleavage despite the military vest. Linda wouldn't give a rat's ass what Jessica said, so she was glad she'd ended up with this bed.

Natalya sighed, "Please tell me that you didn't yell at him."

"No. But he yelled at me."

"Did you deserve it?"

"I dunno," Jessica dragged the covers over her head. "Maybe," she told the darkness.

"Heard that!"

Crap! She could feel Linda glaring down at her as well.

CHAPTER 4

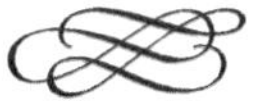

(SATURDAY MORNING)

It was the weekend. Worse, it was damn early on a weekend morning. He should be sleeping in.

Yeah, that always worked well for him. Getting up five days a week at five to help his father at the diner didn't exactly train him to relax on a sunny summer morning. Greg knew that the Judge, a creature of habit, wouldn't stir from his bed before eight on a Saturday—the end of the BBC morning news.

Greg headed out for a run to clear his head. The beach was chilly despite the promise of a warm day. The fog had moved close ashore and though the sun had cleared the Coast Range, it wasn't high enough to clear the bluff and most of the beach still lay in cool shadow.

As was usual, he trotted south to the base of the cliffs atop which stood the Orca Head lighthouse. He did some stretches against the rock.

He glanced up at the Lamont place. That and his family's were the two great Victorians of the town, like side by side beacons; together they were as commanding of the shoreline as the lighthouse perched hundreds of feet above him.

He'd spent much of the night puzzling about why Jessica's question had ticked him off so much.

What the hell, Slater?

Seriously, what the hell? He'd practically drooled all over her. He'd insulted her for her wanting marshmallows in her hot chocolate and run hot and cold through both the dinner and the conversation afterward.

Hi, babe. Haven't seen you in fourteen years, but you're the love of my life. Wanta do it?

Okay, he hadn't been that bad…he hoped. But he sure hadn't been good.

Nine days—eight now—if he wanted to do something about it before she once again left Eagle Cove.

He leaned into his hamstring and felt the stretch tug all the way up to his exhausted brain.

After last night, wasn't much chance of that happening. *Let's impress her by yelling at her and calling her an idiot.* Actually, he was fairly sure that he'd been calling himself an idiot, but it probably hadn't come out that way.

He tried the other hamstring which was no better after tossing and turning through most of the night.

Well, it wasn't going to get any better than this.

He heard a faint call caught on the breeze.

Greg scanned the beach, but the nearest person out this early was Clarissa and Emilio Thompson a half mile down and tossing a ball for their dog.

The call was repeated, a little louder. It might have been his name.

He tracked it to the veranda on the Lamont place. A tall slender figure with blond hair was shouting his name and waving him over.

A thread of hope shivered through him, as chill and cutting as the fog that hung close offshore.

Run down the beach and ignore Jessica for eight days? Or go all in and see just what he could do to explain himself from last night in hopes of patching things up?

Well, since he'd already broken some eggs, he might as well see what he could make with them. Besides, no matter the danger, he didn't want to risk not seeing Jessica for another fourteen years. He had to try.

Acknowledging that he was probably being an idiot, Greg began trotting across the beach toward the stairs that led up the bluff to the Lamont's house.

JESSICA JOLTED out of a dead sleep, the kind that only happened after her brain refused to shut off with the lights. Like a combination of drunk, hungover, and three-day old dishes. She'd laid awake for hours in a mashed-up collage of her stumbling career, the amazing meal, and Greg's harsh words—that she'd thoroughly earned. He seemed like a nice guy doing his best to be honest and she'd slapped him with "What the hell, Slater." Real nice. Jessica heard the grandfather clock downstairs chime two before she'd finally plummeting into true sleep.

She tried to shake off the dream that someone had been shouting Greg Slater's name. Someone with her own voice. Jessica really had to file a complaint with the dreams department for writing such a crappy story. Guy dreams were supposed to be about handsome and sexy ones who flowed with charm. Instead she'd woken from a dream of a handsome and sexy guy who scowled like a ticked-off golden retriever—all happy, then all sad, then all happy, then…

Scrubbing at her face did little to break the mental back loop; she did *not* want to be thinking about Greg Slater first thing in the morning.

A quick glance showed Natalya was already up and out. The window was open and the air was warm so Jessica dragged on some shorts, waved at Linda all armed to thrash some poor Terminator's ass, and headed downstairs in search of cocoa—with marshmallows, goddamn it, and to hell with Greg Slater.

Aunt Gina had an instant hot water tap, so Jessica went with powdered mix and stumbled out onto the porch clutching onto her mug for dear life.

Mom was standing at the porch rail looking down at…Greg Slater just climbing the last steps up from the beach.

Greg stopped and had that same damn smile that had earned him a plate of hash browns down his pants just yesterday. Short memory if he'd forgotten the dangers. He'd forgotten. His eyes tracked down her body.

"Sorry, but you can't blame me for smiling at this. You just can't, Jessica."

She looked down at herself. Her oversized nightshirt was dark blue with a faded pink declaration: *I'm a woman. What's your superpower?* And it was just long enough, barely, to completely hide the fact that she was wearing shorts—shorts that didn't hide all that much more than Greg's running togs did. He wore lime green Nikes, gym shorts that did reveal a very nicely muscled set of legs, and a t-shirt that said: *The rules of the kitchen: 1. The chef is always right. 2. See Rule #1. 3. See Rule #2.*

"Is that so?"

Greg looked down to see what t-shirt he'd dragged on and then grinned back up at her, "Ab-so-tively!"

"And…" she loved it when guys just set themselves up for failure, "…since we're not in a kitchen, does that mean that you're always wrong?"

"Jessica!" Mom said it more as a sigh than a reprimand. "I called Greg to come up to talk about the wedding."

"*You* called him?" She sipped her cocoa and the heat tried to kick start her brain. She'd started to wonder if he'd appeared in answer to her dream calling him, but it had been her mother. That was some comfort to her firm belief in how the world worked. Just as strongly as being in Eagle Cove chipped away at that world view.

Greg went up on his toes and leaned in close to peek into her mug. "Are there marshmallows in there?"

"Of course!" Then she glanced down, she'd forgotten them in her sleepy state. "Damn!"

Greg dropped back on his heels just too damn pleased with himself.

For being a woman she wasn't feeling very superpowerful this morning. She wasn't going to retreat, well not far. She settled onto the porch swing.

She considered doing the whole making-a-show thing of slowly crossing her legs and…being a complete bitch. Her mother had left a rumpled quilt on the swing and Jessica pulled it over her legs as she sat.

Greg settled at a small table by the rail.

Mom patted Jessica's knee through the cover.

Jessica sipped her cocoa and offered Greg her most pleasant smile as her mother offered coffee and went in to fetch it.

Now her question had changed to *What the Hell, Baxter?* She should be teasing him and making him suffer for thinking that a ludicrous high school crush could possibly still mean anything so many years later. But she *was* touched.

And she had even less idea *what the hell* about that, than her career.

GREG DIDN'T KNOW which was worse, having Jessica's long legs out in plain view, or having her wrapped up in the green-and-gold quilt, her sleep-tousled hair the color of the sun, and clutching her mug of cocoa like a life preserver. It was impossible that someone could look so good right after they woke up. It made it far too easy to imagine waking up next to her the morning after; then the one after that and…

Mrs. Baxter came back out of the door and dumped a handful of tiny marshmallows into Jessica's mug. She looked up at her mom with the radiant smile of a woman who loved her mom with all of her heart.

He knew—in that single flash of an instant he knew—that no matter what real-world facade of disaffected urbanite she wore, Jessica Baxter would do anything for her mother. She'd just revealed that the Jessica Baxter he'd fanaticized about all his life was real, not some illusion that he'd been fooling himself with. He might not know her, but he certainly knew what sort of person she was.

Greg forced himself back to the present as he thanked Mrs. Baxter for the cup of coffee, a nice contrast to the morning's coolness. Eight days. Yes, he could think of a lot of things to do over the next eight days. It was plenty of time. And if it wasn't enough, maybe his new restaurant would open in Chicago.

He looked away from Jessica, because he didn't want her to see what he was thinking about "their" future—not even a little. It was utterly insane, but he couldn't seem to stop himself, so like a good chef, he'd follow his instincts.

"We were going to keep it a simple affair," Mrs. Baxter sat shoulder to shoulder with her daughter, but declined to duck beneath the quilt making Jessica look even more cozy. "But May Conklin at The Brass Plover Pub is incredibly overbooked for any catering next weekend. Frankly she was overbooked for this weekend and was only going to do the wedding as a favor to me. So, I was wondering, Greg. Could you possibly cater the wedding next Saturday?"

"Sure," he agreed appreciating the way Jessica's face was relaxing as she sipped her cocoa and watched the ocean. "I'd be glad— Huh?"

Jessica smirked without even turning to look at him. She clearly knew what effect she was having on him...and didn't seem to mind, which gave him a sliver of hope.

He did his best to force his attention back to Monica.

"Well, her Scottish pub makes her the biggest restaurateur in town. Cal Jr. at The Blackbird Bakery is handling the cake, but I'm desperate for the food. You'll take care of that for us?"

"For how many?" He'd been invited, he was fairly sure of that. Living back in Eagle Cove a calendar had become less and less meaningful. Five days working for the Judge, the rest of his time, social or cooking, was typically fluid on a daily or even hourly basis. "How elaborate? And for how many?"

Mrs. Baxter looked ever so innocent as she said, "Nothing fancy. It's an afternoon wedding, so just a friendly sit-down dinner right here." She waved a hand to indicate the grounds of the old Victorian. The large grassy yard sprawled out to the sea cliff.

Jessica's eye roll told him one degree of the trouble he was in.

"And I think we only invited twenty or thirty."

Fewer than he'd fed last night so—

Jessica practically snorted her cocoa with laughter and gave herself a coughing fit that had her mother suddenly solicitous.

"How many invitations did you sent out, Mom?"

She shrugged delicately, she was a softer version of Jessica. Was that time or was Jessica merely a more sharply edged person? Jessica cut a far sharper picture in the world.

"Thirty."

"Anyone turn you down?"

"Just your aunt, but since Gina is going to be my maid of honor again, I know she's just teasing."

Jessica turned to face him. "That's thirty *families.* Plus, knowing Mom, anyone else she happened to be chatting with or sold a house to or..."

Greg blinked hard. Mrs. Baxter wouldn't have thought a thing about inviting people. She had an outgoing warmth that made her one of his favorite people in town completely aside from her role as Jessica's mother.

"Maybe you should start with an elk," Jessica teased him.

"Too bad the gray whales are done migrating," he shot back. Every spring they shrimped their way up the coast, returning each fall. But this was July and he knew nothing about cooking whale anyway.

"Or tourists. No one would ever miss a couple of tourists."

"And I thought I was the one getting ghoulish," Greg grimaced.

"No tourists," Monica Baxter stated as if it was a rule rather than disgust. "They're the ones who buy weekend residences and hire out my Ralph for day-trip fishing. I refuse to cut into the family businesses for this."

Greg laughed as Jessica looked at her mother as if she'd grown a second head. He leaned back in his chair and enjoyed the moment. He knew exactly what she was feeling. It was just three years ago that he'd come home and discovered that his mother and father were not the people he'd thought they were—they were better. He recalled the shock of seeing Judge Slater so shattered by the loss of his artist wife.

That's why he'd stayed in town and his father had appreciated it, not that either would ever say a word on the subject of course. Apparently Jessica had been unaware of her mother's sense of humor.

"I'll do it, Mrs. Baxter. We'll need a better estimate of how many I'm cooking for, but I'll come up with a couple of menu ideas for you."

"Oh you sweetheart. I always knew you were a good boy," she leapt to her feet and offered him a hug and a kiss on the forehead. Then she turned to her daughter, "Well, I have a house-showing out at the Carson place in half an hour, so I have to run along. Natalya and Gina went out with Ralph to spend a day together on the water, so you have the run of the place."

And in an instant he was alone with Jessica Baxter and a sudden awkward silence descended on the porch.

Greg nursed his coffee but couldn't think of a thing to do to break the silence. He'd abandoned her on the beach last night. Yelled at her about him being an idiot. Great. He'd found a way to be insulting to both of them. And if he sat here like a dumb mute much longer, he'd blow any chance of—

"You were going for a run?"

He looked up to see Jessica was still gazing out at the ocean. "I was."

"Give me a minute," and she rose to head indoors, leaving him to contemplate her undressed look as she walked away, and the rumpled quilt now abandoned on the porch swing.

In moments she was back. The shorts were no longer, but they were now visible as the loose nightshirt had been replaced by a form-clinging t-shirt in fire engine red that declared: *Journalist!* in a head-line bold font followed by: *Mess with me and I'll spell your name wrong.* The t-shirt wasn't made out of the thickest material.

"Go ahead, spell it wrong, please!" Greg teased her. "I'd bet anything that it would be completely worth it."

Her laugh was merry as she rested one of those long legs on the porch rail and began stretching out. A last sip of the coffee did nothing to jog his brain to life. He knew how to talk to pretty women, had earned himself a bit of a reputation for how easily he could sweep up a tourist. He just didn't know what to say to Jessica Baxter and she absolutely knew it. He retreated to the kitchen to rinse out his mug and buy himself a little space.

BY THE FIRST hundred yards along the beach they were pushing the pace enough that no spare breath remained for conversation which was fine with Jessica.

When they reached the docks at the two-mile mark and moved up onto the streets, she picked up the pace another notch. Her long legs could run most guys into the ground, but Greg not only kept up, but began pushing her. Up Beach Way, she saw his shoes and socks still on the porch of The Puffin Diner, looking as if their owner had been teleported out without his footwear.

What the hell, Slater? Was that really what she'd said about such a fine meal?

No, that's what she'd said about a man with a boyhood crush on her. Well, she'd only be here for one week, then she'd be safely gone. They couldn't cause *too* much trouble in such a short time.

They ran out to where the town tapered down into the single road. At the final intersection before it headed up into the Coast Range she turned them onto Gull Way. It looped along the backside of Eagle Cove, making the longest possible running route.

In high school, it had been a straight 10K: Aunt Gina's down the beach, through the heart of the town, up and down the short hard hills of Gull Way, cut back along Shearwater Lane and out LBB Lane. She'd usually started the loop at the high school on Shearwater, but had run it from Aunt Gina's often enough that it was like coming home to run the loop.

Out on Shearwater, Greg slowed and waved at someone.

Jessica waved out of habit, but almost stumbled as she took in the image. It was a double-wide manufactured home, just where she'd pictured Greg, Dawn, and a passel of kids. But the home was clearly well tended with a cheery paint job and colorful hollyhocks. In front of a large add-on garage were parked a newer minivan and a beater pickup. But what made her stumble was that Vincent, Dawn, and the twins were all working together in the garage workshop on a beautiful-looking bookcase. Not at all the sort of place she'd pictured them ending up. It looked…cozy.

She started paying more attention to the town they ran through. Growing up here, it had all turned into the blur of "home." Being gone, that memory had turned into rundown and sad. There were still those types; "white trash" places piled with mossed-over trailers, salvaged materials that would never be used, and lopsided picnic tables. But there were also the crisp lawns that marked retired military and the toy-strewn yards of new toddlers.

She almost commented on it to Greg, but then they hit the top of LBB Lane and now he kicked it up a gear.

Two miles to go, he was clearly trying to run her into the ground. Well, that wasn't going to happen. Not to Jessica Baxter. Especially not on her home turf.

"Elmer," she gasped out, finding it easier than she'd like to sound completely winded.

Greg nodded. That was their finish line.

Elmer was the massive Douglas fir that ruled over Aunt Gina's property. It had been there when the house was built and would probably still be there when the Victorian fell down from old age. Elmer was a two-hundred foot-tall old growth, easily seven feet through the trunk.

She let her stride open up and shifted her focus from the houses onto the end goal, calling up the techniques that had gotten her to the regionals if not all-state.

Pictured it in her mind's eye. Not the stretch of road ahead of them or the stiff climb as the road ascended from beach to top of bluff. Not the point where tar shifted to gravel on the final stretch. Jessica firmly planted the image in her head of arriving at Elmer far enough ahead of Greg Slater that there would be no question that she hadn't only beat him with some final sprint; she'd crushed him.

Chicago's biggest hill was the freeway bridge over the river, but she'd balanced out that lack of elevation with longer miles along the lake's edge which was totally paying off at the moment. Running was one of the few things she'd taken with her when she left Eagle Cove and the chance to run here was such a pleasure that it made her feel like she was flying.

Greg did his best, he really did, but she could see that he had nothing left to dredge up when she kicked into her final sprint as they passed the Slater's. She felt a dozen feet tall as she crossed Gina's lawn in first place.

She didn't so much reach Elmer first, but rather ran square into his massive trunk braking with only the last step. Jessica tagged the tree and then splayed herself out against the rough bark so that she didn't collapse to the ground. Maybe she wasn't in quite as good practice as she thought. A moment later Greg did the same—he must have found reserves somewhere to finish just a single step behind her. Good thing she'd been trained to never look back. That simple action might have cost her the race.

Rich pine and dusty bark overwhelmed her own sweat. Salt dripped down to sting her eyes and flavored her lips when she licked them.

"Damn. Jessica," Greg gasped out. "But you. Can. Really run. Damn!"

Laughter bubbled up and almost choked her as she still couldn't get enough air.

As soon as they could stand without Elmer's support, they began walking circles around the tree, shaking out legs, and walking it off.

"C'mon," Jessica nodded toward the kitchen.

They staggered up the broad front steps together—knees loose, bumping shoulders and laughing as they went. It was a good moment, one Jessica realized that she'd treasure for a long time.

***

GREG HAD a whole lot of thoughts as they leaned back against opposite counters in the Lamont B&B kitchen, guzzling monstrous glasses of orange juice. The kitchen had been utterly modernized, in ways that made it look traditionally old. Black appliances, walnut cupboards with brass handles, and dark granite counters. The hardwood oak floor was finished and sealed. The indirect and discreet lighting was unneeded as the sun was currently streaming in through the eastern windows lighting Jessica's hair as she leaned by the sink. She was positively a shining beacon offset by the lush warmth of the décor.

He was no longer thinking of the woman with the amazing body. Well, not only. He was also seeing the woman who never bowed to a challenge but instead grabbed it with both fists and her teeth besides. Someone who understood that there was nothing as funny in this world as people, especially the ones you cared most about. He was telling her about the courtship between Dawn and Vincent with full DVD-extras commentary: Vincent hadn't stood a chance, but Dawn had made him think that he was the one making all the "right" moves.

"He only figured out how to court her because she told him when to ask her out for dinner. When the first kiss was okay. Half the time she fed the tips and cues through me without me realizing it either. She led him like a puppy dog each step of the way," Greg tipped his head side to side like a dog just trying to figure out what was happening to him.

Jessica's merriment had her snapping her fingers and slapping her hand against her bare thigh, calling out, "Here, boy. Here, boy."

Eight days. Don't do anything stupid...at least not too stupid, one side of him admonished.

To hell with that! Greg's other half answered. He had a bad habit of listening to that side and he decided that this time wasn't going to be an exception.

He set down his glass, circled three times in place like an excited puppy dog with big galumphing steps, moving closer to Jessica with each turn as she laughed and kept clapping her hand.

At the end of the last circle, he stepped between her spread feet, leaned in and kissed her.

Fifty-fifty he was going to earn a slap. Forty out of the remaining fifty he was going to get shoved back on his ass hard. Ten percent odds seemed pretty good for a chance to finally kiss Jessica Baxter.

He caught her mid-laugh.

She felt better in his arms than he'd ever dreamed. Her slender frame let him wrap his arms right around her back. Her lips tasted of salt sweat and sweet orange juice, and her laugh continued for a moment as a vibration that shifted into a thoughtful, *Hmmm.*

Greg didn't feel thoughtful at all. He was wholly focused on the way the length of their bodies pressed together, of her arms slipping around his neck as the kiss deepened. Unable to resist, he pressed himself against her. His hands slid up and down her back appreciating the curves and shapes. No bra strap obstructed his investigation, not that Jessica's build particularly called for one. She was sleekly perfect.

Her kiss was shredding his recipe for how this might possibly go. The blood pounded in his head as he held her closer.

Then he felt a cold trickle, almost icy cold.

Right on the top of his head.

He tried to pull back to see what it was, but Jessica had her arm locked tightly about his neck...one arm. She even wrapped one of those infinitely long legs around his waist which was very distracting.

But the cold trickle continued. Then the first ice cube bounced into his hair as chilly orange juice spilled down his forehead and stung his eyes.

"Hey!" (which came out more as "Mgrph!") He tried again to escape and she held him even tighter.

That laugh was back in her kiss, but she didn't release him.

Well, two could play that game.

No they couldn't. His glass was over on the opposite counter.

Fine. Then he'd play it for all it was worth.

He tipped her back against the counter just enough that the juice was trickling down both their cheeks and spilling between them rather than running down his back.

The laughter slipped back out of her kiss—damn, there'd never been anything like kissing Jessica Baxter. Once the flow of orange juice and ice cubes stopped, she fumbled for a moment to set the empty glass on the counter and then both hands grabbed onto him.

He brushed a hand upward, appreciating every muscle. Relishing the softness of her hair and the curve of her ear. Then, as casually as he could, he collected the ice cubes that had perched in his hair rather than tumbling to the floor. With just as smooth a move, he ran his knuckles down her cheek, her neck, and managed to slip the ice cubes inside her shirt collar.

This time it was her turn to struggle and squirm and his to laugh into their kiss. He kept their bodies close enough that the ice cubes couldn't slip past her breasts.

When she finally freed a fist and pounded its side against his shoulder, he backed off. With a judicious grab on his retreat, he managed to yank forward her shorts just as the remainder of the ice cubes slithered out the bottom of her t-shirt.

Jessica yelped as the ice cubes slipped into her underwear.

Life was so good. "Paybacks are hell, aren't they, Ms. Baxter?" He dropped back to lean against the counter—where he'd been standing before all of this had started—and admire the view. Orange juice dripped from her bangs and face. It plastered her already clinging t-shirt tightly to her figure, now forming little more than a sheer overlay. Very admirable.

She reached down, pulling aside her shorts and shaking a leg. The slender ice chips that remained, shattered with soft pops as they hit the kitchen floor.

"You have no idea about paybacks, Mr. Slater." Jessica glared across the kitchen at him, "You have no idea at all...yet."

"Nope!" he agreed as pleasantly as possible. "No idea at all. But I can't wait to find out."

She headed toward him, her sneakers splashing a little on the few puddles of orange juice that hadn't soaked into their clothes. Jessica was moving like a cat on the prowl, swinging hips, eyes locked on his. He didn't know if he could move, but he didn't want to so it didn't matter; this was far too much fun.

But he wasn't paying close enough attention to what else was going on and realized it too late.

She leaned up against him and for a brief moment he once more tasted the orange juice on her lips. But before he could cradle her back against him, she was easing away.

Easing away and—

She'd grabbed his own glass of iced orange juice from where he'd set it on the counter behind him. She didn't trickle it atop his head this time…she dumped it! The cold was breathtaking.

He managed to grab her as she danced back—her bright laugh filling the room—but lost his balance, his sneakers turned to ice skates on the suddenly slick hardwood floor.

In moments he was down, but he didn't lose his grip…not until she landed atop him.

His breath escaped him in a whoosh as her hip crashed into his gut.

Straddled over him, she looked down at him with a puzzled expression.

Any thoughts about what it might mean were washed from his brain as she lay down upon him and kissed them away.

She was right. Paybacks were hell; his kind of hell.

ONCE THEY'D CLEANED up the kitchen, and they'd showered—separately—Jessica sent Greg trotting home in his rinsed-out clothes and squishy sneakers. He could have stayed in a towel while his clothes tumble-dried, but she didn't mention that option. He'd be right back, as she'd promised to make brunch for him, but she wasn't ready to face a naked Greg clothed only in a bath towel.

During the run, she'd worked on her mental man-list a bit. She wasn't an intentional tally-keeper and it definitely wasn't well thought out, but every now and then she'd run into something and add it to her list. Most items she learned about men landed solidly in her no-way-in-hell category. Some fell into her wouldn't-that-be-nice-even-if-she-was-never-gonna-find-it category. Very few items fell into the required category.

She started the bacon and scrounged some smoked salmon, then thin sliced a local white cheddar and found some crumbly gorgonzola to balance it.

Greg had added "fellow runner" to her preferred list. A good sense of humor had been on the required short-list since forever, but she nudged it up a few notches in his honor. And fun! When had she lost sight of the importance of fun? Dad had a decent sense of the ridiculous but Mom's first divorce had kicked the crap out of Jessica's taking joy in it. She couldn't remember the last time she'd had as much fun as wrestling with Greg among the orange juice. Had she ever? There was another thought she wasn't ready for.

Some flour tortillas and she mashed an avocado—making poor man's guacamole with a scoop of store-bought salsa and a sprinkle of cayenne.

Someone to hold her as if she was more special than she knew she actually was would be a great bonus. And the way that man could kiss...

"You're awfully intense when you cook."

Jessica yelped in surprise. Greg stood mere inches off her elbow.

"I like that in a woman." He looked just as good in jeans and a button-down shirt as he had in running shorts and a t-shirt.

"I bet you're one of those guys who likes anything that's female." She cracked four eggs into a bowl, added a splash of cream, some shaved cilantro, and salt and pepper, then began beating it while the pan heated.

"Give me some credit," Greg complained.

"Like what?"

"Well, having a preference for beautiful ones who are cooking for me. I'm a chef; cooking women are a major turn on."

Jessica dumped the beaten mixture into the pan and intentionally nearly rammed him with the fork and bowl as she turned to put it in the sink. She definitely needed a few more feet of space. Greg Slater *was* a major turn on, even if she didn't want him to be.

She stirred the eggs with a spatula, crumbling in the bacon and smoked salmon. It was going to end up tasting very smoky. Jessica spotted a lime in a bowl on the table and squeezed it to drizzle through her fingers to catch any seeds. Then she folded in the cheese. She zapped the tortillas for twenty seconds in the microwave, spread a line of guacamole then sour cream down their centers, and dumped the egg-cheese-salmon-bacon mixture in. With a quick flip it folded into a breakfast burrito.

She dropped a tub of yogurt and a bowl of blueberries on the breakfast nook counter that faced toward the woods then sat on one of the stools.

"Brunch!" She announced.

"Where's the orange juice?" Greg complained rather than complimenting her food.

"Careful, or you'll be wearing what little is left." She made a fake shudder, could still feel the stickiness that hadn't seemed to come out of her hair in the shower. "Not sure I could face it right now."

"Me either now that you mention it. Two glasses of milk coming up," he went to the refrigerator and served them both.

He bit down on the burrito and looked at her strangely.

"What? You're supposed to compliment your hostess' food, even when it doesn't deserve it. Where are you manners, Slater?"

"My manners—"

"Clearly don't include not talking with your mouth full."

"—are being blown away by your cooking. I figured you'd turned into some helpless city girl whose idea of cooking is choosing which takeout to get."

"Trust me, I wish I was. But I'm broke," and she sure as hell hadn't meant to let *that* slip out.

"I...hmmm," Greg thought while he chewed, thankfully swallowing before continuing. "Last night. You mentioned that, but it didn't make sense. I read your writing, you're really good. And you're in a half dozen markets which..." he tapered off and then concentrated on his breakfast burrito.

"You've read my writing."

He nodded.

"But I write mostly for the Chicago market."

He nodded again, spooning up a small bowl of yogurt and blueberries as if it was the most important thing in the world.

"The *Chicago Tribune* has a paywall."

"Maybe I subscribe," he was adding more yogurt, building such a mound that she finally stopped him by resting her hand on his.

He froze in mid-scoop, but his hands were warm and strong beneath her fingertips. She pulled back but the sensation didn't go away.

"Maybe I subscribe to every market that an online search turns up with you in it." He dished half of what he'd served himself over into her bowl.

Jessica rested her chin on her palm and her elbow on the counter. It put her closer to Greg than she'd anticipated, but she felt no need to pull back. "I'm going to repeat a question, but try not to be mad."

He shrugged an easy acceptance.

"What the hell, Slater?"

"I know," at least he had the decency to grimace. "Kind of cyber-stalkerish."

"Kind of," she was torn between agreeing and being touched.

"It's become almost a joke, a joke on myself. Look, Jessica," he turned those dark brown eyes on her, "I know I'm an odd person. I know that I'm at least as bizarre as Vincent or Dawn or the twins will be some day. I'm holding a torch for someone I never expected to see again. And all those fantasies?"

"What?" she asked despite her better instincts.

"They aren't a touch on the real woman who can write the way you do, cook a damn fine breakfast burrito, or feel so amazing in my arms." No matter how odd he might have thought he was, Greg didn't look aside for a single moment of his confession.

Jessica knew it was a mistake even as she reached out to take his hand.

"I'm implying nothing beyond now," she managed a whisper.

His brow furrowed briefly as she rose and gently tugged him to his feet. Feeling more overeager seventeen than her usual coastal twelve or Chicagoan thirty-two, she led him away from their half-eaten meal and up the carpeted, creaking stairs. She closed and latched the door behind them.

Jessica ignored Xena the Warrior Princess' smile of approval from her place on the back of the door.

When Greg laid her down on the bed, the only sound in the room was the ocean surf moving the sand infinitely back and forth far below the open window streaming with sunlight. Sometimes clichés—something she assiduously avoided in her writing—had their place. Jessica decided this was one of those as she gave herself to the moment.

CHAPTER 5

"Well," Jessica's voice was pleasantly husky and smooth as a slow-pouring honey, "that was fun."

Fun? "Sure was." She was the queen of understatement.

Greg now knew what heaven felt like. It felt exactly like this. The warm ocean breeze rippling over the woman wrapped against him. Only a thin sheet and a glow of well-earned satisfaction covered them. If kissing Jessica while swimming in orange juice had been merely wonderful, making love to her had been fantastic. It hadn't been a merry wrestle like the kitchen. Instead it had been a surprisingly tender voyage of discovery.

Not that there was a coy bone in her body. She'd given herself thoroughly, abandoning herself to the act. He had done his best to return the favor and between them there hadn't been a single word, but there'd been no mistaking the shudders of pleasure that had shaken both of them. His pulse had long since recovered, but his head was still spinning pleasantly at the wonder of it all.

Her fingers traced lightly back and forth over his chest and he allowed his own fingertips to linger on her arm. This he could get used to, very used to. And one way to make sure that happened, was by being considerate.

"We need calories. Someone, brilliantly I might add, interrupted our breakfast. I'm feeling seriously depleted." She slid a hand down and cupped him, it elicited only a marginal external response, though it made his breath catch and his eyes would have crossed had they been open.

"Uh-huh," was her only observation.

"So," he managed, "I shall sally forth and recover the rest of our breakfast."

"Sally? Like in a shining knight?"

"*C'est moi!* Breakfast in bed sound good?"

"Mmm," she agreed, but she didn't release him. Instead she burrowed her face into his chest and they started all over again. Thank god he'd taken the risk and brought a strip of protection back with him. Next time he's bring several strips, long ones.

When they were finally finished, again, she lay back and groaned. "Food. I need food."

Food? He lay fully upon her with his face buried in the pillow beside her head. He needed to never move again. *And what kind of a shining knight does that make you?*

He forced himself to action until he was standing, a feat he'd thought beyond him. Reluctantly, he pulled the sheet over Jessica, but her soft sigh made him feel noble and he'd return in moments.

Jessica did manage to force an eye open to watch Greg's naked behind heading out the door. It was a very nice one that went just fine with the rest of his body. The muscles she'd dug her hands into as she'd struggled to pull him closer, gave way to a strong back and nice shoulders. They weren't broad and powerful, they were just very, very nice.

No, the powerful part of Greg Slater was his hands. They had the finesse of a chef and the strength of one as well. He'd found ways to make her—

She heard a microwave cycle on in the distance.

He was even reheating their breakfast.

Then in quick succession she heard: the slap of the screen door, a very male yelp, and feet pounding up the stairs.

Greg burst through the door in a state of wild panic, slammed it behind him, and leaned back against it. Xena looked over his shoulder, apparently approving of this as well. Greg now offered her a very nice chance to admire the front view, if she hadn't been laughing quite so hard.

"Who?" She choked out.

His eyes merely bulged in panic.

He spotted his clothes and dove for them as somewhere in the background a microwave beeped four times calling for attention.

He was mostly dressed by the time steps sounded up the stairs.

At the soft knock, he grabbed a stray sock, one of hers, and bolted into the bathroom.

"Yes?" Jessica managed to call out without choking herself. She sat up and pulled the sheet up under her arms so that she was decent.

"I was coming by to see if you wanted to go out for lunch, dear." Her mother spoke through the still-closed door. "Apparently not. But someone left your tray in the kitchen, dear. I brought it up for you."

"Come on in."

There was a brief hesitation before she did. After a quick glance around the room she smiled, a little more wickedly than Jessica would have credited Monica Baxter being capable of.

Jessica pointed at the bathroom door, and Mom's smile only grew bigger. She didn't react at all to Jessica's complete *dishabille* nor the stray clothes scattered across the floor that showed she had been a little distracted by other concerns on her arrival.

Her mother set the tray on Natalya's bed, winked, and headed back out the door.

Jessica really needed to rethink her relationship with Mom. No lectures. No scowl. Quite the opposite in fact.

With the door almost closed, she stuck her head back into the room and called out, "It's safe to come out now, Greg."

"Thank you, Mrs. Baxter," sounded through the bathroom door.

Then she was gone. Jessica could get to really like her mom in addition to loving her. To avoid laughing again at poor Greg, Jessica reached out and snagged her burrito. She had time for several bites and some leisurely chewing before a very red-faced Greg Slater emerged from his bolthole.

"Some shining knight you are." He still held her sock.

"Give me a break, Baxter," he sat on Natalya's bed and picked up his own burrito, still uncertain quite what to do with the sock in his other hand.

"Of course, you did moon my mom," hopefully he'd been facing the microwave which was on the opposite side of the kitchen from the door. "I suppose that counts for something." Jessica didn't like the fact that she didn't like Greg sitting so far away, as if two feet of difference should matter. Normally she liked her men to keep their distance; it made casual sex so much more…casual.

"I'd rather face a dragon," he mumbled as he bit down on his reheated breakfast.

"I'll find one for you. Now come back to bed."

He eyed the closed door over his shoulder, then shook his head.

Jessica released the sheet from under her arms and let it slide back down into her lap.

Greg's eyes widened, without even tracking down. Then he smiled, tossed her sock over his shoulder and, taking one last bite of his burrito, began undressing all over again.

Gods but there were times she loved men.

CHAPTER 6

(SUNDAY NIGHT)

Greg sat in the Baxter's kitchen, as modern as the Lamont B&B's was classic. It was also one of the most efficient layouts he'd ever seen in a home kitchen, clearly Ralph Baxter's doing. However, Ralph wasn't here at the moment and Mrs. Baxter was making his head spin almost as badly as her daughter did.

For the last day and a half, he and Jessica had rarely been more than an arm's length apart. And now, when he could really use her help, she and Natalya had gone off to do "girl things." They'd actually said it that way, "Girl things." What the hell were those? Well, the itch between his shoulder blades told him the topic of their conversation even if he didn't know where they were or what they were doing.

Instead he was sitting with Monica Baxter, her sister Gina Lamont, and a moderately battered yellow pad on which he'd been scribbling down menu ideas for next weekend's wedding.

Page one through four had been the seafood draft. The three of them had worked out the details of the courses and the flavor progression, shifting dishes to match the bride's tastes and her sister's practical bent from running the Lamont B&B.

Then Ralph Baxter had wandered through with a set of socket wrenches in his hands. Just in passing he'd remarked, "Be nice if it wasn't fish. Spend all the damn day out on the boat with fish." And he'd been gone again.

Greg had sighed and folded the pages under, starting again with a French menu.

They were most of the way through when Ralph Baxter came back in carrying about a third of an outboard engine.

"Not on my kitchen table, Ralph Baxter," Mrs. Baxter declared moments before greasy machinery met bright oak.

"Not your table until you marry me again, honey, but I take your point. Wasn't thinking. I'll get some newspaper and do it in the living room." Then he glanced over Greg's shoulder.

Greg gave him long enough to absorb the first page, then flipped to the second one. He didn't have a chance to turn any of the next four pages before Ralph spoke again.

"Thought you wanted something light, honey. That's some serious cuisine Greg's got going there." And he lugged the engine through the arch into the living room. His fiancé scrambled to her feet and after grabbing a garbage bag and a couple of issues of the Newport newspaper—at a few dozen pages it was the thickest one on the coast—raced after her husband.

"That man," she sighed as she returned to the kitchen.

Taking his cue, Greg folded the pages of the French menu under. Well, at least he had some good ideas for the next couple Irregular Fridays at The Puffin.

"Mediterranean?" he suggested.

Gina Lamont's eyes shifted from him, to her sister, to the bright tick-tick-tick sound of the socket wrench coming from the living room. "Yes, but Greg…if Ralph comes back in, don't let him see the menu."

Greg considered for a second, then scrawled a one-page menu in large letters before turning it for the sisters to see.

Burgers and beer!

They all shared a laugh, then he flipped the page over and started working on an Italian four-course meal. It pieced together quickly.

Jessica would like this meal. A Tuscan white bean soup, which was a little heavy for the season, but he could offset that with seasonal greens and a tomato base. A crab-artichoke ravioli would follow served with a side of arugula and a basil-infused vinaigrette.

He knew he was on a roll by how few additions Gina was making this time.

And then…

He pictured Jessica eating this meal. It would be delicate, light…it was a lover's meal. A meal he might spend a day making just for the two of them. Or perhaps a Couple's-only Night at The Puffin. It wasn't a meal of celebration, it was a meal of wooing and love.

It was an absolute certainty that's what was happening to him. Yes, his fantasies about her had been so wrong; Jessica Baxter was no longer eighteen and leaving for college. But the grown woman was a revelation of her own in attitude and style.

He'd enjoyed their quiet walks and talks on the beach as much as he had when they tumbled together and lost all of their words. He couldn't imagine ever getting tired of either side of Jessica.

"Greg?"

"Hmm? Oh," his attention slowly returned to the women planning a wedding celebration.

" 'Oh'?" Gina winked at her sister. "I know that look."

"Counting the days, Sister," Monica agreed.

Jessica had told him of her mother's peculiar no-sex-outside-of-marriage rule. She had scoffed, but Greg had rather liked it. While he wouldn't trade back a single second of the time he'd spent in Jessica's arms these last few days, a part of him wished that they had waited. Wouldn't that have been a glorious wedding night?

A true celebration.

A celebration.

He slowly flipped back a few pages to the note he'd scrawled pending Ralph Baxter's return to the room.

Burgers and Brew!

"The exclamation point says it all."

"What does it say?" Monica leaned in.

"A celebration," he looked up at her. "Which do you want, Mrs. Baxter? A lover's meal or a celebration?"

"Duh!" Gina chimed in. "Fourth time's the charm!"

Monica looked down at the three words in front of him for a long moment. And then she smiled a long, slow smile that her daughter had inherited straight down the matrilineal line and only used when she was particularly pleased with something.

He flipped to a fresh page and began writing and talking at the same time.

"Sage and rosemary Dungeness crab-stuffed mushrooms. Sliders of Marv's grass-fed beef with Eric's brie-and-bleu cheese melted in the center served between thin slices of baguette garlic toast—light on the garlic because it's a wedding. Maybe topped with a paper-thin slice of prosciutto. Tiny-potato, skin-on French fries with a balsamic-ketchup drizzle."

Greg could feel the excitement growing at the table.

This was how Jessica made him feel. He'd spent far too much of his life struggling to make fine food. Last Friday's halibut service had been the pinnacle of that progression. It had been true fine dining in a coastal diner.

But that's not who he was, or at least not all of it.

He was the man who could make Dawn laugh even in the moment when she was ready to execute Vincent. He loved teasing the twins until they were lost in fits of merry giggles. Entertaining the Judge's sleepy breakfast customers was always a bright start to his day.

"I love making her laugh." Then Greg froze. He hadn't meant to say that aloud. Especially not to Jessica's mother and aunt.

They were both looking at him with sympathy, but it was a male voice that spoke first.

"She needs that," Ralph Baxter, his hands smeared with grease, including a couple of stripes on his face, stood in the doorway to the living room. "Lord alone knows she had little enough training in doing that. Most serious girl there ever was. I was good in school, but I was never driven the way she is."

Greg pictured an orange-juice soaked woman laughing with

delight in the Lamont kitchen and wondered. It seemed such a natural part of her in that moment, but it was true that he hadn't seen much of that particular aspect of the woman before or since.

"I'll do what I can, Ralph."

"Easy enough to see that you love her as much as I love my gal," he stepped the rest of the way into the kitchen and leaned down to kiss Monica on top of the head. Then he checked the back of his knuckles before smoothing them down over her hair.

"You get grease in my hair, Ralph Baxter…" she left the threat hanging.

Ralph just grinned at him over Monica's head, still brushing her with the clean back of his hand.

Greg couldn't help but return his smile.

"I don't think he heard what you said," Gina told her sometimes brother-in-law. Her radiant smile left no doubt about what she was referring to.

She was wrong. Greg had heard it loud and clear.

Easy enough to see that you love her as much as I love my gal.

Greg just didn't see any point in arguing with the truth.

GIRL THINGS.

Today's girl things included going out to visit Becky Billings Blue-Bird Brewery and sample the beer; which had turned into sampling a lot of beer.

Bluebird had been Becky's nickname ever since Jessica had tagged her with it in kindergarten during a chorus practice. Bluebird could sing circles around the rest of them even at five. Jessica was quite proud that the nickname had stuck and been transferred into the company name. Becky had grown up to be one of those women who made short and curvy look like a serious amount of fun. Her thick brown hair fell straight down past her shoulders and the top of her head barely matched Jessica's chin. She was also strong from physical labor and it showed in all the best ways.

"I'm selling from Tillamook to Coos Bay and I just opened into Eugene. Time to hire some help I guess."

"Make sure he's a cute one," Natalya chimed in.

Jessica nodded her agreement and then wished she'd been a little less emphatic in doing so. Becky's brewery swirled and wobbled for a moment after she stopped moving her head. The big steel tanks and pipes visible through the large window behind the tasting bar were momentarily unstable.

The tasting room itself was rustically elegant. When Becky's dad retired, she'd sold the cattle to a farmer up near the Tillamook Cheese Factory, rented out most of the fields for hay, and converted the barn to her one true love, the brewing of beer. She'd started with root beer in junior high and never looked back. The tasting room itself had been the old calf barn—a friendly, cozy space. Remnants of stalls along the back wall divided stacked cases of bottled beer into different sections, probably so they didn't fight with each other.

At the moment Jessica was too comfortable to watch beer bottles heaving caps at one another in pitched battle. She turned her attention back to the counter once more. It was lined with small glasses. They had been drinking four-ounce tasters; the problem was that Becky's beers were so...tasty.

Jessica started giggling.

"What?"

"We're testing Becky's tasty tiny tasters."

"You're drunk," Becky announced.

Jessica started to nod but thought better of it.

"She's also getting happy sex," Natalya told Becky. "As if she wasn't obnoxious enough to begin with."

"Excellent. Anyone we know?"

"Greg," Jessica battled with an incipient hiccup and won, "Slater."

"Oooo," Becky made it a long, salacious noise.

"It's not like that," Jessica protested and picked up a tiny glass of Hummingbird Ale—a bright, cheerfully fizzy beer.

"It's totally like that!" Natalya leaned against the bar a little harder. It was a classic long bar: heavy wood, a line of stools on her and

Natya's side, a row of taps on Becky's side, with the windows to the darkened brewery behind. The room was dim and quiet on a Sunday evening, but it was easy to picture a party here—a crowd of happy tourists plucking cases of their favorite brew from the stacks scattered in their stalls. She resisted giggling at the on-going alliteration.

"Should have the wedding here," then maybe she'd spend it drunk and not have to face being second bridesmaid to her own mother. Aunt Gina had been the first bridesmaid every time. *Ha!* And she'd been there every time as well, even if the first time she'd been in her mother's womb instead of in a dress.

"Your wedding?"

Jessica scowled at Natalya, "No! Mom's. Duh! That's never going to happen with me."

"Not even to the handsome Greg Slater?"

"Not even."

"She's just using him for sex," Natalya confided somewhere in Becky's direction. Her words were slurring as well and she looked distinctly blurry.

"It shows," Becky agreed.

"What shows?"

Neither of them answered her. Instead they both gave her "significant" looks. She wasn't that drunk.

"Nuh-uh! Nothing different about this girl, nothing changed by Greg or his hot body."

"I knew it!" Natalya crowed.

"Don't care what you *know*," Jessica tried to make little air quotes with her fingers but ended up with something closer to air Cheerios. Or perhaps air Fruit Loops. "Marriage is not something you'll ever catch this girl doing."

Again the two "significant" looks.

"It's not like marriage means anything." Nothing but layers of paper stuck to the breezeway door. Divorce, marriage, what was the difference? "Not a thing," she insisted.

She rested her chin on her crossed arms and stared at the mug that Becky set inches from her nose.

"What's that?" It was dark. And it was steaming. "Are you trying to serve me hot beer? That's disgusting, Bluebird Becky B."

"Nope, it's coffee."

Jessica burped, keeping it as soft as she could. "Rather it was beer."

"She'd rather it was Greg Slater," Natalya stated like some goddamn know-it-all.

"And who is getting into *your* knickers, Natya?" It was the best retaliation she had at the moment. It didn't help that her best friend was right. Greg was acting like a drug on her system, one that there was no way to get enough of and she didn't like that at all.

"Knickers. Getting awfully arcane there, Baxter." Then Natalya sighed sadly. "No one is getting in them at the moment."

"I know the feeling," Becky's sigh matched Natalya's.

The perfect chance for revenge, "Greg is getting into mine every chance he has." She resisted adding a *Nyah, nyah, nyah!*

"We already know that," Becky growled.

Aw, what the hell. She gave them her best, "Nyah! Nyah! Nyah!"

"Maybe we should steal him from her. I don't think she appreciates what she has."

"Sure, Natya. Fine. Whatever," Jessica would have waved a dismissive hand, but her head felt too heavy to raise off her arms. She settled for a finger flick like brushing away dust, but no one saw that because she did it on the wrong side. That was the problem with crossed arms, it made everything confusing—like she didn't have enough of that already.

Except she didn't like the idea of giving up Greg. Not even a little. She...liked Greg. Not just in bed either, where he was proving to possess an endless amount of resourcefulness and creativity with a very nice helping of stamina when it really counted. She really did like Greg out of bed a lot. She actually could picture him more easily with his clothes on and a laugh on his lips than she could naked with her against his lips.

There were times she could imagine being with him for more than her eight days in Eagle Cove—

Whoa! Not a chance that was going to happen! She shook it off.

She needed to make sure that didn't happen because it just wouldn't do. Her life was enough of a mess right now. Between her career, her mother's wedding, her return to Eagle Cove...Greg was definitely one too many things to deal with.

She squinted to focus her eyes on Becky and Natalya. They were reminiscing about some of their high school sweethearts. There was laughter and lightness. She felt like an orange-juice soaked rag: damp and starting to smell a little...off. They were clean and fresh because they were unencumbered. But she was trapped between great sex with a nice guy versus some chance of dealing with everything else going on in her life. It was a tough choice, but she knew what she had to do. Time to take action.

Jessica pushed herself upright, shoved aside the coffee, and knocked back a four-ounce tiny taster of Strawberry Stout. Fumbling out her cell phone, she was surprised to find Greg had been added to her contact list. When had that happened? How was he suddenly so far into her life?

She punched the "call" icon on her third try.

It was ringing.

"Hello there, pretty lady," Greg's voice was warm, smooth, an intimate caress.

"Hi, honey," her mom called from somewhere in the background. Okay, so much for the intimacy of their moment.

"Hi, Greg."

Natalya and Becky, caught in mid-sentence, both turned to look at her.

"We're just sitting here and planning the wedding dinner. What can I do for you?" There was something funny in his tone.

"You aren't talking about the wedding. You're talking about me," Jessica could feel the blood rushing from her brain to heat her face.

"Guilty."

"With my mother!" The horror of it rose up and tried to choke her.

"And your aunt and father."

Jessica couldn't breathe. Her heart was racing faster and faster. Just her and Greg she could deal with. Adding on Natalya's and Becky's teasing only made it feel like old home week; they were her inner circle ever since preschool days.

Her parents and aunt took the story to a whole other level. She didn't need to be an interview journalist to know where this was heading and it was scaring the crap out of her. *A good journalist never shows their emotion, but instead reflects the emotion that will lead the interviewee to say more.*

"Are you still there?" Greg's question told her that she was blowing this.

"Uh-huh," was the best response she could dredge up despite her vaunted emotional control.

"Is there a reason you called?"

"I called?" Oh, right. *She* had called *him.* To…oh!… "Yes," she tried to clear her throat and instead the hiccup she'd fought down before snuck back up. "I—"

I what…?

"I just wanted to tell you…" There had been a reason she'd felt the urgent need to call Greg right away. It was… "that we're through." Natalya and Becky gasped in surprise. "It's been great fun, Greg. But enough is enough. Let's not sp—" the hiccup finally escaped in a cliché-sized *Hic!* "—oil it. Great se—*hex.* Se-*hex* has been great. Was great. One of those things. Thanks. Bye."

She ended the call even as Greg shouted something in a panicked tone. Jessica looked around the bar top for something to celebrate with.

The phone in her hand rang and vibrated almost making her drop it.

Greg.

She stared at the display through three rings until she could be sure that she was hitting the off button rather than the answer one. For good measure, she turned the phone off and dropped it on the bar. Then she found another tiny glass of she couldn't tell which beer. At least it wasn't black and steaming.

Jessica raised it in a toast to her friends, "Too free-*he*-dom!" Free-he-dom! Perfect! She'd drink to that.

When it didn't look like they were going to join in, she downed the beer in two swallows and thunked the glass back on the wooden bar top.

"I forgot," Becky studied her, "that you're the stupid drunk of this crowd. Thank god I'm the happy one."

"Stupid?" Natalya was practically yelling. "Idiotic!" She'd always been the rational drunk—which really shouldn't be allowed when drinking was going on.

"Shush!" Jessica waved a hand for them both to calm down. "It makesh per-*her*-fect sense," which was almost as good as Free-*he*-dom. "Though I will mi-*hish* that body. Did I tell you that Greg Sl-*hate*-ter has a wonderful body?"

"We don't want to hear it," Natalya groaned.

"Knows just what to do-*hoo* with it too."

"I'm going to call Greg back and you're going to apologize."

"Don't you dare!" Jessica clutched her shut-off phone to her chest and hoped that Natalya didn't have his number.

"I want to hear about his body," Becky protested. "Give us all of the details. Now that you've dumped him and are in the no-guy zone with the rest of us, we should at least get some fun details."

Dumped him? Had she just dumped him…right, she had.

It was all for the best.

Too bad it felt like the worst. Which was fine. Everything else in her life was feeling that way too and now Greg fit right in.

For lack of anywhere better to be, Greg had spent the evening and well into the night sitting quietly on the front porch of the half-filled Lamont B&B. As it was obvious over the phone that Jessica was drunk, or well on her way there, he'd scouted around town. But Jessica wasn't at the Bobbin' Red Robin Tavern or the Brass Plover Pub. He'd even checked to see if she'd decided to party on the after-deck of her father's fishing boat. Greg ignored the fear as he rushed there that she'd had too much, fallen overboard in the middle of their conversation, and been washed out with the tide, because that was just a little too psychotic even for him. The boat rested dark and quiet at dock.

Natalya was also nowhere to be found which made him feel a little better. It was always better to go on a bender with a friend.

Imagining Jessica drunk had passed some of the time. Was she a giggler? Hard to imagine. Thankfully, Jessica as a morose drunk was even harder to picture—though he'd met plenty of those back in his restaurant days; that type was practically epidemic in professional kitchens.

He checked his watch. Two a.m. He had to get up in three hours to help the Judge with breakfast service, but he knew there was no sleep waiting for him if he gave up his vigil.

There was an honesty to the occasional drunk that worried him. Chronic drunks were often chronic liars—first of all to themselves. But the occasional drunk would lose their inhibitions and say things they never should have said in the first place no matter how true they were—a problem Greg had thoroughly demonstrated a few times in high school. That was how Vincent knew about the true depths of Greg's infatuation with Jessica Baxter.

Well, he was stone cold sober—and fairly cold as well sitting out here on the porch all night, waiting for a crazy woman who had broken up with him over the phone.

It couldn't be real. It just couldn't. He wouldn't let it be. He'd never fought for a woman before, but this time he'd—

A brightness filtered into the trees. He double-checked his watch, 2:03 (three whole minutes later than the last time he'd checked). So, it wasn't sunrise.

The light flickered and brightened: car headlights approaching from a distance, stray beams scattering through the trees. It took a curiously long time for the car to appear. When it finally did, he understood why. It was moving very slowly. Becky Billings' van finally crunched to a stop on the gravel driveway close beside the front steps. Damn it! He'd never thought of going out to Becky's brewery.

Greg scrambled down the stairs.

The passenger door opened and Natalya climbed out.

Before he could do anything about it, Natalya stepped into his arms, gave him a very sound kiss, and then snuggled up against him.

"Hmmm," she let out a long hum of delight that he could feel rippling down her body. "Jess is right. You have a very nice body, Mr. Slater." She squirmed more tightly against him and giggled at his body's reaction. She was warm, soft, and clearly quite drunk.

"Keep your voice down, lots of people are sleeping here. Uh, where's Jessica?"

"Spoilsport," Natalya mumbled but didn't move away.

For lack of any better tactic, he scooped her up into his arms, her head never moving from his shoulder.

Becky had climbed out of the driver's side. "Has she passed out yet?" Her speech wasn't exactly clear either which explained the painfully slow and careful driving.

"Close enough," Greg traded smiles with her. But awake enough to supercharge his body. "Where's the other one?"

"She's out cold," Becky hooked a thumb toward the back of the van. "I'll watch over her while you dump Natalya in bed."

Greg nodded and entered the B&B as quietly as he could. The main staircase was barely wide enough and each creak had him wincing, but by twisting sideways at the turns, he managed to carry Natalya up to her room. He lay her on the bed and pulled off only her shoes before covering her. Undressing a beautiful drunken woman was not going to be on the list of things he'd done this night and would have to explain in the morning.

He went back down and circled to the rear of the van. Becky had the door open and a dome light revealed Jessica sprawled on a horse blanket. She wore a flirty summer dress, that had ridden very high up her legs.

"She was very emphatic about us not calling you," Becky cracked a smile that made him feel better than anything else had this evening. "Sorry about that."

"It's okay."

Becky turned and sat on the edge of the van's deck, facing the night.

As there was no way to move the sleeping Jessica while Becky sat there, Greg turned and sat beside her, shoulder to shoulder. Actually, she was short enough that it was more his shoulder to her ear. They remained there a long time before Becky spoke.

"She's very fond of you, Greg."

"Thank god." He'd prefer more than fond, but after all of his worries this night he'd take any tidbit he was offered.

"More than that…"

"Double thank god."

"…but she's got some shit going on. Not my place to say, not that she said all that much. Jess always did play her cards close. But you and I go back a ways and I want you to know that I'm rooting for you."

"You always were a good friend." And she had been. He ran a hand down her back and kissed her atop the head. They'd dated for a few months when he'd first returned to Eagle Cove. It had been fun, but it hadn't turned into anything serious. She'd become a good friend since, one he counted on for far more than her fine hand at brewing.

"We talked a lot and some things are obvious—at least to Natalya and I if not to Jessica. So, I'm going to say this with the love I have for both of you: don't let her slip away. She's going to try very, very hard. Don't let her, Greg."

"I won't." Not a chance. No one knew about the patience and tenacity necessary to achieve a goal like being a chef.

Becky looked up at him.

"What?"

"I've had just enough to drink to say this. There are times I wish things had worked out between us. Even back three years ago you were something; you're way better now. Don't get all cocky, but don't forget it either." Then she pulled his head down and gave him a long, hard kiss. It was enough to remember all of the things that had been good between them without interfering with what was amazing between he and Jessica.

There was a soft, "Hey!" from inside the van.

He could feel Becky's grin before she broke the kiss. "You said you dumped him and he's fair game now," she said to Jessica without releasing her arms from around his neck.

"Oh. Right. Sure. Go ahead," each word from Jessica slid closer and closer to a sleepy mumble.

He and Becky both turned in time to see her once again collapse into sleep.

"It's a good thing that I love her so much, Greg Slater, or you wouldn't stand a chance."

"Woman as good as you, maybe I wouldn't want one." And while he knew it wasn't quite true for either of them, it would have been nice if it had been.

She pecked him lightly on the lips before letting go, "Let's get your girlfriend out of my van. What you do with her after that is up to you."

He held her in place a moment longer. "Whatever man you end up with Becky, if he forgets for a moment how goddamn lucky he is, just let me know. I'll come over and pound some sense into his thick skull."

Becky giggled, "Very kind, Mr. Slater. And an absurdly male offer."

He shrugged; it probably was.

"Besides, can you see me needing help to drive common sense into a man's head?"

"Nope, I bet you can handle that just fine, but my 'absurdly male' offer stands." Then they stood and he scooped Jessica into his arms. Unlike Natalya who'd been all clingy and sexy, Jessica was as lively as a sack of potatoes.

"Lucky bitch," Becky whispered in her friend's ear and then kissed her on the temple. "Shoo! I've got to get home to my cold and lonely bed." And she was creeping the van out the driveway before Greg reached the porch.

He was half tempted to carry Jessica back to his house; it was just the next one toward town on LBB Lane. At least there he could curl up against her for a few hours before he had to go to work. But that probably wasn't the best choice. First, she'd probably wake alone while he was at work. Also, ultimately, he had to straighten out the fact that she'd broken up with him before he made any assumptions.

Greg crept up the stairs and lay Jessica on the bed. He removed her shoes and did his best not to think about how cute she looked in the flowered summer dress by what moonlight was wandering in the window. Maybe she'd wear it for him to dinner one night and he could take it off her then. Actually, there were liberties he was willing to take with her for her comfort that he wasn't willing to do for Natalya.

He slipped off the dress, doing his best not to admire the body he was only starting to learn about. He could spend a lifetime exploring it and never be bored. Again, all she wore beneath the dress were panties—these were covered in cheery miniature sunflowers. He turned to dig in the dresser for a nightshirt, then thought better of it. The woman might be fussy about a man digging through her underthings.

Then he had an idea. Greg peeled off his own t-shirt, slipped it over Jessica's head, worked her limp arms through armholes, and tucked her under the covers. There was a brief reaction to his goodnight kiss, but brief was the key word there; a pleased hum in the back of her throat and then a slide back into drunken sleep.

Natalya hadn't wiggled so much as a finger since he'd tucked her under.

He turned out the light and crept out of the house. Without his shirt, it was a cold trot home, but it would be totally worth it.

Greg just wished that he could be there to see her face when she did wake up.

CHAPTER 7

(MONDAY)

A pillow slapped into Jessica's face and her headache exploded to life.

"What the hell?" She barely managed to fend off the next blow.

"You're such a bitch," Natalya dropped the pillow back on her bed with a thump and groaned.

"Why am I a bitch?" Jessica managed to crack open one eye to look at her cousin sitting on the edge of her bed with her head hanging down in her hands.

"First, you break up with Greg."

Oh crap! She had, hadn't she.

"Do you really still think that was smart?"

She did. She didn't have to like it, but it was the right choice. He was being an Eagle Cove chef and she was returning to Chicago in just five days. Everything was getting too close and intense when she already knew how it was going to end.

"Second, you just *had* to tell us quite how amazing he is in bed."

"I didn't," please tell her she hadn't. But Jessica could remember snippets of doing just that. She pulled her own pillow over her face to hide her embarrassment. "I did," she mumbled into its depths.

"You did. In thoroughly decadent detail and we were drunk

enough to listen," Natalya's voice shuddered as if she'd never purge the images. "And then third, the part that makes you a total bitch, you got all drunk and miserable and sad like the little puppy dog you are. That made me feel as if someone should keep you company with your drinking." Natalya groaned again. "How was I supposed to know just how much you'd drink?"

The way Jessica's head felt, she'd didn't want to know the answer to that question. She raised a corner of her pillow and caught sight of Sigourney Weaver aiming a massive rifle at a slobbering alien. She looked ready to conquer the universe and Jessica doubted she could conquer a piece of toast at the moment.

Natalya flopped back onto her mattress, "I swear, cousin or not, I'm going to kill you if I ever recover." She still wore the clothes she'd had on last night, though they were now much the worse for wear from sleeping in them.

"Um," the last thing she really remembered was Becky's tasting bar and a shockingly long line of small but very empty glasses. "How did we get here?"

"Don't know," Natalya flopped back on her bed and dragged her own pillow back over her face to shield against the sunlight slipping through the *Harry Potter* curtains featuring a very ticked off Hermione Granger wielding her shining wand.

Maybe she knew a magic spell for hangovers. *Curiatus!* No, that was too much like the *cruciatus* curse presently throttling her skull from the inside.

"I remember kissing someone," Natalya posed it as half statement, half question.

"It wasn't me, was it?"

"No. Male. Very male. Good kisser too."

"I'm a good kisser, too," though why she was arguing about it was beyond her. "But I'm not male." Jessica didn't remember kissing anyone. She wished that she had. Someone who could help her purge Greg Slater from her system. Even thinking of him made her feel all mushy inside and that absolutely would not do.

There was a soft knock on the door.

"Go away. There's no one alive in here," Jessica called out then really wished she hadn't as her headache explored previously undiscovered levels of awfulitude.

"I have coffee and hot chocolate," a male voice answered through the door.

"Coffee!" Natalya moaned from beneath her pillow.

Hot chocolate. Right at the moment, she would kill for some.

"And aspirin," the muffled voice called out again.

"Ohh!" Natalya moaned with delight.

"Enter oh god of the day," Jessica called out. "Just do it softly."

It wasn't until he was opening the door that Jessica realized who the voice belonged to. She really didn't want to see Greg, especially not after breaking up with him over the phone—a rather abrupt pronouncement that had not been kind. But it was too late on both accounts: the breakup and the permission to enter. He was already through the door, smiling in at them.

"It is noon. I thought you might want to get up."

Natalya still mumbled from beneath her pillow. "Noon. Sun at brightest. Must hide."

"Cof-fee," Greg teased and Natalya emerged slowly and took the mug Greg was holding out.

Jessica continued to watch him with the one eye she'd uncovered. She'd rather hide, but she did enjoy looking at him.

"Here," he held out a mug of steaming hot chocolate with a dozen tiny marshmallows bobbing merrily on the surface.

Her father had told his little girl that marshmallows were signs of pirate treasure lying below the surface and each must be swallowed up to reach the prize. She'd always drunk her cocoa that way ever since. He'd told the truth. At the bottom of every mug lurked a treasure of extra-rich chocolate that settled so warm in her stomach.

She struggled upright, shoving and pushing until she could lean against the headboard, a carved relief of King Kong. Natalya's was of Fay Wray, the woman who had brought about the downfall of the great beast. The carving was just deep enough to make a good backscratcher. Her nerve endings were universally fried and appreciated the gentle massage.

Greg was grinning at her as if she was naked and had once again just dropped the sheet to expose her breasts and entice him back into bed. But she wasn't. She was wearing a t-shirt, a nice roomy one that wouldn't show anything.

Natalya turned a bloodshot glance in her direction and then nearly snorted her coffee.

"What?" Jessica looked down. This wasn't one of her t-shirts. In fact, the last thing she remembered wearing was the dress presently spread over the back of a child-sized captain's chair that belonged on the bridge of a miniature *Enterprise*. No, *Star Trek Voyager*. Jessica recalled a stuffed Captain Janeway doll was perched in the seat, even though she was presently giving orders from behind flowered cotton.

It took Jessica a few tries to find the hem of the t-shirt and hold it out far enough that she could read it upside down.

All men are created equal...then the very best become chefs.

Greg's.

She pulled out the collar and peeked down her front. No bra, though she hadn't been wearing one with the dress either, so she couldn't really blame that on him. Her panties were still in place. Jessica looked back up at Greg's smiling face.

"Cad!" She put some heat behind it as a tease, but he took it seriously—a flash of pain that slid across his features then vanished. She didn't know quite how to take it back.

"Proud to be," his cheery response showed just how decent he was as he dug deep to offset Jessica-the-bitch.

Her alter ego mixed with her headache in a very not-cheery way.

Natalya looked down at her own rumpled blouse and skirt, "Not enough of a cad." She looked at Jessica, "Stingy of you not to share, Cousin."

Then a funny look crossed Greg's face and a blush. Jessica had never met a man who blushed so easily.

"I think, Cousin," Jessica called over to Natalya but didn't look away from Greg's dark eyes. "I think I have found the male who kissed you."

"Wha—" Natalya hesitated. "Hmm," a thoughtful sound. "Maybe."

"Actually she kissed me," Greg mumbled then smiled at Natalya. "Quite thoroughly."

Jessica winked at her cousin, "Told you he was a good kisser."

"Hmmm," this time there was more the sound of pleasure than thoughtfulness in Natalya's tone.

"Though," Jessica stirred up the best glare she could and aimed it at him, "I seem to recall you kissing Becky too. But not me."

"*You're* the one who broke up with *me.*"

And in that instant, even the marginal joy of teasing Natalya went out of the conversation.

She could see Greg's hurt at her reaction, but she couldn't hide it. Even in full journalist mode, Jessica could no longer hide what she was thinking from Greg—a skill that had served her well with previous lovers.

"Can we talk about this later?" She plucked at the t-shirt which suddenly felt so tight and constricting that it threatened to choke her. She couldn't seem to get any air.

He froze for a long moment, then spun to his feet and was almost out the door before she could think to call after him.

"Greg!"

"What?" It was more a snarl of pain than a question.

"I wasn't saying that to avoid talking about it. Just give me long enough to shower and change."

He didn't turn and his shoulders didn't relax as he remained braced in the doorway. "You aren't denying it either," his voice was rough.

She wasn't. "Please?"

And after another long moment, he growled, "I'll be on the beach." Then he was gone.

Natalya looked at her.

"No. I don't know what I'm doing," Jessica admitted. "I wouldn't mind some brilliant advice."

Natalya just shook her head. "Sorry, Cousin. I've got nothing this morning. You'd be better off asking one of them," she waved at the science fiction heroines who populated the room.

She looked at the triptych of framed posters hanging along the far wall: Katniss Everdeen of *The Hunger Games* and Neytiri in her *Avatar* blue separated by Natalie Portman as Isabel in *Your Highness*. All were pictured with bow and arrow fully drawn, their eyes clearly focused on the target. They were all such strong, fierce women. She was just a lonely struggling journalist. Not a lot of help there.

She hurried into the shower not sure how long Greg's patience would last. Jessica left the hot chocolate cooling on her nightstand, its marshmallows now melted into a congealed mess that was slowly sinking into the muddy liquid. No treasure there today.

GREG HAD SOMEHOW CONVINCED himself last night that Jessica hadn't really meant it, which only proved what an idiot he was. When he'd put his t-shirt on her last night, it *hadn't* been some attempt to mark his territory, conscious or otherwise.

And then he'd seen her final expression change. Jessica's face was such a subtle one. Like a great actress, there was no single identifiable change, yet her face had completely shifted without moving at all. It had happened while she was tugging at his t-shirt as if she was going to rip off the vile thing whether or not it would leave her naked.

What it all translated to was that she'd meant every word on the phone last night, drunk or not.

How had she greeted him with such seeming pleasure on his entrance this morning and then so cruelly dashed his hopes? He dropped onto the sand, scowled at some tourist's dog that came trotting over for a sniff, and barely resisted yelling at its owner for not keeping it to heel. The beach was dog heaven and they should run free here. There were waves to dive in, endless seagulls to chase but never catch, and high-lobbed tennis balls flicked from their owner's launchers to arc down the beach or out into the waves. But why should a goddamn dog be having such a good time when he was—

"Hi." Jessica came up beside him.

How deep was the black hole that he'd been moping in that she'd had time to clean up and come find him? A pretty deep one.

She shifted from bare foot to bare foot, but showed no signs of settling.

With a sigh he patted the sand beside him, "Sit down. I won't bite." Maybe if he'd been friendly with the dog, it might have bit her for him.

Jessica hesitated several very long moments before sitting. She wore a wide-brimmed straw hat with a blue strip of gauze tied about the crown; it fluttered in the soft breeze as if it was trying to reach out to him—the only part of her that was. She stared straight out to sea with her legs pulled up tight against her chest. She looked pale, even by her fair-skinned standards.

Much to his surprise, she was still wearing the oversized chef's shirt.

"Why don't you take that damn thing off?"

"I was going to. I did to shower. But I…" she inspected him closely from behind her dark shades, then shrugged when he gave no sign. "But I didn't want to."

"Whereas taking me off and casting me aside, that was as easy as a phone call." The depth of his anger surprised him. Last night he'd been planning Monica and Ralph Baxter's wedding, but without any realization on his part, he'd also been planning his and Jessica's at some unknown future date. He didn't notice that until it was taken away.

Shit!

He'd thought Vincent was the goofball, Dawn the smart one, and him somewhere safely toward the Dawn end of the spectrum. Turned out he was the idiot of the gang. Perfect!

"No," Jessica's soft voice barely intruded on his thoughts. "It wasn't easy. And the way I did it wasn't kind, but I still think it was kindness."

"You're going to have to explain that, Baxter. Use simple words.

I'm just a dumb chef, not some brilliant, straight-A school vale-dictorian."

She dug her fingers into the sand and let it trickle back through her fine fingers and dribble over her bare feet.

Fingers that could make him feel so—*Shut up, Slater!*

"Your infatuation with me—"

"I'm done with that, Jessica. I get it but I'm goddamn done with it! Now, I'm—" he bit down on his tongue to stop himself. He wasn't going to spread the carcass of his sad past out on the sand for the gulls to pick over.

"I was going to say that your infatuation with me ended up starting something wonderful."

So, shutting up had been a good choice. Would have been nice if he'd done it sooner, but it was too late to help that.

"This isn't about you. It's about me."

"That's a pretty damned pat answer. We are—were in a relation-ship. As in two people, not just you. How is it *not* about me?" His voice kept rising and he couldn't stop it. He also still couldn't bring himself to look at her.

"You're right. I'm sorry."

In his peripheral vision he could see her hand reaching out, but then she pulled it back.

"My life is in freefall. It's already more than I can deal with. You're wonderful, Greg. Really. I barely know you, but I strongly suspect that you may be the best man I've ever been with."

He liked the way "best" sounded. He badly wanted to be Jessica Baxter's "best." Greg dug up a fistful of sand himself, but when he started dribbling it out it immediately began filling his sneakers. Dusting off his hands only spilled sand into this pant cuffs. If that was "best," maybe she should keep looking.

"You're handsome, smart, and funny. You cook like a goddamn god and having sex with you is more fun than a girl could ask for. More than *I* ever thought to ask for." She said the last line more to herself than to him, but he couldn't leave it alone.

He reached out and took one of her hands. He wondered if

Natalya had alerted her mother and they were both atop the cliff looking down at them through binoculars. A glance down the beach revealed his father on one of his post-cooking constitutionals, but he was too far down the beach to matter. Tourists who hadn't brought picnics had headed into town for lunch, so this end of the beach was relatively quiet.

She was rubbing her thumb back and forth across the back of his knuckles, looking down at their joined hands so that her hat hid her face. He'd rather keep his mouth shut, which had been working well so far, but he had the feeling that if he didn't say something, Jessica might never speak again. He remembered what Becky had said last night, or rather this morning: *Don't let her slip away. She's going to try very, very hard. Don't let her, Greg.*

"Okay." If he didn't speak, he was afraid that neither of them would. "I'm going to steal a question from a very smart person."

He didn't continue until she looked up at him. He reached out and slipped off her sunglasses so that he could see her shaded eyes—those brilliant blue eyes that missed nothing, yet he had so enjoyed making sightless with passion.

"So, if this really isn't about me, then my question is this. What the hell, Baxter?"

JESSICA WANTED TO HIDE. She wanted her sunglasses back to hide her bloodshot eyes from the glaring sand. The typical bank of dense summer fog was lurking a few miles offshore, obscuring the horizon but leaving the beach bright and clear, so no help there either. She wanted to look away from the beautiful man whose brown eyes somehow saw past her defenses, yet didn't turn away from the mess that poured out of her. And most of all she didn't want him to stop holding her hand because it felt like the only thing that was keeping her from shattering into a thousand pieces.

"This is Monday, Greg. My parents' fourth wedding is on Saturday," as if there could be a more meaningless act. But, if it made them happy, more power to them. "On Sunday morning Natalya drops me at the Portland airport and I'll be in Chicago that night."

"Uh-huh."

She could use something more useful than a male grunt as a guidepost, but she guessed it was all the help she deserved at the moment.

"We had a couple of great days." A couple of utterly *amazing* days and a night in between them that she wouldn't forget for a long time.

The small guest house on the Judge's property where Greg lived was her idea of perfection. It was a grand Victorian shrunk to the perfect scale for a small family who thought that being in each other's way was a good thing. It was too easy to imagine such things when she was there. It was one of the reasons she'd scared up Natalya and gone to Becky's. Part of the reason had been to get the old gang back together, but part of it was so that she didn't crawl into that house with Greg Slater as if she'd never leave—when she knew full well that she would have to.

"I grew up with parents who were in love, but can barely tolerate living in the same house. Mom has this whole separate residence through that breezeway. When Dad started building it, it was supposed to be an office for her business on one side and a workshop for Dad on the other. His workshop became a bedroom, den, and kitchen as well—then Mom doesn't understand why his projects end up being done all over the house. And Dad built it for her as if it was okay that his wife didn't live with him part of the time. Or lived with him, but—" she didn't know what.

She struggled to her feet, couldn't tolerate sitting still any longer. Greg didn't let go of her hand and their connection pulled him to his feet as well. They began walking down the beach, like lovers holding hands, not like two people trying to resolve a fight before one of them left to never come back...and after the way this week was going, she was *never* coming back to Eagle Cove.

They walked down to the sand hard-packed by the retreating tide. It was the main thoroughfare up and down the beach. Sitting in the deep sand higher on the beach, they'd been left to themselves. Here they were having to constantly shift their path to avoid clumps of kelp, gaggles of children, and couples who actually might be lovers walking along together. The locals had all hit the beach hours ago, jogging or walking the sand while the tourists were still abed. Now it was midday and she didn't recognize anyone—not a soul to distract her from the hard task of explaining herself to Greg.

"I don't want that. I don't want marriage. I'm open to living with a guy, the right guy." She saw Greg's questioning glance. "My roommate is single and straight. *She* has a cat. I've never had a male *roommate.*"

"I've had female roommates," a fact that Jessica wished he'd kept to himself. "But that's all they were. We were broke sous chefs trying to make ends meet while we served our time as kitchen slaves."

"But when does it end? The kitchen slave part of it." She'd served her time. And her career was more down the hole than it had been five years earlier.

"You always keep learning."

She got that.

"But your industry is getting kicked out from under you," Greg added before she could say something nasty.

"I seem to have noticed that. No suggestions for the sad journalist with a blistering hangover who just kicked a handsome good guy out of her bed?"

He gave her the laugh she'd been looking for and she felt better. "Not a thing."

"Thanks a bunch."

"But I'll give it some thought."

Jessica stopped and squinted at Greg. He actually would give it thought. "I was right. You *are* a good man, Greg Slater."

"Shh!" he glanced up and down the beach quickly. "It's my first time and now you're going to jinx me."

She couldn't help herself, she kissed him.

It was supposed to be a friendly peck of thanks, but somehow she melted back against him. Wrapped her arms around him hard and held on as if she were clinging for dear life.

When at some point—maybe after the tide had turned or the world had spun on its axis a few times or something—she was no longer kissing him but instead lay against him with her head upon his shoulder, she knew she wasn't going to stay away from him while she remained in Eagle Cove.

"If this is how you do it," Greg nuzzled her ear as he spoke, "let me just say that you're really lousy at this whole breaking up thing. I'm liking your way of making it up though."

"You're a guy. You just want make-up sex."

"I *am* a guy, so of course I do. Doesn't mean I'm crass enough to ask for it though. Especially not with the shape you're in."

"What's wrong with my shape?"

And he groaned at the trap he'd just sprung but just held her tighter. Jessica lay against Greg's chest for another timeless amount of time. It was a place she didn't have to think, could just be. People wandered by. Some laughing, some chatting. A pair of surfers went by in dripping wetsuits from tackling the short, hard surf just out from the long facade of The Sleepy Owl Hotel. One of them said, "Get a room, you two," as he walked by.

Jessica could think of many things she should do. Go spend some time with Mom or Dad. Catch up with friends she hadn't seen in years and might never again. Get online and see if there were any developing long-lead stories that she could do research on and maybe track down a few inside contacts before she got back. But they would all require that she let go of Greg and she didn't like the idea of that. Not at all.

Get a room had stuck in her head.

They hadn't walked all that far past Greg's house.

"I could maybe be talked into a little make-up sex."

"You're joking," Greg made it a statement.

But… "Actually, I wasn't."

"But that means…what?" Greg didn't pull her away from his chest to look at her, but instead just kept holding her as if this was the normal state of being for them.

Jessica gave it some thought and finally had to admit, "I don't know. I'm lost here. I broke up with you and I wish I hadn't, but I don't know what that means either. However, having make-up sex sounds better than not having it and it's all I have to go on."

"That almost made sense," Greg teased her a little before his tone went more serious. "You scared the crap out of me, Jessica."

She nodded against his shoulder, "I know. I'm sorry. Scared myself too." Scared at just how deep her attachment to Greg had become and how quickly.

"So, no-commitment make-up sex?"

Against she nodded, hoping it was the right choice. "You'll have to be gentle though, I feel as if bits and pieces of me are constantly on the verge of passing out again."

"I'll be very gentle."

And he was. He was very gentle…and *very* thorough. And for one of the first times in her life, Jessica did nothing but lie on his bed and let the sun shining in over the ocean wash across her as a man made her feel utterly amazing.

CHAPTER 8

"*S*he emerges."

"Eat shit, Natalya." Okay, maybe she had lost Monday afternoon to Greg making lovely sex with her. And maybe, after they'd both slept for a while, she'd spent a fair portion of the night doing her best to give back as good as she'd gotten.

And maybe there'd been a quick round of wake-up sex during breakfast—kitchens seemed to fire up Greg's imagination; *hello, he's a chef. no big surprise.* It had made an incredible finish to the make-up sex. And she was going to pretend that it wasn't only people who were dating or were couples who had make-up sex. After he headed to the restaurant, she'd slept another few hours. They hadn't spoken, not much. Which was just as well because as good as her body felt, her brain was still mostly mush.

"Let's see," Natalya took a piece of paper off the nightstand. "Your mom won the pool."

"What pool?" Jessica started digging in the drawers for a fresh t-shirt. All Greg had were chef ones and for some reason she'd ended up wearing the fuzzy face of the Muppet's Swedish Chef declaring "Kiss the Chef!" Jessica had kissed Greg—very much had—which made it seem appropriate when she had pulled it on. But now it conveyed a degree of coupleness that was uncomfortable with. She felt like a story element out of its proper context.

"Well, you didn't give us time to make a pool on how long until you got back together. Instead we took bets on how long your make-up sex would last."

Jessica stopped with a t-shirt in her hands that said: *I'm a journalist! To save time let's just assume that I'm never wrong.* She shoved that one hard into the bottom of the drawer and found an old Northwestern University t-shirt to wear instead. Once properly protected from complete ridicule by being clothed as herself once more, she turned back to face her grinning cousin.

"My mom bet on how long Greg and I would have sex?"

"She nailed it within twenty minutes. Aunt Gina thought that you'd try to slip in before dawn so that you didn't technically spend the night. Bluebird was always a romantic and bet you'd play house for another day."

Jessica flopped onto her unused bed, face down into the pillow. The coolness of the not-slept-on Wonder Woman linens only emphasized her heated cheeks. So much for not feeling farcical. "What was your bet?"

"You don't want to know," Natalya sounded like she was gloating.

Jessica sat up enough to reach out and grab the piece of paper before Natalya could stop her. Across the top in bold letters she'd written: *When will J. reemerge? ($5 to enter.)* There were a dozen names with dates and times. Her dad even. And names she didn't even recognize that might be guests at the B&B.

Maybe she could get a flight back to Chicago tonight. Too bad the antipode of Eagle Cove lay somewhere deep in the Indian Ocean or she'd go there to be as far from here as possible. NASA really needed to get the whole flights-to-Mars things going…now.

Down by Natalya's name, rather than a day or time, she'd simply written: *Never!*

"What the hell, cousin?"

Natalya shrugged. "I'm on your side. And I can always hope."

Jessica planted her face back into the Wonder Woman pillow.

THE HIGH WHINE of Vincent's table saw made speech mostly impossible this afternoon and Greg was thankful for it.

He'd started the morning feeling high as a kite. The thoughtlessly complete welcome he found in Jessica's arms had blurred the last twenty-four hours into a single, very pleasant memory with a thousand little highlights. The possibility that he might have the chance to wake up day after day to discover Jessica wrapped about him had been a vision of the future that overwhelmed him. The sex had been fantastic, but it was the holding and companionship that were rapidly becoming his favorite aspects of their relationship. He'd never imagined her as the kind of woman who snuggled, but she absolutely was.

There had been so little time for talking. He had the sneaking suspicion that was the important part and he'd better be careful not to neglect it.

Throughout the Judge's breakfast service, he'd pondered that more and more.

He'd promised to think about her problem but then proceeded to not be able to focus. The trouble with thinking about it was that he knew nothing about journalism. He was one of those people who actually knew almost nothing about the news. Other than restaurant reviews, if Jessica Baxter didn't write about it—and her niche was special interest not world news—then he knew squat about it.

He fetched boards for Vincent from the stack and caught them as they came off the saw with a nice forty-five degree bevel down their length. A quick flip and another cut for a double bevel. Goggles and heavy earmuffs made for safety but prevented most conversation.

It was a real problem talking with Jessica at all when the other option was getting his hands on her.

"Are you covered for all of this lumber if the client flakes?" Greg shouted in between cuts. There was thousands of dollars of hardwood stacked here and weekenders were notoriously unreliable customers.

"They paid half of labor up front and all materials on their account, not mine. Forty percent on installation and the last ten percent on acceptance."

Greg shot a thumb's up and went for another piece of oak. Clearly Dawn had negotiated the contract no matter how unhappy she was about what it was doing to her family life this summer.

Actually, he and Jessica had talked plenty in between bouts of sex, but it was all about the past and the Judge's offer to bankroll the start of his restaurant. None of it was about the subject of her future...a topic she seemed to be avoiding.

Did journalism work like the Kriegson's contract ? Half up front? He'd wager not. Especially not for a freelancer like Jessica. She'd started full-time at the *Chicago Tribune,* but had become a stringer since then. He'd tracked down her writing in a dozen different places, but even that seemed to be tapering off.

A chef who had a restaurant paid his employees first, his vendors second, landlord third, and then prayed there was enough to pay himself. The good restaurants could always do that. Feeding people was steady work. *Focus on your people and the menu,* he'd been told by any number of chefs, *then the rest works out.*

"Yo!" Vincent shouted at him and Greg got back in motion. Staring at the lumber wasn't helping Vincent.

None of that would be of any help to Jessica either—just staring at the problem was useless. But there had to be some way that she could get paid up front, even half.

He picked up another length of 1x6 oak and delivered it to Vincent.

"SINCE WHEN DO MOMS HAVE NERVES?" Jessica asked and the whole group started laughing.

Knitting was a serious business in Eagle Cove and anyone who could get away met at the Lamont B&B's verandah Tuesday and Friday afternoons, or in the period-decorated parlor when the weather was less friendly.

Her mom was all in a fuss over wedding details that clearly had nothing to do with the details and everything to do with a barely controlled state of panic.

"Just wait until it's your wedding, young lady. Then I dare you to be calm about it."

"Double dare you!" Natalya jumped right in.

It was lucky that Becky was out doing deliveries today. Jessica wasn't in the mood to face a triple dare.

Tiffany stopped knitting on her Fair Isle leggings long enough to hold up three fingers. *Triple dare! Crap!* At least Tiffany's name hadn't been on the sign-up sheet for the Jessica-and-Greg betting pool. Jessica sighed, she'd probably only missed it because she hadn't come down out of her woods while the pool was running. Tiffany returned to her knitting and Jessica did her best to follow her example.

"Your mother is right, dear," Mrs. Winslow patted Jessica's shoulder. "I was a complete wreck. Of course I only did it the one time." She aimed an arch look at Jessica's mom who appeared completely oblivious to it.

"It's hard to imagine you being a complete wreck." Mrs. Winslow was more of a Rock of Gibraltar type of woman.

"Oh, it turned out well enough, but on the day of, I would have taken a one-way ticket right back into Saigon even if the war had not been over by then." She'd come to Eagle Cove almost straight from reporting on the Vietnam War and married an older retired-Navy man who taught junior high math. Her two boys had been finishing high school by the time Jessica and Natalya had reached Mrs. Winslow's class and Jessica only barely remembered them from occasional visits home.

She let the conversation move on without her as she focused on her knitting. A stripe of butterscotch gold and another of light woodland green. She had plenty of scarves and had traded in her long straight needles for four shorter double-pointed ones to start again, because you could never have too many pairs of thick warm socks. Once she'd started knitting again it had come back easily. Anyone could make a pair of socks—though she might need some help remembering how to turn the heel. She wasn't too proud to ask; she'd just sneak a look in Aunt Gina's *Vogue Knitting* book the next time no one was around. It had meant pulling out a dozen rows of scarf but a woman was allowed to change her mind, wasn't she?

Change her mind.

Like her break-up, make-up, wake-up with Greg Slater. She froze as she recognized the pattern of her last few days. Please god, someone tell her that she wasn't like her mother.

She glanced at Monica Baxter. Having given control of the wedding meal to Greg, she was now worrying about the rehearsal dinner. *Just a judge's civil service wedding on the B&B's lawn. Get a grip, Mom.* Gina had offered to do a big BBQ for the dinner, but because Greg had gourmet sliders on the main wedding menu, Mom wanted to change everything Aunt Gina had planned for the rehearsal.

Jessica turned back to her scarf-turned-socks and focused as hard as she could. Chatting was usually one of the joys of knitting. Except when doing a tricky section or detailed lace work, her hands could run along mostly on autopilot allowing for other enjoyments like conversation. But now she was trying to avoid both the conversation and her own thoughts and the sock was not providing the haven she so needed. She was out of the gold ribbing, which had at least offered an alternating knit-purl for a minor distraction, but now it was just a dozen rows of knitting green in a circle without even a purl in sight.

Change her mind.

Why was that thought sticking around? Like maybe she should change her mind about being a journalist.

She dropped a stitch, then saw that was because she'd dropped one on the prior row. She tried to pick up the dropped stitch in the prior row and only managed to cascade the loss back another row.

Jessica stilled her hands, rested the whole thing very calmly onto her lap, but wasn't paying attention to the needles. One of them had only a single stitch on it—you never let go of a needle in such a state. There wasn't enough yarn friction to hold it in place. The needle slipped out, dropping yet another stitch in the current row, and fell onto the porch without making a sound, which was odd. There should have been a bright *Ping!* drawing all attention her way. Leaning over, she couldn't spot where it had fallen.

She glanced at Tiffany, who of course again hadn't missed anything. She pointed straight down. Jessica looked again by her feet, then Tiffany pointed downward more emphatically. Jessica eyed the dark gap in the old porch decking—too narrow for even a stiletto heel, but big enough for a single knitting needle if it fell perfectly.

"Swish," Tiffany said softly.

Jessica stared at the narrow gap once more. She hadn't climbed under the porch since she was a little girl. It was a dim, cool space filled with garden snakes, old cobwebs, and—at least it was easy to imagine no matter how unlikely—zombie corpses. She looked around, but there wasn't a single small boy running around the yard that she could send in after it. She gathered her knitting, losing another three stitches in the process, then pulled the three remaining needles out. She snapped the ball of yarn off with a sharp tug and then threw the sock disaster into Aunt Gina's rose bush.

Tiffany looked sympathetic.

Natalya just roared with laughter.

GREG FELT a close kinship to the abominable snowman by the time Dawn and the twins returned from the beach. The sawdust that clogged every pore was brown rather than white—maybe he was more akin to a sasquatch.

They both were.

He and Vincent were coated in a thick layer of wood shavings, sawdust, and a half dozen of the inevitable splinters until their hair, face, and clothes were all of a common oak-dust color. Even the white dust masks looked more like furry Chewbacca muzzles. Vincent tugged his mask down around his neck and tried to hug his wife, who kept him at fingertip distance with a firm hand in the middle of his chest as their lips brushed together.

To balance the scales, Greg pretended he was a goggle-eyed

monster and began chasing the twins around the yard with roars on his part and eardrum-shattering giggles on theirs. He finally caught them and gave himself a big shake like a wet dog, completely coating them in sawdust. Soon they were having a sawdust-ball fight with the thick piles that had accumulated under and around the saw. Fistfuls of sawdust flew back and forth—exploding into fine clouds just moments after they were thrown.

One of the twins caught Dawn on the butt.

She turned one of her fierce scowls on the girls and then on Greg. It was enough to cow them all into silence. One of Dawn's strict rules for her husband's furniture making business was: *No Sawdust in the House.*

Ever so calmly, she reached out and gathered a large handful of shavings from the backside of the table saw's fence.

Greg prepared himself for disaster.

Instead, she eased up to Vincent, laying against him and guaranteeing that her front would be coated in dust. She wrapped him into a kiss and just as he leaned in, she rammed her fistful of shavings down the back of his pants eliciting a yelp of surprise.

Dawn jumped back, leaving three moderately clean spots where her breasts and hips had pressed against her husband. Vincent however had other things to concentrate on as he danced and shook his legs trying to shake the itchy shavings out of his pants.

Greg had just started to laugh, when he felt two much smaller hands at his back. They found just enough slack in the back of his own belt to dump fistfuls of sawdust down the back of his own pants.

The twins!

He spun as they rushed away, laughing as high and fast as chickadees.

"Crap! That really itches." In moments he and Vincent were doing similar dances to clear out their underwear. Vincent had already opened his pants, holding them aloft with one hand and digging out the sawdust with the other.

Itching too much to be embarrassed, Greg did the same and began digging great scoops of shavings out of his underwear. How could so much have fit in two such small hands?

He heard a car door slam hard in the opposite driveway.

He turned in time to see Dragon Winslow standing by her car and staring at them. She looked such foul daggers that he was surprised they didn't fall down dead.

Oh perfect.

Then Jessica climbed out of the passenger side and grinned across the street at him.

He tried to close his pants, but instead they slipped out of his fingers. As he reached for them, Dawn gave him a sharp shove. His fallen pants trapped his ankles. Greg fell over sideways and was lost in a puff of sawdust.

Greg decided that he'd just stay here. His best option now was to lie still and wait for the fall rains to come and wash the sawdust and his embarrassment down the ditch and out to sea.

"THAT BOY, REALLY?" Mrs. Winslow asked Jessica once they were inside, but there was a glimmer in her eye that said it was at least partly a tease.

Jessica looked back out the living room window. Greg and Vincent were both down and now being inundated by the three McCall women. Then Dawn discovered a large garbage bag that must have included previous rounds of sweepings. With the twins' assistance, she dumped it over the two men, then walked off around the house—quickly, a very tactical retreat—waving the girls ahead of her. Probably to hose themselves down in glorious victory.

"That boy, really," Jessica replied, perhaps a little more dreamily than she'd intended. As a matter of fact, it wasn't a reply she'd expected from herself at all.

But she and Mrs. Winslow had sat in the car and watched him playing with the twins. It was clear that the girls loved him. It was also clear what an incredible father he would be. He had a good mind *and* a great heart. Who knew?

"I wouldn't worry, Mrs. Winslow," she turned from the window because she didn't want to keep seeing where her thoughts were going. "I've never found a man worth keeping for long." But if there was one—

She absolutely was not going to be completing that thought.

"Best be calling me Marjorie now or I will have to start calling you Ms. Baxter and we have both been through too much to start that."

"Thanks, Marjorie." It felt wrong on her tongue, but it warmed her through. Mrs. W—Marjorie was like the Judge; her merest presence commanded respect. Being on a first name basis with her after all these years was a mark of approval or acceptance that affected Jessica more deeply than it should for a thirty-two year old worldly woman.

Marjorie led her back into the kitchen. At the end of Tuesday knitting, she'd invited Jessica home for dinner with a simple, "Time we talked a bit and it will be a nice change from eating alone."

Throughout the meal prep she kept Marjorie on the topic of her early years in journalism. She hadn't taken a journalism degree and then simply flown into Saigon to begin filing stories from the front lines as Jessica had always pictured.

"I was working at the *Chicago Tribune*,"—one of the main reasons Jessica had applied to Northwestern University in Chicago and also applied to the *Trib*—"when the son of my editor was killed. She was in such agony, knowing nothing of what happened, that it was tearing her apart. I finally filed for an assignment to go get some hard facts and maybe we would get a couple of good articles out of it. I never found out more about her son, but I spent three years filing from there. Just as in any new job, I began with human interest stories, but things happen fast in a war zone. Soon I was reporting from forward bases and camps."

"But you just came home and stopped," Jessica didn't want to stop. She loved the writing and the connection with readers. She just wanted to be paid for it.

Marjorie Winslow shrugged and set out plates and a bottle of wine with glasses as Jessica set out napkins and silverware to carry out to the back garden.

"Why?"

"Oh, I did another few years. But by that point I was a 'civilian veteran,' if you will. There are things that a twenty-six year old girl born in Portland, Oregon was never supposed to see. I suppose that now it would be diagnosed as PTSD, but all I know was that Chicago —the same Chicago that I had no problem reporting about during the '68 Democratic Convention as a freshman-year student project—felt more and more oppressive until I felt I was being squeezed to death."

Jessica wasn't feeling squeezed. She was feeling...she didn't know what. Her job was to elicit and capture the feelings and experiences of others and interpret that for her readers. She'd done such a thorough job of taking Jessica Baxter out of the equation that even when she did want to know herself, she couldn't find a ready answer.

"My family used to come here for summer vacations," Marjorie continued as if Jessica's psyche wasn't busying thrashing the crap out of her like one of Dad's landed but not-yet-dead fish. "I knew I needed to escape the city, for at least a few weeks. I came here and met Harvey Winslow, local boy retired from the Navy. He was good for me and I for him. We did not talk much, but we understood that talking did not heal things that love and time in a small town could. I never did go back to Chicago; had a friend forward my things."

Jessica slid the two pieces of baked chicken onto the plates as Marjorie added a side of roasted Brussels sprouts. Wild rice completed the dishes and they carried them out back.

It was only then that Jessica realized she'd never been here, never even been in this house before. She was sure of it because there was no possible way to forget the garden.

If Jessica had been asked to speculate beforehand—a practice she'd honed as a journalist so that she was prepared for most eventualities —she'd have expected an orderly vegetable patch, or perhaps a neatly ordered rose garden. Instead, it was an English garden wild in its lushness and lack of conformity. There were trellised roses—though how Marjorie managed that in the harsh coastal climate was hard to imagine. But there were also flowering vines, foxglove past their peak and dahlias just entering theirs, rhododendrons and dozen others. She could see where spring plantings of daffodil, iris, and tulip had died back and where sunflowers were turning to the sun.

"Oh. My. God." Nothing less would suffice.

Marjorie smiled and led her to a small redwood picnic table where they sat. Jessica kept staring about her in wonder.

"I'm in Fairyland."

Marjorie looked about, a calm smile making her look far younger. "This is where I come to play. I missed the lushness of Vietnam's flora, but I also did not want a constant reminder of those times by using tropical plants, even if any would have grown here. This was my compromise and my joy."

Jessica's joy was a fifteen-year-old VW Beetle, battered by its life in Chicago, and one-half of a two bedroom apartment. She'd once had a Ficus plant named Atticus, but it died when she'd forgotten to water it between successive four-week assignments back when she could still afford to have no roommate.

"So, Jessica," Marjorie's tone shifted enough for Jessica to regress right past the twelve-year-old Eagle Cove version of herself into the seven-year-old second-grader sitting at her little desk—her gangly frame already too long to fit properly.

It was that tone that Mrs. Winslow had always used when Jessica wasn't performing up to her potential. Or more typically was busy distracting Natya or Becky because she'd already learned the lesson herself.

"We have heard everything from your mother's shortcomings— which she knows full well and does *not* need her daughter reminding her about."

Jessica had already caught herself on that and stopped doing it.

"—To the limitations of Eagle Cove, which those of us who live here know far better than you."

Jessica needed to stop doing that.

"Have you noticed all of the 'For Sale' signs? Or the 'Vacancy' sign on the Sleepy Owl even though it is July?"

She had, but not enough for the implications to really sink in. Some investigative journalist she had become.

"We are too small and remote. People do not even consider visiting here. Cannon Beach, Lincoln City, and Newport are all right on Highway 101 with major feeds over the Coast Range. We are an obscure little town."

Jessica didn't like that at all. The town had always made her a little crazy, but this trip had surprised her at how much she missed it. She certainly didn't want to see it die off like so many of the old lumber towns along the coast.

"But that is all irrelevant to my primary inquiry. Why have you not once mentioned a single thing about your career?"

Crap! She'd been trying desperately to avoid that, but should have known that Marjorie Winslow was a journalist first before she was a teacher. Jessica sawed off a bite of chicken, which was moist and tender so it took no time at all to cut. She stared at a particularly robust sunflower which was peeking over Marjorie's head.

She gave in.

Jessica laid it all out. The successes and the long slide toward impending failure and eventual doom that she hadn't noticed until...well...

"I don't think I understood just how bad it was until I returned to Eagle Cove. Seeing all of these people who I love so much and having no fatted calf to show for my victories. Instead I'm a battered soldier returned upon her Roman shield, except there was no glorious combat to make it an honor."

"Combat is never glorious."

Jessica sighed. She couldn't even get away with a weak metaphor. What was her world coming to?

"But I take your point. Though why you felt that those who love you would think less of you for all of this is beyond me."

"Failure breeds contempt—"

"Is a cliché that is beneath you, Jessica."

Metaphors weak. Clichés failed. What next? Basic grammar? She sawed off another piece of chicken that was tender enough she could have cut it with the edge of her fork. Soon her plate was filled with tiny bits of cut-up chicken, like food prepped to feed a toddler. She dropped her knife and fork on the plate with a clatter as a lost cause.

Lost cause.

She'd say it aloud, but she feared that even analogy was slipping out of her grasp.

"Well, it sounds as if we have a project on our hands this week."

Jessica looked up from her plate to inspect Marjorie Winslow and the sunflower nodding agreement over her head. "We? You can't tell Mom. She has enough going on."

Marjorie dipped her head in consent, "You mother was never the most focused of women."

Jessica poked at her chicken, then managed to eat a Brussels sprout, roasted until it was crunchy-leafed and sweet. "Greg offered to help."

Marjorie looked at her speculatively, "That boy?"

"Yes," Jessica noted the sudden glint in Marjorie's eyes and sighed. "Yes, that boy."

"Man has more sense than I granted him if he managed to unearth before I did what you were hiding so carefully."

"Well," Jessica took confidence from Marjorie's softening expression, "I have spent a lot of time with him these last few days."

"I might have noticed."

"It's almost a pity that I'm leaving in just five days."

"Hmmm," Marjorie Winslow made it a thoughtful sound before returning to her meal.

GREG HAD KEPT an eye out on Mrs. Winslow's house through dinner. He'd thought he was being subtle until Dawn rolled her eyes at him. He shrugged back. How was he supposed to not be distracted by thoughts of Jessica when she was so nearby? Vincent was oblivious of course.

As the evening progressed toward dark and the lights remained off in the house across the street, he finally gave up; he must have missed Jessica's departure.

He was busy losing at some new board game that the twins were ruling through a combination of lucky dice rolls and twin-telepathy—they'd clearly chosen the shared goal of cutting Greg down to size—when Dawn nudged his arm. A light had come on deep in the Winslow residence. Even as he watched, the living room blinked to life and the two women were revealed walking toward the front door: the dauntingly solid Mrs. Winslow and the slender streak of light and air that was Jessica.

If he said goodnight, he didn't recall. He didn't even remember how he came to be waiting at the end of the driveway as Jessica emerged onto the front stoop then turned back to hug Mrs. Winslow. He hadn't known that the old battle-axe was capable of affection, but she held Jessica closely for a much longer moment than mere politeness or even friendship would imply.

Then she looked at him over Jessica's shoulder, because of course the old bat could see in the dark. Her gaze was just as daunting as it had been in second grade. And he still couldn't read what he had done to earn it.

Jessica was most of the way to him before she picked him out of the shadows. She didn't speak or seem surprised. Instead, she walked into his arms, rested her head on his shoulder, and held on tightly. Resting his cheek on her hair, he cradled her and tried to figure out just quite how he'd gotten to heaven.

Back in her doorway, Mrs. Winslow watched them closely for a long moment before closing the door and shutting off the light.

Greg decided that he must be losing his mind because for half a second it looked as if she smiled at him. Not possible.

Now they were shrouded in darkness by the shadows of the late evening and the soft glow of lights from Vincent's windows. Others were awake along Shearwater Lane, but trees separated most properties.

Then the strangest thing happened, Jessica Baxter began to cry. It was soft but there were some things that were difficult to miss with her body pressed hard against his through a thin blouse and slacks. The ripples of gasping breaths down her back, and the warm tears dampening his neck and shirt collar were another sure giveaway. She was the strongest woman he knew, with the possible exception of Mrs. Winslow. Even Dawn had her weak moments.

That Jessica Baxter was crying against him was both startling and oddly enticing. She trusted him enough to cry on his shoulder and it made him feel very strong to be the one she'd chosen to lean upon.

Over the years he'd slowly developed a recipe for dealing with weeping women. In hindsight, it was a little startling how many of them had sought him out when they were sad, but he was thankful for the practice now. He'd learned that trying to stop them only led to harder weeping or, more typically, anger. Instead, he applied a soothing hand slowly rubbed up and down her spine. He had tried the application of a wide variety of meaningless murmurs over the years and had settled on, "Easy now. Easy." And like a good risotto, he just kept his hand moving slowly.

He hoped whatever was making her cry wasn't him. Well, probably not as she'd come to him in order to have her cry.

When she calmed, he gently asked his question, "Is it anything I can help with?" It always earned him a headshake, but it often led to an answer as well. It had even worked on Dawn on the few occasions when she was too frustrated with Vincent to speak to him without bitter words she could never take back.

Jessica, true to form, didn't follow the patterns of other women.

"I thought that you were already working on how to help," her voice was a little rough, but less so than he'd expected.

Help? Help with what? All he could think about was how amazing she felt in his arms and how much he wanted to drag her down on the nearest bit of lawn to...

Oh.

Her career. In tatters. Was that why she'd been in Mrs. Winslow's house? He vaguely remembered that the woman had been a reporter of some sort before coming to Eagle Cove. Something she and Jessica would have in common. Perhaps that had stirred up things.

"I did give it some thought," and had gotten nowhere. But rubbing the tip of his nose through her fine soft hair, he had an idea now.

"Anything useful?" Her voice came out somewhere between a desperate plea and begging as she remained snuggled against him.

"Maybe," he rolled it around on his tongue and liked the way the idea tasted. "Yes, I think so." He breathed her in deeply. There would be some very definite benefits, for both of them.

She waited with held breath, he could feel her diaphragm stop moving.

"You know that I have the money now to open a restaurant."

Jessica nodded uncertainly, then pulled back enough to squint at him in the darkness, only the slightest bit of light from Vincent and Dawn's front window revealing her waiting look.

"I'm thinking that I should open it in Chicago. We can share living expenses and you could help out in the restaurant between jobs. We could—"

One moment she was calmly curled in his arms.

The next moment she was struggling to free herself, shoving hard against his chest to get away.

Greg let her go and took a step back…but there was—nothing there.

He tumbled backward into the roadside ditch. Thankfully it hadn't rained for several days so it was dry and the thick grasses at the bottom cushioned his fall, mostly.

"You are *not* moving to Chicago because of me," Jessica stood at the edge of the ditch, fists on her hips. He was sure that she was glaring down at him.

"Why not?" He leveraged himself up until he was only sitting in the ditch rather than lying in it.

"First, because I won't be a kept woman."

That wasn't what he'd meant, but she continued before he could begin to explain.

"What we have is great—okay maybe better than that—but I'm not shacking up with you here or in Chicago. I thought I'd made it clear that there's no long-term for this girl."

Greg had enjoyed enough short-term flings to know that what was between he and Jessica had nothing to do with those. However, he again recalled Becky's admonition that Jessica would be looking to get away. He decided that pointing out that there was something major between them wouldn't be the best next move.

"Are you okay?"

"Fine. This is a very cozy ditch. I highly recommend it if you are ever out looking for one to sit in."

"Sorry," she moved forward, then stepped back, unsure how to help him up. "I needed a little space, but not that much."

"Sure you don't want to join me?" He assumed not and, clambering to his feet, climbed back up until he was level with her. He shuffled a few respectful steps farther from the ditch.

"Is moving to Chicago to replace my disaster of a career the best idea you've got?" She moved around him, brushing off bits of leaves and dirt.

"So far," he stopped her with a hand and carefully pulled her back into his arms.

She brushed at his chest, but allowed herself to be embraced.

"I'll keep working on it." Then, after placing one foot back to brace himself against another shove, he leaned in to whisper, "but long term still sounds like a grand idea to me."

She growled, but didn't complain or try to get away, when he kissed her.

CHAPTER 9

(WEDNESDAY)

"What am I supposed to do with him?"

"Why ask me?" Natalya protested. "You're the one getting all of the delicious sex."

Perhaps Jessica should have kept more of the details to herself, despite Natya's hectoring. But the morning run through the forest with her cousin was beautiful and the sex last night with Greg had been delicious. Literally.

She and Greg had been walking home together from Marjorie's when the cool sea fog had slipped ashore. She'd forgotten that the coast was like that. During the summer a few blocks inland could be ten or twenty degrees warmer than the beach itself; at times the line of demarcation was a mere fifty steps wide. Last night it had caught up with them when they turned onto Beach Way. At her shiver, Greg had guided her into the restaurant to grab a couple of jackets. But since they were there…

It had started innocently enough; he'd made her braised pears with a cinnamon-honey glaze and a tiny scoop of impossibly lush vanilla ice cream. A dribble of glaze on her chin had led to a very flavorful kiss which in turn had led to… She'd guessed and been proven right about chefs and kitchens, but chefs and commercial kitchens were a new combination for her and took the experience to a whole other level again. Once he'd peeled off Vincent's "World's Okayest Carpenter" t-shirt—his own clothes were apparently still in Dawn's dryer—Jessica had been as eager as he was to see what trouble they could get into. Her naked chef had quite the imagination and her body was pleasantly sore in so many interesting ways. Some had involved chocolate, others honey, and some just a raw heat that neither of them could seem to sate.

She'd declined spending the night with him; she had too much to think about and he did have a five a.m. start to his day with the Judge. Though they had parted on *very* good terms. Instead of thinking anything, she'd plummeted into a deeply languorous sleep—until Natalya had smacked her awake with a pillow again to go for a run.

"You're not helping," she told Natalya as they both jumped over a thin alder that had fallen across the road. She didn't need a reminder of last night's sex; she needed a solution to, well, everything.

"Wasn't trying to," Natalya admitted happily. This time they were up into the forest and running on logging roads. The night's fog had clung to the beach, but up here in the hills it was significantly warmer despite the trees' shade. The spruce and scrub oak were thick with birds. Stellar jays, so majestic with the black face and crown and bright blue body, dominated. Flickers rattled their beaks against old trees sending echoes through the forest. A red-tailed hawk swooped down through the branches, inspected them a moment, then soared back aloft through a tiny gap in the trees.

"Well try," Jessica did her best to not beg. "That's what cousins and best friends are supposed to do."

"If I'm you're best friend, you must be in more trouble than I thought."

"And don't I know it." Natalya didn't look the least put out by Jessica's jibe. Instead she eased off the pace before replying. They trotted in side-by-side ruts along the road. Thick grass and two-foot-tall alders had taken over the hump between them. It had been years since the last round of logging out here.

"I have advice, but you won't like it."

"Have I ever?"

"Nope. But that doesn't make my advice any less right."

Jessica would feel better if Natalya was a little less on the mark about that in general. "Okay, go ahead. Try me."

"Worry less."

"That's it?" Jessica lengthened her stride to clear a low spot. "Worry less? That's your grand, sage advice that I had to drag out of you?"

"Yep."

"So, I should just give in and enjoy the sex while it lasts."

"Yep."

"And let Greg give up everything that he has going for him here—family, friends, and restaurant—and follow me to Chicago so that he can play Mr. He-man and rescue the helpless waif?"

"Well, no, though he wouldn't be so bad in the role. Besides, since when did you turn into a helpless waif?"

Jessica had no good answer to that one. It didn't sound like her. She'd written lead articles in national publications. She'd won a few regional press awards with hopes of more. The sad thing she'd learned about awards was that the payoffs of winning had been less than the cost of the new dresses to accept the damn things. There'd been no magic rise in her freelancer's fee rates that had fallen out of the sky and into her bank account; no new magazines had appeared begging her to write for them. Actually, it had cost her money in the long run as several of her smaller markets had decided she was too important and expensive for them now that she'd won, even though she'd never hinted at a rate change.

"So, Waif Jessica. What are you going to do now?"

She checked her watch. There was enough time…just.

"I'm going to turn around and beat your ass to the front door of The Puffin Diner and you're going to buy breakfast for two for being such a loser."

"Not a chance."

Jessica opened her mouth to renew her challenge.

Natalya took advantage of the momentary hesitation to shove

Jessica sharply off the trail and send her tumbling onto a bed of moss and pine needles. Then Natalya turned and bolted down the hill.

Jessica leapt to her feet and hurried after the hastily retreating figure.

She'd forgotten that Natalya played dirty.

Greg had his hand on the "Open" sign, ready to turn it to "Closed," when the front door slammed open and sent him sprawling onto the diner floor. The small bell on the back of the door clattered like a fire alarm.

The few remaining diners all jumped in their seats.

Jessica stormed in and started doing a victory dance in the middle of the room. Natalya raced in three steps behind her. Jessica whooped and gasped and danced and gasped some more.

He knew from personal experience that she had splendidly long legs, but lying on the floor looking up at her with her thin runner's shorts and body-hugging Lycra top made them look even longer and more incredible than usual.

Natalya was as scantily clad, a study in dusky skin and powerful curves on a frame as lean as Jessica's. The two of them were dripping with sweat and their morning run had caused their muscles to show more than usual proving that these were two very strong women.

Cal Sr. and a couple of other old timers had been lingering over coffee and debating the advantages of Cummins versus Detroit diesels for different types of fishing boats and were now all watching the show. Karen Thompson, who had dropped her book with a loud thump and a cry of surprise, was now shaking her head and searching for her page.

"Can I help you?" Greg struggled for some dignity as he sat up on the floor.

"What are you doing down there?" Jessica gasped out and grinned at him, "Again!"

Natalya ignored him and called back to the Judge, "Are you still serving? Please say no."

Greg glanced up at the big clock and knew the answer…they'd cleared the door with fifteen seconds to spare.

"Of course we are," he echoed the Judge.

Natalya cursed, "Crap! She won, so breakfast is on me."

Then Jessica placed her fists on her hips like Wonder Woman and looked down at him. "Are you just going to sit there or are you going to kiss me and show us to our table?"

As he rose he noticed his father's attention was very focused on him. He didn't much care, in fact…

Greg took his time about kissing Jessica. She struggled only briefly, stopping and leaning in even before he could see if she really wanted to escape. He heard the hoots and hollers from Cal's crowd and could feel his father's continued close inspection. Karen he knew would spare them a glance and return to her reading.

When they did finally pull apart, she whispered beneath the on-going applause, "Damn but it's a pity *you* aren't on the menu."

For a kiss like that from Jessica Baxter, every day, he'd put himself on the menu anytime she asked. Price, one golden ring and happy ever after. Her "No way! Never!" stance didn't worry him any longer. At least not as much.

No.

It *didn't* worry him. He knew what he felt and he knew what Jessica felt. And if anyone ever knew what being tenacious meant, it was a chef.

He escorted the two of them to a table and delivered menus with all the finesse of a Michelin-star *maître d'.*

When he reached the kitchen to hand across their order, the Judge had a smile on his face. "You haven't won the case yet, Son, so don't get cocky," he rumbled softly. "But I'd say that you are absolutely on the right track."

He traded a smile with his father and headed back to their table with a small pot of herbal tea and a big mug of hot chocolate with plenty of marshmallows.

CHAPTER 10

(SATURDAY)

*J*essica's last few days had gone by impossibly quickly.

She'd spent Thursday afternoon out on the boat with Dad, a glorious day of bright sun, large fish, and happy tourists. The sole damper on the beautiful day was that it was the high season and her father's boat hadn't been full. Those two empty spots had glared at her for the entire trip as if she somehow had the answer. Money, family, sightseeing, fishing... It was wrapped up in there somewhere, but she still couldn't find it.

Friday afternoon knitting had turned into an extended state of panic for her mother; it was all Jessica could do to keep Monica Baxter distracted from her nerves. Aunt Gina had even abandoned teasing her sister by providing first-night cautionary tales for new brides.

"It's not like you haven't married him before," had turned out to be the most soothing thing to say. Not because it soothed, but rather because it briefly shifted her mother's near panic into a sigh about her own daughter's shortcomings.

Something had shifted for Jessica during her race to the diner with Natalya on Wednesday. It wasn't just that she liked winning, she did. It was a more that she liked the memory of winning but had forgotten what it felt like. Her career had backed her into a corner so slowly that she hadn't noticed until she escaped to Eagle Cove.

And if she wanted to win, she had to get back in the game. The game may have changed, but it was time she took responsibility for her own career.

The afternoons were for Natalya and the rest of her family and the nights were Greg's, but the mornings were hers. Greg had been busy on the wedding prep anyway as the true scale of Monica Baxter's guest list became apparent.

Wednesday after breakfast in The Puffin Diner and then both of the following mornings, after Greg had gone to serve breakfast, she had climbed the steep ladder to the top story of his Victorian house's circular turret.

With the trap door closed behind her, there was just a small couch that was luxurious for one and would be cozy with two, and a circle of windows filled with the most spectacular view imaginable. Beach, water, and sky to the west. The big main house wrapped in trees commanded the view to the south, backdropped by the towering heights of Orca Head and the lighthouse. The sun-dappled forest lay to the east.

She sat there as cozy as a cat in the sun and doodled on a pad of paper. Marjorie Winslow had taught her an appreciation for the blank sheet of paper. She lived with a recorder, a backup recorder, a laptop, a tablet computer, a cell phone...her purse was more about chargers and cables than wallet and makeup. But her favorite tool for thinking was still a pad of lined yellow paper.

Jessica had started with a list of her clients: past, present, and possibilities for the future. The list was a tapering funnel that was going completely the wrong direction, like down the toilet; of course, just when she really didn't want it, the too appropriate metaphor cropped up.

Now recognizing her current career for what it was, and not being fragile—she had to keep reminding herself to purge her secret inner waifishness—she started on building a new plan of attack. She began listing her skill set, then brainstorming alternate markets that she might be able to apply those skills to.

Television news was turning into social media feeds done by the masses which made that industry just as much of a pending disaster area as special-interest journalism.

Intriguing companies, new artists, and innovative thinkers were all doing their own marketing in websites, blogs, newsletters, and again the ubiquitous social media.

Jessica had been a freelancer for so long that she hated the idea of going in and becoming some cog in a corporate marketing department. She'd keep that idea in reserve.

She seriously considered Greg's offer. But it was a senseless. She thought of him without his father, the restaurant, and his friends who greeted him on the streets each morning.

He belonged here, right in Eagle Cove of all crazy ideas. She could finally see that it was true.

By Friday morning, as she sat and watched the tourists wandering the beach, she began sketching Greg's picture in different poses until she found one that she'd liked. Not the naked lover, but the chef serving fine dining. Of the look on his face as the entire restaurant had burst into applause after that amazing halibut dinner. There was a humility there, but there was also a pride. The pride of achieving something long sought after.

There was a catch.

He couldn't run the kind of restaurant he wanted to one or two nights a month. And Eagle Cove didn't have the tourist volume to justify more. It hurt her heart picturing him having to leave this town, leave his home.

Her sketches were starting to form into…she wasn't sure what. She still only had the idea that there was an idea by the time the Friday afternoon knitting session arrived. The sketches were still rough, but she'd thought that the concepts were good even if she wasn't sure yet how they fit together.

She'd showed them to Marjorie anyway.

Marjorie Winslow hadn't said a word. Instead, she'd sent Jessica inside for a glass of ice tea and been gone before Jessica returned. A cautious phone call had elicited no response and no return call. Jessica had hoped that Marjorie would have some piece of sage advice for her career as well, but apparently that was hoping for too much. Now she merely hoped that she hadn't somehow damaged their friendship.

Clearly she'd left so that she didn't have to tell Jessica what she'd really thought of them. That hurt so horribly, that she didn't mention anything to anyone. She stuffed the drawings and all of her scribblings away, would have torched them if it had been a cooler night and the fireplace had been burning.

Friday night it had been an utterly exhausted man who had collapsed beside her in his bed for a few hours of sleep before he had to return to complete his prep for the Saturday wedding. She had briefly considered showing her ideas to him, but he was too biased— he kept insisting that his move to Chicago somehow made sense—and too exhausted. And she already had Marjorie Winslow's feedback, she certainly didn't need another body slam like that.

Instead, she wrapped around him and held on tight while he slept.

In the morning, they both arose early and parted with little more than a kiss.

She would miss her final private morning in the small tower, but Marjorie's verdict had proved that it wasn't helping anyway. Still, she'd miss it.

Jessica went home. Both of her parents were morning people, so the Baxter household was already on the move by the time she arrived.

Dad was in the kitchen making bacon and omelets, Mom was toasting thick slices of Cal Mason Jr.'s slow-fermented sourdough bread. The Blackbird Bakery's sourdough had been built on a starter his father had brought from San Francisco after a stint there in the Coast Guard. Father and now son had been nursing it along ever since and Jessica had never tasted better in any of her travels.

Dad handed over the spatula and whispered, "Keep your mom busy for a minute," then he sauntered out of the room.

Her mother poured her a mug of hot chocolate and leaned back against the counter, "I finally feel calm this morning. It's as if this whole last week hadn't happened."

"Maybe as if the last two years hadn't?"

"Maybe," Mom's smile showed that maybe that was the case. "But I think it was watching you these last few days."

"Me?" Jessica almost dumped the eggs she'd been beating for a third omelet onto the hot stove. "I've been a train wreck these last few days." Damn! She hadn't meant to say that, especially not on the morning of Mom's wedding.

"No. You might have been a train wreck the first few days you arrived here, but something is shifting. I don't know what because you always hold your thoughts so close, dear. I don't even know if it's because of Greg Slater or not. It made you a troublesome child to raise."

"Troublesome?" In hindsight she'd always thought she was too well-behaved as a child. She'd acted out a little as a teen, but she'd been such a good girl that her idea of acting out had been remarkable only in how trivial it was.

"Perhaps troubl*ing* is a better word. You choose; words were always your gift."

As if Jessica was having such luck explaining herself to herself this week.

"We never knew what you were thinking. Someday you'll have a child—"

Jessica bit back on her desire to argue the point.

"You will, honey. And you'll be an amazing mom because you won't be able to help yourself. I just hope for your sake that she doesn't keep her thoughts so carefully hidden."

"It wasn't on purpose, Mom." Only a little. Monica Baxter had always seemed a little frantic and Jessica had never wanted to add to her mother's burdens.

"I know that, dear. Start your omelet. It's just the sort of person you are. Even as a baby in the crib you tended to just watch and think."

She started her omelet and wished she was someone different, but she wasn't exactly sure who. Becky had always been the exuberant one. Natalya had been somewhere in the middle between them. If she herself became any quieter, she'd end up like that girl Tiffany living alone in the woods with her animals, only slipping from her cloister on knitting days.

Jessica poked at the omelet a bit. "You must abuse your omelet," Julia Child said on her cooking show, an episode Dad had made her watch whenever it was rerun. Jessica had never quite had the flare for it, but omelets were his thing. He and Judge Slater often debated omelet technique as if it were a difficult legal case. When it was nearly done, she dribbled some smoked salmon and shredded cheese down the center, then folded it onto a warm plate and slipped it into the oven.

Her father stuck his head back into the room, "Come along you two. I have something to show my girls." Then he was gone again.

"That man," his bride huffed after him. "He can't even sit down to a wedding morning breakfast without starting some project or other. Come along, Jessica. We'll never eat until we admire whatever he's done this time."

They dutifully trooped down the hall, past the master bedroom that would once again hold a married couple tonight...Jessica crossed her fingers on that one so that her thoughts didn't hex it. Past the gym that had been her childhood bedroom and then her father's office.

The breezeway door opened at the end of the hall. There was a lace cloth hanging over something on the wall right beside the door that opened from the breezeway into her mother's wing of the house.

The first thing Jessica noticed was that the stack of notices were gone from the center of the glass door. The taped-down layers of divorce filing, topped by marriage license, topped by divorce filing, and so on—each layer going backward more and more yellow with age—were gone. It took giving her mother a gentle nudge and pointing circumspectly before she noticed the change.

"What are you up to, Ralph Baxter?" Mom's tone was a mix of curious and cautious.

Like a magician, Dad yanked aside the bit of lace.

A large frame hung there. Tasteful, modern, a sea-blue mat around the edges, and nothing in the center of the display.

"That," he pointed a callused finger, "is where our last ever marriage license will be encased tonight for any and all to see. I know it will be the last because my beloved fiancé told me so."

"Oh you," Mom stepped into Dad's arms and held him so tightly. It was a type of hug that Jessica recognized, the embrace of a woman who never wanted to be anywhere else.

An embrace that felt very familiar.

Her father beckoned her forward and soon the three of them were holding onto each other. Jessica didn't cry for a second time, something she hadn't done in years before her episode in Greg's arms, but she came very close.

But this wasn't why her parents' embrace had looked familiar.

Being in Greg Slater's embrace was exactly like what her parents had been doing…and that was the most disconcerting thought of the entire week. If she felt that way in Greg's arms, and Greg truly belonged in Eagle Cove, where the hell did she belong?

That question haunted her for the rest of the morning.

THE MIDDAY SUN was warm as Greg began unloading his last load of trays into the B&B's kitchen. It felt as if his entire future was riding on this meal, even more than the halibut dinner that had won him his father's financing. He needed the money if he was going to make a splash in a big city, though he wished there was some way to avoid taking it.

But this wedding dinner, a far simpler menu though far more complex in the execution due to the number of diners, was for Jessica's mother. But it wasn't Monica Baxter he was thinking of.

He hadn't even had time to cook one last dinner for Jessica. This evening's post-wedding feast would be tonight's meal and tomorrow morning Natalya would be driving her to the airport.

Dawn pulled him aside on the porch. Vincent had the girls so that

Dawn could help him with the prep. Peggy and the Judge would be at the wedding and had both agreed to pitch in with the cooking and service.

"Talk to me, Greg."

"I don't have time for this," he turned back toward the kitchen, but Dawn shifted to stay between him and his goal. He tried to head for the van to unload another big tray of stuffed mushrooms, but she headed him off there as well. What was it with women when he was in a hurry? First Peggy and now…

Realizing that the only way out of this was through it, he dropped onto one of the benches and Dawn sat beside him. She took his hand and held it tightly.

"Shit," was all he could think to say and he couldn't even conjure up much heat behind it.

"There's got to be a way that the two of you can—"

"There isn't! Okay?" He dug his free hand through his hair and barely resisted the urge to start tearing it out. "She's more than I ever dreamed."

"We're not talking pedestal action here, are we? Took me forever to kick out the one Vincent had me on."

"No. It was. But it isn't. Not anymore. I remember, Dawn. I remember when you gave me my first-ever kiss as my fifteenth birthday present and you told me that you were going to marry Vincent so I shouldn't read anything into it. I know that about Jessica Baxter. I know it just as deep as you knew it about Vincent back then."

"Then it's going to happen."

"I don't see how tha—"

"No!" Dawn cut him off sternly. "You listen to me, Greg Slater. If you feel that deeply about her, it's going to happen. Probably in some way that neither of you expect, but it will."

Greg latched onto what hope he could, "You really think so?"

"I *know* so. And remember, I was always the smart one of our group, so you're going to have to trust me on this."

Greg closed his eyes for a long moment, became aware of the

warm midday sea breeze brushing over the porch. *Yes. There had to be some way that it was going to happen, so it was time to just believe that.*

He opened his eyes and looked at one of his very closest friends.

"You're the best, Dawn."

"Remind Vincent of that on occasion and we've got a deal."

"Oh, he knows it, but I'll keep reminding him anyway. Besides, I happen to know that you're an amazing kisser and even he isn't dumb enough to walk away from that." He kept it light as that was only one of a thousand reasons his friends belonged together.

"Want to know a secret?" They leaned back on the bench together, holding hands and looking out to sea. For this moment, his need to hurry had sprinted off without him.

"Sure."

"I was scared to death. You were my first-ever kiss too, but I wanted someone to practice on before my first one with Vincent."

"Well, it was great. I still remember it well."

"Want to know another secret?" Dawn's voice was little more than a whisper.

"You're on a roll," he prompted her.

"I've gotten better. Lots better."

Greg could only groan. "Lucky bastard doesn't deserve you."

"Greg?" She asked after such a long pause that his urgent need to hurry had found its way back to him.

"Yeah?"

"I know another great kisser who has probably gotten loads better since his fifteenth birthday. And it is going to be a very lucky girl who gets such a man."

He squeezed her hand hard in thanks. "You might try reminding her of that."

"Nope," Dawn stood, yanked him back to his feet by their linked hands, and led him back toward the kitchen. "You're the one who needs to remind her until she finally realizes how damned lucky she is."

Greg would have to work on that. But at the moment he had a wedding to prepare and cook for.

JESSICA WALKED down the lawn-green aisle between the admiring crowd as she headed toward her father. It was her, then Aunt Gina, then Monica Baxter, the bride. "Her Mom the Bride." She'd be truly grateful to never have to hear that phrase again as long as she lived.

But for the moment it was just Jessica and her father beneath the sun-dappled coast pines. For a man in his late fifties, he cut a dashing figure. Strong from the fishing and the projects he was always doing. He'd stayed fit. His best man, Danny McCall looked small and rumpled by comparison.

What would it be like to go walking toward the man waiting for her? Walking on her dad's arm up this same pathway to trade vows with—

Erase! Eradicate! Extirpate!

But her commands to herself didn't work and she glanced aside from the moment she'd been sharing with her father and saw Greg Slater. He hadn't worn a jacket, but he looked just fine in a dress shirt and tie. His collar-length hair, that was such fun to play with, lay tucked back behind his ears. His beard, soft and ticklish, was freshly trimmed short and neat.

He was watching her just as closely with those dark, dark eyes of his. There was no smile, but neither was there a frown. If she had to label his expression, she might be forced to go with "awe." Her bridesmaid dress was a cheerfully frivolous thing that she'd stolen from her mother's closet. Enough of a cleavage for her necklace to lie on bare skin, short sleeves, and a flirty skirt just above the knees.

She passed him by, doing her best to track her eyes forward, but it was hard; far harder than it should be.

The ceremony passed in a blur, as did the meal.

The former a blur of pageantry in true small-town style. There was an equal mix of summer dresses, slacks, and tattered jeans. T-shirts outnumbered blouses or dress shirts and only the wedding party itself was done up to the nines.

The meal was a blur of stunning flavors, succulent dishes, and the mayhem of a hundred people all eating buffet style. The Judge was flipping burgers on a massive grill and Peggy was toasting buns and grilling stuffed mushroom caps close beside him.

In the midst of it all Tiffany slipped up and handed Jessica a small clear food storage bag. Inside was the partially completed gold sock back on its three needles. The dropped stitches had been fixed and the fourth needle lay in the bottom of the bag.

She hugged Tiffany who squawked in surprise, but then hugged Jessica back fiercely before melting away into the crowd. Jessica took it upstairs and tucked it carefully in her carry-on luggage.

Luggage.

She was leaving in the morning.

Jessica sat on the bed a moment and wondered how she could leave. But her life wasn't here no matter how much Greg's was. She'd figured out how to help him, how to help the town a little too.

Or at least she thought she had.

She pulled out the pad with her sketches. She'd develop the idea more this morning, but it wasn't going to pay any bills. It was just an act of—

There was a sentence she wasn't going to be finishing any time soon no matter how true it might be.

The soft knock on the open door behind her had her yelping in surprise.

"Sorry. I should not have bothered you."

Jessica rushed around the foot of the bed and threw her arms around Marjorie Winslow. Marjorie patted her on the back like she was calming an upset child.

"You looked like you were thinking so hard that I almost turned around, but I did not want to climb those stairs again. Getting hard on this old woman."

Jessica held her tighter.

"I suppose that I am glad that I did not."

Jessica was torn between laughter and tears, but managed to go for the former. "You always talk exactly the way you teach second grade, no confusing contractions. I remember you explaining that to me when I asked."

"Third day of class. And you are still the only student I ever had who noticed that I do that."

"It's also probably why you still scare the crap out of Greg and Vincent. I asked, they're both terrified of you."

"Good!" Marjorie turned her and they sat on the bed together. "Keeping those boys on their toes has made them better men. Though Vincent is awfully sweet with his wife and those twins, makes it difficult at times."

Jessica still clutched her yellow pad.

"Those are good, Jessica," Marjorie tapped the pad without looking down. "You have a good eye. You need to give the copy another polish, remember that it is—" she hesitated then enunciated carefully, "*it's* marketing copy not an article."

Jessica nodded. That's exactly what was wrong with it. She flipped through and could see exactly what she needed to do now.

Marjorie made her slow down and they went through the new sketches together.

There were ads for the Judge's breakfasts at The Puffin Diner and Greg's "Evenings at The Puffin." Another spread for her father's fishing trips and her mother's real estate business. Becky Billing's BlueBird Brewery, the Blackbird Bakery... Once she'd started them, she hadn't been able to stop—the pad was half full of advertising ideas featuring the businesses of Eagle Cove. Those had then started turning into ads promoting the coastal town as a destination spot.

"I had a few ideas of my own," Marjorie held out a sealed manila envelope. "Do not—*don't* open it until you're on the plane."

"Okay," Jessica tucked the envelope into the back of the pad and slipped it into her carry-on.

"Now is the time to celebrate a joyous wedding," Marjorie pushed to her feet, brushing off Jessica's attempt to help. "Not that old yet, girl, so do *not* pamper me or I may start to feel that way."

Jessica stayed close beside Marjorie for a long time, their arms linked together in friendship if not support.

THE ONLY WAY that Greg convinced himself to approach them was already knowing his other option. It was either face Jessica and Dragon Winslow or have Dawn kick his butt for being such a wimp.

Food service was long over except for the two dozen pies he'd made. Cal hadn't had enough warning to make a bigger cake, so Greg had added pies and everyone received a piece of each. He'd made them in all different flavors. He should have made more blueberry, as they were peaking right now on the coast; he'd remember that for next time. Seasonal. Just like his restaurant would be. Yes! He liked that. Whatever was absolutely the freshest.

Dancing had begun. A local band had come together. Vincent's dad Manny sang sweet vocals and Peggy played a mean guitar. Becky had a drum kit and the Judge plucked a stand-up bass. And that odd girl Tiffany was cradling a small Celtic harp. He hadn't even realized she was here.

Greg gave himself one more stern talking to, ignored the inexplicable smile that Tiffany sent his way, and headed for Jessica and the Dragon. There were two very different expressions watching him approach.

Jessica's was everything he hoped for.

The Dragon looked ready to slice, dice, and sear him on the highest heat.

"I'm sorry to interrupt you ladies, but I was hoping for a dance."

"Took you five numbers to talk yourself into that, young man," Mrs. Winslow's tone was accusatory.

"I'm afraid so, Mrs. Winslow." He hadn't thought he was being that obvious.

"Good!" She shared an enigmatic smile with Jessica, untucked Jessica's hand from around her elbow, and held it out to him as if Jessica was a mannequin.

He reached out and took Jessica's hand. The shock of contact rippled up his arm and had his heart skipping.

Without further comment, Dragon Winslow retired from the field of battle and, by some miracle, he still lived.

Jessica slid into his arms, half-time slow dancing despite the band tackling a Doobie Brothers song with some success. She rested her head on his shoulder and wrapped her arms around his neck.

"She likes you, you know."

"That'll be the day. I can't stand that you're leaving tomorrow."

Jessica tensed in his arms, definitely the wrong thing to say.

"How about," he tried again, "we just dance and let tomorrow take care of itself?" It must have been the right thing to say, because she slowly relaxed once more until there was nothing but her in his arms and somewhere, seemingly far away, the sound of music and laughter.

Late in the night, as they lay together in his bed not wanting to sleep and miss a moment before the dawn light, she whispered to him.

"You can't follow me, Greg. Please. It's the one thing I ask of you, don't follow me."

"Will you come back?"

The silence stretched forever.

"I'll try."

For now that would have to be good enough. What he wasn't going to tell her was that if she didn't return soon, he was damn well going to follow despite her order. And he had the sneaking suspicion that almost everyone would be on his side with that decision, perhaps even Dragon Winslow.

He spent the rest of the time before dawn doing his best to make this a night she couldn't forget even if she wanted to. And he knew for a fact that she didn't want to, she just didn't know it yet.

CHAPTER 11

(A WEEK SUNDAY)

The ads had started appearing on that first Wednesday after she was gone. They slipped out into social media channels. By Thursday the town had a promotional website. It was slickly functional but friendly and welcoming. By Friday it was the talk of the morning breakfast crowd, the only talk.

Greg was as stumped as everyone else, almost everyone else. The Judge was in on whatever was happening, Greg was sure of it, but he refused to be pinned down.

The reviews hit on Friday, a week after Jessica's departure. Write-ups appeared in *The Oregonian,* the Newport *News Times,* and even the *Seattle Times.* The bakery in one, Ralph Baxter's fishing trips in another, and reviews of both of the meals that he'd cooked while Jessica was visiting.

He knew she had to be behind it. The initial ads had sounded like her, but with a very different flair. It wasn't until the reviews came out that he knew for certain. Those were definitely in her prose style; that powerful writing voice he'd so appreciated in her early days.

The big splash hit on Sunday.

"Puffin Days at Eagle Cove!"

There was a roster of events.

Puffin boat tours!

A special weekend opening of the Puffin Diner, along with the Judge's menu.

Brewery tours.

And right in the middle of every ad, a massive announcement of the opening of "Evenings at The Puffin." Gourmet food Friday and Saturday nights only.

He'd finally confronted the Judge with it over Sunday dinner in the big house.

"Well, that is interesting," his father had inspected the ad at leisure. "I suppose you had better start planning a menu. You have a restaurant to open."

"No! I have a woman to go see. I was going to fly to Chicago next weekend and track Jessica Baxter down whether she wants me to or not."

The Judge just nodded sagely. "Guess that you know more about opening a restaurant than I do, but it looks to me as if you're setting up to disappoint a potentially large clientele."

The Judge slid across a reservation sheet. Across the top it said "Evenings at The Puffin." Beneath that were columns of names. Two seatings on both nights. It was already a packed house.

Damn it! Jessica was just trying to make sure he didn't leave Eagle Cove. It would help if it wasn't the perfect solution to almost everything. He already had the restaurant and a local group of patrons. They couldn't sustain him for a full restaurant opening, but they could certainly provide a solid base for his launch. With everything that would be in place, including his living expenses, he wouldn't need a cent of his father's money. His savings would cover it all. Hell, with four sold-out seatings he might be adding to his bankroll rather than depleting it.

It was perfect except for the lack of Jessica Baxter in his life. But she'd trapped him and she knew it; he couldn't leave.

"You thought much about a ring when you do finally see her?"

Greg startled. If his father thought he needed a ring, then maybe, just maybe there was a way this could work.

"I was hoping that getting on my knees and begging would be sufficient. I figure Jessica is the sort of woman who would want to choose the ring herself."

"Still got a lot to learn about women, Son." His father reached into a pocket and pulled out a small box. His expression was tight and unreadable as he slid it across the table with just his fingertips.

Greg opened the box carefully…and knew right away there was no better ring to be found.

The two stones were the emerald green of the forests and the blue sapphire of the sea. The forest and the sea met here in Eagle Cove as they met nowhere else.

It was his mother's ring.

He stood and walked around the table. For the first time since her funeral, Greg hugged his father and just held on as the Judge patted him on the back.

CHAPTER 12

(AND ONE WEEK MORE)

Jessica's VW Beetle made it over Maxine Pass without too many complaints. It had been a hard three-day drive from Chicago, crossing the endless expanse of the Great Plains, through the heart of the Colorado, Wyoming and Utah Rockies before turning northwest into Oregon. But she could practically coast from here.

The car felt as if it knew the way. Somewhere in the last two weeks since Mom's wedding the control of her future had slipped out of her hands—or at least any future she had recognized.

She'd slept for most of the flight back from Portland to Chicago, only remembering Marjorie Winslow's envelope an hour before landing at O'Hare. There were only a half dozen pages; the first page was a hand-written letter on lined yellow paper:

My dearest Jessica,

I could not be more proud of you if you were my own daughter. You have achieved so much. And you did it while staying true to your heart and your ideals. That is a truly rare achievement.

The market has changed out from beneath you, now it is time for you to be brave and change with it.

Know that whatever you decide after reading the enclosed, you could never disappoint me.

I love you very much.

Marjorie

Jessica had cried for a second time in as many decades, right there in seat 24E.

What she felt as she read through the rest of the envelope's contents was neither sadness nor joy—it was wonder.

The Coast Range stream that had run beside her mother's car just three weeks ago, once again raced her down through the trees. The Doobie Brothers song that she and Greg had danced to played over the car's stereo.

The contents of the envelope revealed why Marjorie Winslow had rushed away from the Friday knitting group. She'd approached the town's merchants. They had all, each and every one, chipped in to finance a contract. Mom's Eaglet Real Estate had been first on the list and her father's Eaglet Fishing and Charter had been next. It wasn't much, at least not in the first year—though there was a very respectable bonus structure if her efforts were successful.

It was a contract for Jessica. The merchants of Eagle Cove wanted her to entice tourists to their town.

The final sheet had been one of Marjorie's sheets of yellow paper. Unlike the friendly letter, it was concise and to the point. So concise that there were only two words inscribed on the entire page:

Think festivals!

It had been a vote of absolute confidence that with that two-word hint she would know what to do.

And she did.

Every skill she had learned as a freelance journalist responsible for making her own career translated perfectly into marketing a town like Eagle Cove.

"Puffin Days" was the first festival—a starter test case for her future concepts. It was also the best she could do on two weeks' notice. If all of her efforts had worked, it should be in full swing by now.

Nerves shivered up her body. In another dozen miles she'd know. And if it did, Puffin Days would become the recurring anchor point of the summer season. In her file, resting on the Beetle's passenger seat, were sketches for fall, winter, and spring events.

She slipped into town and couldn't find parking anywhere—the place was packed. Her nerves kept climbing. Not even the salty sea and the mossy forest could calm her.

Jessica found a space out by Marjorie's house and left the car. It was enough of a signal for her friend to know that she'd made it into town. It was packed with all of her worldly belongings—everything that hadn't fit in the tiny car, she'd sold or given away. Not quite "the clothes on her back," but close. She should knock and say hello, but she couldn't be delayed.

She walked into town, tracing the path toward The Puffin that a very different woman had walked a mere two-and-a-half weeks ago holding hands with Greg Slater after knocking him into a dry ditch. Exactly as planned, it was just at the start of the Saturday dinner service. Her mother and father had made a reservation for three without explaining why to Greg.

So many things now made sense that never had before.

She didn't feel twelve at all.

Jessica felt like a grown woman.

And there were choices that a grown woman could make. As much as she loved her mother, Jessica knew that she was different. Once she'd made her choice it would be forever.

It was finally as clear as the summer sky just turning orange above the crowded and busy streets of Eagle Cove. As clear as the bright sound of the bell on the back of The Puffin's door.

Tonight, either she or Greg was going to go down on bended knee.

And tomorrow the rest of their lives would begin.

Together.

Draft Back Cover Copy

Jessica Baxter cherished her big city dreams. If only they were actually coming true. When her mother's fourth wedding to Jessica's father draws her back to the small Oregon Coast town of Eagle Cove, she discovers that dreams come in many sizes.

Greg Slater left Eagle Cove to become a world-class chef. When he returns to Eagle Cove, he discovers home and family. Finally his cooking dreams lie almost in reach. When Jessica walks back into town, he wonders if he will have to choose between home and his life-long love.

Neither of them expect that the answer might lie in Eagle Cove.

RECIPE FOR EAGLE COVE

*A*n air of delighted mischief pervaded the room as Becky and Natalya changed out of their bridesmaids dresses. Jessica Baxter had always sworn she would never marry. Instead she was the first of the three friends to go down…and they were going to make her pay for being so fortunate.

Becky peered out the second-story window; it was easy to pick Jessica out of the crowd which spread across the B&B's broad lawn. The stately Victorian stood well back from the high bluff above the rolling Pacific. The bride was long, blond, sleek, and gorgeous in a simple white lace gown. The Sunday afternoon sun of the warm September day—because *of course* it wouldn't dare rain on Jessica's wedding—sparkled off her as if she was half elf and half fairy. Both of which Becky had always suspected to be true.

And Becky couldn't begrudge one of her best friends getting Greg Slater because the two were so perfect together. But she could be envious. And the only proper way to deal with envy was merry revenge.

She couldn't suppress her giggle as they were changing. Natalya flashed a grin back at her; Jessica's first cousin was like the anti-Jessica. The two of them were both tall and slim, but Natalya was dusky-skinned, brunette, and had all of the curves that Jessica had whined about not having since forever. It had been Natalya's idea for them to change into little black dresses for the wedding reception, as if they were mourning Jessica's demise. Pure pixie, always a tricky lot, Natya was the strategist of their childhood trio.

Becky had fashioned matching corsages for them out of black tissue paper. Those dozen years of schooling had finally paid off, even if it was just in crafts projects from the first grade. She preferred the down and dirty school of hard knocks that had spanned the last fourteen years since graduating from Puffin High.

She turned back to the room and saw that she had another problem. Natalya in a little black dress was going to gobsmack every man around and Becky didn't think that was much more fair than Jessica looking so ridiculously happy.

Becky checked herself in the mirror, not that it did her much good. Natalya lived three hours away in Portland, so she was staying in the Writer's Room of her mother's Victorian B&B. It was an airy, lofty-ceilinged room typical of the old architecture. This room was filled with books, images of writers, and the décor was pure Jane Austen-era Georgian. That meant that the mirror had a massively ornate, gold-painted frame. Yet despite its imposing presence, it was actually small, round, and set far too high for Becky's five-four. That her two best friends since kindergarten were both five-ten was just another injustice. What she'd lacked in stature she'd made up for in curves, "lush Italianate curves" her similarly-shaped mother had always said—which made perfect sense with their pioneer-stock, Gold-Rush era, boringly Anglo-Saxon heritage. Not!

She was... Becky had never been able to pin down what she was. Imp? Garden gnome? The right metaphor always eluded her. She sighed, standing on tiptoe didn't help either.

Unable to see her reflection much below the generous cleavage that even the most conservative little black dress gave a woman of her shape—and this dress was not meant to be conservative—she turned for help.

"Your mom's stupid mirrors. Help me, Natya!" It was an old problem that didn't need explaining.

Natalya whirled a finger and Becky did a turn on the ornate Persian rug that looked as if it had been snatched out of the Hogwarts Gryffindor Common Room, making the bedroom warm and cozy. J. K. Rowling watched Becky from her portrait over Natalya's shoulder. Emily Dickinson considered one profile and Jane Austen the other. Maya Angelou may have been inspecting her shoes. She'd pulled on her bright red cowboy boots with the pretty black stitching. The low heel was good because of dancing on the lawn. Besides, Becky held a firm conviction that high heels on a short woman were just a lame form of sucking up. And whatever James Tiptree, Jr. was thinking about Becky's shoulder-length auburn hair, she was keeping to herself, just as she'd kept her gender hidden through two decades of writing science fiction. Georgette Heyer merely hung on the wall and looked magnificently 1920s as she always did.

Natalya shot out a thumbs up. "Men are going to whimper!"

"Yes!" Becky offered a fist pump and did a little circular stomp dance on the rug. "That is if they notice me with you around."

"Since when have you ever had to worry about that?"

"Since Jessica looks so damn happy dancing with Greg." Together they turned to look back out the window. Becky half wanted to collect the writers' pictures from the walls so that all the women in the room could look out together.

"It *is* a little like she's bragging, isn't it?"

Becky could only nod. Jessica was draped shamelessly against her new husband, slow dancing to an up-tempo Backstreet Boys song. Three months ago Jessica returned to Eagle Cove after a decade working as a Chicago journalist. She was supposed to be here just a week and then return to her whirlwind urban career. Instead, she'd stayed as the town's new marketing manager and was kicking ass at it. Tourism was at its highest level in years. That was good news for the Lamont's B&B, the real estate business of Jessica's mom, and it certainly hadn't hurt Becky's brewery.

"Time to go break up all of this unmitigated happiness." Natya declared firmly. It was. And Jessica was right, Natalya was always the sneaky one of the group.

"First dibs on cutting in on the bride for a dance with the groom," Becky declared just as Natalya was opening her mouth to do the same.

"Damn!" Natalya's curse warmed her heart.

To secure her victory, Becky raced for the door, offered an air high-five to Nora Roberts' picture above an entire bookcase filled with her writings, and beat Natalya to the stairs. But she was blockaded from escape at the bottom of the stairs...the kitchen was packed. She was in the midst of the mayhem, when across the impenetrable mob, she saw Natalya slink down the old servants' back stairs and out onto the porch. Her wicked grin showed exactly where she was headed—to claim the second dance from the groom.

"Damn!" All she could do was echo Natalya's heartfelt curse of a moment before. Becky stomped her foot in frustration; growing up in this house gave Natalya an unfair advantage.

<hr />

HARRY YELPED MORE in surprise than pain as someone tromped on the toes of his Oxfords. The kitchen was so noisy with a dozen simultaneous conversations that no one particularly noticed his cry. It took him a moment to spot his attacker, but when he looked down he discovered an astonishing sight.

The first thing he noticed was the impressive swell of exposed breasts. It wasn't that they were all that uncovered, they were just very...impressive. *Ah yes, his lawyerly finesse with words. Sad.* But it was hard to be completely coherent when faced with such an exceptional view. Then he forced himself to focus on the owner's face.

"Becky!" He ignored her smirk that said she knew exactly where his attention had first landed and gave her a quick hug that she returned after a moment. "It's like old home week." Everyone had turned out for his little brother's wedding. The fact that Greggie was marrying, *had* married, the first woman Harry had ever kissed didn't bother him...too much. He and Jess had been almost done before they started during freshman year. Wasn't it just backward justice that Greg was the one who'd always had the big crush on her without ever admitting to it.

"Old home week only to you foreign types." Becky Billings smirk had shifted to tease, something he recalled her excelling at. Her light brown eyes practically twinkled with delight. He also recalled that among other things, she'd absolutely ruled every class debate in high school. He might have ruled the soccer field, but her quick mind and quicker tongue had ruled the verbal playing field.

"Foreign as in a hundred yards down the road," he gave it his best shot. His family's homestead was the other grand Victorian of the town. The two old houses stood at the head of the beach and commanded the best views in Eagle Cove.

"Foreign as in you live in New Orleans and are just here slumming."

"Care to do a little slumming with me?"

"You call that a pickup line?" Becky snorted out a laugh and slapped him hard enough on the arm to send him ricocheting off Cal Mason Jr. who bumped into Cal Mason Sr. in earnest conversation with Jessica's father. Cal Sr. shoved Jr. back into him and the two of them ended up tangled together against the stove, both struggling not to spill their beers all over each other.

"Sorry, Cal, Becky just—" he pointed, but the spot where she'd been was empty. Cal gave him a look as if checking his mental capacity: low, after the view of Becky's chest had drained the blood out of his brain.

He looked around and caught occasional glimpses of the top of her head as she moved through the tight-packed kitchen crowd, her liquid-oak hair floating lightly behind her. The crowd parted just enough to offer him a full view as she stepped out the far door and onto the sunlit porch.

She might be short, barely up to his chin, but her industrial-grade curves and trim waist looked damn good on her. And that dress. *Holy wow!* Spaghetti shoulder straps, clinging material, and a flirty flare high enough on her thighs to reveal that there was no excess load on that frame. She was no runner, couldn't be with that body, but they were damned amazing legs. Then with a exuberant "Yip!" of excited greeting, loud enough that he could hear it over the music and the overlapping chatter, she raced out into the sunlight and was gone.

Harry rubbed his shoulder where she'd hit him. He'd forgotten how strong she was. He'd have to remember that the next time he caught up with her. And the way she looked, he definitely had some catching up to do. But he didn't want to appear overeager either. So, he leaned back against the stove with Cal. They'd been the forward strikers on the soccer team back at Puffin High, finishing the season ten-and-two, a new pinnacle for the Pufflings. Cal Sr. and his own father, Judge Slater, had chosen the ridiculous baby seabird as the school mascot most of half a century before. He'd never found out quite why, so he and Cal Jr. worked on their beers and rehashed it some for old times' sake.

But what he really wanted to talk about was Becky Billings and the way that woman looked in a clinging black dress with chili pepper red cowboy boots.

BECKY SNAGGED her dance with Greg once she'd dug Natalya's claws out of him. She did a turn with Vincent McCall while Greg danced with Vincent's wife Dawn. Then after Becky twirled and giggled with Dawn's twin girls, the three of them raided the wedding cake for second pieces and wolfed them down as if they were about to be caught for being naughty.

Becky and Natalya made sure to point out their black mourning frocks to Jessica at every chance and the damn woman just nodded, giggled—which oddly didn't looked ridiculous on a thirty-two year old woman—then sighed happily. The whole black-dress ploy would have been a complete waste of time except they were drawing the attention of every single male, even snaring a few of the married ones into receiving eye rolls from their spouses. She pitied the male of the species. Around women like the three of them, the male gender didn't stand a chance.

Throughout the reception Becky had been keeping a weather eye on eligible men as she moved back and forth across the lawn, up onto the big porch that wrapped around the house and was so crowded with merrymakers, and back out onto the lawn. The problem was that she knew these men too well. Mick, Zander, Alex…it really *was* like old home week.

It was one of the only drawbacks to a small town. Every man her age she'd either dated, hated, or just knew too much about to do either. How did you find a man like Vincent or Greg while living in a small town? She and Greg had even taken a test spin around the track a few times when he first returned to Eagle Cove, but he'd clearly been looking for something else, as was she. Now he'd found it, but she still hadn't.

Evening was settling over the yard. The sun was turning brilliant orange as it descended into the fog bank that so often lingered a few miles offshore. It had been a perfect day for a wedding. Probably one of their last warm and sunny days until next spring.

Already the older generation was drifting inside to pack the kitchen, the library, and the parlor. The evening chill was rolling in off the Pacific so she'd be headed that way soon. Little black dresses offered no defense against the night sea air.

Actually, she already was chilled, standing alone and watching the endless waves roll in and hammer down on the sandy beach far below. Deciding to retreat, she turned abruptly for the house and rammed her nose into the center of a broad chest.

"Was looking for you." Harry Slater. He looked nothing like his brother or his father. The Judge, as everyone called him, was a large, imposing man. Greg was lean and darkly handsome just like his mother had been.

Harry stood as tall as his father, a little broader than Greg, and as blond-haired and blue-eyed as his brother and father weren't. The last time she'd seen Harry was at his mother's funeral three years ago.

"Looking for me?" Why was he looking for her? And if he was, why hadn't he done it sooner? "Took your time, foreigner. Waiting until the dancing was done?"

"Saw you dancing before."

She liked his voice. It was low and smooth—more like a distant freight train than a rumbling diesel engine. He had the kind of deep voice in a lawyer that would make a jury want to trust him. And his accentless Oregon had picked up a hint of Southern-smooth from his years in the Big Easy.

"Can't imagine how I'd keep up with that."

"Like this," she slid up against him and wrapped her arms around his back. A jazz sax was playing somewhere in the distance. She wasn't really sure what had come over her; not that much champagne had passed her lips. Becky might run a brewery, but she drank very little even on major occasions like today. Maybe it was how gorgeous he looked in his gray designer suit. She'd never known she was a sucker for men in great suits.

Harry hesitated for a long moment before wrapping his hands slowly around her shoulders. She didn't have to really duck to lay her head on his chest. His chin rested lightly on her hair and she let herself be swept up in the moment.

Just a moment.

She was in the arms of a handsome, successful, single man. Lying against his chest with her eyes closed as he guided them about the lawn to a deliciously slow cadence.

It was magical.

It shouldn't be.

Harry was just the groom's brother at a wedding, but she could pretend that he really had sought her out.

And maybe she him.

As long as she was pretending, maybe this was what "magical" actually felt like in real life. The music slipped by and the world melted along with it.

A slow shiver slipped over her arms.

"You okay?" Harry whispered it against her hair.

"Um, I think so." Why didn't she know? "You?"

"Oh yeah," he said in one of those deeply satisfied male ways.

She pulled out of his arms enough to look up at him. Without her noticing, the sun had set…long enough ago to make his expression hard to see. They were alone near the high bluff above the beach. Harry had kept them away from the few remaining dancers and some of the younger kids running about with sparklers flaring bright in the falling darkness. Twinkle lights which hung from the lower branches of the towering Douglas firs near the house cast a soft glow over the remnants of the party.

To the north, two miles of white sand beach stretched off to where the Eagle River entered the Pacific. The lights of the town of Eagle Cove were sparkling to life. The very first stars were also putting in an appearance. The ocean had gone nearly black, only marked now by the steady whump of the waves landing on the long strand in a never-ending cascade, There was the smell of salt and the promise of a fresh, amazing world.

High above the south end of the beach, perched atop a rocky headland that blocked any view in that direction, Orca Head Light cast its bright beams out to sea. It was just possible to see the path of the automated light sweeping across the waves far below. When the fog rolled in, it was a dramatic sight.

Even at the moment it was fairly breathtaking.

Speaking of breathtaking, how long had she just been lost in Harry's arms?

Simple answer: too long. It had been forever since she'd gotten *lost* in a boy's arms. The last time had been back when boys were still *boys* and not patented and certified *men* like one Harry Slater.

"That was…" *Lovely* was too mundane, even worse, too predictable. "…kinda pleasant coming from a foreigner."

HARRY GROANED.

It had been a full half an hour that he had held Becky Billings—close. At first it had been friendly, cozy, and arousing as hell. Becky was a sweet package to cuddle with. When he held her, he knew that he was, without question, holding a woman. And she had abandoned herself to it, letting whatever parts of them come together to do just that. When she stepped back, he could feel the cold replace the warm outline of her upon his chest.

"I'm used to a different kind of woman."

"What? Standoffish ones? No, you don't have that problem, do you? Tall ones? Beautiful ones?" She bit off the last strangely.

"I'm used to ones that I don't accidentally speak my thoughts aloud to." That was a given.

"Objection: irrelevant. The court directs the counselor to please answer the original question."

Harry could only stare down at her in astonishment.

"Well?" Becky demanded, her tone completely proper for a disdainful judge.

He looked out to sea for along moment, listened to the breaking waves through three or four landings upon the beach, but found no better answer out there.

"Spit it out, Counselor Slater. Keep this up and I'll find you in contempt."

"Okay…" No woman had ever even thought to speak to him in his own language and Becky Billings, Eagle Cove's pint-sized brewmaster was doing exactly that and doing it well.

Then he caught the hint of her smile despite the darkness. Having fun with him, was she? Well, he wasn't a courtroom lawyer for no reason.

"Contempt, huh?" Harry crossed his arms. "What's the fine if I fail to comply? As a counselor I am honor bound to protect the reputation of—"

"—of all the hot women you've bedded. Well," she crossed her own arms to mimic his position, which only emphasized the magnificence of her chest. "I will offer the counselor a choice of two options to offset the charge of contempt."

"Proceed." This had to be the strangest conversation he'd ever had with a woman that he'd—

Except he hadn't.

All they'd done was dance. No date, no drinks, no…well, none of that either.

"Your first option, Counselor, is a sharp poke in the ribs for being an over-confident, self-assured, *foreign* interloper."

He remembered how hard she'd hit his shoulder. "Not my first choice." Besides, if she did that, he just might tumble off the cliff and it was a long and very steep way down to the beach from the Lamont B&B. The access stairs were twenty or more paces to the north on the line between the Lamont and the Slater properties. Probably too far to make a break for it.

"Second option, pay the fine."

"The fine? Perhaps I should opt for the sharp poke in the ribs after all."

"Your call: answer the question about what type of women you're used to, a sharp poke, or pay the fine. The court has ruled."

He was having a very hard time not smiling. The muscles tugging at the corners of his mouth felt unfamiliar. There hadn't been a great deal to smile about lately in his life. It was almost as if he'd forgotten how, but Becky was rapidly reminding him.

She offered no clue as to what "the fine" might constitute.

But he most certainly wasn't going to answer her question about available women. His looks and his job did indeed make picking up women a simple task; he was never alone on a night he didn't want to be. Though lately he'd spent far more nights alone than with someone. He hadn't really noticed it until this moment. He wasn't bored with the sex, but there had been nothing special about it lately either.

"Well," he had to tease her a little, "I'll admit that you aren't as tall as most women who I've…"

He managed to dodge that poke in the ribs as much by luck and darkness as by light-footedness. Her laugh was awfully merry for a judge on the bench. Didn't he just know it. His father, Judge Slater, had never in his life spoken an unnecessary word to his wife or either of his sons.

"What the hell, why not. Okay, Judge Becky Billings, I'll take the fine. Nothing risked, nothing gained."

"My thoughts exactly."

BECKY STEPPED FORWARD until she was once again pressed against Harry Slater's splendid body. The yard had emptied while they'd sparred. They now owned the entire bluff from house to ocean.

Then she had a crazy, dumb idea after she was already stepping into his arms. She'd thought to cop another dance…

The man had been arrogant, a long time ago back in high school. But not any longer. It was as clear as the night sky that *that* had been kicked out of him somewhere along the road since he'd left town. He also wasn't happy, and that wasn't right.

Some trifecta of pity, a little champagne, and just how wonderfully he'd held her collided. Reaching up, she pulled him down to her and kissed him hard.

As she'd expected, a man who looked like Harry Slater had found plenty of opportunity to hone his kissing skills as well as his lawyering skills. As a matter of fact—she wished to hell she had worn spike stilettos with high platforms so that she could get closer to his kiss—if he was as good a lawyer as a kisser, he must be a kajillionaire.

His hands didn't wander much. Most men went for her breasts and never looked back. Harry wrapped one arm around her waist and the other around her shoulders and pulled her in until her feet were light in her boots.

He *was* foreign. His sharp gray suit that smelled…well, she wasn't sure, but it definitely wasn't Eagle Cove. He'd been the snappiest dressed man in the entire wedding, discounting only Greg's tux and the Judge in his magisterial robes as he performed the ceremony. Harry still wore a silk tie that he hadn't loosened.

As he continued his efforts to melt her bones, she slipped a hand up onto his chest and loosened that tie. Then he slid his hand down her back and onto her butt and grabbed on hard, pulling her tight against his thigh. The jolt that convulsed through her had her hand fisting around the Windsor knot.

One of them moaned. She was fairly sure that it was him, but she could feel it echo into her chest and down her body in ways that were going to lead to places she didn't want to go.

She pushed back against his chest. He protested, hung on tighter when she persisted, but finally gave in and let her ease back. Her head was spinning and deep gulps of cool salt air did nothing to clear it. Unable to release her fist, she pulled on the tie; the silk tail slid free as a smooth caress against her palm.

"Careful," Harry's voice was rough.

Careful? Who was he kidding? Careful didn't begin to cover the present dilemma. She started to take one more step—

Harry grabbed her wrist and tugged her sharply toward him. "Cliff," he croaked out before she could protest. A glance over her shoulder revealed that she was a single step from a hundred-foot tumble down to the beach.

"Uh, thanks." This time she was careful to sidestep but couldn't seem to slow her need to retreat from Harry Slater.

"Becky?"

"That's..." she searched for something to say. Something light, even funny. "That's a hell of a kiss you pack there, Counselor. You got a license for that thing?" It came out all whispery and dreamy.

"Nope," she could hear the smile in it even if it was too dark to see. He was regaining control of that smooth voice of his, so why couldn't she do the same with her own. "Unlicensed. Is the court going to fine me again?"

Not if the judge wanted to keep her sanity. "The, uh, court rests at this time. It will reconvene..." when more than two brain cells were firing with something other than the temptation to jump Harry Slater's bones here and now, "...tomorrow." At the very earliest.

She turned abruptly for the house and started to toward it. Even with the low heels of her dressy cowboy boots, she tacked across the lawn in a staggering line. The house practically throbbed with the sounds of the party that had all moved indoors by now: laughter, shouts, conversations, and a stereo pouring out AC/DC's *Back in Black*. With the assistance of the handrail she navigated the half dozen pitching steps up onto the verandah.

"Nice tie," a voice whispered from the shadows. Tiffany Mills sat on one of the porch swings. Her long hair had slid forward mostly hiding her face. It fell almost to her lap. She was knitting by the light spilling out from the living room window.

Becky looked down at her own hands. She still clutched Harry's necktie in a bunched fist. It was green with gold strips. Inside the narrow gold stripes she could see "Oregon Ducks" imprinted in a pale green. What was it with University of Oregon grads that they were such rabid fans of the Ducks even after a decade in New Orleans?

She dropped down to sit beside Tiffany and clutched the tie in her lap. "Thanks, I guess."

"Trophy?"

"I—" she'd never taken a boy trophy in her life. "I don't think so. I just couldn't seem to let go of it at the time."

"I might have noticed."

Becky glanced up. The horizon was invisible in the darkness. Then the lighthouse beam swept across the water. In the foreground, low bushes and the handrail for the beach stairs stood out as dark silhouettes. She and Harry would have been visible front and center in the vista. She watched carefully through a handful of sweeps of the light, but he was no longer anywhere to be seen.

Tiffany had returned to her knitting. Her actions at least made sense for the evening. Several years back Tiffany had purchased and cleared property up the hill, a mile past the lighthouse. She came down to town only for the Tuesday and Friday afternoon knitting sessions at the Lamont B&B and to sell her farm's excess produce. As far as Becky knew, this was the first time Tiffany had come to an Eagle Cove party of any sort. So it made sense that she would be sitting out here, away from the crowds, and enjoying being near rather than a part of the action.

Becky wasn't making any sense to herself at all. She was normally in the heart of any crowd and this was exactly her sort, local. There wasn't a person at the party she didn't know. It was fun and loud.

She barely managed to return a wave from Peggy as the Judge escorted her down the steps and away beneath the twinkle lights to where the cars were parked. Judge Slater was always the perfect gentleman, which was more than Becky could say for his son. She could still feel the warm palm print where Harry had grabbed her butt.

Instead of jumping up to rejoin the party, she was sitting out here in the cool darkness clutching a man's tie like a lifeline.

What the hell?

WHICH WAS EXACTLY the same question Harry Slater was asking himself as he stared through the trees from his old bedroom window toward the shining lights of the Lamont's Victorian B&B.

He should be over there. If not picking up a bit of fun for the night, then at least catching up on some drinking with his old pals.

The big Douglas firs and a small copse of alder that rose between the properties were outlined by a thousand pinpricks of light from Jessica's party. It was a familiar sight. Gina Lamont, Jessica's aunt, was known for turning everything into an occasion. Sure, the bed and breakfast served up a fine and generous breakfast—he and Greg had slipped through the trees to avail themselves of leftovers any number of times. But guests were often in during the evenings as well. Rum cake, brandy, and boisterous euchre tournaments. Homemade chocolate chip cookies the size of a person's head and a murder mystery game that used the entire B&B grounds and every guest. He'd played the clumsy young sidekick to Gina's suave-and-sexy redheaded inspector any number of times back in high school.

He'd kissed Jessica for the first time on the widow's walk. A tiny space high on the roof of the B&B. Visible to no one, but open to the sky. He'd always thought his first kiss would be something stolen in a dark, cramped, and hurried way. Instead it had been an amazing exploration. Okay, an amazingly clumsy one, on both of their parts, but nothing like he'd ever imagined. And then Greg had impossibly popped up to completely ruin the moment.

He reached up to loosen his tie, and grabbed nothing but air. Where had it gone? He didn't remember taking it off earli—

Becky. He'd lost it somewhere while kissing Becky Billings. Well, no wonder he couldn't recall misplacing it. That kiss had seared everything else right out of his brain. She'd been apparently unaffected. Instead she'd stood at the cliff's brink—hip cocked and her broad smile shining in the darkness—*"You got a license for that kiss, Counselor?"*

No, but he was definitely going to find out where to register.

Harry dropped down onto his bed to stare up at the darkened ceiling. His room had been preserved like some crazy shrine. Plastic trophies were still scattered over the shelves. Photos of the Pufflings soccer team at regionals, crowded close together in their white-and-black uniforms. Their noses were all grease-painted like bright orange Puffin beaks—the fact that the beaks of the seabirds who roosted out on the big sea stack turned orange only during mating season was merely added motivation for a group of high school soccer players.

There was also the college memorabilia layered on through four years of visits home. School books from University of Oregon, even his third-string Ducks shirt—which had been for track-and-field as they didn't have a men's soccer team. Maybe it was just as well. He'd dated a wing-back on the women's soccer team for a while and, watching her play, he'd discovered just how small-town the Pufflings really were. He'd thought himself and Cal as fine athletes, which they'd been in the world of small-coastal-town sports. But that was a whole different scenario than the Pac-12 Ducks. Being a wing-back, Chrysse did have incredible stamina, which Harry had appreciated even if he could barely keep up with her.

Maybe he should look her up. He still wasn't sure what had happened there. They'd been hot and heavy for the last two years of school then he'd gone into law and she'd just...gone. Her parents were local, weren't they? Portland maybe? Wow! There was a dead brain cell.

His whole identity (and ego, he ruefully admitted) in Eagle Cove had been athletics…until he barely qualified for the Ducks' track-and-field team. And his top grades, only bested by Jessica Baxter, had been in a class of merely thirty-four students. Freshman year at U of O had been another harsh shock. It had taken six years of hard work to fix that. He'd graduated number two in his law class, but it had been a long hard climb to get there.

"Shit!" He was getting all morose. He went to shove himself out of bed. Anything would be better than lying here and being stupid about the past.

Instead, he closed his eyes and drifted toward sleep.

It wasn't the six-foot of chocolate-skinned wing-back who came to mind.

Nor was it the five-ten of a brilliantly blond and ever-so-happy Jessica Baxter.

He fell asleep only aware of the imprint that the short but bountiful Becky Billings had left on his chest.

*B*ecky had risen at five a.m. and watched the sunrise as she drove across the Coast Range—the long line of three to four thousand foot hills that separated the Oregon Coast from the Willamette Valley. The fog had been gentle, only dusting the hollows as she climbed and descended through Maxine Pass and on into one of the richest farming regions anywhere. Mostly thirty miles wide and running a hundred and fifty miles from north to south, everything grew in The Valley—as coasties referred to it.

But what she cared most about was the hops and this was one of the premier hop growing areas anywhere. Becky doggedly had cultivated her own special suppliers.

The sun was now clear of the high Cascade Mountains that climbed to the east of The Valley and was already warming the fields. As she wound her way along ever-narrowing roads, she rolled down the windows to her van. It was painted as dark brown as a stout beer, with "Becky Billings BlueBird Brewery" and "The 5B" in gold lettering as light as a cream ale. It was actually one of her prized possessions, the first thing she'd ever bought with her beer money. And she'd paid cash.

Her dad had left her the farm, one of the only ones squeezed into

Eagle Cove, before he and Mom had gone snowbirding off. Unlike most snowbirds who went south to Tucson or Cabo during the long, damp-and-chilly months of a coastal winter, they'd gone north to Alaska. He was always sending her funny postcards: a cluster of a dozen or more polar bears and his note on the back, "Miss my cattle, taking up herding PBs. No nastier than Mr. Wooster." Mr. Wooster had been the orneriest bull anywhere in Coast County and it often cheered Becky to know he was now safely up in Tillamook a couple of counties to the north.

She'd sold Mr. Wooster and most of the dairy cattle to a farm close by the Tillamook cheese factory, and used that money for her first tanks and full set of gear. During the lean startup years she'd sold the farmhouse as well, and built herself an apartment in the barn loft. She spent most of her time there anyway to be close to her brewery.

With the addition of several new fermenting tanks, she could keep five types of beer in process at any time. This was only her third season experimenting with atypical flavors and this year she wanted to really break out into something interesting.

Cherry had to be rejected because once she'd had a Walking Man Black Cherry Stout from up in the Columbia Gorge and she knew there would be no matching it.

She briefly wished she had access to some of the ropical, but local and fresh was a key element of her plans for The 5B; so no mango porter or papaya lager for her. Not that she lacked for ideas... September was always a problem for her. She wanted to do everything. The tail end of the blueberry season was hanging on, a nice sweetener for an ale. Cantaloupe was also beckoning to her as she drove past fields with huge wooden crates being filled with melons by migrant workers. A melon malt. Strawberries were long gone but late peach and nectarine were still around.

She'd start with Tovar Farm and then see what else she had to do. She'd warned them she'd be coming and was greeted by a wave from the back kitchen door as she pulled her van around.

"Good morning, Valeria," Becky called out as soon as she reached the door. "Alejandro please tell me you have some of your excellent coffee brewing." Valeria Tovar was Becky's height and just as full-figured. Alejandro was a lean whip of a man no taller than his wife with the first spots of gray in his dark black hair. They both had the dark skin, prominent cheekbones, and broadly open faces of their far south heritage of Oaxaca.

Alejandro rarely spoke to her but he served up the best coffee in the Willamette. At first she'd felt hurt by his silence, as if she somehow wasn't good enough or was too crass or maybe he thought women were a lesser lifeform. But one day Valeria had whispered that he was very shy around women. "Especially beautiful women like you." Becky knew better, but after that she always made a point of being extra nice to him.

Valeria offered a broad wink and let Becky in through the kitchen door—apparently she'd hit the right note in her cry for Alejandro's coffee. The ranch house looked like any normal triple-wide from the outside. A line of cherry, apple, and Willamette oak trees offered a wind and sun break to the west and south. To the east and north stretched several hundred acres of land that the Tovars had purchased and cultivated for twenty years now since they'd earned enough as migrant workers to stop.

Inside the manufactured home it was almost like stepping back into Mexico. The sun-yellow kitchen was accented with warm reds of thick clay cookware, hanging spices scented the air almost as thickly as the dash of chili in the brewing coffee, and a big table filled the middle of the room. Three bleary-eyed teens were shifting focus between plates of food and checking their packs for school.

Alejandro set stoneware mug of aromatic coffee in front of Becky as she sat. Valeria followed it moments later with a plate of *huevos rancheros*. She'd given up protesting years ago. When you entered Valeria's kitchen, you were fed. Tortillas and eggs, both fresh this morning. Alejandro's black beans, salsa from just-picked tomatoes…

"I'm moving in," Becky said as she always did. The flavors exploded in her mouth: rich, strong, powerful. Just like—

Becky nearly choked as she tried to reconcile dreamy thoughts with sharp salsa.

Just like Harry Slater's kiss. She'd expected the memories of that kiss to keep her awake all night trying to figure out what they meant. Instead she'd been sent straight to sleep with a happy smile. This morning it had been easy to discount it as "a moment at a wedding." At least she hadn't slept with him. But the powerful flavors had brought back that kiss with a body slam.

It exploded out of her more as a gasp than a choke. Unable to help herself, she turned to look over her shoulder back toward Eagle Cove. What was Harry Slater doing right now? And would he still be there when she returned?

"Who is he?" Valeria patted her on the back and thumped a glass of water down on the table which Becky took several quick sips of before regaining control of her breathing. Alejandro was eyeing her curiously.

"Who is who? All I did was choke on a chili." She went for her best innocent look.

Mara rolled her eyes. When a half-awake fifteen-year old girl rolls her eyes at you it couldn't be good.

Becky shrugged, "An old friend, back in town for a visit." Except that wasn't quite right. They'd never been particularly close during high school. He was a jock and she'd organized dances and the talent show. She'd even managed to put together a half decent production of *The Sound of Music* senior year, using the school gym for a stage. She'd tried to cast Jessica as Maria because she looked most like Julie Andrews, but was shouted down because Becky had the best singing voice in the class. Instead Jessica had played the baroness and she'd conned Cal Mason Jr. into the Captain's role. He wasn't a great singer, but he'd looked great onstage. He also hadn't been the least bit shy about practicing for the big kiss scene either.

But she'd never thought of Harry Slater much one way or the other. Too arrogant for her taste, which had only made him a likely target when she needed someone to pith. The Harry Slater *she* knew…

Except he wasn't. That much had been clear last night. First he'd stared at her breasts, which—to be fair—had been part of the purpose of the little black dress. But he'd recovered well, looked her in the eyes after that. She'd caught him staring at her from across the kitchen. There'd been a very satisfying heat in his eyes that had cheered her at first. But when he hadn't followed, too damn sure of himself had been her conclusion. Right up to the moment she'd slid into his arms on a whim.

An arrogant man would have groped, grabbed, or at least gone for the kiss. Instead he had held her and they had danced. Even a night's sleep and sixty miles away, it had her sighing. He'd been so…

Mara was watching her with a big smile on her face.

"What?" Becky asked.

"I know that look."

Valeria's big wooden spoon whacked down abruptly on Mara's plate startling them both.

"*Oye!*" She aimed the spoon at her daughter's nose. "My fifteen-year-old daughter, she does *not* recognize that look. *Comprendes?*" Then Valeria sighed and lowered her spoon, "At least not in your mother's hearing, *por favor. Si?*"

"*Si,* Mama," Mara only looked a little abashed.

Then the spoon swung around and centered on Becky's nose, "But I too know that look."

"Well, I don't!" Becky glared at the enormous spoon hovering inches from her nose. She was not having that look about Harry Slater.

Mara skipped offering another eye roll and went straight to smirk as she shouldered her school bag. Her brother and sister did the same, thankfully without eye contact. Those two dutifully kissed their mother and father on the cheek before rushing out the door to catch the bus. The distant throb of its diesel engine was clear over the quiet fields. Mara stopped by Becky's chair and gave her a hug that took Becky by surprise, she barely had a moment to return it.

"I so know that look," Mara whispered in her ear. "That's a really good look," and then she was gone.

Becky tried to catch her breath as Valerie and Alejandro joined her at the table with plates of their own.

"She's amazing."

"*Sì!*" Valerie agreed. "She's just like I was at that age and that is to be the death of me."

"I was already in love with you by that age," Alejandro whispered softly.

The look that the two of them shared took Becky's breath away.

That was what she wanted. She wanted a man to look at her like she was the most important thing in his life, just as he would be the most important thing in hers.

And that certainly wasn't going to happen with Mr. Harry Slater of Eagle Cove and New Orleans.

She turned to her breakfast and to the business at hand. "I need a half ton of your malted barley, of course. But I'm really hoping for some Mt. Hood hops. Please, Alejandro, tell me you grew some this season. And maybe a few hundred pounds each of Super Galena and Perle. Why is everyone growing Fuggle this year?"

Of course just because Harry wasn't a happy-ever-after sort of guy didn't mean she couldn't have some fun while he was still in town. If he was still in town.

HARRY STROLLED ALONG LBB WAY, headed for The Puffin Diner. It lay in the heart of town. Which was something of an overstatement as the Eagle Cove business district was just five blocks long. The whole town was caught between the beach, the broad bay fed by the Eagle River, and the Coast Range forest.

LBB Way was the longest road in town. The woman who had platted the seaside part of the town had used all landside bird names and Little Brown Bird Way had been her nod to the myriad species that she didn't have enough streets to honor. It was almost two miles from the lighthouse and the two Victorian manor houses to the town. The lane snaked along the shore connecting houses and beach along the way.

He'd headed for his car this morning and then noticed that Dad's and Greg's were still parked at the house even though he knew they'd both be down at the diner. It was a fine clear morning, so he grabbed a light jacket and walked into town instead.

New Orleans was a walking city—in the tourist sectors only. You actually needed a psychiatric checkup if you were crazy enough to try and drive through the crowds in the French Quarter.

A lot of the locals walked most places as well, but that had never worked well for him. His firm's offices were in the downtown core and within a mile of every major courthouse, making all of them an easy walk under normal conditions.

The problem was, that his Oregon Coast blood had never thinned out to Gulf Coast weather—the Big Easy was thirty degrees hotter and far more humid. A half-mile walk could leave a man in need of a half gallon of Gatorade. Worse, it *would* leave him soaked through an eight hundred dollar suit. He exchanged Christmas cards with his Gravier Street dry cleaners; Eagle Cove barely had a dry cleaners (a pickup-and-deliver service that Trey ran out of his basement along with a towing and taxi service, if the old man hadn't died or his beater tow truck hadn't dissolved into a pile of rust yet).

Walking was how people got around Eagle Cove when it wasn't raining.

There were fewer For Sale signs along LBB Way than he remembered from his last visit three years ago—it had taken his mother's funeral and now his brother's wedding to drag him back to this town.

Jessica's mother, the town's real estate agent, must be busy. There was a new life to the town that showed itself in little ways. Emil's yard had been cleansed of the car he'd never gotten around to restoring as well as the stacks of salvaged building supplies that were never going to be used for anything. He'd actually mowed it for a change. Mabel's sign advertising fresh eggs had received a new coat of paint and a fifty-cent per dozen bump in price. The Sleepy Owl Hotel had several cars in the lot despite it being a September weekday.

Greg had said something about his wife being hired as the town's new marketing manager. Seemed an odd choice for a Chicago journalist who had wanted out of this town as badly as he had. Maybe it had just been an excuse for Jessica and him to move in with Dad.

Though it wasn't like they were cramping Dad's style. The Judge lived all alone in the big Victorian that had belonged to the town's founding family. The Lamont's place had belonged to their daughter and, if town history was to be believed, never a civil word traveled between the two houses.

Ma had passed three years before and Greg had taken up residence in the guest house, a charmingly compact copy of the main house. Now Jessica was living there with him, but apparently they had dinner most nights with the Judge. Better them than him.

Harry tried to imagine a more excruciating choice, but had trouble coming up with one. Despite being most of the way to retired, the Judge still ran his household the same way he'd run his courtroom, with absolute and iron control. Never a misplaced word was spoken, never a statement was made without carefully considered content, and never, ever was a voice raised—not in anger and not in joy.

Harry kicked a stone out of the road and then cursed as his toe throbbed. Instead of sneakers he should be wearing shit-kicker boots like Becky had last night. The ones…

No! She'd already cost him a night's sleep. He was not going to waste any more time thinking about her.

It was a cool morning. The sun always took a while to make its appearance over the Coast Range, not striking Eagle Cove for an hour or more after it had lit the sky. The beach below the bluff would be in shadow for another couple hours after that. As the road dipped down he could see a few tourists huddled about in their shorts and sweatshirts wondering why they'd ventured to the shore. The few locals up at this hour for their morning constitutionals were dressed in jeans, warm coats, hats, and gloves. Harry's light jacket wasn't up to the morning beach chill, so he stayed with the road as it climbed back up toward town.

He turned onto Beach Way. Flamingo Apparel was having a tiny tots display, backed by Eagle Cove t-shirts. He hadn't seen those before. It was a good design. He might even get one himself before he went back home. He went over for a closer look, which was safe because they weren't open yet. It was…one of Ma's eagles. Mom (a.k.a.

Ma Slater) sold her paintings all up and down the coast and somebody had co-opted one of her distinctive eagles right here in her hometown.

His blood pressure was rising. How could someone steal her work? Goddamn, but he was going to sue somebody over…

In a corner of the window display hung a small lithograph of the same eagle. A sign advertised "Ma Slater reprints available for purchase in Grosbeak Gallery." Okay, maybe he wouldn't sue anybody. Reprints? That was smart. Continued use of copyright. He should have known that the Judge wouldn't miss a trick. It struck Harry as a damned bloodthirsty act, turning a buck by degrading Mom's work.

This end of town was still awfully quiet. He checked his watch, six-thirty. Too early for a decent body to be awake, except his was on Central Time. By eight-thirty he was typically well into his workday, unless there was a hot case on and he'd probably been there right through the night.

Merganser Weavings actually had a couple of tourists sniffing around. Danny McCall's wife had a gimp leg from a teenage boating accident and Danny had set her up with a shop in the front room of their house. She spent most of her time at a big loom close by the window. On warm days, she would slide the window wide and was practically weaving out on the porch. She always had time to chat, but not this morning.

Then Harry blinked, the name had been changed: Merganser Tours and Weavings.

Tours? In Eagle Cove? Taped to the glass were a couple of nice aerial shots of Danny's and Ralph Lamont's fishing boats. Bright banners declared: "Whale-spotting in Season!" "Deep Sea Fishing!" There was even a "Scenic Plane Flights" poster that showed a Stearman 4 soaring above the coast. Peggy Naron must have finally finished restoring that old biplane.

Something was going on in this town and it was disorienting. Nothing ever happened in Eagle Cove.

Cal would give him the lowdown. And maybe he'd find a way to ask about Becky Billings, except Cal's Blackbird Bakery had a line out the door. In September. *What the hell?*

The town was...busy. Half of the parking spots along Beach Way were taken despite the early hour. Next thing you knew they would put in parking meters.

The Flicker's marquee, at least the part not blocked by the massive chainsaw art flicker woodpecker clinging there, declared a "Northwest Local Film—*Overboard*." He'd barely been born when Goldie Hawn and Kurt Russell had done the filming just up the coast in Newport, but he knew the Newporters talked about it still. They really needed to get a life. Of course locals up there also talked about the filming of *Sometimes a Great Notion* along the Siletz River from even a decade earlier and it was...the "Coming Soon" attraction.

God spare him from small towns.

The Puffin Diner commanded the far end of Eagle Cove, closest to the boat docks. It was the oldest building in town—or at least the oldest foundation. The original log cabin trading post had washed out to sea in the "Great Gale" of 1880. Its loss was still referred to in the present tense even if it had only been a solitary fur trader's hut at the time. However, when it had burned at the turn of the century, the city founders had fought back with a stone foundation made of large boulders and mortar. Early photos showed a third grand Victorian had once stood in the town, but heavy rot and a builder with no imagination leveled it shortly after the Great War and a two-story in the American-foursquare style now stood there.

The Puffin Diner's deep verandah was supported by well-spaced columns guarding the large front windows without darkening them excessively. It was painted white with black trim and had a bright orange door, just like its namesake. The Judge really did like his Puffins. It was almost as if...but Harry knew that the man had no sense of humor.

Quite why Harry was seeking out The Puffin Diner when he could have had a quiet breakfast at home eluded him. But he climbed the steps, swung open the front door, and stepped into chaos.

"I LOVE YOUR FARM, ALEJANDRO."

He had led her out into the hop fields. Most were harvested, but a few of the later-maturing varieties still stood. Becky was glad she'd gotten here before the final harvest and had a chance to walk the fields. She liked remembering the smell of rich earth and blooming plants later when she brewed.

At either end of the rows were tall wooden poles leaning outward and driven deep into the soil. Wires anchored straight down from their high tops and into the soil. Between each pair of outward-slanting poles a high wire stretched down the length of the field with only occasional supporting verticals along the way. In between the poles, green hop vines climbed up vertical lines that dangled from the high wire.

There was a serenity among the graceful towering plants. All of her worries seemed miniscule in comparison. Every vine climbed, reaching for the sun with a slow, undeniable patience. Its tri-form palmate leaves twisted to catch every bit of light. The tight clusters of hop flowers, looking like small green pinecones the size of her thumb, grew in thick clusters.

"There is a peace here," he acknowledged after a while.

She closed her eyes and imagined her toes turning into roots to dig down into the soil for nourishment and water. She turned her face until the sun shone, green and bright through leaves and closed eyelids, as if she too could be energized by sunlight.

Alejandro let her have her moment.

It was almost as if she was slow dancing in the arms of…

She dragged herself back to reality long before she wanted to. "I need a flavor, Alejandro." *And a subject change for my thoughts.* "Something that tastes of fall. Others do cherry well and yet it feels too early for melon to be as rich and sweet as I'd want."

"Come," was all he said and led her deeper into the towering rows of the fields.

She felt at home here.

This is where she came to life: in the fields and also in her brewery. There was a serenity to working the process. Every little thing changed the beer. She scrubbed her steel and copper mercilessly because that gave her a known baseline—something in the process that never changed. Then she tuned and altered. Cooking the mash, changing the ratios, late addition of more wort; everything affected the final outcome. And her brewing notes had to be as meticulous as the tanks. She would spend hour upon hour studying what she had changed and how it had been expressed in the final product.

They emerged from the end of the long row of hops and Alejandro moved beneath a pear tree to pluck a fruit. No, beneath an Asian Pear tree.

She too took one and bit into the round flesh. The light brown skin broke easily and it crunched like an apple. The smooth fruit was a kiss on the tongue, and yes she would let thoughts of Harry drift in with that luscious flavor: soft, sweet, melony. But it wasn't the punch of cantaloupe or the juice of watermelon. It had the warmth of honeydew and the slightly foreign cast of Crenshaw both backed by the hint of pear. Like home and wild lands combined.

"Oh, this," she couldn't help but moan. "This, Alejandro, is exactly what I've been missing in my life."

He handed her a fruit picker, the long wooden pole felt warm against her palms—worn smooth by a hundred thousand pickings. The small cloth collecting-bag and the broad claw-like fingers let her pluck the pears one at a time. He took up another pole.

As the morning warmed, the two of them harvested the very best off the tree until she had several bushels of the perfect fruit.

THE PUFFIN DINER was in as much of an uproar as Harry had ever seen it. The dozen and a half tables were packed. Several people milled about, craning their necks looking for an open seat. Ten people were at the counter which only had six stools. Yet more of the weary-blue Formica tables were empty of food than sported plates. The hunter green-and-mauve linoleum, that had probably been out of style even before *Overboard* was filmed, sported a scattering of tourist beach bags, dropped napkins, and a shattered plate with a tall stack that had been discreetly shoved into a corner rather than being cleaned up.

He was a gifted courtroom lawyer, able to gauge the judge's, the jury's, and even the crowd's mood.

This was an unhappy crowd on the verge of tipping over into anger.

A hand reached and in moments Cal Mason Sr. had one of his meat cleaver-sized hands clamped around Harry's upper arm. "Don't stand there gawking, boy. Go be useful for a change." He practically launched Harry across the dining room with a sharp shove.

The Judge intercepted him near the swinging door and was guiding him toward the kitchen with a hand on Harry's back. He could count the number of times on less than ten fingers his father had touched him. His hugs didn't count. They were offered only at the moment before departure and consisted of a side-arm hug accompanied by an awkward fist thump on the back.

"Can you cook?"

Harry took one look at the big commercial griddle. On the black surface there were several sets of pancakes, eggs, bacon, hash browns…the last more burned than cooked. The roar of the big fans didn't quite move enough air to hide the smell. Maybe long ago he could have, but he'd lived in New Orleans for the last eight years. The food was so good there, from street carts to gourmet eateries, that Harry didn't even have butter or eggs in his kitchen for a morning-after treat. "Not a chance."

"Then you have front of house."

Harry turned to look out through the wide, stainless steel service window. Rather than a neat spinner with orderly tickets and a line of plates to be delivered, it had become the depository of dirty dishes as anxious customers strove to clear the tables.

His father threw an apron at him, "Put that on. Good luck."

"Where's Greg?"

"Having the first morning of his married life. Tomorrow, he's back here whether he's done honeymooning or not." The last came out as close to a growl as Harry had ever heard from his father. A judgment had been made and the sentence delivered. Once the Judge did that, nothing ever changed. *Tough luck, little brother.*

"But—" Harry had never done waiting staff jobs. He'd worked through high school mowing lawns. And been a tutor to make spending money in college and law school. "Cooking and restaurants was always Greg's thing, not mine."

"When all good people shall ride to the aid of those we owe," the Judge decreed.

"I'm a lawyer. I only do that for a large retainer fee," but he strapped the apron around his waist.

The Judge almost smiled as he waved a spatula in Harry's direction and turned to salvage what he could from the grill.

Harry tried to place the phrase. Constitution? Declaration of Independence? The Magna Carta? Didn't the phrase start with "In times of war," or maybe "tribulation" was in there somewhere?

Taking a deep breath, he grabbed a battered gray plastic washtub, an order pad, and a stack of menus. The Judge stopped his progress long enough to hand him a pen so he could write down orders on the pad.

Right.

Harry swung through the doors and into the fray just as he identified the source of the quote. King Theoden of Rohan speaking to Gandalf in *The Lord of the Rings*. And if he remembered correctly, the line was quite different in meaning. "Why should we ride to the aid of those who did not come to ours? What do we owe to Gondor?"

It was too late for Harry to ask why him and what did he owe.

He went for the coffee maker first and started figuring out how to brew more.

*H*arry more collapsed than sat in the chair. It was almost noon. He knew the Judge always closed the doors to newcomers at ten. Eleven had gone by before either of them noticed. And it had taken another hour to take care of the last customers and send them on their way with a full belly and a smile.

His father slid two plates onto the table and settled his big frame into the chair across the table. A pair of the Swiss cheese-mushroom omelets, bacon, English muffin, and the inevitable hash browns. The Judge looked even more haggard than he felt.

Harry forced himself back to his feet. Rather than filling two mugs, he grabbed two of the last clean empties and brought the whole coffee pot back to the table. Just before he sat he remembered that the Judge liked cream and had to go all the way back into the kitchen's big walk-in to find some. The kitchen looked as shattered as the front of house. Eggshells had long since overflowed the trashcan and clustered all around its base, dripping onto the tile floor. Splatters of pancake batter were strewn across every surface. And the stack of burned product overflowed onto one of the prep tables.

He fetched the cream and carried the whole carton back out to the dining room.

They ate in silence for a long time. If he felt like this at thirty-two, what must the Judge feel like at sixty-four? Harry didn't like that thought. No more than he liked that no trace of pepper remained in his father's salt-white hair. Or the heavy lines on his face.

"Why didn't you get a substitute if you were going to let Greg sleep in?"

"Underestimated him."

He'd just married the beautiful Jessica Baxter: valedictorian, journalist, marketer, the #1 "get" of Harry's senior year at Puffin High. Everyone had underestimated his little brother, everyone except apparently Jessica.

"I ran the Puffin Diner myself for years. I would just call out the orders and the people would come and pick them up. I considered that today would be no different."

Harry waved toward the front door and then flinched. A tourist was peering in through the glass while his wife pointed to the hours posted on the door.

"Are you open?" The man shouted through the glass despite the "Closed" sign and the one beneath it that read "Monday to Friday, 6-10 a.m." The Judge didn't open on weekends because he notoriously didn't much like tourists.

"No!" Harry did his best to not make it a cry of horror, but the couple scurried away as if he'd been a shrieking demon. He turned back to his father, "They were lined up out the door. You never had a chance."

"Ever since he came home three years ago, Greg has taken care of the front of house. The income has risen four-fold, and that was before Jessica started her marketing campaigns to attract more tourism to the town. I never really appreciated all that he does now. I should have."

"Well *I* do. That was insane." And he was going to have to take his clothes out to Trey. The khakis might machine clean, though the ketchup and the grease stains were worrisome. But his Hugo Boss shirt was a wreck. Damn, it was one of his favorites. He'd worn it in case…in case he ran into Becky Billings. How sad was that?

"What happened here?" Peggy Naron's voice rose indignantly from the kitchen. She must have come in the back door which he hadn't thought to lock. In moments she was at their side glaring at them. She wasn't much taller standing than the Judge was sitting, but her glare was fierce enough to have both Harry and his father easing back away from her.

"We were a little bit…overwhelmed," the Judge stated.

"Utter goddamn catastrophe," was Harry's take on it.

"I'm just glad that Harry showed up when he did or I might have had some trouble."

Harry could only gawk at his father. If he could have, he'd have pinched himself, but the shock was too great. As kids, he and Greg had called their father JRB, for the Wild West's Judge Roy Bean—the self-proclaimed "Law West of the Pecos." The hanging judge wasn't exactly one to hand out praise. Harry wished there'd been a court reporter present so that he could review the transcript, but he was fairly sure that a compliment had just been perpetrated.

"What are you gawking at?" Peggy was five-six, had a shock of dark-red hair pulled back into a bushy ponytail, and her figure was the only small thing about her. She owned the local airport and gave helicopter and plane rides. A hundred exploits had been attributed to her by the kids of the town and she'd never denied a one. The crazier they got, the more likely they seemed; it was just the sort of woman she was.

"Um," Harry looked at his father, but he was watching Peggy intently. "Nothing, ma'am." And that wasn't just Southern politeness; she was the type of woman you said ma'am to.

"And you?" She turned her laser-powered glare on the Judge. "You were in trouble and you didn't think to call me?"

Why would his father call Peggy? Old friends, he supposed. The two of them went back forever.

"Sorry, Peg. Wasn't even thinking by the time my boy arrived. But we got through it okay."

"So I see," her sarcasm lay almost as thickly about the room as the detritus of the last meals. There wasn't a single thing in order. "Well, let's get it cleaned up, boys."

Harry rested his forehead on the table and whimpered.

A sharp knock rattled the front door.

"We're closed!" He shouted without looking up.

Peggy smacked him on the back of the head, driving his nose sharply against the dirty Formica.

"Ow!"

He heard her walk over and snap open the lock. Harry turned to see Natalya standing in the doorway. Now that was a serious looking woman. He tried to remember why they hadn't hooked up in high school. Bethany Garber's blond hair and blue eyes came to mind. As deep as a mud puddle, but she'd fed his ego just fine and his hormonal whims just fine too. Besides, Natalya Lamont had been dangerous as a teen and looked even more so now. Still, the challenge could be—

"I'm headed back to Portland."

Figured. His luck was running true to form, all bad.

"Becky called and needs someone to drive her van back. I'm not going to bother the lovebirds, so you're my next pick, Harry. Which means I must be desperate."

"Next pick for what?" Was he really such a bad choice? How bad was his reputation?

Natalya just looked at him with those dark eyes of hers. Apparently plenty bad. A pity that he couldn't argue it being wholly undeserved.

"Right. Why does she need someone to drive her van back? Where is she?"

"She's at the hospital in Salem. Seems she busted her leg or something. I couldn't tell because it sounded as if they had her on some pretty good pain meds. Let's go," she shook her car keys at him. "I have a meeting in Portland in four hours and there's three hours of road plus delivering you to the hospital between here and there."

"Becky's hurt?" Harry was already in motion, trying not to imagine the worst. Pain meds. Big ones? Maybe she'd been in a car accident or... "What the hell is she doing in Salem?" He'd assumed that she was simply somewhere around town. He'd been planning to swing by the brewery after breakfast, just to see what she was up to out there.

He was half out the door before he recalled the disaster he was leaving behind.

He considered counting himself lucky and just making good his escape.

But he didn't like the way that felt.

Harry turned back and started to speak, but got stuck somewhere between starting his sentence with "Dad" and "Judge" simultaneously.

" 'Bout time!" Peggy scoffed at him. "Now you can go."

Harry still hesitated. The restaurant was a real mess and his father looked…old. He wasn't ready for that. "I'll—" he didn't know what. Arnold Schwarzenegger had ruined the "I'll be back" line for all time.

"Don't worry," Peggy rested a hand on the Judge's shoulder. "I'll help him."

Harry nodded and rushed after Natalya. It was only as he was climbing in her slick little Mini Cooper that he wondered about that gesture. Judge Slater was not a man to be touched lightly, but he hadn't reacted at all.

───────

BECKY OPENED her eyes when someone poked her on the nose. "Hey, Natya! Sho nice to shee you." She could feel her voice slurring, but couldn't find the energy to be interested in fixing it.

She was still in the Emergency Room. Curtains turned her personal, private corner of it into an eerily dangerous place seen in too many television shows. But she wasn't hooked up to any of the machines which she'd take as a good sign. Well, except for the one giving her an IV drip of painkiller and she didn't mind that one at all.

Then her eyes focused on the man looking down at her over Natalya's shoulder. "Ooo! Pretty! You brought me a pretty!"

And Harry Slater was very pretty. He hadn't inherited much from the Judge, but like his father, Harry's face had more character than… Indiana Jones. If you took Harrison Ford, made him blond, changed the color of his eyes…he'd still look nothing like Harry. The man looked like…himself. She was really having trouble connecting thoughts.

"What did they put me on?"

"I don't know," Harry grinned down at her. "But by that smile, I want some."

"Sure. But then who would drive me home? You'd have to crawl into this hospital bed with me."

Harry's smile lit up in a way that made her giggle. Damn but he was cute; every thought moved so clearly across his features.

Natalya rolled her eyes, "I should have brought the Judge instead."

"No! You brought me a pretty. I wanna keep my pretty."

Natalya looked quickly at Harry and then back at her before narrowing her eyes. Then in one of her lightning quick mood changes, she smiled brightly and Becky almost forgot that momentary look of suspicion. "So, what did you do?"

"Hish fault," she pointed an accusing finger at Harry, careful to use the arm without the IV in it. "I stood up too soon as I stepped out the back door of my van. Shoulda ducked longer." Right. Her head. Reaching up, she found a bandage taped high on her forehead. Even through the drugs she could feel a sharp pain when she found the gigantic lump. "Then I fell, but snagged my boot on a crate of Asian pears. My knee made an awful noise. All crunchy."

Harry winced and paled.

"Like dropping a bag of pretzels on a concrete floor. Crunch! Crunch! Crunch!"

Harry went sheet white. Natalya knew exactly what she was doing and just offered her an evil smile that Harry wouldn't be able to see as he still stood behind Natalya.

"Valeria and Alejandro wanted to stay, but they have barley on the malting floor. I forced them to leave as soon as we found out it was just a really bad sprain and you said you'd bring the cavalry. Didn't know the cavalry was so pretty." Even to herself she was sounding fairly stupid, but the drugs just made her happy to go with the flow.

"How…" Harry swallowed hard and looked about the curtained corner of the E.R.

Becky checked. Still not hooked to any machines. Good.

"How is this my fault?"

"Thinking 'bout…" the drowsies were coming back, "…you. 'Stead of my head." Her eyes drifted closed though she fought against it. "Sh-cared poor Alejandro spitless."

NATALYA'S sudden grasp on Harry's arm was painful. She'd hit a nerve junction of some sort.

"Hey! Ow!" He tried to shake her off which only hurt more. In moments she'd dragged him out of the E.R. and into the parking lot. Salem was twenty degrees warmer than Eagle Cove and the sun felt bright and hard unlike the way it shone softly on the coast.

She pushed him up against the side of Becky's van before releasing him. She did it hard enough that he bunged his elbow right on the funny bone.

"Cut it out, Natalya!"

She poked a finger into the center of his chest, "Can I trust you?"

"What are you talking about?"

Natalya growled. It was a dangerous sound that didn't make him think of dog or cat; it was pure pissed-off woman.

"What am I missing?" It was one of his better skills that nothing took him by surprise. He could adjust faster than most lawyers and better than any witness to changing circumstances. But he had no insights in this situation.

"That," Natalya jabbed a finger toward the E.R., "is one of my very best friends. I don't know what you did to her last night. She was all strange after the reception and now I know whose fault that is. Don't even think about going there, Slater. She's drugged out and she's going to be hurting. You so much as blink wrong and I'll know. I'll come down from Portland and castrate you with a rusty butter knife."

"Christ, Natalya! What sort of a man do you take me for?"

She hesitated, then shifted back onto her heels, giving him a little breathing space. "I don't know you anymore, Harry. I've barely seen you since we both went to college. But I most certainly knew the shallow troll that was Harry Slater."

"Well," he wished that description hadn't once fit him so well, but there wasn't much point in arguing. "Even then I wasn't the sort who takes advantage of a woman under pain meds. You have my word as a member of the Bar Association on that one." He wasn't quite sure why he felt compelled to add that last. In New Orleans there'd been no past to live down. He'd simply arrived and made himself into the man he was today. If asked before the last two days, he'd have said he did a halfway decent job of it. But the women of Eagle Cove were definitely keeping him off balance.

"And you find Becky attractive?"

"Shit, yes!" And only after he answered did he catch her change in tone. He hadn't been ready for a friendly, casual question in the midst of a cross-examination. Hadn't meant to speak that truth to a woman threatening him with bodily harm. "Damn but you'd have made a good attorney, Natalya."

Natalya checked her watch and then cursed. "I'm going to be late. You take care of her, Harry. Can you do that for me?"

He raised three fingers in a Boy Scout salute, "Scout's honor." He'd been a lousy Boy Scout.

She rolled her eyes at him, because of course she knew that about him. Couldn't get away with crap in a small town. Then with another curse she checked her watch again, rushed over to her Mini Cooper, and cranked it to life. She backed out of her spot until the driver's side window was close beside where he still leaned against the van.

"Don't screw it up, Slater, or you're dog meat!" Then with a harsh chirp of her tires, she was racing out of the lot and back onto Mission Street.

Harry headed back into the E.R.

Becky was waiting for him in a wheelchair. They must have given her a wakeup med, because her eyes were bright. That too-bright of over-medication. He was used to seeing it from his days defending low-lifers back in criminal court. He'd escaped to civil court as fast as he could, at least corporate clients didn't try to knife you when you asked for your fee.

He didn't like the bandage on her forehead either. She wore a denim workshirt that still sported a couple dribbles of blood that some E.R. nurse had been kind enough to try and sponge off. Her right leg was wrapped in a brace and propped up on the wheelchair's raised leg support.

"Nice skirt," it was all he could think to say to cheer her up. He didn't like seeing Becky Billings looking sad as she fingered the top of the leg brace. And the skirt was nice; as different from last night's little black dress as you could get. Bright splashes of color: reds, blues, and golds, as if she'd pulled on a flower garden.

"Valeria's. The woman thinks of everything. Even as they were loading me into the ambulance, she knew I wouldn't be able to get back into my jeans." On cue a nurse handed him a bag. It contained a pair of battered work boots, socks, folded up jeans, and a set of bright blue panties covered in giant sunflowers. Which meant that under her skirt she was wearing—

Harry could feel his breath growing short as the nurse handed him a pair of crutches. Which worked as thoroughly as a cold shower.

The nurse rattled off a set of instructions about time off the leg, time on the crutches, follow-up appointments with the local doctor, and so on. He should be taking careful notes, and under normal conditions his mind was a steel trap for such information. But Becky: sad, battered, yet still sexy as hell in a wheelchair, was the ultimate distraction to his thoughts.

"Here," the nurse flapped a sheaf of papers as thick as a trial pleading under his nose. "This covers everything I've just said. Take these top two sheets to the pharmacy down the hall to get the prescriptions filled."

"Okay." In a daze he was wheeling Becky down the hall. The view wasn't all that different from his first look down at her in the kitchen last night. But instead of a jaunty attack on the world, her head was tilted sadly down. He raised a hand off one handle and stroked it down the long flow of golden brown.

"It'll be okay, Becky."

She nodded in a very unconvinced manner.

And then, because he'd only kept one hand on the handles, he practically rammed her into a wall.

When she didn't even tease him about his driving, he really began to worry.

BECKY LAY back in the passenger seat and tried not to scream at her leg. It was throbbing through the narcotic, which was making her stomach churn through the anti-nausea drug, which made her so...*angry* at the world.

She didn't have time to be hurt.

The van was filled with almost a ton of malted barley, dried hops, and Asian pears at their peak of ripeness. She couldn't afford to miss one day, never mind the ten that the nurse had told her to stay off her leg. Truly couldn't afford it. Part of being a supplier was that her clients, taverns and restaurants, expected a steady and reliable supply. If they ran out of 5B beer, they'd just roll someone else's keg into place and she'd have to fight like a demon to get the slot back by offering special price incentives that she could ill afford. She was being a success, but lately that was a seventy hour-a-week proposition with time off only for best friends' weddings.

And the Asian pears didn't have ten days either. They were picked at the moment of perfection and were now scenting the van with their soft, sweet tease. If they weren't in boiling copper within two days, she might as well throw the whole mess away.

"Talk to me, Harry. About anything. So far you've just driven in silence clutching the wheel like a concentrating drunk. Anabelle is a sweet girl and only needs a light hand."

"Anabelle?"

"Go ahead, tell me that your Beamer or Porsche doesn't have some testosterone laden name. Max from *Mad Max* or Luthor, from Super-man's arch enemy."

"Clive, my Mercedes Roadster—"

"SLK or SL?"

"SLK. The 350," he said it cautiously. Harry looked over at her for the first time since they'd gotten her into the van and buckled into place. He hadn't taken even the tiniest bit of advantage as they'd brushed and bumped together while figuring out how to maneuver her from wheelchair to the front seat.

"Wimp!" For two reasons, but she wasn't going to mention the second one. Even if she hadn't been in the mood for flirting, it would have been nice if he'd at least tried.

"I'm a wimp for owning an SLK?"

"C'mon," she loved that her tease was working. "The SL has half again the horsepower."

"And twice the price tag."

"Wimp!" All that time she'd spent online daydreaming over a hot driving machine a few months back hadn't turned out to be a waste of time after all.

Harry drove for another mile down the freeway in silence before turning once again and sticking his tongue out at her.

"Bring that here and I'll kiss it for you."

"Not a chance, Billings." With that he returned his attention to the road.

Not a chance? Sure, kissing Becky Billings had been fun at a wedding reception, but not good enough for every day. Especially not for a man like Harry Slater. Double especially not now that she was broken.

Well, he wasn't going to see her crying over it.

She closed her eyes and let the rocking of the heavy-laden van combine with the narcotic fuzziness and nausea to transport her away from this moment. Away from the heat burning in her eyes. Way far away.

———

THE SUN WAS WELL to the west by the time Harry was creeping the van toward Becky's.

"Not the house," she murmured, her first words in a hundred miles. It had been lonely, but he was glad that she was sleeping. Must have had a hell of a day and sleep was probably the best thing for her.

The house was nothing much. Just a small two-bedroom place at one end of the fields. A truck and a minivan were parked close beside it. Somehow he'd had the impression that Becky lived alone.

"Had to sell it in the early years to get going."

Oh.

Past the house stood an old hip-roof red barn. Becky's family had kept forty head of cattle, mostly dairy and some beef. His family's freezer had often had half of a Billing's cow done up as steaks, roasts, and burger. There was nothing like grass-fed beef. He'd forgotten how much he missed that flavor.

But no longer. The fields were all deep in hay from the house out to the barn near the little airstrip. The hangar with Peggy's truck parked beside it stood only a hundred yards way.

"The barn?"

"Around the side," Becky's voice was rough, probably from just waking up.

The driveway led to a well-mowed and tended parking area capable of holding ten or more cars. The old calving barn had been spruced up. It was a single story extension off the side of the main barn perhaps thirty by forty feet. Cheery clumps of mums and *Rosa rugosa* grew to either side of a broad double door with diamond-shaped glass panes. The siding had been painted the same colors as Becky's van, dark brown with golden lettering: "Becky Billings Blue-Bird Brewery, The 5B's Tasting Room." He'd forgotten about her nickname of Bluebird.

"Do you still sing?" She'd had far and away the best voice in the school. Her Maria in *The Sound of Music* had been great. A little...actually a lot sexier and sassier than Julie Andrews, but it was Becky Billings after all.

"In the shower," she bit off the admission.

"Pity." And it was. He didn't know much about singing that he didn't pick up from the playlist on his phone. It wasn't as if she should have pulled up and gone to Nashville, but there'd always been merry humming or singing whenever Becky was around. "Your singing was always a really happy sound."

She looked at him strangely. Again his training failed him and he couldn't make any sense of it.

This whole side of the barn had been fixed up. She waved him toward a big cargo door for loading hay that stood close beside the converted tasting room. It had a person-sized door built in.

"Back in."

He eased the van into place, shut it down, and came around to help her. By the time he reached her she was a tangle of seatbelt, crutches, and frustration. He tugged the crutches from her hands and stood them against the side of the van. Then he unraveled the seatbelt.

She wouldn't look up at him. Embarrassed? Sorry to have been a burden? Or just because she was hurt?

Unable to stand the tightness in his chest from watching her, he leaned in and scooped her up into his arms.

"Hey!" Becky started to squirm.

"Don't do that, unless you *want* me to drop you?"

She went absolutely still for a moment and then relaxed enough that it felt as if he was carrying a woman and not a mannequin. Thankfully he'd kept her keys in his hand and was able to unlock the brewery door without having to set her down.

As they crossed the threshold, Becky reached out and flicked a light switch. Harry could only stop and gawk. The stalls had been ripped out and walls raised to create a sealed room. There were rows of gleaming steel tanks—some tall, others squat. A big copper kettle shaped like an upside-down wine glass from the bowl to halfway up the stem dominated the center of the room. Stainless steel piping connected tanks with big valve handles along the way. A control panel fit for an aircraft carrier stood off to one side.

"Holy shit, Billings!"

"Beautiful, isn't it?"

"Beautiful? No. Scary maybe," he made a show of peering about cautiously. "Any monster creation I should know about, Dr. Frankenstein?"

"Not a one." For the first time since they'd left the E.R. the tease was back in her voice which was a major relief. "Well, maybe one or two little ones, just, you know, knee-high maybe. I'm still starting out."

Harry gazed at the bewildering array of shining equipment. "If this is just starting out, I'm completely humbled."

"It's way easier than what you do."

"Law? That has got to be simpler."

"You don't need seven years of schooling to do this. You can put me down."

"Well sure, but they don't teach lawyers anything about alchemy and magic, especially not with such high-tech cauldrons." He wasn't ready to set her down yet. She was trim. And while that didn't make her weightless and his arms were tiring, he liked the feel of her curled against his chest.

"I do have a book of secret formulas."

"Can I see it? I promise not to understand a single thing. I'm merely a little curious about what real-world magical formulas look like."

"Maybe. Now put me down, Harry."

"Sure, where?"

She pointed toward a set of rough stairs that led up to the hayloft, "I have an apartment up there."

"You have a bum leg remember. That's not going to happen."

"I— Damn it, you're right. I hate that you're right."

"Me personally?" His arms really were aching. He spotted a battered couch that looked well lived in and set her down on the cushions.

"No, the fact that I can't even go home," she looked toward the stairs again and appeared about to cry.

He was certainly not ready for that.

Now he saw that the couch was part of a small living area set in the corner of the brewery. It had all of the basic amenities: couch, an equally well worn and cushy armchair, coffee table, a tiny two-burner kitchen area, and most importantly a bathroom. It was…he surveyed the area…it was for the nights when she had to pay attention to some critical stage of the brewing process. That meant that he'd set her down wrong.

He shifted some of the couch pillows and patted them. "Here," he supported half her weight as she moved to the other end of the couch, and ended up facing her vast array of brewing apparatus.

She was scowling up at him with a look of deep concentration.

"What?"

"When did you become so observant?"

"Lawyer, remember. Part of the job description."

"And so thoughtful?"

"Oh, well that part of it is just a mistake. I won't let it happen again."

That finally earned him a Becky laugh. It was a short one, but he could detect none of the earlier bitterness in her tone.

He glanced at his watch, "Crap!" He rushed out to the van to retrieve her crutches and her drugs. She was past time for the next painkiller and the nurse and the pharmacist had warned him about not getting behind on the pain meds for the first couple days.

***

BECKY LET HIM PAMPER HER, mostly because she didn't have a choice. Her emotions were in such chaos that she barely knew which way was up.

Harry had made it clear that he didn't want to kiss her again. Hadn't said a single thing during the whole drive while she fought back tears.

Then he carried her about as if she was a fairy princess rather than a broken garden gnome. And he'd admired her brewery. Not just, "That's nice," like most people, but he'd been seriously impressed.

What she really hadn't been ready for was the perception that somehow told him that she would always choose to face her brewery. Then he'd rushed back in from the van as if being twenty minutes behind on her meds was an international crisis. Actually the way her knee was feeling half an hour later, those twenty minutes were at least of statewide if not national concern.

"Perhaps I should call out the National Guard."

"Don't need them. You have me," Harry startled her as he came back into the brewery. He'd said that he would be right back after watching her take the meds, but then had driven away in her van and she had no idea why. Harry held aloft a brown paper bag. It smelled of…

"Oh my god!" She couldn't keep the squeak out of her voice.

"Yes!" Harry did a little dance step. "The man nails it!"

"Screw that! Gimme!"

And in moments he had a pair of May Conklin's burgers from the Brass Plover Pub and a massive load of onion rings spread out on the small coffee table. He perched down past her feet.

She grabbed the burger that he held out.

"I brought Cokes because you can't have alcohol with your meds."

She didn't point out that she had several hundred bottles of cider, root beer, and other 5B sodas sitting on the shelves not twenty feet away.

"What inspired you to such perfection?" She took a monstrous bite and closed her eyes to appreciate the good beef, Mr. Greene's garden-fresh tomatoes and lettuce, and May's trademark sauce.

"Because you don't have crap in your fridge," he waved a hand toward her kitchenette. "Don't forget. You're supposed to have food with your meds."

"My kitchen," she mumbled around another mouthful, "is upstairs and very well stocked. Not that I'm complaining."

Harry gazed up at the ceiling for a long moment as he chewed. "Right. Forgot about that. I'm not much of a cook anyway."

"You just haveta have the right kitchen."

And again with that fine perception of his, he glanced over his shoulder at the brewery rather than back at the ceiling.

"Come here."

He eyed her carefully as if trying to gauge her intentions.

As if she could be any more obvious. It was as if she'd misread him again, but she didn't think so.

Harry inspected his half-eaten burger but didn't take another bite.

"If it's not me—"

"It's not you," Harry cut her off.

"Then what?"

"Look," and she could see him trying to pull on his reasonable-lawyer cloak. "You're hurting and you're on Schedule II narcotics. If I took advantage of that, I'd be no better than…than dog meat."

"Dog meat? That's Natalya's favorite threat. She cornered you, didn't she?"

Becky could see it on his face.

"I love Natalya to death, but for this I just might have to kill her. Is that the reason you've been acting so strangely around me all day?"

"Her points on decent and proper behavior have a valid basis—"

"Counselor, shut up!"

It took him a moment, but he closed his mouth. Then a grin slowly formed. It didn't start at his lips, it started with those ocean blue eyes.

"The court has ruled. I am not Natalya's little sister despite my size. And being of sound mind and body, I hereby order you to kiss me."

"Well," the grin had reached his lips. "I can't speak to the mind, but that is some body you have."

"Stop quibbling."

And he did.

It wasn't a scorcher like last night, or maybe that was the buffering of the drugs, but Harry didn't leave much else to complain about. It was just lip to lip as they both still held their burgers, which made it only the second best kiss ever committed…anywhere, ever.

Her head was spinning long after he leaned back and resumed eating his burger with a cat-and-canary smile.

"Don't need any drugs as long as I have access to that," she muttered to herself.

"I have a supply in stock."

"Good, give me another dose."

"I'm busy eating."

She couldn't wipe the smile from her face as they continued their meal. Okay, she had a blown knee, a knot on her forehead the size of a quahog and a brace most of the way up to her crotch. But she did have a whole lot to smile about at the moment.

Then she looked up at her vats and tanks. The latest fermentations needed checking. And the mash tun and kettle were both empty— waiting for the ton of product stacked right now in the back of her van.

She decided to worry about all that in the morning.

She barely noticed when strong hands tucked a blanket around her.

The kiss on her forehead was a soft caress.

CHAPTER 4

The cell phone ringing eased Harry awake with all of the grace of an electric chair. His nerves were jangling as he managed to answer it.

By a dim worklight in the brewery, he could see that Becky was still asleep on the couch. And his back could feel every second of sleep he'd managed while slumped in the armchair.

He didn't want to disturb her and hurried out the door before speaking. It was still dark and a chill bit at his bare arms.

"This had better be good," not his most gracious greeting. Especially not if it was one of the partners at Parrish, Merryfield, and Roland operating from another time zone. Harry was in the final year of the partner track—the one senior associate that everyone knew was a shoe-in. They rarely tapped more than one a year, but the firm's director had made it clear he was in, without making promises of course.

"Peggy has a flight this morning and Greg and Jessica left town," the Judge began without preamble.

"Why didn't you stop him?"

"I had told him to take the week off and I have never been one to go back on my word, despite my ill-spoken sentiment yesterday morning."

"And you're calling me because…" Please tell him he was wrong.

"Your assistance this morning would be appreciated. Am I correct in assuming that you're in town?" His father was careful not to ask where he actually might be as he hadn't come home last night. "Passed out drunk on Cal's couch" had been too likely a response to that question in his younger days. There was no point lying about anything in a small town, especially not in the Judge's house.

"Yes," he was in town though he wished he could have said no.

"Fine. We open in twenty-eight minutes."

And Harry was holding a disconnected phone. "I never agreed to help, you arrogant prick!"

Shouting at a cell phone in the middle of the night. Really useful; but it was more than he'd ever managed or would manage to his father's face. Twenty-eight minutes. Okay, it wasn't the middle of the night. It was five thirty-two in the morning. Because, if the Judge was anything, he was punctual.

There wasn't time to get home, shower, and change. Eagle Cove wasn't big, but LBB Way wasn't exactly a raceway and Becky's was on the far end of town.

He tiptoed back into the barn-turned-brewery.

Upstairs he discovered that a section of the hayloft had been walled off. It was a single space that was both cozy and rustic. Windows to one side opened onto darkness, and to the other they revealed the unfinished section of the hayloft, still partly stocked with large bales of sweet grass.

Becky had wrestled a king size bed up the stairs, it was covered with a quilt made from all the colors of the sea. It started dark in one corner and went through a storm-tossed transition of intricate piece-work before finally emerging in the lighter tones. A good kitchen made of salvaged materials dominated the other end of the room: a large cast iron sink, refinished planking thick enough to park a tractor on, and odd-sized cupboards that looked more appropriate for animal tack than human food.

In a corner stood a toilet and clawfoot tub. What was it that women had against showers? The clawfoot had a curtain on circular rod, but the spray nozzle was a handheld on a steel flex-hose coiled about the faucets.

All open plan. Becky either never entertained up here or she had no modesty around her partners. He very much liked the image of a naked Becky cooking in the kitchen in easy view from the bed. He didn't like the image of Becky here with another man. Possessiveness wasn't really his thing, but he didn't like it anyway.

Something was missing and it took him a moment to figure out what. The loft apartment had no living room. No desk. Becky might sleep, cook, and bathe up here, but she lived downstairs close by her brewery.

He shed his clothes, trying to ignore the intimate sensations of being naked in her bedroom, and washed himself quickly. Just like the plumbing in the brewery downstairs, it was perfect—hot and plentiful.

There was nothing else to change into other than yesterday's clothes. They felt clammy and grimy. They were still stained with grease and ketchup from yesterday's diner disaster.

"And today is looking so much better." Maybe instead of dry cleaning he'd just have them burned. He found a toothbrush still in its packaging and used that.

He left a note and things she'd need where Becky couldn't help but see it and kissed her lightly on the forehead. Unshowered, injured, and hurting, she was about the damn cutest thing he'd ever seen all tucked under her blanket with little more than her hair showing.

He resisted, just as he had last night, his urge to do so much more. Natalya had been right to trust him, even if she didn't. But he could at least wish he was a little less honorable.

BECKY WOKE to the start of her van's engine. It was dark except for the nightlight she kept on in the brewery—she'd banged her shin more than once when some overpressure alarm had gone off in the early days or a timer had run out. Now her living room was never truly dark.

It was so quiet that she could hear the gear shift lever dropping into place and the parking brake clunk off.

Someone was taking her van.

She heaved the blanket aside, swung her legs off the couch—

And landed in a heap on the floor between the couch and the coffee table on which she banged her elbow.

Her knee. A leg brace. And as she lay on the floor, a slow cascade of pills rolled off the edge of the table and began piling up inches from her nose.

Pain meds.

She'd blown out her knee, which used that moment of awareness to start hurting like mad.

But that still didn't explain her van.

She sat up as well as she could to stem the flow of pills. The concrete was damn cold through her thin skirt. Valeria's skirt.

A quick sniff of the air told her that the brewery was okay. No scent of overcooked mash or a fermenting tank having outgassed yeasty air through an overpressure valve. No scent of warm copper from a working kettle either. In fact, the kettle was cold because…all of the product that was in the back of her van was currently crunching down the gravel drive and off into the distance.

As she gathered pills, she spotted the note.

Gone to help Judge with breakfast.
Rest easy. Take meds with food.
I'll bring back lunch.
H.D.S.

H.D.S.? Oh, Harold Davis Slater. Or was it Harold David? She didn't even know.

He'd left a container of yogurt, a banana, and an energy bar on the table for her which was awfully sweet. The last time a man had made a meal for her had been her father making waffles the morning before climbing into the RV and heading north. It wasn't much of a meal, but Becky wasn't going to tell Harry how many bonus points it had earned him.

She opened the yogurt, but there was no spoon. And her crutches were…she scanned around…leaning by the door a good dozen steps away.

"Missed that one, didn't you, Harry?"

Becky leveraged her cold butt back onto the warm sofa. From there she achieved her feet and immediately wished she hadn't. The brace didn't compensate nearly enough for putting weight on her bad leg. Raising it so that she could hop across the room wasn't much better; she more ran into the rough barn wall than reached it.

She added splinters to her list of woes. Harry was rapidly losing those bonus points. With her crutches she made it to the bathroom, fetched a spoon and a juice in the kitchenette, and hobbled back to the couch. Breakfast and taking her meds lasted about two minutes.

She checked her phone, rather she tried to. It wasn't anywhere to be found. She could almost picture it…on the dash of the van. Crap! The big clock above the brewery's control panel read six a.m. Harry would be back in about five hours. What in the world was she supposed to think about for five hours?

Certainly not Harry Slater.

Her other option was staring her in the face. She could think about all of that gleaming hardware standing there doing nothing.

She'd be better off thinking about Harry.

HARRY DECIDED that he'd be better off dead.

He had the coffee maker figured out, so that part of it was okay. And to replace the soiled Hugo Boss the Judge had found him an Eagle Cove t-shirt with more of Ma's art on it. He only wore t-shirts when he played racquetball and it left him feeling strangely exposed. Ma's art made him feel like a walking billboard for opportunistic exploitation. Didn't the man respect anything about his wife's legacy? Every local would recognize it and know that her son was wearing…

Least of his problems.

It took him a while to understand that the Judge had very specific rules of the kitchen, which really shouldn't have been a surprise, but it was.

He offered omelets five different ways that weren't written down on the menu; thankfully the locals knew them and Harry soon had those down. Pancakes came in two different-sized stacks. And oatmeal apparently only ever existed in one, single form: with sliced dried apricots and diced apples. Everything came with a side of farm sausage and hash browns—neither was optional. Marshmallows in hot chocolate were also considered a punishable crime for anyone tall enough to rest their elbows on the table without a high chair.

Harry ignored him on the last point because the other option was whipped cream from a can. When he found the stash of several bags of tiny marshmallows hidden in the server's station he decided that just maybe Greg was an okay little brother, even if he did marry Jessica Baxter and then skip town just because it was his honeymoon.

The problem was that the Judge's omelets were absolutely incredible and everyone in town knew it.

That meant the tables filled rapidly and stayed that way. Every time he looked out the big front windows, he saw another person walking toward their end of town along Beach Way. It was like a zombie apocalypse or something; they just kept coming.

Because they stayed mostly full, there were seventeen wrong tables that he could deliver an order to, using the process of elimination. His average hit rate of the correct table was awful. He finally started marking the tickets with quadrants of the room: north, east, south, west.

"Greg has the tables numbered," the Judge kept offering him service tips across the pass-through window. This time it was accompanied by three omelets and a tall stack that went to one of the five tables of four people each in the west corner by the door, but he had no idea which one. Or did it go to the two sets of two. If the Judge offered more variety, it would be easier…but he didn't…so it wasn't.

"How are they numbered?" He had already proven that a tray was a bad idea in his hands, so he grabbed the first two plates, then cursed. It was about the hundredth time this morning that he'd forgotten to use hot pads. The Judge served his plates very well warmed. His father's hands might have calluses of iron, but Harry's didn't.

"No idea," the Judge actually looked chagrined. "He just makes it work."

"Thanks for the helpful tip." He grabbed the two plates again using hot pads and went in search of their owners.

BECKY SPENT the morning going quietly insane.

Thoughts of Harry distracted a woman only so long when she had nothing more than a pair of nice kisses and a slow dance to base them on. Her reading material was upstairs, as was her laptop. She eyed the climb several times, but her antics of the morning were still having repercussions. There was a demon poking at the inside of her knee with a sharp knife, and every time she stood up the room gave a nasty spin that sent her plummeting back to the cushions.

If she was her old self, dressed in jeans, she'd just scoot up the stairs on her butt. However, ruining Valeria's beautiful skirt was not an option and the inevitable splinters that would jab through the thin material and into her behind didn't sound like much fun either. The tasting room didn't have hours today, so she didn't need to worry about that.

If she had her goddamn phone, she could call Peggy for help. But her phone was…where? Oh, parked down at The Puffin Diner. Maybe if she wrote a note to herself she'd remember that for more than fifteen minutes.

Harry's score had slipped below par and was rapidly sliding down the cliff and being washed out to sea.

For lack of anything else to do, she managed to fetch her recipe books. They were her prized possessions and she kept them locked in a small fire safe she purchased for just that purpose. So far there were four thick, leather-bound journals in the series. She had to make three trips to get back to the couch. Why four books hadn't taken two or four painful, weaving trips rather than three was something she couldn't figure out at the moment.

Each one had been horridly expensive, especially in the beginning. Custom hand-tooled leather outside and handmade paper within. Barry did such beautiful work and she'd forked over the cash for each one because she wanted her business to be a real and serious business. No fooling around, no cutting corners. One hundred percent the best the whole way. She brushed her fingers over the hand tooling, "5B" with roman numeral volume numbers worked into the soft leather. She loved holding the journals. These were her children, for now. At least until she found the right man.

There was a laugh. If Harry Slater was anything, he wasn't the right man. Worldly, handsome, living the high life in New Orleans with his Mercedes-Benz roadster. She could see him back in Eagle Cove as easily as Jessica. Except Jessica had come back, surprising everyone including herself.

Becky turned to the journals, knowing Harry was never coming back to stay.

Integrating the Asian pear was going to require a new approach. The texture would behave like an apple, but the flavoring profile was so much more subtle than anything she'd used before that she hardly knew where to begin. She was halfway to her feet to fetch one so that she'd have the flavor on her tongue as she thought about it, when she remembered that the produce was with her cell phone. In the van parked a mile away. She plummeted back down into the couch and her knee screamed. Crap! She sat very still until the pain eased back down to merely intolerable.

She went back to Volume I.

The first journal covered the pre-beer years, but she flipped through it anyway for nostalgia. Pop had started her off at the age of eight brewing a demijohn of root beer. The five-gallon glass vessel had exploded and nearly killed one of the barn cats. That's how she'd learned about pressure relief valves.

She paged through the learning years. By twelve she made more spending money than most of her friends' allowances selling off her root beer, twenty-five cents a bottle and a nickel back when you returned the glass. Cider and ginger ale had come next. She'd taken over a whole bay of the farm's equipment shed by the time she was sixteen. The second journal contained the years of research on the brewing process. Eventually, there were sketches of the basic system design that she hadn't had a chance to build it until she was twenty.

Pop was frugal and Mom was good with money and they'd trained her well. She never borrowed, never used credit. Becky took no action until she had the cash in hand.

Instead of giving her the money they'd set aside for her college, they gave her the farm in exchange for a ten percent share of profits. They'd taken her college fund and their savings and moved to Alaska. So far all they'd received for their faith in her had been ten percent of the fee she collected for the pasture she rented out for hay; a hundred percent of the brewing money went back into the business. For now.

The second journal ended with the results of her first batch, a simple pilsner. No special flavoring, just a clean, single-fermentation brew.

As she studied the third and fourth journals, she couldn't seem to get comfortable. No matter what she did, her brace was awkward and uncomfortable and her knee throbbed. Every time she thought she had an idea about how to make the Asian pear come to life, a new twinge sent it slipping away.

It was hurting badly by the time she remembered she was supposed to stay ahead of the pain. She popped a pill and tried to cheer it to action before it could possibly have reached her stomach.

Food, she was supposed to have food with it. But again, there was nothing here on the ground floor. She'd never really used the kitchenette, just the mini-fridge for cold sodas.

The recipes in the journals were blurring together. Two bushels in the mash, but scrape off the skins early? Or should she core them to avoid any bitterness from the seeds? Maybe…

There were no maybes. Not until she got the product unloaded and had the malt headed into the mash tun.

But she had no product.

It was in the van.

It would be here soon. It had better be or Jessica was going to be out one brother-in-law and Becky didn't care if it was during her friend's honeymoon.

And when the van finally did show up, she'd need help unloading.

Zander was her best bet. Normally she'd just call Peggy. They went back and forth across the hundred yards separating the barn and Peggy's hangar all the time to give each other a hand lifting a wing, installing a new fermenting tank, or just to share a meal. She was as close to a second mom as a girl could have. But this was getting past friendship and family. There was hard work to be done and there would be more to follow. And if he wasn't available—

She reached for the phone…and swore for the hundredth time today. She couldn't call anyone; her phone was still in the damn van.

When she finally heard the tires crunching on the gravel, she grabbed her crutches and bolted for the door. Then almost did a face plant crossing the high threshold.

From fighting to stay upright her leg was screaming as Harry pulled up in front of her with a wave.

The crutches were wobbling and her knee almost let go despite the brace.

As the van stopped, Becky knew what was about to happen and there was nothing she could do to stop it.

She was about to utterly humiliate herself.

HARRY SCRAMBLED but he was too slow.

Becky collapsed to her knees. Tangled in the crutches and with one leg out of commission she went down hard on the grass. The retching sound that ripped from her had him rushing forward.

He pulled her hair clear barely in time and did his best to support her as she heaved long past dry before collapsing against him.

"Wow, Becky." Harry didn't really know what else to say.

"I'm done utterly barfing my guts out now."

"Yeah." He never met a woman who could laugh at herself when she was in complete misery—not that he usually hung around for such moments, but it was still impressive. "Yeah."

"Sure. Fine. Whatever." She flapped a hand indicating the mess she'd just made.

"Nothing a hose won't fix. Let's get you back on the couch," he scooped her up into his arms.

She curled there and he could feel the shivers coursing through her as her body reacted to the abuse. He seemed to be holding and carrying Becky a lot in the last forty-eight hours. He resettled her on the couch, found a damp cloth and a glass of water, but she wouldn't look up at him. While she cleaned up he fetched her toothbrush from upstairs, loaded it up, and handed it to her without comment.

"So," he did his best to keep his tone light, "what was *that* all about?"

"I don't like those pills," she mumbled.

He eyed them and noticed there was only one bottle. "Where are the others?"

"What others?"

He started looking around and found them under the edge of the counter on the far side of the living room as if she'd heaved them there, "These. Anti-nausea."

"Now they tell me."

"With food," he lowered his voice into that I'm-a-lawyer-so-don't-mess-with-me register.

"The only food was upstairs and my knee was hurting too much to try the stairs."

And now he was the one who felt like eight kinds of an idiot. "How long ago?"

"An hour, maybe."

"That means most of it's in your bloodstream," he hoped, he wasn't sure. "Let's give you a buffer of some food anyway."

He went back out to the van and grabbed the bag that the Judge had prepared for him. It had been a real surprise. He'd cleaned up the front of house at the diner as the crowd tailed off, but he really wanted to get back to Becky. However, he didn't want to leave the Judge high and dry again as there was no sign of Peggy.

"Here," his father had held out a bundle of small bills. "Half tips from yesterday and today. Actually one-third from yesterday as I felt that Peggy earned her share."

There'd be no argument from him on that judgment. Harry had riffled through the wad of crumbled green. Nice for a breakfast place he supposed, but not much more than he was paid per hour, which was a quarter of what his firm billed him at per hour. "Greg makes a living on this?"

"He also receives free rent and utilities at the house along with a small salary. And he now serves fancy sit-down dinners Friday and Saturday nights."

Then his father had handed over a bag warm and heavy with food. "Lunch for two. It's a good thing you're doing, helping out Becky."

And his father knew what Harry was doing because there were no secrets in Eagle Cove. He hadn't known what to say other than "Thanks."

On his way back into the barn with lunch, he gathered up her crutches and set them inside the door.

"No!" Becky called out without even raising her head. "Not way over there, Slater."

It took a moment to realize what she'd meant, but it took him no time at all after that to feel like an utter idiot. He'd left her without food and without crutches.

He sat down across from her, "Are you ready for some food?"

Becky smiled at him, "God you are so cute, Slater."

"I am?" He'd earned "handsome" often enough that it had become a meaningless non-sequitur. "Cute" was new.

"I barf my guts out all over you—"

"Actually you missed. Better luck next time."

"—and you have the decency to be the one acting guilty about where you put my crutches."

"But that was unforgiv—"

"Like I said, very cute." She took the to-go container.

Inside were bags of chips and egg salad sandwiches built on thick slices of Cal's sourdough bread. He didn't think after a second morning working at the diner that he'd ever want to face an egg again, but the sandwiches tasted even better than they looked.

"Your dad can make a mean sandwich."

"He can." He also wasn't quite the person that Harry was expecting. He was as gruff and dictatorial as ever with all of his little rules. But he'd also paid Harry for his troubles and it sounded as if he'd worked out a fair deal with Greg. And he really cared how Becky was doing. Not enough to ask outright, but enough to make a nice lunch for her.

"Once we're done eating, I need my cell phone from the van."

"You couldn't even call for help? Shit!" He dropped his sandwich and rushed out to grab it right away. Couldn't he do anything right around Becky?

She took it with a simple, "Thanks. I need to call around and find a pair of hands to hire. Nothing good is happening to all of the supplies in the back of my van by baking them in the sun."

"Who are you—" *Wrong question, Counselor.* "How about if I help you?"

"I thought you were on vacation? Frankly, I kind of expected you to be gone by now. You never visit Eagle Cove for long."

"I'm rather surprised myself." His normal limit was forty-eight hours. Some visits he spent longer in transit than he actually did in Eagle Cove and that suited him just fine. "This trip I don't seem to be in a hurry to leave." He'd actually planned to fly down to Vegas for a couple days and have a hedonistic week before heading back into the grind.

Becky was looking at him and he could see she was thinking hard.

"Penny for your thoughts," he asked her.

"Cheapskate."

"I'm a lawyer. Why are you surprised?"

"A lawyer who drives an SLK350."

"I'm not a stupid lawyer, just a cheapskate."

"Well, I can't pay more than minimum wage. Maybe a bonus for good behavior."

"Good behavior, huh?" He'd certainly liked the way she thought about court orders last night and fines for contempt the night before. "Bonuses sound very tempting."

"This will be really awful for you, so just know you can call it quits at any time and I'll start calling around."

"Deal. Where do we begin?" Her radiant smile of relief was payment enough right there. A beautiful woman who smiled at him like that not because she was manipulating him, but just because he made her happy. It was a hell of a charge to his system.

"Open the big door and back the van in."

BECKY HAD NEVER APPRECIATED the benefits of having a willing man-servant before. Especially not one who looked so nice after he worked up a sweat and stripped off his t-shirt.

"Whatever you do down there in New Orleans, it suits you well, Counselor," she called from her couch. He was heaving fifty-pound burlap bags of malt and hops out of the van and stacking them in piles by the malt hopper. She hated not having her hands on her own prod-uct, but watching a real-life Harry Slater sweat on her behalf was better than Bradley Cooper in the movies.

"Racquetball mostly. Some gym time," he grunted out as he dropped another bag on the pile. And he'd been surprisingly kind after she'd barfed all over him, or at least right in front of him.

Her knee was starting to hurt again. She reached for her crutches and Harry materialized in front of her and squatted down until they were eye to eye.

"What do you need?"

"Well I'm done with that," she waved her hands at the bottles of drugs. "Over the counter for this gal."

"And I'm guessing that they're upstairs, so nope. Put those crutches down."

He was so close that she could smell him. The hint of new clothes from the t-shirt had left him, and there was a small tear in his khakis that he hadn't noticed yet but would probably give him apoplectic fits when he did. He wasn't ugly sweaty, just sort of heated and glowy and smelled so positively male that she wished she could brew a batch with just that heady scent. She wouldn't sell it, she'd just crack a bottle on rare occasions when her spirits needed bolstering after he was gone. His breathing was hard enough from the workout to have his chest and flat gut doing their own beautiful workout. Tempting the fates, she leaned in.

"I'll get them." And he was gone, trotting up the stairs in what he probably thought of as his slumming around shoes, two hundred dollars' worth of Nikes.

He came back down, tossed her a bottle, and kept going.

All she could do was gape. She wanted to be holding a gorgeous chunk of man and instead she was clutching a little white bottle that rattled when she shook it.

Those fates had a nasty sense of humor. She should know that garden gnomes must never tempt the fates.

Of course, Becky Billings wasn't a girl to give up so easily.

"WHAT'S NEXT?" Harry didn't know the last time he'd felt so jazzed. Each of the fifty-pound sacks individually had almost done him in, yet now that they were unloaded and stacked in neat piles, he couldn't wait to do more.

"You've lost your mind."

"I must have," he collapsed back into the armchair and knocked back most of a cold bottle of water that felt so clear and good going down. Water never tasted like that in New Orleans. A cold bottle of water there was bitingly cold in contrast to the thick heat—more likely to give you stomach cramps than soothe a thirsty soul. And as soon as it was out of the refrigerator, it grew thick with condensation that then dripped onto silk ties and Ike Behar suits.

"You are going to be so sore tomorrow."

He flexed and knew she was right, but it didn't mean he wanted to stop.

"The next step starts a process that I have to monitor closely for two to three days. It's not something I can just stop when you decide you get bored. I'd better try to call Zander."

"No. Wait," he rested his hand on hers. She'd already grabbed her cellphone. He always told people in the Big Easy that they knew nothing about moving slow if they hadn't been to small-town coastal Oregon. Becky was the clear exception to that rule. Everything about her was so fast and focused.

"What?"

"Just..." he didn't know why, "...wait. Okay?"

Becky didn't huff in exasperation or roll her eyes. She simply sat like a princess propped on the pillows of her beater couch.

He looked at her for a long time and she let him. Beneath that buxom and flouncy exterior was a very sharp woman. It wouldn't surprise him if she'd assembled every single piece of equipment behind him herself. And maybe done the rebuild upstairs somehow making it comfortable rather than utilitarian. And if he was looking for a woman who was nothing like the sharp-edged women who prowled New Orleans bars and jazz clubs hunting lawyers, doctors, and oil magnates, she was sitting right in front of him.

He should be out of here. He'd timed his arrival Sunday morning to just a few hours before the wedding. It was now Tuesday night, twenty-four hours after his planned departure.

Harry had never considered himself to be a particularly deep guy, but the fact that he hadn't bolted out of town at the first opportunity must mean something. He hadn't caught up with Cal except a little at the wedding. They needed to sit back and crack a few brews. He knew a couple other high school friends still lived in town, maybe more that he didn't know about. Hell, Bethany Garber was as often out of marriages as in them. If he remembered, her social media said that she was over in Salem and between men at the moment. It might be fun to revisit some of that for old time's sake.

But he knew that wasn't why he was still in Oregon.

The reason he was still here was the fragile, broken, beautiful, and tough-as-goddamn-nails woman sitting across from him. Fragile? Who was he kidding? If he hadn't been here, he'd wager that she'd have tackled unloading the van herself despite the drugs and blown knee.

"Your look of angelic innocence and patience isn't fooling anyone, Billings."

"Damn! And I was trying so hard."

But she wasn't. No, erase that. It was clear that she worked harder than anyone he knew. But she made it *look* easy. Around her he felt... good. Like there was hope and purpose above and beyond the daily grind of the law and how far could it be bent. It was a game he excelled at, but one that he'd wager Becky wouldn't like at all.

He wanted...

Just that. He wanted Becky. Not just the way he felt around her, but the way she'd felt against him too.

"Okay. I'd like to cut a deal with the court."

"The court is listening."

"Three days you say?"

Becky nodded.

"Okay. I'm willing to trade three days, except for the hours helping the Judge. My question is: what does the court have to offer in exchange?"

Becky's face remained unreadable as she considered his offer. She always *seemed* to be so open and outgoing and...obvious. Most women were the last no matter how they thought they hid it from him. He could read a blond within three seconds of entering a bar and a brunette before she had time to cast a second glance his way. But he was rapidly learning that Becky Billings was anything but obvious.

What surprised him was quite how much he was vested in her pending answer.

"The court notes," her tone was worthy of any trial judge, maybe even his father, "that she is partially incapacitated by a leg brace."

"So noted and entered in the record."

"The court therefore inquires if the counselor is willing to bear one more burden this evening."

"He's willing to take it under advisement," Harry couldn't stop himself from smiling. No matter the verdict, because it was Becky he knew it would be fun.

"If the counselor would help deliver the court to her bedroom so that she might freshen up, because she rather suspects she smells like a herd of swine, our conference could be continued at a more suitable…" She finally broke and blushed a brilliant red.

"The counselor," who was suddenly having problems with the fit of his slacks, "would like to file a Motion for Change of Venue."

"Passed without objection," Becky managed to gasp out.

Harry strode over and scooped her once more into his arms and headed for the stairs.

"Hey!" She protested.

"What?"

"You're supposed to kiss the court before you drag her away and have your way with her."

"I'll take your pleading under consideration," he continued up the steps. "But due to purported odor similarity to swine, that will take long and careful consideration."

She thumped the side of a fist against his shoulder, then wrapped her arms around his neck and snuggled against him. He buried his nose in her hair as he reached her upstairs apartment. To him she smelled like heaven.

Then he spotted the clawfoot tub and realized that her brace couldn't be immersed.

That meant…a sponge bath. Now that was a judgement he was truly going to enjoy administering.

CHAPTER 5

*H*arry's creativity with a wet and soapy sponge had started out incredible and expanded greatly with practice.

For three days he had completely lived up to his word. Together they had made a mash, cooked it, and run it through whirlpool filters and heat exchangers before getting it run into the fermentation tanks.

And the payments had been…breathtaking. She was supposed to be giving payment, not taking it, but her new lover gave her little choice.

Modesty had never been one of her issues, but that first sponge bath had pushed her limits. He'd put a chair in the tub, propped her bad leg on one rim, and then taken what felt like hours to unclothe and wash her. Her beautiful blond hero was meticulous in his investigation of her body. Not a single curve went unwashed or unappreciated. He had caressed, tasted, teased, and cleansed until her breath had sounded in shocky gasps. His research left no place unaddressed from ticklish nibbles on her insteps that had her in whorls of laughter all of the way up to a deep scalp massage and shampoo that had her melting in place.

The towel rub had sent shockwaves through her and after a little experimenting, they'd found a position on the big bed that worked in amazing ways. Since then they'd run through her meager supply of protection and he'd had to make a run for more.

Tuesday night had now rolled into very early Friday morning. She was almost as proficient at horizontal maneuvers as he was and her latest efforts had left both of their bodies humming.

Now she curled against him. Dr. Fairchild had upgraded her from a full leg brace to spending part-time in just a knee brace the prior afternoon which made their present position possible. Her leg now lay across Harry's hips, her head on his chest, and one hand slipped down between his hips and her thigh to cradle him.

"You make a fair brewer's assistant, Counselor Slater."

"As long as you don't move your hand, you'll find no complaints from me."

She lightly massaged him with her fingers and received exactly the groan she'd been hoping for.

"Okay," he gasped out, "you can do that, but only under one condition."

"Name it."

In answer he rolled her onto her back and shifted down to nuzzle her breasts. He certainly did enjoy them and she'd always figured that the main point of having such prominent ones was to have a man nuzzle them.

That or a child.

"What?" Harry looked up. He was so aware of her least little shift in mood.

She hadn't meant to freeze at the unexpected thought. She brushed her hand into his hair and guided him back to what he'd been doing, while her mind went elsewhere.

A child. She'd never particularly thought about it one way or another, at least no more than the next woman. It wasn't a driving force in her life, but she was the age her mother had been when she'd had Becky.

A child. With Harry Slater? Well, that was never going to happen. Over the last three days his suitcase had migrated from the Judge's house to her bedroom, but he'd turned down the dresser drawer she'd offered. She could almost make out the fine leather in the darkness. It sat on a chair close by the bed absolutely declaring the transient nature of this relationship. Was he even aware of what a monogrammed J.W. Hulme distressed leather bag that he insisted was a "duffle" —as if that made a fifteen hundred dollar suitcase more casual —filled with only designer-labeled clothes said about a man? It wasn't that she didn't appreciate fine clothes, it was that he'd come to the coast without a single piece of casual wear.

She'd known all of that going in, so why was she disappointed? Three days was all that he'd promised her and he'd delivered. But that meant that by tonight she might once again be sleeping alone.

He continued to work his way down her body. And between his skill and her affinity for him, her hips were arcing up to press harder against him as her heart drove madly against the inside of her chest.

She might love him, more than might, but this would be no more than a dalliance for the high-powered lawyer. In a matter of weeks Becky would be no more than a good last-trip-home memory. In a few months she probably wouldn't even be that.

But for the moment, this wonderful ecstatic moment of raw joy, she gave herself completely and knew that she would treasure it forever. This time the waves slamming through her body rose as much from her heart as from her hips.

HARRY LAY with his face pressed into Becky's stomach. One hand was trapped beneath her buttock when she'd finally collapsed back onto the bed. With the other he reached up to gently massage the nicest breast he'd ever held. Her good leg, which had latched across his back as she rode over her peak, was still draped lazily around him.

He no longer asked what he was doing here.

What was the point of asking? He'd be gone soon.

He couldn't invite Becky to go with him. He'd seen her as they worked the brewing process. Her passion for this place that she'd built with her own hands was as undeniable as the passion she brought to their sex. She'd spent hours poring over her recipe books and making notes as carefully as he'd ever studied precedent when building a case. They really did look like alchemy texts: the leather worn by a thousand handlings, the pages covered margin to margin in Becky's draftsman-quality lettering. He could read it easily, not that the words made much sense. "Overly dense wort." "Excess raffinose production in lager about 12 degrees C." "Dusty mouthfeel with acetaldehyde foreground and catty aftertaste."

There was nothing here for him. It had been fun, though he would never be more than a mediocre assistant. He'd called in for another week of vacation and, since they owed him several months of untaken leave, they hadn't argued for long. He'd just come off a large case and didn't have anything on his desk that one of the junior associates assigned to him couldn't handle.

But he hadn't told Becky about the extra week. He could see she was involved, more every day. She was a decent and fair woman and hadn't once referred to any future in their relationship, but she must be thinking it.

"That..."

Harry pushed his face deeper into her belly. He didn't want to hear it. Every time she spoke he braced himself, trying to be ready for the shoe to drop.

"That was absolutely spectacular, Counselor. I'll return the favor if my heart rate ever drops back down below stratospheric." She languidly shifted and moved against him, somehow snuggling him tighter against her.

Her fingers began playing with his hair and he groaned. It felt so good that he never wanted her to stop.

No. He definitely couldn't tell her about the extra week. If they were like this after three days, what would it be like after ten?

Vegas. He'd go back to his original plan of Vegas. Pick up a showgirl or a recent divorcée and purge Eagle Cove and Becky Billings from his blood.

Greg would be back tonight and making one of his fancy dinners at the diner. Harry would take Becky out for a special dinner, let her know it had been a wonderful time, and be gone in the morning.

He could work with that.

Becky's breathing shifted, the rise and fall of her flat stomach against his cheek slowing until he knew she was asleep. He now knew her mood by how she breathed or smiled or laughed. He knew that she sang when she was happiest, making them a meal while balancing on crutches in the kitchen or working at even the most mundane chores. That her world narrowed to such a tight focus when she was working on her brewing that her singing stopped and the rest of the world ceased to exist. He'd tried to seduce her while the heat exchanger was…exchanging heat or whatever it did. He'd had no luck until the whole batch had been safely moved through and into the CCV fermentation tanks and a proper dose of yeast added.

The instant the temperature was set she had jumped him and they'd ultimately done it like animals gone mad right against the still warm curves of the copper kettle.

There was one other thing he knew as he lay against Becky in the midnight darkness; he was utterly, completely, and most of all metaphorically screwed.

CHAPTER 6

*H*arry knew he still had a smile on his face when he reached The Puffin Diner at precisely five minutes to six to help with breakfast service—pushing the limits, but still on time.

Becky had insisted on paybacks when his alarm went off, but had respected his limited schedule. By habit he didn't wake quickly and his body hadn't completely shifted to Oregon time. By the time the snooze alarm buzzed, she'd teased a part of him to life and he became fully awake already deep inside her. Midway through, a frantic slap at the clock bought him another nine minutes. She kissed him as their bodies struggled to get closer than was physically possible, and she didn't stop. Her tongue was ravaging his mouth just as thoroughly as he was ravaging her in other places.

She swallowed his groan as the release slammed through him. He knew it was a good one for her because when he got it especially right, she didn't moan, she hummed. Literally. He'd never been able to pick out the tune, but the stronger it was, the happier she was. He could feel it where her breasts pressed hard against his chest. Her powerful, working-woman's, and thankfully with close-cut fingernails, hands dug into the muscles along his shoulder blades as she hung on for the ride that coursed through her body.

He'd barely finished shuddering out his last when she finally eased back a half-inch, "You're going to be late, Counselor." And then she rolled free and was gone from the bed.

He'd lain there dazed past speech as he watched her hobble over and take a quick sponge bath. By the time the second snooze jolted him to action, she was already over in the kitchen making herself a protein shake and still wearing nothing but her leg brace.

It was a sight he could watch all day. Then he checked his watch. He could watch all day only if he wanted to make the Judge even more prickly than he typically was. In fact, he'd had to hurry enough that it had left very little time to enjoy the scenery before he had to bolt out the door.

A classic September coastal drizzle greeted him, but he was too late to turn back for his jacket which was upstairs. If he did go back inside to fetch it, he'd see Becky wandering about her apartment as if all goddesses did indeed grace the earth with their nakedness. Worse, he might see her dressed in her jeans and flannel shirt and be faced with the choice of whether or not to get her back out of them. Instead, he slogged through the mud and managed to get into his rental car without stepping in any puddles that might soak his sneakers.

He was shivering by the time he came in the back door of the diner. His shirt clung to him and his hair was dripping. He'd completely forgotten about coastal microclimates. The distance from the shore to Becky's place was a difference of barely a mile. Yet a light drizzle there was a deluge here.

The Judge was at his griddle and the air was thick with bacon and coffee. He eyed Harry carefully before stating, "No Oregonian is ever caught without a jacket."

"And no goddamn New Orleans' lawyer would ever need to remember that."

The Judge regarded him a moment longer, then turned back to his griddle.

Peggy was also there.

Harry's first reaction was to be pissed. The old man had his phone number and could have called to say he already had help. Harry could still be warm, dry, and in bed with the sexiest woman he'd ever laid hands on. Could have taken the time to show her just how much he appreciated her.

Peggy was hunched over the old waffle iron. Damn thing hadn't worked in years, what was so important about fixing it now, that she couldn't have covered breakfast service? Every menu had a wavy black line drawn through "Waffles (with blueberries when in season)" so it wasn't like there was a sudden rush.

"Need some parts," Peggy closed it back up and was gone before Harry had a chance to protest.

"Time," the Judge intoned like his griddle was a judicial bench. Harry was surprised he didn't rap his spatula on the cast iron like a gavel. He'd retired five years back from the judgeship up in Newport. Since then he'd run the diner in the mornings, held office hours—mostly for weddings and wills—in the afternoons, and took weekends off. Five years off the bench and he still—

This time he did bang the spatula, making the metal ring loudly enough to hurt Harry's ears and make him jump.

Harry grabbed an apron and order pad, turning on lights as he moved toward the front of house. He stopped to turn on the coffee pot to set the first pot brewing. He could feel the Judge's eyes boring into him as he did so, even though there wasn't a soul waiting on the porch. The big clock said six-oh-three when he unlocked the front door and flicked on the porch lights.

" 'Bout time," Cal grunted as he pushed through the front door.

"Eat shit, buddy."

Cal merely grinned in response and made a point of clipping him hard shoulder-to-shoulder as he passed by. Cal Mason Jr. was the size of a Mack truck—several inches taller and wider than Harry. How he'd been so fast on his feet back when the two of them had ruled the Puffling soccer team was still a mystery. His big frame meant that his brush against Harry had sent him stumbling backward and crashing into a table.

"Oops! Did you run into me? That always happens with little people. They run into me and just kinda bounce back off. So sorry."

He almost delivered the whole line with a straight face, but it slid off sideways into a self-satisfied grin that had Harry bracing to commit a charging penalty in turn.

Cal moved aside fast enough to get clear without looking like he was hurrying before Harry had a chance to untangle himself from the chairs he'd collapsed into. Cal continued blithely toward his standard spot at the counter. Cal's day had started hours earlier at the Blackbird Bakery across the street and he was always first in for breakfast as soon as the lights were on.

The Judge would have his standard order ready, but wouldn't serve it up until Harry hung a ticket. He scribbled "Cal" across a ticket, tore it off, stuck it in the spinner, and turned it to face his father.

"Junior or senior?"

As if the Judge wasn't less than five feet from Cal because Cal always sat at the counter that faced the service window.

Harry spun the ticket back and yanked it free. A corner of the ticket tore off. The bit fluttered down and managed to land in the mug of coffee Harry had already poured for Cal. He dumped the coffee down the service sink, but splashed a lot of it on his Nikes. The blazing hot liquid ran right through the mesh and caused him to yelp at the sudden sting.

He slashed "Jr." across the ticket and managed to not write, "Asshole!" as well, stuck it back in the spinner, and slapped it around to face his father. The Judge slid across the plate with what might have been a smile—as if the man ever smiled.

Harry grabbed the plate, adding a seared hand to his morning's complaints, but slung it across the gap anyway and nearly dumped the Western omelet, hash browns, bacon, and English muffin in Cal's lap.

"Smooth, buddy. Real damn smooth. Did you forget everything I ever taught you about how to handle a hot ball?"

Before Harry could come up with a good comeback, he always found that hard when he knew his father was listening, Ralph Baxter came in with seven tourists. Must be an early start to a fishing trip. He tried to remember what was running in late September and came up mostly blank. Cod? Halibut? Was salmon still running?

Whatever it was, Jessica's father was one of the best fishermen on the coast and there'd be a lot of happy tourists by end of day. Happy people spent more around the town which was good for Eagle Cove and...

And why the hell was he wasting a single brain cell on this sad little place? Rather than attacking his father or Cal, Harry grabbed a fistful of menus and stalked off.

"Smile," Cal whispered as Harry walked past him.

"Fine!" He plastered one on and turned back to Cal. "Better?"

"Sure, if you want them to think you're going to kill them rather than serve them."

Harry tried to take a deep breath to ease down. He knew that Eagle Cove always made him crazy. Another breath.

It wasn't working.

He gave up on the smile and figured he'd let the tourists dine here at their own risk.

BECKY WISHED she could think of something other than Harry. He'd marked her property more thoroughly than any dog worried about the sanctity of his fire hydrant. And she knew it was completely unintentional. Worse, that he wasn't even aware of it.

The beautiful leather suitcase on the chair in her bedroom. A couple of shirts and the Michael Kors suit he'd worn to the wedding—the gray of a spring sky just before a long-awaited rain—hung at the end of her closet bar. Toothbrush and hairbrush at the sink. A second towel air-drying beside hers near the tub.

The tub had made her blush every time she looked at it after the first day that they became lovers. She'd never been one to parade around unclothed, not even when she was alone. But after that first sponge bath, modesty had seemed out of place.

Harry had taken right to it, complimenting her open floor plan. As if she'd meant it that way. She had just been being cost-efficient. Interior walls took planning to lay out the rooms and then time and money to build, wire, and finish. They also made a place feel smaller and the room wasn't that spacious to begin with. She could expand to the whole loft, but couldn't imagine why she'd ever need it.

A family someday?

Sure, maybe in some other century.

Living alone in a renovated hayloft she'd dropped in four walls and a ceiling and called it good. Her closet was a heavy wood dowel hung from screw eyes in the ceiling by some old rope.

Going to pee the first time would have been mortifying, except for the way Harry looked at her. With him watching as she crutched her way from bed to bath, she'd felt beautiful rather than like her usual garden gnome. She knew he liked her curves, but over the last three days his attention had shifted more and more often to her face as she stumped around the apartment with all the grace of a lumberjack.

Once they'd spent the desires of their bodies, they'd spent hours in bed, on the downstairs sofa, or just sitting on the bench outside her front door when the sun warmed it, and talked. Often about nothing at all, just leaning together and chatting about the day, old friends, and new dreams. In retrospect it had been about *her* new dreams. Maybe slick, successful lawyers didn't dream about the future.

Maybe he didn't have to.

He'd soon be full partner at a prestigious law firm. All dug in with his high-rise condo and fancy sports car. He talked about cases, all corporate law now. Defending construction contractors and large corporations against the inevitable actions brought against them. His firm handled the cases that were too big and messy for their own in-house counsel. Sometimes guilty and sometimes innocent, it was his job to defend them and it sounded to her uneducated ear as if he did it well. It also sounded as if it wasn't much fun, but who was she to judge someone else's choices. She'd chosen being a brewer over college and wherever that might have led.

He'd left reminders of himself everywhere. The tub, the bed, the couch downstairs, even in the brewery...he'd left behind memories as deep and thick as an unfiltered stout.

Once she'd managed to crutch her way downstairs, she brushed a hand over the copper kettle. No man had ever even kissed her in her brewery. Now and forevermore she'd think of how their shared cries had tangled among the equipment as he'd taken her hard against this now cool metal. Every batch she cooked would incorporate the memory.

She was so pathetic.

How could she possibly think that they'd be good memories after he was gone? How many batches of beer and cider would she flavor with tears?

"None, Becky Billings! Not a single, solitary one!"

She listened and didn't like what she heard.

Instead she strapped on the big walking brace that would keep her knee immobilized, then fished out the long-handled brush and a hot-water hose to clean up the equipment in preparation for the next cooking. Perhaps a ginger stout with some of the leftover Asian pear as a sweetener.

Even over the thumping of the high-pressure pump she could still hear the echoes of their passion.

"No tears, Billings," she tried to drown out the echoes with little luck.

She turned to her work, but it was a long time before she felt any of the usual peace doing the task.

PEGGY SWUNG back through and finished tinkering with the waffle iron.

The Judge watched her intently, almost as if she was hurting him rather than helping him. He was so focused on her that he botched a couple of orders that Harry silently slid back across the service window for a re-do.

When Peggy finished, she'd patted the Judge's shoulder with an easy familiarity before leaving again.

The Judge's idea of a lowered voice carried easily across any room, but this time Harry barely heard the old man when he sighed and spoke to himself, "Well, that's that then."

Then looking up, he caught Harry watching him.

"Waffles will be back on the menu come Monday," he made it sound unimportant, but Harry could see that it worried him.

Unable to ask why, Harry simply nodded in acknowledgement and moved off to bus some more tables. Monday would be Greg's concern, not his.

The crowd was thinning before Harry thought to add his own name to his brother's dinner reservation sheet. He'd taken any number of calls during the week, but it wasn't until he was staring at the page on the clipboard that he began to be impressed.

How many people had he already told on the phone that both of tonight's seatings were already sold out?

Sold out. Two seatings.

There was no menu, but he'd seen the jar with the sign that simply said, "Fifty Dollars. Drinks included. Tips welcome."

Fifty dollars a person was high on the coast. He could think of only a few other places anywhere along the shore that charged more. Yet his little brother didn't lack for reservations.

But he'd wanted to bring Becky here.

He turned to the next sheet. Saturday's first seating was gone as well. On the second seating he scribbled his name down and put a "2" after it. Only space for one more couple.

"Sweet!" Greg looked over his shoulder.

Harry startled at Greg's sudden appearance, then hit his brother on the head with the clipboard.

"What the hell are you still doing here?" Greg thumped him on the arm—hard enough for it to be payback for being hit with the clip-board rather than a friendly greeting. "I was sure you'd be gone before I got back."

"Old man trapped me." Then he glanced past Greg. "You don't look so good, Jessica."

"I don't?" She was raising her hand to her fair complexion.

"Nope. You look absolutely incredible," he brushed Greg aside much the way Cal had shoved him this morning, and pulled Jessica into a brief hug, then he stepped back again.

Her light blond hair was highlighted with droplets from the rain. Her blue eyes were sparking with joy and her smile was huge. She'd always had a killer smile, but it was over the top now. She positively shone against the backdrop of the gray day going on outside the window. She was sleek and slender unlike Becky's generous curves, but she…

"You do look amazing. How in the hell is that possible? I mean you married my little brother, after all."

"I'm just continuing an old family tradition."

"That," Harry puzzled at it for a few seconds, "doesn't make any sense at all."

Greg just grinned at him, "Oh, but it does."

"Come on and I'll tell you and the Judge together," she nodded toward the kitchen.

Harry turned to check on the patrons. No one else had snuck in while he was distracted. It was just ten minutes to the ten o'clock end of service and the few remaining guests were all served. He followed Greg and Jessica back into the kitchen.

The Judge waved a spatula in greeting to Greg and Jessica, but didn't leave the grill.

"Judge," Jessica smiled up at him.

He tipped his head to show that he was listening.

"You know my family tradition."

"Seems that I do," he checked under the edge of an omelet but decided to let it be for the moment.

"Some parts of it are repeating, and no, I'm not going to be divorcing your son."

Jessica's mother had married Ralph Baxter four times and divorced him three, without ever moving out of the house. If it wasn't that…

Harry didn't know what was happening, but Jessica now had the Judge's full attention.

"Are you…" he trailed off.

Harry had never known the Judge to be at a loss for words.

Jessica simply nodded and smiled. No, she nodded and glowed. Not only did she look incredibly happy, she also…

Greg leaned close and whispered, "Her mom got pregnant the week before the wedding, though she didn't realize it at the time. We started trying, but didn't expect it to happen so fast."

Harry was still having trouble adjusting to Greg and Jessica being married. And now she was pregnant and—

"How do you like the sound of Uncle Harry?"

At a complete loss for how else to respond, he punched Greg in the arm hard enough to send him flailing into the big steel door of the walk-in refrigerator.

The Judge's response was wholly unexpected. He stepped up to Jessica and wrapped her into his arms as if he was holding something precious. The Judge didn't hug people, ever. But he hugged Jessica Baxter.

Harry shook his head to clear it, but it didn't help.

Then Greg's counterstrike caught him hard enough on the shoulder to send him tumbling out through the swinging door to land on the dining room floor.

Greg stuck his head out and grinned, "You've got customers."

Harry looked up into the face of Cal's father. Cal Sr. looked down at him with a stony gaze. The water dripping off the brim of his hat pattered in Harry's face.

"Tall stack and coffee if you're done lying around, boy." Then he turned and headed to his favorite table. The way he'd said it took Harry right back to high school days.

Cal Sr. was more of a father figure than the Judge had ever been. That wasn't quite right Harry thought as he climbed to his feet and dusted himself off. He'd been a more *active* father figure. As coach of the soccer team, he'd had an eye on things that the Judge didn't due to his commute an hour each way four days a week up to the Newport courtroom.

The first time Harry had felt up a girl, Cal Sr. had somehow known. He'd hauled both his and Jr.'s ass out on his fishing skiff and lectured them but good on what he'd do if they ever went all the way with a girl without protection. After scaring the crap out of both of them, he'd handed each a box of condoms.

His first sick drunk, Sr. had once again hauled him out onto the glaring water on sixteen-feet of rocking aluminum. It had been an abuse that had his eyes, head, and gut vying for the title of Most Willing to Die First.

"Did you touch a girl in this state?"

"Girls didn't want anything to do with me."

"More sense that I thought they had. Good for them. You make stupid mistakes when you're drunk. Doing them to yourself is one thing, doing them to another, that's not right." Then Sr. gave the drunk driving lecture even though neither Harry nor Jr. had their license yet.

And when he and Jr. had been star forward strikers for the Puffling soccer team and didn't think, but both *knew* they were better than gods, Sr. hadn't said a single word in praise. That was perhaps the hardest lesson and one that Harry had taken years to understand. "Being good is one thing. Being good enough that others say it without you saying it first is what counts."

He filled out Cal Sr.'s order and spun it in.

The Judge handed the plate across, already made up.

Harry delivered it without comment to Sr. and received not a word back, just a nod of thanks.

"Seriously, bro," Greg popped up at his elbow once more.

Little shit had always been able to do that to him. Even that first time Harry had kissed Jessica when they were both fifteen—Greg had just happened to check the widow's walk of the Lamont's B&B at that moment. Partly because they had never been able to get clear of Greg it hadn't gotten far enough for him to earn Sr.'s "feel up versus fuck" lecture about Jessica; that had come later.

"Why're you still in town?" He tugged the order pad out of Harry's apron pocket, scribbled down a pair of orders, clipped and spun them around to the Judge himself.

"Dad needed help."

"Like that would be enough to make you stay in Eagle Cove for an extra five minutes." Greg filled a coffee mug and made a hot chocolate with marshmallows and carried them to a table where Jessica was just sitting down. So much for the Judge's "only children get marshmallows" rule.

Harry followed along with two sets of silverware and napkins, "I was also helping Becky."

"Since when," Jessica asked, "did Becky Billings need help with anything. I swear she is the most capable woman on the planet. I find her completely daunting."

"Since she blew out her knee. I've been her hands and strong back all week."

Greg choked on his coffee. "You? When was the last time you did manual labor?"

"All week, asshole."

Jessica was on her feet and clutching onto his forearm. "She was hurt? Where is she now?"

"Out at the brewery. She's fine."

"I gotta go!" She looked desperately at Greg.

He tossed her a set of car keys and she bolted for the door.

"Jessica," the Judge's voice boomed out bringing her to a screeching halt.

It was the same tone that had electrified Harry with raw terror every single time. He remembered his last Christmas visit home at twenty-two. He'd been upstairs in his room working on his undergraduate thesis, when his name had rung through the old Victorian. He'd almost lost his laptop to the floor as he'd jolted off the bed in a cold sweat wondering what the hell he'd done wrong this time. He'd raced downstairs only to have the Judge ask him to hold some boards so that he could cut them more easily.

Jessica didn't look the least mortified, though Harry could feel an adrenal shock just as a by-blow from standing nearby the Judge's call.

"Here," the Judge slid across a pair of to-go containers. "Greg, I'll have to recook yours, give me a minute."

"Thanks, Judge," Jessica waved and bolted out the door.

" I, uh," Harry looked back at Greg and tried to remember what they'd been talking about. He never lost the thread of a testimony or cross-examination. He could pick up a thread days later that the jury had forgotten all about and impress the hell out of them with his masterful understanding of such a complex case.

"Why you're still here?" Greg helped him out as he settled back in his chair.

"Right. I couldn't leave the old man to himself, could I?"

Cal Sr. was eyeing him from a nearby table, almost as if he didn't recognize Harry all of a sudden. Was it so damn weird that he'd lent a hand where it was needed?

"And Becky was really hurt and drugged senseless on major painkillers." And fun as hell. Somehow the morning had been so busy that it slipped by without her really being in his thoughts. But she'd still sort of...been there. *Again with the words, Counselor.* He could practically hear her tease and it made him smile.

Right up until the moment Greg's fist crashed into his jaw and sent him falling into Cal Sr.'s lap. The old man put a hand on his back and heaved him toward Greg hard enough to hurt.

Greg got right up in his face, "You fucked Becky Billings while she was on painkillers?" His roar stilled the diner. There wasn't so much as a fork clink. The latest pot of coffee brewing broke the silence with that dry-sucking burble when the coffeemaker had sprayed the last of its water on the grounds.

"No, I didn't!" Harry roared back at Greg as soon as he caught his breath.

Greg remained poised with both fists clenched.

"Goddamn it!" Harry rubbed at his jaw.

It hurt like hell.

"What we...did," he really didn't enjoy announcing it to the whole world. It had been something private between them. More than that, it had been precious and now it was sullied by his little shit of a brother.

Greg shifted his weight, readying another blow. Harry was so goddamn sick of everyone pushing him around today that he'd welcome it right now.

"Why the hell couldn't you have stayed on your goddamn honeymoon until I was gone? What we did was *after* she was off the drugs and it was very, very mutual. And then I spent the week busting my ass to help her because she asked nicely. Now you can go and fetch your own damn breakfast, asshole."

Harry peeled off the apron, and jammed it into Greg's hands, barely resisting the urge to paste him in the jaw. Instead he shoved him at Cal Sr.—hard!

Sr. slid his chair out of the way and let Greg tumble by to crash into another table, one still filled with dirty dishes which clattered to the floor and broke. Water glasses tumbled and shattered as chairs skittered away to knock into other patrons' tables.

Harry took one look back at the Judge who offered the same neutral expression every single time his sons fought.

To hell with both of them.

Sr. again had that look as if he didn't recognize Harry standing right in front of him. Then he smiled slowly as if inordinately pleased with some inner reflection.

To hell with all three of them.

Harry slammed his way out the front door and strode into the chill September rain.

"DID HE REALLY?"

Becky could only laugh with delight. She so loved having Jessica back in town after the fourteen years she'd been living in Chicago.

"He did. Right over there," Becky pointed at the copper cooking kettle. "I never knew how wonderful it was to make a man lose all control because he's so desperate to have you."

Jessica's smile was huge in turn, "Isn't it though."

They worked their way through a pair of the Judge's smoked salmon omelets as they sat side by side on the couch.

She remembered the first time Harry had sat there while they ate burgers from the Plover. The sweetness of that kiss, so warm, soft, and gentle. And no matter how hard she'd worked her hands and body—which her knee was really complaining about despite wearing the full brace all morning—she hadn't been able to block the thoughts about Harry and how soon he'd be gone from her life. And—

Before she knew what was happening, Jessica had set their to-go containers on the small table then slid close to wrap her arms around Becky.

Becky buried her face in her best friend's shoulder.

"He's never going to stay here. And he knows that it would be like ripping out a piece of my heart to ask me to leave."

"I know. You so belong here."

"It doesn't help to have that confirmed. I swore I wasn't going to cry over him." Which was a completely pointless statement as she was now weeping and couldn't seem to stop it.

She could feel Jessica's nod, "I said the same thing."

"It doesn't work," she barely managed to choke out, "does it?"

"Nope," and Jessica ran a soothing hand up and down Becky's back.

She'd thought that barfing her guts out at Harry's feet had been the worst, but this pain was unending and there was no solution except to give up everything she loved. "And that's if he even wants me," it came out as a sob and more tears.

Jessica pushed her back until they were face to face, "If he doesn't realize that you're the most incredible woman on the planet—"

"Besides you!" Jessica always looked so slender and perfect.

"Well, of course me," Jessica's smile was warm and teasing. "If he doesn't realize that you're the second most incredible woman on the planet—"

"And Natalya!" Jessica's cousin was the darkly sexy version of the blond beauty currently holding her.

"Becky!" Jessica gave her a shake. "You are beautiful and incredible and have done amazing things. If Harry doesn't know that you're the best thing he's ever going to find, then he's an idiot. And if you don't get that about yourself...well, shit! You scare the crap out of Natya and me all the time."

"I do?" Becky liked the sound of that though she couldn't imagine how it was possible.

"Duh! Look at this!" Jessica waved a hand at the brewery. "You did this. I managed to create a failed journalism career and I'm now trying not to weep with terror as I scrape through my startup year as the town's marketing manager. An effort, I'll remind you, that is partly funded by Becky Billings BlueBird Brewery."

"But you're great at it. I knew you would be. You can do anything."

"Hello!" Jessica waved at the brewing equipment again.

And Becky looked at it, really looked. Over two thousand gallons of beer were working their way through the fermentation tanks. A line of bright steel kegs, filled and ready for delivery, were lined up along the wall. She'd have to figure out how to do deliveries, because they were due to go out next week for Tillamook down to Coos Bay and two new clients inland in Eugene.

She'd dreamed a dream when she was an eight-year-old girl and it was real. Right there. In front of her. She turned back to Jessica.

"Hello!" Jessica waved again at the brewery.

Becky nodded. "Right. So...if Harry doesn't get what he's missing then..." she wasn't ready, couldn't bring herself to say to hell with him. "Then..." she still didn't know what was on the other side of that statement.

"Then," Jessica grinned at her, "we'll just have to make sure he figures it out."

She had no idea how to do that, but she liked the way it sounded.

"Now," Jessica gave her a napkin to wipe her eyes with, "I happen to know exactly what you need." She pulled out her phone and began dialing.

HARRY WAS a hundred feet from the Slater Victorian when a car headed into town splashed to a halt beside him.

Gina Lamont, Natalya's mom and Jessica's aunt, rolled down the window.

"Do you need a ride, Harry? Where's your coat?"

"Forgot it. I'm almost there."

"You sure?"

He looked into the car. Gina was a tall, statuesque redhead and beside her sat a smaller woman who gave the impression of being almost entirely made up of flowing light brown hair. Gina wore a stylish rain jacket and the other woman was dressed in a well-worn yellow slicker and a rain hat with a wide enough brim to mostly hide her face.

"I'm fine."

"Okay. Take a hot shower quick." Gina rolled up her window and drove away.

Harry made it five more steps before he stumbled to a halt ankle deep in a mud puddle. He'd stopped caring about how wet he was before he had even turned off Beach Way. He kept his hands jammed in his pockets and his shoulders hunched against the on-going deluge. Another two degrees colder and he'd be shivering. He was just warm enough to be totally and completely miserable.

He came to a halt when he realized that he'd been aimed to the wrong place. And he'd been in such a head-down, foul mood that he'd walked two miles in the rain before he noticed. He had no clothes here at his childhood home, they were all out at Becky's. He'd go to the guest house and steal one of Greg's jackets for the long walk back to town to fetch his car.

Except their house was locked. He looked at the sodden driveway. Greg's truck was parked in the carport. And he'd seen Jessica take off from the diner in a ten-year-old VW Beetle. There were no recent tracks in the mud, meaning Jessica and Greg were only just returning from their short honeymoon. He trudged across the yard but the big house was locked as well.

Putting his head down he turned and slogged back toward town.

Now, when he needed a ride, no one passed along the lane. It was as if the town had emptied with the gray Friday morning.

That reminded him that there was a rhythm to a small coastal town. Friday morning is when everyone did their shopping and other errands so that they didn't have to fight the weekend tourists who would start cluttering up the store aisles by two or three in the afternoon. So everyone would be out for a while, then they come streaming back but all going in the wrong direction.

Sure enough, he was most of the way back to town when the first cars passed him, heading out of town not into it. Each older person waved. One or two of the high school-age ones who were headed home for lunch aimed at the mud puddles, sending huge gouts of cold muddy spray his way. He'd done the same himself as a kid. When you saw a tourist being as stupid as he was, they were marked as fair game.

Paybacks were hell.

He and Becky had made a whole game out of paybacks. Those hadn't been hell. They'd been the best time he'd had in—

He stumbled to a halt in front of The Puffin Diner. It was almost noon and the windows were dark. He splotched muddy footprints from his ruined Nikes up the steps and across the porch.

Locked.

He trudged around to the back.

Locked.

By shading the glass he could just make out where the apron he'd worn all morning hung. In the pocket were his car keys. After that final round this morning of feeling up a naked Becky as she leaned back against the kitchen counter and moaned like a lost soul, he'd been running so late that the keys had still been in his hands as he'd grabbed the apron. It had been natural to dump them in one of the pockets.

He turned around to stare at his rental car.

It was pointless, but he went down to check it anyway.

Big city habits, he'd locked it.

The joke on the coast was that you locked your car only during zucchini season. It was so that local gardeners didn't slip in a couple of the overgrown monsters that they didn't have the heart to compost.

He looked up Beach Way. No one to ask for a ride really.

Cal was a possibility, but Sr.'s truck was parked close beside Jr.'s and he didn't think he could take more of the old man's disapproving looks right at the moment. God forbid if he had some lecture on tap this morning.

Harry had already walked two miles out to the house and two back. One more mile to Becky's wasn't going to kill him.

It only felt as if it would.

He considered calling her, but then she'd probably feel obliged to come fetch him in her van and he didn't want her driving with that knee yet. Besides, he could see his phone right there, on the locked car's dash.

He pulled up the sodden collar of his Peter Millar sport shirt and began trudging out of town.

Jessica had been absolutely right, this is exactly what she needed.

The brewery was alive with a dozen knitters. Every Tuesday and Friday afternoon, everyone who was available met out at Gina's lovely B&B for knitting. Tuesday Becky had been drugged out of her mind. No, she'd been off the drugs by then, and busy admiring Harry unloading her truck. Then the sponge bath and... She'd been busy.

So, this afternoon wasn't as good as last Tuesday's, but it was wonderful in every other way.

Today, the ladies of the town had brought their knitting group to her. They pulled chairs and stools out of the tasting room and made a merry circle with the couch and armchair. She'd had Jessica pull out a case of cider and another of a cream soda she was rather proud of. Gina had brought ham-and-turkey roll-ups. Monica supplied veggies and hummus. And Becky had sent Tiffany up to her apartment to raid her secret stash of a giant bag of Fritos. Tiffany had chortled with glee and the two of them feasted on their newfound shared passion for crunchy salt and high fat content.

The saga of her leg was the first topic as everyone pulled out their knitting projects. She herself was working on a scarf of a ridiculously sparkly and floofy yarn of gold, reds, and oranges.

"It is autumn after all," she defended her choice to the traditionalists in the group who poo-pooed "novelty" yarn. She'd chosen an eyelash yarn which had a thousand little strands sprouting from the main thread like brilliant fireworks. It was fun, ticklish, and it was very easy to imagine teasing Harry's body with it because it was so soft. Not that the scarf would be done before he was gone, but it was still nice to imagine.

"Harry? He's really helping out?" Marjorie Winslow's question was enough to shock the multiple conversations into a single ply.

"He was always such a cocky boy, no pun intended." Gina said it in such a way that it was obvious that the pun was wholly intended which earned her a round of laughter.

The whole town must know that the two of them were shacked up together, but still Becky couldn't stop the blush that led to catty calls for details.

"No," Becky defended him. "He's not. Except in the way you actually mean it of course."

Gina threw her head back and unleashed one of her big laughs. It was a good offset to Becky's earlier tears on Jessica's shoulder.

"Seriously though," Marjorie Winslow, who had been the best second-grade teacher ever born, narrowed her eyes in concern, "I remember him as a rather arrogant boy."

A murmur of agreement rose.

As the younger women told different tales of when he'd tried to date them, or the older ones of when he'd gone after one of their daughters, Becky had her own memories to think over. She hadn't done that much, being too wrapped up in enjoying the present.

With a senior class of only thirty-four students, it was hard not to know everything about everyone. Yet even in so small a group, her and Harry's circles rarely overlapped outside the classroom. Even in retrospect, she saw less of the arrogant boy and more of someone trying to prove himself to the world.

The Judge was such an austere and powerful man, it was hard to imagine what it would have been like growing up as his eldest son. He set such a high standard to live up to. And that had been contrasted with his wife. Ma Slater, as absolutely everyone called her until finally that's how she began signing her paintings, had been a reserved yet warm woman. She was someone that you could take your troubles to and always receive good advice. If Becky hadn't had Peggy living so nearby, she'd have missed Harry's mother badly.

Now that Becky knew the man grown, she could see the elements of his past so clearly.

"No," she interrupted a particularly ribald story. "He isn't arrogant anymore. He's...lovely."

As if on cue, the front door slammed open and an apparition trudged through the door. Harry was drenched, covered in mud, and visibly shivering.

Dumping her knitting out of her lap, she raced over to him as fast as she could wearing the leg brace.

"Are you okay?"

He looked at her out of haunted eyes. Filled with a pain so deep that she almost recognized it as her own.

———

HARRY GLANCED over Becky's head at the circle of women who had frozen in place at his entrance. He was greeted by a wide variety of expressions. Some smiling, Jessica the most prominent among them. Some scowling, led by the town's terror of a second grade teacher— given a choice, Marjorie Winslow was one woman he would *not* want to catch up with while visiting Eagle Cove. Gina and her sister Monica looked amused. And the one he'd seen in the car with Gina, the woman with the long flow of wavy brunette hair, just watched him carefully—as carefully as he'd ever watched a key witness. Not judging, but not trusting either.

"Are you okay, Harry?" Becky rested a hand on his forearm but snatched it back from the wet and cold.

"So not." Standing still he was starting to shiver. "Looks like the jury hasn't reached a consensus on me yet either." He kept his voice low.

Becky glanced over at the circle of women as they began to return to their knitting but were clearly paying attention to the drama unfolding by the door.

"Of course we have," Gina Lamont called out proving he hadn't kept his voice low enough. "Off with his head!"

"Great." He wasn't sure that he'd argue the verdict at this point himself. He began peeling off his shoes and socks so that he didn't track the mud all through Becky's place.

Becky reached out again and he stepped back.

"No. I'm disgusting." And he hadn't meant it quite the way it came out, but it had been a long, wet mile from town. And his thoughts had become as sodden as his underwear. He didn't want Vegas. He didn't want some needy, leggy blond trying to prove she was still attractive fresh off a divorce. He wanted this stunning, amazing, pint-sized woman standing not three feet away.

And what was he going to do about that?

He was going to take her out to dinner tomorrow night (only because he couldn't get a reservation sooner), and then leave her on Sunday morning to go lose himself in something he absolutely didn't want. And he was going to leave because the one thing he knew for certain was that Becky Billings deserved something way better than Harry Slater.

"Go back to your friends," he whispered to her. "I'll be fine."

"Hot bath," was all she said. Then she leaned in and raised up on her toes. He could see by a brief wince that the motion was hurting her bad knee, but she didn't withdraw.

Not wanting to sully her, he didn't reach out to drag her against him and hold on tight against the storm he could feel coming. Instead, they traded a soft and gentle kiss before he turned and splatted his way up the rough stairs.

Harry climbed into the tub and sat down in it still fully clothed. He cranked open the faucets and tried to ignore the slowly rising murmur of voices below.

The sooner he was gone, the better off she'd be.

The shakes came on as the water rose past his ankles and he couldn't seem to make them stop.

BECKY RETURNED TO THE COUCH, favoring her bad leg. That last move of raising up on her toes had almost driven her back to trying to hop again. But he'd looked so hurt and lost that she would do it again.

She made it back to the couch and Jessica helped her get resettled. Tiffany regathered her knitting from where she'd dumped it on the floor and handed it over. Becky focused on getting restarted. One of the drawbacks to eyelash yarn was that it was so busy that it was almost impossible to tell whether or not you'd dropped a stitch. She carefully checked the main ply and welcomed the familiar rhythm once she could restart her knitting.

The conversation slowly resumed around her, a soft wash of friendly voices as pleasant as the rain on the barn's tin roof.

She'd had her fair share of lovers. Some were after just the sex, others willing to give more. A few had lasted a single evening, one had lasted a year before she'd realized that the sex was good, but there wasn't much else there for either of them. Even Greg, when he'd first returned to town three years ago, had been sweet. Neither of them knew it back then, but his high school crush on Jessica hadn't gone away and it had been enough to ultimately send them on their separate ways.

And in all that time, Becky tried to think of the most romantic moment any time in her history. The slow dance at Jessica's wedding had been incredible. The moment when Harry had swept a broken garden gnome into his arms and carried a princess upstairs to bathe and bed her had been completely swoon-worthy.

She looked up at the faces of her friends.

Gina's booming laugh spilled like an ocean wave, brightening multiple conversations. Peggy's late arrival was greeted with waves and catcalls of just what man had she been busy with that she was so late; a question she declined to answer with even one of her sharp comebacks. Tiffany, in her silent way, watching everything with a soft smile and missing nothing.

The most romantic moment in her entire life?

When a beautiful, sodden, grimy, frustrated man had come home to her, and then kissed her in front of her closest friends as if it was the most normal thing in the world.

What had Jessica's advice been?

"We just have to make sure that he figures it out."

Apparently he had. But there was still the old joke: a garden gnome could love a lawyer, but where could they live together?

Having no good answer, she let the conversation swirl around her without jumping in as she normally would.

Becky waited a long time, hoping that Harry would come back down to join her. She could understand why he didn't with all of the women gathered here. But that didn't stop her wishing that he would.

CHAPTER 7

*I*t had taken a lot of hot water before Harry's hands worked well enough for him to strip off his clothes. He'd squeezed them out as well as he could while sitting chest deep in the tub before dumping the sodden mass onto the bathmat.

When the shivers finally stopped, and the water was brown with the mud that had sluiced off him, he'd dried himself off and crawled into Becky's bed.

He could hear the laughter downstairs. He tried to pick out Becky's laugh, but couldn't. Another sign, as if he needed one, that something was wrong. If you couldn't recognize the laugh of the woman you were having sex with...that had to mean...something. Though he'd be damned if he knew what.

What a group of friends Becky had. A dozen people gathered together from different walks of life by a common interest: a brewer, a real estate agent, a teacher, a B&B owner, the owner of a movie house, and others. Did he even know a dozen people outside of his office and his clients? Because clients certainly didn't count as friends. He'd guess that the waiters and bartenders at his favorite restaurants didn't count. Gina's big laugh boomed out again from below and others joined in, but he still couldn't pick out Becky's.

He pulled the covers over his head to block out the sound of cheerful conversation. It went on forever.

He kept thinking about New Orleans. In September and October the heavy summer rains were tapering off and the temperature was easing to where it was tolerable for even an Oregon boy. There were fall film festivals, the three-day utter-culinary-mayhem of the Annual Louisiana Seafood Festival. Hell, even the Southern Decadence was a hoot to watch. Called the "Gay Mardi Gras," it made one hell of a party. Sure, he'd get his butt pinched, but hordes of straight women showed up for the festivities as well.

Instead, he was cowering under the bedcovers in an Oregon hayloft.

Sure, like New Orleans is so great.

He wasn't sure where that voice had come from, but he didn't like it much. He tried to think if he'd actually gone to a single festival in the last year and couldn't come up with one.

Instead his life was bounded by the cool silence of his air-conditioned condo, quiet restaurant meals mostly eaten alone, and the frantic pulse beat of the law offices. Yet another contractor looking for ways to force through a million-dollar change order on a client because they'd low-balled their cost estimate to get the job, and now needed to make it up in other ways. Yet another class-action lawsuit for criminal negligence in an oil spill that was soaking into the water table. Yet another massive embezzlement case at one of the casinos. Yet another CEO fighting molestation charges that were probably only too true but they were such a major corporate client that a personal criminal defense had to be mounted.

How many people had he defended that he'd rather see raked over Satan's coals for a few millennia?

Too many.

But that was part of being a lawyer.

Didn't mean he had to like it, though he loved the *challenge* of it. The law was interesting. It was a living, organic body of knowledge that was a blending of intent versus word of the law. There was a visceral joy in unraveling how case law and precedent affected the legal code. But it was the courtroom that he found most fascinating. Many thought courtrooms were impersonal, but his greats victories had been because he understood just how personal they were for plaintiff, defendant, jury, judge, opposing counsel, witnesses, and even the onlookers.

But he wasn't feeling terribly inspired by the whole mess at the moment.

He curled deeper into the flannel pillow and sheets, decorated with little beer steins, that smelled of the nearby ocean and the most amazing woman he'd ever bedded.

One he was going to hurt more than any woman he'd ever been with.

Peggy hung back as the others left, returning chairs to where they belonged and collecting cream soda empties.

Becky lined up the empties in the washer racks that would strip the labels and sterilize the bottles for the next usage. She really should go upstairs, but she wasn't sure what she'd find. A part of her wondered if Harry would be dressed and packed, just awaiting the end of the knitting group to say goodbye. Some irrational part of her wondered if he'd gone out through the hayloft and down the back stairs. Even though she knew that he'd never do anything so cowardly, a part of her had to clamp back on the panic of that possibility.

She finally came to a halt by the mash tun. There was still a full pallet of barley that Harry had unloaded and stacked that should be processing now...but wasn't. She sat on the big, burlap bags and wished she could chop off her leg and replace it with a new one that wasn't throbbing. The over-the-counter pain killers were upstairs and it had been too long between doses. She hadn't thought to bring them down this morning because Harry always took care of such things for her. After thirty-two years of taking care of herself, she was turning into a totally dependent, lame, weakfish of a woman who—

"Enough with that look, Becky." Peggy sat down on the next barley bag over and wrapped an arm around her shoulders.

Becky huffed out a breath hard. Then another trying to clear the negative thought maelstrom out of her system.

"That's better," Peggy gave her a small shake. "Doc says you're doing a good job of staying off the knee. Do it for another week and everything will be back to normal."

Becky winced and managed not to look at the stairs.

"Men however," Peggy didn't need to be a mind reader to see her thoughts, "move at their own pace, unless we nudge them along."

"Is that what you do?"

"Some men need more nudging than others. The Slaters were never the quickest lot." Peggy was gazing intently at the empty mash tun.

"Is there something that *you* want to be telling *me?*" Though Becky didn't feel like she had much in the way of advise for anyone, especially not as cool and together a woman as Peggy.

Peggy actually startled before squinting at Becky for a long moment. "Just look at...what Jessica had to go through with Greg."

"That's an evasion, Peggy, and you know it. Jessica was the one who Greg had to nudge along."

"True, but Harry is..."

"Yeah," Becky admitted when Peggy didn't continue. She let herself look at the stairs this time and wondered what she'd find waiting for her. "He really, really is." Wonderful. Amazing. And completely not part of Eagle Cove.

Peggy squeezed Becky's shoulders again and then rose to her feet. "Best foot forward, Becky. That's the best we can do. We put our best foot forward and we hope. Actually..." Peggy stared off toward one of the barn walls for a long moment. "That's good advise, just might take it myself." Then with a final hug, Peggy was gone.

"Wait!" but she was too late. Whatever Peggy had evaded saying, she'd very neatly taken with her.

Becky climbed to her feet and grabbed her crutches. Well, at least there was no question about which was her best foot to put forward. So, she'd do that and hope for the best.

Becky managed to slowly navigate the steps with one crutch and a plate of leftovers. She almost lost them and herself down the stairs. She was glad that neither Peggy nor Harry was around to watch her struggle—they'd have been pissed. But she finally managed to reach the loft still intact and would count that as a triumph of the day.

Her best case scenario was to find Harry reading a book or watching a movie on his tablet, basically hiding from the clouds of estrogen that had been sweeping through the brewery. Instead she found a bathtub with dirt still smearing the drying bottom, a mangled pile of clothes that was worth more than her entire wardrobe, and a lump under the covers—hidden except for a small tuft of Harry's golden hair.

Romantic moment number fifty-six: beautiful, sweet man lying under the covers and waiting for her.

For her.

It was hard not to giggle in delight, though she'd striven to train herself out of giggling. What looked charming on tall blond women like Jessica, looked flat out childish on women of small stature.

She hobbled over, her crutch and brace clunking as she went.

No response from the bed; he must be asleep.

She set the platter on the nightstand, and stripped down to t-shirt and leg brace. She shed the big brace, but kept the underlying knee support in place. She wanted to lose it as well, it was the only part of her that had never touched Harry, but she also wanted to heal as fast as possible so that they could do so much more once she took it off.

A voice whispered in the back of her mind that the speed of her healing was going to be outstripped by his departure, but she chose to ignore it as she watched him sleeping.

He was here. In her bed. It was a good thing, better than anything else she'd imagined, and there just had to be some way to make it last.

Peggy was clearly cheering her on. And Jessica thought it was possible even if she didn't know how.

Becky figured that she could take that one of two ways. Either

Jessica was so happy about marrying Greg that of course she'd wish it to be true for everyone around her. Or second, maybe there was some semi-mystical thing that married women knew when they looked at an unmarried couple. Somehow they could see that it was simply right and they really knew it just was going to work out fine.

Her inner voice whispered to be cautious, to protect her heart.

Becky kicked it to the curb.

She decided to bank on the mystical power of married women, peeled her t-shirt, and slid under the covers. She snuggled up close behind the sleeping Harry. She was too short to be on the outside of the spoon, but she lay gently against his back and slid an arm over his ribs. She knew it wouldn't disturb him, he was a deep sleeper, but when he did wake up she wanted him to know that she was there beside him.

The moment her hand slid onto his chest, he clamped a hand over hers so fast that she gave a little squeal of surprise. He pressed it hard enough against his heart that she was half afraid she was hurting him.

He didn't uncurl from his near fetal position. He didn't turn to her. He just held her hand over his heart, never once easing up on the pressure.

Not knowing what else to do, she stroked his hair with her free hand, and whispered to him, "Shh. It'll be okay. It was just a hard day."

His hair was so clean and soft. It smelled of her own shampoo. She guessed that she was leaving imprints on Harry's life just as he was leaving them on hers.

"I built us a hell of a trap, didn't I?" When he finally spoke, his voice came out rough with anger and soft with resignation. Any lesser man would have denied it, or not spoken about it in the first place, but not her Harry.

Her Harry. Gods but that sounded glorious.

Becky smiled against his shoulder blade as she kissed it, "I think I might have helped with that one."

"I'm so sorry. So sorry," he gasped it out. With her hand on his heart, she could tell he wasn't crying, might not be able to. But he was really hurting.

She knew it was stupid and dangerous, but she couldn't help being happy about it. She'd thought that she was the only one foolish enough to fall in love in this relationship. They'd been together from a Sunday night dance to this Friday evening. Five days. Just five amazing days.

"Falling hard," was such a cliché, yet she'd done it. And now, for the first time, she began to have a sliver of hope that the same thing had happened to Harry. It didn't mean that there was a future for them—she still couldn't see that—but it meant she wasn't alone as she dangled by this thin twist of yarn.

She could feel the pain coursing beneath her hand. More surely than she could feel when a brew had cooked enough just by the sense of it.

"I don't have any answers," he clamped even tighter onto her hand.

She kissed his shoulder blade again, "If it makes you feel any better about it, neither do I."

He choked a bitter laugh, "No, actually, that doesn't help."

"C'mon," she pulled at him to get him to roll over. He resisted. "Come on."

He was reluctant at first, but finally rolled.

"We're not going to talk about it right now," she kissed him lightly on the lips. It was miracle enough for tonight that this wasn't just some five-night stand to him.

She pulled his face down between her breasts and cradled him there. Not as she would a lover, but simply to comfort his aching soul. She slid both of her hands into his hair and propped her bad leg on his hip as they lay side by side.

He stayed there a long time with his arms wrapped around her. He let her hold him for what seemed like hours before they made love. And when they did, it was a slow, gentle, silent act in which they were both far kinder to one another than any time before.

CHAPTER 8

"Rise and shine, Counselor." A hand smacked down on his butt, jolting Harry awake. "I want pie."

"Pie?" His mumble was absorbed by the pillow he was face down in.

"Yes, pie. Up and at 'em!"

Becky. Definitely Becky. She began poking at his ribs. Probing until she found…

"Shit!"

He tried to roll away but he was snarled in the sheets and couldn't seem to escape her fingers.

"Damn it, woman!" His ticklish spot was very ticklish.

He made a grab for her, but she made good her escape.

Opening one eye, he surveyed the situation. Beautiful woman wearing clothes (damn it), one crutch, and an evil grin. She stood in a pool of sunlight that made her dark-blond hair shine.

"The court wants her pie and she wants it now."

Woman in sunlight. Sunlight? "Shit!" He twisted around to look at the clock, but became only more snarled in the sheets and quilt. He tumbled off the edge and hit the floor with a loud thump. "I'm late for the diner."

"It's Saturday. The Judge is closed Saturdays and Sundays, his anti-tourist policy."

"It's Saturday?" He'd been in Eagle Cove almost a full week? He should have his head examined.

"Does your father really strike such terror into the heart of a grown man?" Becky was a smart woman and was keeping enough distance that he couldn't drag her down onto the floor with him.

"No." *Absolutely.* "At least not when you ask it that way." *And completely.* "Does he make me feel like a freaked-out kid who just screwed up, again, every single time he looks at me? If you ask it that way then," he tried to shrug it off and clipped his shoulder on the base of the night stand hard enough to hurt. "Yeah."

"He's used to scare me too," Becky nodded, backing up another step to remain at a safe distance. "He is always so proper that it seems that all of us mere mortals could never live up to his standards. But not anymore."

She was mostly upside down from his point of view, but her answer appeared guileless.

"Well, not really," her smile gave her away.

"Knew it! Though he certainly seems to like Jessica a lot," the only person on the planet the Judge had ever hugged. Harry untangled himself from the covers and heaved them back onto the bed.

"Everybody likes Jessica."

"Whereas everyone flat out loves you."

"Bull!"

Becky had perched on a kitchen stool with her crutch planted like a "No Crossing" sign between her knees, so Harry headed over to brush his teeth and get dressed. Then he spotted the still sodden mass of clothes by the tub. He hung them over the shower curtain rail and wondered if they'd ever be useable again. Eagle Cove was being awfully hard on his wardrobe. The tub was a mess; he'd clean it up for her later.

As he brushed his teeth, he began poking through his duffle. He went for dry underwear, the Santorelli trousers, and his last Hugo Boss shirt.

"Seriously," he spit and rinsed, then began dressing. "What do you think yesterday was about? You should have seen Jessica bolt out the door of the diner when I told her you'd been hurt. Every one of those women came rushing here to take care of you."

"They came to knit. They were just being nice."

"Allow me to quote the court's earlier statement: Bull!" His Nikes were still a mess; he should have taken them into the tub with him to rinse them out. That only left him with the Allen Edmonds Oxfords that he'd brought for the wedding. At the rate he was going, he'd have to replace those as well after he got home.

He looked up to see that Becky was squinting at him.

"You didn't see that? Well, it was obvious to me." Habit had him reaching for a tie and jacket before he caught himself. "You could see it in their faces. Marjorie Winslow was ready to have me dragged out and beaten on your behalf at the least provocation. Of course she always was an absolute terror. Jessica had one of those dreamy looks as if—" And Harry wished that he could cut out his goddamn tongue. He couldn't turn to look at Becky, so instead he knelt down to retie his Oxfords.

"As if," she picked up in a whispery voice, "she hoped for us what she found with your brother."

"As if," he finally agreed. But Harry couldn't bring himself to look up.

She slid off the stool and thumped over until she stood close in front of him and he was forced to look up at her face.

He tried to read what was there, but with Becky he always had to ask. However his throat was too dry to form words at the moment.

"I hope for it to."

Harry couldn't even breathe.

"But it isn't what I expect. What I expect is..." And the tease was back in her voice, but he couldn't make sense of it in the middle of this conversation.

"What?"

"What I expect is for you to take me out for pie."

The laugh burst out of him. All the terror of last night about how he would hurt her and the impossibility of their situation laid out this morning just flew out of him like an Oregon Coast windstorm.

Becky Billings was the most amazing and startling woman anywhere. He knelt before her and pulled her tight against him, his arms around her fine butt and his face buried in her stomach. She stroked his hair and he could feel her grin even if he couldn't see it.

He jumped to his feet, kissed her lightly but resisted the urge to do more, then bowed deeply. "Come, my lady. Your chariot awaits and I shall chauffeur you wherever you wish to go."

"Well, the first thing I need is my other crutch from downstairs if I'm going to navigate the descent."

"You—" Harry bit down on his tongue. She'd come up the stairs with only one crutch?

"Why would you—" Then he remembered the cold meal they'd shared in the middle of the night by the moonlight streaming in through the skylight and windows. The empty plate still rested on the nightstand on her side of the bed. *Her* side of the bed? That meant that he had a side and—

"You crazy woman."

She shrugged but made no denial.

Rather than fetching the other crutch, he scooped her off her feet and enjoyed every second she clung to him as he carried her down the stairs.

BECKY ALMOST LET HIM DRIVE, just to save his shoes. But it was too silly. It was less than a hundred yards from the back door of her brewery to Peggy's airplane hangar, but it would be a half mile drive or more to reach the airport entrance and double back. The path was well-trodden—either she or Peggy tromped along it several times a week and at least once every Saturday morning—and it wasn't too muddy from yesterday's rain. The path ran through this corner of the broad field of hay. Her father had put a gate in the fence years ago. Becky still latched it every time out of happy memory of her father's cows who always thought the airport grass looked so much sweeter. Every chance they had, they broke out, much to the consternation of pilots trying to land on the grass and gravel strip.

The airport itself consisted of the main hangar that Peggy used and five others that were enough to hold the aircraft kept permanently in Eagle Cove. They huddled with their back walls toward the ocean storms and the front walls open like carports for airplanes. Only Peggy's had actual doors that slid across. The runway itself was freshly mown. A sun-faded windsock dangled limply from a high pole —not a breath of wind to disturb the day.

The air was cool and damp, washed clean by yesterday's rain. There was a magic to a sunny morning after a rain. It felt as if the whole world had been scrubbed until it shined.

"Why are we going to the airport?" Harry eyed the path with clear distaste.

"Peggy said there's a thing among private pilots. They're always looking for an excuse to go flying."

"Which has what to do with pie?" Harry began picking his way around puddles and soggy spots like they were populated by alligators.

Becky splashed ahead in her single rubber Wellington, though she did have to be careful to keep the tips of her crutches from sinking in too far and to not dip her sock-and-brace clad foot into any puddles. "They fly to some airports for their sandwich shops or superior burgers. Some runways are right along beaches or up near great hiking trails."

"So we're going flying?"

"Well, we can if you want to and Peggy has time, but I'd rather have pie."

She glanced over. Harry was so confused that he stepped right in a muddy spot then jumped into the tall wet hay as if he'd been bitten. Roland Greene who rented and worked this field for the hay had gotten most of the field harvested and stored before the rains came. His mower had broken down though and this one end of the field had gone unharvested. Unless there was an unusually dry two weeks very soon, this section would be knocked down by the weather and he'd just have to plow it under for the spring.

By the time Harry returned to the path, his trousers were soaked from the calves down. He was even cuter than she'd thought, which was pretty damned cute.

"On Saturday and Sunday mornings Peggy serves the best pie for like a dozen counties around. Fliers from all over come in for it."

As if to prove her point, a small plane buzzed above them before turning to line up on the runway. She pointed a crutch and Harry looked skyward, this time having enough sense to stop walking while he looked up from the path across the field.

They reached the big hangar. She led Harry through the people-sized door that simply said, "PIE. Saturday and Sunday while it lasts."

HARRY STUMBLED while crossing the high threshold.

High windows let light into the big interior, but most of it was in shadow. A monstrous yellow biplane dominated the space. It had two open cockpit seats with tiny window cowlings and pointed it nose to the sky because its tail rested on a tiny rear wheel. The struts between the wings and the trim were painted a gloss black. Even in the shadows, it gleamed. The last time he'd seen it had been a dozen years ago when it was a stack of exposed frames, a mostly-intact fuselage, and pallets of metal parts. It now glistened.

Beyond it was parked a small helicopter that seated four or six and was painted in the same brilliant colors. Across the nose of each was painted "Naron's Goldfinch Air." Of course, her aircraft were the colors of the little birds.

On the far side of the hangar was parked a moderate-sized RV. It had its stabilizer pins down and he could see that full hookups had been run out to it. Peggy must live there. It was one of the cut-above brands, he'd seen enough go by as bankruptcy assets to know. It would be very comfortable inside.

The front corner closest by the door had broad and generous bay windows facing out onto the airfield.

He watched the high-winged, blue-and-white Cessna 174 that had buzzed by over their heads drop down onto the tarmac with an amateur's hard bounce before settling into a smooth roll. A couple of big picnic tables were tucked up close to the big bay windows.

"Quick," Becky called to him. "Pick your flavor before they all get here." Through the thin walls he could hear the plane pulling up to the hangar as well as car doors slamming nearby.

To the side of the door there was a counter filled with pre-cut pies all neatly labeled. Several apple-rhubarb and peach pies sat beneath a warming lamp. A cherry cobbler and five pumpkin pies sat on open glass shelves, and a glass-fronted refrigerator case held several lemon meringue and a chocolate-peanut butter with a crunch topping. Every pie had a server under the first piece, except for the apple-rhubarb which was missing several pieces already. In the refrigerator case there was also a line of whipped cream canisters, the good kind that restaurants used with nitrous, not the pre-packaged ones like at The Puffin Diner.

There was a stack of paper plates and plastic forks next to a jar that said, "Five dollars a slice. Whipped cream included. Must eat here."

Becky noticed where his attention had gone. "People used to buy whole pies and she'd run out in the first ten minutes."

"Smart lady." He shoved a twenty-dollar bill in the jar.

"She only asks for ten for both of us."

"I want my Becky to have two if she feels like it. If they're as good as they smell, I certainly am." He hadn't meant to add the possessive to her name. Maybe she wouldn't notice.

Her brilliant smile was far too bright for a treat of two pieces of pie and showed that she had absolutely heard it.

He'd never been possessive about a woman in his life. *My Becky.* Well, if there was ever one to feel that way about, she was dishing up a slice of apple pie and another of pumpkin. He'd always had a weakness for lemon meringue, a pie Mom had been especially good at. He took a slice of that and would decide what else to try later.

He was carrying Becky's pieces, the pumpkin nearly lost in a mound of whipped cream, over to the table she had crutched to when the hangar door slammed open. Two guys in their forties stumbled through the door, "I'll be damned, Josh wasn't leading us on. That's a nice change."

Close behind them Cal Jr. walked in.

"Buddy!"

Harry barely had time to set down Becky's slices before Cal came over and wrapped him in a bear hug with a bone-bruising thump of greeting on the back.

"Hey Beck! Peggy got any of her rhubarb?"

"She sure does."

"And you're not having a slice? That is so wrongheaded, girl. Almost as goofy as shacking up with some sharpie N'Orleans lawyer type. So high and mighty he doesn't even remember who his drinking buddies are on Friday Poker Night."

Harry had completely forgotten. Cal had mentioned it back at the wedding, but as neither of them had expected him to still be in Eagle Cove, he'd hadn't bothered to pay it much attention. Besides, last night he'd been curled up in a fetal ball like—

"Totally my fault," Becky rescued him. She even said it with a grin as if there'd been nothing but wild sex.

"Lucky shit!" Harry managed to absorb some of the shock of Cal's next congratulatory buffet with a sag and twist. "Save me a seat."

The two fliers sat at another table as two more planes pulled up in front of the hangar.

Harry doubled back to the big urn of coffee and slipped two more dollars in the jar. Becky was a cream-and-sugar woman, easy to remember because she was so bright and sweet herself. He pulled himself up sharp for a moment. That was the kind of trick he always used to remember a date's preferences so that he looked more attentive than he actually was. Hell, after the first trial break he could tell you how every single juror drank their cuppa and he wouldn't forget. He didn't like using those kinds of games on Becky.

You know how she likes her coffee. That's all that matters, Slater.

And it was.

He arrived back at the table just a single step ahead of Cal which was all that secured his seat directly across from Becky. He'd thought of sitting beside her, but decided that the chance to play footsie and just look at her made sitting across a better choice.

Cal sat beside him rather than beside Becky. "Guy's gotta sit where he can be in the glow of a smile like that one. He's really lighting you up, Beck. Looks good on you."

"Feels good too, Cal. We have to find a girl for you."

Cal grimaced and took a forkful of the apple-rhubarb. "Not a lot of girls who think a grown man who goes to bed at eight and gets up by four to bake bread is a whole lotta fun."

"But it's such gooood bread, Cal." She drew it out with enough sexual innuendo to have Harry's body heating up. She caught his reaction, fluttered her eyes closed and groaned in a way he'd learned was an indicator that he was doing something really right.

He could see Cal swallow hard and the two flyboys stop eating for a moment to look over and see just what was causing her to make that sound.

"Just like this is such gooood pie." Under the table she ran her good leg up the inside of Harry's.

Harry's pulse picked up another couple notches until Cal shoved his shoulder against Harry's hard enough that he'd have gone off the end of the bench if it wasn't up against the wall.

"Damn Beck, cut that out," Cal complained. "I'm a single guy for crying out loud, not even getting it regular like some lawyers."

"Shut up and eat your pie," Harry told him, then whispered, "Loser!" as he held his forefinger and thumb in an "L" against his forehead.

And that set the three of them laughing.

He'd missed Cal. Good friends like him didn't come along every day. He'd seen him half a dozen times in twice as many years and he felt like his brother more than, well, his brother. Nothing that wrong with Greg, but he and Cal had been close.

"So what you're saying is I gotta find a girl who loves me for my bread?"

"Hey, you think I'd have caught a lawyer without my beer?"

"It is damn good beer," Cal agreed. "Mighta had some of it last night."

Odd. Harry only now realized that he had yet to have a taste of it. Jessica had apparently served Becky's beer at the reception—which he'd carefully flown in too late for—but only champagne and cider for the wedding.

While he wasn't watching, Cal stole the last forkful of his lemon meringue.

"You need to make lemon meringue beer, Beck. Just stir in some of this pie and do whatever it is you do."

Harry laughed, but he could see Becky go thoughtful.

"It would have to be a lighter beer."

He should know by now that brewing was the one subject she never joked about.

"A pale ale, like an IPA," Cal suggested.

"A lager," a deep voice declared like law from the end of the table. The Judge stood there holding a piece of the lemon meringue. "Anything heavier would overwhelm the subtlety of Peggy's pie. As good as your ma's," he pointed a plastic fork at Harry's chest. "May I?" he nodded toward the seat beside Becky.

"Please," she patted it for him to sit beside her.

Just as Cal had been wanting in on facing a package as cute as Becky, now Harry was faced with his father and wanted nothing to do with it.

"How's the leg doing, Becky?"

"Good as can be, sir. Your son's been taking good care of me."

Cal turned to waggle his eyebrows meaningfully at Harry.

"He'll never be a great brewer, doesn't have the passion for it, but he's been a very handy assistant."

Cal knocked his knee sideways into Harry's.

Harry knocked his knee back against Cal's.

Then Becky kicked him sharply in the shin with her Wellington—hard enough to make him yelp—at the same moment she was smiling up at the Judge. A glance down showed a big muddy boot print on the leg of his last clean slacks. And he wouldn't be surprised if a blood stain formed there in a moment. She'd kicked him hard.

HARRY MIGHT BE a successful lawyer and an incredible lover, but there was still a major dweeb in the mix. It really was like watching the two high school stars of the Pufflings soccer team fooling around in the back of the classroom rather than paying attention. And between them they'd just banged her bad leg hard enough to hurt.

Unlike Harry and Cal, who sat with their backs to the hangar, she'd seen the Judge's approach. She'd almost missed it, as he'd circled around behind the aircraft, but he could only have come from Peggy's RV. Which also explained why Peggy had avoided answering the tease about her late arrival to knitting yesterday afternoon. *What man had she been busy with that she was so late?* Gina's barb had hit dead center even if no one knew it. It seems that Peggy had taken her own advice after knitting last night.

The Slaters were never the quickest lot. Now Peggy's comment made perfect sense.

Becky wondered what that bit of information would do to Harry's presently adolescent brain. But if Judge Slater wanted to be discreet, she wasn't going to spoil it for him.

Peggy came out of the RV with a loose-hipped saunter that Becky would absolutely be doing if it weren't for the crutches and leg brace. At the moment Becky knew she was about as sexy as a forklift, but Harry wasn't complaining so she shouldn't be either. A couple of the fliers stopped Peggy at the Stearman biplane. They were obviously geeking out over the restoration. It was just as well because the Judge's reaction was as plain as day.

His attention hadn't just drifted to Peggy, it had zeroed in, and one of his quiet smiles eased the lines on his face. Thankfully neither of the boys noticed.

Becky rested her hand on the Judge's arm to distract him. It took him a moment to shake off his thoughts and turn to her. Now that he had, she didn't know what to say.

"Are you looking forward to being a grandfather?" It was the first and dumbest thing to come into her head.

The Judge's look acknowledged that without having to say aloud, "Is there anything that *you* want to be telling me, young lady?"

Then he smiled softly as if setting the question aside.

"As I consider it, I find the thought to be rather new. I am deeply sorry that my wife didn't live to see how happy they are."

"You can be happy for them too, Dad," Harry's voice was harsh.

Becky spun to look at him.

Harry's face had taken on a grim set. The Judge merely looked sad. She'd seen that anger before between son and father, but hadn't seen it so blatantly displayed.

Becky shot for another subject change, "Will you be ready for Salmon Days?"

"I do not understand why I must open on the weekend for tourists," the Judge looked relieved at the subject change. "But my daughter-in-law insists and I agreed to follow her guidance in order to promote Eagle Cove."

"Salmon Days?" Harry's look slowly shifted from aggressive to puzzled. A good change.

"Pay attention, dude!" Then Cal smacked him on the back of the head.

Harry's expression shifted to a different kind of irritation—now aimed playfully at Cal instead of at his father with a load of anger. Thank goodness.

Cal continued as if Harry's attitude was utterly meaningless to a man of his size. "Your sister-in-law is a marketing genius. Why do you think the town is so busy? She did a whole number on the snowbirds using September to travel down the coast toward their winter homes. The campground is solid with RVs and the hotels are mostly full even though tourists have to go out of their way and cross a pass to reach us from Highway 101. Next weekend is the first weekend in October, time for the big Fall celebration: Salmon Days."

"And we," Becky held up a palm to Cal who smacked it with a high five, "are going to kick ass!" She got a high five out of the Judge as well which surprised her and apparently shocked his son.

"Doing what?"

"Beer tastings!" Becky called out. "And a beer garden at events."

"Amazing baked goods!" Cal declared.

"Feeding tourists breakfast on the weekend," the Judge's tone was dead dry but his smile gave him away.

"Airplane and helicopter rides!" Peggy sat down next to Cal, playing it a little coy by sitting opposite the Judge. Becky half wondered if they'd soon be playing footsie under the table, though it was hard to imagine the Judge doing something like that. Then Peggy smiled over at her in a way that said the Judge might not have a choice on whether or not that happened.

"Greg is doing his gourmet thing," Becky started ticking off on her fingers. "Salmon Fishing Derby for the biggest fish, the youngest and oldest fisherman to make a catch, and a couple of other things. Wood chopping contests with a raffle to benefit community hall projects, not to mention firewood for the town's old folks. Sunday we have a chainsaw art demonstration that is drawing carvers from all up and down the coast—they each get an eight foot section from Saturday's Jack and Jill handsaw event. We have a couple boats coming down from Depoe Bay for the weekend to do gray whale spotting tours during their winter migration south. The whole town is really doing it up."

"Huh," was Harry's thoughtful input.

Actually, *Huh!* was appropriate for her, too. She'd only cooked a single batch of beer, and too many things had gone by the boards this week. Next week was going to be a hard push to get ready.

Time for play was almost over.

It hit her like a punch to the chest. She tried not to look at Harry, not directly, but time for play *was* over. Or near enough. By Monday she'd have to be in full scramble mode no matter what shape her knee was in.

Maybe, if she was careful and didn't mind not sleeping much, she could carve out the rest of the weekend with Harry, but their fling really was coming to an end.

It ripped at her heart, but being a practical girl, she'd have to face that.

Really soon.

But not quite yet.

CHAPTER 9

*H*arry spent the day doing his best to make everything perfect. He took Becky for a drive along the coast. They had a chilly picnic at the stone gazebo perched high on the cliffs above Yachats. They drove up the Alsea River just because Route 34 along the valley was so beautiful in the fall where it wandered through the Siuslaw Forest.

At the Alsea Mercantile, the only real store in the town of a hundred-and-sixty, they worked on naming the twelve-point Roosevelt elk whose head was mounted above the front door along with a display of old saws and rifles. They bought a pint of Tillamook Caramel Toffee Crunch ice cream and wandered up and down the hardware aisles making up purposes for bizarre pipe fittings. He took turns feeding himself and Becky by the spoonful as she still had her crutches. The game was a little spoiled because Becky knew everything about almost anything hardware, whereas he was stumped by even the simplest item.

"I'm a lawyer, not a brewer, so sue me," he grumbled at one point. He wasn't used to environments where he knew less than anyone else in the room.

"Deal. Can I hire you to sue yourself?"

"Sure." The way he was feeling, he might sue himself just on general principle.

"Good, come here." They were somewhere between sump pumps and engine cleaners that smelled as sharply oily as the water had when he'd had to personally visit the site of a coastal spill. She pulled him down into a sloppy, sweet, caramel-flavored kiss that had him curling his toes it was so good. He cursed that his hands were filled with ice cream and spoon so that he couldn't take more advantage of the moment before she broke it off.

"What was that for?"

"Down payment. Consider yourself hired. Defendant is one Harry Slater. Go get him, Counselor!"

"How do *you* do that?"

"What?" She crutched off into ducting and air conditioning. How did anyone sell air conditioning in coastal Oregon?

"The legal talk thing."

Becky did one of her cute-as-hell blushes, "Dylan McDermott in *The Practice.* Total dreamboat during my lonely teen years. I own the complete set, all eight seasons. How do you do it?"

"Do what?"

"The legal thing."

"By shutting off my heart."

She stuttered to a stop in switches and turned to face him. This aisle smelled vaguely of burnt rubber. Or bad electrical smells. Carbon arcing or some such.

His spontaneous answer lay there between them on the scuffed cement floor mud-tracked to a dull brown. Harry closed his eyes. He so didn't want to face this. He enjoyed his job and he was damn good at it. Honestly he did, especially as long as he kept telling himself that.

"Ehhhh!" Becky made a harsh, penalty-buzzer noise. "Try again, Counselor. This girl knows better. Frankly, if I was you, I'd sue the dude who said that. Now give me another bite of ice cream. I think you've been hogging it."

He dipped in the plastic spoon and fed her another bite.

"Yum!" Then she turned and continued their slow pace along the aisle, leading him away from the site of his vomiting out his darkest secret. It *was* how he got through so many cases. *Focus on the law. Precedent, code, procedural errors. Ignore the facts because attorney-client privilege protects the client no matter how much you know them to be guilty.* How many times had he held proof of fraud in his hands and tried to figure out a way to be sure that opposing counsel didn't know it existed but without, quite, breaking the rules of discovery? Probably about the same number of times as opposing counsel had done the same.

Becky Billings had just told him he still had a heart, and then made no big deal out of it.

All the way back down to the coast and out to Eagle Cove he tried to juggle the facets of the situation, but they weren't coming together. Normally he was the one who could take the turbulent mass of evidence, testimony, and the law and find a way to create a coherent presentation that an everyman jury could follow and at least think they understood.

How he and Becky Billings could possibly fit together was not one of those situations.

By the time they arrived back at the brewery, there was just time to clean up and go to their fancy dinner. He was thankful that there was something to occupy them.

He dressed in the suit he'd worn to Greg's wedding, and felt moderately ridiculous, but it was either that or beige wool gabardine on which you could still see the outline of a Wellington boot print.

Harry half hoped that Becky would opt once more for the little black dress, even if the evening was chilly for that. He really would enjoy taking it back off her later tonight.

Instead, she dressed in a black satin blouse and form-hugging slacks that made her legs look long and her hips look almost as sexy as he knew they were. She only wore the lighter brace, which had disappeared under the slacks. She accented the outfit with…

Harry laughed. He couldn't help himself, it was just knocked out of him.

Becky wore his missing Oregon Ducks silk tie. The greens and golds somehow drew out the color of her eyes, her lips, and her hair. She wore it like a loose cravat before it disappeared into the blouse. It was only too easy to imagine the tie running out of sight down her cleavage.

"Inside or outside the bra?"

"*That* is a question that you'll have to solve later, Counselor, if you get lucky that is."

"Well, if my little brother cooks even half as well as everyone says, I have high hopes."

"He cooks better." Then Becky groaned with disgust as she picked up her crutches.

Harry hurried forward to get ahead of her going down the stairs in case she lost her balance and needed rescuing.

She didn't.

But she did look spectacular climbing into his car.

"I DON'T KNOW how to do this." Harry held the car door for her, but Becky didn't climb out. She didn't know how to face her friends through a whole dinner at The Puffin. She didn't know how to sit across from Harry and not have every emotion in her heart splatter out for all to see.

"You release the seatbelt. Then you swing out one leg. After that—"

Her baleful glare apparently got the message across.

He squatted down so that they were eye to eye. Damn, he had to be a considerate guy on top of being kind. She couldn't find any anger against him. Against the circumstances that surrounded them? Easy! But not against Harry Slater.

"For days I've been looking forward to taking you to a fine dinner. The fact that it's made by my little brother," he made a grimace like he'd bitten a lemon, but he kept the tone light and funny and added a wry smile that made her want to kiss it so that she could be a part of that smile as well, "is an issue that can't be helped."

"Why?"

"Because dining out with a beautiful woman who I care so much about just sounds like a really good idea."

Who I care so much about. She studied his eyes and ignored the curious looks they were receiving from others walking along the sidewalk toward the diner. He did care about her; she knew that. So why did it keep surprising her? A man like Harry wasn't likely to use any stronger words. That seemed to be part of their unspoken agreement —she hadn't used the L-word either. Heaven help her though, she couldn't imagine ever loving another man the way she loved Harry Slater.

"So, I have an idea," he continued to balance easily in a squat she couldn't even do any more.

"Thank god."

"There are two legal terms I can think of to apply to this matter," again that melting smile of his, "should it so please the court."

It took an effort, but Becky pulled on the mental cloak of their game of her being the court and he the counselor.

"The first," Harry continued apparently oblivious to how hard this was, "is *de novo.* It means 'as if new.' An appellate review *de novo* is one made without consideration of the trial judge's ruling. The other is *pro tem* which is a fancy way to say 'only temporarily.' What if we declare tonight to be dinner *de novo pro tem?*"

Or maybe Harry did understand how hard this was. Maybe he too felt the pressure of the outside world that was squeezing in upon their idyll.

"Dining *de novo pro tem?*" She like the way that sounded. Dinner as if new, at least for the moment.

He nodded and held out his hand to assist her from the car.

"Just us. Ignore the world."

"Just us," he took her hand and with that connection made, she could do nothing other than slide free of the car.

Unable to take her hand because of the damn crutches, he instead looped a hand about her elbow as they proceeded to The Puffin, climbed the steps, and went inside.

———

BECKY'S GASP of wonder almost pulled Harry out of their fragile bubble. It was as if he could see the edges crackle, and then ease back together.

The battered Puffin Diner had been transformed into The Puffin. Instead of bright fluorescents, twinkle lights were draped across the ceiling like stars. The Formica tables, so scuffed with age that they were almost colorless, had been lined up into two long communal-style tables and covered with tablecloths of midnight blue. Fat white candles set on crystal dishes cast small pools of light over shining silverware and pale blue linen napkins.

Harry ducked into the back room to grab a footstool to support Becky's leg, and helped her settle in the seat farthest from the service window and kitchen. For a moment he was afraid that some local would take the next set of seats along the table, but two out-of-town couples sat in the next four chairs. It was rapidly apparent that they were friends on their journey south, enjoying a fine meal before getting on the road again. They were as content to ignore he and Becky as they themselves were glad to be ignored.

He scooted one of the candles until it lit just their portion of the table and left a line of soft shadow between them and the rest of the long table. With the darkened window to their other side, they were almost alone in the entire restaurant except for their candle-warmed reflections.

"Haven't you been here for dinner?" Becky was looking around like a child gawking at a circus.

"Only in the beginning. Greg started out by inviting a few friends over to test dishes on. We'd all kick in ten bucks, except me, I'd kick in a case of beer. But since he took it upscale, it's out of my price range."

"Methinks the court is fibbing." Her tone definitely didn't ring true.

She fiddled with a salad fork but didn't answer.

"You came!" Greg blasted through the side of their little sanctuary. He was almost unrecognizable in his immaculate white chef's coat. He clasped Becky's hand in delight then turned to Harry, "Good job, bro. She's been very resistant. I'm gonna knock your socks off, Becky." He gave her hand a final squeeze and disappeared again.

"Now I know the court is fibbing."

Becky toyed with her fork some more, but finally answered. "Greg doesn't serve his meals with wine, he serves them exclusively with Billings beers. I used to come and do the 'beer talk' at the dinners, but as he got better and better, I felt more and more out of my league. I finally begged off."

Which Harry's courtroom sense told him was only half the story, so he waited.

"Well look," Becky finally looked up at his eyes, but gestured down the table.

He did and it only took a moment to see what she was talking about. There were a few family groups, but this was definitely a couples' restaurant. He'd run into those in New Orleans and learned the power of taking a date to one that felt like this, but she was right— he never ate in them alone.

"Point taken. But tonight is good, isn't it?" How pitiful was it that he was begging to have his ego stroked that he was doing this right?

And her radiant smile did exactly that. "It is, Harry. This is very good."

The first course arrived. Delicate sushi rolls of crab, salmon, and butternut squash. It seemed an odd combo until dipped into the spicy black bean sauce. It was paired with an ale so light and delicate that it was almost saki-like in its clarity and was served in tiny coffee cups.

"Yours?"

Becky nodded, then closed her eyes. He could practically see her comparing and cataloging flavor profiles.

"Need a notebook?"

Becky almost snorted the beer as she tried to cover her laugh.

"No. I think I'm fairly happy with this one. I'd like to find a few more floral notes, but I'd be afraid to ruin it."

"Rose petals," he teased her.

"No, but maybe dandelion."

"I forgot. You don't joke about brewing."

"Never," she sipped again at the tiny cup of beer. "What don't you ever joke about?"

"Well, by the very nature of my job I'm the butt of the largest segment of jokes ever told. But I've learned that there are certain topics not to ever joke about with others: money with corporate types, and guilt or innocence with the obviously guilty. Though that isn't a bad way to find out if your client actually is guilty when they're playing coy."

Becky's laugh was appreciative and the bubble of their little sanctuary grew stronger and more solid. When they were served the butternut squash soup with wild mushroom and pancetta tortellini and paired with Barn Door Red Ale, it barely impinged on their awareness. The nuttiness of the beer complemented the hint of walnut in the pasta.

He tipped his beer toward her to acknowledge it.

"What else?" Becky bowed her head briefly at his accolade. She had a real modesty about putting herself forward, but none about the amazing quality of her beer.

"Never joke with anyone about the fact that the increased idiocy of their case is only going to augment the exorbitant size of your fee—no matter that it's absolutely true."

Becky was the most willing of listeners.

"And never, ever, under any circumstances, joke about a woman's hair, clothes, or anything whatsoever to do with marriage."

Her expression froze despite the warm candlelight.

And if he could remove his foot from his mouth surgically he would do so.

He could see Becky dig in and struggle to bail him out of his own stupidity, but there was no helping him this time. He'd shattered the illusion and they were once again sitting in an old diner built in a ridiculously small coastal town. The buzz of conversation along the two tables only made the stark silence at their end all the more painful.

BECKY HADN'T LET herself think that word. She'd built fortress walls around it every time she looked at Greg or Jessica and saw how insanely happy they were. It was fine for them, but she couldn't imagine it for the Becky Billings of the world. The bolt of raw envy knocked her speechless.

Harry had given her a glimpse of what was possible. It was no more than that, but it was like a tiny taste of a perfect beer, and then never again being permitted to have any.

But this dinner, this moment was so precious that she didn't want to mar it with her own issues. She scrambled around for a tease and felt a wave of relief when she finally found one.

"What's wrong with my hair?"

Harry's jaw simply dropped. He didn't laugh like he was supposed to, or struggle to backpedal which also would have been okay. He didn't even take the obvious opportunity to pay her a compliment. She had been too self-conscious with him in the room to spend much time fixing it up (another disadvantage to an open floor plan), but still she'd thought it looked nice brushed out over her shoulders with a simple copper barrette holding it back to one side.

Instead, he looked at her with such warmth that she could feel heat rising into her cheeks.

"You are, without contention, Becky, the most amazing woman ever."

She had to look down at the table and study her empty bowl. Between one eyeblink and the next, the bowl was slid away and a fillet of bright pink-orange salmon surrounded by crab-stuffed mushroom caps took its place. A light sauce of rice wine vinegar and dill was balanced by the tartar sauce built into the mushrooms.

The unexpected pairing of her sweet and malty Deep Ocean Bock was…incredible.

"This is how you make me feel," she forced herself to look back up at Harry.

"I do?" He inspected his dish with a puzzled frown.

"Yes, you do. You make me feel incredible enough that I can almost believe it."

"You should. You absolutely should."

The rest of the meal passed in soft tones and meaningless conversation.

And the rest of the night passed in soft tones and meaningful love-making that permanently changed the way she'd ever think of herself again.

*H*arry woke early on Monday. It was dark and the rain that had been a soft background to their Sunday had been replaced by a heavy drencher. It pounded down on the barn's tin roof and pinged off the glass of the skylight. Stiff gusts of wind slapped it against the seaward windows like a thousand ball bearings dumped on a sheet of steel.

He didn't need to reach out to know that he was alone in Becky's big bed; it felt different when she wasn't there.

Saturday night after the dinner, he'd kidnapped the stout white candle from the table.

Becky had accused him of malfeasance aforethought and he hadn't denied the charge. But she'd also cooed with pleasure when he'd relit it in her hayloft apartment. He'd made love to her—there was no longer any way he could just call it sex—trying to outlast the slow-burning candle.

It was still burning when they finally slept curled tightly together.

Sunday they'd left the bed only for food and a shared bath in the big tub. They'd stretched out together and watched a half dozen episodes of *The Practice* on Becky's computer and he had to admit that with the attractive distractions of LisaGay Hamilton and Kelli Williams, the show wasn't that far off the mark.

At dusk, they'd relit the candle, but neither of them had been up for much, neither physically nor conversationally. Mostly they'd lain together and held on tightly.

And now, Monday, he'd woken alone. The candle had burned out and the only light was a soft glow coming up the stairs from the brewery.

He felt positively somnolent as he moved through the morning's actions: making the bed, brushing his teeth, getting dressed, packing his bag. It was as if someone else was performing the actions, especially the last.

Harry didn't want to go, but it was time.

I get through it by shutting off my heart.

So he did. Each piece of clothing held a memory. Ripped khakis from unloading her truck. A bleached spot on a dark blue Armani shirt where cleaning solution had splashed while he helped her scrub one of the tanks. The dried mud that had filled every little hole in his Allen Edmonds Oxfords. At least the Nikes were dry, mostly.

He barely managed to hold it together when he found the Oregon Ducks tie tucked into the pocket of his suit. He'd worn it to the wedding as a tease to his brother who had gone to culinary school rather than college, but it had become a real thing with Becky. It was the only clothing she'd worn for most of their stolen Sunday together. He zipped it into the suiter bag along with the Michael Kors gray two-piecer that he'd worn to that cozy dinner.

He'd been using the extra toothbrush that he'd found that first night while Becky had slept on the couch below. The decision on whether he should take it or leave it was nearly the final straw.

I get through it by...

Talk about a sucky mantra. Those things were supposed to be uplifting, weren't they?

He moved down the stairs quietly and set his bags by the door before going to find Becky. He located her deep in the brewery. She was leaning against the copper cooking kettle right where they'd taken each other like it was the best thing in the—

I get through it...

He stopped only a few feet away, but couldn't move closer.

She faced away from him. Her head hung down and her shoulders were shaking.

What was he supposed to say?

Should he take her in his arms? He half expected that she'd strike out at him if he did and he wouldn't blame her. But if he touched her, how was he ever supposed to let her go?

"Becky?" He could barely hear his own voice over the low hum of pumps and heaters.

But she heard it and flinched as if he'd slapped her.

He didn't know what to do or what to say. He caught himself shuffling from foot to foot, a habit that his first defeat during a law school mock trial had trained out of him. "Student projected a deep lack of confidence with body language, particularly with the constant shifting of weight from one side to the other."

She leaned her forehead against the kettle.

"I—"

"Just go!" Her shout blasted out. "Look, Harry. It's been wonderful, but now you need to just go." Her voice was ragged and thick with pain.

He took a step forward.

"Don't!"

He froze. And when she moaned he didn't know what else to do.

He turned and left the brewery. At the door he stopped for one last look around the living room. He could hear the echoes of her friends' laughter, could almost see the women who loved her.

They would take care of her. Some day she'd be glad that he'd gone. She deserved so much better.

He hated that thought, but didn't know what else to do. He took his bags and went.

Becky didn't hear him go, but she felt the pressure change as the front door opened and then closed again. A chill breeze slipped into the warm brewery and set her to shivering.

The silence was impossibly deep, far quieter than when her lover had been sleeping upstairs, even if she'd no longer been able to tolerate lying beside him.

She braced her hands against the cool copper kettle, so warm when the two of them had lain naked against it.

Enough. It was time to do what must be done.

As she tried to stand up straight, her knee twinged. It wasn't bad, but she didn't have the energy to overcome even the minor ache.

Instead she let herself fold down onto the cold concrete floor. There, she curled into a small ball and let herself weep.

Becky wept through pain and tears. She wept until her eyes were dry and her chest ached as if it had been crushed, and still she couldn't stop. She curled more tightly around the agony and it only hurt worse.

Dying would be less painful; it just had to be.

Harry parked at the back of The Puffin Diner.

He wasn't sure why he was here. Habit? To say goodbye? Something for the road? The rental's dashboard clock read 5:50. Time to go to work. No… But it was…

Having no better plan, he tugged the collar of his jacket more tightly around his neck, and hurried in through the back door.

The normalcy was comforting. The Judge at his grill, giving the immaculate surface a final scrub with a bronze wool pad. The familiar odor of the first pot of coffee on to brew.

"Hey, bro!" Greg swung by and punched him on the arm. "Come to lend a hand?"

"I guess." Not really.

"Could use some more silverware sets."

Harry didn't take off his jacket, but stepped out of the kitchen and over to the service station. He began taking a knife, fork, and spoon, rolling them in a paper napkin, and putting a sticky strip around them.

He made up sets until he ran out of forks and then stood there with no idea of what to do next.

Greg dumped a pile of plastic-covered menus at the service station.

Harry read down through the options until his eyes hit the wavy black line drawn through "Waffles (with blueberries when in season)."

"You'll need to reprint these," Harry marveled at how normal his voice sounded.

"Why?" Greg stopped hurrying around and was being so cheerful that Harry wanted to club him with the coffee pot.

"The waffles."

"What about them?"

"The waffle iron got fixed."

Greg grabbed his shoulder and twisted him around, "Say what?"

"The waffle iron. Peggy fixed it. What's the big deal?"

"Of course you wouldn't get it."

Greg's hand clamped harder and harder on Harry's shoulder as he slowly turned to look through the service window at the Judge.

"Peggy *fixed* it?" Greg asked their father.

The Judge was watching them, but didn't say a word.

Goddamn reticent asshole. Harry couldn't find much heat to put behind the thought though. As a matter of fact, he couldn't find any emotion about anything.

Harry tried to shake off Greg's hand; it was hurting. He finally clubbed it aside hard enough to make Greg yelp.

"Ouch! Damn it, Harry!" Then Greg squinted at him. "You look like shit. What happened, Becky finally grab some common sense and dump your sorry ass?"

Harry's fist connected with Greg's chin hard enough to smash his brother against the counter. With a roar that ripped at his throat, Harry dove at his brother.

Greg's counterstrike hit hard enough to hurt, but not enough to slow him down. Silverware scattered to the floor. The pile of menus flopped over and spread out across the linoleum. They made the footing as slick as an ice skating rink.

Harry didn't care.

He pounded his fist into Greg's gut and earned a very satisfying grunt.

They fell.

His attempt to knee Greg in the balls caught him on the thigh.

Greg managed a grab onto Harry's jacket and used it to throw him against the line of stools bolted to the floor. The pain blew sparks into Harry's vision.

His little brother was almost clear when he managed to grab an ankle.

Greg lashed out with his other foot and caught Harry on the shoulder, but Harry didn't let go.

This time. Once and for all. He'd really—

Pain sliced through the red haze over his vision.

Someone had his ear and was yanking on it hard.

It hurt too much to even fight against.

He had a brief vision of a small woman with curly red hair dragged back in a ponytail.

Peggy...was hauling him toward the door by his ear.

Greg managed a brutal gut punch that cost Harry the last of his air, leaving him barely able to stumble where Peggy was dragging him.

"I've got the other one," a male voice boomed just as Peggy led Harry out onto the porch and over the railing. He tumbled head over heels to land flat on his back in a mud puddle.

A moment later a crushing weight slammed into him as Cal Jr. dropped Greg over the porch rail and right on top of him.

Harry tried to groan, but didn't have enough air.

Greg managed a groan, but little more. He finally flopped off Harry until they were lying side by side in the puddle. The Puffin was exposed to the beach and the heavy rain was backed up by a lashing wind. It was like ice cold acupuncture against every bit of uncovered skin.

Harry shoved himself up to a sitting position and managed to lever himself against the stone foundation of the porch. From here the steps afforded a little protection from the slicing wind.

Greg forced himself around until he too was leaning against the porch with Harry.

Harry punched his arm. Greg punched him back. Neither of them were able to make much out of it.

"Who the hell bit your ass, Harry?"

"Why do you care so damn much about a fucking waffle iron?"

Greg slicked back his hair and then made a vain effort to wipe the rain off his face.

Harry didn't even bother trying. He was starting to feel where Greg had caught him. His ribs weren't going to be playing racquetball anytime soon.

"You say Peggy fixed it?"

"Sure, on Friday. Took her about ten minutes other than getting some parts."

"Shit! I could have done that. Hell, it was so easy, you could have done it."

Greg jostled his shoulder but Harry didn't care enough to do more than jostle him back.

"The waffle iron broke the same day that Ma died. Neither of us could face touching it."

"Can't believe the old man even noticed she was gone."

In moments Greg was straddled over him and had a fist pulling Harry's jacket collar choking tight. "You don't know shit, asshole. You didn't watch him cradle Ma in his lap for hour after hour, day after day. You didn't see him age twenty years the day she died. Why the hell do you think I stayed in Eagle Cove? At least at first it was because I couldn't bear the thought of him being alone." Greg shoved him hard against the foundation before flopping back into the mud to sit beside him. A gust blasted along Beach Way hard enough to make waves in their personal, private mud puddle.

Harry had always assumed that his father was just a cold son of a bitch. But he *had* aged. He remembered the change at the funeral. He'd almost walked past the Judge he'd been so changed. If Harry hadn't been so wrapped up in his own misery, maybe it would have meant more at the time.

"If he had fixed the waffle iron," Greg stared up into the rain, "Maybe it would mean that he'd finally accepted Ma's death or something. But that Peggy fixed it... I don't know."

"They're sleeping together," Harry knew it was true as soon as he'd said it. All of the little pieces fell into place. The way she'd rested a hand on the Judge's arm. Saturday morning getting pie, the Judge hadn't been there when Harry and Becky had arrived. But he also hadn't come in the door that Harry had been facing. That meant he had been in the RV with Peggy.

"No way!"

"Count on it, baby bro." His father had moved on and found another woman as if anyone could measure up to Ma. On top of that, he'd commercialized Ma's art, selling it on t-shirts, hats, posters, and all of that other tourist crap. He wasn't cherishing her memory no matter what his brother thought.

"Well," Greg wiped at his face again as the water continued to drip off his nose. "Ain't that something. So what's up with you and Becky anyway?"

There were some things that Harry didn't want to talk about.

He forced himself to his feet, ignored the charley horse where Greg had kneed his thigh. He patted his pockets. Good, he'd managed to keep the car keys.

He crossed to the far side of the puddle then stopped and turned to look down at Greg.

"That was a hell of a good meal, Greg. And you have an amazing wife. Take good care of her."

Then unable to face what he could never be to another amazing woman, Harry trudged around the diner to his rental car, climbed in, and drove out of Eagle Cove.

CHAPTER 11

$\mathcal{H}$arry hit the discount department store out by the Portland airport. He bought the first jeans he'd owned in a decade, a t-shirt that didn't have anything to do with the coast or Oregon at all, and a pair of cheap shoes that felt like they were trying to reshape his feet. The dressing room trash bin he filled with the Nikes and everything else he'd been wearing—it wasn't even worth the effort to see if any of it was salvageable.

He skipped Vegas and flew home on the first flight he could find.

Tuesday, he checked in at the office. After a couple of meetings, he was told to take the rest of the week off and enjoy himself. There was a complete laugh. He hadn't even slept since leaving Oregon except in fits and naps filled with ugly dreams.

Wednesday he walked into the local shop for strong coffee and beignets. He took his usual chair at one of the open tables crowded onto the sidewalk and tried to focus on reading the newspaper. He must have missed some interesting local cases, but he couldn't make his mind focus on the printed words.

All he could picture was the woman who wouldn't look at him as he left.

While he'd been in the air, his phone had picked up a voicemail—a vitriolic diatribe from Jessica. Apparently Greg had called her right after Harry left town and she'd rushed out to find Becky. He considered trying to call back, but there was nothing to explain.

Harry closed his eyes. If he could feel any worse…but it wasn't possible.

He opened his eyes as a big man lowered himself into the other chair of the small table.

"What the hell are you doing here?"

The Judge merely sighed.

Harry rubbed at his eyes, "Okay, not my best effort. But seriously, Dad, what the hell are you doing here? Who's cooking breakfast?"

"Gregory has that well in hand. Peggy is assisting him."

"Are you and she…" he didn't even know why he asked. "Sorry, none of my business."

"She's a remarkable woman, Harold. As remarkable as your mother, in different ways."

"Why? Does Peggy have something else you can display on tourist crap for money like Ma's art?"

Again the sigh from the Judge.

Harry was just about to lash out or maybe he should just storm off, but the Judge held up a hand as if calling for silence in the court.

Old habits died hard; Harry waited. He was barely aware of the tourists rushing by, always in such a hurry, already working up a sweat though it was still early morning. The locals stood out in their relaxed, easygoing pace, one that Harry had never been able to match. He would always be an outsider, just by how he walked.

"I do not sell your mother's artwork for the money, Harold."

"Then why?"

"Because I want others to see the wonderful things she did. Her art is done. It died with her and nothing new will ever be created by her. But I remember her so well from even the least brushstroke. I didn't want that to die with her. Even if others cannot appreciate what they see, I do with every single t-shirt or gift bag that comes through the diner."

Harry leaned back in the chair, almost tipped it over backwards.

Would have if not for the big man seated close behind him. He apologized then turned back to his father.

It was the longest speech he'd ever heard Judge John Slater make except from the courtroom bench. As a kid he'd often gone to court during summer breaks to listen to the cases and hear his father administer justice—a memory he'd almost forgotten.

His father's explanation also meant that Greg was right, the Judge missed his wife. Surprisingly, he had a heart...which was more than Harry could claim.

"That still doesn't explain why you're in New Orleans."

The Judge took one of Harry's beignets and bit into it. He chewed a long time for such a soft pastry, then finally set it down and looked right at Harry.

"Do you love her?"

"Do I what!" It came out loudly enough to make the people seated nearest to them jump in their seats.

"Becky Billings. Do you love her?" The Judge was wholly unfazed.

The coldest-hearted man the planet was asking him if he loved...

Shit!

Harry shoved away from the table, tossed his paper down on his chair, but didn't make it even a dozen paces down the sidewalk. People jostled and bumped against him as he stood there with his head down. Looking up at the sky didn't help either. It wasn't that brilliant rain-washed blue of the Oregon Coast. Nor the roiled gray of a storm sweeping through. It was the washed-out blue-gray of a city tinged with heat haze and too many people.

"Do you love her?" Harry asked the sky. *How the hell am I supposed to know?*

He trudged back to the Judge with all of the enthusiasm of a defendant approaching the bench for sentencing. It was almost as hard as walking away from Becky just two days ago in a land thousands of miles away.

He collapsed back into his seat, "Do I love her."

"That is the question under consideration," his father sounded so much like Becky that he was torn between laughter and tears.

"I really hurt her, didn't I?"

The Judge nodded. "Luckily, when they love us, women are a forgiving lot."

He couldn't even forgive himself for walking away from her. For getting so involved in the first place.

"Parrish, Merryfield, and Roland offered me a full partnership yesterday."

"Very respectable," the Judge nodded. "I always knew that you'd do well."

"No you didn't. You thought I was an arrogant prick who would crash and burn."

Impossibly, the Judge began to chuckle. "Well, I will admit that I certainly feared that to be the case."

"What changed your mind?"

"Two things," the Judge was suddenly serious.

"Which were?"

"One, the way you assisted me at the diner. An arrogant boy would have wished me luck and walked away, but instead you did your very best day after day."

"It was the right thing to do."

"It was," the Judge nodded in agreement. "But it was no less unexpected. The second was Becky."

"What about her?" Harry was surprised at how desperate he was for any word of her.

"She is one of the most sensible women of her generation. She has a generous heart that she gives freely, but only so far. She gives to her friends more than friendship would normally call for. But for herself she gives nothing…until she met you."

Harry slouched lower in his chair. "If you're trying to make me feel any worse, you're succeeding."

The Judge picked up his beignet and took another bite. He looked about at the pedestrians and the thick traffic along the street.

Harry in turn looked at the Judge and wondered that he was here. Yet it wouldn't be hard to find Harry, he was a creature of habit and a call to his secretary would reveal where to find him at this hour each morning. If there was any doubt, she could always access his phone locator software. He'd given her access because he was always losing the damn thing. But that the Judge had come all the way to New Orleans. There was more than just local-girl-made-sad-by-big-city-lawyer going on here. He really cared about Becky. And by extrapolation, maybe he cared about his eldest—

There was a train of thought about to jump off the track.

"Partner at Parrish, Merryfield, and Roland is quite an achievement," his father only ever repeated himself as a point of emphasis.

"I'm so glad you approve," Harry couldn't keep the sarcasm out of his tone. He knew it was a big deal without being told by the ever so popular,   elected-to-six-terms-with-no-one-daring-to-run-against-him Judge Slater. PMR never recruited below top three and only from the best schools. Only one in twenty associates made partner.

"Have you accepted yet?"

"Have I—" Well, he hadn't actually. Not in so many words. He'd thanked them when they took him out to lunch at the club yesterday, but he hadn't actually said yes. "Why? Do you have a better idea?"

The Judge laced his fingers together as he always did when delivering a verdict, whether from the bench or at the dinner table. This time he kept his two forefingers pointed outward and tapped the tips together as he only did when he was uncertain of his choice of words.

"Just spit it out, Dad."

He grimaced, but stopped with the damned finger tapping. "There is an upcoming election for the 17th District Circuit Court in Newport, Oregon. There is a certain gentleman who is running uncontested for my old seat who is…"

"An incompetent boob?" Harry offered into the Judge's silence. His father had notoriously little patience for weak judges.

"An ambulance chaser has more savvy."

"It's way past time to file even if I wanted to be on the ballot."

"And yet you have retained your membership in the Oregon State Bar." An easy fact for the Judge to look up. It simply surprised Harry that his father had cared enough to do so. Yet he'd cared enough to travel all the way to New Orleans.

"Fought too hard to earn it, just to let it go."

"You are a sensible man." The Judge managed to say it without sounding too condescending.

"And you'd suggest that I do this how?" He was actually rather flattered that his father would suggest Harry run for his old seat. Actually, it was tempting. Perhaps even very tempting.

The Judge slipped a large envelope across the table.

Harry opened it and half expected a snake to jump out at him.

Instead there was a campaign sign. Eye-catching. Sharp design.

Vote Slater for Judge (Write it in!)

"Your sister-in-law's work," the Judge nodded approvingly.

"But she hates me. Told me so at length on the phone." However, it was a chance to help dispense justice rather than spending his life trying to trick it. It would be a hell of a cut in pay, but he lived the high life now and it had done less for him than… Than a week with Becky Billings.

"Yes, Jessica is a passionate woman." The Judge pulled out his phone, dialed a number, and handed it to Harry while it was still ringing.

Oh crap!

"Hi, Jessica!" Harry tried to put on a cheery tone, then winced in preparation for the reply.

"Asshole! Natalya and I still want to cut your balls off!"

"I'd rather you didn't."

Jessica huffed at him over the phone. "But if you love Becky—"

"I do!" And the statement shocked him into silence but didn't slow Jessica down for a second.

"I know that, asshole brother-in-law, I'm just glad that you finally do. Okay, here's the plan that I have put together so far." And Jessica began rattling off promotions, ads campaigns, appearances at grange halls and Kiwanis meetings, and more that he couldn't even begin to follow. "You're kicking off your campaign on Sunday at Salmon Days, so you'd better get your ass back here by then." As if his compliance was a foregone conclusion.

And Jessica was gone.

Harry slowly handed the phone back to his father.

"That is a very determined woman."

"She is," the Judge agreed.

"I like that in a woman," because he'd never met a more determined woman than Becky Billings.

"So do I," his father nodded, obviously talking about the new woman in his life.

Oddly, for once, Harry didn't need to prepare a thing to make his decision. The jury didn't even have to leave the room for him to know his own verdict.

*B*ecky knew something was up. But she didn't have time to think about what it might be. This week had been both wonderful and horrid beyond imagining.

Among the worst moments was that she'd been able to overhear what Jessica had yelled to poor Harry's voicemail over the phone. She loved her friend, and appreciated her staunch heartfelt support, but Harry had done nothing to deserve it. He had promised nothing and in so many ways given her everything.

All of the good things this week had kept her too busy to hurt for long.

After a few calls around, she'd hired Alex away from Cal Jr. "Let's hope he makes a better brewer than he did a baker," had been Cal's gruff statement after practically forcing Alex on her with high recommendations. The 5B Brewery had finally grown beyond anything she could manage herself. Alex drove deliveries, picked up product, and helped her with the heavy hauling work around the brewery. He seemed genuinely excited by the process. But even with his help, it had been a miracle that she'd been ready for Salmon Days at Eagle Cove.

The tasting room had been swamped, and not just with tourists.

Four different pubs and three restaurants over in The Valley had come in for a tasting and left her with their cards to contact them about standing orders after Salmon Days was over. Peggy would have normally pitched in to help, but she'd been assisting Greg over at The Puffin Diner for most of the week. And now that it was the weekend, she had flights booked for almost every minute of daylight.

Becky had managed to corner her friend briefly over pie this morning, but Peggy had been very close-mouthed about why the Judge was out of town, suspiciously so. However, she had been completely open about how she and the Judge had hooked up. Becky had just assumed it was Peggy's doing, but couldn't be more wrong.

He'd come out to the airport one day over a month ago, with no one the wiser, and asked for a plane flight. He'd brought a picnic lunch and they'd landed on the sand of a remote cove.

It was hard to picture the Judge wooing a woman, but it sounded as if he'd done an excellent job of it, plying her with Becky's non-alcoholic cider, and homemade crab sandwiches.

"He spent a whole month courting me. It was only after I spoke to you on last Friday," she had the decency to offer a sympathetic squeeze of Becky's hand, "that I realized he was waiting for me to take the final initiative. 'Woman's prerogative,' was all he said when I asked. He doesn't say much, but the way he says it..." Peggy had looked very pleased with the results. "He was a little flustered that you caught on. You're the one who outed us."

"But I didn't tell a soul."

"No, but you proved to him that secrecy was not so crucial. He's not demonstrative, except in private, though he's very demonstrative there."

Becky offered the best smile she had, and struggled not to think of Harry. He too had been demonstrative and he hadn't been shy about being seen with her in public. Except now he was back in New Orleans.

The Saturday afternoon crowd had cleared out all the cases of two flavors entirely. She was trying to calculate if she had time to run a couple of batches through the bottler when Jessica and Natalya dropped by.

"Natya! I didn't know you were back in town for this."

"Just managed to get in. How's the knee?"

"Doc says that I was so good about wearing the big brace that I can probably lose it permanently Monday. Then I've got six weeks of physical therapy, but I should be good. I hate to ask this, but can you finish up here in the tasting room? I've got to get some bottling done."

Jessica and Natalya didn't even hesitate, they both jumped right in and shooed her off.

She came up behind each one and hugged them hard for a moment, "I love you both so much."

"Likewise, champ. Now go!"

Becky hurried back into the brewery and after about twenty minutes had the bottler running her Rushing River Stout into dark brown glass with her trademark bluebird-colored caps.

There was a clack and rattle as the bottles were jostled into position, filled under pressure, and capped. The labeler made a smooth slick sound and she taught Alex how to slide them into cases.

Peggy and Greg showed up while she was checking the progress of the next batch in the malt tun.

"Aren't you guys busy?"

"Dinner at The Puffin isn't for a couple of hours," Greg poked at a couple of gauges that he obviously knew nothing about. "I'm taking a quick break. Thought I'd come out and see my wife."

Peggy just drifted over and started inspecting the gauges on the CCV tanks, knowing exactly what she was looking at. The two of them often geeked together over plane engines and the brewing process. She soon had a wrench and was tightening fittings on the whirlpool filter that Becky had been meaning to get to all week. Peggy made her feel calmer just by being here.

Tiffany wandered in, which was unheard of on a Saturday. In her typically odd way, she simply sat on the couch and without a word pulled out her knitting. Even though it was Saturday rather than Friday, others soon joined her: Gina, Marjorie…

Becky didn't have a moment to go over and ask what the heck was going on, not with the bottler running. The machine was awfully fussy and had to be watched over like a hawk to keep it running smoothly. She started teaching Alex the tricks to making it behave.

Jessica came in the back, "Crowd is thinning in the tasting room. Natya's shooing the last ones out the door."

"Thank god!" Becky loved the income she'd just received. She'd probably banked the next month of Alex's salary just from the sales that the tasting room had generated, but she really needed for everything to just slow down for a moment. Tomorrow was going to be even crazier.

"Someone just handed me this," Natalya came in and shoved an envelope into Becky's hands.

There was no address or marking.

She started to pull it out and swore. It was a legal document with the line numbers down the side and the header block of a lawsuit title.

"I don't have time for whatever this is." She really, really didn't want to know what else had just gone wrong with her life.

She tossed it aside.

Jessica retrieved it and shoved it back into her hands.

Becky pulled it out from the envelope and began reading.

"Pleading for Forgiveness," she read aloud. "What the hell?"

"Keep going," Peggy prompted, suddenly at her elbow.

"The party of the first part, hereinafter named Harold Davis Slater..." Becky lost her breath and leaned back against the copper cooking kettle. It was warm. She'd started heating it earlier so that it would be up to temperature as soon as the mash was ready for cooking.

Natalya snatched the document from her nerveless fingers and continued reading aloud, "...hereby petitions the party of the second part, hereinafter named Becky Billings—fool doesn't even know that you're really Rebecca—for consideration of this motion being placed before the court."

Becky would have slid to the floor if she hadn't been wearing the big leg brace which kept her pinned upright with her back against the kettle.

"Do you want me to keep going?"

"Yes!" About half the people shouted, which was good, because Becky couldn't seem to catch her breath. The brewery felt so full with her friends all about her.

"How about if I finish it?" The Judge's deep voice sounded from the back of the crowd that had gathered. He moved up to stand beside Peggy.

"No," Harry stepped around him. "Let me."

Becky couldn't move, she couldn't breathe. She could only watch as Harry stepped into the brewery.

"It has been pointed out during a long drive across the country," Harry scowled at his father, but Becky could see there was humor behind it. "That counsel is not the sharpest lawyer there is. That title obviously goes to Dylan McDermott."

Becky almost choked herself on a half laugh.

Harry kept coming. Other than the bottler rattling away in the background, the room was dead silent.

"But he begs the court to consider the changed circumstances."

"What—" Becky had to cough to clear her throat. "What changed circumstances?"

"First," Harry came to a stop and took her hands. He held them tightly, rubbing his thumbs over her knuckles.

Even that simple gesture sent shivers up her spine. Really good shivers filled with hope.

"I appear to be the hot write-in candidate for the 17th District Circuit Court."

"Which is where?"

Harry smiled down at her, "Which is here. Newport anyway, but very commutable as my father proved for years."

Becky couldn't even breathe so it was a good thing that Harry continued without prompting.

"Second," and he kept her hands in his as he knelt so that she was the one looking down at him. "In front of these good friends and this copper kettle, I wish to state that I love you."

She could feel the tears running. They were the kind of tears with which a beer should be flavored. It gave her a recipe idea for a new brew that she'd think about later.

"Please, Becky Billings, please tell me that you'll have me, for without you, I'm lost."

Becky leaned back against the kettle, letting the warmth radiate through her and chase away the chill that had sunk into her body all week and threatened to freeze her heart forever.

"The court has a condition, Counselor."

He smiled up at her, "Name it. Anything."

And Becky knew that was true.

"The court demands," and she brushed a hand through his hair, before cupping his cheek and coaxing him back to his feet.

"The court demands that you kiss her here and now to prove your intent."

And Harry pressed her back against the warm copper and kissed her as the room erupted with cheers and applause.

LONGING FOR EAGLE COVE

"This is…different." Natalya Lamont had been to a number of friends' weddings, but none like this.

"But it is *very* Becky," her mother agreed. That had them both smiling because it was absolutely true.

The double wedding, which appeared to be the first in Eagle Cove's history, held in what had once been Becky's father's cow barn, added an extra layer of merry confusion to the event. The best man for both weddings was the same person—one groom's brother and the other groom's son, as it was to be a father-son double wedding this actually made some form of common sense. Greg's brother Harry was marrying Becky and his father, three years after his wife's death, was also marrying again.

Natalya had come down from Portland to the Oregon Coast for the weekend to help set up and decorate, and it was going to be surprising…surprisingly wonderful.

The reception after the pending ceremonies would make this an even more Becky-esque event. She was a top craft-beer brewer, so there was beer rather than champagne. In addition to being best man twice, Becky had twisted Greg's arm (which hadn't needed much twisting), to cater it. His restaurant had just been named the best on the entire coast, making both the Whale Cove Inn and the Heceta Head Lighthouse Bed & Breakfast rather tiffy, and promise of his food might have helped account for the amazing turnout.

But most especially of all, the barn setting that was no longer a barn was completely Becky.

A classic January storm was rattling the Oregon Coast hard with intense winds and curtains of lashing rain. Eagle Cove in mid-winter didn't offer a lot of venues for weddings.

The Grange Hall—which for a while had also doubled as the Unitarian Church (which now held service in The Flicker movie theater)—had recently been converted into dog kennels and a training area for Catbird Service Assistance Dogs. Catbird had offered the use of the training space which was big enough, but since it smelled of wet dog...

Her mom's grand Victorian B&B, commanding the head of the beach, had hosted weddings in the past but couldn't accommodate the scale of Becky's. It seemed as if half the town had turned out for the doubled nuptials today. So maybe the draw was more than Greg's food.

"Doubt if you'd get a dozen people at my wedding," Natalya whispered to her mother as they waited for the first ceremony to begin.

Her mother threw her head back and laughed. Gina Lamont had the best laugh; she always gave in to it completely. The people around them joined in with bright smiles even though they couldn't have heard the conversation. Mom's laugh just did that to people. Natalya had always envied her mother's laugh.

"You'll have more than you think, dear. We'll invite Becky and she'll bring her friends."

"Thanks a lot, Mom."

"That is if you bother to marry one," her mother plowed on completely ignoring Natalya's sarcastic tone. "You know my advice."

She did. Her father, only ever referred to as "That Unholy Disaster," had been gone before Natalya was born and her mother had never remarried. A few months ago a stray comment had made Natalya suspicious enough to ask whether or not they'd ever been married in the first place. Her mother had slyly avoided answering by wielding a fresh batch of her irresistible macadamia nut-chocolate chip muffins.

She turned to ask again now, but at that moment Becky's mom, who was as short, blond, and buxom as the bride, made her way between Natalya and her mother like they were pool table bumpers.

"Sorry," she gasped out and waved a cherry-flavored ChapStick as an excuse before plunging back into the crowded "bride's room."

The main room for the wedding was packed, but the smaller space where the two brides were getting ready was utter mayhem. Natalya and her mom had retreated to the big side-sliding door that opened into the main area just to avoid being trampled by the herd. There was no questioning Becky's power to win people over.

And it *was* her influence.

Harry, her fiancé, was a high school troublemaker only recently returned. The other couple, Peggy and Judge Slater, were quiet fixtures of the community and had been for decades.

But everyone adored Becky.

Her mother too won people's hearts effortlessly. Another gift Natalya had failed to inherit along with the big laugh. It was actually okay with her; Natalya often found the social whirl tiring. She had her good friends, and that was enough for her—except they were all here in Eagle Cove while she lived three hours away in Portland.

In another way, Natalya *had* followed closely in her mother's footsteps, taking a lover when she wanted one and only keeping him until he became boring—which never seemed to take long. But now the second of her two best friends was tying the knot, she was less sure of her choices.

First Jessica and Greg. Now Becky and Harry. That left Natalya and…nobody. She didn't even have anyone to invite as a wedding date, never mind someone with potential for longer term. That wasn't good. But a quick flip through the mental contact list of past affairs also didn't unearth any regrets. Which was good. But it should tell her something…only she couldn't think of what.

However, it was impossible to feel too morose in the glorious mayhem that was a Becky Billings' event. Her friend absolutely knew how to throw a party.

"Aren't they starting yet?" Becky's father came up and asked for the twentieth time in the last ten minutes.

"Check your watch, Max," her mother told him for the twentieth time.

"Oh," he looked at it. "Right." And he was gone again.

"Do you think he actually saw the numbers this time?" Natalya asked.

"Not a chance." Her mom waved at Carl Parker then jabbed a finger in Max's direction. "They'll be talking cows and hogs in seconds."

"No," Natalya shook her head. "The weather." And sure enough, both men turned to look out the nearest window being splashed with rain. They'd been the two big farmers in town before Max Billings had given the farm to Becky and retired to Alaska.

Eventually, the winter venue options had come down to The Flicker movie theater (awkward and nowhere to dance afterward), Peggy's airplane hangar (chilly even with the big heaters running and presently mostly filled with a disassembled 1930s Beechcraft Model 17 Staggerwing that she was restoring), and Becky's barn (so much more inviting than it sounded even before they started dressing it up).

Becky's barn had won the day.

Over the fifteen years since they'd graduated high school together, Becky had converted the cow barn into one of the best craft-beer breweries on the Oregon Coast. The milking stalls had been replaced with a giant copper cooking kettle, massive fermenting tanks, a bottling machine, lines of kegs, and all of the other strange and magical equipment Becky used to practice her art. She'd walled in a part of the upstairs hayloft as an apartment, which was a very cozy space combining bedroom, kitchen, and bath. They'd recently taken over another section of the hayloft for Harry's home office.

The old, ground-floor milk processing room had been converted into their living room. From there Becky could keep an eye on any batches she was brewing. She'd made it into a homey and comfortable space...that was now a whorl of bridal-prep mayhem.

Bridesmaids, best friends, well-meaning wedding guests, and family were all crowded about them in what had been the milk processing room and was now a very comfortable living room.

The wedding proper filled the former calving barn to capacity. Becky had turned it into a tasting room. She'd refinished the inside wood so that the Douglas fir planking glowed warmly under a wash of indirect lighting. A long oak bar took up one end of the big room. It now served as a backdrop for the ceremony.

Behind the bar were lined up a dozen beer taps, from Windy Wheat Ale at one end to Rushing River Stout at the other. And there was always a pony keg of Becky's Original Root Beer hooked up as well, a brew she'd started selling for a dime a bottle back in fourth grade. The taps were all shaped like bluebirds for Becky's childhood nickname, with the flavor clearly marked on each bird's wing.

Above the bar at the far end of the room was a massive painting of the town of Eagle Cove as if seen from a plane flying offshore.

It was one of the best things Natalya had ever worked on. It was also one of the last paintings she'd ever done. Her life in Portland was web and product design, and she'd only picked up her brushes a few times in the years since she'd helped do this.

The town filled the two-mile stretch of beach from the rocky headland of Orca Head with its proud lighthouse to where the Eagle River arrived after a rushing descent out of the Coast Range mountains into the broad reach of Eagle Bay. The town proper was nestled where beach met bay and backed by the start of the dense state forest that covered the rugged slopes. No town history explained why it was called Eagle *Cove* when there was no cove to be found for miles around.

Natalya wondered how the Judge felt about that painting—and that he'd be married beneath it. It was based upon a photograph taken by his wife-to-be. But it had been painted by his late wife and Natalya. It was one of the last works that Ma Slater managed before the cancer drove her to bed. She'd been such a guiding hand for Natalya's own art. She didn't know about the Judge, but it certainly made her own heart hurt.

Ma had used the detailed style that had made her famous up and down the Oregon Coast to render the town she'd so loved.

Natalya had then painted the framing foreground of massive Douglas fir and coastal pine to the sides. She'd added the three-masted schooner *Wawona* that had transported massive loads of Oregon lumber and fish down to San Francisco in the late-1800s—though getting the perspective and rigging right had almost made her crazy. She'd had much more fun adding the mother-daughter team who had platted the town at that time. They had both been very fashion conscious so it had given Natalya a chance to render them in full Victorian style, her absolute favorite era, though it had been hard to resist steampunking them up a bit. Unwilling to mar the composition with their animosity (history told that they hadn't spoken once in the last forty years that they'd lived in side by side houses) but also not wishing to rewrite history, she had arranged for them to be looking in different directions.

The two women also had been avid birders. So they had divided the town, through intermediaries: the seaside half of the town to have streets named by the mother for land birds and the landward half by the daughter named for seabirds. Hence, the single question that the Eagle Cove Chamber of Commerce received the most often. They'd divided the town's naming right down the middle of Beach Way, Eagle Cove's main street, then moved into the two grand Victorians at the end of town. Natalya and her mother were direct descendants of the daughter and the Slaters had bought the mother's property when she passed.

Natalya wished she'd worn a watch so that *she* could check it. With the bride's father happily catching up with his old friend and neighbor, Natalya was now the one impatient for the first ceremony to begin. Her own antsy feelings didn't extend to the crowd's though. Probably because Becky had the foresight to post Alex her assistant behind the bar. He was busy making sure that everyone had a brew to sip while they were waiting. A beer sounded good at the moment.

She turned to her mom to see if she wanted one, but she was busy catching up with Becky's mother—still clutching her unopened cherry ChapStick.

So much history here. Natalya had to try hard again to shake off the sadness. Eagle Cove was so rich and full; it had a texture and depth like a fine painting…and yet she lived in Portland rendering websites and marketing products.

It's a good job, she reminded herself. *You love your job,* she wished her internal voice had sounded more convincing on that second point. Natalya made her living from techno-retro design. She led a whole team of web and product designers specializing in it at ORTech4U2. Her Victorian division of Oregon Tech For You Too accounted for over a third of website and product designs, both period authentic and steampunk "updated." They were on the verge of breaking into film. It should be exciting, riveting, consuming…well it was certainly the last one. She'd definitely feel the pinch of taking off an extra day tomorrow. Tuesday was going to be hell.

By force of will, she focused back on the room itself.

To the sides of the long beer-tasting/wedding room stood an odd assortment of twenty tables and a hundred chairs that had been borrowed from The Puffin Bay Diner and other places around town. Because Becky had cleared out the cases of bottled beer usually offered for sale, there was plenty of room for the dancing afterward.

But first there were two weddings to manage.

"Which of us is first again?" Her mom turned back as Becky's mother rushed away once more. It wasn't like her mother to be spacy about anything. She was a statuesque redhead with an easiness that Natalya had never managed to even emulate never mind possess. Yet being bridesmaid to Peggy Naron, who had been one of the other long-term single women of the town, had definitely put Mom off her game.

"I'm a bridesmaid first," Natalya reassured her. "See?" she pointed to the Judge standing in front of the bar-soon-to-be-altar. He was an imposing man even without his black magisterial robes. In them today, with his shock of white hair and somber expression, he looked truly grand. If he was there, ready to go, then it was Harry and Becky's ceremony first.

Her first cousin Jessica arrived in a flurry. She instantly started fussing with the gown Natalya was wearing. It was a long black sheath that matched Jessica's—it had become tradition among them for the bridesmaids to wear black as they "mourned" the fall of another of their childhood trio into marriage.

Natalya had wanted to shift over to black steampunk. But Jessica had vetoed that—her own marriage had turned her into some kind of a spoilsport, though she and Becky had still been in favor of the black dresses.

Instead Jessica was now fussing with Natalya's flowers (a beautiful bouquet of yellow winter jasmine and red poinsettia—which Natalya had successfully dubbed as Becky's *Ironman* colors), her hair (dark and worn loose past her shoulders, nothing like Jessica's trendy layer cut—though Natalya was the one stuck living in a big city), and then rearranging where the spaghetti straps crossed on her back. Finally Natalya had to slap at her hands.

"Stop it, Jessica. Is Becky ready?"

In answer, Tiffany—who had eased into the role of wedding manager as quietly as she did everything else—gave them both a light shove from behind and between one breath and the next she and Jessica were headed up the aisle, making way for Becky, the bride. Becky's mother and father had come down from their Alaskan retirement to escort their only child. Becky had needed the steadying hand of both of them, so both parents were currently flanking her as they went up the aisle.

Except there weren't really aisles. Some chairs had been moved to the front by the bar-altar to accommodate the elderly, but it was more a friendly gathering than anything organized. Bride and groom sides were utterly meaningless in the packed house.

"We're like plowshares," Natalya whispered as she and Jessica forged a pathway from the bride in the back to the groom waiting up front. She had to shoo Dawn and Vincent's twin girls out of the way several times because they somehow kept popping up in successive layers of the shifting crowd.

"You're next!" Jessica whispered. Then the last of the crowd fell silent as Becky began walking up the aisle.

Natalya didn't get a chance to tell Jessica just *how* unlikely her being next was, though it did make a certain amount of sense. At least by the process of elimination.

The three of them had been best friends since, well, birth. After today she'd also be the last one to be "cheerfully single" as they had all proclaimed over the years.

But there wasn't a soul on her horizon. There were always men hanging around, but none of them were interesting enough for more than a dalliance.

Was it any surprise? She'd never fit in.

Jessica and Becky were like younger twins of their mothers. Natalya's brunette and dusky skin nothing like her friends, her mother, or the few photos of "That Unholy Disaster."

They both had fathers to walk them down the aisles. Natalya could barely remember her father's name most of the time. "T.U.D." her mother would say when referring to him until his name might as well be Tud. A missing "r" was always implied by her mother's tone.

There was no more sign of Tud in the crowd than there had been over the last thirty-two years and Natalya didn't miss what she'd never had. Not much anyway. She'd never really dreamed about finding a permanent man in her life, but her friends were planting the idea.

The crowd finally parted enough for Natalya to now see Harry Slater standing at the head of the aisle, vainly trying to catch a glimpse of his wife-to-be. Becky was six inches shorter than Natalya and Jessica's five-ten. She and Jessica shifted together so that their shoulders were brushing, just to make it harder on Harry; the move earned them a pained smile. His brother Greg stood close beside him in his new suit; his eyes were only for his four-months pregnant wife.

"You should be banished," she whispered to Jessica as they neared the head of the aisle.

"Me? Why?"

"Looking too damned happy."

"You'll see," was all the frustrating response that her friend offered as she looked back at Greg all goofy-happy.

Natalya didn't want to see. She wouldn't mind a man someday, but they'd have to be cut out of a different cloth than any man she'd ever dated. But if she hadn't found one in all of Portland, she certainly wasn't going to find one here in Eagle Cove.

Now that the wedding party was all assembled—and Alex had served the last beer from behind the "altar," at least until after the ceremony—it suddenly felt very real. The second of her two best friends was about to be married.

For a moment, Natalya wished there was someone here to look at her the way the groom and his best man-brother were looking at their wife and wife-to-be. The second groomsman was leaning down and chatting with the groom. He towered above both brothers and even the Judge.

Cal Mason Jr. was built on as massive a scale as the suit that actually looked damned sharp on him. Cal was the sort of guy you wouldn't think owned a suit but the charcoal gray three-piece looked amazing. Light-haired and blue-eyed, he could be the twin of his father. He'd crossed six foot in junior high and by the time he and Harry were lead strikers for the Puffin High soccer team, he'd topped out at six-four. He had a Nordic reindeer-herder sized frame more appropriate for football, though Natalya could still recall how agile he'd been as he raced up and down the field. Harry might have thought he'd ruled the games, or that it had been a cooperative effort, but Cal was simply in another league. The problem was that he'd known it—not arrogant perhaps, but still too cocky for her taste.

She could see him joking with Harry, probably being "bar" shallow even though they now stood at an altar. The instant Harry spotted his bride, Cal Jr. might as well have been babbling away on some other planet. *Tough luck, Cal.*

He caught on quickly and began scanning the room. His eyes slid past Natalya with as much recognition as—

He jolted and turned back to look at her. Not Jessica. And not Becky. Definitely her.

She made a point of shifting to a preoccupied expression and looking away as if he didn't exist. At least that was the plan. But Cal's attention had riveted on her and she couldn't ignore her reaction to that familiar smile that spread across his features. In fact, Natalya almost bumped into the groom at the head of the aisle, because she was having trouble looking away from Cal Mason Jr.

Only when Jessica pinched her, rather more sharply than Natalya felt was called for, did she veer to the bride's side. Even the Judge looked at her a little oddly.

WHAT THE HELL was up with weddings?

Cal wanted to ask Harry, but he was all busy with responses, vows, and the biggest shit-eating grin ever worn by man. Of course, marrying Becky Billings, it was hard to blame the guy. She was damned cute. Wedding white did absolutely nothing to hide how hot the woman was. It also didn't hurt that her smile was just as ridiculously oversized as Harry's.

After a bit of debate, Harry had chosen Greg to do the actual best man dance, carrying the ring and all that. It was fine with Cal; nice to see the two brothers getting along for a change. He'd have bet that to last mere minutes after Harry had moved back into town, but whenever they started getting out of hand one of their women stepped in and shut it down before it descended into one of the wrestling matches that had been their standard form of communicating. They got along better, so he'd have to admit that was one benefit of marriage. Just an unexpected one.

With nothing much else to do, other than make sure Harry wasn't dumb enough to nerve out at the last moment, Cal had set himself to surveying the crowd.

Not a soul from New Orleans for the groom's side. Man had been a hot-shit lawyer down there for a decade and he didn't even have the decency to invite a cute Creole "hot mama" paralegal for Cal.

As for the townies who'd shown up, Cal knew every one of them and had dated more than a few. He knew Dawn—who'd been a total babe since fifth grade—would give him a dance, but her husband would hog her most of the time—lucky bastard. And the way Greg was looking at Jessica, there wouldn't be much cutting in there either.

But even pretending he didn't already know, there was no question where he was going for the first dance. Which took him back to his original question: What the hell was up with weddings?

He'd known Natalya Lamont since before they'd done the old: if you show me yours, I'll show you mine. They'd been six and they'd both chickened. When they were old enough for that question to take on a whole different meaning it had never come up again. She'd blended into the scenery of Eagle Cove until he'd no longer really seen her.

Oh, his hormones had tracked her whenever she'd crossed a room, her and every other girl of their thirty-four person high school class— a field of just eighteen women. Yet for reasons beyond him, he'd never so much as touched Natalya.

Then today she'd come walking through the brewery crowd with her hair the color of dark chocolate and shiny as a new penny, swept down over her shoulders. And those deep eyes catching the Christmas lights Becky had strung everywhere. If he could ever find someone to explain what it was that happened at weddings, he'd also ask them what was up with grown women and "twinkle lights."

As the bride and groom were doing the "Until death do us part" thing, he had to glance over Greg's head to check out what Natalya had been wearing. Somehow that hadn't even registered as she'd come up the aisle. Just that hair and face and those deep eyes that stared straight back without even blinking. It was unnatural how long that woman could go without blinking; like she was casting a spell or something.

Jessica and Natalya wore long black straight dresses complete with black, paper flower corsages.

He got the joke right away. The death of another life of singlehood. Cute. Damned cute. No, that had described Becky Billings. It even described the sleek and shining blond Jessica. It so didn't cover the long shapely woman with smoke-dark eyes.

Natalya had never looked so…

"You can kiss the bride now, Son," Judge Slater told his eldest and Cal had missed his chance to mess with the ceremony just to tease his best friend by protesting when the call for it was made. But he wasn't low enough to screw with "the moment" for his buddy. That didn't mean he was above trying to tap in on the first dance.

Though, if he *could* arrange to slide onto the floor with Natalya Lamont for the first dance, maybe he'd leave Becky Billings and Harry Slater to themselves.

RATHER THAN THE couple returning down the aisle to cheers and congratulations, there was a marginally pre-orchestrated reshuffling that happened during the generous applause.

Becky gave Natalya a quick hug hard enough to drive all of the breath from her lungs, gave a gentler version to the pregnant Jessica, then laughed and raced back up the aisle. She hiked up her skirts to knee high in her hurry, exposing her favorite bright red cowboy boots. She abandoned her new husband with no more than a wink. Though the kiss she'd left behind at the end of the ceremony had definitely been something to behold. Damn, but Natalya could feel envy about that one.

Jessica gave Natalya a nudge to remind her of their wedding rehearsal move. Right. The two of them moved aside from the impromptu altar and turned to join the leading edge of the crowd. Their role in Becky's wedding was complete, they were now in the audience for Peggy's.

After carefully not looking at the groom's side of the altar for a long moment, Natalya stole another glance. Every time she'd peeked at the groomsmen, Cal Jr. had been looking at her over the tops of the others' heads. It had unnerved her enough to not join in the happy tears streaming down Jessica's cheeks.

They ended up standing close beside Mrs. Winslow—their second grade teacher. She was a notorious stoic who had taken on the personal responsibility of shaping the youth of Eagle Cove since forever. But even *her* eyes were misty. Natalya had liked to think that she, Jessica, and Becky held a special place in Marjorie Winslow's heart.

"I'm just being hormonal," Jessica wiped at her face with one hand as the other rested on the slight bulge of her waistline that would have been invisible if the dress weren't so clingy.

Mrs. Winslow handed over a handkerchief. "No, Jessica. You, my girl, are turning into a mush. Never would have thought it of you."

Jessica had been a notorious non-crier until she married Greg. Even the harrowing breakups of high school had seemed to slide by her like wind past a seagull on the beach. Natalya kept her tears to herself, except a few times when one of her best friends or her mother stumbled upon her at the wrong moment, but Jessica had none of those. Becky wept at heartfelt commercials on TV, especially ones with the puppies and the Clydesdales.

Jessica dabbed at her eyes and for a moment rested her cheek on the shorter woman's gray hair. "I never would have thought it myself."

"Wimp," Natalya whispered.

"You, Natalya Lamont," Mrs. Winslow had that you're-about-to-be-sent-to-sit-in-the-corner look. "We shall wait until marriage and pregnancy happens to you. I think that shall be very interesting."

"Not likely." And for perhaps the first time in her life, that answer didn't sit well. Her mother was the embodiment of how joyous a single woman could be...but that sat equally uncomfortably at the moment.

Searching for a distraction from wedding-goofy women and Cal's constant attention, she found one at the bar-turned-altar. The newly married Harry Slater stepped up to his father and Natalya was still close enough to hear him.

"Okay, Dad. Hand them over."

The Judge actually looked worried. It was a look Natalya had never seen on his face before. Ever. She'd seen brief bouts of fear when his wife had been dying three years before, but never worry.

Natalya started to look away to see where Cal Jr. was, in order to make sure that he wasn't still staring at her, when Jessica nudged her in the ribs.

"What?"

Jessica just nodded back toward the altar.

Harry actually held his father's hand in a two-handed clasp, a degree of closeness that was still very unusual to see between the two men who'd been estranged for so long.

"You'll do fine, Dad. It's me I'm worried about. What if I screw this up?" He made it funny. Something he and Becky shared, always having the right thing to say in just the right tone to put others at ease. It was another skill she envied, and didn't possess even a shade of.

"Son," the Judge's voice rumbled out, carrying easily to where Natalya stood despite the rising chatter of the crowd anxious for the second ceremony. "You'll do fine. Weddings are one of the very best parts of being a judge."

"Then hand them over," Harry repeated himself and plucked at his father's robe. "Pops!"

Judge Slater had served over thirty years on the county bench before retiring to cook at the local diner and hold lawyer's office hours here in Eagle Cove when needed. Harry had just been elected to his father's former judicial seat in November and was now fully instated.

The room slowly fell silent as Judge John Slater removed his robes and helped Judge Harry Slater don and settle them. The passing of the mantle, literally. Until three months ago, Harry had barely come home in the fourteen years since leaving for college. It was like looking into a new reality to watch the two of them interact at all. That they were exchanging roles—the father officiating the son's wedding and now the son officiating his father's—meant that somewhere along the way the space-time reality in which Eagle Cove existed had shifted.

Natalya felt momentarily lightheaded. So much so that she briefly wondered if, when she drove back to Portland Monday evening, the city would still be there or had the whole world changed along with Eagle Cove.

When Judge Harry Slater was dressed to Judge John Slater's satisfaction, the two men embraced. Natalya glanced aside and saw she wasn't the only one sniffling this time. Marjorie Winslow and Jessica leaned against each other for support and others were doing the same.

"Now, get over there," Harry gave his father a gentle shove until the Judge—for that would always be the elder's name—was standing where Harry had been just moments before. Cal Sr., almost as big as his son and nearly as imposing as the Judge, came up to shake his hand and thump him on the shoulder. Greg shook his father's hand as well before he and Cal Sr. stepped into the bridegrooms' positions.

"He is a good boy," Mrs. Winslow declared quietly.

"You didn't always think so. You never liked Greg," Jessica complained to her old mentor.

"You have brought out a new and good side to that boy. His brother was even worse as a child, but Becky appears to have done him some good, too."

And they all three turned to look at Harry, now standing tall in his magisterial robes. He noticed their attention and he waggled his eyebrows and shot them a smug grin.

"Or perhaps not," Mrs. Winslow said in her driest tone.

Harry looked quite discomfited when the three of them burst out laughing.

Someone started the music and Harry did his best to compose his expression, then he looked up the aisle and jolted as if he'd been electrocuted just like the time Natalya had wired his chair to a hidden car battery in tenth grade science class.

Natalya turned to look back down the aisle. This time it was her mother and Becky who were "plowing" the aisle clear for the bride and the two judges were both rapt.

Natalya couldn't see Peggy in her wedding white except as a flurry of curly dark red hair just visible over Becky's head.

But she could most certainly see Cal Mason Jr. across the aisle. He'd eased back against the far wall so that he wouldn't block others' view of the ceremony. He slouched comfortably there as if he was dressed in jeans and t-shirt rather than a three-piece suit.

But he wasn't watching the ceremony.

He wasn't watching Becky, still in her wedding white, nor Natalya's mother, looking like she was ready to gather up a whole crowd of men with her statuesque figure. Her mother had liked the bridesmaids' slinky-black-mourning-dress idea, but between a knockout figure and short hem, she also looked like one of those classic redheaded Italian models in it.

But Cal wasn't watching Gina Lamont either, though most other men were.

And he wasn't watching Peggy, standing as bride, who barely reached the groom's shoulder when she finally stood beside him. Peggy did look every inch of the woman she was—one who built and flew planes, had climbed the highest mountains on all seven continents, and won transoceanic sailboat races.

Cal Jr. was watching her. Natalya. He wasn't staring, not exactly, but neither was he looking aside. If she had to label his expression it might be...confusion? She wanted to go over and shake him and shout, "What are you looking at?"

***

CAL DIDN'T HAVE a goddamn clue how Natalya had got her hooks in him. She hadn't even done anything.

He tried to recall the stick that the girl had been, growing up like a weed before she...grew out. Always overshadowed by her friends.

It wasn't that Natalya Lamont was some sort of weakfish—even as a girl she'd had a spine made out of steel. It even showed in her dancer's posture, so poised that she made everyone else appear to be slouching just a little. Too bad Frau Schmidt, the only decent dance teacher for thirty miles around, had died when Natalya was still a kid or she might have really become something.

No, it wasn't that she was overshadowed.

It was more as if her two friends were such amazing distractors.

Becky was just so out there, a whirling dervish of energy and ideas. She'd started brewing and selling root beer while they were still in grade school. Now she was a hell of a craft-beer brewer. Focused and as ambitious as hell. Once she'd set her sights on Harry Slater, Cal's best friend hadn't stood a chance.

Since birth, Jessica was always blond, elegant, and so damned smart. She'd been able to speak her words as well as write them and always won every argument. He remembered class debates in social studies where she'd pick the crappy side of the argument, yet so dazzle everyone with her words that her team was inevitably the winner. She used to start arguments just so she could win them.

Natalya had always been the quiet one. But not shy kind of quiet. It had taken him a long time, and some bitter experiences that now made him smile even if they hadn't then, to understand that she was the hidden ringleader of the Terrifying Trio. The three of them were always in trouble—no, they always *were* trouble. And any man watching would swear that it was Jessica's or Becky's doing, Natalya just along for the ride.

Unless you caught her quiet smile. She didn't need to brag or show off to others, but she did love stirring things up.

Like the last soccer game of senior year, his final time ever on the field and everyone had known it. Most of the town had turned out, they'd never had such a winning season. He'd long since announced that he was joining his dad in the family bakery straight out of school —didn't need some fancy degree to enjoy himself—though he'd been bummed to have no chance at college soccer.

For that final game, he and Harry had decided that the Eagle Cove Pufflings were going to go out victors even if they had to kill the other team. That it was against their archrivals from just down the coast, the Siuslaw Vikings, would make it all the more satisfying. Then the Terrifying Trio had arrived in homemade cheerleader outfits so goddamn cute and skimpy that it was impossible to look away. However, they had made their costumes up as Viking maidens complete with fake fur and horned helmets and were cheering for the other side. It was so messed up—and classic Natalya. No thanks to them, the good-guy Pufflings had won…in overtime…barely.

Well, Natalya was sure stirring up some things for him. Not just memories, but definite ideas.

There was a roar from the crowd and he blinked. He'd missed Harry doing his first official gig as judge, which was too bad; would have been fun to give him some shit about it later. Maybe he would anyway, though maybe not.

It was cool seeing the Judge unwind enough to lean down and kiss Peggy in public—even if they were…older. The Judge didn't go quite as far as Harry and Becky—making a man wonder if they were going to do it right there on the altar—but he did a fair job of kissing the bride and it was just a little uncomfortable, like the time he'd caught his dad necking with Melanie Andriessen in the back of her own movie theater. It had been long after Mom had flaked and run off with that Corvallis stockbroker but it had still been weird. He knew sex wasn't just for young people—he hoped to god that wasn't the case—but it didn't mean that he wanted to think about it either.

It had taken Cal years to understand why his dad had told Cal's mom to go to hell when she'd tried to come back two months later. It had taken Cal even longer to forgive him. But as far as Cal knew, his mother had gone and done just that, all the way to hell. No birthday or Christmas cards, squat. Damned bitch! No wonder his dad had never remarried. Women were good for only one—

"WHO ARE YOU SO PISSED AT?"

Natalya might have resisted Cal's attention.

But oddly, his inattention had been what finally dragged her through the doubly celebrating crowd and across the room. She'd watched him change right through the ceremonies.

First, during Becky's wedding to Harry, he'd watched her with a very clear and, she'd ultimately decided, flattering interest. Then there'd been the puzzled gaze through Peggy marrying the Judge.

It had shifted abruptly afterward. She'd felt a chill as his deep blue eyes had gone ice-cold. Rather than joining the happy congratulations flowing to the two new couples, she'd become aware of the January storm lashing against the barn's tin roof so hard it might have been hail. The two windows that Cal leaned between were dark with the late afternoon and rain streaming down the glass in thick rivulets. She shivered in her thin dress as she stood before him.

"Guess I'm not fit for man or beast," he continued to glower down at her. She should have worn heels. His six added inches of height seemed a long way at the moment. She wasn't used to looking so far up at a man.

"Since when is that news, Mason? You look like some demon god, glowering here in the shadows."

It earned her a bark of laughter, "Well, at least I'm consistent."

That made her smile in turn. She'd forgotten about the drawing. After one of her inevitable teenaged clashes with her mother—back when she'd still cared about not having a father—she'd stormed off into the woods with her sketchpad. She was always doodling in her notebooks and on napkins.

This time, she'd started drawing the Demon Mother, Destroyer of All Hopes, when Cal had come sauntering by in that way he had. She'd started first with the drawing's background, filling it in with the darkness worthy of Rodin's *Gates of Hell* and Michael Jackson's *Thriller*.

"What you at *now*, Gnat?" He'd called her that since kindergarten, like she was the one who was an annoying bug.

She'd slashed her pen in a dozen quick strokes to fill in the demon's face and slathering jaws with Cal's face rather than her mother's.

He'd looked down and, somehow judging her mood perfectly, had said, "Damn! I *am* handsome." Which had oddly cheered her up.

And he was handsome. Even pissed at the world, Cal Mason Jr. dressed up in a snappy suit was a very fine sight—a very tall one, but remarkably fine.

"So," she looked up at him and batted her eyelids, "are you going to ask me?"

"What?" He blinked at the sudden shift in topic.

She'd thought he was sharper than that.

Then his smile shifted and she realized that his thoughts had gone somewhere she'd never intended.

"Dance, Mason. Are you going to ask me to dance?"

"Shit, Gnat, I've just been waiting for all the goddamn weddings to finish to ask you."

And before she could even draw breath, he pushed himself off the wall. He didn't lead her out onto the dance floor, there was no transitional moment to catch up with his mercurial change from demon to lecher to dashing groomsman. Cal simply swept her into his arms and between one heartbeat and the next, they were dancing.

Stairway to Heaven, much to her mother's distress, had come back into style and Becky and Peggy had agreed on it for their combined first-dance music. Natalya had resisted the urge to save a copy of AC/DC's *Highway to Hell* or Mozart's *Requiem Mass in D Minor* with the *Stairway to Heaven* filename onto the playlist because she'd actually looked forward to watching the two new couples dance. Becky had been so happy and she was one of those people who completely deserved every good thing that came her way. Like Gina's laugh, it was something Natalya deeply envied and wished for herself.

She thought to glance around and see just who was dancing, but Cal's mood was a little manic and he bore careful watching. His shoulders were also broad enough that he thoroughly blocked a wide range of sightlines.

"You need to always wear slinky black, Gnat."

"Only for your funeral, Mason." Because wearing it for the weddings had clearly been a mistake. Cal's hands felt as if they were on her bare skin, even though they were merely at her waist. Next time she'd wear a parka...with a bulletproof vest under it. She didn't quite remember sliding her hands up around his neck, even if it was appropriate for the slow dance rhythm.

"Aww. Didn't know you cared enough to come to my funeral. I'll start a guest list."

"Invite Becky. She always draws a crowd." Natalya wasn't very happy with the way that tone had come out.

"I thought I was the one in a grumpy mood, Natalya."

"Don't do that."

"Do what?"

"Call me by my real name."

Cal didn't ask or pry. He just offered a brief squeeze where his hands had somehow wrapped around her back. "Sure thing, Gnat."

She didn't know why it bothered her. She and Cal had never been close. With a graduating class of just thirty-four there had been some point or other where everyone had been friends...or enemies, and it did make for a certain degree of connection no matter what.

But Cal had been outside that norm. They'd never dated, rarely even danced together at the various high school parties (which she was rapidly learning was a mistake, he was a good dancer). He'd never really ticked her off, especially not with the skill that his best friend Harry Slater—correct that, *Judge* Harry Slater—had done, but then the younger Harry had ticked off almost everyone and done it frequently.

More than once, Cal's apparent unawareness of her had made him the target of one of her schemes. Like the time she'd discovered clear casting resin, and rather than embedding a small flower or shell in the clear plastic had encased all of his schoolbooks in it before returning them to his locker. Though she hadn't been able to bring herself to do that to his prized letterman's jacket which had been the original idea.

Her connection to Cal was that he'd always been there at significantly odd moments of her life. Like that day in the woods. Or today when the second of her two best friends became married, forcing her into the unmarried minority. Then he would pop up in her awareness and nudge her out of whatever mood with a joke or a sly tease.

"Say something funny, Cal." Natalya rested her head on his shoulder and enjoyed the way he held her so close yet so carefully. She felt she was floating along the floor as if they were the only dancers.

Say something funny? And said in a whispery sigh of a voice close by his ear. It was so unlike Natalya and about the sexiest damn thing he'd ever heard. Who the hell was she kidding?

Cal knew he'd held women this closely, but he couldn't remember when or who. They were dancing as if their bodies were one. His arms wrapped around her until her ribs on opposite sides lay beneath his fingers. Her chest against his... Her head on his shoulder with her nose brushing against his neck... The slightest tip of his head brought her thick wash of hair against his cheek...

This was definitely *not* a time for humor. This was a time for heaving a woman over his shoulder and dragging her back to his cave.

He guided her past Harry and Becky. Harry didn't glance up for a second, but Becky interrupted her bridal ecstasy long enough to stare at him, or rather to stare at him dancing with Natalya.

He mouthed a, *What?*

Becky just shook her head like she was trying to shake off a hallucination and kept an eye on them as her infatuated and oblivious husband spun her away.

Greg and Jessica actually stopped dancing to look at them. Greg was smiling his ass off. He pantomimed like he was catching a bouquet and sniffing the flowers with a goofy smile.

Cal was so not "next."

Jessica's eyes narrowed as she watched them, for a moment looking almost as dangerous as Natalya did.

Say something funny?

"How about surreal?" he finally whispered when he was clear of Jessica's baleful inspection.

"Sure," again in that slow, throaty whisper. What the hell *was* it with women and weddings? How had he ended up dancing with the most dangerous woman here—most dangerous one in Eagle Cove for that matter?

"My dad. Your mom."

"What about them?" A lazy mumble that was more fitting as an invitation for morning-after sex than a dance floor.

"They're dancing almost as close together as we are."

Natalya raised her head sharply. She caught his chin with the top of her head and clacked his teeth together hard on his tongue.

"Ow, shit!"

"Sorry," she went up on her toes and kissed the point of his chin. "All better now."

Which it absolutely wasn't. His tongue was throbbing with serious pain signals, sharp enough that he'd barely had time to be aware of how her soft and warm lips felt against his skin.

She was looking for her mom, but in the wrong direction.

"To your left."

He managed to keep his chin clear as she twisted to look the other way, but her motion left him with his face buried in her hair. It smelled as if it had been clean washed by the ocean air. That's when he realized that had always been her smell. Not the sea salt and seaweed of the beach, but standing atop the rocky cliffs of Orca Head at the base of the big lighthouse. Ten thousand miles of fresh-scrubbed Pacific Ocean air and you were the first person to breathe it since Japan.

That was Natalya. Impossibly fresh. Impossibly alive in his arms. It made him—

"What the hell?" Gnat sounded pissed. That whispery sigh that had him thinking of a soft bed and a naked woman beneath him was gone. Cal felt a bit of sadness; he hoped that he'd get to hear it again. Soon. He'd have to work on that.

He brushed his nose through her hair, slowing for an extra moment to enjoy himself, as he turned to face in the same direction she was. He could see their parents over Dawn and Vincent's heads. It took a moment for them to dance aside and reveal a really clear view.

Gina Lamont wore a black dress as slinky as her daughter's, except flirtatiously short rather than elegantly long. And in three-inch heels that she definitely still had the legs for. It also made her almost as tall as his dad's six-two. She and Cal Sr. didn't quite cling together, though there was little air between them.

Gina's head was thrown back in one of her infectious laughs, her shoulder-length red hair dancing about as if it too was laughing.

Dad was…smiling. He wasn't a grumpy man, but his smiles weren't exactly the most common thing around Eagle Cove.

In sixth grade he and Gnat had once had a class project together—bird spotting. They'd spent a long cold March week getting up early and staying out late, working to make sure they had the longest species list of their class. They'd even kept a tally of how many times they saw each breed. Natalya had an artist's handwriting, whereas he had a doctor's, so she'd written up their final list in count-of-sightings order. The paper had come back with a "90" on it rather than the "100" he felt they deserved, below Harry's "95" too, which really sucked. The last item on the list was circled in red and a "–10" slashed next to it. Gnat had added a final entry to the species without his knowledge: "Cal Mason Sr.'s smiles. Count: 0."

Gnat had dubbed him "The Master of the Dead-Pan Expression," which had stuck among Cal Jr.'s friends for years. "Hey Cal. Heard that The Master of the Dead-Pan Expression kicked your ass out fishing on Saturday." His dad's salmon had weighed half-again what Cal's had, so it was hard to deny. And his father hadn't so much as smiled in triumph to lord it over his son so that Cal could be angry about it.

Then Gina Lamont leaned in and kissed his dad. It wasn't some friendly peck; it was a joyous smack of lips that his dad appeared to enjoy thoroughly before the Judge and his new bride Peggy swung into the foreground and blocked the view. The kiss was a surprise, but other than the instinctive "Eww!" factor of grown parents having such thoughts, it didn't bother him any.

He turned his attention back to Natalya. He eased her close again, moving them in the opposite direction through the crowd as he could feel her attention still wasn't where he wanted it to be.

She slowly came round.

hat was it with weddings?

Natalya lay in the dark and wondered how the hell she'd ended up here. For there was no question where "here" was—not with Cal's arm draped lazily across her in the monstrous California King bed.

She'd never actually done this at a wedding: jumped into bed with a groomsman. Once or twice with a wedding guest, but only when he'd been particularly charming.

Cal hadn't been charming, he'd been…Cal. They'd danced, shared a beer, danced some more. They'd switched off with Greg and Jessica once and Harry and Becky another time—the five-four of Becky with six-four of Cal had their whole group laughing.

Much to Natalya's surprise, Tiffany had taken a turn with Cal as well. She was an odd, quiet woman who had hacked a farm out of the Coast Range forest a mile past the lighthouse. It had taken a long time before she'd started coming to the twice-weekly knitting groups and coming into town to sell her fresh produce and meats—mostly to Greg for the high-end restaurant he ran on weekends out of the Judge's diner.

Tiffany had orchestrated the two weddings with hardly a word spoken, and done it well. Not much taller than Becky, she could only clasp her arms around Cal's waist as he reached down over her shoulders to rest his hands on the back of her long brown hair.

As Natalya had watched them, she could feel the warmth of the way Cal held her so close. She'd gone eagerly back into his arms for the last dance. And that had somehow crawled into her brain...or her brain had shut down all together. Because it was a brainless maneuver to land in his bed.

No, actually. The way she felt at the moment, it hadn't been brainless at all. Neither of them had been good for much. They'd danced until the last dance, past eleven, then helped clean up so that Becky wouldn't face a disaster in the morning.

Cal had made multiple runs in his bakery truck to return the borrowed chairs and tables to the bakery and the diner. Rather than closing the Puffin Bay Diner while on his honeymoon, the Judge had arranged for Greg to cover for him starting tomorrow morning, so they had to put it back together tonight.

Jessica and Natalya had cleaned and swept and gathered empty bottles, glasses, and plates until were both staggering with exhaustion.

But when she'd been done and ready to leave, her mother was already gone, clearly forgetting that they'd carpooled here. How she was supposed to get back to her mom's B&B on the far side of town in a bridesmaid's dress on a cold winter night?

That's when she'd spotted Cal. He'd been leaning on a door jamb. Shed of his suit coat and tie, and with the top couple buttons of his dress shirt undone, he'd looked a little dangerous. He'd been watching her intently with his dark blue eyes.

"Hey, Cal," was the most intelligent greeting she could muster at that late hour.

"Coming home with me, Gnat?" He'd asked it so casually as if it didn't matter at all. In a fit of pique she'd simply slipped her arm around his elbow and nodded that she was.

They hadn't even done anything. He'd showered first and been asleep by the time she was done though she hadn't taken long. She should have backed away, gone home, or at least gone in search of a couch to sleep on. It wouldn't be a big search.

He lived above the bakery on Beach Way in the heart of the town. It was a big comfortable space. A great room with a bedroom to either side. The set of steps climbed into the middle of the U-shaped layout and they'd passed through the living-dining-kitchen room on their way to the master bedroom.

She could have gone through the door and slept on the couch.

If only he hadn't looked so nice in the shadowed bed. And he'd folded down the covers on the near side and even been thoughtful enough to set one of his t-shirts there all folded up. A shiver as the storm continued to batter the coast had her tugging on the t-shirt. It was big enough that the neck could almost slip over both shoulders and it reached down past mid-thigh, longer than many of her dresses. The material was warm and thick—thicker than the sheath dress she'd worn to the wedding anyway. Taking a deep breath, she'd ducked into the inviting bed and been asleep in moments.

She didn't know how long she'd slept—amazed that she'd slept at all—when Cal had rolled and wrapped his arm over her as if she'd always been there.

And now she was wide awake, in the middle of the night, and her body was buzzing. So much so, that she was amazed it didn't electro-shock Cal to life. Well, she'd be damned if she was going to lie here like this in his bed. Her mother was always telling her to seize the moment. This time she'd follow that advice rather than slipping away.

She turned beneath Cal's arm, thankful for the protective feel of his oversized t-shirt, and faced him. It was only as she slipped her arm over him that she realized Cal slept without a t-shirt. She tentatively slipped her hand down to his waist—nor underwear. It must be some kind of guy thing, as if showing off. "Hey world, check this out." She'd sleep safe inside her t-shirt, thank you very much...except that it was Cal's.

Natalya was about to chicken out, pride be damned, and slip from the bed when Cal slowly nuzzled his face between her breasts with a low, "Mmmm." Suddenly his t-shirt didn't feel so thick and protective.

"You're supposed to kiss a woman before you do that." They hadn't even kissed last night. She'd simply come home like a...besotted bridesmaid. Besotted by a handsome man who had held her so close while they danced, and gone out of his way to make it clear that it was *her* he wanted to be dancing with.

"Mmmm," he mumbled into her cleavage. "Give me a moment on that." And he tightened his arm around her keeping her in place.

Well, she had brought it on herself. Besides, it was nice to hold a man close. His hair, which was so short it should have been prickly, was fine and soft beneath her hands. She hooked a leg over his hip and let the arch of her foot ride up and down his calf muscle.

"Mmmm," Cal was sounding more awake as his hand slipped down over her hip and cupped her behind.

It was—

A high-pitched tone blasted from his bedside nightstand.

A synthesizer note whistled up and down the scale piercing right through her skull.

Cal didn't even flinch; he continued holding her tightly. He did mumble a brief, "Aw shit!" between her breasts.

Natalya covered her ears as the Beach Boys started singing *Wild Honey*. "What the hell, Cal? Can you stop that?"

"Only if I'm willing to let go of you," she could barely hear him.

"Why is it playing?" She tried to reach out herself but the bed was too big and he had her very thoroughly pinned.

"Alarm clock. Four a.m. Baker's hours. I start early. Need time for dough to rise."

"*Wild honey?*" She echoed the Beach Boys as they hit the refrain hard. "Four a.m.?" She never got up at four a.m.

"Honey. Common ingredient in baking. Part of my alarm playlist. Random foodie hits." He still hadn't let her go or raised his head. His voice was a buzz against her sternum, nose to chest.

"How long do we have?"

"Eight minutes."

"Eight—" she'd never set an alarm only eight minutes before anything in her life.

"I could stretch that a few minutes," he squeezed her bottom suggestively.

"I'm not here for some quickie, Mason." She grabbed his pillow and clamped it over her head to block out the whining synthesizer and over-orchestrated track.

He sighed and held onto her through two stanzas and the final refrain before he pulled his head up. She could feel him squinting at her in the dark and eased back off the pillow as the song thankfully ended.

It would really help if he didn't feel so good.

"Why *are* you here, Gnat?"

"I—" But she didn't have a good answer.

"Not that I'm complaining."

Then a blast of trumpets, a big band intro, and the Andrews Sisters broke in with *Hold Tight, Hold Tight (Want Some Sea Food Mama)*.

"Maybe I shouldn't have asked."

"I—" Again she stalled not knowing what was around the next turn. "Not for a quickie," she went back to her original premise.

"Not what you deserve anyway." He rolled away and slapped at the off button just moments before the Andrews Sisters were going to make Natalya kill herself with an oyster shucking knife.

"What *do* I deserve?" That's a question she'd like answered…in a couple of different areas of her life. Work wasn't satisfying any more —busy but not satisfying. If it ever had been. She hadn't had a decent lover in far too long. And she missed Eagle Cove, Portland was three long hours away. What she "deserved" wasn't even on the radar.

Cal rolled to his edge of the bed and flicked on the bedside lamp.

Natalya was about to cover her face with the pillow again to stop the stabbing light, but Cal had continued his roll and was now parading stark naked around the foot of the bed headed for the bathroom. He'd lost none of the grace that he used to display on the soccer field. Come to think of it, on the dance floor as well. It had been so natural that she hadn't given it a thought as she'd followed his lead, thoroughly enjoying herself in the hands of a skilled dancer.

Over the years he'd also added some muscle, some very nice

muscle. Wrestling great quantities of dough every day had given him powerful arms and shoulders. His legs said that he lived on his feet, and the view from behind as he crossed into the bathroom was very nice. Then, in plain view, he planted his feet apart and began to pee. At least he lifted the toilet seat first, but he needed to learn when to close a damned door.

She dragged the pillow back over her face and groaned. This had to be the craziest situation she'd ever been in.

He clomped back into the room. Bracing herself, she went for another peek but had waited too long. He'd already dragged on a black t-shirt, underwear (tighty whities that clung particularly nicely to him), and then slid up jeans.

"It's four now. I get breakfast at six at the diner if you'd like to join me." He dug a set of keys out of his pocket and dropped one on the dresser. "That's for the Vette if you want to get back to your mom's." Even asleep on his feet, he'd remembered that this had all started because her car was at the B&B.

"You'd let me drive your Corvette?" She'd lusted madly for the car the moment he'd held the door for her last night and she'd climbed in. Somewhere in the last six months he'd traded in his practical, red beater pickup for that amazing machine—probably his best friend Harry's fault for returning from New Orleans driving a BMW SLK roadster. The Vette was old enough to be affordable without having become a classic yet; a gorgeous piece of muscle car that had made Natalya feel like a total hot-rodder's babe for the lazy mile drive from Becky's.

"Huh!" Cal looked down at the key, then looked up at her with some surprise. "Yeah, I seem to be willing to do that for you. Nobody but me has ever driven her, so treat her nice."

Natalya sat up in bed, but kept his pillow over her chest in addition to his t-shirt. "Nice? Hell, Cal. I'm going to kidnap it and take it home with me. I'm going to name her Priscilla. You can have my MINI Cooper."

"Yeah, like I'd fit in that tiny thing. And if you try to name her

Priscilla, I'm taking back the key." But he left it and started out the door. "Would really like to see you at breakfast," then he was gone.

Nice of him to say, but there was still no kiss. No hug. No second attempt to talk her into a fast romp. What was wrong with him?

Knowing she wouldn't get back to sleep—it felt too strange being in a man's bed who wasn't her lover—she too climbed out. All she had was her black wedding dress and rain jacket. Cal's wardrobe didn't offer any more likely options. He wasn't fat, at all, anywhere, as he'd just proved by strutting about naked as a jaybird, but she could practically go camping using a pair of his pants as a tent.

She peeled up the t-shirt but it was so big and sloppy that she got it all snarled around her head and arms, and hooked over her elbows.

The door crashed open.

She bit off a yelp of surprise and managed to find a hole in the tangle to peek out of.

"Forgot my music player." Cal walked across the room, unplugged it from the nightstand, rammed it into the back pocket of his jeans, crossed back, and closed the door behind him. She could hear him clomping back down the stairs.

What the hell?

* * *

CAL MADE it five steps down the stairs when the vision slammed into him. He stopped so quickly that he almost tumbled the rest of the way to the bakery. He had to clamp a hand onto the wooden handrail to save himself.

Natalya Lamont, stark naked from the shoulders down.

He'd thought that the wedding dress was so sleek on her that there couldn't be any surprises. Stupid assumption. There were famous movie stars who didn't look half as good out of their clothes. Her dusky skin traveled all of the way down to her toes. Her breasts were goddamned magnificent—not overly big, just full and perfect for her slender frame. And her hips said "Here is a Woman"—with a giant capital W. She had runner's legs that also fired his imagination about how they'd feel wrapped around him as he—

Cal looked back up at the closed door at the head of the landing. Not much to see as he hadn't bothered turning on the lights. It was just an old, wood-paneled hall with a battered front door at the small landing.

Natalya Lamont stood up there, behind that door, naked next to his rumpled bed.

The bakery lay the opposite direction at the foot of the stairs.

He'd had his face buried between those firm, soft breasts...and done nothing.

His body leaned upstairs while some cursed, overly responsible part of him that should still be fast asleep continued downward.

He had held her not for sex but just because she had felt so perfect against him. But the part of him that desperately wanted more of that wasn't in sufficient control to turn him around.

So, he trudged downward and with each step he could only conjure one thought:

Coffee.

Coffee.

Coffee.

He'd thought there was no better way to wake up than between a woman's breasts, but between Natalya's just made it even better. Too bad he wasn't awake yet.

He really, really, really needed coffee. Coffee. Coffee.

Natalya slipped quietly out the side door at the base of the landing, the one that didn't lead into the bakery. She could hear the distant rattle of pans through the wall, but there was no way in hell she was facing Cal at the moment.

The heat on her face should be enough to light up the night despite running a cool washcloth over it. She didn't know whether the fiery blush that wouldn't go away was at being caught naked, his non-reaction, or imagining him standing naked himself in the bathroom while she changed in there with the door closed and locked. And another thing, he may have raised the toilet seat, but he hadn't put it back down when he was through, which evoked memories of both his nonchalant attitude and his magnificent—

Nope! She wasn't going to be thinking about that either.

She floundered through a couple of puddles on the driveway, which her dancing shoes discovered by instantly filling with ice cold water. She made it into the doorless garage where the Corvette was parked next to a small white delivery van with Blackbird Bakery emblazoned in bold letters down the side, with four-and-twenty blackbirds fluttering about. Natalya stood at the passenger-side door for a long moment wavering with exhaustion before she remembered that Cal wasn't going to be coming by to hold the door open like the gentleman he wasn't.

She was more tired than she thought. Four a.m. for god's sake, was it any surprise? She circled to the driver's side.

For one thing a gentleman would have kissed her before taking her to bed, and he'd have stayed awake until she'd joined him there. For a third, he'd have had the decency to say something complimentary about catching her naked—even just an "Excuse me" of embarrassment. But no, nothing. Or he'd at least have put the toilet seat back down.

Climbing into Cal's Corvette was like climbing into...Cal. The cockpit—they actually called it a cockpit he'd informed her last night —was deeply luxurious and surprisingly big. It felt that way partly because Cal had the seat about eighty feet back from the pedals. She scooted it well forward—then decided that she'd leave it there when she returned the car. Maybe she'd stick around long enough to see how he dealt with adversity. He was only six inches taller; by where he'd had the seat, he must drive with the tips of his toes.

Her MINI Cooper was small, spunky, and she'd purchased the sport version so it moved very nicely when goosed. The Corvette rumbled to life with a low throb that barely touched her in the deep leather bucket seat.

She reversed out onto the alley, checking clearances very carefully as she went. She'd wager that even the slightest damage to his precious car would eradicate any chance of a dalliance. That's assuming that she was still interested in having one.

It was an interesting question, even at four in the morning on a drizzly Monday in January. If it had been anyone other than Cal, there wouldn't have been a question—an absolute and emphatic "Bring it on!"

But with Cal there was history, even if it was a lack of history. He was a friend even if he wasn't a former lover. Or perhaps he was a friend because he *wasn't* a former lover. She loved Eagle Cove, but it wasn't where she lived. She liked the purity of the experience when she came home to visit. Her mother's welcoming hugs and bedding down together if all of the rooms in the B&B were full. They'd talk the night away like lifelong girlfriends. And with Jessica's return, her two best high school friends were here in town as well.

If she did let Cal take her to bed…

Natalya suppressed a sigh.

If she did let Cal take her to bed and they actually *did* anything, she'd have to face him when it was over. If they'd made love last night, it would have been uncomplicated post-wedding sex. But now, it would be something more. There'd have to be planning and a mutual agreement that that was what they both wanted and…

And if she sat in this car any longer in the dark, Cal would find her asleep in the alley.

After a brief struggle with unfamiliar controls, she found the windshield wiper. Clutch, first gear, and she eased down the alley. The Corvette felt like a rocket ship begging to be unleashed, but she only let it idle down the narrow lane, veering to avoid lined-up trash bins and muddy potholes.

Out on the main drag, she opened it up to about ten miles an hour. Its engine climbed to a dull, aching roar before she found the shifter and the clutch in the dark. She found second and the purr shifted back to a mellow throb that a lion might make the moment before it pounced on an antelope. She wondered just how fast this car would go.

In the rearview mirror, which she also adjusted and wasn't going to move back, the only light she could see on Beach Way was the bakery. Nobody else in town would be up for at least another hour; not until the Judge came in to prepare the Puffin Diner for its six a.m. opening. Except the Judge had just gotten married last night. So it would be Greg.

She turned right on LBB Lane. Little Brown Bird Lane dipped down toward the ocean before turning south and heading toward Orca Head and the Lamont B&B.

She went for third gear and the car whimpered about her going twenty on a one-lane road when the car wanted to go a hundred. Why did Cal even own a machine like this? From Becky's and the airport to the B&B was three miles: the two opposite corners of town. It was a town fit for MINI Coopers and scooters—most people walked everywhere on the nicer days. Though January wasn't big on nicer days at the moment.

About a mile out, she spotted a car coming toward town. Unable to imagine who it might be at this hour, she scooted over as far as she could. She recognized Cal Sr.'s beater pickup truck—he was a Dodge man and it was always fun to watch when a Ford or Chevy fan made the mistake of trying to correct his "uninformed" ways.

It was only as he pulled slowly by her that Natalya knew if she recognized his truck, he would certainly recognize his son's car. He offered her a very startled expression during the brief moment their driver windows passed one another. Startled and none too happy about it.

Great. She'd done nothing but sleep and now she'd ticked off Cal Mason Sr. What repercussions that was going to have she was definitely too tired to think about.

She eased the car up to the B&B as quietly as she could despite all of its throbbing and grumbling. The back porch light was on, which was unusual, and the kitchen light as well. Her mother was a creature of habit on one account: she was never, ever up and about before 6 a.m. Breakfast at the Lamont B&B was served hot at seven, warm at eight, and put away at nine.

Natalya managed to park beside her MINI and shut down Cal's "machine"—it hardly seemed right to call it a car. She squished up the steps in her sodden flats and discovered her mother at the kitchen table. It was a small table with a pair of bench seats. It could squeeze four, but had been perfect for a family of two. Natalya had spent endless hours looking out the now-dark window at the thick forest of Douglas fir and spruce while she painted, drew, and even occasionally did homework.

"Mom?" Only the light above the stove was on, so the shadows were thick about the kitchen. Gina sat at the table with a mug of hot chocolate and a croissant. She wore her winter bathrobe of thick, dark green terrycloth and her fluffy white sheep slippers with black noses, floopy ears, and black button eyes.

"Natalya. Are you up late or early? Water's still hot."

Natalya crossed to the stove and debated between hot chocolate and coffee. Hot chocolate meant warmth, comfort, and she'd be headed to bed—her bed. To sleep alone. Coffee would mean that she was going for the jolt of caffeine so that she could stay awake long enough to meet up with Cal for breakfast at six at the diner. Or maybe she should opt for green tea and let her body decide which way it wanted to go.

Wimp!

Never one to turn away from a challenge, Natalya fished out a packet of the gourmet instant coffee, Italian Roast, and poured the water over it. There was only half a cupful in the kettle. She could make more water or drink it like espresso which would mean... And if she waffled on one more decision this morning, she was going to hate herself.

She carried the half full mug over to the table and sat down across from her mom.

"I'm not sure," she tried to answer her mother's question. "I think I'm up early."

"Not me," her mother's smile went a little wicked. "I'm up late. Still have time for a couple hours sleep before I have to start breakfast. Only three guests at the moment so it shouldn't be a problem."

"You and—" Now she knew exactly where Cal Sr. had been, though that didn't shed any light on his perplexed and irritated expression as they'd passed each other on the road. Unless it wasn't about her and he just didn't like being caught.

"Absolutely! I'd forgotten what a good dancer he is. Both on the dance floor and—"

"I don't need to hear it, Mom." Natalya took a sip of her warm sludge-like brew and could imagine she felt the concentrated caffeine bite into her system.

"You always were private about such things," her mom brushed her fingers through her tousled red hair. "Certainly didn't get that from me."

"Maybe I got it from Tud."

"Not damn likely. Oh, your father was pretty enough, ever so pretty. And hands that could—"

"Mom!"

"Sorry. He was a complete hedonist. Made me look like you in comparison. Of course what Cal Mason Sr. can do with *his* hands—"

Natalya groaned...loudly.

"Yum!" was her mother's conclusion as she grinned over her hot chocolate. "So tell me about your Cal."

"My Cal? He's not mine."

"Then maybe I shouldn't ask where you've been the last four hours or why his Corvette is now parked in the driveway," she nodded out the window.

"I— We— He and I— We fell asleep, damn it!"

"Seems like a waste of a perfectly good wedding to me. Maybe if you'd had sex you wouldn't be in such a contrary mood."

Natalya didn't even bother to answer. If she'd had sex, her body would be loose, her emotions mellow, and she wouldn't be winding herself up about leaving in an hour and a half to meet Cal for breakfast. He hadn't invited her back to his apartment for breakfast. Again it had been that casual, *don't really care if you're naked* attitude of his. *I get breakfast at six at the diner if you'd like to join me,* he'd said, without so much as a suggestive leer implying that he was just after a quick tumble.

Her mom's oversized yawn and loose-limbed stretch weren't helping matters.

"Are you going to see him again?" Natalya went for a subject change. "Or was it just post-wedding sex and you're done with him." Exactly as she'd been with every man while Natalya was growing up.

"It wasn't post-wedding sex; it was *great* post-wedding sex. Sure. We live in the same town. I'll probably see him this afternoon as I'm running low on sourdough bread," her smile was teasing as she purposely misinterpreted Natalya's question then climbed out of the seat.

"Seriously, Mom."

"Seriously?" She filled her mug with tap water and left it in the sink. "I can't particularly see why I would. He didn't ask when he left either. Just gave me a kiss and a very friendly squeeze, then went on his way."

Simple sex. Even with an old friend. Why couldn't she have had something like that?

"But Natalya," her mother came over and wrapped her arms around Natalya's head and shoulders and pulled her into a tight hug. "You shouldn't be planning your life by my standards. Your father may have been That Unholy Disaster, but he gave me you and that was worth everything to me. That's all I care about."

Then her mom was gone and Natalya was left with a quarter cup of cooling sludge in the semi-darkness.

For lack of a clearer decision, she knocked it back, left the mug in the sink beside her mother's, and headed upstairs for a shower and fresh clothes.

CAL HAD all of the bread dough rising and had started building the pastries when he heard the back door open and close.

Natalya had driven away before he'd even finished the morning rounds. He liked the daily ritual of preparing the bakery. Starting the first pot of coffee. Firing up the glass-doored ovens that his father had installed in *his* father's bakery, which lit off with a low wump of gas. One of these days he was going to put in a wood-fired oven, but it would require a complete renovation to fit it in, maybe even knock out a wall and he wasn't ready to face that.

While the coffee brewed, he had circled out to the front of the house. Here the steel kitchen with its thick rubber mats on red tile flooring gave way to worn oak hardwood that dated back to when his third-great grandfather had built the bakery. He flicked on just one light out in the seating and customer area that would warm the windows for anyone passing by. A glance showed that everything was in place—he'd made sure of that when he brought the loaners back from the wedding.

The wedding.

He'd closed his eyes for a moment and imagined Natalya once more in his arms. Neither t-shirt clad and snuggled close nor mostly naked in his bedroom, but rather sweeping across the dance floor in his arms, swaying to the music as if caught in a kind breeze.

And if he didn't get some coffee soon, he'd sway one time too many and crash to the floor.

Back in the kitchen, he had plugged in his player and kicked off his baking playlist. Unlike his alarm music, it emphasized rock and roll—some his, a lot of his father's. They'd always baked to rock and his dad's taste for the classics had become his own. At the moment Pat Benatar was cranking out that *Love Is a Battlefield*, which Cal rather felt defeated the whole point. Love was supposed to be better than that, though he hadn't given the matter a whole lot of thought.

He hadn't heard the car's return over the music, but the jolt of her arrival had him spraying a smear of raspberry filling over a half-dozen Danish, utterly ruining them, and a long splat right across the stainless steel prep table. He wouldn't even be able to scrape that up and use it because he'd had cornmeal spread down the table for kneading out some rolls that the Brass Plover Inn had ordered to go with their lunchtime chili.

He looked up. "You're—"—not Natalya.

"Morning, Junior."

Cal tried to reply, but nothing much came out.

His dad looked down at the Danish. "Guess you were hoping someone was bringing your Vette back. You know she took it, right?"

Cal nodded.

"Just checking. Driving it like a girl."

"Well, she is one," he finally found his voice. "What are you doing here?" Dad was off on Mondays and the only early mornings he worked any more were Cal's day off on Saturdays. Cal opened the other five days. The shop was closed Sundays.

"Found myself awake. Thought I'd lend a hand."

Benatar finished rocking out and declared her victory.

Dad looked down at the mess Cal had made of the prep table. Rather than scowling, all he did was smile to himself.

Blake Lewis cranked up his beat-box cover of Bon Jovi, declaring *You Give Love a Bad Name.*

"What are you doing up at this hour?"

His dad's smile didn't change. "Just enjoying life, boy." Then he turned up the music blocking further conversation, poured himself some coffee, and they both got to work.

The next couple hours flew by in an easy rhythm. Cal had started working in the Blackbird Bakery when Mom had bolted during third grade. After that, the school bus had dropped him off here just as the bakery closed at two. He'd learned clean-up tasks really well. By high school he was doing prep with his dad for a couple hours before school every morning and worked most Saturdays—except when there was a soccer game. When he went full-time, they'd conferred and added a lunch menu. Simple at first, but over time they'd added homemade soups and hot sandwiches.

But it wasn't until this moment that he missed all of those mornings working side by side with his dad. They never spoke much, not unless Cal was getting in trouble—often Harry's fault back before he'd taken off to be a New Orleans lawyer. But Junior and Senior side by side pounding down and shaping long lines of bread loaves was a happy memory and now a good moment.

If Cal ever wanted to do this with his own son, he'd have to stop goofing around and find himself—

A glance at the clock showed straight up six. He was usually at the diner's door at six sharp to grab breakfast.

"Shit!" He had his apron half off before he stopped. They were in the middle of bagel prep. His father's help had thrown off his timing. He normally had everything quietly rising or baking while he ate his breakfast. But they were ahead this morning. It was also mid-winter on the coast, so it was a much smaller bake than a summer tourist weekend.

"You worried about breakfast?" Senior asked him in between the verses of Boston singing about it being *More Than a Feeling.*

"Not just."

"Maybe worried about your Vette?"

"Kinda." At least about whether or not the woman driving it had come back into town.

"Well go, boy. I got this."

There was something about his dad's smile that Cal wasn't going to hang around and ask about. Come to think of it, he'd been damned cheerful, for him. Especially considering how late they'd all danced last night and how early it still was this morning.

His dad noticed his hesitation and shouted out over Boston's rocking drum riff, "If you're going, go!"

Cal went.

The storm was back, but Cal's jacket was all the way up the stairs and he wasn't going to waste the time. While Cal wasn't soaked, he was definitely cold and wet by the time he'd crossed the street from the Blackbird and hustled down three doors to the Puffin Diner. He bolted up the steps, but stumbled to a halt at the big glass doors.

The diner was empty except for Hector Jackson; Cal was usually second in and Hector was already at his corner table working on *The Oregonian* newspaper's daily crossword. Cal could see Greg back in the kitchen and Jessica leaning against the big steel opening that separated it from the dining area. The dozen tables that Cal had helped Greg move back from the wedding were all neatly arranged without a soul at them. The six stools along the counter were vacant as well.

No Natalya. He felt bad about leaving during the bagel prep. He fought off a shiver. Maybe he should just return to the bakery and—

"Will you quit blocking the door? It's cold out here." A hand shoved lightly at his back and warmth spread from that point of contact.

"Hey, Gnat. Just waiting for you." Without looking back at her, not wanting to reveal his smile of relief, he pulled open the front door. At first he'd thought to hold it wide with a doorman-style bow to usher her through. Then he thought better of it and stepped through himself and, as a tease, didn't hold the door by reaching back until she could grab it.

The spring, strong against the winds that ripped along the coast, slammed the door shut on his heels.

"Hey, Jess. Harry," he waved as the bell on the back of the door tinkled sharply when Natalya yanked it open. He moved up to his normal spot at the counter, dropped down on the stool, and called out, "The usual."

An apparition in a sopping raincoat, citified and stylish enough in a hot blue to completely evoke Natalya's sexiness, came to a stop beside him.

"You've got the manners of a moose, Mason."

He turned to her, primed to offer some pithy comparison himself, but she took his damned breath away. Even angry, and her cheeks and nose scattered with raindrops, she was absolutely breathtaking. In a struggle not to let her know, he shrugged. Before he could come up with something appropriate, Jessica cut him off.

"Tell me something we don't already know. Becky was worried that Cal would drag Harry into his old ways after he moved back." She winked at Cal to show it was just a tease, so he winked back.

But there was a problem there. His best friend was back, but it was all somehow different now.

Harry had been one of the stars of the Eagle Cove Pufflings soccer team. In high school they'd been inseparable, often in trouble with Dad, but inseparable even then. Harry hadn't been close to his own dad, especially not with the Judge commuting up to Newport every day. But Cal Senior made no bones about teaching them both his strict former U.S. Marine Corps moral codes on every topic from girls to drunk driving to girls to drugs to girls. He and Harry had double-dated, gotten drunk, played video games, conquered the soccer field, and played poker together. They'd also never driven drunk, done drugs, or failed to use protection with a girl—Cal Senior had given them each their first box of supply after first delivering one of his lectures.

Then, after bailing for a decade, Harry had come back for one of his infamous twenty-four hour visits, stayed two weeks, and then moved back from New Orleans—leaving what was like the ultimate party town—to become a judge and marry Becky Billings. It just wasn't right. Had they even gotten drunk together once since Harry had come back? If so, Cal couldn't pin it down. Hell, had *he* gotten drunk himself in that time? Shit! When had he stopped having fun and become responsible? He'd better get over that and get over it soon.

Jessica slid across a menu, but Natalya waved it off. The Judge offered a very limited selection and Natalya was local enough to know it by heart.

"Omelette with green pepper and onion and an English muffin." No need to specify the meat, Greg would either be serving bacon or sausage, depending on which Carl Parker had delivered fresh from his farm. And hash browns were not an option. They were a fixture, even with Cal's tall stack of pancakes.

"Coffee?"

Natalya shuddered. "Hot chocolate. No whip."

He'd thought she liked coffee. He couldn't start his day without it. If two people couldn't even agree that the planet was fueled by coffee…

Dumb, Mason. Real dumb. There wasn't anything between them except a bit of wedding night lust. Of course, having held someone as hot as Natalya once, he felt a definite need to do it again. Soon.

He'd start with peeling her out of that raincoat.

He focused on his coffee.

How in the world did a woman manage to look sexy in a wet raincoat?

"So, what is the queen of the night doing up at this hour?" Jessica slid over a cutlery set wrapped in a napkin along with her cocoa.

Natalya glanced sideways at Cal, but didn't have a good answer. Her design team in Portland started their day at nine only under duress. They had enough East Coast clients where it was already noon, that they had to. But she still preferred working at night and often did—they all did.

Six a.m. was an hour always safely buried somewhere deep in her REM state. Add in the blast of thick, lukewarm coffee at the B&B and her system didn't know whether to panic or shut down, leaving her jittery and off balance.

And then there was Cal. Pouring on enough maple syrup to drown his pancakes rather than flavor them. If she ate even a bite of that, her system would go sugar-shock catatonic in a moment.

She'd driven her MINI back into town, not trusting herself to drive Cal's car in her current state. Parking beside the diner let her approach mostly along the covered, wraparound porch. It had also let her see Cal rushing across the street wearing nothing but a t-shirt despite the storm. He'd been in a real hurry, more than could be explained by a cold rain.

For her. He'd been in a hurry for her. At least that's what she'd thought until he'd slammed the door in her face. Well, if he wanted to play that game, so could she.

"Heading to sleep after this," she told Jessica, "just haven't gone to bed yet. Had some ideas for a project at work and wanted to get them up on the server. You know, Jess," she kept her voice as nonchalant as possible while keeping a weather eye on Cal as he started to dig into his tall stack. "The weekend was so crazy that we didn't get a chance to do anything but the wedding. What are you and Greg doing for dinner tonight?"

Cal froze with his fork caught between his teeth.

Jessica and Greg traded shrugs. "*Nada.*"

"Great! The *three* of us should get together for a meal."

Cal choked loudly on his pancakes. So, he had assumed that she'd be spending the night with him without his even asking.

Jessica had looked puzzled at Natalya's emphasis on just the three of them. Then her expression shifted while Cal coughed and gagged. When he gasped as he tried to rinse it all down with a slug of blazing hot coffee, it was one clue too many.

Jessica had always been sharp. At the moment, as she turned to stare at Natalya, too sharp. Without even looking, Jessica poured a glass of water and thunked it on the counter beside Cal's coffee.

Then she smirked. Over the initial shock, she saw right through the tease of Natalya asking Greg and herself to dinner.

"Man doesn't even know how to eat pancakes without hurting himself," Jessica picked up some menus and went to greet the latest arrivals.

Natalya reached over kindly and pounded a side-fist against Cal's back as hard as she could. It was a mistake. Her fist merely bounced off all that solid muscle which only reminded her of how his bare shoulders had felt beneath her hands while he'd been curled against her. Most of her lovers had been urbanites like her: programmers, designers, gym-machine buff at best. Cal was in a whole different league and it had felt surprisingly good—like finally getting to Italy and understanding that's what gelato *really* tasted like.

An awkward silence slipped between them. Greg was only ten feet away, but the grill and the windowed opening gave some feeling of distance. Also, the big overhead fans made it hard for him to overhear them. He checked on them occasionally, but it was just a chef watching out for his restaurant. He'd missed what was going on. Jessica would fill him in soon enough.

"Hey, Gnat," Cal was decent enough to be the one to break the silence.

" 'Hey, Gnat?' That's all you have to offer after..." Jessica came back to the window with another order and Natalya cut herself off.

Cal waited too, until it was obvious that Jessica was lingering.

"Nothing happened, Jess!" Natalya snapped at her best friend but was too confused to care much. "We danced and we slept together, as in sleep. That's it."

"Which totally doesn't explain why you're awake at six in the morning and are being so flustered." And she walked away not even waiting long enough to leave a smug smile along with Natalya's omelette.

"Crap!"

"Sorry, Gnat." And Cal did sound sorry.

"Yeah, Cal," she patted his big arm and wished she didn't have some need to keep patting him. He was cold to the touch and wet, and not in a happy, healthy dog's nose way. "Me too."

"I can't even stay long. I left Dad making bagels on his day off. Guess he just woke up full of energy today."

"Or never went to sleep," Natalya mumbled to herself.

"What was that?"

"Nothing."

Cal worked through a whole section of his tall stack, a daunting task with how big the Puffin Diner served their pancakes, before speaking again. "I was thinking maybe you and I could have dinner."

"Pizza and a quick tumble?"

"Wouldn't find me complaining."

"I was being sarcastic."

"Yeah, your tone kinda said that."

Natalya took a bite of her omelette.

"How about a burger and brew at the Plover?" Cal offered as a compromise. He was many things, but stupid wasn't one of them.

Once he'd calmed down, he too had understood the tease of her pretending to ask Greg and Jessica to dinner. This time his tone was kind.

"My treat. I feel bad about last night. Tried to stay awake. Heard the shower go on, but never heard it turn off. My schedule's a little weird, baker's hours and all. I usually have dinner at five and I'm asleep by nine, not dancing up to midnight. But we could eat anytime you'd like. What time do you eat in the city?" He was rambling a bit. Which meant he was nervous. Nervous about her reaction. At some level he actually cared about her as well as the sex.

It was decent of him. That was another of the things Cal was. He might tease her by letting a door slam in her face, but he hadn't pushed about not having a quickie though she'd been lying against him barely clothed in his bed.

And he'd loaned her his beloved Corvette.

"Portland isn't Paris."

"Which means what to a boy from Eagle Cove?"

"It means I don't eat dinner at ten at night."

"That's a relief."

"More like a nuked burrito at one in the morning."

He groaned, just as she'd planned.

"But five sounds great."

Cal smiled down at her, his face lighting up for the first time as it had at the wedding. "Maybe a tumble afterward?" Pure tease.

"Don't count on it, Bagel Boy."

He tried a pout and she brushed a hand along his cheek for being so cute. Unlike his shoulder, it was dry, warm, and soft with just a hint that he hadn't shaved this morning. He might be six-four of powerful man, but he *was* cute. Maybe he wasn't totally foolish in his hopes of getting her into bed tonight.

"Ha!" It just burst out of her.

"What?"

She shook her head and focused on her omelette.

"What?" He said it in a soft, warm voice as if trying to coax her out of her clothes here and now.

Well, he'd already done that once. Besides, she'd originally planned to drive back to the city this afternoon before it got dark. Yet she'd just answered her own question about Cal when she'd agreed to go to dinner with him without a second thought. It meant that she'd be driving back to Portland tomorrow morning before work.

If he used that low, sexy tone on her tonight after dinner, it just might do what he intended. She'd give him fifty-fifty odds at the moment that she wouldn't be leaving from her mom's B&B in the morning.

CHAPTER 4

Cal went up to the front to close the Blackbird Bakery's curtains. The day had continued wet with a steady Pineapple Express storm slamming in from the general southwest direction of Hawaii. It wasn't a particularly big storm, and while it wasn't raining at the moment, the air was almost as wet as the streets. The cinnamon rolls had been slow to rise in the high humidity and the traffic in the store had been low. Still, he'd estimated fairly well and the day-old rack wouldn't be too full tomorrow.

One of the changes he'd made over the last decade and a half was how much of the bakery business was over the counter. His dad had developed recipes and built up the bakery, but Cal was building a business. He'd made deals to provide toast bread to the Puffin Diner, dessert tarts to the Brass Plover Inn, and even cookies to the snack counter at The Flicker movie house. Blackbird Bakery bread was featured next door in Jane's Warbler Market and he'd had inquiries from Coos Bay and Yachats, but he wasn't interested in doing wide area deliveries. Their orders would have to be big enough to hire a driver, and they weren't.

Sunset had only been ten minutes ago, but it had been behind dark, thick clouds that were promising more rain. The sky was already night-black. The Flicker's marquee was the main light in town, making the eight-foot tall chainsaw-art flicker woodpecker clinging to the sign's side appear to glow in the dark. The Bobbin' Red Robin Tavern, being a land bird, was on the same side of the street as his Blackbird Bakery and The Flicker. Except for the Brass Plover Inn, the other side of the street went suddenly dark even as he watched. Merganser Weavings and Tours and Sandpiper Hearth and Home Supply just closed shop for the day.

There was some debate, on particularly slow nights over a beer at the Plover, whether Bird Beak Taffy belonged with the seabird side of the street or over with the land birds. To add fuel to the fire, Celeste recently—well, while Cal was still in high school so recent enough— had painted a great blue heron on her sign, chewing away on a piece of bright orange taffy. At least most everyone agreed it was a great blue which was a land bird, placing her on the wrong side of the street. But as Celeste's art was abstract at best (really just kinda funky), there was a small but verbal contingent that thought it was a black-necked stilt.

Celeste wasn't saying which she'd intended, which offered everyone at least one point of consensus: they all agreed that Celeste had always been a troublemaker. If only because she made the very best taffy on the coast much to everyone's, except the dentist's, remorse.

Cal closed the curtains to block out the darkness.

He hadn't a clue about what had inspired him at the last minute this morning to ask Natalya to meet him at the closed bakery at five rather than at the Brass Plover Inn, but was glad of it now. Maybe enough of his brain cells had finally been firing to do something right around her for a change.

He had one of the tables set with actual silverware and wine-glasses. Unable to scrounge up anything better, they'd be stuck with paper napkins. The place was still warm from the heat of the ovens that had been turned off at noon—except for the small one set to warm with a tray of the Plover's lasagna in it.

Cal wanted to get some private time with Natalya. Going to the

Plover felt too public. Everyone would know they'd gone out to dinner together, an event that hadn't happened since group pizza outings in high school. And they'd conjecture many things if he and Natalya crossed the street back to his apartment together afterwards.

He wouldn't mind. Hell, a man who got to lay beside a woman as fine as Natalya definitely had bragging rights.

But he wanted to give Natalya some option about how public she was going to be.

Though it wasn't like they were doing anything. Two old friends having dinner, that's all. Of course after the way they'd been dancing together last night, the whole town would be making assumptions about—

Cal grabbed the door frame ready to pound his head against it to make his whirling thoughts stop when he spotted automobile lights through the door's window. Natalya's MINI cooper slid to a stop at the curb right in front of the darkened bakery's door.

No mistaking who climbed out of that car. Not with those graceful dancer movements and the stylish raincoat. They way she looked as she hurried around the car was—

"What the hell?"

She ducked across the street and headed toward the Brass Plover.

Cal yanked at the door.

And cursed as the deadbolt stopped him.

He undid the bolt and yanked again.

Too hard, the doorknob slipped out of his clumsy grasp and slammed against a table he kept meaning to move. It had one of those wire tourist brochure holders that was always getting knocked askew. This time he bashed it hard enough that it spilled to the floor and a hundred glossy, one-third page cardboard flyers sheeted across the floor mixing Ralph's Eaglet Fishing Tours with the Newport Aquarium and Peggy's Albatross Air Tours with the Sea Lion Caves.

The wind gusted in and began stirring them about.

He grabbed the door handle, but before he could shout out to Natalya a blast of rain slapped him in face. When he could see again, she was gone.

"Shit!" He yanked the door closed behind him as he raced out into the night and across the street.

Natalya had stumbled to a halt when she entered the Plover. The warmth was almost a wall to hold you up after ducking through the cold rain.

May Conklin had decorated the Brass Plover like a British pub. Comfortably battered booths lined the walls. Tables small enough to be easily dragged into larger groupings were scattered over most of the floor in a pleasantly disorderly jumble. The walls were covered with pictures of the Queen, the royal family, British Navy ships, beautiful coastlines, and a whole section dedicated to the princes—especially William: in his military helicopter, with Kate, and with the kids. Princess Di was also prominent, though Charles was rightly nearly invisible and Camilla nonexistent.

The lights were set low enough to give the feel of oil lamps without quite tipping from cozy into dingy. The dark wood bar— supposedly shaped from the decking of a three-masted lumber schooner that had wrecked on Orca Head over a century ago—ranged down one wall. She had several imported beers, but most of them were Becky's.

The pub's wall of warmth and coziness after the chilling winter storm was built on a foundation of the rich smells of comfort food. May's kitchen served up a mixture of English fare including: fish and chips, shepherd's pie, and bangers and mashies as well as burgers. The burger meat varied by what was fresh: grass-fed beef, venison, elk, and occasionally buffalo. She also, in honor of her great-great-grandfather who had wagon-trained out of Buffalo, New York, and down the Oregon Trail, served lethally spicy chicken wings.

A dozen or so people had come out for a beer or dinner. Locals were used to the heavy rains of the coast, so it would take more than this storm to stop them coming out. Instead they'd used the foul weather as an excuse to gather at the Plover.

Natalya spotted Greg and Jessica, but there was no sign of Cal.

She checked again, but her eyes were dark-adapted from the overcast evening. She hadn't missed him, not that it was possible to miss a man built on his scale.

Greg's wave drew her to their table. "Hey there, Natalya. Dinner was a great idea. Jessica was so glad of a chance to catch up with you." He said it as if her morning ploy to tease Cal by going to dinner with Greg and Jessica had been serious.

But Jessica knew—

And that's when Natalya saw that Jessica absolutely *did* know that Natalya had been teasing and this was supposed to be a date with Cal. Worse, Jessica hadn't informed Greg because he'd be too decent to butt in. Not Jessica.

Resigned, Natalya shed her coat and slipped in to sit across from her.

"Bitch," she mouthed.

Jessica smiled happily as if it was a compliment.

Greg missed it all. He was busy waving toward the door, "Hey Cal! Well, this will be a great meal."

Natalya waited until Cal stood at the end of the table before turning to look up at him. Then she laughed in his face.

"What?" It came out as deep, irritated-as-hell man-growl.

"You're all wet again." His light hair was darkly wet and plastered to his head. The black t-shirt clung to every curve of muscle. It had a big heart of white lettering in the center of it made up of baking words: vanilla, honey, flour, cinnamon, and more. Her fingers itched to take it off him, squeeze it out, and wrap him in a warm towel. He looked so sad and bedraggled.

"You *weren't* kidding." Cal glanced at Greg and Jessica then looked back at her. She could see that he was about to turn and go, thinking she'd actually planned this.

"Yes, I was. Jessica is just a buttinski."

Cal glared down at Greg who finally put two and two together and realized that it equaled two people too many on a date. "Shit, man. Sorry. I didn't get it. Come on, Jessica."

He started to rise, but Cal just pushed him gently back into his seat. He glared down at Natalya until she became aware of the hardness of the seat and that her hair lay wet against her back.

"What?"

"Then why did you come here instead of to the bakery?"

"The bakery?" And then it clicked. As he'd walked her back to her car, Cal had asked her to meet him at the bakery. Had some plan...that she'd screwed up by coming here instead.

"Oh god. I'm sorry, Cal," she reached out a hand and rested it on his damp forearm. "If you're going to date me, there's something you have to learn. You can't be telling me something at six in the morning and expect that there's any chance in the world I'll remember it."

"Ah ha!" Jessica crowed. "You two are dating!"

"Not yet," Natalya looked up at Cal carefully. "Unless you want to sit down and share dinner with me."

"Truth, Gnat?"

"Absolute truth, Cal," Jessica answered for her. "That's why I was so shocked to see her at the diner this morning. At that hour she usually can't remember her own name."

"Truth, Cal," Natalya answered for herself. "Never anything but."

"She also can't lie to save her life," Jessica pointed at the open chair in a peremptory gesture. "That's why she never tries."

Cal sat. Close enough for Natalya to feel his cool dampness though they weren't quite touching.

"Why do you think she had to perfect that ever-so-innocent smile?" Jessica was happily carrying the conversation which was a relief at the moment.

Natalya wondered just what plan of Cal's she'd messed up. Well, she had a few plans of her own for later and was hoping that she hadn't messed those up herself.

"If she spoke," Jessica continued, "you'd know she was fibbing."

"That so?" Cal seemed to have forgiven her brainlessness, which was awfully decent of him. She definitely owed him.

"Sure," Natalya admitted. "Learned that the hard way when I tried to pull one over on Mrs. Winslow back in second grade. I then made the mistake of trying to talk my way out of it."

"Didn't go so well, huh?"

"Don't you remember the three weeks she spent in the corner wearing a dunce's hat?" Jessica was having too much of a good time at her expense, but Natalya couldn't think of what to do about it. Besides, it had only been for three days.

"Old lady Winslow had it in for me," Cal explained.

"Me too," Greg put in. He'd been three years behind the rest of them, but Marjorie Winslow was still a fixture in the Eagle Cove school system. "She was—"

"Don't you say a word against her," Jessica warned her husband. "She's wonderful."

"Teacher's pet," Natalya got her back a little.

Jessica stuck out her tongue.

"Only thing I remember about you in second grade, Gnat, was you were always borrowing my notes, but when you gave them back they were in mirror writing. Took me forever to learn how to read them." Cal laughed at the memory. It was a good laugh and Natalya liked that he used it more and more as they enjoyed their meal together.

CAL LED Natalya back to the bakery at a dead run. She'd offered to hold her coat up as an umbrella for both of them, but he knew the rising wind would snatch it aside and soak them both for spite.

They crashed into the door together—which was odd because he'd grabbed the latch before they hit.

He tried it again as Natalya laughed about the mad race through the rain. But he knew it wouldn't do any good; the deadbolt had snapped into place as he'd slammed the door behind him in his rush to intercept Natalya before she entered the Plover.

"C'mon, Cal. It's cold out here."

"Quit griping, Gnat. At least you have a coat."

"At least one of us has some sense of self-preservation. What's the holdup?"

"My keys."

"What about them?"

"They're on the hook beside my jacket in the back."

"In the back of what?"

Cal looked down at her and wished he was somehow smarter around her. But he wasn't. Natalya brought out the stupid in him.

"In the back of what?" She repeated her question.

"Of the bakery."

She looked from his face, down to his hand still on the door, then back up to his face. For a long moment he couldn't read her expression, then she laid her forehead against his chest and burst into laughter.

Taking a risk, he slipped a hand around her back. Even through the cold, damp raincoat she felt so amazing.

"Running a hell of a seduction here, Mason."

"Yeah, a screwed up one. Of course it was all on track until you went to the Plover by accident."

"And you locked your keys inside. Don't you have a spare hidden somewhere?"

"Sure," Cal could picture it easily even though he'd never used it. He didn't lose or forget things, except around Natalya. "It's in my Vette."

"Which I left at the B&B." Her laugh climbed until it was almost enough to warm him despite wearing a wet t-shirt in a forty-degree windy January night.

He rested his cheek on top of her wet hair, but he couldn't suppress the first shiver.

"C'mon," Natalya pulled back then tugged on his hand, leading him toward her MINI Cooper at the curb.

Cal glared down at the car that barely reached his sternum. Natalya slipped into the car with a, "Try it, you'll like it."

He groaned and bent down to open the door just as Natalya leaned over to slide the seat all of the way back. Cal folded himself up like a pretzel and eased down into the tiny car.

"Sit up, Mason."

Cautiously he raised his head. When it didn't hit, he looked up and saw he had at least an inch to spare. Easing out his legs, only his toes hit the firewall.

"Small car for big people. I'm five-ten, Cal. I like having some space to move around in."

"I'll be damned."

"That's a given," Natalya cranked the engine as he pulled the door shut.

"Heat would be good," he fought down another shiver without much success then buckled in. He might be able to fit in the tiny car, but maneuvering around for seatbelts had him bumping and jostling against Natalya. He could get to really like this.

"Thought you'd be plenty warm from being damned. Besides she's cold, too. Give her a moment. We don't live in Minnesota so I didn't spring for the heated seats."

"Cheapskate," at the moment he'd really appreciate it if they were. "Besides, 'I'll be damned' is future tense."

She eased back from the curb as he cupped his hands over the heater vent. Even the marginally warm air was an improvement.

"Ready?"

"For what?"

She goosed the engine and dropped into first. The car actually chirped its tires despite the wet pavement. She fishtailed once, but handled it expertly and in moments was bolting up the long empty stretch of Beach Way.

Cal hung on as she did a four-wheel slide turn onto LBB Lane and hit the narrow, winding lane like a motocross course.

"Shit, woman!" For half a second he thought she'd miss the last turn south, and instead they'd launch right off the high bank down to the sandy beach and out into the pounding ocean. Third to second, handbrake turn, hard on the gas, back to third, then fourth. They flew off a rise, leapt over potholes, and slalomed through curves.

Somewhere along the way she passed Greg and Jessica despite their significant head start back. The two grand Victorians of the town stood side by side at the very end of LBB Lane: the Lamont B&B and the only slightly less impressive Slater residence just one driveway earlier. She passed them so fast that Cal barely had a glimpse of Greg's alarmed expression.

They covered the two miles to her mom's B&B before the heater had a chance to warm up, and definitely before he caught his breath.

A hundred yards out, she backed off the gas, dropping into a quiet coast, and bled speed until she was parked close beside his Vette. The porch light was blurred by the rain.

"Did you do that to my poor little car?"

"Absolutely! Though I found it kinda sloppy in the turns." And Cal could hear it. "Kinda" was one of his words, not one of hers.

"Jess was right."

"That's news," Natalya turned off the car. "About what?"

"You can't lie for crap."

Natalya sighed, then leaned forward as if to pound her head on the steering wheel. "Frankly, your car scared the daylights out of me and I don't think I made it out of first gear. I knew if I put a single scratch on it, you'd kill me."

"You always were a smart woman, Gnat."

"What?"

He repeated himself more loudly, as the gods had yanked open the heavenly sluice gates and the rain pounded down against the car in solid sheets. The porch light was visible now as little more than a bright spot in the mass of water dumping out of the sky.

They sat quietly for a long moment listening to the pounding rain before she spoke again, nearly shouting, "Well?"

"Well what?"

"Are you going to get the spare key? I'll follow you back to your place if you still want me to." She held out his Corvette's key.

He took it but made no move to get out of the car. The cloudburst continued to pound on the roof.

"Well?"

He leaned forward to look out the front windshield and up. "Maybe we should just stay in the car and neck until this cloudburst moves inland."

Natalya poked a finger against his chest. "Ew! You're still cold and wet."

"Sure are picky, Gnat."

He looked up again at the grand Victorian B&B. "This place here looks pretty warm and cozy. Think they have any beds?"

"I think there's an open room if you want to sleep here. Single or double occupancy?"

"Double." He tried to make light of her joke, but it came out rough and needy.

"Just can't wait, huh?"

He turned to look at her, shadows and shapes as she too leaned forward and looked upward, the curve of her neck making his fingers itch to touch. "To hold you, Gnat. No! I can't wait."

"Last one loses."

"Huh? Last one of what loses wha—" But he was talking to himself. She was out the door and racing across the wet lawn. Cal shoved open the door and almost strangled himself before he remembered the seatbelt.

When he caught up to her in the kitchen, she wasn't waiting for him. He'd expected her to be facing him and had been planning on scooping her up, over his shoulder, and dragging her upstairs.

Instead she was over at the basement door and looking down. It was open, the light was on, and there was a string of loud, heartfelt, female curses sounding up the stairs.

***

"Mom? Everything okay?" The exhilaration of racing Cal into the B&B, the anticipation of having him in her bed, faded away abruptly.

"No!"

Natalya made it halfway down the stairs before she saw why. Six inches of water was flowing through the basement. It was an old problem that she'd forgotten about over the years. A French drain around the outside had diverted some of the water and a sump pump usually took care of the rest, but this whole side of Orca Head and the surrounding forest wanted to drain right through the B&B's basement tonight.

Her mother was standing in the middle of the mess wearing coveralls, waders, yellow dishwashing gloves, and a foul expression. Thankfully, they'd had the problem before so the lowest level of all of the shelving around the room was empty. But if it kept rising, it could be disastrous.

"The sump pump clogged or failed. Or maybe it just drowned. I can't tell."

Natalya wouldn't be of any help. Mechanical things and she didn't get along very well. She was well known at her job for her ability to break computers that worked fine for everyone else.

Cal had come down the stairs behind Natalya and was surveying the scene. Without a word, he gently pushed her to the side and continued down, wading right into the water in his tennis shoes.

The next few hours were a scene fit for a Victorian steampunk disaster.

Natalya had fetched a second pair of her mother's boots, more gloves, and soon the both of them were dipping up buckets of water and dumping them down the laundry sink.

The chill water kept rising until it finally tipped over the tops of her boots as often as not, and it was a race to save the furnace and water heater which weren't on the floor, but weren't much above the water either.

Natalya's arms burned with the workout. Bits of paper and plastic junk floated along the surface and they were soon clogging the sink. She was cold, wet, and on the verge of telling her mom to either call the fire department for one of their pumpers or find some dynamite to blast a hole in the seaward wall to let it all drain out.

All the while she and her mom had been bailing, Cal was squatting half in and half out of the water, often reaching down shoulder deep to work on the pump which sat another foot below the floor in a sump.

Then a hum sounded, a deep, powerful hum. One she could practically feel in her bones.

And Cal was standing there, calf deep in the water, soaking wet, and grinning like a fool as he stared down at a small whirlpool in the water. In moments she could see the surface water flowing toward the pump as it dug in and did its job.

Her mom shrieked with delight and grabbed Cal in a hard hug.

Natalya could only stand and watch.

A man with skills. There was something about a man with skills. A big, handsome man whose head almost brushed the low basement ceiling that just made her knees go weak.

They all stood and watched as the water level dropped until finally, it was just little trickles and puddles on the concrete floor. With a self-satisfied burp, the pump shut down. With a broom, Cal swept the larger puddles toward the sump. It cycled on automatically for a few seconds and then shut down again finding the job too easy.

It was when they were climbing the stairs that Natalya understood quite how weak her knees were, and it wasn't just Cal's macho influence.

* * *

CAL FOCUSED on putting one foot in front of the other. The water had been damned cold. And he had to keep ducking down into it. The pump's float switch had broken and he'd pretty much had to rebuild it under water.

Up the basement stairs. It was a vast relief when the door closed and they were done with the basement. He passed up Gina's offer of hot cocoa or tea in favor of a shower. Besides, Natalya was staggering, so he slipped a hand around her waist as she led them up the stairs. The two more stories up the stairways of the B&B took almost all she had left, but he didn't think he was up to carrying her right at the moment. And if she hadn't liked that he'd been wet before, he was thoroughly soaked now.

Just like him before, Natalya didn't bother to turn on lights. However, the flight to his apartment was one clean shot. These stairs were bent on pitching him overboard with twists and turns in odd places.

He knew the ground floor well, of course. Gina Lamont's parties were notorious and he and Dad had tried to never miss a one. Though the last one had been a while. It had been Greg's wedding to Jessica three months ago, an event that had packed the house, the porch, and spilled out over the lawn. It was also when Harry—back visiting for his little brother's wedding—had fallen for Becky Billings.

As if he'd needed proof that weddings were dangerous.

"Do you live in this place or one top of it?"

"Third floor," Natalya led him up the last few steps. "Mom always said that just because we lived in a B&B didn't mean we were supposed to have the crappiest rooms. She's always had the suite on the north-west corner of the second floor, three rooms which has one of the balconies facing out toward the ocean. I've got third floor, southwest corner, view of the beach and Orca Head lighthouse. Mom rents it out last of all, so I usually get to stay in my old room during the off season."

The third floor hallway wasn't really wide enough for the two of them but he wasn't willing to let her go. Didn't know if he dared—half afraid that she'd evaporate into thin air and more than half afraid he'd slide bonelessly to the carpet if she did that.

He'd never been up here on the top floor. In all the years he'd known her, he'd never been up to her room. In the darkness, their path indicated by a few small nightlights that illuminated no more than the floral green runner and the dark oak floors, he felt as if he'd wandered into *The Adams Family* and Uncle Fester would come stumbling out the next door along the hall at any moment.

He could just make out the sign on the door to the last room at the end of the hall: The Victorian Room.

"Victorian, huh? Curtained four-poster and chintz curtains?"

"Not quite," Natalya turned on the lights and guided him over the threshold.

The bed wasn't a four-poster, but it did have an ornate, padded headboard, which would have given him a few ideas under different conditions. And it did feel "classic" with dark wood and a broad oriental rug on the hardwood. But then he focused on the rest of the décor.

Rachel McAdams inspected him from a Sherlock Holmes movie poster in which she played the sexy yet dangerous Irene Adler. Selma Hayek wore a stunning Victorian dress in the terrible *Wild Wild West* remake.

"I started when I was about ten, collecting Victorian and steampunk images."

Winona Ryder as Jo Marsh was hunched over her writer's desk, feathered quill in hand, scribing out her own story in *Little Women*. He'd gotten snookered into watching it while on a Kirsten Dunst movie binge. Nicole Kidman in *Moulin Rouge*, not the sad but fallen woman, instead the grand beauty caught mid-laugh.

There were also drawings of steampunked women. Their garb half Victorian and half mechanical. Their powerful expressions undeniable.

But that wasn't what captured his attention as he forgot for a moment quite how cold he was. Mixed in among the posters were sketches and paintings. Some were pen and ink, others were fine creations on canvas. And he knew the hand of all of them.

Natalya.

She disappeared into the bathroom as a shiver shook him. He crossed his arms over his chest and kept inspecting the walls. He could see the evolution of the artist. Early drawings of elves and princesses had been preserved. They'd given away to occasional monsters, he recognized a far more polished version of the one she'd drawn of him that day in the woods—not recognizable as either himself or her mother, but now artful. Steampunk and Victorian women abounded. Many had a breathtaking beauty. Not that every one of the images was pretty, but these were strong women whose very expressions were forces of nature.

Natalya reemerged from the bath long enough to toss a towel over his head. She was now wrapped in a towel. Thinking back, he had heard her taking a lightning fast shower.

By the time he pulled off the towel, she was gone again. He scrubbed the towel at his hair and face for a moment, then began peeling off his soaking wet clothes.

His attention drifted back to the most recent paintings. They were different. Still the same artist, but the content had shifted again. The Oregon Coast replaced the dust and grime of the Victorian era. They were portraits. Sometimes from the back, but they were again of women. Each one...belonged. He didn't have a better word for it. Having seen them in their setting, they couldn't be anywhere else.

"Hey, Gnat. These are really—" He turned his attention to Natalya and completely forgot what he'd been about to say.

Wearing a long t-shirt that was far skimpier on her than his had been, she was sliding into the bed.

"Damn you're a vision."

If she heard him, she didn't acknowledge it, instead pulling the covers over her head and huddling beneath them.

Cal hurried through a scalding hot shower. Even his underwear was wet and he didn't want to wear it anyway. Naked, he slid under the covers and reached out to pull Natalya against him.

Except she wasn't responding. She wasn't just asleep, she was out cold. The wedding, only a few hours sleep last night, and two hours of mucking about in freezing water.

"Crap!"

He curled up behind her and buried his nose in her hair—which was cold and damp and had him jerking back.

Giving up, he collapsed onto the pillow and was out.

CHAPTER 5

A low cello started out somewhere in a dream about tiny cars with giant blackbird wings swooping over a field of baked goods—diving like raptors to clutch giant blueberries.

A pair of violins joined the flight and Cal came fully awake in time for a viola to join in and for the MINI Cooper to steal the last berry before his Vette could get there, leaving nothing but a stray sunflower seed behind.

The cars were gone, but the music continued—upbeat, energetic.

Cal didn't know this one. Didn't recall putting it on his playlist.

He reached over to see what it was and bumped his arm on someone curled up close beside him. Some—

Natalya! Again they had slept together and not crap else. This was really starting to suck.

"Mrumph!" was all she gave him in response.

Damn it! He didn't want stolen seconds with her. He wanted time to enjoy himself and make sure that she did the same.

All he'd had a chance to do yesterday morning was hold onto her for a few minutes. Last night he hadn't stayed awake long enough to even do that. It looked as if today he was in for another serving of the same. He'd take what he could get.

Her back was pressed against his arm, so he curled up behind her and wrapped an arm around her waist. He'd always been partial to long and slender, and Natalya was definitely that.

A drummer joined the quartet and the energy climbed again. And not just the music's.

She woke enough to push back against him. She rested her head on his extended arm, which let him nuzzle his face into her hair, and then she shifted the rest of her body up against him. When his rousing interest pressed up against her backside she made another noise; one that he'd judge as contented rather than bothered.

He ran a hand down over her thigh and, after only the briefest consideration, came back up under her t-shirt rather than over it. Most women on a cold night were like a good sports balm after a hard soccer game. Natalya Lamont, warm and sleepy beneath the covers, was in a whole other league. Of its own will, his hand stopped spread across her flat belly, long before it reached his actual target. He became mesmerized by the feel of her breathing.

He buried his face deeper in her hair—soft and dry now—inhaled the ocean clean scent of her, and pulled her even harder against him.

This time it earned him a definite happy sound.

She lay on his bicep, so he took advantage of the moment and bent his elbow around to gather himself a palmful of breast through the t-shirt fabric with his left hand while his right remained on her stomach.

A sleepy sigh and she slipped a hand over his. Rather than moving it, she just rubbed her palm lazily up and down his arm.

"You're killing me, Gnat. You're just killing me."

"Good," it was a soft, quiet whisper, but she sounded very pleased with herself.

Without enough time, he again wasn't going to get more than a quick feel. Which sucked, because it was a really amazing feel. To back off from his need to just take her now and the consequences be damned, he asked her about the music.

"All-girl string quartets," her voice was part sleepy mumble and part breathy seductress—at least that was his body's response. "Mostly

Bond, some Escala, and a few others. And why are you clamped onto my breast but we're suddenly talking about music?"

"The alarm. I have to go to work."

"Sure," and she paused maddeningly. "In an hour. I set the alarm an hour early, and I want you to remember quite how big a sacrifice that was for me. But since you're so interested, let me tell you about the four women of Bond. Australian and British. Two tall, two not so much."

An hour! "I had no idea you were brilliant in addition to being beautiful." He could really get to appreciate this woman.

"Two blond, two brunette," she continued as if she hadn't heard him.

Cal could do plenty with an hour. Not near what he wanted, but it would be a good start.

"Their videos—"

"Please tell me you have some protection here. I don't want to waste the time dragging you back to my place."

"Of course I do, Mason. I'm not some idiot who locks himself out of his own house. Now, Escala's music videos are good, but Bond's are awesome, very sensual yet still all about the music itself. Amazing marketing. You should watch them play."

Cal held onto her tightly and tried to make sense of what in the world she was talking about.

"Here, let me grab my tablet, I can show you some," and she moved to get out of a bed.

He almost let her go. The woman was an absolute primal force.

Idiot! She's just messing with you!

Two could play that game. So he let her get half away, then three quarters. He could feel her hesitating as he continued to call her bluff. Then he felt the shift from teasing to ticked. That was his cue. He lunged out, grabbed, and scooped her back against him so hard that it knocked some of the breath out of her. He took advantage of the moment to flip her over so that they were face to face.

"Maybe another time," she managed on a gasp. "Though I bet you'd like the little Asian cellist. She's—"

The only way he could think to silence her was to kiss her, hard. As she opened to him, she might have mumbled, "About time."

After that her focus was absolute.

Against a background of soaring, exotic music, they explored, played, and gasped in shared delight. When he finally took her, or perhaps she took him for he was the one flat on his back, the world went quiet.

Somewhere in the far distance the music continued, but the world of sensation overwhelmed and he was only aware of the searing heat where she wrapped around him and the lovely light weight of her as he supported her with his palms cradling her breasts.

Her hair teased over his chest as she hung her head and gave herself to the dynamic building between them. She didn't cry out or moan.

Instead, she whispered as the release wracked through her body, "So good. Oh, so good. So...good."

As her words dissolved into odd mumbles and finally a shuddering silence, it made him feel as if maybe he really was a good lover. To have the power to drive Natalya Lamont beyond the ability of speech must mean he was doing something right. So very right.

And the more he felt that, the more true it became. She drove her hips down hard against him again and again until all he could do was arch up into her and lose himself as well.

When Cal finally found his way back to reality, Natalya lay upon his chest, her knees alongside his hips, and his hands scooped around the nicest butt he'd ever held.

"Damn, Mason."

"Damn yourself, Gnat. That was...unreal." Best he had. And it was true. He and sex certainly weren't strangers. He'd had more than his fair share of the locals over the years and was thankful for every one. There'd been any number of cute tourists who were willing to offer their buns for a little quick kneading. He'd thought he knew all that it could deliver. Not really. Not even close. Natalya had just completely redefined the reality of sex.

"We definitely have to do this again," she planted a kiss on his chin.

"Uh-huh," he couldn't agree more. "How much time do we have?"

She turned her face into his shoulder and giggled. He'd never heard her giggle. Natalya Lamont smiled quietly when one of her pranks worked, which was pretty much every time. She laughed quietly at a good joke. But now she lay on his chest and giggled. Cute on top of gorgeous.

"Okay. Not enough time."

"Hell, I'm ready to do that all over again, Mason. You could almost convince me that waking up in the middle of the night is totally worth it. But you're a guy. What are we going to do about *that?*"

Well, parts of his body weren't up for a rematch, but he wasn't ready to let go of her yet. He lifted her off him, and set her down on the bed still face down. Then he sat up and began running his hands over her. Training as a baker had given him a real awareness of texture and pressure through his fingers. He'd been told by more than a few women that he should have been a masseur.

So, he turned his attention to learning about Natalya's body. Unlike others he'd been with, he felt no hesitation in what he did and didn't touch. You could stroke a woman's ass all you wanted during sex, but not during a massage, even if you'd just had sex. Somehow those inhibitions didn't apply here.

CAL'S STRENGTH as he simply lifted Natalya aside knocked her speechless. She wasn't overweight, but she wasn't a size zero model either, yet he'd picked her up as easily as a tray of bread. She wasn't ready to be done with him and was about to protest until Cal began running his hands over her as if he were a bow to her fiddle—which was still playing in the background. It was a long playlist; she'd never been one to wake up quickly.

Then Cal drove his fingers deep into her hair and began massaging her scalp. Absolute heaven. She buried her face in the pillow and gave herself up to the experience.

She could feel her whole body tingling in anticipation when it became clear he wasn't going to stop there.

Her shoulder muscles gave way beneath the onslaught of his baker's hands. During sex she'd been busy appreciating so much that his hands had blurred into the background, except to notice that they were gentle despite their immense strength. Now they probed and eased tight muscles. He slipped his hands between the sheets and the front of her shoulders to loosen pectoral muscles already gone liquid. When he used the opportunity to cop an extra feel of her breast, she rocked to the side to make it easier for him.

Her lower back, often sore from too many hours in the computer chair, eased and loosened. When he dug strong fingers into her behind she considered protesting, but the steady assurance of his hands working her muscles brushed even that consideration aside. Also, the pressure against the mattress was such a very nice reminder of how it had felt to take all of Cal into her.

It had been a submission on a grand scale, but also an empowerment. To let a man invade past the boundary of her skin had always felt like a slightly unjust twist of evolution.

Yet, to have Cal inside her, to feel such a deep connection and to hear his breath catch with her every movement, had also made her feel so strong. The galvanic clenching of his body at the moment before his release—wound tighter than a coiled spring powerful enough to run the world—had created a shocking contrast to the moment he let go and poured all of that energy into her. For a brief moment, riding atop the wave of his need, she had been the ruler of the world.

Cal had—

Oh god.

Almost without her awareness he'd slipped a hand between her legs and slid it between her and the sheets.

Too late, unable to stop herself, she rubbed and thrashed against his kneading palm until, unanticipated, another release shot through her. Not nearly the scale of having him buried to his hips inside her, but absolutely breathtaking for being so soon after the first experience.

As she rode it out, or rather as it rode through her again and again, Cal slowly lay back down beside her, leaving gentle kisses and nuzzles as he went.

She clamped her legs together so that he couldn't pull that hand away. Not yet, please not yet. That it forced him to lie awkwardly against her side wasn't her concern. Just the incredible sensation of being held so intimately, so strongly, yet so gently—that's all that mattered.

He nuzzled his nose against her where the side of her breast met the sheets.

She really hadn't been kidding, and if she ever recovered her breath and her mind, she'd have to tell Cal.

They definitely had to do this again.

Cal left her with a kiss so sweet that it almost lulled her back to sleep, and a slap on her bare ass that had completely ruined the effect.

Natalya made the bed, because the mussed sheets made her wish Cal was still in them. She then plunged into the shower so that she wouldn't be one of those pitiful women listening for the sound of his car driving away at four in the morning. She did come out of the bath wrapped in a towel, just in case he'd returned, forgetting who knew what this time.

Instead of Cal, her mother was sitting on the quilt, leaning back against the padded headboard, and sipping from a mug of coffee—her favorite, declaring, "It's True! Redheads *ARE* Hotter!" in little flaming letters.

"Um, hi."

"Um, yourself. Saw Cal on the way out, gave him some coffee. Did you have fun?"

Natalya decided to ignore the palm print she could still feel on her behind, and simply nodded her head. Natalya toed the pile of her clothes, all wet.

"I brought you fresh ones," her mom pointed toward the suitcase by the door. She'd put it in the car last night, assuming that she'd be leaving from Cal's this morning. "Cal said you might need them. I caught him headed back up the stairs with them."

"Uh, thanks." She supposed that their intentions had been made clear enough last night that any embarrassment this morning would be wasted effort.

"Coffee for you, too," her mother rightly assessed Natalya as being momentarily overwhelmed and pointed to a steaming mug on the nightstand. It declared, "Brunettes Are Da BOMB!" complete with an explosion in the background.

"Thanks again. I need that."

Natalya settled on the bed and tucked her legs under the quilt. It was a crazy thing from high school days. She'd gotten into the scraps box and decided to teach herself a dozen quilting patterns from a book. Each block of the quilt was different, each themed with crazily mismatched fabrics: Monkey Wrench, Log Cabin, Bear's Paw, Flying Geese. Friendship Square (pieced in her, Jessica's, and Becky's favorite colors), Mother's Dream (which looked nothing like her mother or a dream, but a much younger Natalya had liked the name…still did).

Her mom rose off the bed just for a moment so that she too could tuck her legs under the quilt. This was familiar; this was family. Just her and Mom together.

Somehow Gina Lamont always knew when Natalya needed a Mom-dose and just showed up.

Natalya's first kiss, not counting Jessica when they tried to practice on one another before trying it out on a boy—which had turned out to be beyond weird and could still set them both giggling. The first crush followed closely by the first heartbreak when she'd been dumped a week later. The first time she'd given herself to a boy. Even when something had gone terribly wrong as an adult living in Portland. Mom would somehow know and…show up. "I had a few city errands to run," which they both knew was a lie. Then they'd sit together and she'd remember that the Lamont women always had each other.

"Do you ever regret it, Mom?"

"What, not marrying Tud? Not for a second."

"Okay, not quite the question I was asking."

"Still, you're twenty-nine now, it's about time I answered it. You were conceived, baked, and born out of wedlock and I don't regret it for a second because you were worth every second of it…well, maybe not the seventeen hours of labor, but otherwise totally worth it. But what were you asking?"

"I'm thirty-two, Mom. And I was asking if you were sorry that you didn't ever bring someone home to keep."

"No daughter of mine will ever be more than twenty-nine. Makes me feel too old." She sipped at her coffee for a bit.

Natalya did the same and felt the smooth warmth slide down into her—two sugars and a splootch of cream just the way she liked it. " 'No daughter of yours?' Any half sisters I should know about?"

"Not a one. Unless you count my twin sister's kids that she had with Tud."

Natalya almost bobbled her cup.

"Just joking. I know Viv slept with him a couple times—a lot of women did and probably a few men. Not your other aunt though, Jessica's mom. My little sister Monica never did have much imagination when it came to men."

Jessica's mother had married Ralph Baxter straight out of high school. Between them they had three divorces and four marriages—all to each other.

"As I said," her mother continued, "Tud had no scruples but was so very pretty. Of course that was before my twin's plane went down in New Guinea and she was eaten by those cannibals."

Natalya knew that Aunt Viv had died in a car crash in Italy when Natalya was two, but her mother was always giving her sister strange and spectacular ways of dying, though the fictitious offspring were new. Perhaps it was her mom's idea of a gift to the dead, keeping her twin's story alive and ever changing. As much as Natalya loved her mom, it was hard to imagine what Eagle Cove had been like with two of her in it. A pair of statuesque redheads with big laughs and a devil-may-care-but-women-didn't-need-to attitude.

Natalya supposed that she never should have asked her question in the first place.

"So, are you that serious about Cal Jr.?" Her mom took advantage of Natalya's silence for her own question.

"What? No! We only had sex once. I'm not enough of an idiot to think that means anything."

"Then where were you two nights ago?"

"Sleeping." Natalya groaned at having to explain it again when she could barely explain it to herself. "Just sleeping."

"But with Cal Jr."

"Yes, with Cal Jr."

"And was it wonderful?"

"He gets up at four a.m. to an alarm playlist filled with early Beach Boys and Andrews Sisters singing about food."

"Probably includes Dean Martin singing, *How D'ya Like Your Eggs in the Morning.*"

"Doris Day, *A Bushel and a Peck.*"

"Harry Chapin, *30,000 Pounds of Bananas.*"

Natalya tried to think of a one-up to that but the giggles caught her again which was okay, she couldn't think of one anyway. "Imagine waking up to that!"

"Stay with him long enough, and maybe you will."

"Eww!" Though it had been awfully nice waking up next to him this morning.

Her mother bumped her shoulder to shoulder, but didn't say another word.

"Okay!" Natalya struggled out from under the quilt and began dragging on dry clothes. "Yes, I'm thinking about seeing him again. But right now I have to get back to Portland for a nine a.m. meeting. Sure he was fun, but I don't see any software companies opening major divisions in Eagle Cove."

"Not this week anyway."

She eyed her mother. Natalya couldn't always read her mom, but this time it was merely a joke. "Besides, I don't want a weekend relationship. I want someone to curl up next to every night." Which surprised the crap out of her now that she'd said it.

"You always did have that in you, Natalya," her mother got up and tugged the quilt back into shape. If a guest needed the room, it would be cleaned and sheets changed then. Probably through the whole stormy winter it would just be Natalya's. "That desire for stability." Natalya didn't like the flash of sadness across her mother's face and circled around the bed to hug her hard.

"You gave me great stability, Mom. Maybe *that's* the problem. I grew up in this house, in this community. I'm thir—twenty-nine and I still have my own room most of the time complete with my old art and the crazed quilt."

Her mom looked down at the quilt. "Yep! Natalya's brain on quilting. Still makes me wonder sometimes what it must be like living inside your head."

"Very cluttered."

"Well, declutter it now. You have a long, dark drive ahead of you. Be extra careful and text me when you're off the road."

"Love you too, Mom." She gathered her things and headed out the door.

The rain had stopped, which was a good thing. Driving over the twists of Maxine Pass in the dark was challenging enough to Natalya's dreamy state without being blinded by the rain as well. The eight-hundred-and-three foot crest was one of the highest that punched through the Coast Range. The rain down below had turned into snow up here.

She considered doubling back down to Highway 101 and chasing north to one of the lower passes, but the only sure way around the snow was way out to Astoria. She didn't have the extra two hours it would require to go so far north before doubling back on Portland. Instead she caught up with a sanding truck and stayed just far enough back to not have her windshield pinged with sand and gravel.

The road through the mountains was usually the fun part of her drive. The MINI Cooper digging in and growling its way around the sharp curves like a grumpy basset hound—low-slung and surprisingly quick. Not today.

Leaving Eagle Cove behind was being much more difficult than usual. And oddly, the hardest part of all hadn't been driving away from the lone light still shining out her mother's bedroom window at the B&B, but rather driving out along Beach Way and seeing the light in the Blackbird Bakery.

She knew stopping in wouldn't be a good thing to do—but for the whole climb up and over the pass and the descent back out of the snow as she reached the Willamette Valley she was wondering how she knew that to be true.

"*D*eal 'em!" Cal chewed on a Red Vine. Greg had brought a fat plastic bucket of the damned licorice whips and they'd all been chowing down on them.

The big round table in the center of the closed bakery looked like a bomb had exploded on it. They were playing around the corners of a couple of well-decimated pizza boxes from Carrier Pigeon Pizza, which didn't deliver despite their name, except to Cal. It had been part of the deal he worked out because they used his big mixer when making up fresh batches of dough and he made all of their garlic bread. It wasn't a real burden as they were only two doors apart, sharing a covered porch with the Bobbin' Red Robin Tavern in between.

None of them were heavy drinkers any more, but it was Friday night and each had a beer and an empty or two that no one had bothered to clear off. A roll of paper towels was partially unraveled because no one had wanted to get up for the paper plates Cal had forgotten to grab. They all wore a couple of layers, turtlenecks and flannel shirts or fleece vests. Rain slicks and empty pizza boxes were piled on the other tables near them.

Harry riffled the cards again. Then set them down to take another bite of his Cowboy Special, which was a whole lot of good, greasy meat.

"Wipe your hand before you—Aw shit!"

Harry offered him a literally cheesy smile and went back to shuffling the cards with slimy fingers.

"Asshole!" Just for that, Cal wasn't going to tell him about the cheese caught in the ridiculous two-week mustache he'd started while on his honeymoon. There were a lot of bets around the table as to who would make him shave it off first, his new wife or his father because "such an affectation would not be appropriate for the bench."

"Take any advantage I can get."

"Not gonna help *me* any." And nothing was tonight. Even though it was a low stakes game, Cal was down at least twenty bucks. Greg was up five, Vincent about ten. His only consolation was that Harry was down even more than he was.

The one sweeping the damned table was Alex.

"Damn it! You used to work for me! And this is how you pay me back?"

Alex raked in the latest pot, putting him up at least forty for the night. "Well, you aren't paying me any more, Becky is. Only way I got left to take money off you."

"You were always a crap baker anyway," he grumbled though they both knew it wasn't true. He'd been good enough, but his heart wasn't in it. Becky had needed help and he'd sent Alex her way. He'd taken to brewing like a seal to a sunny sandbar.

"Bastard is shacked up with *my* senior prom date," Greg sounded irritated, but probably by the fact that Alex's flush had just beaten his straight.

"Crap, Greg! You're married to Jessica Baxter and you're complaining?" Harry cuffed his brother on the back of the head.

"Not for a second. But," Greg slapped him back, "aren't you supposed to be thinking about *your* new wife?"

Harry sighed happily and started dealing the next hand, "I am, Brother. I really am."

That was when it struck Cal that he was the only single guy left at the table. Greg and Harry were recently married. Vincent had somehow captured the awesome Dawn way back in high school and they had two of the cutest twin girls imaginable—perfect seven-year-old copies of their stunning mother. And Alex had just "shacked up" with Vicki Highland. The main reason Cal had sent him Becky's way was so that Alex and Vicki's work schedules could mesh—Alex was saving for the ring before popping the question even though they were all after him to hurry it up.

But no one wanted a guy working baker's hours.

Not even Natalya Lamont.

Two weeks and not a peep. No e-mail. No phone call. She hadn't come back to town last weekend as he'd been hoping.

Maybe he'd head over to the B&B later, ask Gina for Natalya's phone number as casually as he could. Maybe he'd just take the Vette out for a spin up to Portland and knock on her door, if he knew where she lived.

Cal checked his hole cards: two of clubs, nine of hearts.

He should just fold, lose his fifty-cent ante, and be glad he got off easy.

Being a complete sucker, he threw another quarter in, bad money after good because sure as dough rose, he held a losing hand.

Natalya stood in the shadows of the Blackbird Bakery's porch and looked in at the game.

It was *such* a guy moment.

It gave her an idea for a painting, not that she'd really had time to do that these last couple years. But maybe this weekend she'd fish out her easel and give it a try because the image was so pure. Not the softness of watercolor. No, this would best be rendered oil…no, acrylics. The dark of the wooden table, the brightness of the lights, and the flashing tiny cards. Contrast the warm mid-tones of laughing faces and easy banter. The green fleece of Harry's vest and Cal's red-and-black flannel shirt as if he were a rough lumberjack rather than a man who shaped puff pastries for a living.

She'd been surprised into stopping when she saw the lights on in the bakery despite it being eight at night.

Fibber. That wasn't what had happened at all.

She sighed. She'd gone to work early (arriving at the office at the obscene hour of seven in the morning) so that she could leave early to beat the weekend traffic south—which hadn't paid off as well as she'd hoped. The three-hour drive had taken almost five as there'd been dumping rain in Portland and ice up in the pass. The coast was a dry and balmy forty-five.

Natalya had driven by slowly, trying to decide on whether or not she really was going to stop and knock on his door. Not as if he'd be expecting her. Showing up with a "Hey, that was some amazing sex, let's have more," was too schoolgirl. Too needy. But she'd slowed anyway.

She'd even braced herself to find another woman's car parked at the bakery. After all, they'd made no promises. But when she spotted four cars and the downstairs alight, curiosity had mixed with caution. She'd parked in front of Carrier Pigeon Pizza and casually walked back to peek in the window.

Harry was hooting with laughter, jostling his brother in his triumph. Vincent and Alex tossed their cards in.

Cal sat with his back squarely to the door. All she could see were his broad shoulders and the back of his head. She remembered how it had felt to wrap her hands about him as they'd danced, how those shoulders felt when she—

Disgusted with herself, Natalya turned and strode back to her car.

You didn't drive five hours for sex.

Then why did she?

It was a question she still hadn't answered when she pulled up to the B&B. The lot was packed.

In January?

That made no sense. Not until she recognized a couple of the vehicles. Mrs. Winslow's, Andrea Martin's, and others. Peggy's car, normally identified by its "Eat. Sleep. Fly." bumper sticker, now boasted "Live. Love. Fly." Is that what marriage did to a person?

Why were they all—

It was knitting night!

Tuesday afternoons and Friday evenings were knitting time in Eagle Cove. It was when the knitters of the town came together. It used to always be here at the B&B, but Tuesdays had moved out to Becky's when she'd torn up her knee and the group had never moved back.

Natalya raced up the porch stairs ready to throw herself into their midst.

This is why you came home. Except she hadn't packed her knitting. For that matter she was still working on the cowl she'd started last summer. She could really use that cowl now.

Again she stopped on the porch and looked in through the parlor windows. Everyone was gathered. Unlike the national disaster area that was the boy's poker game, there was an order here. Glasses of wine and cups of tea. Small plates bearing the remains of her mom's lemon cheesecake with the deep purple of Marionberry syrup sat nearby. Napkins and dessert forks all in place. The raucous laughter of the men that she'd been able to hear through the double-paned glass at the bakery was much softer...even one of her mom's laughs that rang out and set everyone off was milder. It was also gentler—not the laugh of card-game triumph, but friendly, inclusive.

This scene Natalya would paint in watercolors. Again she'd start with the rich browns and golds of the classic Victorian furnishings rather than the well-worn tables and scuffed bakery flooring. The bright colors of the yarn, almost distracting the viewers' eyes, but not quite. The heart of the painting would be in the soft joy of the women.

Perhaps even mount the two side by side.

Or a single work that transitioned, melded, and morphed. Dark wood furniture flowing into a dark bakery table. Delicate desserts colliding with surrealistically garish pizza. Both sides would reveal joy: the rough happiness of men undisturbed by having to behave around women, women quietly glad to be with each other.

Then, wholly unlike the bakery, Tiffany happened to glance through the window and spot Natalya beneath the porch light. She waved.

Natalya waved back.

And in moments she'd been swept inside: receiving hugs, having a dinner plate of lasagna made up, and soon tucked in between Jessica and Becky on the big couch.

This was *exactly* why she'd come home.

Except it wasn't.

CHAPTER 8

$\mathcal{S}$even a.m.

Ridiculously early. Especially considering she'd woken up at six the prior morning to get her workday done early so that she could drive down to Eagle Cove.

Yet Natalya was awake and was having a hard time denying it.

Saturday! She scowled at her foggy reflection after she'd showered.

Your day off! Her pillow teased her. *Stop making the bed and crawl back in it.*

Instead, she smoothed the quilt, and worked her way downstairs in a plush robe and her elk slippers (complete with brown fuzzy sides, soft ears, and tiny antlers). She heard voices, but they must be in one of the guest rooms as they stopped the moment Natalya creaked one of the old stairs. The B&B was about half full, but the guests wouldn't be stirring outside their rooms yet.

Her mom was just starting breakfast.

"What in the world are you doing up?"

Natalya kept her head down and drove straight for the coffee pot. "I have absolutely no idea." She poured her cup and prepared it with sugar and cream, then held it up to her nose, close her eyes, and just breathed it in.

She leaned her elbows on the counter, and when she felt she could open her eyes again with a chance of seeing anything, looked out the window at the woods as she cradled her warm mug. It was still dark out there. The towering Douglas firs, that she noted with some chagrin still had the common sense to be asleep, were little more than shadowed impressions.

"It's still night out there."

"That's what happens when you get up before the crack of noon," her mother was slicing strips off a slab of Parker's farm-fresh bacon. Natalya couldn't find the energy to help.

"Okay, I do feel bad about that." She buried nose in the coffee again. She often came down from the city so stressed that the main thing she did when home was sleep.

When home.

But she hadn't lived here in over a decade. Four years at Portland State then straight into the local job market. She had a nice one-bedroom apartment—a third-floor walkup in a century-old bricker right in the heart of the Northwest District. Her street was lined with massive heritage trees—tagged, numbered, and protected by the city for their historic majesty. She even had a territorial view to the south and east from a living room smaller than her bedroom here.

But home was Eagle Cove. How had she missed that?

Deep thoughts for seven in the morning. This morning just kept getting worse and worse.

"Mom?"

"Uh-huh?"

"I—"

"What, honey?"

The sympathy, the understanding without even needing to understand had Natalya setting down her coffee and wrapping her arms around her mom. She buried her face in the fluffy kitchen towel Mom always wore over her shoulder when cooking. Natalya had always wondered if it was a holdover from when she'd been an infant.

The soothing hand stroking down her back was just too much and Natalya started to cry.

"Shh, Baby. Shh," her mother rocked her and cradled Natalya's head. The easy familiarity of the motion definitively answered the question about the fluffy towel.

"I don't even know what's wrong," it came out as a choking twist in her throat that was dangerously close to a sob. Natalya dug deep and tried to reel it back. She knew that for Gina Lamont this was maybe a little too real. As much as she loved to laugh, tears always kind of freaked her mother out. Natalya finally clamped it down but hung on for a while longer simply enjoying the feeling of being held.

"You'll figure it out, honey. You always do. Maybe you should take the week off and just stay here."

"I can't do that."

"How much sick leave do you have built up?"

Natalya was never sick and they both knew it. They owed her for weeks of time—it would be months, except sick leave didn't roll over year to year. She *could* log in from here for critical meetings...

"Next weekend is Stormy Days at Eagle Cove—Jessica's latest promotion for the town. Everyone could use an extra hand. You call in sick and we'll go from there."

"I..." Could she? "I've never done anything like that."

"Well," her mother patted her briskly on the back which told Natalya that the hug was now over. "What you're going to do now is sit down while I cook breakfast and all of us will figure it out together. Okay?"

"I guess," Natalya felt as if she was twelve again. "Who is 'all of us together'?"

Her mom just patted her back again, whispered, "Surprise!" and let her go.

Natalya opened her eyes and looked over her mother's shoulders, straight into Cal's eyes. He sat at the table, to her back as she'd gone for the coffee. An empty mug was clenched in his big hand.

"Hey there, Gnat."

"HEY THERE?" Natalya's voice came out as a tight squeak.

He shrugged. "Don't really know where else to go with it, Gnat."

"You could have said something when I came in the room."

"Like what?" He could see her building up a head of steam, but didn't know how to defuse it. Though he did figure it wasn't quite the right moment to point out that her robe had slipped open enough for him to tell that she wore neither t-shirt nor bra.

"Like, oh, I don't know. How about, 'Hey, Gnat.' Would that have killed you?"

"Not a problem, if I could have spoken." Because sleepy-eyed, elk-slippered, and wrapped in a terrycloth bathrobe as dark as her eyes, she'd knocked the wind right out of him. Twice he'd gotten to hold her and wake up beside her. And it wasn't until this moment that he understood quite how amazing and unusual a gift that was for a big lummox like himself.

"Don't see your muzzle, Mad Dog Mason. Seems to me you could have spoken just fine." She was up on her toes and leaning toward him. In a moment he'd find out if she was wearing underwear under that robe or not.

"Kinda *like* that." He wasn't going to give her the satisfaction of the truth that she could steal his voice as well as having filled every waking thought for the last two weeks. "Mad Dog? Yeah! It works. Though Mad Baker might be more accurate."

And she growled just as dangerously as one.

"Sit down, Gnat."

"Or what?" Except for the thin line of the belt and an equally thin line of black cotton behind it, he now had a clear view that went from her ridiculous slippers, all the way up one impossibly long leg, a curve of hip he remembered—that dip just inside the hip bone that fit the stroke of his thumb so well—and clear up to her throat showing his kind of cleavage.

Cal grinned, he couldn't help himself. "Or at least close your robe before I'm forced to throw you over my shoulder and drag you upstairs."

She looked down, cursed as her mother turned around in time to see and unleash one of her big laughs, then Natalya yanked it tighter around her neck than a formal kimono.

"Now will you sit down?" He did his best to sound as if he was coaxing a three-year old.

She didn't miss that and looked around for some other option, but apparently didn't find it so she dropped down onto the other bench seat of the small breakfast booth. Even when pissed she moved with a smooth grace that was a miracle to watch. It had him shifting in his seat trying to get comfortable without being obvious about his body's reaction in front of a couple women.

Gina set Natalya's abandoned coffee mug on the table along with one of the chocolate-filled croissants Cal had brought with him as a bribe to get Natalya's phone number. Gina rested a warm hand on Cal's shoulder and squeezed encouragingly.

"A word of advice for the future, she's always snippy until she's eaten something."

"Mom! Not true. Besides, Cal does not need to know things 'for the future.'" But Cal noted that her fingers were ignoring her protests and had already torn off a bite-sized piece of the croissant.

Gina squeezed his shoulder again and returned to the stove and her breakfast prep.

"What are you doing here, Mason?"

Grab the bull by the horns? Sure, he liked living dangerously. "Looking for you."

"No, you weren't." A second bite disappeared fast after the first.

"Sure. Thought I'd..." but among things he didn't want to reveal was that once he'd gotten her phone number, he'd been planning to drive to Portland before calling it. Then he'd seen her MINI Cooper parked out front and been prepared to haunt the B&B's kitchen all day if necessary. "...I'd see if you were around and wanted to go for a walk or something."

She turned to glare out the window. The Coast's changeable weather was favoring him at the moment and a quiet sunrise was occurring beneath clear skies. She might be upright, and vibrating with emotions, but she wasn't awake yet. In a few more minutes she'd be awake enough that so simple an evasion wouldn't have succeeded but he'd take what he could get for the moment.

"Beautiful morning out there," he prompted.

"No, you didn't come here for a walk."

"Okay, Ms. Telepathic Lamont, why *am* I here?" He went for more coffee because her robe was slipping open about the neck again and he really needed to adjust some things. And getting coffee also gave him a moment to keep his own balance.

"You're here because you want me to be your sex kitten this weekend."

He poured slowly, trying to find a way to breathe despite that image slamming into his nervous system. Her mother's sly, sideways smile at him didn't help matters. He took his time walking back to the table.

"Maybe," he nodded thoughtfully as he sat then sipped his coffee. "At least that was the initial plan. But I think your mom's right, she's a smart woman."

"I am!" Gina declared. He'd noted that she was working her pans and the big griddle particularly quietly so that she wouldn't miss a word. "About what?"

"Yes, about what, Mad Baker Mason?"

"I think you should definitely call in sick."

"So that I can be your sex kitten for the whole week instead of just a weekend?"

"Well," he made a point of glancing down at her chest.

She followed his gaze and snatched her robe closed again. Damn but he could spend a whole lot of time teasing Natalya Lamont and counting it all as well spent.

"No. I was thinking that you could do something other than that."

"Like what?"

"Not sure. I mean at some point we'll have to sleep, I suppose."

"Someone save me," she cast her glance to the heavens, or at least the kitchen's ceiling. Thankfully, she'd kept a hand clamped around the neck of her robe which was the only thing saving him at the moment.

She finished her coffee and croissant in silence, all one-handed.

He took the time to appreciate sitting with her as the rich smells of a B&B breakfast filled the kitchen. Frying bacon, individual salmon quiches in the oven, and strawberry smoothies made with fruit Gina had put up in the freezer fresh-picked at the height of the summer season.

Again he was having problems.

Sure he wanted to bed Natalya, because talk about the best sex ever…whew! He just *had* to find out if that was all real or merely his imagination.

But he'd also woken up alone for two full weeks and caught himself each time reaching to see if she was beside him. And he still hadn't washed the pillowcase she'd slept on the night of the weddings when they hadn't had sex. He was eight kinds of pitiful; there was no way it could still smell like her, but he kept imagining that it did.

He had it bad and couldn't figure out how he was going to take care of that. Unless the next time they had sex it was awful, but even then he'd—

"Do you still run?"

Cal shrugged. "Not like when I was in school. But yeah." A baker had to do something or he'd turn into the size of two bakers. Since he was starting out at six-four with a Swedish farmhand build, it wouldn't be a pretty sight. And just breathing the air could be fattening in the Blackbird.

She leaned over to look under the table. "In those shoes?" Her bathrobe, forgotten again, slid open as she did and his blood pressure which had been spinning down skyrocketed back up.

"Good as any."

"Okay, give me a couple minutes."

Natalya rose and headed out of the kitchen, her bathrobe sliding off one shoulder. No, she hadn't forgotten about it for a moment. At the doorway, just before she disappeared up the shadowed stairs, she glanced back at him over her shoulder. The motion caused her bathrobe to practically slide off one whole side, exposing her shoulder, waist, one cheek of her butt, and the back of her leg all the way down to her brown fuzzy slippers.

That's when Cal caught sight of that smile of hers.

Then she was gone.

"Holy mother of god," Cal flopped against the back of the bench seat and rubbed his eyes.

Right. Natalya had always been the dangerous one.

Her mother's knowing smile wasn't helping him at the moment.

***

NATALYA CHECKED the mirror and decided that revenge was such a fun game. She'd see how Cal survived this morning's run. He may "still run" but in Portland she'd taken it back up with a vengeance.

Six months ago, despite a slightly dirty head start on Natalya's part, Jessica had outrun her by three paces for the prize of breakfast at the Puffin Bay Diner—exactly as Jessica had done to her at their final high school meet, though that had been a fair start and the prize had only included a cheap blue ribbon and bragging rights. And she could still remember just how much mileage her cousin had gotten out of the second part of that prize.

After half a year of running almost every day, Natalya figured she could run Jessica into the ground, even if she wasn't four months pregnant.

Cal was about to get an education.

She trotted down the stairs in her running gear. Skin tight and lime green swirled with dark chocolate brown. Her Nikes, from a trip with a former boyfriend (who liked to pretend they'd get back together someday even though he knew they weren't) to the Nike campus employees' store. Wrap-around shades. Her hair back in a ponytail. Cardio band on one wrist; Mace spray on the other. She'd left her music player behind since she'd be running with someone. Well, at least briefly, until she'd dusted him on the trail.

Natalya stepped into the kitchen and suddenly had a challenge of her own.

Cal had a gym bag at his feet; it must have been in his Vette. He still wore a close-fitting turtleneck, but he'd pulled on runner's shorts. His legs were massive, powerful pistons that looked like they should be bolted into the earth, except he was dancing lightly on his toes, warming up. Instead of beat-up tennies, he wore a pair of ASICS.

He looked her up and down once, very slowly, which didn't harm her ego any. All he'd be seeing after this was her backside.

"Who you gonna Mace, Gnat?" He tried to sound casual but she could hear the roughness in his voice as he struggled with her body-hugging outfit.

"A rabid seagull, a porpoise with a foul purpose…maybe a Mad Dog," she shrugged. "You never know what you'll find around here."

Mom breezed into the kitchen with an empty tray and began filling it with quiches. "Just don't Mace him in my kitchen. I have guests."

Natalya peeled the canister off the Velcro patch and tossed it on the counter. Then they shifted out onto the porch to finish their stretching.

The sun was up now, though not high enough to light more than the tops of the ridge. It wouldn't clear the Coast Range for another ten or twenty minutes. And the high bluff bank would shade the beach for a couple more hours.

But the morning was a fine one. Mid-forties, the air had a nice freshness to it without the sharp snap of thirties. And there was no taste of snow on the air.

Watching Cal stretch and warm up was backfiring on her plan to make him suffer. If it went on much longer, she'd be the one to suffer. In silent consent they headed off the porch and finished their warmup with a slow side-by-side start.

Cal started for the stairs down to the beach, but Natalya turned instead for the slender track up to the lighthouse. LBB Lane was paved from the town out to the two grand Victorians at the end of town: the Slaters where the Judge and now Peggy lived in the main house with Jessica and Greg in the guest house, and the Lamont B&B. Past her mom's house, the unpaved one-lane wound up the side of

Orca Head, twisting through the thick trees. It was driven only once or twice a month by service personnel checking on the automated light and Marty the town cop drove up there a couple times more. It was a common stop for outdoor teenage adventure—Natalya had certainly led a few boys astray up here—but as long as you were discreet and didn't leave any garbage behind, Marty didn't seem to mind.

Natalya used to run up here all the time in high school for the workout, but it had been years. The gravel was hard-packed in the tire tracks, though tall grasses grew between them. It made her glad of her leggings, which got damp from the grass, but Cal's bare legs were soon dripping with water.

It was only half a mile up to the light, but it switchbacked twice and maintained a stiff grade. Her legs could definitely feel it as they wound through towering conifers and scrub oak. The forest was alive with complaints at these strange two-footed intruders. Squirrels scrambled up vertical trunks then chittered at them from high branches. Stellar jays swooped over to see who was interfering and dozens of little brown birds, flitting too fast to be identified, shot aloft.

Thankfully Portland was built against the base of the Tualatin Mountains which had been preserved as a five thousand acre park. Less than ten blocks out her apartment door lay seventy miles of forested trails. It was perfect for a former cross-country team co-captain. Cal's workouts for soccer in high school had been mostly sprints and flat track work, so this was another edge in her favor.

They burst out of the trees at the old lighthouse keeper's cottage and stopped to look. The cottage itself had seen better days but offered a commanding view both north and south. It sat at the end of the woods a hundred feet shy of the light itself.

To the north, Eagle Cove trailed along the beach from the B&B two miles up to the mouth of the Eagle River where the bay met the ocean. Beyond that was untenanted forest land, no neighbors just across the bay. To the south, tall sea crags dotted the shoreline. Small cove beaches, accessible only by boat, and more forest. The next town was invisible around a point less than ten miles away, but would take thirty miles to reach by road.

The rocky clearing was dominated by the three-story tall lighthouse. In the quiet morning she could just hear the soft whir of the motor that spun the stepped Fresnel lens which cast its guiding light out to sea. Actually, it wasn't a guiding light. It was a "Caution! Do not approach!" light. The guiding lights were small flashing green and red beacons marking the channel into Eagle Bay.

"Interesting choice, Gnat." Cal was still trotting in place to keep warm. Here atop the bluff they were in the first sunlight of the day to reach the coast and it was warm against her face.

"Why?"

"Well," he nodded toward the base of the light. "Might have lost my virginity to Allyson Chaney right over there."

"Allyson? Really?" She'd been one of those purer than bleached cotton types that Natalya had never understood, always looking down on everyone who wasn't as pristine as she was.

"Oh yeah," Cal sounded far too pleased with his memory of the experience.

It was also uncomfortably close to where she and Nicky Vance had their first, then second and final times together.

"Well, isn't that amusing." Cal read her far too easily. And the changing shape of both his smile and his running shorts showed exactly where his thoughts were going.

"Not a chance, Mason." She turned to follow the trail that led up into the logging roads—and nearly flattened Tiffany. They both yelped in surprise at the narrowly avoided collision.

Tiffany was dressed far more sensibly than either of them. She wore her usual battered hiking boots and jeans. She also wore a warm jacket and a Bohemian wide-brimmed floppy hat that would shed rain, block sun, and made her face a little difficult to see as she was several inches shorter than Natalya. Her long brown hair was in a French braid flipped to the front so that it wouldn't be caught in the heavy backpack she wore.

"Not many people come up here. At least not in the winter." As usual, she spoke barely loud enough to be heard. Every conversation she'd ever had with Tiffany required leaning in to be sure to hear her soft words. Up here, with the wind blowing up over the bluff and the cry of a pair of seagulls soaring on it, her voice seemed doubly soft.

Natalya had forgotten that Tiffany had homesteaded somewhere up here in the forest. Since her boyfriend had bailed on her and taken her truck with him, she'd remained aloof and alone out here in the wilderness. She only came to town for knitting days and to sell her produce in town, always afoot no matter the weather. She probably couldn't afford to replace the missing truck.

"We're just out for a run."

Tiffany tipped her head up enough for her gray eyes to become visible. "You don't seem to be running."

"We stopped for a moment to admire the view," Cal spoke as if to a child.

But Natalya knew from past experience that Tiffany's comments might sound simple at times, but that she was actually very sharp and missed nothing.

"The view is best on the other side of the light," and she offered one of her enigmatic smiles to Natalya as if she'd been there fifteen years ago to see exactly where Natalya had given herself to Nicky.

Then Tiffany turned and started down the trail toward town.

"She's right you know," Cal said. "She's strange, but right. Let's go see."

"Not interested in revisiting the site of your old conquests, Mason." Nor her own. She bounced on her toes a couple of times and headed for the trail that climbed up into the woods.

"Nothing wrong with making some new conquests there," Cal grumbled, but fell into step close behind her.

NATALYA MUST BE part mountain goat and part jackrabbit. She ran as fast up steep trails as she did down them. But she was giving him a fine motivation for keeping up, because her running togs hid almost nothing other than the color of her skin. Many women he'd seen in tight leggings really shouldn't go there—but the whole concept had been designed with women like Natalya in mind.

Women like Natalya. *How many of those have you met, Mason?*

Could count them on one finger and her name was Natalya Lamont.

She set a pace that excluded conversation. A couple of times she'd tried opening up the lead on him. The first time she'd added a dozen paces before he'd caught on and closed the gap. After that, he hung solid, three paces back.

He might be breathing too hard to talk, but he could still think. It had taken a mile past the lighthouse before he managed to think about something other than her body. The image of taking her up against the lighthouse with only ocean and sky as witnesses was a very powerful one.

But somewhere in the second mile he also started thinking about the sleepy-eyed woman he'd watched this morning. The one that had left him unable to speak when faced with that unexpectedly quiet and serene version of Natalya.

Only not so serene.

Her tears may have discomfited her mother, but it had left him with a lot to think about.

I don't even know what's wrong.

About the only thing he could think of that was wrong with his life was that he wasn't curled up in a bed with Natalya at the moment. He liked baking. There was a sameness to each day's tasks, but there was art there as well—what baked right one time might not work the next. Baking was advanced chemistry, a class he'd done particularly well in because of that understanding.

The business was taking off well enough that he'd had the extra cash to buy the Corvette outright. He had poker buddies, the occasional lover, and afternoons and weekends off to enjoy the beach, get in some fishing, or go for a run. He and Dad shared dinner as often as not. Cal had never had big dreams and was doing fine with that.

They hit a logging road that led back down toward town, and

Natalya picked up the pace. He leaned into the run to keep up with her, but didn't try pulling alongside because he knew that would just goad her on. With the way she looked running, as graceful as if born to it, he wondered if just maybe she could dust him.

There were others like him who were doing well here: Vincent building fine furniture out of his garage, Becky and her brewery, Dad, Gina Lamont, the list went on.

Some had big, out-in-the-world dreams. But it was as if they were coming home to roost. The Judge had never left, though he'd commuted to Newport for thirty years before staying home and opening the diner. Harry had been a hot-shit New Orleans lawyer for a decade before coming back to take his father's place on the bench. Greg's high-end restaurant, open only on Friday and Saturday nights, was good enough he could have made a go of it anywhere. But he hadn't; he'd opened it in Eagle Cove.

Jessica was in yet another category. Her journalism career had collapsed along with the newspapers. She was now the town's marketing guru and kicking ass at it—just as you'd expect from Jessica. He really needed to talk with Dad about bringing on some help before the summer because if the tourism kept picking up at the rate Jessica had it increasing, they'd need it.

Then there was Natalya, who had shifted up the pace another notch. Thankfully his body enjoyed the view and had kept close while his thoughts wandered. Though if she took it much faster, she just might leave him behind.

Natalya's career was rocking. He looked up her company online in the two weeks he'd spent trying not to think about it. Their backdated press releases announced any number of new clients, the employment opportunities listing was long, and Natalya was often mentioned in the newsletters.

Yet she'd wept on her mother's shoulder this morning.

I don't even know what's wrong.

Yeah, he'd really like to have Natalya in his bed for a whole week—his initial reason for agreeing that she should call in sick. But he'd bet there were other reasons too. More important ones.

"Hey, Gnat. I think—" he started to speak to her, but she wasn't there. She'd slipped away once they'd hit the up and down hills of Gull Way. He spotted her half a block ahead, kicking hard as she turned onto Shearwater Lane. They hadn't called a finish line, but she was going after it like she had one in mind.

Cal dug in and sprinted hard. He blew by Vincent's, not even bothering to wave a hand at the shouted greeting. Besides, Vincent had finished in the money last night, going home fifteen dollars heavy—Cal had to hold a grudge on that for at least a day.

By the end of Shearwater, she was still way out in front. Along Egret Hollow he gained a little ground. She skipped Sandpiper Circuit, but now he guessed at her direction. He took the turnoff, but didn't follow the second half of the circuit. Instead, he raced through Andrea Martin's landscaping business (clearing several rows of blueberry bushes like a line of hurdles), shot across Beach Way, through Sleepy Owl Hotel's parking lot, and came at her sideways on the sandy beach.

"Cheater!"

He swung in close beside her. Two miles to her mother's B&B. It would be a hard race, and a good one. But her mom was there and had a houseful of guests. He wanted Natalya to himself.

Cal squeezed in on her, edging her toward the water. In a hundred yards he had her dancing along the edge of the surf without realizing it. Then he did a move he'd perfected on the soccer field. He made as if to stumble and turn abruptly while actually pushing just a little ahead. Without any contact, no illegal pushing of the opponent, he used her own instinctive reaction to make her stumble into the ocean to avoid his pretended fall.

"Goddamn it, Mas—"

That's when he tackled her.

Full body hug, he threw them both into an oncoming wave, though he did twist to take the brunt of the fall himself.

"What the—" the breaking wave crashed over her face and left her gasping and sputtering out sea water.

"Sorry, Gnat. Guess I tripped." When the icy water dragged back to sea they were both drenched through and sitting in only about six inches of water.

A husky, who'd been romping in and out of the waves after a Frisbee, rushed over to see what was happening. He shook his coat off in their faces, then bounded away to his owner's call.

Cal wiped the water off his face. "Gotta get me one of those someday," he teased her, wishing his life was a little different so that he actually could. It wouldn't be fair to lock a big dog up while he was in the bakery all day.

"Great! Then I can always smell like wet dog. I knew I should have brought my can of Mace."

"You wouldn't Mace some poor dog?"

"Never! But you I'd spray in a heartbea—"

He rolled her down into the next wave just for the hell of it.

"Now you don't smell of wet dog anymore," he said when they resurfaced. "Besides, I thought you might be overheated from your run."

"Well now I'm freezing!"

"I know a place close by where we can go to get warm."

She glanced up the beach. "You should be hung, drawn, quartered, and hung again!" But she was grinning at him. His apartment was only one block over.

The next wave had her leaping out of his grasp, pushing off hard against his shoulder to get clear. Unable to make it back to his own feet in time, the icy wave drove into his face and knocked him flat. It also dragged a massive load of sand up his shorts.

THE BOTTOM of the tub was all gritty beneath her feet. It seemed no matter how much Cal rinsed, there was more sand to be found. Her hair was an unruly snarl of seawater and sand as well.

One moment they were giggling and washing each other like a couple of children beneath the steaming spray. The next moment Cal had her back slammed up against the shower wall, his body pressed hard against her, his face just an inch from hers.

"I've got an awful need for you, Lamont." But he didn't take. No matter how badly he wanted, he didn't take.

She brushed her fingers over his cheek. The image of sex out at the lighthouse had gotten planted deep in her brain by Tiffany's knowing smile. And then to have Cal pace her through a half dozen miles as if he was her shadow only heightened the thought until the image had become a searing need. She'd waited long enough for the idea to plant itself distractingly deep in Cal's thoughts as well and then pulled away by stretching out her stride without changing the speed of her steps. People always fell for that trick. They'd match her pace, until it was like a metronome to them. That's when she'd stretch out her long legs —a trick which had won her any number of races. Only Jessica never fell for that, as her cousin's legs were just as long as Natalya's.

And Cal had decided that race be damned, he wanted her more than he wanted to win.

His blue eyes were watching her, desperate with need. He was taking no advantage despite having pinned her to the wall. She could push him away with no more pressure than to move a feather. He made it clear that the choice was hers, that the power was hers.

That was a heady tonic she couldn't resist.

As she pulled his head down into a kiss, Natalya wondered if he knew that. Even if he was manipulating her, it was to right where she wanted to be.

CHAPTER 9

Natalya lay alone on Cal's big bed listening to Hank Williams crooning out *Jambalaya*. She felt both wrung out and thoroughly energized.

They'd woken to *American Pie* which she'd argued really shouldn't be on his list because it wasn't about food. He'd mumbled in between her breasts—his favorite place to wake up—that even songs about food were mostly about other things. ABBA came on next with *Honey, Honey* to prove his point. When he'd tried to leave to go bake, she'd pulled him back and they'd had that quickie he so wanted, to Maroon 5 belting out *Sugar*. Though they'd finished to The Monkees' *Tapioca Tundra* which had them groaning for multiple reasons.

Two days. Despite her protestations, she had spent two straight days being Cal's sex kitten. Of course he'd been a sex *god* so it was hard to complain. It hadn't all been sex, but they hadn't gone out either. As predicted, they'd slept some. They'd watched a couple of Jason Bourne action movies while eating delivery pizza on the sofa. And they'd taken turns reading aloud chapters of the latest Lee Child thriller—after all, Cal was built on the scale of Jack Reacher and she'd ad-libbed certain lewd comparisons as she read.

Now it was Monday.

Time to leave her little two-day idyll and start thinking again.

First, she'd have to go home and get some clothes. All she had here was her running togs. For the entire weekend, when she'd worn clothing, it had been nothing but a big shirt that declared "Bakers Do It With Chocolate"—a truth Cal had very thoroughly proven upon her willing body. And he'd left her this morning with an evil grin while wearing a "Darth Baker" t-shirt, though she'd kept her butt safely under the covers so that he didn't smack it again in his glee.

Second, she'd have to decide about taking the week off "sick." Within the next hour she either needed to get in her car and drive, or call in. And she needed to make the decision on her own before her mother had a chance to argue her point once again. Mom was such a primal force that Natalya had learned—shortly after childbirth probably—that she had to make the really important decisions on her own.

This week's schedule was—

Even thinking about the office made her feel a bit ill.

She flopped face down as Harry Belafonte broke into *The Banana Boat Song (Day-O)*. It was the same position she'd been in two weeks ago on Monday morning: her bones just as liquid as they were now, her face once again buried in Cal's pillow which smelled mostly of him and, this time, a little bit of chocolate.

She wasn't going to call in sick just so that she could keep having amazing sex.

Tempting, but no.

Again the thought of going to work…

Her gut clenched.

Well, if she didn't want to go to work, then what did she want?

That answer wasn't forthcoming as she dressed and made the bed.

She didn't find it going down the stairs either.

At the bottom, the door into the bakery was open. She turned in.

Cal was there, of course, like a hulking demon in his laboratory. The bright worklights made the floating flour dust sparkle in the air as he smacked a bread loaf. Sugar, jam, and, yes, chocolate assaulted her nose. He stood before a great counter of stainless steel working methodically down the row kneading massive balls of dough, slapping them with flour, and setting them aside to keep rising. Behind him, the big ovens were heating up.

She watched him for a long time before speaking. He was so beautiful. His big muscles rippling as he manipulated bags of flour and giant mixers, turning out giant piles of dough. He was power embodied, but also finesse. She could watch him all day.

"Everything in your world is so orderly, Mason."

He didn't jolt. Cal simply looked up at her and smiled. He brushed his hands together releasing a puff of flour. "Baking is an orderly process otherwise it doesn't work."

"I'm rather envious." Because her world, that looked so orderly from the outside, was a screwed up mess inside her head. A mess she couldn't seem to get a handle on. She only knew that it hurt.

Cal came around from behind his counter. He paused a moment to look her up and down, with that lusty smile she'd come to know so well.

"Not helping, Cal."

"Sorry, Gnat. But you are an incredible sight in or,"—he leered —"out of your running gear." Then his expression sobered. "And the gift you've given me these last two days, well, it's something that just makes a guy happy."

"I suppose," she saw the hurt at her vague response as soon as she said it. She placed a hand on the middle of his chest. "No, Cal. Don't go there. You're all a woman could ask for and then some. And I'm sorry that I'm a damned bitchy one at four in the morning."

"Can I get you something to eat?" His smile was a teasing reminder of her mother's instructions to him, but she could still see the hurt there that she hadn't repaid the compliment. She searched inside but couldn't find anything to say.

"No. I just need to get home."

Cal went cautious, "Home here or home Portland?"

"I don't know yet."

He nodded slowly. "Let me give you a ride home in the van." Both the Vette and her MINI were still at the B&B.

"Your dough," she waved a hand toward the table.

"I can spare ten minutes."

She nodded, didn't know what else to do. It would be a long cold walk in her tights and she was sick to death of running. Especially when she didn't know if she was running away or running toward something.

CAL DROVE the delivery van slowly, giving Natalya time to think, but she still hadn't said a word. He finally understood that if he didn't speak, no one would.

"Hey, Gnat?"

"Yes, Cal," she sighed in a tolerant tone. He debated but decided that it was best to keep using her nickname.

"As a friend, not as the guy who loves having you in his bed…"

"Uh-huh?" her tone was carefully noncommittal.

He slowed the truck at the Slater's, finally pulled over and doused the headlights, but left the engine and heater running. Was he about to step over some line? They'd spent an entire weekend together and not once talked about anything important. Not a single word.

"What, Cal?"

"I just think," he turned to look at her shadowed face barely lit by the B&B's porch light filtering through the thin line of trees that separated the properties. "I think you really should call in sick. Not to spend with me, though you know I wouldn't mind that."

"Wouldn't *mind?*"

"Okay, a part of me is down in the footwell," he thumped his sneaker on the van's floor for emphasis, "trying to sell his soul to the Devil to get you to stay with me." There wasn't quite enough light to tell if that earned him a smile or not.

"And the other part?"

"The other part thinks his friend Natalya should take some time for herself. Some time to think about this last weekend."

"This weekend was all about sex, Cal. Awesome sex, but that's all it was."

"That's my point. I'm gone on you, Gnat, you know that. You want to shack up and never leave, I'll be a happy man. But all weekend you didn't say a single word about what had you crying on your mom's shoulder. Never seen you cry before, Gnat."

"I—" her voice choked off. "I don't do it much, Cal."

"Well, something's in there. If you go back to Portland, you'll get busy as hell and not think about it. I'm just saying maybe you should hang out here. See me or don't. But you ripped us both apart with that weeping. You're so goddamn amazing, neither of us knows where that came from."

"That makes three of us. I don't know either, Cal. Not that it's any comfort."

He reached out and took her hand which was far colder than could be accounted for by the bakery van's lame heater. "That's my point."

Natalya remained still and silent, but did squeeze his hand back when he squeezed hers before he let go.

"I'll drop you off now; my dough can't wait much longer. But if you need to talk, you let me know. Call me from Portland and I can be there in three hours. Okay?"

No response.

"Okay?"

"Yeah. Thanks, Cal. You're the best. In many ways."

He dropped the van into gear and drove around the last clump of trees. He didn't hit the headlights because he didn't want them to shine in some sleeping guest's window at four-thirty in the morning.

On the porch in the glow of the porch light was a sight unlike anything he'd ever seen.

Gina Lamont stood there, her bathrobe wide open where she was pressed against a man that she was kissing hard. The man's arms were inside the robe, clearly holding her close.

Then they turned in unison to face his van.

"Dad?"

NATALYA AND CAL SR. nodded cautiously at each other as they crossed paths at the bottom of the steps. Senior moved to the van driver's window as Natalya stepped up onto the porch.

"Close your robe, Mom."

"What? Oh." She wore a light cotton nightgown underneath the robe...very light and quite short. It didn't hide anything about her mother's generous figure. "Sorry. I'm just a bit..."

"Breathless?"

"Yes."

Natalya wasn't sure if she'd ever seen her mother made fluttery by a man before.

Together they turned to watch the two Cals. The men spoke too softly to be overheard, so Natalya decided to fill in the script.

"Hi, Dad," Natalya did her best to imitate Cal Jr.'s deep voice, though she kept it to a whisper so only her mother would overhear.

"Hey, Junior," her mother answered in kind, imitating Cal Sr.

"See you at the bakery?" Natalya offered as both men looked away from one another.

"Sure, son," her mother finished. And that must have been fairly accurate, because Cal Sr. turned on his heel and clambered into his pickup.

Cal didn't move. Natalya could feel him looking at her. She'd known and hadn't told him. She'd figured it was her mother and his father's business, but now she wished she had.

She raised a hand, but didn't see an answering one before he backed in a half circle, turned on the headlights, and headed into town. Moments later Cal Sr. was gone as well.

"Did yours wave?" Natalya asked her mom.

"Not sure. But he did a few other very nice things."

"Too much information, Mom."

"Anything you want to be telling me?"

"No."

"Stingy!" Then her mom laughed, though quietly because of the guests, as they entered the kitchen. "Bet you twenty dollars the two of them spend the whole morning baking together and never say a word about it."

Natalya smiled. "No bet." And then her smile slipped away. Wasn't that what Cal had just pointed out to her, that she hadn't shared a thing about herself? But if she had, she just might have started crying again and that wasn't going to solve anything. And if it started again, she was half afraid that she wouldn't be able to stop.

For now she'd keep her peace and head up to her room.

Three hours later, that's where she still was. Sitting on the foot of her bed, watching the walls as the darkness outside began lightening toward day.

At eight, she pulled out her phone and called in sick with a bad flu. Dan's sympathy, and telling her to just lie low and get better because he'd handle any meetings that came up, didn't make her lie sit any better. But she truly didn't feel up to the long drive back to Portland.

By nine, sunlight was poking over the Coast Range and the first squares of brilliant yellow were slipping through the south window. The first thing they lit was her demon sketch from that day in the woods, or at least the final evolution of the idea. Cal might no longer be recognizable in the finished work, but she saw him there none-theless.

The demon who was doing strange things to her. The demon who looked like a magician in his bakery and like...she didn't know what... as he rode down upon her until they were both writhing with the pleasure of it.

Natalya went to the footlocker that any guest would assume was merely decorative. She reached around the back and took the key off the tiny hook there. Inside, beneath the iron-banded wooden lid, were her art supplies: a roll of canvas, palette, paints and pastels, a stack of various-sized sketchbooks, folded-up easel, and a couple of stretched canvases.

She didn't need to start with a pencil. The picture had been so clear in her head over these last two days.

Natalya started with the brown acrylics.

First, the poker table.

Well, at least Cal now knew where Dad had gotten his "energy" two weeks before. When he recalled a stray comment from Natalya, Cal almost punched a hole in the pie dough he was rolling out for Scottish pasties intended for lunch service.

He woke up full of energy, Cal had said.

Or he never went to sleep, Natalya had declined to clarify her mumble.

And Dad had commented about seeing Natalya driving his Corvette. But Dad didn't live on LBB Lane. When he'd given Cal sole possession of the apartment for a high school graduation present, he'd bought a small place out on Gull Way, not far from the airport.

Cal's first instinct was to be pissed. At Natalya. At his father.

Even if Natalya had decided it was none of *her* business, it was his father and that was part of *his* business. Except, it really wasn't. Senior had just as much right to his privacy as Cal did. Hell, Cal and Natalya had just spent two full days in a love nest right upstairs while his father ran the bakery Saturday.

Still didn't sit quite right.

"Sleep much?" Cal couldn't stop himself.

"Not a wink," Senior was clearly bragging as he rolled out the bagel dough and started bending it into circles. "You?"

"Not much," then he knew how to get back at his father for all of those times he'd caught the bigger salmon, snagged the bigger burger, or found the better deal in a flea market. "Of course, it was two straight days and nights. Had to sleep a little."

His Dad just nodded and stayed focused on his bagels, but still it felt good.

WHEN SIX HIT, they had the bagels boiled and baking in the oven.

Cal headed over to the diner. No sign of either car. But the diner wasn't empty even right at six. Cal was always first in as the doors were unlocked. Excitement rose—until he saw that it was Jessica, not Natalya, sitting at the counter.

The Judge was back in place in the kitchen and Greg was running the front of house again.

Cal dropped down on his stool, "The usual."

Greg wrote it up just that way ("The usual"), put it in the spinner rack, and slapped it around. The Judge immediately set a fully dressed tall stack of pancakes on the service ledge and pulled down the order slip. It was all ritual now between the three of them, had been for a long time. Cal liked the comfort of it. The steadiness.

"Hey, Jess."

"Hey, Giant." She didn't have a meal in front of her. Instead she had notebooks and printouts and was scribbling notes on a pad.

"What's all that?"

"Stormy Days at Eagle Cove."

"Oh, when's that?"

"When's that?" Jessica spun to face him. "When's that!" She now had Greg and the Judge's full attention. "It's in five goddamn days, Mason! I've been working on it for three months. I've been giving you updates and timelines for three damn months. You're going to be open this coming Saturday *and* Sunday. Special cupcakes and custom cookies. You're doing a 'Storm Watcher's Box Lunch' if there actually is a storm, a Bird Watcher's one if there isn't. I've already got over a hundred pre-orders for those. I even got Old Man Jaspar at Grouse Hardware to roll over and promise me those individual hand-warmer things—two per lunch order so people can keep both hands warm. You promised me special pastries. You've got to get your shit together, Mason, or I'm going to kill you."

"Oh, that," Cal picked up a piece of bacon and bit down on it. "Yeah, Dad and I have that covered."

"You—" Jessica sputtered.

"Aren't you supposed to be careful about your blood pressure, Jess? You do know you're pregnant, right?" He turned to Greg, but pointed at Jessica with his bacon as he pretended to whisper. "You did tell her she was pregnant, didn't you?"

"Aaaaaaaaa!" Jessica buried her face on her crossed arms.

"Or is it some hormonal thing and you don't want her in on the secret yet?" He kept talking to Greg. "Hope I didn't mess you up, buddy."

Greg rolled his eyes, but he had got the Judge chuckling which was hard to do. He absolutely doted on his two daughters-in-law, but it was clear that he had a special weak spot for Jessica. Besides, Becky was so strong and independent that she was harder to dote on.

Jessica sat up and glared at him. "Next time we'll have *you* be pregnant. We'll start you out with three months of morning sickness and barfing your guts out for breakfast and then see how damned funny you think it all is." She pointed at a plate with a half-eaten piece of dry toast.

"Well, okay. That part doesn't sound so great, but I'm not the one who gets to give birth to a kid and create a new human being."

"Birth. Labor. What a joy *that's* going to be!" She didn't look amused. "I'm going to get you back for this, Mason."

He wasn't worried. It was a pretty empty threat...unless she teamed up with Natalya the evil genius.

The bell on the back of the door rang and Cal spun, but it was the McCalls. Every Monday morning, as a treat before starting their week, Vincent brought all four of them here for breakfast. It was a good thing. Family moment. Nice. Then the twin girls would go off to Dragon Winslow's class, Dawn would be off to try and pound some science into the empty heads of Eagle Cove's high schoolers (his head had sure been empty then of everything except soccer and girls), and Vincent would be back in his garage-shop making furniture.

He glanced out at the lit porch through the big windows. No beautiful woman in a stylish raincoat. Though he saw Hector was already in place by the window with his crossword, Cal hadn't even heard him come in. He'd made Eagle Bay Marina his home for the last three winters, renting a slip for his Pearson 42 sailboat. His biggest fear appeared to be someone getting to the crossword puzzle before he did.

"Hey, Cal," he offered a nod when he noticed Cal looking his way.

"Hey."

"Seven letters. A baker's mistake. Got an 'O' in the middle of her."

"Stupid-ass clue," Cal had heard this one too many times. " 'Bloomer.' It's a UK word for a mistake. Separately, it's a UK word for a really large loaf of bread."

"Gotcha," and he went back to his puzzle. Greg headed over to the McCalls with menus as Cal turned back to his breakfast.

Still no Natalya through the front window.

"So, where's Natalya?" Jessica asked as if she was reading his mind. "I didn't see her all weekend."

"I did. Like every minute for forty-eight straight hours," and the instant he said it he knew it was the wrong thing. What had worked on his dad came out like he was bragging about seeing her when Natalya's best friend and first cousin hadn't. "We spent a fair amount of time together," he went for the backpedal, but knew it was too late.

"And where is she now?"

"Wish I knew. Either at her mom's or halfway back to Portland."

"And you don't know?" Jessica sounded completely disgusted. "How can you say you're in love with her and not know?"

"Look, Jess. I don't like it either. She's trying to deal with some shit and I'm trying to help. She's—" And Cal froze. "Wait! What?"

"Don't try to deny it, Mason, or I'll think less of you than I already do."

"I—" He couldn't deny it, but it wasn't true either. Natalya was amazing. She was far and away the best time he'd ever had. And he hadn't been totally joking when he said he'd be glad to shack up with her long term if she was, you know, in the mood for that. These women were making him into a blithering idiot. He—what? The L-word didn't happen to Mason men, not unless it was spelled L-U-S-T.

His dad and Gina Lamont.

She'd always been the ultra-hot mom of the town with her bright red hair, her tall, amazing figure that had only improved with time, and her infectious laugh. That's what lust looked like, this morning on the porch. The better part of naked, her breasts beneath filmy fabric still rising and falling with her rapid breathing after the kiss Dad had been giving her.

But lust wasn't what he felt for the dark beauty that was her daughter. Not all of it. Maybe not most of it. When she'd waved at him, he'd been unable to respond. Despite the pain that he knew lay below the surface, she had stood so poised, so perfect. No one would ever know she wasn't, except maybe him and her mom. And that's what made her so captivating. She was—

Jessica was still staring at him.

"I'm not confirming or denying shit, Jess."

The bell on the back of the door rang twice more while Jess merely studied him.

"Okay, Cal." And he could see what she was thinking.

"Look," he lowered his voice so that no one would overhear, not even Greg delivering new orders to the window. "Go easy on her, Jessica. She's having a real hard time at the moment. Don't go trying to corner her on shit like..." he shrugged indicating what she'd just done to him. "Right now I think she needs a friend."

"You know what, Mason?" Jessica sat up, patting him on the arm.

"No. What? Maybe I don't want to know what."

"You just might be okay after all."

"Huh." He couldn't think of what to say.

"But don't let it go to your head. Now eat your tall stack and get back to your baking. You've only got five more days."

"It's okay," though he did start eating again. "Dad's helping out this morning."

"On a Monday?" She was local enough to know it was Senior's normal day off.

"Yeah. He and your Aunt Gina were—" And he bit down on his tongue, but again it was too late as Jessica choked and gasped in surprise.

"Your father and my aunt?" She clamped her hand painfully onto his forearm. Her nails weren't long, but she had a strong grip to drive them in with.

He nodded.

"And you and Natalya?"

"We're not a foursome freakshow, Jess."

"No. No. I didn't mean that. But still, it has to be…strange."

Cal nodded. That didn't begin to cover half of it.

THERE WAS a sharp knock on the door that had Natalya jolting. Thankfully she'd just pulled the brush away from the painting to daub up some more cadmium red.

It wasn't her mom's knock, so she just called out, "Go away!" and returned to the painting that had absorbed her attention all morning.

Whoever it was rattled the doorknob, but Natalya had locked the door. She was back to working on Cal's shirt before the footsteps tromped away. Too light to be Cal's, but it didn't matter. She wasn't in the mood to see him either.

The painting had come together so fast. She'd considered moving Cal to the other side of the table so that she could see his face, but that felt too intimate, too personal. Though his face was hidden, he was the dominant figure in the foreground, commanding the canvas. His head was tipped slightly up and back, his joy reflected in the faces of others around the table. She'd shifted the faces so that they weren't recognizable, but anyone who knew Cal would know him in an instant. Her every effort to change that had failed, and she had scraped off and painted over until she'd given in and let him be himself.

She'd also shifted the women's side. The two realities had blended so smoothly: the raucous men's half circle and the quietly peaceful women's half. The rustic bakery and the neatly Victorian parlor.

Except, just to the right of center. There Natalya had placed herself, seated hard against the shadowy disjunction between the two settings. She alone, of all of them, was quiet.

Natalya set down her brush and stared at the painting attempting to puzzle out the expression she'd given herself.

A shadow passed across the sunset's orange light washing into the room—when had it gotten so late? Then a sharp rap on her balcony door had her jumping. She spun to see Jessica opening the door and bringing in a cold blast of air with her.

"Jessica!" Natalya was appalled. She knew exactly the way Jessica had gotten in: climbing the heavy iron mesh from the porch two stories below. The original Lamont daughter had installed it and trained climbing ivy upward to make a home for birds. After a century, it was a thick mass of leaves and vines. In the spring the ivy wall was so raucous during the day that it was impossible to sleep past sunrise. It had also provided a handy escape for teenage outings which didn't pass by her mother's room.

Jessica looked quite pleased at the surprise she'd just created.

"You're pregnant! You can't be doing things like that!" Natalya rushed over to check on her friend.

"Just four months. I'm not a feeb yet," she pushed away Natalya's hands just as she'd done to Jessica when she was fussing at the wedding. "Greg is already hovering, and Mom asks twice a day if I might want a 'nice lie down.' So don't you start."

Natalya backed off and dropped onto the bed. Jessica did look incredibly healthy. The fair skin of her face pinked by the exertion of the climb. The happy smile that so mimicked the one Natalya had given her in the painting. "You're looking good."

"Just happy I guess." Jessica shrugged. "You'll see when it happens to you."

"A lot of good Greg sex?" Natalya teased going to a subject change. She especially didn't like the appraising look in Jessica's eyes.

"Totally," Jessica sidetracked—at least for the moment. "He's gotten even sweeter since this," and she rested a gentle hand on her own belly.

Jessica had shared, well, entirely too much information during her and Greg's chaotic courtship. Of course she and Jessica had been rooming together at the B&B at the time, so Natalya had been "primary confessor" just as when they were teens. Even from Day One Greg had always been a sweet and gentle lover.

Natalya couldn't help but draw comparisons. Cal wasn't gentle. Not that he was rough, he simply enjoyed sex and threw himself into the act. And sweet was a word she'd never apply. Sex with Cal was an active and energetic exploration of everything that was good. His manners were as frank in the bedroom as they were in public. She glanced over at the painting. He ruled it, though his face was the only one completely hidden. Cal Mason Jr. was emphatically male.

"Hey! This new?" Jessica crossed to the painting.

"Still wet. Don't touch."

Jessica looked at it. And then she went quiet. She stared at it for so long that Natalya's nerves forced her to her feet. Sitting back on the stool in front of the easel, she started to reach for her paints.

"It just needs some—"

"Don't you dare!" Jessica slapped the back of her hand hard enough to sting.

"Ow! What?"

"If you do anything to that painting other than signing your name, I won't speak to you ever again."

"Don't tempt me."

Jessica leaned against her, waist to shoulder, and gave Natalya a sideways hug. Of course she'd know it was an empty threat.

"Really?" It didn't feel finished. Though she couldn't think of what else to do to it. Maybe it was. But it wasn't a comfortable painting.

"Really," Jessica confirmed. "Sign it, now. Before you change your mind."

She stood silently while Natalya took a fine brush and filled in the blocky "N. Lamont" that she'd worked out across the corners of a hundred science- and math-class notebook pages. She circled behind it and knelt to paint her full name and the date on the back of the canvas. After a moment's thought she added, *Joy* and then set down the brush and palette.

"What did you call it?"

"Joy."

"What about her?" Jessica pointed at Natalya's image of herself. She couldn't tell if Jessica didn't recognize Natalya's self-portrait or if Jessica was being kind because the figure didn't fit in with the rest of the painting.

"That's why I wasn't sure if the painting was done. I wanted to make, uh, *her*...happier. But she didn't seem to want to go there."

"Well she's the complete focus of the painting."

Natalya had thought Cal was, dominating the foreground, his head back in laughter.

"It's perfect, Natalya. She's the figure that turns it from a kinda cool painting into an emotional gut punch. The contrast. The ultimate outsider." Then Jessica turned to face her and simply pulled her into a hug and whispered into her ear. "And if that's how you see yourself, you're an idiot."

Natalya held on and Jessica let her. No sob resurfaced. No fiery pain burning in her chest. But over Jessica's shoulder she could see the woman staring quiet-eyed out of the canvas. It was a look she found every morning in the mirror.

CAL LAY in bed wide awake in the dark, second-guessing himself. He knew he'd better get some sleep...but insisting on that wasn't working.

He hadn't gone out to the B&B to see if Natalya was still in town. The Corvette still parked out there had given him the perfect excuse for an afternoon walk, but he hadn't gone. Part of him didn't want to know if she'd left town or not. Another part didn't want to intrude if she hadn't.

He was still fairly certain that Jessica had just been yanking his chain at breakfast, but the question had stuck with him.

Did he love her?

Was he even capable of such a thing? And that was assuming the emotion even existed.

Love wasn't a mother who cheated on her husband with a Corvallis stockbroker and then abandoned her son. But it might be he and Dad baking silently together in the early mornings.

He'd said it to enough women over the years, it seemed to be what they wanted to hear—they'd certainly said it easily enough.

But saying something like that to Natalya Lamont wouldn't be some light, flirtatious, groaned-out-during-sex kind of thing. Around Natalya words were more important, had more meaning. Too bad he didn't know crap about things like that. He'd squeaked out of high school and been glad to be done with the whole mess. His dad and most of his friends hadn't gone to college.

Harry had law school, but Greg only had culinary school. Vincent built great furniture and Alex was learning to be a brewer. Gina Lamont and Jess's parents had never left town for college and were some of the best people he knew.

Maybe Natalya was just having fun with him, because there was no question how much fun they had together; she'd be swept away by some degreed city-boy later. He wasn't inclined to complain about the situation, as he was getting great benefits from it at the moment.

But he didn't much like it either.

Which would make some sense if he was falling—but he wasn't— in love with her. Because love probably didn't even exist…

And shit! He was right back where he'd started.

He yanked the pillow over his face, the one that now very much smelled like Natalya after their two days together, and screamed into it.

Then he froze as he heard a key in the downstairs door. The door opened and closed softly. He pulled aside the pillow and could just pick out the creaking of the stairs as someone ascended slowly. His father's tread would have practically shaken the building, but these steps were light.

He'd left his keys at the B&B when they'd gone for the run and had yet to retrieve them.

The apartment door creaked open and closed again.

Maybe…please…maybe…

"Cal?" the softest whisper in the dark.

"Natalya." The relief breathed out of him with a happy sigh.

Without another word, she moved up beside the bed. He listened to her undress. Scrabbling around on the floor to his side, they had sides now, he found his t-shirt and held it out into the darkness.

She took it from his hand and moments later slipped into the bed beside him. So silently that it was almost as if she wasn't there, she eased against him. Head on his shoulder, her hand resting lightly on the center of his chest, she came to a stop.

"You okay?"

He could feel her uncertain shrug. Cal almost asked if she wanted to talk about it, but suspected that if she wanted to she would. So instead, he kissed her on top of the head and squeezed his arm around her shoulders.

She turned her head enough to kiss his shoulder and then went quiet.

It wasn't long before she fell asleep.

Cal continued to hold her for a long time.

He didn't like the question of whether or not he loved her. However, he was so happy that she had come to him, even in silence, that it didn't really matter. And that thought actually answered the question he was avoiding in the first place.

Which had him smiling.

He considered waking Natalya to tell her, but decided against it. She slept as if exhausted. The morning would give him plenty of time.

The only drawback was that it really sucked that Jessica was right.

So, her he wouldn't tell.

CHAPTER 11

*N*atalya woke to darkness before the alarm.

Cal wasn't just asleep, he was out. She'd learned the difference during their weekend together. When he was this far under he could sleep through the apocalypse, which would explain why his alarm music was so loud. Maybe that's why she was awake so early, self defense against being alarmed out of her common sense.

That still didn't explain why she was here, because this made no sense at all.

"Just to return his car," had been her excuse to herself as she'd climbed into Cal's Corvette…because naturally that's the most important thing to do at ten at night.

"Merely dropping off his keys," had led her upstairs despite no lights on in the apartment…sure, why not, just stroll into someone's house while he slept.

"For sex," had led her between the covers. Or perhaps that impossible relief she'd heard when he'd whispered her name so hopefully into the dark.

But none of that had turned out to be true.

"To be held!" It had certainly worked. After the wracking exhaustion of creating that painting, it was what she really wanted. To be held. To belong somewhere.

And she had.

Cal had welcomed her without hesitation. Opening his bed and his arms. If he'd asked for sex, she'd have given it. Gladly because she suspected she was a long way from running down Cal's imagination. But somehow he'd known what she really needed and simply let her lie beside him.

Unsure what drove her, she slipped from his bed while he still slept. She had his shirt half off before she changed her mind and pulled it back into place. It was way too big, but it smelled like him.

Tugging on jeans and jacket, she stuffed her bra into the jacket pocket. Unsure how to thank him, she left her own t-shirt on her pillow. It would at least let him know that she wasn't just walking out on him. She tried on one of the hats he had hanging by the door but it dropped down over her eyes and she hung it back up. Rather than trying on any others, she headed out into the night for the two-mile walk home before she could second guess herself back into his bed.

The air was crisp and cool. It smelled of night woods and ocean.

A hat would have been good. She tightened up the front zipper and pulled her hair forward over her ears.

Was she avoiding Cal?

Maybe, if he had started asking things last night, she would be. She wasn't ready for questions yet. Not from Jessica. Not from him. Not from her mother. Hell, she wasn't even ready for them from herself yet.

Where LBB Lane dipped down close to the ocean before climbing back atop the high bluff beach, the background roar of the waves divided into individual crashes on the beach. At any distance, the ocean sounded like a nearby highway. Her Portland apartment was a half-dozen built-up blocks from I-405, but she could still hear the traffic as a deep and steady roar. Similar sounds made by such different worlds.

She could tell the tide was low by how loud the surf was, crashing in on the hard wet sand rather than the softer, quieter sands that had drained dry higher on the beach. Forsaking the road, she followed the moonlight down onto the beach.

The entire length of the beach lay dark but for the lunar nightlight and Orca Head Lighthouse flashing out its warning at the far end of the beach. From Grouse Hardware to the Lamont B&B the entire town slept. She wore no watch and had oddly left her phone at home, so had no way of telling the time. No way to know if Cal had been "alarmed" awake yet and wondering where the hell had she gotten to.

Rather than puzzling at how she felt about doing that to him, the ocean lulled her into not thinking at all as she walked along. Just like Cal had last night. She'd felt so wound up inside, ready to fly apart in a thousand directions at the slightest touch. Yet the moment Cal had wrapped his big arm protectively around her and kissed her atop her head, a peace had washed over her.

She wasn't used to peace.

Portland was about working herself until exhausted, crashing into sleep, then doing it again the next day. When the team went out for drinks—which was a couple times a week—they always hit the hot clubs, and closed them too. Work hard, party hard, pass out hard. That was her life in Portland. In an entire weekend together, she and Cal had each had one beer, because having pizza without beer was just so wrong. But that was it.

Eagle Cove seemed to clear her head of the storms of Portland.

Natalya looked up at the moon. It had a faint glowing ring. Not bright enough to block the brighter stars behind the halo, but it was there. Incoming weather.

She'd have to remember to tell Jessica, she'd be pleased. Maybe her Stormy Days at Eagle Cove festival would bring in some much needed mid-winter business.

Climbing the long flight of stairs up from the beach, Natalya felt as if she was climbing out of the darkness and into the light though it was still hours to sunrise.

At the head of the stairs, she turned and watched the moonlight shining off the foamy wave crests until it looked as if they were glowing. She smelled the air again. A storm *was* brewing out there.

Natalya turned and hurried inside, not even pausing when she saw Cal Sr.'s truck parked out front, except to see if her mother's light was on or off. It was off and the B&B was silent. She wasn't the only one who'd wanted to be held in the quiet of the night.

She tiptoed up to her room and pulled out her biggest canvas.

Looking down into the sea chest, she surveyed the possibilities. Oils.

She hadn't worked in oils in years.

"She's still in town," Cal told Jessica as he sat down beside her.

"Duh!" Jessica didn't even look up from her small laptop. He could see that she was updating the town website that she'd built half a year ago and been expanding ever since.

Greg was waiting expectantly, "The Usual" already written on an order slip.

Cal was half tempted to order an omelette just to screw him up, but that would mean messing with the Judge as well. Finally he just nodded, "Do it."

Greg hung and spun the slip, but rather than simply setting the plate on the ledge, the Judge was watching him carefully. When Cal nodded it was okay, the Judge slid across the tall stack and pulled the ticket. Greg served it across and set the butter and warm maple syrup by his plate bearing bacon and the inevitable hash browns without noticing anything amiss in the "usual" routine.

Jessica might be working, but he could feel her waiting for him to say something more. So he didn't and instead set to eating his breakfast.

Besides, he didn't know what to say.

He'd woken up alone, wondering if he'd dreamed her beside him in the night. It wasn't until he was dressing that he spotted her t-shirt over the pillow.

"All women are created equal, but the very best become web designers."

He had a quick mental flash of her walking home naked, then he'd missed his own t-shirt and couldn't help laughing despite his confusion. His had said, "God created man and woman, then he did the hard work and created bakers."

But while he was encouraged by the curious gift, because there was no way he could wear it, he still didn't know what to make of it. Well, now he knew she was in town, he'd just wander out to the B&B after work and maybe find out what was up.

"Not saying much, Giant."

"Not to you, Jess." Passing on Natalya's silence felt good. A little bit of payback in the confusion department.

She eyed him carefully, but didn't argue the point.

Cal finished his breakfast, waved his thanks to the Judge and Greg as he left.

He'd feel a little better if Jessica had looked confused rather than finally nodding as if he finally was doing something right.

WHEN THE KNOCK came on her door this time, Natalya didn't snap at whoever it was to go away—not if there was a chance it would make a pregnant Jessica climb the ivy arbor again.

She called out, "It's open," before she came out of her reverie enough to recognize her mom's knock.

"Oh, you're painting again. That's wonderful, honey."

"Am I?" It didn't feel like she was "painting." It wasn't something she was doing because she liked the process, which she did. The images were simply too clear to keep inside her head. Actually this one was still only part of an image, but it was being too insistent to deny.

"Don't know what else you'd call it," Mom moved closer.

Neither did Natalya, so she didn't argue the point.

She pointed to the *Joy* painting propped on her dresser to distract her mother from the work in progress. Especially because she didn't know where it was progressing to. She dropped her brushes, flipped a cloth over it, and went to stand beside her mother. Natalya glanced out the window and saw that it was early afternoon. She'd been painting since…well, she never had looked at a clock. Since very early.

"That's…" Her mother stopped for a long moment continuing to study the painting. She usually just said, "Oh that's lovely" or the equivalent. She'd long ago confessed that for her, art was mostly about covering empty spots on walls. Which partially explained the B&B.

Every room was heroine-themed by genre.

Natalya had made hers Victorian, but there was the writers' room, kick-ass movie heroines' room, romantic comedies, great woman leaders…ten unique statements about powerful women. But that made the decoration choices simple: mostly framed posters and pictures.

She stared at the painting as long as Jessica had yesterday. Then she turned to stare at the walls, cluttered with the best of Natalya's other efforts.

"What are you looking for, Mom?"

"I'm not sure. This one is…different." Natalya had filled in the spaces around the Victorian women in order. She'd started at one side of the bed and worked her way around over the years. It was her progression as an artist.

Natalya tried to study it with a critical eye. There were a few child-hood drawings that showed a nice understanding of color if little skill. There had been a dramatic shift when Ma Slater had taken her in hand and given her technique to go with the images in her head. Another change when she'd discovered boys—emotion had taken more of a role. Love found, love lost, and all the chaos of being a teenage girl for sure. But also friendship, solitude, and a host of others.

Then through her twenties the number of paintings had thinned. What there was showed a thoughtfulness, perhaps an over-conscious one. She'd been attempting to manipulate the images to say something she thought was important. That she "thought." The emotional turmoil of her teenage paintings had slowly been filtered out. Steam-punk. Traditional Victorian. Studies rather than emotional paintings.

On the wall by the door, her latest, there was a shift back. One she barely recognized as her own. Rather than fantastic settings, she now used more of the Oregon Coast. Sometimes in the foreground, sometimes the background, but it was undeniably here. The emotion had swirled back in on the waves and in the wind. Sometimes it was Victorian set—the pioneer era of the Oregon Coast—sometimes modern. But they were thoughtful portraits of…

"They're all women," her mother exclaimed.

Natalya checked. And almost all of them were, but that wasn't the point. It was—

"That one isn't," once again Mom faced Natalya's latest work.

She'd forgotten how hard it was to complete thoughts around her mother. She'd almost understood something but it had slipped away. It didn't stop her mother from being right. *Joy* wasn't just women. Not with Cal dominating the foreground with his laughter. There was a balance to the image, but—

"That one isn't just lovely, dear. It's powerful, too. I want to be in the group, laughing and enjoying myself, but I also feel that the lone woman in the middle is who I am inside."

"You?" Her mother was one of the most gregarious women on the planet. She'd been born to run a B&B and be the life of the wonderful parties she hosted.

That brought out her mother's big smile, "Me! You captured what it feels like to be a woman, Natalya. That's amazing!"

Natalya stared at her self-portrait again. Maybe "lone" had been the wrong adjective. There was also a peace to the woman.

"Now get out of your t-shirt," for some reason that tickled her mother no end. "It's time to go."

"Go where?" She looked down. She still wore Cal's baking t-shirt. Oversized, comfortable, fallen off one shoulder…and totally ruined. She'd stained it with a dozen dabs of multicolored oils that would never wash out. "Crap! I owe him a new t-shirt."

"Oh, just let him see you wearing it like that now and then and he'll consider himself well repaid. It looks very sexy. As a matter of fact, maybe I should steal one of Cal Sr.'s. Now change."

Suddenly exhausted by her hours in front of the easel, she did as her mother said, first cleaning her fingertips with turpentine and wrapping her brushes in plastic because she knew she'd be back to them soon. "Where are we going?"

"It's Tuesday," her mom breezed out the door as if that told Natalya anything.

Natalya was almost never in town on a Tuesday afternoon. The last time had been six months ago when Jessica had come home for her mother's fourth wedding to her father. On Tuesday they had… Natalya turned to her painting. Knitting in Eagle Cove was a twice-a-week affair. It felt a little odd as if she was about to step into her own painting. On her way out the door, she snagged the knitting bag her mother had thrown together since she hadn't brought her own.

They were halfway to town when her mom slowed the car.

Natalya looked up and saw someone walking toward them along the narrow lane. It was…

"Cal! Stop the car, Mom."

Her mother didn't. Instead she simply waved at Cal as they drove past him.

"Mom!" Natalya twisted in her car seat to see him looking after them in confusion.

"Don't worry. He'll still be around after knitting," and she drove on.

CAL WATCHED the departing car as Natalya once again looked back at him.

She hadn't waved. Hadn't stopped.

Hard not to be disappointed, but she was going somewhere with her mother, and it wasn't out of town. Her MINI would still be out at the B&B. Still, he'd already walked a mile of the way out to see her.

Cal looked up at the sky. Horsetail clouds. Thin, wispy and still way up there, but weather coming. But when he looked out to sea, it was all clear—a rare crystalline blue sky descending right to the ocean without even a hint of sea mist.

Greg lived down this way with Jessica. He liked Greg well enough, but if Jessica was home, it would get awkward. Especially if the conversation turned to Natalya...which Cal guessed was who he wanted to talk *about* since he'd just lost his chance to talk *to* her. Harry wouldn't be back from his judicial duties in Newport until six. Alex was busy at out at Becky's brewery. And that's where Harry would be coming home to.

For lack of anything better to do, Cal turned and headed that way —a mile back to town and another out to the brewery. Becky was always good for a laugh, too. On his way back through town he'd raid tomorrow's day-old rack of some apricot Danishes he hadn't sold.

She and Natalya had been friends since forever and Becky was far less tricky than Jessica, especially when bribed with a Danish or two.

———

NATALYA HAD ABANDONED the socks she'd started Friday night. She'd only started them because she could do socks in her sleep and it had kept her hands busy while everyone talked around her, mostly about Becky's honeymoon in Hawaii.

Instead of continuing the socks, Natalya had poked through the skeins in Becky's converted gun cabinet. She'd bought the glass-fronted mahogany piece for ten dollars from the fire hall's annual garage sale, when everyone in town exchanged their junk with each other and the rest went to Goodwill in the Valley. Natalya had walked right by it but with typical Beckyness, she'd seen more. Dusting it off and changing out the rifle rests for shelves, she'd made a beautiful yarn cabinet where Natalya had just seen garbage.

She stole a ball of honey-colored worsted weight and borrowed a set of number eight sixteen-inch cable needles. She'd also fished out a scrap of blueberry yarn that would be big enough to knit "Baker" in big letters across the front of the hat. She sat on a love seat next to

Tiffany and cast on an extra six stitches for Cal's big head and started knitting.

Peggy arrived and she and Becky began comparing notes about the Judge and his son in overly happy tones. Andrea Martin complained about it as did May Conklin. Mrs. Winslow of course kept her own counsel on such matters.

Curiously, her mother didn't join in. Normally Gina Lamont would be at the center of teasing the two new brides for salacious details. She was listening, joining in, but she wasn't poking fun at them. Natalya was going to have to have a sit-down talk with her mom very soon. She'd been so wrapped up in her own world that she hadn't given much thought to anyone else's. But the middle of the knitting circle in Becky's living room wasn't the time or place, so she kept her questions to herself for now.

It wasn't as if she lacked questions of her own.

It was only after she was well started that Natalya wondered what it meant that she was knitting clothes for Cal. Okay, only a hat, and she'd knit them for boyfriends before. Or maybe, more accurately, she'd knit hats and sometimes mittens for lovers before. A lover was someone you had sex with. A boyfriend was more personal. Or had living in the city somehow screwed that up and gotten it backwards? A "lover" was supposed to be more important, but they'd somehow become less important. And boyfriend? Is that what Cal had become while she wasn't paying attention? Thinking of Cal as a "lover" was a whole diff—

Tiffany leaned over and looked at what Natalya had knit. On the relatively big needles the inch of knit-purl ribbing had gone quickly. She'd slowed down when she added in the second color to knit in the lettering and only had the bottom two rows so far.

"I don't think you're spelling it right," Tiffany said quietly. Other conversations continued among the knitters.

Natalya looked down but was fairly sure of her spacing. She'd done enough graphic design that she didn't need to map it out on graph paper for only five letters.

"You left out two of the dashes. Dash dot dash dot. Dot dash. Dot dash dot dot."

"What are you talking about?" The bottom tips of the five capital letters made a different pattern: dash, four dots, dash, and two dots.

"Morse code," Tiffany tipped her head sideways so that half of her face disappeared beneath her thick hair. "Sorry. I thought you were writing 'Cal' in Morse code."

"I—"

"If you went back and put in two more dashes, here and here," she pointed a slender finger, "you'd have it."

"I was spelling 'Baker.'" And wished she hadn't said it aloud because it made it too real. "In English."

"Oh," Tiffany nodded. "That makes sense then. In that case I think you need another stitch between the B and the A to get the spacing right."

Natalya considered and realized that the bulge of the B *was* going to end up too close to the A. She began ripping it out back to the ribbing, then stopped. She glanced at Tiffany who was back at work on a hat of her own—and intricate piece of Fair Isle knitting on number one size needles which meant it would be beautiful and take forever compared to her own number eights.

Tiffany had just assumed that Natalya was knitting for Cal. Did that make them a couple?

No, you've just been sleeping with him and having mad sex with him because he's a total stranger.

She really, really had to get her shit together.

She'd just managed to get the ribbing back on the needles without dropping any stitches when Tiffany spoke again.

"Now everyone will know."

"Know what?" But Natalya looked up. In the big double door that stood open between Becky's living room space and the microbrew tasting bar, stood a massive shadow. So big that it could only be Cal.

Out of the corner of her eye she could see her mother jolt in surprise and then sigh sadly. For an instant, she'd obviously thought it was Cal Sr. She and Mom definitely had to have a talk.

"Hello, Cal," Tiffany's raised voice slashed an abrupt silence across several overlapping conversations.

Everyone turned to look at her in shock. She'd never spoken so loudly.

Tiffany ignored them. She simply waved, then looked at Natalya.

"Get up, go over, and greet him," her voice was once again as soft as ever. "You know you want to," a barely audible whisper.

Natalya felt like a stick figure puppet as she stumbled to her feet. Someone, Tiffany, slipped the knitting out of her hands and then gave her a little shove. She managed a stumbling step and now, with everyone watching her, she couldn't very well stop.

She crossed past the low coffee table covered in knitting patterns and tea mugs. Slipped by her mother *without* looking down at her. Exited the circle of knitters, briefly resting a hand on Mrs. Winslow's shoulder for balance, and came to a stop in front of Cal.

"Hey, Cal."

"Hey, Gnat," he looked as flummoxed as she felt.

Then he held aloft a white bakery bag.

"I brought apricot Danish."

"Is it safe to come in?" Cal looked over her head at the circle of women watching him. All except Tiffany, who after shouting out a greeting was now quietly knitting again.

Natalya turned as if to survey the watching women before turning back. "Enter at your own risk."

"Mad dog in the yard, huh?"

"There is now," she teased and he felt better. He'd almost turned around when he saw all the cars. It had been weird that the brewery tasting bar was so busy on a Tuesday afternoon in January. But he'd already walked three miles to get here, then he saw Gina Lamont's car and poked his head in to investigate. The bar had been empty, so he'd followed the sound of voices.

Still, he hadn't anticipated walking in on an entire knitting circle.

He'd planned to bribe Becky for information. Or guidance. Or something. Maybe even just hang out, have a beer, and catch up with Harry when he got home from playing judge.

"C'mon. You've entered the lion's den, might as well make a job of it." When Natalya reached out to take his hand, it was somehow the most natural thing to enter the circle.

The small couch that Natalya had been sitting on was empty. He was fairly sure Tiffany had been there, but now she sat on the far side of the group, looking as if she hadn't moved a muscle all afternoon.

Conversation was slow to restart, though when he remembered the bag of Danish, much to Becky's delight, it kicked back to life.

Unsure what to do next, he turned to Natalya. "What are you knitting?"

"Socks," she gasped out at him.

He didn't know much about knitting, but a glance around the circle revealed two or three people making socks and they were much smaller. Tiffany sat with her head tilted so far forward over her knitting that her long hair was practically a shield across her face. But it was shaking like she was laughing silently at some private joke.

"Damn big sock you've got there, Gnat."

"Wrong needles."

"Oh." But she wasn't doing anything about it either.

He looked up at the brewery tanks on the far side of the glass wall that divided Becky's odd living room from the works, wondering how long he could pull this off.

When he looked back down Natalya was bent over almost as far as Tiffany. The "sock" was gone and something much more sock-sized lay in her lap. She was being very careful not to look at him and Tiffany was still giggling to herself.

Cal settled back. Maybe this was going to be fun.

"How you doing, Ms. Lamont?"

Natalya's mom blushed bright red before answering.

Definitely fun.

475

"WHAT KIND OF AN IDIOT ARE YOU?" The instant Harry had entered the door, he dragged Cal away from the women and up the stairs.

"Smart as a whip, Slater. Comes from not hanging out with you for a decade."

"You can't just," he waved down the stairs, "just…those women are dangerous."

Cal leaned back in one of the big armchairs in Harry's upstairs office. "Nice place you've got here. Weird, but nice."

Becky had built herself a one room apartment in the barn's old hayloft. Kitchen, bed, bath, all in one space. She'd punched skylights out through the barn roof and placed a long line of windows which opened into the hayloft. When Harry had moved back, they'd extended it. He had a majestic oak desk, comfortable leather chairs, even a nice rug. It could have been a big city lawyer's office, if the view wasn't bales of hay stored just past the windows in one direction and the funky little Eagle Cove airport out the other windows.

"Mason. What the hell are you doing here anyway?"

Cal tipped his beer in Harry's direction. "That's a fair question, Judge."

"That's my dad," Harry complained.

"Get used to it, Judge. You're right, too confusing. Judge Harry, that works." Then Cal shifted trying to find a comfortable position in the big chair. "It's a question that I'm not quite sure how to answer. It has to do with Natalya."

"What about her?"

Okay, this wasn't going to be as easy as Cal had thought.

"Wait a minute," Harry thumped his beer down on the desk, planted his elbows, and leaned forward to glare across at Cal. "You and Natalya?"

Cal shrugged.

"Holy shit!"

"Yeah," Cal agreed.

"But she lives in Portland. You aren't moving to Portland, are you?"

"Wasn't planning on it."

"Well from what Jessica and Becky have said, she's kicking ass and taking names up there. Big promotion last fall, stuff like that."

"Shit!" It was worse than he'd thought.

"You and Natalya," Harry slumped back, taking his beer with him. "I'll be damned."

Yeah, that about covered it.

"Mom! Talk to me."

"Keep your voice down, honey."

"It's a car. There are two of us in it. Nobody cares if I can be overheard." And Natalya had gotten into her mother's car rather than going to find Cal because…she was a coward. Or maybe because she just wasn't ready to talk to him yet.

Sleep with him? Yes.

Relate to him? No.

Real nice, Lamont.

"What is it with you and Cal Sr.?"

"What is it with you and Cal Jr.?"

Natalya collapsed back in her seat. "I don't want to talk about it."

"There you go," her mother shrugged.

Natalya scrubbed at her face and did her best not to scream. After a series of deep breaths she didn't feel any better.

"It's your fault actually."

"*My* fault?" Natalya turned to look at her.

Uncharacteristically, her mother had both hands on the wheel and was staring straight ahead as if navigating Eagle Cove was impossibly challenging. Mom always talked with her hands, her contact with the steering wheel often marginal at best. And she always glanced over whenever they were talking. Now her normally expressive face was slightly clenched and aimed straight ahead.

"My fault?" Natalya forced her voice to remain calm.

"At the wedding. The way you two were dancing. I've known Cal Sr. my whole life. He was sweet on me in high school, but then all the boys were. And Tricia, she was something to see. Ended up, an idiot for kicking Cal to the curb and then abandoning her son, but still a total knockout," Mom shrugged. "Never really gave him any thought until I saw him standing as best man to the Judge and then the way you and Junior were dancing, I thought…why not."

"My fault," Natalya felt like a parrot repeating herself. "Is it serious?"

Again the shrug. "He's a fairly serious man. Hard to have casual sex with a man who makes everything seem so important."

Natalya considered that as they turned off Beach Way and onto LBB Lane. The road dipped and curved down toward the ocean. Then Natalya figured she should do her thinking aloud because her mother had been kind enough to break the deadlock.

"Cal, my Cal…not *my* Cal. Cal Jr." She had turned into a babbling idiot.

"See?" Her mother declared. "That's why I didn't want to talk about this. It's hard."

"Cal *Jr.*," Natalya tried again, "doesn't make things serious."

"So it's just casual sex?"

"It—" but the confirmation wouldn't come out. Someone you were having casual sex with didn't hold you silently all through a night. He didn't track you all over town and when he finally found you was content for an hour on the couch while joking with a circle of knitting women. She, and everyone else there, had been intensely aware of Cal's arm stretched comfortably along the back of the sofa, never quite touching her shoulders but commanding the space as if he ruled the world. It hadn't been possessive, at least it hadn't felt that way, he just…sat that way. So comfortable with his maleness. So at ease by her side.

"See?" Her mother prompted.

"I wish I didn't. If he's serious, then it gets insanely complicated."

"Uh-huh."

"At least you two live in the same town."

"Sure," her Mom practically snapped out. "I see him almost every day. And what happens when this falls apart and we still have to live in the same town? Tell me that one, Natalya."

Natalya stared over at her mother. She'd never heard her mom have so much emotion about a man. Not even That Unholy Disaster evoked such depth of feeling.

Her mom took the turn at the ocean and began driving up the long climb to the B&B.

"And what if it *doesn't* fall apart?" Natalya couldn't help asking. Once she said it, she didn't know if she was asking Mom about Cal Sr. or herself about Cal Jr.

Her mother drove in silence the rest of the way. When they were parked in the driveway, she still didn't move.

Natalya rested her hand over her mother's where it still clenched onto the steering wheel. She continued to stare out the windshield. When she spoke, it was so soft that Natalya could barely hear her.

"What do you think is scaring the crap out of me?"

Okay. That Natalya could relate to.

CAL DIDN'T KNOW what kept driving him.

Despite all of his plans, he couldn't quite ask Becky about Natalya. Even over dinner, he had kept the subjects on town news, the growth of both of their businesses caused by Jessica's effective promotions, and the upcoming Stormy Days event. They even cooked up a few new ideas that they could do to cross-promote more. Beer bread that he'd send her way with a supply of New York style giant pretzels for the tasting bar, and she had a spare display cooler that he'd install at the bakery to sell her wares by the bottle: beer and soda.

But not a word about Natalya until he and Harry were almost out the door. It was dark and the temperature rapidly dropping, so Harry had offered him a lift back to the bakery which he appreciated.

At the brewery's threshold, Becky had given him a surprisingly strong hug then whispered, "I can only wish for the two of you what

Harry has given to me." Then she was gone and he was out in the wind.

Like it was serious between them or something.

Which maybe it was, because after Harry dropped him at the bakery and made sure they were on for poker Friday night, Cal hadn't gone upstairs. Instead, he'd climbed into the Corvette. Sometimes at night he'd take it for a spin up into the hills just for the fun of it—at night the road up to the pass was quiet and Marty the town cop would long since be tucked in with his wife. Tonight he drove out to the B&B.

Halfway out he spotted Gina's car coming toward him. He pulled to the side as much as he dared without risking his paint job on the scrub salal, and rolled down his window. Seeing that, Gina stopped across from him and rolled down hers as well. The clouds were thickening up enough to make the moon a hazy patch in the otherwise blank night sky.

"Going to town?" Was the best he could manage.

She actually blushed a bit, which told him exactly where in town, then nodded. Then she said, "She's in her room. Just go on up."

Which had him doing the blush and nod in return. Uncomfortable with the moment, he offered his best smile. "Have fun, Ms. Lamont."

"You too, Cal," and for a brief moment her smile went huge.

By mutual consent, they rolled up their windows and drove off in opposite directions without another word.

He ran into a couple of guests trying to find decaf tea in the kitchen. He gave them a hand and then headed upstairs.

Asking to get hurt? Maybe.

Was Natalya worth the risk? Now there was the dumbest-ass question he'd ever asked himself in decades of stupid questions.

He knocked, and at her vague, "Uh-huh," swung open the door.

The image was a hard punch to the gut. Every light in the room was on, an additional pair of stand lights illuminating the canvas she worked on. He couldn't see it from this angle, sideways on, but Natalya in profile was stunning.

She had her hair back in a ponytail that exposed the fine lines of her features. She wore his baker's t-shirt, smeared and splotched with bits of color like a painter's smock. It had slid off her shoulder, one of the things he loved about the times Natalya wore his shirts, revealing a splendid expanse of her dusky skin. She was so intent that she didn't even turn to look at him.

"What is it, Mom?"

"Your mom isn't here."

Natalya didn't startle. She simply turned to look up at him for a long moment.

"I passed her on her way to Dad's."

"Oh," was all she said. Then after a long moment turned back to the canvas.

Well, if she wasn't going to be upset by it, he guessed that he wasn't either.

She continued with the painting almost as if she'd forgotten he was there. But he knew that wasn't the case; he could feel her attention tracking him even if her eyes weren't.

Not wanting to completely distract her, he began to circle the room, really looking at the art. Art never did much for him, but he could really see things in Natalya's works. Enough of Ma Slater's paintings had been displayed on the bakery walls for sale over the years that he recognized when a young Natalya had tried to imitate her. He could then see when she moved away from that and began developing her own style. By the time he'd reached the later paintings and sketches, he decided that he'd know her work anywhere. Not because he knew her so well, but because the voice of the images was so purely Natalya.

That's when he found the poker and knitting circle painting. It was something new, related, but new. Though the faces had been shifted, he knew every one of these people. Not Alex, Vincent, Harry, and Greg, but rather the younger, the softie, the joker, and the forthright. The women were equally distinctive. It took him a moment to see himself, so big in the foreground. It had to be him, she'd made his shoulders almost cartoon large. The peace of the woman watching him, seated in a different place, in a separate group, but not separate. The connection between.

Natalya came to stand close beside him, still holding palette and brush.

"You're breathtaking," and as he slid his hand around her waist and pulled her close he didn't know if he meant the woman in the painting, the painting itself, or Natalya as she tipped her head onto his shoulder. They remained that way for a long time, rocking gently.

"Make love to me, Cal." She whispered the request. Not "let's go to bed." Nor did she simply grab his hand and drag him over there. She leaned against him, perfectly still.

He disengaged the brush and palette from her clenched fingers and set them aside. Cal considered sweeping her up in his arms and crashing them down into the bed together. Or tossing her in the shower much as he'd tossed her in the ocean forever ago.

But she'd said, *Make love to me, Cal.*

So he did. When he pulled her close, Natalya ducked just enough to tuck her head under his chin, her nose brushing his collar bone. As they stood in the middle of the brilliantly lit room, he began giving her a standing backrub, working his fingers deep into tight muscles. Her body swayed against him as he applied pressure to particularly tight spots.

He soon had his hands under her t-shirt…his t-shirt, and her skin was so warm and soft against his palms that he simply stopped and held her tight for a long time. Her arms hung lifeless. But it wasn't as if she was unwilling, but rather unable to do more.

When he slid his oversized t-shirt off her slender frame, she didn't assist or protest, but leaned back into him as soon as it was out of the way. After he shed his own t-shirt, she turned just enough to lay her cheek on his shoulder, her arms slowly locking about his waist.

He'd never had a chance to study her, at least not under an artist's bright lights. Now he did, learning every curve that his hands had come to know so well. As he knelt before her, she wrapped her arms tight about his head, pressing his face into her belly.

For a moment, just a moment, he wondered what it would be like if a child was there, his child. It sent a shiver over his skin.

Would Natalya just leave, abandon her own child?

He looked up at her. Her head hung forward, her hair a loose shower framing her face as she swayed side to side, her smile so soft.

No. Not her. Natalya was not his mother. Natalya Lamont would be an incredible mother.

Something opened inside him. Like finding the surprise filling when opening a stuffed bread or biting down on a blueberry muffin only to find a strawberry jam center—which was a good idea, he'd have to remember that one.

He wasn't about to make love to Natalya Lamont.

He was about to do so with the one woman for him. She'd slid under his skin forever ago, playing her merry pranks on him. He now knew, beyond any doubt, that he had been the target and Harry was only caught in the by-blow because they'd been such buddies. Becky and Peggy's double wedding two weeks ago had only been the tipping point. It was as if all these years she'd been the only one for him and he was just now realizing it.

As he slid her pants off her lovely hips, he hoped to god it was true for both of them.

Sex had always been good. Even when it was bad, Natalya found that it was good in some way.

Never before had sex been devastating.

Of course she'd never asked anyone to make love to her before. And even if she had, which she hadn't, that person hadn't been Cal Mason.

She curled up against him as if she could somehow get closer than they'd already been. Cal had shattered her with his gentle mouth and strong hands. Then, with a frantic need previously unknown to her, she'd laid down right in the middle of the carpet and dragged at him until he was atop her and sliding inside until he had no more to give.

She'd clung desperately, wrapping him tight in her arms and legs, as he drove them both into ecstasy. When at last he'd collapsed onto her, she'd welcomed the weight, unwilling to let him go for even an instant.

Beyond words, they'd simply lain there beneath the bright lights clinging to each other. When they finally released one another, he'd swept her up in his powerful arms and carried her toward the bed, shutting off lights as he went. Now it was just the two of them and a small bedside reading light that he'd insisted stay on.

Still not speaking, he'd stroked and traced her eyebrows, cheeks, nose, lips, and chin as she clung to him. She'd felt as if she herself was being painted, cast into art, one fingertip stroke at a time.

What if it doesn't fall apart?

Then Natalya decided that her mother's fear was right

What if this is real?

Cal woke in his favorite place, with his face planted between Natalya's breasts and her arms wrapped around his head. They were amazing breasts, as he'd taken great opportunity to study last night, but that wasn't it anymore. It was the intimacy of his nose pressed against the center of her chest. She smelled warm and ocean clean. She smelled of sex but she also, somehow, smelled of passion. Of heart.

She had given herself completely to him last night. It had been intimate but it had also been true. There was no longer any denying what there was between them. He needed her even more than he needed to bake. Besides, he didn't have to be in Eagle Cove to bake. There were bakeries in Portland, good ones, places he wouldn't mind working…if they weren't in Portland.

"Hey, Natalya."

"Hey yourself, Cal." She didn't protest about his using her proper name. She was no longer an annoying Gnat. She was his Natalya.

He'd been thinking of saying that he'd come visit her in Portland and check out some of the bakeries up there. He didn't want to, but he wanted her more. However, he changed his mind at the sound of her voice so thick with memories of last night. Definitely not the time to bring up any harsh realities. Instead he planted a firm kiss in the center of her chest and pulled back to look at her eyes.

Last night he'd never managed to reach the bedroom light on her side of the bed, as she'd fallen asleep wrapped about him and he'd been unwilling to disturb her. Now it let him see her eyes.

Her voice might be thick with soft memories, but her dark eyes were wary, glancing aside to avoid hard questions. Three-thirty in the morning didn't seem to be the time for confronting anything serious, so he kissed her on the tip of her nose and pulled her head down against his shoulder.

She nuzzled in against his shoulder and he enjoyed the sensations as her body slowly came awake against his. She slid completely beneath the covers, leaving him to look at the room as she roamed a line of kisses across his chest, her smooth hair sliding behind as if its passage permanently implanted the memory of each brush of her lips.

As he looked at the walls, he had the start of an idea.

It was crazy, but maybe it had some merit. Just maybe it—

She slid her lips and hands lower down his body and the thought skittered aside.

He took a deep breath and repeated his idea three times quickly to himself to make sure he had it firmly in mind. Then he gave his full attention to the delightful torture that Natalya was giving him beneath the covers.

"You want what?" Natalya wasn't really paying attention to Cal's words. Watching him dress beside her bed had her attention quite well occupied.

"Some of your paintings. We haven't had any good art on the wall of the bakery since Ma Slater died and everything was bought out. I'd like to put up some of yours." Sliding up his jeans didn't decrease her distraction, instead it made her think about sliding them right back off.

"Uh-huh. Sure." She attempted to focus on his face, but he hadn't pulled on his turtleneck yet. Natalya was more than a little mesmerized by his left shoulder, right there was where she'd slept so peacefully. "What are we talking about?"

"I want to put up some of your stuff for sale. Good for the bakery's look. Good for you if anything sells."

"Uh, okay. I guess. Sounds stupid to me, but if you think you can get anything for them, go for it."

"Thanks," he pulled down his turtleneck and shrugged on his jacket before turning to the paintings.

"Hey!"

He looked back at her, then smiled down. In two steps he had her pinned down, a hard kiss driving her back into the pillow and a none too gentle hand clamped onto her breast through the thick covers. Neither was quite hard enough to hurt, but both clearly demonstrated that last night had only heightened his need for her.

As quickly as he'd begun, he let her go, leaving her gasping for breath.

"A man's gotta bake."

"And birds gotta fly," she murmured because she couldn't think of anything more sensible to say with the heat he'd rekindled in her body. Rekindled hell. If she'd had any control of her muscles she'd jump him right now.

He grabbed three paintings, seemingly at random, then glanced at her as he stopped in front of *Joy*.

She shrugged. It was the painting of it that mattered to her, not the owning afterward. But it wasn't a wholly comfortable feeling.

"Don't just give that one away."

He nodded and picked it up, "I promise that I won't."

Then he was gone.

The bare spots on the wall bothered her.

But not as much as the painting that she'd carefully covered while Cal had prowled the room last night. His inspection had made her feel both terribly exposed and immensely appreciated. Her awareness of him had grown until he'd consumed more than her thoughts or emotions. Somehow, she'd needed to feel she was a part of him and he was a part of her.

And that's exactly what he'd done. Deeper than thought, deeper than her heart, they were a part of each other.

She'd been able to see it in Cal's eyes this morning. Knew he was going to say something stupid.

I'll give up Eagle Cove and Blackbird Bakery for you. It had been there, so clear just below the surface. It was a truth and a lie. She didn't doubt that he would, and she didn't doubt that it would kill his heart to do so. Even if he didn't realize it, she did.

How had they become so important to each other?

That jolted her from the bed and had her moving back to her canvas. She looked at the storm-torn seascape for a long time before reaching for her palette knife. Then she began methodically scraping everything she'd done off half of the painting.

CHAPTER 13

Wednesday and Thursday passed in chaos. And Friday wasn't starting out much different. There was a line in front of the bakery when Cal had returned from breakfast and the diner itself had been hopping.

Jessica hadn't put all of the events in the actual weekend. She planted teasers for several days before the Friday night kickoff to Stormy Days at Eagle Cove and man oh man were they working. The town had started filling up on Tuesday and was packed by Thursday night. The weekenders were in their houses days ahead. Vacation rentals were maxed out. The Sleepy Owl Hotel had its No Vacancy sign lit and the Lamont's B&B was booked out as well, including Natalya's room.

He'd offered Natalya his second bedroom as a studio, mostly filled with sporting gear he no longer used. No time to put it up for sale, he piled it to the side and she'd moved in there. Perhaps moved in was too strong a word—just an easel, her paints, and the one canvas that she wouldn't show him—but it changed everything. It had been his until his dad had given him the apartment and moved out, but he didn't tell her that in case it made her uncomfortable. Personally, he liked having Natalya working in his old bedroom.

At night, they'd crash into bed together, too exhausted to do more than cuddle. But they rose together and she'd go and close herself in that back bedroom.

Living together.

He'd never done that before. Some clothes and a toothbrush at each other's place, sure. Even the suitcase on the chair wasn't all that unusual when he'd dated the occasional tourist. But that one slender, hidden canvas made it so much more. Though it wasn't as if he saw much more of her than if they were living apart. Friday knitting and Friday poker were cancelled as the town hit capacity and struggled to keep up.

The Flicker movie house was running a winter film festival, without one Christmas movie among them. *Perfect Storm, The Eiger Sanction, Cliffhanger, The Ice Storm, The Day After Tomorrow,* and a list of others. Twenty-four hours of films running in a different order each day. You could either show up for a full day or purchase a time slot or two across successive days.

After eating at Carrier Pigeon Pizza, he'd gone back into their kitchen and tossed pizzas for them for an hour or two to help them catch up.

Cal barely had a chance to breathe. Dad stopped making excuses and simply showed up to help with the early morning prep, and they both stayed late.

"Gonna break your streak, Dad?" Cal didn't look up as he rolled out rye dough into a long thick snake on the floured marble block.

"Be damned if I know, Junior." His dad was doing the detail work of rolling up croissants: plain, chocolate, and almond. He was better at the fine pastries while Cal liked forming the larger breads and baguettes. Though custard fruit tarts were a lot of fun and he enjoyed doing those when they were in season.

Cal began chopping his dough snake into three-inch chunks. He rolled each into a fat ellipse and dropped it on a Silpat-lined baking sheet. They'd have to rise another half hour and then they'd bake up as hearty sandwich rolls.

"They're certainly defining new levels of confusion," his dad finished sheeting the croissants and shifted over to apple crisps.

Cal hadn't considered that. "You think it's a Lamont woman thing?"

His dad shrugged uncomfortably.

"Well, that would explain some stuff, wouldn't it?" Cal took a break long enough to slug back a mug of orange juice. Between the big ovens and intense work pace, he was sweating it out faster than he could drink it.

"It would," his dad stuck with water.

"So if it's just Lamont women—"

"We're both either lucky as hell or totally screwed and I'll be damned if I know which."

Cal didn't know either, so he pulled the sourdough out of the proofer and began setting the loaves up for baking.

But he was leaning toward lucky as hell.

CHAPTER 14

The storm slammed into Eagle Cove on Saturday morning. Thankfully it wasn't a Pineapple Express, like the one that had lashed the coast during Becky's wedding. Those storms were unrelentingly wet on top of the major wind blasts. Instead, this one was curling up the California coast where all of the worst windstorms came from. The powerful blasts ripped huge waves out of the ocean as it hammered the coast.

The drama was incredible, but by some miracle the power lines were holding up and the rain wasn't heavy enough to drive the tourists away. Instead, they ducked out for a few awestruck minutes watching the thirty- and forty-foot waves crashing down on the closed beaches, then scuttling inside. Which was right where the merchants wanted them.

Natalya had watched it all happening outside her win—Cal's window. The second bedroom that she was using as a studio was on the north side of the building and offered her a view up Beach Way, past the Puffin Diner, out to the breakwater. Eagle Bay had been formed by a narrow rocky spine that had resisted the Eagle River's efforts to move it out to sea. On the inside was a small dockyard where a half-dozen fishing and tour boats huddled. On the outside, waves were slamming into it and shooting up high enough to see over Grouse Hardware's roof.

She didn't even look at the painting.

It was done.

Out in the living room, Cal had an incredibly tacky poster over the couch of a husky dog carrying a six of beer in its jaws. It was curling with age. It was easy to see that Cal didn't really live here. He slept here, but he lived for the bakery.

During the two days they'd holed up in the apartment together last weekend, she'd gotten the impression that they'd used the living room more in two days than he had in any two months prior. A comfortable chair and a TV were all he typically bothered with.

Neither the apartment nor his living room was hers to change—no matter how much it needed it—but she took the risk that he might like her painting more than the husky. The poster was so old that it cracked and split as she took it down. If he really loved it, she'd paint him a new one.

In its place, she hung the painting.

Again, she couldn't bring herself to look at it.

She cleaned up, changed, and slipped out of the apartment.

At the bottom of the stairs she detoured briefly into the bakery. It was, she checked her watch, two o'clock. Closing time, but they were packed. Cal Senior was working the counter; her Cal was in the open kitchen making sandwiches.

She slipped into the kitchen side of it.

"You doing okay?"

Cal looked at her a little wild-eyed, then grinned hugely. "Am now!"

She went up on her toes and gave him a quick kiss not wanting to slow him down.

He went back to his sandwiches, "You look pretty wrung out yourself."

"Flatterer."

"Is it working?"

"No, I really am wrung out. I finished the painting."

"Really, that's great. Do I get to see it now?" He made it a pout which was cute enough on a six-foot-four baker to make her smile.

"Sure. Upstairs, whenever you want. I'm gonna go home."

Cal froze and turned slowly to look at her.

"Just to help mom. I'm sure she's slammed too."

"But you'll be back tonight?" His whisper was desperate, barely louder than the hubbub of the packed bakery.

She nodded. He was so sweet about it, a nod was all she could do. She wanted to wrap herself around him and just hold on until the storm abated: the one outside, the one in her chest, and the one on the painting.

"Okay."

She waved and was halfway to the door when he called out to her.

"Oh you were right. I screwed up."

"How?"

"I underpriced your paintings."

"That's okay. It doesn't really matter. You actually sold some?" She hadn't expected that at all. She glanced out at the bakery walls but didn't see anything that was hers. Of course through the milling crowds it was hard to tell. There. The only one she could spot was *Joy*.

"Yeah," Cal came up to her and looked in the direction she was facing. "I told them that they couldn't take that one until tomorrow night. After the Stormy Days Festival is done."

"That one too?" Natalya had told Cal she was done with that painting, but maybe it wasn't done with her.

"We always had a deal with Ma Slater, one third-two thirds."

Sounded good to Natalya. Even at crappy prices it was the first time she'd ever sold her own art.

"Okay if we cut you a check on Monday?"

"I was—" her throat went dry. "I was going to drive back to Portland tomorrow."

Cal opened his mouth to protest, but was decent enough to close it again and nod. "The storm is probably dropping snow in the passes. You'll want to do that in daylight." His voice came out rough, almost hard.

"I don't want to leave either, Cal. You've got to get back to work. We'll talk tonight."

"Okay," he nodded to himself as if trying to gather energy. "Okay. And I'll cut the check for you tonight. Two grand."

"You joker," she went on her toes to kiss him again and headed out the door.

CAL WATCHED HER GO. Watched his heart walking out the door.

She waved, and was gone.

He went back and finished the latest sandwich order and delivered it to his father.

Something was itching. Something he didn't like.

"Dad, I'll be back in a minute."

"Don't have time for that right now, Junior." It was a tease, an actual tease from his dad.

"She's just gone out to help her mom."

"Oh. Okay. Did you tell her to say hello for me? Haven't had as much time as I'd like to pay attention to Gina this week."

Cal clapped his hand on his dad's shoulder in reassurance. After all, *they* both lived here and had all the time in the world. Natalya lived three hours away.

"Gonna take your damned minute anytime soon?"

"Oh, right," and Cal raced up the stairs to the apartment. He turned sharply for the second bedroom, but it was clean. Pristine. The easel had been folded. The paints and brushes tucked back into their small wooden case. The only sign of Natalya being here for the last five days was the dissipating odor of turpentine.

He stepped back into the living room and ground to a halt.

The stupid beer-toting husky that Harry had slapped up there in high school was gone. In its place hung what could only be Natalya's painting.

It was a self portrait.

Actually, it was many self portraits.

The background started as a murky, dark storm on the left. Slowly, agonizingly, it clawed and fought but was ultimately driven back by a lightening to the right. A tiny patch of blue sky, not quite at the top of the painting, but continuing off the right edge, promised hope and sunlight after the storm.

But that was the background.

Across the foreground was a woman. Repeated over and over. The leftmost figure, as tattered by the storm as the violent surf, looked to be on the verge of losing all hope. Survival was only a glimmer of a chance. Nothing more.

But as her repeated image moved across the storm, slowly crossing toward the viewer as she proceeded to the right, she became more and more well realized. More and more alive. And the rightmost figure looked out of the painting much as Natalya's self portrait had looked out of *Joy*. He almost hadn't put *Joy* up for sale because he didn't want to lose that image, but here it was again. Clearer, more fully detailed.

There was space for one more figure, but there wasn't…

But there was.

Faint within the clearing sky. Barely visible. The hint of a woman, not a full figure like the others, but just of the face. And the more he looked at it, the more clearly he saw her. It wasn't some suggestion of Natalya—it *was* her.

And she was smiling. Smiling at him with love in her eyes.

He stumbled back downstairs.

"Damn long one minute, Junior. I'm buying you a watch."

Cal blinked.

The crowds were still going strong but he couldn't really hear them over the ringing in his ears.

"Sorry, Dad. I just found out I'm going to marry Natalya."

His dad stopped and turned, right in the middle of taking an order. "She know that yet?"

Cal could only shake his head. "Doesn't make it any less true."

"Damn it!" His father scowled, but not at him. Maybe he wasn't the only one making a leap.

"Like son. Like father?"

His father realigned his scowl at Cal. "Just go make me three roast beef, two turkey, one with extra cranberry sauce, and a goddamned ham and Swiss sub with double meat and extra mustard."

"Sure thing, Pops." Cal felt like dancing as he returned to his station.

Dancing.

Maybe soon there would be another wedding to dance at with Natalya. Their own.

It just had to happen.

AT THE LOW point of LBB Lane where it dipped down to the beach, the cars were parked so thickly to either side that Natalya could barely sneak her MINI through the gaps. It was worse than July 4th. And then she saw why.

Vincent McCall wore his volunteer fireman's gear as he stood before an orange cone barrier strung with "Do Not Cross" tape and a "Beach Closed" sign. A hundred or more people in parkas and slickers were huddled together for support as seventy mile-an-hour blasts tried to knock them off their feet.

And beyond them, the tide was coming in.

This stretch of the coast always had five- to six-foot breakers. Storms kicked that up into the ten- to twenty-foot range. These monsters were running consistently at the high end of that range with a few even bigger. When they landed she could feel her car shake in the heavy thunder.

A tree stump the size of a small RV was being tossed about by the pounding surf. Forty-foot logs, long since stripped of all branches and bark didn't just roll, they tumbled.

Everyone had a camera out. Which they were going to find to be a very costly mistake. The spray, sheeting landward with the wind, would be thick with corrosive salt water. Even by coastal standards this was a big one. What the tourists didn't know was that Monday, after the storm had passed, that's when the truly monstrous waves would come crashing in.

She spotted Jessica wearing a huge grin.

Yes, this was a Stormy Days at Eagle Cove that would be talked about for years to come. The one that all future festivals would be measured against.

Natalya waved, wasn't seen, but it didn't matter. She continued to the B&B.

Her mother was out, but everything was in order. There were even little lemon custard tarts and Murchie's tea set out in the parlor for teatime.

There were guests staying in Natalya's room, so she headed for her mother's. It was actually a cozy suite of three rooms on the second floor with its own balcony. Instead of the powerful-women theme that defined the rest of the B&B's rooms, her suite was like the parlor: cozy elegance. It had been the private quarters of the daughter of the town's founder and Natalya's own mother had preserved it in its original form.

A living room big enough for entertaining six but not eight had a large fireplace, a tiny kitchenette, and a sweeping view of the coast and ocean for miles to the north and west. The bedroom to the north side was an aerie in the trees, looking toward the state forest. Her mother had made it into a comfortable office from which she conducted the B&B's business. But it was also a library of books and movies with a moderate-sized screen hidden tastefully in a mahogany armoire.

Natalya went into the master bedroom and sat on the quilt—an elegant heirloom piece in dusky reds and deep golds. The private balcony was accessible only from here. And it faced due west into the storm.

She watched it shred the waves for a long time.

CHAPTER 15

*C*al looked at his father slumped across the table from him. They were in the back corner of the Brass Plover, nursing a burger and a beer. It was packed to the limits, but May had found a spot for them close by the kitchen.

"Tomorrow's got to be easier."

"Sunday," Cal agreed with a groan. "Tourists leave early on a Sunday."

"Why were we greedy enough to stay open on a Sunday?"

"Wasn't greed," Cal shook his head.

His father eyed him as he sipped his beer.

"Okay. It wasn't just greed. Did you want to be the one to tell Jessica no?"

Senior didn't have to consider before shaking his head no.

"I got a new side business."

That got his father's full attention. His father had never thought much beyond baked goods, but Cal was always adding new ideas and the bank balance growth had convinced his father to start doing the same. They were almost big enough to buy out the Plover when May decided to retire. Side by side eating establishments; they'd make good.

"Put up some of Natalya's art."

"Uh-huh."

"Sold it."

His father just watched him.

"All of it. All that she gave me."

That earned him one of his father's rare smiles. "Seems I remember something about your grandpa doing the same for Ma Slater. Gave her a start back when she was younger than you and the Judge was courting her."

"That's where I got the idea."

His father held up his beer in a toast. "Guess I didn't raise no fool."

"Nor did Grandpa," Cal toasted him back.

They both drank deep and set their glasses down in unison.

"Now about these women…" his father started up again after finishing his fries.

"Yeah," Cal couldn't agree more.

"Yours come back yet?"

"Not that I've seen." And Cal had been sitting where he could just see his apartment out the window. Not a single light had come on.

"Haven't seen much of Gina either."

"Nope," Cal agreed.

"Guess we oughta go find them."

"Make sure they're okay," Cal nodded. "What with the storm and all."

His father just snorted. "You ever met two more capable women?"

"Hey," Cal protested as he polished off the last of his beer and stood. "I just need an excuse, not a reason."

His father actually laughed, then slapped him on the shoulder to lead the way.

"I found her in here. Graceful as ever."

Natalya was vaguely aware of someone speaking. She cracked

open one eyelid and saw her mother silhouetted in the doorway, with two faces looking over her shoulders. Two men. It was—

Someone flipped on the bedroom light.

Natalya yelped and covered her eyes but it was too late, the image of Cal's evil grin was seared into her retina.

It took her a moment to get oriented. It was evening, darkness had fallen and the storm still raged against the glass doors to the balcony. Her mother's bed. She'd fallen asleep; didn't even remember curling up and hauling a corner of the quilt over herself.

When she dared squint her eyes open again, her mother and Cal Sr. were gone, but Cal Jr. still leaned lazily against the door jamb.

"Get out. Just give me a minute."

"Sure thing, Gnat," he flicked off the light and closed the door.

"Jerk."

They were all sitting in the suite's living room by the time she staggered out, still half asleep and squinting against the brightness. She went to the small fridge in her mother's kitchenette. She found a bottle of pear juice and a piece of cold fried chicken. She sniffed it. Her mom's homemade. Major score! A plate and a paper towel and she was set.

She joined the others in the living room, but sat on the armchair beside her mom rather than on the couch by Cal. Natalya needed a little distance from him. Something more than inches. A whole afternoon worrying at the problem of her being stuck in Portland had served nothing except to wear her into exhaustion.

Reaching out, she took her mom's hand.

"Eww! Greasy!" Her mom yanked her hand away. "Use the towel first."

"Sorry," Natalya wiped her hand, but returned to eating. The problem was, everyone else focused on her eating as well.

"Talk about something," she waved a hand at them.

"Okay," Cal Senior spoke carefully. "Let's talk about long-term plans."

Natalya glanced at her mother, but she didn't know what was

going on either. Then her eyes widened just as Natalya's own suspicions kicked in.

"No!" She blurted out, spraying flaky fried chicken crumbs all over her lap. "No. We're not talking about that."

"Oh, but we are," Cal agreed with his father. He slumped down on the couch, lacing his fingers behind his head and looking ever so relaxed.

"I'm listening," her mother said softly.

"You're what?" Natalya slapped a hand over her mouth as a few more bits of crust came out. "Sorry," she mumbled through her fingers. "Didn't mean to shout." She sipped some pear juice and swallowed to make sure she'd swallowed it all.

"At least *I* am," her mother replied. "I at least want to hear what they're thinking."

"There isn't a *they*. There can't be a *they*. The world doesn't work like that."

The two Cals watched her through narrowed eyes, then looked at each other. Whatever silent father-and-son conversation was going on, it had them both grinning.

"Besides," Natalya already knew the answer. She hated it, but could find no other. "My answer would have to be 'no.' So please don't ask."

At least Cal stopped looking so damned relaxed, but his father didn't even bat an eye.

"You got something against Eagle Cove, girl?" Senior made it sound like a crime.

"God no! I love it here. My mom," Natalya wiped both of her hands on the paper towel and then reached out to take her mom's hand, who inspected it briefly before accepting the handclasp. "My mom is here and I miss her. Why do you think I come back so much? But my job is in Portland."

"Pretty attached to that job?"

"What is this? The Spanish Inquisition?"

"Comfy chair next," Cal agreed, but his father's glance quelled him before he could continue the old Monty Python routine.

"Pretty attached to that job?" Senior asked again.

"I'm most certainly attached to the paycheck."

Cal Sr. nodded thoughtfully. "Can't do it from here? Remote… whatever they call it?"

"Telecommuting and distributed teams. Not really. Don't even want to do it much anymore, but they pay me really well."

For reasons beyond her Cal brightened up, but his father hushed him.

"Junior tells me he sold some of your paintings."

"You sold some paintings?" Her mother practically cried out. "Why didn't you tell me?"

"He did it," she waved a hand at Cal. "Just told me this afternoon, so there's no way I could have told you sooner. He sold *Joy* as well."

"Oh, I liked that one."

"It's okay, Ms. Lamont," Cal leaned forward. "Wait until you see the one she replaced it with."

"Did you like it?" Natalya really hoped Cal had liked it. She'd tried to put everything she couldn't say "yes" to into it so that he'd at least have that much of her.

"I'll never take it off that wall unless we move somewhere else."

"Crap! You—" *We?* Natalya dragged a free hand through her hair, the one she hadn't wiped off.

Ick!

"Cal, I just said there isn't a *we*. There can't be. And no, you can't leave your bakery. Your heart would die out there in the world."

Again he leaned back in that arrogantly male way of his, his smile utterly denying the truth.

"I did mention that I sold some of your paintings," he repeated himself.

"Sure," Natalya waved a dismissive hand. "Then teased me with some ridiculous number not even worthy of comment. If you're going to make a joke work, you have to at least make it believable."

If Cal's grin got much bigger he'd have pear juice in his hair and the remains of a greasy chicken down his shorts.

"What if I told you it wasn't a ridiculous number?"

"How much was it?" Her mother asked in a whisper.

"But you said it was underpriced."

"Uh-huh!" Cal slouched back even more. "I bet I could have gotten half again for *Joy*."

"What was the number?"

But Natalya couldn't even speak to answer her mother's question.

"Three thousand," Cal Sr. said.

"But you said 'two thousand,'" she accused Cal Jr., finding her voice.

He nodded, "Bakery keeps a third as commission. That's two thousand to you. I'd wager you could make a better living with your art here in Eagle Cove that doing web stuff in Portland."

Natalya didn't know what to say. The idea was too big. Too close to dreams she'd never dared have. Never shared with anyone... including herself. Yet, like some miracle, Cal had found them.

"Now?" Cal asked his dad.

Cal Sr. gave a judicious nod.

Then they both rose and came to stand in front of their chairs: Cal Sr. in front of her mom, Cal Jr. in front of hers.

Her mother squawked as the two men knelt.

Natalya couldn't even manage that.

"Of course," Cal spoke ever so softly. "There is a way to keep *all* that money in the family."

Natalya looked over at her mother, just as her mother turned from looking at Cal Sr. while he knelt before her. Her eyes were glowing with joy. True joy.

The men, in turn, grinned at each other before speaking.

"Do you two ladies—" Cal Sr.

"—like double weddings?" Cal Jr.

Her heartbeat pounded in her chest as if coming to life for the first time and it was an amazing feeling.

Natalya shared a smile with her mom, then they turned back to face their men before speaking in unison.

"We do."

KEEPSAKE FOR EAGLE COVE

CHAPTER 1

*E*nvying other people wasn't something Tiffany Mills had much experience with and she didn't like it. Especially not when they were hugging her so fiercely.

She'd always thought of Natalya Lamont as the calm and collected one of her friends. Well, not her friends, but Natalya's. Maybe it was Natalya's own wedding that had her bubbling like a giddy schoolgirl.

Of course Natalya's mother also was exhibiting similar behavior as it was her wedding day as well—a mother-daughter marrying a father-son event. But Gina Lamont was a generally more effusive type, so at least it was expected of her.

Tiffany wanted to ask Natalya what it felt like to be so happy, but resisted the urge. Delaying a bride making the rounds wouldn't be fair...and, with Natalya's present mood, probably not even possible. It was awfully kind of her to notice Tiffany at all—she was as close to being a friend as Tiffany had allowed in years.

"I really appreciate you being here," Natalya finally let her go, then gave her another quick hug with a loud "Ooooooo" of sheer delight before spinning back into the congratulatory crowd surging through and around the Lamont B&B.

"No, it was my pleasure," Tiffany ended up saying it to herself, always remembering too late to speak her thoughts aloud when she was with others. If it meant she had lived too long alone, she wasn't going to think about it now.

It was a gorgeous day for spring in Eagle Cove, Oregon. The big Victorian overlooking the Pacific Ocean was packed with wedding revelers. The parlor and the kitchen overflowed out onto the porch on the warm May day. That was where Tiffany had retreated to, a small bench on the wrap-around verandah that let her overlook the events on the lawn without getting snarled up in them.

Becky Billings had lobbied to have the event out at her brewery, as her own wedding had been, and they would have moved it there if the weather hadn't cooperated. But it was one of those magical spring days after a long, wet winter that made everybody smile. Natalya and her mother Gina had thrown a lunch—catered by Greg, the town's master chef, of course—then had the wedding, which left plenty of time for dancing on the front lawn. It overlooked the ocean and was well filled with people during the warm afternoon; the cool evening would chase everyone inside, but not for a few hours yet.

Gina and Natalya had both wanted to be wed in the family home, the last house before the big headland that defined the end of Eagle Cove. The town was spread over two miles of shoreline and the town's founders—a mother and daughter as well—had built two grand Victorian houses on the high bluff below the rocky palisade of Orca Head. One house became the Lamont B&B, and Judge Slater owned the other.

Not for the first time, she felt a pinch. Gina and Natalya Lamont belonged here in Eagle Cove, direct descendants of the daughter. They even still lived in the family home, at least Gina did, and Natalya had grown up in it.

Tiffany was connected to the town as well, but it was a connection from long ago and one that she had kept secret for the three years since she'd moved here.

Of course she wasn't exactly in town, which made her feel a little less guilty. She lived alone, homesteading a full mile farther out of town into the forested hills. She had found a small gap between two plat surveys of adjacent state forests and, much to the Oregon Department of Forestry's surprise, had purchased the ten-acre anomaly from the state. She lived in "unincorporated" forest—technically, she wasn't even in a county.

Maybe she should declare her *own* county, or better yet her own country! Occupancy: one human, thirty chickens (unless some more eggs had hatched this morning), a half dozen goats, and her guard dog. There was also an exceptionally lazy cat the black-over-white color of an orca whale—and roughly the same blobbish shape—who kept Tiffany's lap warm on cold nights. Fitz only roused herself for mouse hunting, a task at which she excelled.

Oregon State law had some considerations that might make it implausible to declare independence and Federal law definitely did. Of course, if she did declare her own state, she'd have to decide whether or not to sign onto the Interstate Commerce Commission for fair trade with other states. Would that be necessary for when she sold her chicken eggs and excess garden produce to Greg at The Puffin restaurant in Eagle Cove? As a bonus she could elect a governor. Of course, with only one resident, the choice would be obvious and the balloting blessedly painless.

Tiffany raised her right hand, "And the ayes have it."

"Good. They can keep it," Jessica Baxter stepped up, slapped Tiffany's raised hand like a high-five, then eased herself down on the bench as close as Tiffany had observed best friends often did.

Tiffany's other shoulder was against a wall, so she had nowhere to go.

"If my husband ever tries to touch me again, he's going to get a big-ass *nay.*"

"You're huge!" At eight months pregnant, Jessica seemed to be expanding daily, but she sat so close beside Tiffany, that Tiffany could see Jessica's belly almost from the owner's perspective. Jessica had been the first of Natalya's friends to get married. She'd gotten pregnant right away and every one of those eight months showed on her belly. She was five-ten—Tiffany wouldn't have minded those extra four inches herself—and slender as could be, except for the pregnancy. From the back she looked perfectly normal, as she had one of those pregnancies that went straight forward.

"Tell me something I *don't* know," Jessica groaned with a happy sigh of relief at being off her feet.

"Okay, you probably don't know why your five-times-great-grandmother stopped speaking to her daughter," for Jessica Baxter was Gina's niece and also a descendant of Pearl Lamont. And then Tiffany wished she could cut her tongue out. It was something Jessica wouldn't know, but it said so much more than Tiffany wanted to reveal. Ever.

Jessica blinked at her in surprise.

Tiffany could only hope that it would be written off as "just one of those things that Tiffany Mills says." Her own four-times-great-grandmother's journal was what had led her to Eagle Cove in the first place. Lillian Lamont had been one of the founders of the town. But if Tiffany wished to survive, her past had to stay hidden, cut off, forever.

"Wait." Jessica furrowed her brow as she massaged her back. "Five times…you're talking about the founders of Eagle Cove."

Tiffany really didn't do well with people who lived outside of her imagination.

Jessica, she knew, had been a journalist and was incredibly tenacious. Now that she'd latched onto it, there wasn't a chance that she'd let go. Tiffany didn't want to reveal how she knew what she did or that she had any connection to the town prior to the founding of the State of Tiffany in the woods. She suspected that her normal ploy of shaking her long hair forward and "going shy" while focusing on her knitting wasn't going to work this time. Especially as she hadn't brought her knitting to the wedding. Running might be an option. But if she started, she might never stop. Then where would she—

"Hi."

Tiffany looked up at the man now standing eye-level to them, two steps down from the porch. He was lean and had brown eyes beneath tousled hair of the same color. He wasn't dressed like a wedding guest, but rather in unseasonably early shorts, a plain t-shirt, and hiking boots. He looked like a trekker, certainly had the strong legs of one, but she glanced around and saw no sign of a pack.

"I don't want to crash the party, but I think I'm in the right place. This is the Lamont B&B?" He appeared a little lost and a lot overwhelmed, two feelings that Tiffany knew well.

Grabbing any distraction she could, Tiffany rose to face him as he climbed the last two steps. He was only a few inches taller than she was. "It is. It's also the Lamonts' weddings, both of them."

"Oh, that explains the crowd. Maybe I'll, uh, just come back in a few days." He looked around as if trying to find somewhere to go.

"Did you have a reservation?" Tiffany almost grabbed his arm as he started to turn away. Jessica hadn't moved from the porch seat close behind her and Tiffany was still trying to distract her from the accidental revelation.

"No. Not really. And not yet. I'm a couple days early. Once I got in my truck..." he waved vaguely back toward the long drive clogged with guests' cars, "I just drove."

"I think the B&B's full with wedding guests, but let's go check." Tiffany took his hand and led him inside. At the last second she risked a glance at Jessica, and saw that she hadn't gotten away with anything. But more than that, Jessica was looking at Tiffany as if she was suddenly an alien or something. She grabbed the man's hand more tightly and plunged into the crowd.

———

DEVIN ROBISON HAD RARELY FELT SO OUT of place in his life. He'd slept in the back of his pickup last night in the Boise National Forest. Up with the sun, he'd landed in Eagle Cove nine hours later in the middle of a wedding. It was terribly disorienting, and not just the road-weariness-meets-wedding scenario.

He'd thought that growing up in Chicago had prepared him for great expanses of water. Lake Michigan was Chicago's front yard—three hundred miles long and a hundred wide. He'd even boated on the Caribbean a few times. But as he'd crossed the country, the towering peaks of the Rockies had been as disorienting as if he'd traveled to the moon. The real shock had been when he'd broken out of the Coast Range forest before the final descent into town and seen the entire Pacific Ocean before him; he'd nearly crashed his Toyota in surprise. Unless you happened to stumble on an island, Tokyo was five thousand miles away. The expanse was impossible to comprehend.

Neither Chicago nor the towns he'd driven through in the last four days had prepared him for the tiny size of Eagle Cove. One mile from forest to ocean and two miles along the beach...and it wasn't densely populated. The next town of any size was thirty miles up the coast. He'd been on the verge of turning around from an attack of agoraphobia, the fear of open spaces—or maybe just plain nerves. It was news to him that such obscure places even existed. Eagle Cove was so remote, so wild. He hadn't seen a single fast food place in the town. Maybe they weren't allowed; every business, actually every road except the main drag of Beach Way, had been named for a bird: Blackbird Bakery, Warbler Market, Rusty Pelican Tavern. Strange place.

Devin had come west looking for a fresh start, or at least a break. He needed the latter desperately, but he'd left "middle America" somewhere staggeringly far behind.

Finding the massive Victorian home had been easy. "Find LBB Lane at the far end of downtown," which was their grandiose term for a business district four blocks long. "Go to the end of the road Little Brown Bird Lane. You'll know when you find the right place."

And he absolutely had. The house was gorgeous. It was exactly the sort of structure that had led him into architecture school. Three stories of classic, early-1880s American Queen Anne Victorian. He'd fallen in love the moment he'd seen it. The house was one of the best examples he'd ever seen of that style. Unlike so many of the ones in Chicago, the whimsy had not been allowed to overwhelm the beautiful lines and overall cohesiveness of the design. Yet it was still playful, with circular turrets, balconies, and a wrap-around porch.

A verandah clogged with people.

Devin floated through a kitchen packed solid, anchored in this reality only by the hand of the woman leading him.

The woman leading him.

Few greeted her, though they readily moved aside, allowing her a straight line passage. His first sight of the kitchen had made him wonder if it was even possible to cross. Yet for whoever-she-was, the crowd made way. He was half tempted to guess that it was magic, as people almost didn't notice that they had moved aside for her. They certainly didn't break their conversations for her passage.

He usually at least knew the name of someone he was holding hands with. Had there been introductions? He didn't think so.

He'd headed for the woman on the verandah the moment he'd spotted her. Her nearly waist-long fall of thick tawny hair had acted like a guiding beacon. Only a model had hair like that, not normal people, yet she looked to be perfectly in her element. Then, as he climbed the steps, he'd become aware of her eyes watching him from beneath the wide brim of her felted hat—twin glints of blue-gray carefully hidden by shadow.

Her blouse and skirt were…rustic, for lack of a better word. Perhaps bohemian, as the maroon belt made by a wrapping of fabric defined a trim waist and made her billowy sun-yellow blouse and light spring-green skirt look very nice. Maybe someone's mild-mannered and carefully cloistered cousin. Except for her hands. The one holding his was firm and, even if she didn't hold on hard, the strength of her fine fingers was obvious. And hard calluses. She worked with her hands a lot.

"What's your name?" She didn't look up at him. They'd come to a small nook in the back corner of the kitchen. It felt oddly quiet here though he could hear a dozen different conversations. She let go of his hand to pull out a register. The woman spoke softly, but he could hear her despite the other noise.

"Devin. Devin Robison."

She didn't offer her own, but began flipping through the pages. Then she stopped as if shocked. She looked up at him sidelong.

Yes, more gray than blue, at least the one eye inspecting him.

"Who are you?"

Devin figured that if he could answer that one, he wouldn't be twenty-three hundred and seventy-nine miles away from everything and everyone he knew. "Am I in the book?"

She nodded with a mesmerizing slide of long hair. "Yes."

"Is there a problem?"

This time the hair shimmered side to side.

"And?" What a curious person she was.

"Gina Lamont gave you the best room in the house other than her own. Until today it was her daughter Natalya's, though she's been living with her now-husband in town."

"I take it that's unusual."

She tipped her hat back enough that he could at least see a hint of a smile. "More than a little."

"Maybe we should check with her."

"Wedding day. I think she has enough distractions. Let me show you the way." She took a classic skeleton key from the hook and once again led him away, though without taking his hand this time. He kind of missed it.

Devin wanted to inspect the house as they went, but found himself unable to look away from the *still* nameless woman leading him up the twisting stairs and along a narrow hallway.

She knocked perfunctorily on the door and had the key inserted when someone called out, "It's open."

She eased open the door and peeked in.

"Tiffany!"

At least Devin now had a name for her. It fit. Fragile as glass in some ways, but enduring and undeniably beautiful. Also completely different from any woman he'd met before. The women in his Chicago social circle were consistently sharp, perfectly maintained, and elegantly attired.

A short blonde, dressed in a tight-fitting black dress with a dangerously bountiful cleavage, yanked the door wide and grabbed Tiffany by the wrist to haul her into the room, even though she was already retreating. Then the blonde, who seemed part small tornado, leaned around to look at him past Tiffany.

"Ooo. He's cute. Way to go, Tiff. Natya, check this out. We'll get out of your way, Tiff," she made the last lurid and suggestive.

The room was as classically Victorian as the house itself, high-ceilinged and it incorporated one of the circular towers as a small seating area. A white wedding dress lay spread across a dark quilt on the bed. Art covered the walls. Paintings and drawings of women. Powerful women.

Before he had a chance to notice more, a tall, dusky-skinned brunette spun to look at him. She too wore black. At a wedding? Above her left breast was pinned a corsage of tiny bud roses…spray-painted as black as her dress. Maybe some kind of joke? He was glad Tiffany instead wore the colors of spring; they looked very cheery on her compared to the other two women's, admittedly sexy, black.

The instant she spotted him, the brunette's expression went from surprise to narrow-eyed suspicion. She looked as if she'd leapt straight out of one of the paintings on the wall and was ten times more daunting in real life than the numerous two-dimensional women who seemed to be glaring at him also.

"No, I—" Tiffany was protesting as the blonde pulled her farther into the room.

It was easy to see what was going on and Devin was hard-pressed not to laugh.

The tall brunette stepped up close in front of him and his desire to laugh dissipated rapidly as he looked up at her. She stood at least five-ten and that was, he risked a glance to check, barefoot.

"If you so much as touch her, I'll personally—"

"No, Natalya," Tiffany cut her off. "He's a guest. I'm just showing him to his room."

The tall Natalya glanced over her shoulder, then she turned back to glare at him, her protective ire only slightly tempered.

"Hi, I'm Devin," he held out a hand. "I'm actually not a guest."

Natalya was halfway to shaking his hand, but stopped.

"A Gina Lamont hired me."

"Mom hired you?" The handshake never completed.

So the wedding dress had been Natalya's, Natalya Lamont's—Tiffany had said it was *both* Lamonts' weddings today. At a quick glance he saw that she and the cheery blonde both wore wedding rings. He double-checked, but Tiffany wore no jewelry. Neither rings nor earrings, at least not that showed through her hair.

"Well, isn't that convenient," the blonde said suggestively, winking at Tiffany, who blushed fiercely.

She fist-pumped at Tiffany's reaction.

"Yes! We'll be wearing black for you next. Another one bites the dust!" She began a small stomping dance, her bright red cowboy boots marking a muffled circle on the rich Oriental carpet.

Devin finally got the joke of wearing black—the "death" of another single woman.

Tiffany shook her head fiercely, creating a cloud of hair, but kept her peace.

Natalya's continued glare told him that her interrupted threat was still in place.

Devin felt as if he was suddenly swimming in deep waters. He'd come here for a fresh start, a reset on a life that had gone sideways (way the hell sideways), and he was already in it neck deep.

Welcome to Eagle Cove, buddy.

<hr>

TIFFANY SLIPPED the key into Devin's hand and abandoned ship. She felt bad about doing that to him but she'd suddenly felt so claustrophobic, the room and the two strong personalities crushing in on her, that she had to run.

Downstairs was little better. The kitchen crowd surged into the parlor. Dance music sounded from out on the lawn. Danny McCall on vocals, the Judge (as everyone called the retired Judge Slater) on stand-up bass, and his wife playing a rocking lead acoustic guitar. Becky would be on the drums soon now that the music was gearing up. Tiffany played her harp with them on occasion, but not today.

Through the window, she could see that Jessica was still on the verandah bench. Tiffany didn't dare go out that door or she'd be trapped in a conversation she didn't know how to avoid.

She retrieved her harp from where she'd tucked it behind the basement door and made for the B&B's back door, ready to flee Eagle Cove just as her ancestor Lillian Lamont had over a century before… though Tiffany would only go as far as her farm, not all the way to San Francisco as Lillian had. Tiffany was *never* going back there.

Tiffany made it through the crowd, using the harp in its case as a shield, and opened the back door to escape just as Becky swept down the rear stairs. She hooked an arm through Tiffany's.

"Come on! They're waiting for us."

"There's no need…" Tiffany tried to point out that the band was already playing and people were already dancing on the lawn; therefore, no one was waiting for them, especially not for Tiffany. But she never had the chance.

Becky didn't let go, so Tiffany was helpless to head back to her home in the hills. Instead she was towed out the back door and around the house to where the band had set up under the spreading branches of a big old cherry tree on the front lawn. Becky deposited Tiffany on her usual seat, a nicely carved stump of a tree that had gone down in the Christmas Day Gale of 2005. She knew that because of the date carved by the chainsaw artist who had reshaped the stump.

At a loss for what else to do, she pulled her Celtic harp out of the padded case. The harp stood about three feet tall and had twenty-six strings, exceptional for a harp that she could carry on a shoulder strap and play while standing. As she was seated, she screwed in the lapbar crosspiece that would rest on her knees. The harp was one of her prized possessions, one of only two from her entire childhood—the only two she had brought north with her to Oregon and later to Eagle Cove. From the inlaid Celtic knots of shimmering abalone to the smoothness of the dark walnut wood, she loved everything about it. It was one of only two things she had ever felt to be absolutely and completely hers.

Tiffany listened for the harmony line in the Cat Stevens ballad. She slid in on the beat and kept her head down.

As it always did, the music soothed and lifted. She'd come to enjoy the rare community events when they played in the group. She knew her harp added a warmth to the sound. They occasionally tried to have her take a solo. An offer she always refused except for a few Harry Chapin songs, where she took the soulful cello part, or anything by Sting; she preferred being an accent rather than a statement.

Usually she watched the townspeople. There was always something amusing to learn, something to watch. Some were the great forces that shaped the town: Judge Slater, Gina Lamont, and Maggie Winslow—the town's second-grade teacher and a primal force for decades. Then there was the upcoming generation of Jessica, Natalya, and Becky, the self-declared overseers of the town's future. But there were other, subtler forces at play and she enjoyed watching those as well.

Tiffany had moved to Eagle Cove shortly after Ma Slater's death. Tiffany had seen right away that Peggy Naron was going to be the Judge's next wife...even though it had taken him three years to learn the same. Cal Mason Jr. and Sr., who had just married Natalya and Gina Lamont today, weren't chaotic influences. Rather, the two big men were solid, stabilizing influences to their dynamic women.

But today she didn't watch even though she could hear their laughter, pick out their voices. She kept her head down and focused on the music.

Until the moment a second guitar joined in on a chorus of the Beatles' "Here Comes the Sun." A glance to her left had her fingers jangling on the harp strings.

"Hi," Devin Robison sat cross-legged on the ground close beside her with a beautiful Martin twelve-string acoustic in his lap. He easily picked the backup line, filling in spaces between Peggy's lead and her own harmony.

"Hi," she tried in response but it came out strange and discordantly squeaky. Her fingers found their way back into the music. Once she was solid, he ducked over to the harmony himself, teasing her with a descant to her line, counterpointing the harmony. She responded by leaving him in the harmony and sliding in above Peggy's melody.

He chased her through a tricky round of rock and roll, Maroon 5 and Five for Fighting, which were always a challenge on the harp. She teased him with half harmonies in Jimmy Buffet and Fleetwood Mac, forcing him to fill in around her gaps so that the harmony line wouldn't shatter.

Only when Peggy finally called a break was Tiffany aware of how sore her fingertips were—they must have played at least a double set for them to be so sensitive. They'd played long enough for the sun to slide well down toward the ocean, making it painfully bright to look westward. Somewhere in that shining blur, the crowd began applauding wildly. All of the musicians were bowing. Even Devin had risen to his feet to join the others. Tiffany used the harp in her lap as an excuse to stay seated and simply bowed her head.

The applause went on far longer than normal. When each of the band members made a point of stopping by to shake Devin's hand and tell both him and Tiffany how wonderful their playing had been, Tiffany knew she'd messed up again. She'd always been careful to play simple harmonies, avoiding notice; but with Devin challenging her, she'd played far beyond what she normally let others see. Had her life been different, she might well have accepted the San Francisco Symphony's request for her to audition for them—one of her only regrets about abandoning her past.

As the band dispersed into the crowd, some calling for drinks, others simply heading for them, Devin remained by her side.

"I'm fine," she assured him.

"You are fine. You play wonderfully."

"I meant you can go join the others."

He shrugged as he sat back down on the grass close beside her and she couldn't help but look over at him.

"You have a nice smile." She bit down on her tongue. Tiffany had meant to compliment his playing.

"Thanks. I'm waiting for you to smile to see if you do."

"Really, I'm okay by myself." Was he flirting with her? The whole flirting thing had somehow passed her by without her ever learning how to do it.

"I don't know anyone else here."

"Oh, I'm sorry."

"Why are you sorry? You're the one person I *do* know. Other than Natalya Lamont."

He said it in a way that was funny.

"Oh," he said softly, "you don't have a nice smile."

Tiffany slapped a hand over her mouth to hide it.

"You have a *great* smile. Do it again."

Tiffany just shook her head, but her smile really was incredible. Even over the hand presently covering her mouth, Devin could see her eyes sparkling.

It made him feel as if he'd done something right. As if leaving everything he knew back in Chicago and driving into the coastal wilderness might, just might, not have been the most idiotic maneuver of his entire lifetime. Well, no, the absolutely *most* idiotic moment had been six weeks earlier and *that* had launched him on the path to Eagle Cove. But maybe there was finally a glimmer of light in his personal tunnel.

"I'm sorry I left you with Natalya. She's mostly wonderful," Tiffany spoke from behind her covering hand.

"Except when she's teasing you?"

Tiffany nodded uncertainly, then shook her head, covering half of her face with her hair.

There were television ad shampoo models who didn't have such incredible hair. It was hard to look away from its shimmering length as it reflected Tiffany's every move and mood.

"No, Becky was teasing me. Natalya was..." Tiffany tapered off, looking puzzled.

"Protecting you," that much had been obvious.

"Really?" Her eyes went wide and her hand dropped to clutch the harp that she held against her chest like a warrior's shield. Because he was seated below her, he could see every expression despite the wide-brimmed hat... No, more than that, he could see every emotion. There was a purity that couldn't be real. Humans were never that honest. Not brothers, not ex-fiancées, and not conniving—

He shook his head, trying to shed the sudden, dark thoughts.

"She was guarding you like a mama bear," he said and liked the image though he wondered how the woman in question would feel about the description. "Natalya threatened to feed me to an orca whale."

"I have an orca-colored cat. Does that count?"

Devin laughed. "Absolutely." He almost asked if he could come see that, but decided against it at the last moment. He remembered the way she'd bolted from the upstairs bedroom—her hand had actually been shaking as she pushed the key into his palm. Shy. She was remarkably shy and it again made him wonder that she'd taken his hand in the first place. A momentary lapse? He liked being her momentary lapse.

That smile slipped back. This time he didn't comment on it for fear of scaring it away again. There was no calculation behind the smile, just a brightness to her eyes and a curve to her very nice lips. Again that strange dichotomy as she switched back and forth between seeming just a little simple and then having a quick humor. And the way she'd played, it had taken his breath away. She was beyond performance-level skilled; she should be playing concerts on international stages or something. He tried to remember if his brother's weekend band had ever been that much fun to play with before it all went so wrong, but not that he could recall.

"Excuse me?" Tiffany's voice was so soft that he'd almost mistaken it for a trick of the breeze.

"Yeah?"

"If you don't mind my asking, why are you h—" But Tiffany was cut off by a stern voice.

"Now we'll get to the bottom of this."

Devin looked up and wondered what new disaster was headed his way. The very pregnant blonde from the porch was approaching, arm in arm with a gray-haired battle-ax of a woman.

Tiffany jolted to her feet. But rather than running off, she handed her harp to him and rushed to assist the pregnant woman.

"I'm not an invalid," she protested as Tiffany and the older woman practically forced her into the seat Tiffany had just vacated. "I've got another month of this? Why didn't anyone warn me!"

Devin noted that Natalya wasn't the only over-protective one in this group as Tiffany quickly fetched the padded stool from Becky's drum kit and offered it to the gray-haired woman.

"You will not find me perching on that, Tiffany Mills."

"We'll trade," the blonde began to lever herself up.

"Sorry, Mrs. Winslow," Tiffany whispered as the older woman pushed the blonde back into her seat. "I'll get a chair from the house and—"

"I may be gray on top but I am not dead. I stand all day in the class-room," she folded her arms and glared at all three of them. "I can certainly stand here. Now sit yourself down."

In response, Tiffany sat straight down where she was standing, close beside the stool, but not on it. She ended up on the grass almost close enough for Devin to rub shoulders with her.

He silently offered her harp. She took the instrument and wrapped it protectively in her arms once more. It was as big as her torso, ornately carved, and well-used. The sweeping arch climbed past her shoulder, reaching higher than her head. He wasn't a harp aficionado, but while his Martin was one of the best commercial twelve-string guitars made, it was clear that her harp was a custom piece of a whole other class.

"Now what is this I hear?"

Devin cringed, having no idea what was about to happen.

"Jessica..."

That must be the pregnant blonde.

"...tells me that you have knowledge of what divided our town a hundred years ago."

So this wasn't about him. Still, his nerves were having trouble relaxing. Mrs. Winslow reminded him of too many dictatorial teachers from his past. Though now that her obvious displeasure was aimed elsewhere, he discovered in himself a desire to protect Tiffany just as Natalya had. Though there was something about her, that enigmatic quality to her reactions and the way she'd leapt to Jessica's aid, that made him suspect that perhaps Tiffany didn't need as much protecting as all of her friends thought. And her playing had nothing to do with timidity in any form.

Tiffany nodded reluctantly—he was learning to read her. Like her music, there were complex interactions that were as much body language as facial expression.

"A little bit longer than that actually." Then she rested her chin on the smooth curve of the neck that formed the top of the harp as if to clamp it shut.

"You know that I value our town's history."

Tiffany nodded carefully.

"And yet you did not tell me, though we've known each other two years."

"Two years, eleven months." Then Tiffany actually bit down on her lower lip and stayed very still.

"Is your reason good?" That had Jessica looking up sharply at Mrs. Winslow. She'd clearly never thought there might be a reason.

Tiffany tipped her head, rolling it enough to lean her cheek against the upsweep of the pegboard…then shrugged uncertainly.

"You will not make it too much longer," Mrs. Winslow did not make it a question.

Tiffany shook her head, but Devin could see the deep reluctance there.

The older woman considered them all for a long moment, nodded once, and turned to go.

"No, wait," Jessica called after her. "There can't be any reason for her to not tell us now what—"

"Hector Jackson," Mrs. Winslow said as she walked off, "has asked for my hand in the next dance when the band starts once more. I must find him and confirm if that is still his intent." And she was gone.

Devin couldn't help laughing. "Why in the world does she talk that way?"

"Second-grade teacher," Tiffany said quietly. So quietly that Jessica didn't hear though she sat only a few feet away.

"She was my second-grade teacher," Jessica answered in kind. "Started long before me and still is, though she's past retirement age. She wants to exemplify the English language to her students. She firmly believes that contractions will not communicate the importance of learning the language properly to young minds," Jessica sounded a little like the woman herself. "But after so many years, she can't switch it off when she's out of the classroom either."

Devin could hear the love that poured out of Jessica as she spoke. He was used to home, where people always seemed to have a hidden knife waiting in every conversation. Here people protected one another like, well, he was going to say kin, but experience had taught him that was the least true of all.

"Why would someone choose to teach second grade their whole life?"

Jessica spun on him, suddenly looking as dangerous as Natalya.

Devin held up his hands, "I meant that with nothing but respect. I just remember me in second grade and I was no blessing."

"I'll bet," her tone was as dry as the prairie in August. "Who are you?"

"Devin," he was getting tired of that question. As if everyone already knew everyone. Then he glanced at the number of wedding guests spread across the lawn and guessed that some fair portion of the town's population was here...and knew each other. And if they'd all shared the same second-grade teacher—he couldn't even guess how many second-grade class*rooms* there'd been at Alexander Graham Bell Elementary. That had him laughing again.

"What?" Jessica sounded only a little friendlier than the dangerous bride had been.

"I just realized that my elementary school back in Chicago was a couple times bigger than this entire town. And my high school was ten times that."

"Chicago?" Jessica lit up like he'd just said the magic password. "What part of the city?"

"North, mostly. And central," and it felt like dust on his tongue to even say that much.

"The Gaztro-Wagon," Jessica said with a happy sigh.

"The Southern Mac & Cheese Truck." Devin did miss the food already even though he'd been gone for only three days. To find another fan of the Chicago food trucks out in the wilderness of the Oregon Coast was something of a relief. Maybe civilization wasn't so far away.

"The Mexican-wrestling-mask and sombrero guys," Jessica offered next. "Their truck had a weird name."

"Tamalli Space Charros! Those guys are the best." Devin felt a sudden homesickness so deep he almost felt ill.

"No," Jessica said as if commanding him not to go there. "The Flirty Cupcakes food truck. They're the best."

And he did feel a little better for meeting her.

TIFFANY HAD WATCHED THEIR REACTIONS.

Jessica's acceptance of Devin grew rapidly based on no more than shared gastronomical experiences in a city thousands of miles away. Such simple things to tie people together. Why did she never find that? Her connections were never simple.

Devin, too, was much more complex than he'd first appeared. He shifted between joy at discovering a fellow urbanite and...Tiffany almost wondered if he was going to be sick at other moments. There was some history there that wasn't sitting comfortably. He—

"Where are you from?"

"Nob Hill, San Francisco," Devin's question surprised the answer out of her.

"Well, that explains the long hair," Jessica declared, as if San Francisco was still rooted in the 1960s and '70s.

It wasn't true. When she'd been growing up there, she'd had the same stylish haircuts as the other girls. Eventually she'd learned to dislike the attention they drew, at school and from her stepfather. She'd burned her hip clothes and grown her hair long to hide behind, but it had been too little, too late. Even after she'd managed to have him jailed, which created a major scandal for the global bank he was on the board of, she'd kept the frumpy look. By graduation she'd had the longest hair of her entire school except for two girls from India.

Last night she'd been reading her ancestor's journal that had become her guide on being a woman and come across a passage she had long since forgotten about. It directly contradicted the town legend that the town's streets had been so curiously named because the mother and daughter had fought and were no longer on speaking terms. That was the part that she had referred to when speaking with Jessica. Tiffany liked to remember Lillian's sense of humor when she was feeling sad herself.

August, 1887

Clarence loved to brush my hair. My husband was not an expressive man, but my long hair was an endless wonder to him. Now he has gone and left me with a seven-year-old daughter and a town that is little more than a dozen shacks and a bounty of timber and fish.

We are lost here in the Oregon wilderness.

But it is not in my blood to give up, not when my little Pearl grieves so. To cheer her, I have made a game. Together we have designed how the town of Eagle Cove shall someday appear. No longer a rough logging and fishing camp huddled by the bay.

We have drawn a map. Pearl has run a ruler line down the middle of the main street. "I'll name all of the streets on this side."

"Then," I told her, "I shall name all on the other."

"My half is seabirds," Pearl declared. When I indicated that she had selected the landward side of the town and yet would name it for seabirds, she

did not care. "Don't use any of my names," she has commanded. Taking her instructions to heart, I have named my "half" for land birds.

Eagle Cove is only forest and clearing, so it matters not that her streets wander and curve strangely. In response, I have drawn one that follows the entire shore to the far distant bluff of Orca Head though I cannot imagine the town every reaching so far. I have named my wandering street LBB Lane, complaining that there are too many Little Brown Birds to sort out. That made my daughter's laugh ring once more in our lonely home and we are both happier for it.

The game has served its purpose and distracted her from her grief. A task well done though it fails to distract me from my own worry and grief.

I so miss the man who loved to brush my hair.

Tiffany's own hair was now as long as her ancestor's. Though there had never been a man to brush it for her. But when she brushed her own hair each night, she would pretend it was Lillian's Clarence caring for her. Of course he'd be far too old for her, well over a hundred and fifty if he'd lived, which would have made Tiffany laugh had she been alone. Her cat would appreciate the story; she made a mental note to tell Fitz tonight when she retur—

"How many in *your* high school?" Devin asked.

"Too many!" His question acted as a whiplash out of the past. There had been too many who wanted to take down the rich girl with the long hair. Too many with grasping hands who knew how to corner a shy girl and—

"Man do I know that feeling!" Devin agreed.

For a second she jolted. Had he too been—

"Feels like you're lost in a crowd."

No, he was happy.

Joking.

Which was as elusive for her as flirting.

She did her best to nod as if she'd felt the same about her school days.

After high school she'd changed her name, packed her harp and her several times great-grandmother's diary (her second cherished possession), and taken her trust-fund inheritance with her to Lewis & Clark Law School in the woods of Oregon.

She didn't go back for her stepfather's funeral after he was killed by a couple of lifers inside the jail. He'd probably bragged to the wrong person about his "conquests." Or maybe they just didn't like bankers.

Tiffany didn't go back to her mother's third high-society wedding, either.

And, though she'd considered it seriously, she also didn't go back and confront the harassers and abusers from her high school in a court of law. Though it had been very tempting, she knew that without hard evidence there was little she could do. However, she *had* listed them prominently on multiple molester sites. Several reputations had been destroyed but she refused to feel guilty, especially after other women had begun adding their own accounts to those listings.

In all of California, the only person who knew her present name and whereabouts was a lawyer who utterly despised the family lawyer. Tiffany could trust him to keep her confidence out of mere spite, completely aside from professional attorney-client privilege considerations.

"Won't get lost in the crowd here," Jessica was telling Devin. She had not departed along with Mrs. Winslow but had remained to chat, yet another skill Tiffany could wish for but had never acquired. "My graduating class had thirty-three of us."

"There he is!" Gina Lamont shouted out as she rushed up. "Devin, you made it!"

"Told you," Jessica made it an aside. "No hiding here."

Tiffany had done a fair job of that so far, but she could feel it crumbling around the edges, chipped away by good intentions of kind people. She had roots here now, roots grown from seeds planted by the discovery of the old journal in the family library. But today's revelations were more than—

"Oh good, Jessica," Gina patted her on the shoulder. "You're sitting down. Tiffany, keep an eye on her. Don't let her help with anything."

Tiffany nodded. She wouldn't have anyway.

Jessica groaned in disgust at being pampered, though she made no move to rise either.

Gina turned to inspect Devin, who was struggling to his feet. She did that to people. Her five-ten height was the only trait Gina shared with her daughter. Natalya was a dusky-skinned, slender, and dark brunette with nearly black eyes and a sharp sense of humor. Her mother was a voluptuous, blue-eyed redhead with almost as much joyous energy as Becky. She too had changed into wedding black, but with a sexy, flirty cut that must be making her new husband crazy.

Sure enough, Tiffany spotted Cal Mason Sr. crossing in their direction with his son and his new daughter-in-law in tow. Unlike the Lamont women, the two Mason men were cut from nearly identical cloth—or perhaps baked from the same dough as they co-owned the town's bakery. (Tiffany kept her smile at the apt analogy to herself. Devin noticed far too much, as if from him she had no secrets at all.) They were both well over six feet tall and built like Swedish linebackers. In their matching charcoal-gray tuxedos, they were completely astonishing to look at. They'd have dominated any setting…that didn't have Gina and Natalya in it.

A small husky puppy trotted along behind Cal Jr. It had a good bite on its own leash.

Natalya noticed the direction of her attention, "I gave her to Cal as a wedding present."

"Damn thing is gonna chew through everything in the place," Cal Jr. said with obvious affection as he tugged back and forth on the leash to play with the dog.

Then the puppy noticed the strap on Tiffany's harp case and lunged for it. Cal scooped him up just a moment before she could cry out.

"Scamp! Should name you Gnat Jr. for your troublemaker mom." Tiffany had heard him call Natalya "Gnat"—a nickname that apparently went back to kindergarten.

"You do and you're spending your wedding night on the couch. Alone," Natalya wasn't doing a very good job of hiding her smile while making the threat.

Cal looked at the dog. "Sorry, buddy. Guess you won't get your name until tomorrow. Got me some things to do tonight."

"Such as locking up all of our shoes," Natalya tickled the puppy's nose.

"This the boy?" Cal Sr. ignored his son's and new daughter-in-law's antics as he slipped his hand around Gina's waist and looked Devin up and down. Both women looked ridiculously pleased at the attentiveness of their new husbands.

Would Tiffany look that way on her own wedding day? If she ever found someone she was willing to have a wedding with. It was an event she'd never been able to picture clearly. Lillian Lamont's journal offered little guidance as it was not even the highlight of the day's entry:

March 1, 1879

Wed to Clarence Lamont by the ship's captain before he delivered us and our supplies to this unnamed strip of desolate beach close beside the Eagle River in Oregon. Though the beach is straight, I have called it Eagle Cove because I need some sense of boundary in this terrifying wilderness.

"He is 'the boy'," Gina confirmed, then asked, "Aren't you?"

"I think so," Devin replied calmly despite the arrival of so many new people. It was an equanimity she had never managed herself. "Of course, that depends on who you think I am."

Tiffany had been puzzling at that since his arrival. Had almost managed to ask the question herself before Mrs. Winslow's interruption. Not a guest. Hired by Gina. But he'd been given the second best room in the B&B (Gina lived in the best rooms—her ancestor's master suite). For what? She already had her summer help at the B&B lined up.

"What have you built, boy?" Cal Sr. asked.

"Now, Cal," Gina tried to stop him. "We both asked Devin plenty of questions when we interviewed and hired him."

"That was over the phone," Cal grumped. "I like to judge a man in person."

Tiffany glanced around. Natalya, Cal Jr., and Jessica were all as lost as she was. So it wasn't something that she'd missed by only coming to town twice a week for knitting group and to sell her produce.

"It's okay, ma'am," Devin told Gina, who smiled at being called "ma'am."

Devin waved a hand at the B&B.

"I've never built anything as pretty as that, but I've restored several of them. As to modern houses, I've designed a couple dozen and built them myself, or my crew did—some designs many times. Degree in architecture, but make my living as carpenter and general contractor. Wanted to build my own company to see what it was all about before joining my father's big business."

Tiffany could see the flinch. That last statement had thrown Devin at least as badly as her own admission about knowing a key piece of the town's history. But unlike her own instinct to duck and dodge, Devin continued easily and no one besides herself seemed to notice.

"Doesn't look like this old girl needs much help," he waved again to the grand Victorian, directing everyone's attention there.

But not looking himself.

Tiffany could see him watching the others cautiously, then slowly relaxing. She was glad that he didn't check in her direction.

"Oh," Cal Jr. winced at some memory as he spoke, "she has her issues now and then."

"Wimp!" His wife informed him.

"You weren't the one who had to go swimming in the basement last winter to fix the sump pump. That water was so cold that—"

"Whiner!" Natalya and her mother said in unison, then shared a smile while Cal Jr. sputtered, then Gina patted his cheek in obvious appreciation.

"Maybe I should just talk with the pup," Cal addressed the dog currently shedding fur on his dark tuxedo. "You women are dangerous." Then Cal Jr. looked down at Tiffany. "Tiffany, are you dangerous, too?"

Tiffany could feel her jaw flapping. She hadn't even realized that Cal knew her name.

"Of course she is," Jessica announced, resting a hand on Tiffany's shoulder. "Don't mess with her or you'll regret it."

Tiffany noted Jessica's smile and felt the warm squeeze on her shoulder. Tiffany wasn't dangerous, but she did like the way the tingling sensation of being included felt. Natalya, on the other hand, was the most dangerous of them all and was gearing up to renew her attack on poor Devin.

"What is he here to build then?" Tiffany tried to turn the conversation back to the safer topic. It earned her surprised looks from Natalya and Jessica that she did her best to ignore.

"You can show him on your way home," Cal Sr. dug a key ring out of his tuxedo pocket with one key on it and tossed it to Tiffany. There was a small, stamped-metal label threaded onto the same ring. *USCG Keeper's Cottage—Orca Head.* She showed it to Jessica before passing the key across to Devin.

"We purchased it from the US Coast Guard," Gina announced happily.

"Gonna be a nice annex for my wife's B&B. So you make it pretty, Devin. Deal?"

"Deal," Devin shook hands with Cal Sr. It looked very strong and manly. "But where is it?"

Tiffany pointed up at the lighthouse perched atop the rocky headland of Orca Head. "If you thought *this* house was remote..." And that's when she understood that for the first time, there would be people, well, one person, much closer to her farm than the Lamont B&B.

She was definitely going to declare her own country. And she'd install a large moat and train her cat in border patrol.

"Should I have brought my truck?" Devin couldn't help looking back down the narrow lane as the B&B disappeared from sight, swallowed by the towering pine trees. He felt as if he was never going to see it again.

"Is it a four-wheel drive?"

"Sure. A Toyota pickup." They were walking in side-by-side ruts, up something Tiffany insisted on calling a road despite the deep grass and low brush that was growing between them. The woods were a profusion of thick trees, a half dozen kinds of conifers and a couple more leafy types—the only ones he recognized were maples and some variety of oak. The undergrowth was so thick he wondered if a machete would even be sufficient, though farther in, deep under the pines, the way looked passable, but not along this road/path/track into the wilderness. Even the pine trees looked different than the ones in the parks back home. He really should have traveled more, but he'd never felt a need to leave the city…until it ejected him forcibly.

"Yours is the little blue SR5?"

"Uh-huh," she didn't miss anything. He'd parked among the fifty other vehicles on the far side of a line of trees, yet Tiffany had picked it out through the branches as not belonging.

"You may want to fix the road first, before trying it with that. Peggy has a road grader you can borrow."

"Peggy?"

"Small woman with red hair, married to Judge Slater." He couldn't place her, though the Judge had been hard to miss: as big as Cal Mason Sr., though not quite as tall as Cal Jr.

"And she has a road grader?"

Tiffany looked at him as if he was being stupid. Well, maybe he was. They were hiking into a wilderness that could be filled with wolves or cougars or whatever. All they were armed with was Tiffany's harp in a padded backpack case. He didn't think the Swiss army knife in his pocket would count for much in a life-and-death situation. "Music soothes the savage beast," was a misquote he'd rather not test personally.

And he was being told he could "borrow" a road grader from the Judge's wife? Had he landed in the land of the Amazons?

"I've never driven anything bigger than a Bobcat."

"Oh, I have one of those if you ever need it. Though I'm not sure I could get it from my farm to the lighthouse. I'd have to take some measurements along the trail."

"Your farm. You have a farm?"

She waved vaguely up the hill.

"Up here?" Now Devin himself could hear how stupid he was sounding. He wasn't used to being so out of his depth. Today was being a harsh lesson.

"Farther back," Tiffany didn't explain more. "But this is where you'll be working."

The path crested the ridge and at first he didn't see what she was talking about as the trees to the east were still thick as could be.

But to the west, toward the ocean, there was a broad clearing along the top of the ridge. There were small saplings, the size to be planted in a Chicago suburban front yard to make it look finished. Here they were tiny things that looked as if they needed to be either mowed down or pulled up like weeds from among the tall grass.

At the far end of the clearing, a towering lighthouse utterly commanded the point. It was a classic: circular, white, and several stories tall with a glass housing at the top. Inside, he could see a big glasswork lens spinning. Each time it swung by, there was a bright flash of the light.

"Why is it flashing? It's still daylight."

"It's a navigation beacon, so it's always flashing. At night I like to watch it as it sweeps across the trees then out over the water. When there is a light sea mist, it's an amazing sight, like the beams of light could go on forever." Tiffany's eyes had gone soft and wondering. Again, that simple child inside what he was coming to understand was not a simple woman. She noticed his scrutiny and continued flatly. "White, green, and red every ten seconds. They're all automated now so the keepers don't live by the lights anymore."

Sure enough. He watched the lighthouse through a full minute, two flashes of each color. It *was* mesmerizing. The light itself didn't move or blink as he'd always assumed. Instead, a stepped lens bigger than his torso spun about it, six of them actually, forcing the light into beams. It was the glass itself that was colored.

Then he refocused in the foreground. To the north side of the clearing, providing it with a nice southern exposure, stood the lighthouse keeper's cottage. It was right out of some storybook: two stories tall, a big box with six well-spaced windows wide, all painted in glaring white with a red shingle roof. If ever there was a blank template, this was definitely it. He would need to keep the feel or it would lose its lighthouse charm. But he needed to do something serious, because other than its lighthouse heritage, it was one of the least charming buildings he'd ever seen.

"What do you know about—" Devin turned, but he was alone. There was no sign that only moments ago Tiffany had stood here beside him. He saw no hint in the trees, no flash of color from her dark blue harp carrying case. He scanned again, but he was definitely alone. He couldn't even see any sign of a trail leading away other than the one back to the B&B. A vague hint of what must once have been a logging road switchbacked to the north. Yet she'd waved southeast toward her farm and in that direction there was nothing but a solid wall of forest and dense undergrowth.

Still no sign. He pulled the key out of his pocket and headed over for a closer inspection of the cottage.

Devin just hoped to hell that he hadn't imagined her. He was less concerned for his mental state of possibly hallucinating and much more concerned with hoping she was real so that he could meet her again.

TIFFANY STOOD fifty feet into the trees to the east of the lighthouse clearing and watched Devin Robison.

She knew that her abrupt departure was rude, but she hadn't been able to stop herself. She had spoken more and to more people today than she typically did in a month. But what had finally driven her to escape was how much she'd enjoyed speaking with Devin. Despite his obvious pain over something in his recent past, there was an easiness to being around him. She'd always suspected that her own pain pushed others away and isolated her. Perhaps it was sharing a common theme of broken pasts which had made him so easy to be with.

It was the very easiness that she found so disconcerting.

Tiffany almost called out to him as he kept turning again and again to look for her. It was touching really. When at long last he went into the keeper's cottage, she picked up the compound bow and quiver of arrows—that she carried for protection but never took into town— from where she kept them stashed before turning for home. She brought it with her ever since a black bear had almost caught her. She'd escaped only by shedding her pack of fresh supplies and bolting for the farm. Coming back with the bow had filled her larder with bear meat to make up for the loss of her slashed and chewed supplies, but her pack had never been the same no matter how she patched it.

Keeping to the narrow path she'd forged, little wider than a deer trail and mostly over rock outcroppings, she left little trace of her passage. That had been her goal, her guiding principle since her arrival in Oregon, long before she came to Eagle Cove. She wanted no one to know where she had passed, or how.

At first she had appreciated the privacy. She had attended no functions in town. Spoke with no one and slowly learned to enjoy the peace. Even now, the birdsong soothed her far more than any people. Gray squirrels, little Douglas browns with the tufted ears, and striped chipmunks scattered up trees, saw it was her, and came back down hoping for a treat.

"No treats today, girls. Tuesday, I promise." When she went to town, she normally slipped an extra scone or a few cookies into her pocket, especially the ones with nuts and raisins, but she'd forgotten them in all of the day's flurry. A few of the braver ones followed her the distance of two or three trees before moving away to more fruitful pastures.

Going to town. She'd thought of it as if doing so was a normal thing. When had that happened?

Three years ago her ancestor's journal had led her to Eagle Cove and it had taken Tiffany months to work up the nerve to enter the town. She hadn't wanted to even then, but her assistant had finished his job and left. Everyone had assumed he was her boyfriend and that he'd jilted her and stolen her truck, leaving her abandoned and penniless. Actually, she'd bought him the truck as part of his pay. In exchange, he'd spent three months helping her with the heavy work of getting the farm started—a back-breaking summer before he'd returned to college.

She felt bad about leaving the false assumptions from the rumor in place. But Tiffany had learned the hard way, the true danger of anyone knowing she was descended from the highest tier of the San Francisco financial monarchy. Any misdirection was welcome.

Her four-times-great-grandmother had made a fortune in big lumber in the late 1800s. The guardian of her three-times-great-grandmother had owned the first lumber ship to arrive after the 1906 quake and fire and had quickly chartered two more. Three more generations of women had safeguarded that fortune assiduously. But for her mother's ability to marry well, much of it would have slipped away in the last generation prior to Tiffany's own. But she did marry well, and it had continued to grow. And Tiffany had wanted no part of it.

Her entrance into Eagle Cove society had been tentative. By the first time she came down from the woods to buy some essentials at the Warbler Market, she'd had "eccentric" down (though she wished it felt more like an act than a reality) and had been reluctant to break it.

One day she'd been slipping along the verge of the Lamont B&B's property, she'd stopped to look at it. This was the house that Lillian Lamont had built for her first daughter, Pearl, so that she would be close beside her mother. Lillian had lived in the house next door, now owned by Judge Slater. There was so much history and so many memories here. It was like a lens into the past.

January 1, 1900

New Year's Day

We held the housewarming at Pearl's upon the first day of the new century. Together we have designed and had built a Victorian house close beside our family home so that we may never live far apart.

Each visitor brought a log and we toured through the new house until each fireplace had been filled and lit. The warmth of the air felt almost as great as the warmth of spirit shared by those within these new walls.

My daughter is situated now, though her hopes for Thomas Harrow to join her were so recently cut short by the loss of his fishing craft. Yet we Lamont women put on our cheerful faces and welcomed all who came to wish her well. She is only nineteen, but in the morning she sails to San Francisco. There she shall briefly reside with my aging mother. I have entrusted Pearl with renewing our lucrative timber and fish sale contracts.

It is my hope that she will find a better man than poor Thomas while she is about her duties.

And Tiffany had seen the two layers, both past and present, intertwine that day three years ago as she walked by the B&B. She had been pulled toward the grand Victorian, fascinated by the vision of men and women once so attractively dressed in their Sunday finery, visiting good wishes upon the town's founders. She edged forward, imagining that she could catch a glimpse of Lillian and Pearl Lamont at their very best.

Then Tiffany had stumbled against the first step up to the verandah. The image faded, she was once again in the present, and she stood mere feet from a circle of women knitters, sitting out on the porch in the spring sunshine. The bright clicking of aluminum needles manipulating colorful and patterned yarns was so startling that she couldn't move.

Her hesitation lasted too long and Mrs. Winslow had spotted her. She'd waved Tiffany to sit in a seat beside her in such a peremptory fashion that Tiffany had been unable to refuse. But once there, they had allowed her to simply sit with her hands clenched around a glass of ice tea. The others might have looked at her oddly; she didn't know because she hadn't looked up. They let her just listen, and hear the warm friendship that flowed back and forth between them all.

Weeks later, working up her nerve, she'd come to town on a Tuesday afternoon with her own knitting tucked in her pack. Daring greatly, she'd walked up onto the porch, sat down next to Maggie Winslow, and pulled out her own project. The conversation had died at first, but once it restarted, Maggie Winslow had leaned over and whispered in her gruff way, "Good girl." That had made her Tiffany's first friend in town...her first in *years*. Though it was weeks before she could find her voice to answer back, she'd never forget that day or that kindness.

Tiffany stopped high on the trail leading to her farm and looked back to the north. The trail crested here on a ridge. It was one of the best views there was of the town founded by her forebears. Two miles to the north lay Eagle Bay, where the Eagle River pooled and slowed before finally reaching the sea. Beyond it lay only state forestland, patchworked with recent loggings and more mature growths.

The town stretched for two miles southward along the beach from the docks. The core of town lay nestled close by Eagle Bay. Residential areas stretched a half mile inland then were backed by a few small farms and the gravel-runway airport. The houses continued close above the beach to the south, finally petering out in the last long stretch of LBB Lane, slipping between the ocean and the forest to reach the Lamont B&B.

Her perch was at twice the height of Orca Head here and she could look down on the lighthouse and the cottage. Devin stepped out of the door as she watched and she could imagine him looking for her one more time as he twisted and turned—though he didn't look high enough to see her perch above the ridge—before he hurried down the trail, racing back down toward the civilization of the B&B. Evening was fast approaching and clearly the forest unnerved him. Yet another reason to feel bad about abandoning him.

"Sorry, Devin." It was the first time she'd said his name aloud and she liked the sound of it. Then she felt utterly ridiculous. She'd met many men with wonderful voices and learned that it didn't mean a thing about who they were. Devin's voice was nice—not deep, but nice. Kind with a bit of funny built in.

He disappeared out of sight down the trail after one last look behind.

"Devin."

Perhaps it was ridiculously schoolgirl, but she still liked the sound of his name.

She turned south, crossing over the ridge and out of sight of Eagle Cove. More importantly, out of sight of the lighthouse as well. Tiffany began to trot along the trail despite how it made the harp thump against her back. The farm might not be her own country...yet, but it felt as if it was. Her step always lightened as it came into view.

"Returning to her remote kingdom," she announced to the forest. After all, no one said her new country had to be a democracy.

"By unanimous accolade," she told a pair of seagulls riding high on the updrafts, "she is acclaimed the ruler. Long live Queen Tiffany Mills."

Giggling to herself, she went to feed the cat. Fitz always pouted if she wasn't greeted immediately upon Tiffany's return...or much more importantly, fed precisely on time.

DEVIN TRIED TO RELAX, but he felt twitchy and couldn't seem to pull it off. He kept turning to look over his shoulder as if Tiffany would suddenly reappear out of thin air, just as she'd disappeared into it. It wasn't doing him any good because he sat on the small bench on the B&B's verandah where he'd first met her. And that meant that the only thing over his shoulder was the outside wall of the Lamont B&B. In front of him, the evening had swallowed the front lawn and chased the last of the wedding guests inside.

Light came from the windows behind him and the multicolored twinkle lights wrapped about an old cherry tree that commanded the center of the yard. Lurking in the shadows, great trunks of trees soared upward into the darkness. He'd have to ask what they were… he didn't think redwoods grew here, but what did he know.

Somewhere beyond that was the steady roar of the freeway.

Except there was no freeway, but there was definitely a steady roar. Not a train; the rhythm was wrong. Besides, he'd seen no tracks as he came into town. He twisted and turned before he identified the source.

The ocean! It was a long, steady thunder in the darkness. Yet another strangeness of this odd place he'd landed in. A moment later his ears again told him that they were listening to the Kennedy Expressway as if I-90 was running close by. He wondered when his ears would catch up to the Oregon Coast like the rest of him.

"You're sitting in her favorite spot, you know," Becky dropped down on the bench beside him.

"Whose?" Apparently his brain was still somewhere in Chicago along with his hearing. He could see why Tiffany liked it. It offered a wide view, but it placed his back to a wall, with another to his right because of a jog in the architecture. It was partially protected from the wind…and from people approaching an obviously shy woman from too many directions at once.

"I do so love a wedding," Becky ignored his question and bubbled on. "I never thought I would, you know. But once you have one of your own, it just makes the world seem so much brighter."

Or darker. But Devin had learned to keep such thoughts to himself.

"And a *double* wedding…" Becky sighed happily.

"Are you close?"

"With Natalya? We go back almost to the hospital room. All three of us;. Jessica and Natalya are cousins, which I always envied, and tall, which I *really* envied. And now we're all married. I don't think I could stand it if I was and they weren't. It's so amazing to be back together again."

"Jessica was in Chicago?" Devin had been so pleased to find someone who knew his hometown. And at the same time, it had thrown him badly to be reminded of the places and flavors. In all likelihood he'd be back there in the fall. This was just a summer job after all, but he had no idea how he'd ever face that, especially not in four short months.

"She went and stayed ten years, the dizzy girl. She was following in the footsteps of Mrs. Winslow, who was a journalist there, back when *she* was young…if you can imagine Maggie Winslow ever being young," she confided the last in a whisper and then giggled like a little girl rather than a married woman in her early thirties. "I mean she was probably only my age or a little more when I had her in second grade. And that is a totally weird thought. But to a seven year old girl, all adults are ancient."

"I'm out here shopping for a retirement home myself," Devin tried to crack his voice with age. Though it was hard to imagine anyone thinking of Becky as ancient. She bubbled with enthusiasm, more than most kids he'd met.

"Eagle Cove is the best place there is. I never left, not like Natya and Jess."

"Why?" That came out harsher than he intended. "Aren't you curious what's out there?" He waved a hand, but not toward distant Chicago. Not that he'd traveled or explored either, but Chicago was much closer to the center of the universe than Eagle Cove.

"Sure. But I have a life here, friends, and my brewery, even before I made an honest man of Harry. I'm sure I'll travel someday. I would love to taste the German and British brews in their own locales, but this is home. Why would I look any further?"

Devin didn't have a good answer to that one, because Chicago certainly didn't feel like home anymore.

Behind him, the party continued. The cracked-open windows allowed the sound of conversation and laughter to filter out and join the ocean's roar—his ears must have finally caught up with him. He was just wondering why Becky was out here with him rather than inside with the others when a tall man with blond hair stepped out onto the porch.

"There you are."

"I've been waiting for you," Becky made a sudden show of rubbing at her arms and shivering as if she was suddenly in a chill Arctic winter rather than a warm spring evening. "I can't believe it took you almost five minutes to notice I was gone." Then she stopped shivering and winked at Devin as if he'd been party all along to her little tease.

"It took me less than a minute, but then I had to find your jacket, and after that I had to convince Jessica that I was indeed going to find you if she'd just stop delaying me. Now I want my dance with you."

Becky took the jacket and set it on the bench between her and Devin.

"See why I love the man," Becky told him, then offered another of her happy sighs as she took her husband's hand and bounced to her feet. "If you'll excuse us, we have a tradition of dancing in the dark after weddings. Call Marty if we fall off the cliff edge."

"Marty?"

"He's the town policeman," Harry answered. "I think he's in the kitchen with his wife and Jessica's parents."

And he led her far out onto the lawn past the glow from the cherry tree's twinkle lights. Then the two indistinct shadows became one and they began to dance ever so slowly. Thankfully nowhere near the high-bank cliff over the beach.

The town policeman. Singular. Devin didn't even know how many *precincts* Chicago had.

Devin could practically hear Becky's contented sigh from here on the porch.

And then he had the strangest image of him and Tiffany dancing beneath the stars. He barely knew her. Had never touched her, except —he flexed his hand at the memory—as she'd led him across the kitchen and minutes later when she'd pressed the room key into his palm as she fled. Yet somehow he could easily imagine what it would feel like to hold her against him. There would be a warmth and a genuineness that Devin had rather doubted existed until his arrival in Eagle Cove. She would feel...right.

Not like Rebecca, who no one would ever dare to call Becky. Rebecca Monica Monash of the Winnetka Monashs. When he'd held Rebecca, he'd always been aware that she wasn't to be "mussed up." Apparently there was no tragedy worse than a woman being "mussed up" in public...or in private. Five-foot-five of elegant blonde, an exquisite horsewoman, and always dressed in designer clothes—in public, in private, and even in the bedroom.

In retrospect he had no idea what he'd ever seen in Rebecca Monica Monash of Sheridan Road, except perhaps that she was the woman that everyone wanted. And his family, the Robisons, had the connections and wealth that met her requirements. Devin had been, perhaps still was though he wasn't sure anymore, the heir apparent to the Robison construction empire. That had assured him of Rebecca's juggernaut-strong attention.

Right up to the moment where he'd proven the old adage that it was bad luck to see the bride in her wedding dress. Or at least half in it.

Devin had stumbled upon her just an hour from the altar, her dress peeled down to her waist, her Prada lingerie filmy over her fair skin—one breast elegantly displayed and the other hidden by where his couldn't-keep-a-job older brother's face was buried. And when Rebecca had spotted Devin, she'd met his gaze levelly, still cradling Mikal's head as if to say, "Of course this is a part of our marriage."

Apparently all other men bent to her will.

Devin had considered bowing out and merely leaving her at the altar.

Instead, he'd pulled out his phone, snapped a picture of Rebecca Monica Monash's "mussed-ness" as her expression shifted into shock. He had posted it to his social feeds as he walked out the back door of the cathedral with the caption, "I guess the wedding is off."

The backlash had been immense. The Monashs, who should have been horrified or at least embarrassed, had defended their "little girl." His own mom, who served on several committees with Mrs. Monash insisted he should apologize, announce that it was a "Photoshop joke in bad taste," and then go through with the wedding to make everything right. His dad had shrugged, "Hell, your mother and I have never been saints. Nobody ever said you had to fuck the woman you married. My secretary has the hots for you. Go ease yourself there. Trust me, she's good at that."

Devin shuddered, trying to shake off the image.

The cool Oregon evening *did* suddenly feel cold.

Devin stumbled to his feet. Left Becky and her husband to their intimate dance in the night.

He'd come so close to revealing that he was next in line to the control of one of America's largest contractors, a fact he'd kept carefully hidden even during the job interview. He needed to be away from his family, and from their business and his own. When he'd spotted the tiny ad—"experienced renovation contractor needed, Oregon Coast"—he'd immediately pulled out his phone and dialed.

Only getting lost twice in the odd twists and turns of the Victorian, he found his way to his third floor room and pitched face first into bed.

TIFFANY HAD BEEN in too much of a state last night to do more than lock the chickens into the coop before going to bed. And she hadn't read a word of her four-times-great-grandmother Lillian's journal, something she typically did every night.

The wedding had slid into her veins and made her blood flow faster—or perhaps in tiny whirlpools. Natalya and Gina had looked so beautiful as they stood at the rose arbor, which the two grooms had somehow transported from Mrs. Winslow's cloistered garden for the ceremony. So much joy and hope combined together.

Eagle Cove was no paradise, the Judge dealt with divorces as often as any judge did. But when it was special, there was no mistaking it, and last night had been doubly so.

She awoke with the first light of dawn filtering down from the circular plastic dome atop her yurt. The circular space of her open floor plan was barely visible as she dressed, but the warm woods of the structure were always a joy, even in dim light. The sidewall was made of seven-foot-high latticework that looked far too frail to hold up the structure. But the dozens of polished, long rafters speared up into the central ring to support the sealed canvas roof. So different from Devin's Victorian bedroom at the B&B.

When designing the living space, she had chosen simplicity in style, function over form. A sectioned-off bath was the only enclosed area. With a line of bookcases, she'd separated off a workshop including tools, gardening supplies, and medicines she needed for the goats and chickens. Most of the space was a full kitchen, a queen-sized bed (and she still hadn't finished the new quilt she'd intended for it), and a comfortable living/dining room in front of the two big windows looking out over her meadow and the ocean. A propane stove with a glass front kept her warm and provided a cheery flame.

Fitz watched her with on sleepy eye from the other pillow on her bed for a while before going back to sleep. Morning tea in hand, she stepped out onto the wide deck and descended the redwood steps in the first light of dawn. Her farm was still in deep shadows, but to the south and west the smooth ocean rolled in endless waves to the horizon. Even as she stood and breathed in the pine and sea salt-scented air, she could see the light changing, shifting from dark blue to soft pink along the horizon.

Some mornings the sun lit the entire horizon and this was one. No offshore fogbank today as there would be in summer. No storm clouds building at the first sign of land after their long journey over the ocean—preparing to unleash their load of rain.

She'd built the chicken coop under the raised platform for her yurt —which, she'd learned the hard way, had been a huge mistake. She didn't mind the occasional night clucking of the chickens, but it had required a lot of sound insulation to keep the rooster's call from electrifying her like a Taser every morning. She'd tried any number of solutions, but a yurt's walls were thin and did nothing to muffle sound. The final solution had been to install lightproof shutters over the henhouse windows and remember to close them each night.

Sure enough, the moment she cracked the first one open, Dillinger —he of the lethal crow—let loose his morning salvo. In moments, the chickens were up and about and declaring the start of their day. She opened the door and they poked their heads out to inspect the pen she'd constructed as if they'd never seen it before.

"Brains of a pea," she chided them as they clucked about her feet while she scattered feed. The pen had chicken wire around the sides and fishnet (interlaced with orange tape) over the top.

Jake, the bachelor bald eagle, just molting from his juvenile brown-headed year into his trademark white head, soared low, looking like the raggedy teen that he was. His head feathers were half brown, half white, and always seemed to be sticking out at odd angles. Every day he carefully checked her chicken protection for gaps.

"Get along, you chicken eagle." The tease always worked—Jake soared higher into the brightening day to find easier pickings and was gone. He hunted a lot among the field by the lighthouse, though he could drag twenty inches of salmon out of the bay when he put his mind to it.

Between yesterday and today she'd gained four new chicks. She swiped two fresh-laid eggs for her morning omelette that dressed up nicely with the addition of an early wild morel mushroom she'd found yesterday morning and a sprinkle of homemade goat cheese.

Then she rushed off to check on the goat pen. It was a temporary fence that she moved around the land to wherever she wanted the undergrowth cleared. The Forest Service, not knowing about the mistake in property lines, had clear-cut eight of her ten acres five years before she bought it. This had turned out to be a huge bonus. She had a two-acre buffer of forest from the nearest passable road, and eight acres of cleared land to work.

She simply moved the pen about and the pygmy goats mowed down the tall grass, chomping the salal, blackberries, and alder shoots flush to the dirt. On quiet days she'd take them all out on a walk to some particularly lush area and read a book while they grazed.

With a clucking sound, Tiffany warned Tall Guy that she was coming. The massive Kangal lumbered to his feet. Two and a half feet tall at the withers, the brindle-furred guard dog trotted eagerly up to the fence's gate to await her. She let herself through and he leaned his big head into the center of her chest. She gave him a big scritch, which had him mumbling happily to himself. Then he raised his head to glance wistfully over her shoulder at the steel can outside the fence.

"Fibber! You said you loved me!" He raised his great, sad eyes set in his broad, black face. "Oh, like you're starving to death."

But she scooped up his dog bowl and carried it back out to the can to fill it with dog food. She really needed to write and thank the woman who'd told her about Kangals. Donna had kept the full-sized Nubian goats and a Kangal. They weren't shepherds, they were guard dogs. They could take down a coyote, even a couple of them, and would brave a bear, spooking it back into the woods. The big dogs were quite content to live with their flock, even when the flock was so much shorter than they were. A pygmy goat rarely reached two feet at the withers.

While Tall Guy ate, she circulated among the goats. Her *Little Women* were doing fine. Meg and cousin Flo were about to drop kids. Jo, Beth, Amy, and their friend Annie already had. Tiffany had decided it would be too crass to name her rutting male Laurie; she'd needed a scandalous lout. Horatio snorted at her out of both nostrils, which had earned him his Horatio Hornblower moniker. He swaggered about, firm in the belief that he was somehow in charge of his little harem. With all of the females bearing, Horatio had certainly lived up to his duties.

She started checking the goats more carefully. Trimming hooves, inspecting teeth, and so on. They were used to the routine and it gave her a chance to interact with each one. Only Horatio made any fuss, nibbling at the untucked hem of her flannel work shirt, which he knew was forbidden.

DEVIN HAD WOKEN a dozen times in the night, wondering at the expressway's roar, only to remember he was nowhere near the Kennedy or the LSD. Lake Shore Drive was two thousand miles away. He'd finally watched the moon set into the ocean just an hour before dawn.

He hadn't expected to find Gina Lamont in the kitchen starting breakfast.

"Aren't you on your honeymoon?"

"Nope," Gina handed him a large mug of coffee. "Cal Jr. and Cal Sr. run the town bakery together, so we tossed a coin and Senior and I took our honeymoon the week before the wedding."

"Oh," Devin sipped the coffee and settled at the small booth seat so that he'd be out of her way after his offer of assistance was refused. "I guess that means that your daughter got stuck with all of the final wedding arrangements."

"Exactly!" Gina sounded very pleased as she added link sausages to a hot pan. In seconds, the aroma had his mouth watering. "Though I am keeping it simple this morning. I have some frozen strawberries, which I'm using to make waffles with a mascarpone and maple syrup topping, and a side of Apple Brown Betty."

"If that's your idea of simple, I'm never leaving."

She waved a spatula at him, "Be careful of what you ask for in this town, Devin Robison. Statements like that can lead you in strange directions." She smiled down at her sausages. Goofy morning-after-wedding looked good on her. "My Cal certainly changed my direction and now I wonder what I was doing with the years up until now. I never dreamed that I'd ever marry."

As to dreams, Devin didn't have a whole lot of those anymore, so he didn't think that would be an issue. A few months spent as far as he could get from Chicago was good enough for him.

"What I got for my dreams," Gina continued as she checked the baking Brown Bettys, "was a man who took me on a week-long dogsled tour in Fairbanks, Alaska, and thought it was a great honeymoon surprise."

Devin almost snorted his next sip of hot coffee.

"Worse, it was wonderful! I can't stand that he was right. A man isn't supposed to do something like that to a woman who has been single all her life."

"But Natalya…" was her daughter—at least that's what everyone said. He decided that a subject change was in order. "Tiffany said I could borrow a road grader from someone named Peggy?"

And that was how an hour later he found himself, with a bellyful of waffles and Apple Brown Betty, across town at the small rural airport, knocking on the door of a big hangar.

"Gina called about my grader," was the greeting that met him. "Come on," and she led the way into the shadowed hangar. Peggy was just as Tiffany had described her: short and darkly redheaded. Which had left out everything else. She was at least sixty, had unabashed streaks of gray in her red hair, walked with a rolling gait like a cowboy or a Navy sailor, and had deep blue eyes that he was fairly sure could see right through him.

He knew nothing about small planes, but the assembled biplane just inside the hangar door looked classic and in mint condition. The unassembled one? He could barely tell that it was a plane. The broad hangar floor was scattered with a vast array of bits and pieces. He spotted some metalwork in the shape of wings, but with no coverings on them. An airframe in sections. An improbably large engine half disassembled onto pallets. But it wasn't chaos. It was like one of those exploded views, everything laid out just so. Peggy radiated competence even just walking across the hangar, so he had no doubt that she was the one rebuilding it.

There was also a small helicopter and a large RV parked in the back. The road grader was parked between the RV and the hangar wall. It too was a classic. A Cat 112F, which he'd only ever seen in the equipment junkyard catalogs. It had to be sixty years old, though the paint was fresh and there were no signs of leaking hydraulic fluid anywhere.

"She's one of the first two hundred of the four thousand they built," Peggy patted the big machine as if it were a kitten. "She doesn't have a lot of the upgrades of the later models, but she runs like a champ. I use her mostly to keep the gravel runway smooth. It'll be good for her to stretch her legs out in the hills a bit."

Devin had run small excavators and a Cat D2 dozer, which was little more than a Bobcat in serious need of a weight loss program. They were small, chunky crawlers with enough power to completely reshape a residential backyard. But this road grader was nearly thirty feet long, ten high, with a twelve foot wide scraping blade dangling between the front tires and the rest of the machine. More significantly, the D2 had very little imagination and minimal controls to match. The road grader had a proliferation of controls—the blade alone had angle, depth, tilt, reach, and who knew what else. The back wheels didn't even have to follow the front wheels because there was an articulation joint in the middle so that the main machine could run down the level road while the nose of the beast skewed up hills and over ditches.

His protests were ignored and his suggestion that she might want to do it for him was met with, "Got a flight today." But he wasn't so sure about that. Something in her smile said that he was going to be driving the machine no matter what, so he stopped arguing and tried to absorb everything she gave him in a twenty minute lesson on how to run the grader.

"Last thing," she called out as he managed to find the first of six forward gears, without accidentally finding one of the six reverse gears. "This model doesn't have rollover protection, so if you flip her, be sure to jump well clear." Her face was absolutely deadpan before she turned away. He wondered how long she was going to hold the laugh in...hopefully until he was out of earshot.

He lurched off along the runway and onto the road leading through town.

No question what stories would be told in the local bar tonight. As he drove toward town, every single person who saw him coming started to raise a hand to wave, then froze with a puzzled expression on their face.

Eagle Cove was so small that everyone knew who was supposed to be driving the road grader. He was trying not to feel too self-conscious about everyone staring at him perched atop Peggy's big machine, and that's when he made his first mistake…and then his second.

He managed to find the transmission release and the brake before he could make a third.

Devin's first mistake had been turning onto Gull Way. Not yet comfortable with reverse, he'd forged ahead. Navigating up and down the hills had taught him a great deal about where to find third and fourth gear while going down the hills, and first and second for climbing slower than he could walk.

Mistake Two: to eventually escape the hills of Gull Way, he'd turned onto Shearwater Lane, which was flat but wasn't much wider than the road grader itself. It had deep ditches down one side that he'd bet would roll the machine if he slipped into one.

"Are you lost, Mr. Robison?"

It took him a moment to find the speaker. It was the woman who had practically attacked Tiffany…Winslow. Maggie Winslow, the second-grade teacher, was standing beside her car in her driveway—which he'd just completely blocked. He shrugged uncertainly. The town only had a few dozen roads; everything this side of Beach Way was named for sea birds, most of which he'd never heard of. That made them far too easy to mix up. At least he assumed a shearwater was a bird, because everything else in all of Eagle Cove seemed to be named that way.

"Take a right at the end of the street. That is Egret Hollow. Do not turn onto Sandpiper Circuit until you learn to drive much better than you presently do." With that she climbed into her car, clearly ready for him to move along.

He just didn't know if he dared.

"I'll give you a hand," a man called out from a driveway on the other side of the road. He paused to pat two seriously cute twins on the head and plant a very thorough kiss on the knockout wife that was the spitting image of her children. Or the other way around. Devin's thoughts were getting decidedly scrambled.

"Don't let Dragon Winslow spook you," he called out as he headed down the road ahead of Devin and waved him forward.

"I heard that, Vincent McCall," she called from her open car window.

"Wouldn't have been any fun if you didn't, ma'am," Vincent said it with absolute respect.

Devin found first gear and eased away from the two driveways. With Vincent's help, he navigated the turn without landing in any ditches or running over Vincent. Unwilling to try any of the higher gears or try to fit the big machine into a single lane, Devin walked the road grader mostly down the center of the road and screwed up traffic in both directions.

———

"You grow the most beautiful vegetables, Tiffany."

She kept her silence as Greg sorted her produce atop one of the big steel prep tables in the back of the Puffin Bay Diner. Greg and his father the Judge always made her a bit nervous. The Judge was an austere, silent man, and she felt like a trespasser every time she entered his kitchen. Greg was an amazing chef, or so everyone said; she'd never eaten one of his dinners. And he always complimented her produce.

"Winter beets, spring leeks, fresh spinach, and snow peas. I can't believe you grow snow peas. This gives me some great ideas for tomorrow night, you really must come at least once." Greg had recently added a Tuesday night dinner at The Puffin.

His father served breakfasts at the Puffin Bay Diner five days a week. His son turned it into The Puffin on Friday and Saturday nights —fixed menu, fixed price (very high). But not wanting to shut out the locals who had helped him get started, he'd recently added a "locals only" Tuesday night. It was back to the original tradition: stuff a twenty in the jar, if you can afford it, and Greg took care of the rest.

"Seriously, Tiffany. No charge. Anytime you want."

She nodded, a little abashed by his generosity couldn't figure out how to explain that she had no need of charity, however kind.

When he didn't continue, she tipped up her head enough to see his face beyond the brim of her hat. He was waiting.

"I—" she waved a hand to the south. "My farm. Long way at night." She sounded like a babbling fool, typical of her when in town. It was as if by being silent for so long she'd forgotten how to talk to people at all.

Tiffany heard the big truck engine.

"Will you look at that?" Someone called from the front of the diner. Soon everyone was moving to stare out the front windows. Laughter was beginning to sound throughout the diner.

Not wanting to join the crowd as Greg and the Judge were, Tiffany slipped out the back door and saw the problem...or at least half of it.

The back end of Peggy's road grader was still in the street beside the diner. The front end was out on Beach Way. It sat at a dead stop. Even as she watched, it jerked forward about two feet, slammed to a stop, then stalled.

Devin leaned forward over the steering wheel as if he was going to cry.

Through the open back door into the kitchen, she could still hear the laughter and exclamations from the crowd in the dining room. She could see others gathering on the street to watch him.

Tiffany knew how that felt. The creeping truth that you could do nothing right and the sick feeling that came with it and pressed in while others watched. Her heart couldn't bear to watch his pain.

She closed the back door and slipped up to the open door of the grader's cabin.

"Devin?"

"Just shoot me now, Tiffany. Please?"

"I'll bring my bow and arrow next time."

He raised his head and looked down at her. "You have a bow and arrow?"

Apparently, she wouldn't have said so if she didn't.

"Uh, I'll remember not to upset you. Do you hunt with it, too?"

"Elk and deer. Coyotes if my dog doesn't scare them off. Though I only started carrying it when I had an argument with a bear."

"You argued with a bear?" What planet created women like this? Rebecca Monica Monash of Sheridan Road never argued with anything bigger than a designer label at Fields. "Dare I ask who won?"

Tiffany simply looked at him.

"Okay, you're here. Where's the bear?"

"Salted jerky. I don't have a freezer, so I had to preserve it another way. And I sold some to Greg, a chef in town." She waved to the building behind her. A careful glance and she saw that the audience was no longer pressing up against the glass and the street was emptying once more as people went back to their meals and errands.

"Can I go back to Chicago now?"

"I don't think Peggy would like it if you don't return her grader first."

Devin rested his head back down on the steering wheel. "If that's the case, then I'm not sure I can ever leave."

Devin watched as Tiffany walked once around the grader before coming to stand once more by the cabin door. Her eyes were the soft blue-gray of a hazy summer sky. Unlike Rebecca's coolly perfect blue eyes the color of a frozen winter sky. He felt as if Tiffany was seeing him, actually looking at him rather than her own reflection in his face.

"I think..." she glanced along the vast length of the grader. "I think you should teach me how to drive that machine."

"But I don't *know* how to drive that beast. I can't even turn it."

"I saw," and her smile lit up her face more brightly than the music had yesterday.

"Great." Exactly what his ego hadn't needed.

"Teach me anyway." Then she climbed up beside him.

The bench seat wasn't all that wide. Even though she was slender, they were touching shoulder to shoulder and hip to hip. And rather than being totally distracting, he found it to be a calming, focusing feeling.

"I'm ready."

At a loss for what else to do, he started on the far left and began explaining each control and what it did. And the more he explained, only occasionally redirected by her quiet questions, the better he understood how they interacted.

For half an hour they sat there, blocking the main intersection in town. There were no honked horns. No shouts of complaint. People backed up and went around the block to get by him. He didn't know where he was, but it definitely wasn't Chicago, where he'd be ticketed, towed, and possibly shot by this point.

GINA WAVED as they edged by the B&B. It had taken Devin another half hour to drive the two miles from town and news traveled much faster in Eagle Cove than that.

Tiffany had considered having him shift up to third gear, but if second was all he was comfortable with, she wouldn't push him.

He set the blade at the base of the road up to the lighthouse. It barely knocked down the small bushes and it certainly never touched the soil. After fifty feet, she nudged the blade-depth lever with one finger until it bit in.

"You sure?" Devin asked tightly.

Tiffany glanced down at the blade now scraping across the grass. It clanged loudly on a rock. "I was going to suggest we go even deeper, but I'm not sure." By halfway up she was sure but wasn't willing to change anything as they reached the first switchback.

Devin negotiated it without driving them off the edge and down into a stream's deep ravine.

As they broke into the high meadow in front of the lighthouse, Jake the eagle swooped very low along the other side of the grader to see what had invaded his territory.

"Holy shit!" Devin practically dove into her lap in his effort to get out the door on her side. His abrupt exit had including popping the clutch and stomping on the brake. The engine stalled and the grader lurched, tumbling him out into a windrow of freshly scraped soil.

Tiffany couldn't help herself. The laugh started somewhere deep and simply burst out of her. She couldn't remember the last time she'd laughed.

"Oh, you should see yourself, Devin."

"What the hell was that?" He was scanning the sky from where he lay in the dirt as if the zombie apocalypse was about to land on him.

"A bald eagle. Jake is more show than substance. He only fledged last year. Bald eagles take a while before they become majestic."

Jake decided they were of no interest and caught a thermal to climb up above the ridge.

"He's harmless if you're bigger than a salmon," she reassured Devin who still hadn't moved.

"Am I bigger than a salmon?"

"Most of them," Tiffany managed to keep her voice normal as she told the fib.

DEVIN SLOWLY CLIMBED to his feet, leaving his dignity in the dirt.

Tiffany sat in the cab as if ready to drive the machine herself. Probably could, and better than the mess he was making of it.

"I thought it was a dragon right out of myth and fable. I've never seen one before and definitely not that close. They don't look so big in documentaries." He squinted up at the sky, but the eagle was now little more than a black dot.

"They look small on the backs of coins, too."

That made Devin smile. Ms. Forthright. "Right. The ones on the backs of coins must be a very small breed. Maybe they should put moths on the backs of quarters; they would fit better."

"Moths are lousy at looking noble. Perhaps we need bigger coins."

"Life-size currency? You'd need one of these," he kicked the grader's tire, "to carry it around."

"Graders don't carry things. They scrape things."

That stopped him. She was speaking perfectly seriously. Again that simple woman showed through the fancifully complex one.

"I think I've got this thing figured out now, if I could arrange for eagles to not interrupt my train of thought." He circled around and climbed back in the other side of the cab so that he didn't have to crawl over her lap again. The smell of her was overwhelming as he sat once more beside her. In a world of dirt and a hint of motor oil, she was like a fresh breeze. His train of thought was headed in a direction that had nothing to do with this machine.

"If so, show me."

He almost took her command as an order to kiss her, but caught himself at the last moment and turned back to the controls.

HE'D FINISHED the meadow and cut the road. Tiffany was no more sure than he was about how to cut ditches and widen turns, but between them, they figured it out. When it was all done, he drove out to the lighthouse and parked the road grader with its nose pointing toward the sea. The engine turned over a few final, thudding times after he'd shut it down, then there was only the pinging of hot metal and the ringing in his ears.

Again, the infinite expanse of water spread before him. As his hearing recovered, the low roar of the ocean filled in the background. Then Tiffany's soft breathing in the foreground.

He turned to face her and they were nearly nose to nose.

"Well done," her voice was a whisper of praise that felt greater than any he'd received before.

"I couldn't have done it alone," which was true. She'd pushed him to learn and to be better than he thought he was.

She shrugged as if dismissing the compliment.

"No, really," he raised a hand to her cheek when she tried to turn away. His fingers buzzed from the strong vibrations of handling the big machine. But through his fingertips he could feel the impossible softness of her skin. Her thick hair slid across the back of his hand like cool water soothing a hot day.

Then he leaned in and kissed her.

There was a muffled sound of surprise, but she didn't pull away or push at him. For a long moment they held the kiss, his whirling thoughts stilled by the soft warmth and the simple acceptance.

Then between one eye blink and the next, she was gone. Out of the cab, on the ground, and moving away.

He scrambled after her before she could do her disappearing act again. "Tiffany! I—"

"Don't!" She commanded him to silence, but at least she stopped her hell-bent retreat a single step from the edge of the forest. Standing with her back to him and her head down, she stood still for a long time before turning. It was hard waiting, but he knew it was the right thing to do.

When she did turn, her hair covered much of her face, but he could feel as much as see her steady gaze upon him. There was no sign of the seemingly simple, overly direct woman now.

"I—" he tried again, but she held up a hand to stop him.

"What were you thinking?" She didn't make it an accusation, rather a literal question.

"I wasn't," but that wasn't a sufficient answer. "I was thinking how kind you are to help me learn that thing," he waved a hand back at the grader. "And how heady a mixture it is to find someone so beautiful yet so powerful."

"So you took me out parking on Lover's Lane in a Cat 112F road grader, hoping for second base or a home run?" There was a dead flatness to her tone.

"No, I—" then he turned to look at the grader. This would be an ideal spot for lovers. In fact, he should install a couple of park benches for guests who wanted to sit together and admire the view. Just there, with concrete pads so that it would last. He mentally rearranged the parking lot for the cottage to make a couple of spaces to park facing the view just as the road grader now stood. "No. I didn't kiss you for that reason."

He turned to see her reaction, but was alone in the midst of the scraped-smooth meadow. Tiffany had stepped beneath the trees and had almost faded away completely.

He took a step into the cool shade to follow her, but stopped after that single step. She had changed in the woods.

She now held a vicious looking bow, nearly as tall as she was, with a half dozen arrows in a holder built onto the frame. It was complex, painted in camouflage forest colors, and looked dangerous as hell.

"You really know how to use that thing?"

In answer, she pulled an arrow from holder to string in a smooth, practiced motion. Faster than he could follow, she drew, aimed, and let fly. The arrow whistled dangerously as it passed over his shoulder.

He turned to follow its flight.

It struck a tree on the far side of the meadow, close beside the grader. It made an audible *Thwap!* where it stuck hard and vibrated. He definitely was no longer in Chicago.

"Uh, I'll remember not to upset you while you have that. I kissed you because you are—"

He turned back, but she was gone. In that single moment she had slipped away as if she'd never been there at all.

"—so amazing." He told the listening forest.

When it didn't answer, he stepped back into the meadow. He would respect her privacy and not go looking for her. Especially not when she was armed with that bow.

Only two things proved that he hadn't lost his mind and hallucinated her. A line of woman-sized boot prints upon the pristine soil from the grader to the forest. And an arrow driven into the heart of a tree.

CHAPTER 3

*T*iffany was tired of running away. It seemed as if she'd been doing it her whole life prior to Eagle Cove. And now she was doing it here.

Devin's kiss had been…lovely. She'd spent much of the night trying to find another word for it, but had been unable to.

For a long moment she'd given in, aware only of the lovely kiss. Then she'd snapped out of it as if slapped. Next would come grope, pin, and take! She wasn't going to go there again. Wasn't going to let some man have his way with her against her consent ever again.

Yet Devin's kiss had been…lovely.

Great-gran Lillian's journal didn't help matters either. When needing advice, Tiffany had taken to opening it at random and reading whatever passage presented itself.

March 1900

Ernest is a common sailor, who has just delivered fresh news from San Francisco. My daughter's business efforts on our behalf continue well.

Unknowingly, she has given me the greatest gift when she chose him as the messenger. He may be an unlettered man, but he is wonderfully handsome and such hands he has.

When he unlaced my corset and scooped his rough palms over the most private areas of my bare torso, it was but the beginning of what I discovered that my poor Clarence could never give me while he still lived.

Tiffany slapped the journal closed. She did not need the romance portion of Lillian's long journal. The next weeks of entries, Tiffany knew, would read like the best steamy romance novel, filled with tantalizing snippets and moments. Clarence, the good man, had provided home, daughter, and been a fumbler in bed. Ernest had been the handsome lover who came to her when she was a lonely woman of forty—while her daughter celebrated her twentieth year in San Francisco.

"I'm losing my mind," she'd told Fitz, who hadn't argued the point.

Neither had Tall Guy nor the goats.

But she wasn't going to run any more.

So, when it was time to head down into town for the Tuesday knitting group, she didn't shy off. She also didn't take the path that could have avoided the cottage clearing.

"I'll just wave politely and continue down the road. I'm mature enough to do that." A part of her wanted to take the bow and arrows in case Devin became unruly, but she hid it in the usual spot.

No Devin to be seen. Tire tracks marked the departing grader but no other sign. Nor was there any vehicle parked at the "Lover's Lane" spot beside the lighthouse. Instead there was only the cottage and a half acre of unblemished earth. It would need a flower garden and perhaps an herb garden to make it homey. The arrow that Devin had left in the tree would definitely have to go. Though it was nice that he'd left it in place. He'd probably forgotten about it the moment she was gone…but some part of her knew that wasn't true. He might even be upset if she took it down.

When she turned to leave the barely recognizable meadow, the road was another harsh shock. Other than the occasional US Coast Guard four-by-four truck sent up to inspect the lighthouse, no one else had tried to get a vehicle up here in the three years she'd lived in the State of Tiffany.

Now there was a clear passage down the lower part of the hill. Where there had been a gentle forest trail, there was now a wide and civilized dirt road. It was hard to not think about its surface. She could see each place she had made an adjustment to the cut of the blade. Could remember how it felt to be rubbing shoulders with Devin as they jounced over patches that were still rough in the early passes.

Devin had been so comfortable. Why did he have to ruin it with—

Though maybe she shouldn't lay all of the blame on him. He'd done nothing beyond a simple kiss. She had been the one to overreact. Yet another thing she didn't like about yesterday's memory.

"What are you thinking about so seriously?"

Tiffany was jolted to realize that she'd exited the trees and arrived at the Lamont B&B without first checking to see who might be there. And now that she did, the first thing she noticed was that Devin's truck wasn't here either.

But Gina Lamont was and she had her knitting bag draped over her shoulder.

"Hello, Gina. I'm sorry. My mind was wandering."

They climbed into Gina's Prius together. When Tuesday afternoon knitting had moved from the B&B out to Becky's Brewery near the airport, Gina Lamont had offered her a ride. Her first time in a car in years, it had been bewildering—as confusing as the unexpected kindness. Now she was used to the feel of her typical two-mile walk between the B&B and town sliding by in mere minutes. And Gina extended her kindness to Tiffany every week as if it was a simple "of course" assumption with no idea how rare and precious that was.

As rare and precious as a kiss.

"You're doing that thinking thing again," Gina told her as they turned onto Beach Way. "About something juicy, I hope."

Not a chance that Tiffany was going to answer that. Instead, she watched the stores go by: Merganser Weaving and Fishing Tours, Carrier Pigeon Pizza (that didn't deliver), Blackbird Bakery (that did), Brass Plover Inn, and Puffin Bay Diner anchored at the far end of town close by the water.

Gina didn't push, and for that alone she deserved an answer.

"I'm just being startled by all of the changes happening."

"Like the lighthouse cottage project?"

"And the road. And your and Natalya's weddings."

"What's wrong with those?" Gina sounded suddenly defensive.

"Nothing. That's not it." Tiffany floundered. "It's not what I meant." She tried again. "Your weddings were so beautiful and you all looked so happy. I just…" And she finally ran out of words.

"And you started thinking about your own."

"Right. What? No!"

Gina's big laugh filled the car. "I know. I watched Monica remarry Ralph for the fourth time and I didn't think much of it. But when Peggy married, that was a shock to the core. She and I had been single-type girls together since forever. And there she suddenly was, wearing wedding white and looking as if she owned the world. What woman wouldn't want that feeling?"

This one, Tiffany thought. But it didn't sit well.

"And I can tell you what's even crazier," Gina said as they parked in front of the old cow barn that was now Becky Billings BlueBird Brewery. "It's completely true."

"For you," Tiffany hadn't meant to make it sound like an accusation.

"I dare you to ask Jessica and Becky about that during knitting. Natalya too, if she wasn't away on her honeymoon."

Tiffany shook her head. That was a dare she wouldn't be taking.

Gina's laugh led them out of the car and indoors to join the knitting circle.

DEVIN SURVEYED the airstrip and couldn't help but feel good about it.

He'd driven the road grader back through town this morning, with a minimum of mishaps, though he'd had to stop and pull a parking sign back into position, mostly, at Kingfisher's Court, and had gotten lost again among the seabird roads—they wound and twisted and overlapped as if they were in flight themselves.

He'd started talking advanced grader technique with Peggy, which had turned into a long discussion. Then she'd sent him out to scrape and shape the runway. With her instructions in his head, he'd finally gotten a good feel for the machine and had enjoyed refinishing the runway's surface before she returned from another flight.

"Nice job," she said after landing her Stearman 4 biplane and taxiing back and forth over the surface a few times. "Can I borrow you for a minute more? I have to carry a couple of pies over to Becky's." She nodded toward a barn across a hundred yards of pasture deep in hay.

"It might cost you a slice," Devin warned.

Peggy nodded at the deal.

"What do I owe you for the grader?"

"Nothing. Gina lends me a room whenever my sister comes to visit —which I count as a blessing because she makes me too crazy to have close night and day. Besides, I'll consider the nice job on the runway as me owing you."

Devin sniffed at the pie she placed in his hands. He did it again, deeper. Strawberry-rhubarb. Not a construction man worth his salt wasn't an expert on pies.

He was also getting the hang of how things worked away from the city.

"Smells like a slice of this will set us even there. If it tastes even half as good as it smells, I'll owe you."

"Good," Peggy picked up another pie and a cloth bag in which he could see some yarn and needles. "Because it tastes even better."

There was a narrow path beaten through the hay, which was waist high. Chicago snow had just been melting out at his non-wedding. By the time he'd left a month later to drive west, the hay fields were barely ankle high. They had some kind of crazy growing season out here on the coast. When was everything going to stop surprising him?

Not yet!

That question was answered soundly when he stepped through the barn's side door. He'd seen the "5B—Becky Billings BlueBird Brewery Tasting Room" sign and assumed it was some hobby operation. He remembered the short blonde who had danced in the darkness with her husband after the wedding. He expected a little craft setup.

Through the tasting room door was a spacious area with a dozen tables and a long bar sporting a dozen taps. It was a beautiful space that made him want to sit down and draw a pint.

Up above the bar was a painting of Eagle Cove as it would appear from Peggy's plane, reaching from wall to wall and from bar mirror to peaked ceiling.

"Your photo originally?"

Peggy nodded.

The representation of the town itself looked modern and had been painted by an artist who managed to bring the high view to life. Another artist had painted framing images of an old-time sailing ship and a couple of women in Victorian garb.

"Don't miss this," Peggy called his attention to a long glass wall beyond which stood an immaculate brewery. "I helped Becky assemble most of this. Her work, I was just labor." She didn't need to mention how proud of it she was; it was clear in her voice.

Tall, stainless steel tanks surrounded a big copper kettle and a host of other mysterious equipment. There was one person in back working a bottling machine. The guy waved and Peggy nodded back, her hands full of pie.

Peggy led Devin into a big living room area. A dozen women were gathered in a big circle, chatting happily. There seemed to be three or four conversations going at once and he estimated that his best strategy was to grab a slice and beat a hasty retreat.

Calls of greetings sounded out for Peggy, and then one by one the conversations quieted as heads turned, noticing him for the first time. He'd met Gina, Mrs. Winslow, Jessica, and Becky. He recognized several others from the wedding even if he hadn't met them.

Maybe he'd skip the slice and just beat a hasty retreat.

That was the plan until a person sitting on one end of a couch turned slowly to look in his direction.

Tiffany Mills' hands stopped with their knitting, even as the rest of the room resumed what they were doing. Was there anything she couldn't do? Play harp, knit, farm, and shoot a bow and arrow.

That image had cost him an entire night's sleep.

Tiffany with her feet well planted in the forest, her long hair billowing soft in the breeze, and smoothly powerful in her handling of the bow. Robin Hood would be an idiot if he didn't recruit Maid Tiffany after a single glance. Forget Marian, whether played by Olivia de Havilland, Mary Elizabeth Mastrantonio, or even Cate Blanchett (his personal favorite—true of almost any movie Cate was in). Tiffany wielding her bow and arrow was a revelation.

Peggy took the pie from his hands. "Sit while I slice these up."

Devin headed for the seat over by the brewery's master control board. At least that's what he hoped it was, because if there was another one with even more controls and readouts he didn't want to know about it. These controls were plenty complex enough.

"Don't disappoint me," Peggy's whisper was sharp and private.

Devin looked at her and again was the target of her steady gaze.

"I'm not blind, so don't you be stupid."

Which was exactly what he'd been about to do. Sure he was curious to see what information a brewery reported to its operator. But there was also an empty chair close beside the couch Tiffany was seated on. "For a slice, I'll sit for a bit," he offered loudly enough to be heard.

Peggy rolled her eyes at him, but nodded when he turned for the chair by Tiffany.

Devin had three steps to figure out how to approach this.

Only a pissant would embarrass her in front of her friends.

He could act hurt that she'd bolted.

Or he could pretend everything was normal, as if their last conversation had merely been interrupted.

He sat, smiled at her, and looked down at her knitting.

"Wow!"

He'd never seen anything like it. Intricate designs in multi-colored yarns made beautiful pictures creating a tube that he could only imagine would be a scarf someday. A glance revealed that it was easily the most complex piece in the room. He turned back quickly so that she wouldn't disappear.

"What's that?" He nodded down to her knitting.

TIFFANY LOOKED down at it and she had absolutely no idea.

Devin's unexpected arrival had broken the seams of normality she kept wrapped around herself during knitting.

"It's—" It had been so clear in her head just seconds ago, but like a dropped stitch, it was gone without noticing.

Devin leaned in and traced a finger over one of the patterns.

It felt as if his finger traced upon her cheek, just where he'd touched her before the kiss.

"It looks like a windmill."

"It is," Tiffany gasped out. She remembered that now, the long propellers of a big windfarm on a field of dark blue. "Denmark. Copenhagen. The water is so shallow that they plant them in the bay like giant tulips."

"Have you been there?"

She shook her head. "But I've seen pictures of them standing in the sea." Her family had traveled a lot, but mostly to the Orient, where her stepfather's business interests had been. "This is my anti-trip."

"Anti-trip?" Devin's finger traced over other patterns. "Places you've never been but want to go?"

That had Tiffany looking up at him in surprise. "Yes. Exactly."

"What are the green steps?"

"Vineyard terraces of Liguria."

"And this?"

"Gelato, by the cone and cup."

Devin had her lead him through her fanciful adventure, a bit of Scottish tartan, a classic Fair Isle pattern from the Shetlands and another from the Highlands. It was actually a map of her heritage: Scottish, Italian, a little Norse, and a chambermaid of Henry VIII (at least according to family legend), who'd been banished to Alnwick Castle for producing yet another girl for the king without a male heir. Online, Tiffany had found water sculptures in the Alnwick gardens and included those for the chambermaid.

"F," she explained on the last section he pointed to, a whole row of them connected together in a long chain: black with white block letters. "For Fitzinger the cat."

"The orca-colored cat."

He'd remembered. She wasn't sure if she was charmed or if it felt a little intrusive.

"Why Fitzinger?"

"Leopold Fitzinger was the first to include the killer whale in a genus-species taxonomy."

His laugh tipped her over into charmed.

It was easy to join in.

Then she was aware of the abrupt silence around the entire circle of women. It was as if her and Devin's shared laughter had snipped off all other threads of conversation. A quick peek revealed that, indeed, everyone was looking in their direction with differing reactions. Jessica was scowling at Devin, Becky and Gina were both smiling as if to say "of course." Most were simply surprised. Maggie Winslow looked at her thoughtfully—not at Devin, at her.

Tiffany tried to read her expression, but it was elusive. Neither surprise nor misconceived congratulations, but rather as if she was somehow finding Tiffany's laugh as food for thoughts of her own.

Unable to stand the pressure, she shot to her feet, barely rescued her knitting, and headed out the door.

Devin caught up with her a dozen steps across the gravel parking lot.

"I'm sorry. You should go back with your friends. I'll leave. I'm sorry for making you uncomfortable."

She shook her head, then tried to explain. "It's not you that's making me uncomfortable."

Devin blinked at her several times and then offered one of those glorious smiles she was rapidly learning to appreciate. "Let me guess:

that's exactly what *is* making you uncomfortable. That you aren't uncomfortable around me."

"I—" she shrugged. "No point in denying that, since you're right. You don't have to look so pleased." And he did look terribly happy with his discovery.

"Do you want to go back?"

Tiffany considered the closed door. Her friends were in there. Actual friends. Ones concerned for her and ones happy for her. Actual, real, live people she would count as friends. Then she looked back at Devin. She thought about his kiss and the way his questions about her knitting had tickled up her spine. And oddly, about the arrow he'd left in the tree like some lucky talisman.

Devin waited patiently while she dragged her thoughts back from the four winds.

"I—" She was going to have to find a way to start sentences without stuttering to a stop every time. "I," she pushed through, "would rather spend some time with you." There, she'd said it. Not what she'd expected to say, but still it was true.

He offered one of his great smiles, "I know this great parking spot."

She heard the tease this time and the flirt.

"Hang on," he raised a finger, then turned to the brewery and went back inside.

Tiffany was left to stand in the gravel parking lot, reviewing the conversation to see where it had gone astray. He'd left her to go and…do what?

"We can't miss these," Devin came back out carefully balancing two paper plates, each with a generous slice of pie.

"We'll need forks."

"Crap! Here," he handed her the pie plates so quickly she almost lost them to the gravel drive. Then he ducked back inside and returned wielding two plastic forks. "I had to promise a day of labor in the brewery if I don't return these. I think Becky was kidding." He took back one of the pie slices and then nodded across the hay field toward the hangar.

She could see his little pickup parked there and followed him to it.

It was a totally different experience riding through town in Devin's small truck than Gina's Prius. And it wasn't just the additional height off the road. The last time she'd been in a car with a man had been her assistant three years ago who helped her start the farm. Now a man was driving and she felt as if she was floating. But she was also conscious of the closeness. The SR5 was not a big truck and it felt closed in. Not unsafe, just…as if a pressure was squeezing her gently inward like a dive into deep water.

"Don't lose our pie," Devin's admonition grounded her in the moment.

She held the two plates, one balanced on either knee. They were perfectly safe, why was he—

"I mean, who knows if we can trust the guy who cut this road." Again he made it easy to smile at his joke.

Tiffany had daydreamed herself all the way to the B&B. Devin didn't stop. He rolled out the far side of the little parking lot by the big Victorian and turned up the hill along his newly cut road.

He needn't have worried. The surface was smooth and well packed; his truck climbed it easily.

Rather than parking alongside the lighthouse and facing outward as he had with the road grader, he turned and backed the truck into the same place. Tiffany was now looking toward her path home— across the newly shorn and level meadow and off into the trees. She felt no desire to run this time, but didn't know what Devin was doing. The view was now behind her.

He came around and opened her door as if she was some sort of a lady. "I'll take those," and he lifted away the two pie plates.

Now what was she supposed to do? *Get out of the truck for one thing, Tiffany.* And when she did, she saw that Devin had lowered the tailgate and perched on it facing the ocean. The evening sun was ducking down into the clouds far out to sea, lighting up the sky with warm yellows and soft oranges. The sea was calm; the breakers down below no more than five or six feet high where they crashed into the rocks at the base of Orca Head. The ocean breeze was still warm in the sun, though it would be cool in the shade.

It was cooler here; the tailgate put her at more ease than the close confines of the truck's cab. Somehow Devin had known that. She scooted up next to him and he handed her a slice of pie. They ate together in a comfortable silence and watched the sun's slow progress down into the clouds holding offshore.

"Good pie," she said when the silence had stretched long enough.

"I carried it from Peggy's myself."

"Tough job."

"Glad to do it." Again the silence sat with them for a few minutes before the breeze brushed it away. "So, tell me about your anti-trip. I've never really traveled much outside Chicago."

"My stepfather always took us to the Orient. I speak Japanese and Mandarin...but neither has ever felt right, like my brain and my mouth weren't built for those sounds. I heard a tape of Gaelic and somehow it made sense. It's a crazy language, but it simply fit."

"Which language is hardest? I only speak English and construction-crew Spanish, which isn't presentable anywhere except a build site."

"It depends..." and Tiffany marveled at herself as they discussed language and the travels they each hadn't done. She hadn't understood until this moment how little she'd spoken to men over the last few years. It was as if she'd forgotten how, had fallen out of practice. But Devin made it easy to recall, like a long forgotten sweater that still fit once patched, both familiar and new.

When they finished their pie, Devin tossed the paper plates into the back of his truck, but tucked the plastic forks safely into a pocket and winked at her. Then he continued telling her about his cross-country road trip and how that had made him realize what he'd been missing by staying anchored in Chicago.

If it had been a long time since she'd talked to a man, it had been even longer since she'd kissed one. She didn't really count yesterday's brief kiss. It had been ninety percent alarm on her part and only about ten percent kiss.

"I know I have to go back to Chicago at some point, but for now—"

For now.

Now!

Tiffany grabbed her nerves, wrestled them into submission, then leaned over and kissed Devin. She caught him mid-word, which should have been awkward, but he didn't let it be.

He tasted of strawberry-rhubarb pie.

When he slid an arm about her shoulders and held her close, she didn't feel trapped at all. Instead she was whirled up into a maelstrom of feelings. Her heart was moving blood at an unheard of rate, so fast the sonic boom was making her ears ring. She felt as if she could step off the cliff edge and fly over the sea as long as—

Devin pulled back first and she almost fell forward off the tailgate at the aftershock. She'd never so thrown herself at man in her life. But before embarrassment or confusion could take hold, Devin whispered softly.

"Hot damn!"

"Hot damn?" Tiffany was amazed that she could speak.

"Well, it sounds more western than 'Holy Shit!' or 'Son of a Bitch!' which would be more common in Chicago."

"Properly I'd be 'Daughter of a Bitch!' Which has the advantage of being true."

"Maybe we should introduce our moms. Sounds as if they'd hit it off."

Tiffany's head was still spinning. Moms, amazing kisses, and throwing herself at Devin all collided to leave her speechless. Deep inside she decided that she definitely agreed with his assessment on one point though: *Hot damn!*

"If I'd ever met a woman who kissed like that…" Devin left her hanging for a long moment as he stared out to sea. "I guess I'd never have come to Eagle Cove." It sounded as if he was speaking to himself, but she couldn't feel guilty for eavesdropping. Then he turned back to her, cupped her cheek in his callused palm, and kissed her lightly.

This time all rational thought didn't tumble down to plunge into the sea, but there was still a dreamy sense of rightness as she pressed her own palm in turn upon his cheek. There was an impossible rightness to it.

Maybe now she understood better the long sections of Lillian's journal where she had waxed eloquent upon how a man made her feel. But Tiffany didn't want to use her ancestor's words—this was her time. Her moment.

"Kissing you," she whispered against Devin's lips, "feels as right as speaking Gaelic."

"WE'VE HAD the dessert portion of our evening." Devin was unwilling to let her go yet but they couldn't spend the whole evening sitting on the back of his pickup truck. The wind was picking up and it was turning chilly.

"And the kissing portion," Tiffany agreed.

"Now it must be time for the movie portion," Devin agreed, happily quoting one of the funniest movies ever. "I can't believe you know *My Favorite Year.*"

"The problem is, did you see what's playing at The Flicker? *The Poseidon Adventure.* The 2005 version."

"Ack, gack!" Devin grabbed his throat and made choking noises until Tiffany laughed. Then he remembered Peggy had told him about Greg Slater's Tuesday night for locals and that he qualified. He grabbed Tiffany's hand and dragged her around to the passenger door of his truck.

"What? Where are we going?"

"I think it's time for the dinner portion of the evening, don't you?"

"No! Wait!"

But he knew if he waited, she'd slip away again. He closed the truck door, reached in through the open window, and toggled the lock. Then he rested his hands on the door frame and hoped as hard as he could.

She only would have to move her finger a few inches to unlock the door. And he would open it and let her go if she did. Slowly, ever so slowly, she turned to look up at him. She gazed a long time into his eyes. Then with a soft smile and that same impossibly slow action, Tiffany reached out and took hold of the seatbelt.

Devin held onto the door and hung his head until he heard the soft click of it engaging. He didn't know why it took so much out of him or why he hoped so hard, but it had and he did.

He climbed in beside her and drove them slowly back into town.

TIFFANY HADN'T EATEN in a restaurant in three years. And not in a high-end one since leaving San Francisco most of a decade ago.

Greg had transformed The Puffin. Fluorescent lighting had been abandoned and replaced by twinkle lights and table candles. Sheers had been drawn across the big windows, not quite hiding the main street, but softening it, making it feel far away. Worn Formica was masked by midnight blue table cloths. The individual tables had been pushed into a long line for communal service.

It was in some sort of dreamlike fugue that Tiffany floated through the evening. It became a scattershot of images. Greg's delight at her arrival. He and Devin debating about paying for the meal—Devin had ended up jamming two twenty-dollar bills down the back of Greg's pants when he'd turned away thinking he'd won. When Greg had dug them out and tried to give them back, Devin had raised his palms outward. "Eww!"

Tiffany had mimicked the motion and they had all three laughed together.

She knew many of the people who came; they greeted her as if nothing was out of the ordinary. Greg had seated them at one end and she recognized but didn't know the couple beside them, which was perfect. Mrs. Winslow and Hector at the far end—paying such attention to each other than Tiffany almost wondered if Mrs. Winslow hadn't seen her. She'd certainly made no fuss.

The food was exquisite. Her leeks showed up in the onion soup. The beets had been sliced, roasted to sweetness, and topped with a chilled salad based on fresh-caught crab. Snow peas adorned Asian-spiced rockfish. Fresh-made strawberry gelato with a dark chocolate sauce finished the meal. Becky's beers had accompanied each course in tiny taster glasses that matched to perfection.

There was only one thing in the entire meal that didn't blur together until she couldn't separate one thing from another.

Devin.

They talked movies, books, and even plays. It all meant nothing, and it all meant everything. Not once did he ask about her past, her farm, or even about her. Yet between their meaningless words, she was unsure if she had ever told anyone so much about herself.

THE SUN HAD TURNED the sky red-gold and the sea black by the time he drove Tiffany back to the lighthouse meadow. At the invisible trail-head—Devin had assumed it was just a rabbit track when he'd scouted the edge of the woods two days before, looking for where she'd gone—she turned to him.

No words.

She simply placed a warm hand on the center of his chest, as if keeping him carefully away for a moment. He reached up with both hands to catch her thick hair and brush it back over her shoulders. He wanted a clear view of her face despite the fading light. Her fine lips and strong eyebrows came from her father's Scots heritage, or so she'd said. The slender oval of her face from Italy. The hair and the shy smile, those were completely hers.

Rather than kissing him, she shifted her hand around his waist and hugged him. Hard.

There was no hesitation. No worries that he might "muss up" the woman in his arms. She simply held onto him and he did the same to her.

The crazy synergy of their kiss slammed back in, then built at a steamroller pace. When Tiffany hugged him, nothing was held in reserve. He could feel the soft curves of her body pressing against him as well as the fierce strength of her arms wrapped about his waist. When she rested her head on his shoulder, all he could think about was never letting go.

And then with a smile and a softly-whispered "Thank you," she slipped away into the dark forest. Just mere steps into the trees and she was gone like a ghost.

CHAPTER 4

Wednesday was delivery day and Tiffany spent much of it running her ATV with its little trailer out through the woods. She had a deal with a farm supply over in Eugene for biweekly deliveries of goat and chicken feed, along with anything else she called in. Once her garden had started producing and she'd canned a season's worth of food, her personal needs had been minimal. They also delivered propane whenever the biweekly truck driver noticed it was running low.

Her pick-up point was two miles up an old logging road that had the advantage of meeting the highway well out of town. The driver always dropped the load in a lean-to she'd placed along that road. It was the closest any vehicle bigger than an ATV could travel.

Three years before, after finishing with the heavy equipment, she'd planted a thick patch of native trees across the end of where her access driveway had been. In just a few months they'd blended into the forest until there was no sign that there had ever been a turn-off onto this road lost deep in the woods. A hundred feet before her now-hidden driveway, she'd built the lean-to mostly out of moss-covered logs and branches from the forest floor and topped it with rusted, corrugated metal. It had looked thirty years abandoned by the time it was done—exactly the effect she was after. On the back side, where it couldn't be seen without knowing it was there, stood her propane tank. After each delivery, she used a rake to spread forest floor detritus over her fresh tracks.

The lean-to also kept the feedbags and other supplies dry while waiting for her to fetch them in the thin rain that had moved in overnight. She'd heard it patter on the yurt's roof as she lay awake and considered the effects of her choices.

Three years alone in the woods had definitely been the best years of her life…so far. It was the "so far" that kept niggling at her, like a mischievous angel poking at her with a terribly ticklish feather—a very uncomfortable feeling. For the first time in a long while, a part of her had awoken with a question, a new one.

"What's next?"

She had no clearer idea after she'd pulled on slicks and tromped out into the morning weather.

Rain wasn't a constant on the coast like most people thought; instead it was a whimsical force that often slid in from the ocean with little warning. More often than long steady pours, it arrived as brutal dumps, then moved on. Her rain gauge had counted sixty-five inches last year (three-point-two inches in one day was her record so far) and this year was right on track—January had been chilly and dry, but February had already more than made up for it in sheeting downpours. March had again been dry and surprisingly warm. Only time would tell what April would provide. Her Wednesday delivery day was a "typical" long, slow drizzle, just heavy enough to require she wear slicks and just warm enough that she cooked in them.

She spent most of Thursday, after the storm system had thankfully moved inland and left behind a patchy gray overcast, shifting the goat pen. It was a challenging task as the goats were always so glad to see her that she could barely move as they clustered around. Maybe letting them learn that she always had some treat in her pockets had been a mistake. She doled out bits of early carrot and kale. Why in the world she'd ever planted kale she didn't know. It was healthy, but tough and took forever to cook.

Tiffany didn't mind the crowding. The baby goats were calf-high and bounced about as if their legs were made of pogo sticks. She was out of names from *Little Women*. She considered *Star Trek*, but if she did, she'd run out after Uhura and Chapel and have to name them all for Kirk's women. This year's kids would be from *Fiddler on the Roof*. Soon Tzeitel, Hodel, and Chava were all chasing Motel Kamzoil around the pen. If the last two were girls, they'd be Shprintze and Bielke; all five girls together again.

She'd brought a couple of biscuits for Tall Guy, who she then teased about how she'd met another man. He'd nodded his big black muzzle and huffed out a sigh as if that was only to be expected, or perhaps because she'd only brought two biscuits.

Devin was never far from her thoughts. There seemed to be an amplitude curve—the closer she worked to the west end of her property where the trail led to the lighthouse, the more aware of him she became. That's part of why she was working on the goat pen to the east. She wasn't exactly avoiding him, but she wasn't seeking him out either. That the pen needed moving—well, almost—was only part of the excuse.

Tiffany discovered that it was confusing to be attracted to a man again. It was as if that part of her had fallen so out of practice that the signals were constantly crossing. Social graces had never been one of her strengths but she'd gone out with a few nice guys in college and grad school, and "few" had been just fine with her. But with three years alone in the woods, she'd lost what little skills she'd had.

Lunging at Devin when she'd wanted to kiss him…the memory made her wince at her own ineptness. A woman was supposed to be…what?

"Well for one thing," she told Beth, who had always been her favorite goat, a dainty gray with black boots and a white mask, "she's not supposed to smell like a goat unless she is one." Amy came over— all elegant in her pure, soft silver coat—because she always did when another goat was receiving attention. Tiffany knew that she wouldn't smell of goat, she'd reek of it. She gave in and sat upon the drying grass to play with them and rest from the heavy work of moving the fence. Tall Guy took that as an invitation to come over and sit on her lap to keep her firmly in place.

"At a hundred and thirty pounds, you are not a lap dog," she groaned.

In answer, he began beating her in the ribs with wags of his great tail.

"A woman isn't supposed to smell like a dog either," but she scratched his ear as he kept her pinned to the wet grass.

Another happy thump against her ribs.

"I guess dog is better than goat."

As if she had a choice.

Was there anything else she could do to be *less* attractive to her own species?

DEVIN WALKED into the Puffin Bay Diner as it opened on Friday morning—and was nearly bowled over by Cal Sr. coming in on his heels.

"I swear. This is the last time Junior ever gets to leave town on a honeymoon. That's it. One time only." Cal stormed up to the counter and called out to the Judge working over his grill. "Tall stack, John. And double up on the coffee, Greg," he told the waiter, a slender man who might be the retired judge's son.

"Trouble at the bakery?" Greg poured him a mug.

"Wasn't paying enough attention these last few years. Junior has made all of these little expansions to our business, and dealt with 'em just fine without me really noticing. Now I'm making beer bread for the brewery, sourdough for our lunch service, pizza dough for Carrier Pigeon. Damn list goes on forever. And now Vincent McCall comes in wanting some kind of pretty cake for his tenth anniversary. Damn boy doesn't have a clue what, which tells me that Dawn didn't send him because she'd have included instructions—guess he's finally thinking how to keep her happy, but now it's making me *unhappy* as I can't just call up the girl and ask what she wants."

"Do you have their wedding cake on file?" Mrs. Winslow asked from where she'd come in behind Devin. "Pineapple Upside Down Cake if I recall. A single tier, as they were very poor when they started out. I suggest that you add a second tier as a marker of their success in building a family."

"Great! Thanks, Maggie. You're a wonder and that's the truth."

"Tell that to my students. Are you planning to stand there all day, boy?" She said the last to Devin.

"Uh, no, ma'am." Devin got caught between a smile that said she must be hell on her second graders and a wince at the admonition aimed his way. She waved him to one of the tables and, like a bad little boy, he headed for his corner.

The Puffin Bay Diner was a classic diner plucked right out of the fifties. Worn linoleum flooring. A dozen battered Formica tables of indeterminate color. Fresh paint and a mixture of art on the walls. There were two main artists represented, and the work was exceptional by both. They were almost related, but the vision was so different that they had to be two people. Even Picasso from Blue to Cubism, as he'd seen at The Art Institute of Chicago, you could see the same hand.

These were somehow the opposite. Here were two very different artists painting with a common emotion in a common theme: a deep love of Eagle Cove. He'd never seen them before, yet the art looked familiar…and then it clicked in. They had joined their talents to paint the big mural in Becky Billings BlueBird Brewery.

He'd never been an art collector, that was one of his mother's things. She'd buy exceptional pieces of art and then loan them to the Art Institute as long as they were prominently labeled with "On Loan from the Private Collection of…" But he might have to buy one of these before he left town. Something to remind him of this place. Maybe a second one to give to his mother as a family peace offering once he was less angry at her. If that ever happened.

Behind him, the big plate glass windows were still dark with the morning. Ahead was a six-stool counter and a big service window back into the kitchen.

Gina had told him last night that someone had called to set up a six a.m. meeting at the diner. She'd declined to say who, though of course she had to know. The women of this town were conspiring to make him crazy.

He'd tried drawing the plans for the renovation up at the light-keeper's cottage, but it had been wet and chilly these last few days. When he tried to work at the B&B, Gina had hovered. The library, his usual retreat in Chicago, was called the Wolery here (after Owl's home in Winnie the Pooh, the seat of all wisdom in the Hundred Acre Wood), but was only open Tuesdays and Saturdays from two to four.

For something to do, he'd spent most of the last two days ripping out the interior plaster. It had cracked with age. When he'd discovered there was no insulation behind it and the wiring was all turn-of-century (and not the most recent one), there'd been no further question: it had to come down. The problem with straight physical labor was that it left him far too much time to think.

And Tiffany had offered him a kiss and a hug better than any lover, and then evaporated into thin air. No one spoke of her in her absence. No one thought her invisibility was strange. It didn't bother anyone except him, and it was making him completely and totally—

"I thought you might want some help," Mrs. Winslow sat down across the table from him.

"All I'm doing is mucking out at this point, stripping walls and so on." He was currently working under a local contractor's license, a relationship that Gina had arranged with EC Contracting. He hadn't met with the contractor yet—and couldn't read the hieroglyph that passed for the signature of whoever had pulled the permit, except for an N at the start of the last name—but it didn't matter while he was still doing tear-down work. At some point he'd have to meet whoever owned Eagle Cove Contracting and make sure they saw eye to eye on quality and design. He shrugged, "Not that big a job."

Mrs. Winslow stared at him blankly while Greg delivered a menu, only to him.

"Aren't you eating?" Devin didn't want to be the only one eating at the table.

Mrs. Winslow nodded, "My usual if you please, Greg."

Devin stared down at the menu and ordered the first thing he spotted. "Western omelette, but without the onion."

"Nope," the waiter gave him a smile.

"Nope?"

"Nope. You order it and the Judge cooks it however he wants," then he winked. "Hasn't changed the menu in the six years since he retired from judging. Except the waffles, but they're back now."

"Okay," Devin sighed. Who was he kidding? He wasn't going to get another chance to kiss Tiffany again. The way things were going, he'd be glad to just see her again before he left town at the end of the summer. "With the onions is fine. On the side I'd like—"

"Nope," Greg again said with that smile.

"No options there either," Devin could feel his own smile starting up. "Is it okay if I put sugar in my coffee?"

"Sugar in your coffee, yes. You put ketchup on Dad's eggs and you're outta here."

"Deal." Which left him once more facing Dragon Winslow. He'd heard the nickname only the once when Vincent had called her that, but it fit. If he wasn't careful, he'd be saying it aloud.

The bell on the back of the door tinkled.

Dragon Winslow didn't even turn. "Over here, Hector."

"Just let me get my crossword," a tall, spare man in his sixties with thinning silver hair riffled through a copy of *The Oregonian* by the front door and brought one of the sections over to the table.

"Morning, Maggie. Hi," he held out a hand and offered Devin a crushingly powerful grip. "I'm Hector Jackson."

"Yow!" Devin did his best to shift his own grip to take the unexpected squeeze, but he was too little too late. "Devin Robison."

"Heh! Love doing that to young folk," he told the Dragon as he sat down. "Can't let them think that old people are, well, you know, Maggie."

"Old?" Devin offered.

Which earned him a cheerful, silverware rattling thump of agreement from Hector. Dragon Maggie Winslow gave him a chilly look. But he noticed that she offered Hector a smile just a moment later.

"Well, as I was telling..." he hesitated to make sure he chose the proper honorific, "...Mrs. Winslow."

A darting, dark-eyed glance told him that she hadn't missed his hesitation and probably not what was behind it either.

"I'm still tearing out the old interior. The plaster is too brittle and what's behind the walls needs a lot of work."

"Never worked on a house before. Wasn't exactly planning on starting now."

"Then—" Devin stopped in confusion.

"Do you sail, Mr. Robison?"

"Sure, I've been out on Lake Michigan a couple of times in a sail-boat. Though usually on my family's—" he bit that off "—power boat." Chicago Master Constructors, Inc. kept their ninety-foot motor yacht for entertaining at the family dock during the summer. In the winter, it was driven out through the Great Lakes and the St. Lawrence Seaway down to the Caribbean for entertaining top clients there. It was the only real travel he'd ever done, hopping the company jet down to the boat, and he hadn't done that in years. Oddly, the Oregon Coast looked far more foreign than a Caribbean island viewed from the sweltering deck of the big yacht.

"Stinkpotter," Hector and the Dragon exchanged smiles.

"What?"

"Boats that need engines aren't boats. They're floating pots that make a stink. It has to have a sail, buddy, or it's not a real boat."

Devin couldn't help but smile as he imagined how his father would react to the slur; he loved his yacht more than his wife, and probably more than his mistress. Thank god these people knew nothing about that connection. There was no more than a shared last name with CMC's CEO to link him with one of the biggest contractors in the Midwest. And at the moment he wished there wasn't even that. D.R. Builders was his own firm, even if he'd left it in his foreman's hands for the summer. He liked it that way.

"I believe that you need to fix that," the Dragon was still talking to Hector.

"Fix what?" Devin had missed something while watching the approach of their breakfasts. He could only goggle at the omelette slid in front of him. It was a four-egger, overflowing with red and green bell pepper, cheese, and sautéed onion. And the sausage and ham in the omelette apparently hadn't been enough meat, because there was a healthy serving of farm patty sausage and hash browns on the side. He wouldn't be hungry for a week if he could even finish this thing.

Dragon Winslow's and Hector's portions were significantly smaller.

"Dad knows that contracting is hungry work," Greg explained. "He also appreciates the runway work you did for his wife."

Devin turned to wave his thanks to the Judge, but only received a level gaze in return. He could imagine Peggy and the Judge trading that exact expression back and forth across the dinner table—mutually unreadable. Except perhaps to each other?

"You're looking at his thanks on the plate." Greg shrugged as if to explain that was typical and was gone again. Devin kept an eye out on the next couple of services as the diner was over half full despite the early hour. His meal was all out of proportion with the still generous servings that were sent out to other tables.

The Dragon was watching him.

"What?" Devin had lost the thread of the conversation.

Hector was the one who answered, but continued talking to the Dragon. "Won the Judge's respect his first week in town. Hard to do."

"Peggy walked Devin's new road above Gina's. She said it was respectably done."

News to Devin.

Then the Dragon turned to face him. "Nine o'clock on Sunday. Be at the docks unless there is no wind."

Devin had been here long enough already to know how unlikely that was. Wind appeared to be one of the constant features of the coast.

Then something shifted in her stern face. The Dragon faded and for the first time he saw deep tenderness that he'd wager she revealed to few.

"I think, young man, that you should bring that girl with you on Sunday. If anyone can coax her off her mountain, I suspect that it is you."

"Sunday?" Devin wondered what possible power he had over Tiffany. Or what strange insight did Mrs. Winslow have that he didn't? "She's invisible. I might not see her before then."

"Oh, I would not worry about that. She never misses Friday knitting. Now, Hector," she picked up her fork, "what is the first clue on your crossword puzzle this morning?"

DEVIN SPENT the early part of Friday afternoon loading debris into his truck so that he wouldn't miss Tiffany's passage down to the B&B for knitting. He was white with plaster dust by the time he was done but he'd seen no sign of her. The tiny nails in the lath strips had caught his clothes and skin, tearing holes in the former and leaving him scratched and scraped. It stung, but it was also comforting in its familiarity. Demolition of plaster was a familiar part of renovating older homes.

He checked the trailhead before leaving for the dump, but there were no new footprints coming out of the woods.

On his way back from the dump, he pulled into the B&B, ostensibly for water and an energy bar, though he had both in his truck. He didn't know how he'd speak to Tiffany in her circle of friends, but he had to at least see her.

In complete contrast to the damp morning, the afternoon was warm, almost hot, and the breeze still. The knitters sat out on the porch. A quick scan—no Tiffany. No empty chair with a pile of elaborate "anti-trip" knitting resting on it, awaiting its mistress' return.

Then Mrs. Winslow looked up from her own knitting and spotted him. With pursed lips, she shook her head ever so slightly. It was impossible to miss the look of concern, which slammed him from cheery to fearful.

He scrambled back to his truck with the barest of courtesies and headed up to the lighthouse. The fact that she was obviously a very capable woman did nothing to turn aside his fear. A bear got her. Or she'd broken a leg and couldn't get up. Or…

Devin slammed the truck to a halt close by the woods. He rummaged among the tools in his truck and grabbed a crowbar for defense before plunging into the woods. After the first dozen paces he was hopelessly entangled in the low, dead branches sticking out from the Douglas fir trees. They broke off easily enough, which said that Tiffany had never passed this way.

He traversed back and forth, looking for some sign. On his third try, he spotted a footprint on a muddy spot among the ferns and branches that littered the forest floor. Once he turned onto the track, he could see a clear passage, but not before. It weaved and veered, but it led in the right general direction for the overlook above the light-house meadow.

The shadows jumped at him. A squirrel, far smaller than the big grays of the Chicago parks, chittered at him angrily from where it clung upside-down, far up a tree. Birds scattered away in front of him as if he was hunting them instead of a missing woman. He scanned side to side, at first for signs of Tiffany, then also for signs of bears as he plunged deeper into the woods—he kept his crowbar at the ready.

The forest was bewildering. He'd thought he had a feeling for it from driving through it and working alone at the lighthouse meadow. But nothing prepared him for walking beneath its canopy. The sunlight, almost hot in the still meadow, was a shadowy memory. The occasional glistening shaft would pierce down to illuminate a few square feet of moss, growing on a fallen log, but even that was shad-owed by splayed branches. Looking at the sunny spots was a mistake as it darkened the rest of the forest.

Trees soared upward to bewildering heights. The lower branches sported little greenery, leaving bare trunks to reach forever upward. Smaller trees struggled in the darkness. Ferns grew around fallen trees. Some of the fallen had tipped their roots with them, exposing labyrinths of twisted roots and shedding soil two or three times his own height. At one that looked fairly recent, he looked to see if Tiffany lay beside or partly under it. The trunk ran for a hundred feet or more off into the distance; smaller trees were flattened to either side by the blast zone of the giant's crash.

No Tiffany. He hurried on.

He was moving so fast that he almost ran off the cliff at the over-look. It was a narrow ledge over a hundred-foot fall. Not that narrow, but enough to stop him cold. And she passed this way every day?

Devin had walked the ironwork on plenty of his father's skyscrapers but hadn't felt as exposed as he did at this moment. The sweeping hundred-and-eighty-degree view took his breath away and the hundred-foot fall into Terra Incognita nearly took away his nerves. He edged around the curve until he once again picked up the trail.

And now his goal was clearly in sight. A neat area the size of two city blocks had been carved into the wilderness—ten acres or close enough. Much of it was in meadow. But a circular building with a pointed roof was tucked up against the far trees. It was so incon-gruous that it took him a moment to identify it as a yurt, which he'd only ever seen in photos of the Mongolian nomads. Near it lay a massive garden laid out in neat rows behind a tall fence. There were a few small outbuildings that looked like garages. A large set of solar panels stood on the south slope. The view, he looked over his shoul-der, was a massive south and west vista of untouched wilderness backed by ocean.

He wondered how much help she had tending to it. Some man who took care of it, and her?

No.

Not with the way she'd kissed him. He refused to believe that someone who was two-timing him, like his ex-fiancée, could have kissed him like that. Rebecca Monica Monash of the Winnetka Monashs certainly never had.

Devin hurried down the trail. It plunged back into the forest but was far better groomed on this side of the ridge, as if she had nothing left to hide. A wide lane of tamped earth let him move quickly. In a few places, logs had been chainsaw split and buried flat side up as steps. A small bridge crossed an active creek rushing down a narrow gully from somewhere higher up in the Coast Range mountains.

The woods ended abruptly, practically launching him into an open meadow. And there he nearly flattened her.

———

TIFFANY YELPED in shock as a man burst out of the trees. He was filthy, his clothes torn, his face looked as if some woman in her last desperate moments had dragged her nails over his skin, and he held a weapon high in one hand.

Her past had come back!

Somehow it had found her here in what she'd always thought of as her maiden's mountain fastness, safe from the cruel world.

She dropped to the ground, beside the hole she'd been digging, and huddled there in the dirt.

Her final thought was how appropriate it was that she'd dug her own grave.

"Tiffany?"

She kept her head covered, waiting for the blow, the inevitable crashing slap her stepfather had so loved before the true horror began.

"Tiffany?" This time a hand touched her ever so lightly on the shoulder.

When she flinched it jerked away rather than pinning her harder.

"Tiffany, it's…"

Devin.

"…Devin."

She knew the voice. Not her past—no flashback of foul memories. But she couldn't move. Not yet. Though she managed not to flinch when the hand once more brushed her shoulder.

"I'm sorry I scared you."

Which didn't begin to explain what he'd done. Scared and stark terror had no more relation that a smile and ecstasy. It was a black pit from which there was no return. No way back to—

She did her best to shove that aside.

"Devin?" She hadn't meant it as a question, but her throat was too tight to control.

"Yes." And he was helping her to sit up in the dirt.

Her hands remained clenched protectively across her chest, but her feet swung down into the hole. Into the grave. Into Flo's grave. The little goat had fought bravely through the night and the day to bring her kid into the world. She'd succeeded, but in the end it had cost her own life and it had been beyond Tiffany's skill to save her. It was only the second goat she'd ever lost, and it felt as if a piece of her heart had died along with it.

Her hands were still bloody, her jeans and shirt dark with dried stains of a blood loss she hadn't been able to stop.

"Devin?" This time she managed to turn and face him as he sat on the grave's lip beside her.

"Right here."

He too was a mess. Covered in plaster dust. His face bore a half dozen scrapes that she would now see were minor and not the parallel claw marks left by a panicked woman. One had released a small trickle of blood that had run down his cheek like a tear before it dried.

She'd never seen anything so wonderful in her life and buried her face in his shoulder.

When his arm slipped tentatively around her shoulders, the tears began to flow. And she couldn't stop them. Soon she was weeping for her failure to save Flo and then for her past and then simply because she couldn't stop. Her sides ached with the release, yet Devin simply held her.

He didn't shush her.

He didn't promise it would be alright.

He did nothing but hold her tightly and let her cry. When her tears had turned the plaster dust of his shirt back into muddy plaster, she finally found the ability to rein herself back in before the plaster reset and they became a permanent casting themselves. Her fingers hurt as she unclenched them from their tight fists, and finally patted Devin on the chest in thanks.

That had been her undoing before. After that amazing kiss, she had rested her hand on his chest. It wasn't the strong pecs that had captured her attention, but rather the way he felt. As if her hand had simply belonged on his chest. A warmth. A connection. Like no other she'd ever experienced. And she felt it this time too as she spread her fingers over his shirt.

"Sorry I scared you so badly," he whispered again.

"Not your fault," she managed, and brushed at where she'd been weeping against him. Her efforts did nothing but stir the soggy plaster patch into an even less artistic form than her nose imprint. "Don't take the blame for my past."

And without needing explanation, without asking *what* about her past, he simply hugged her hard against him again, dried blood on her clothes and all.

That's when the laugh started. Small at first, it built inside her until it burst forth, almost as wild and hysterical as the weeping had been. Her sides, already sore, were soon in agony.

Where Devin had unexpectedly accepted her weeping, he pulled back from her laughter.

"What's so goddamn funny?"

"I—" she gasped again, trying to find the air to speak. "I was telling Tall Guy—"

"Tall Guy?"

"My dog. I was telling him…that there was no way…I could make myself…less attractive to my own species."

"Uh-huh."

"That was before I got covered in goat blood," Tiffany brushed at her tears. "God, I'm a mess in so many ways." She found a clean spot on her sleeve and used it to wipe her face and nose clean. "Run, Devin. Take my advice and run while you still have the chance."

"Could do that," he rubbed a hand down her back.

She suddenly really wanted him to stay.

"But I only just got here."

And this time she was able to join in his laugh without lapsing back into man-repelling hysteria.

Then she looked down at their feet, dangling together in the grave, and remembered she had a friend to bury and a newborn kid to nurse.

"IT SEEMED TOO impersonal to use the Bobcat to dig it, but I'm being silly. I'll go get it."

Devin stopped her, picked up the four-foot steel breaker bar, and pounded and levered at the hard soil until the hole was deep enough. She knelt at the edge, scooping out shovelfuls of what he broke free.

Devin was utterly exhausted by the time they finished digging the grave in the hard soil.

The goat looked so small when they put it down in the grave. Once the body was covered, they backfilled it together. Rather than morose words or a dirge, she offered up a song by Little Big Town about all being in the band together. All the while tears trickled quietly down her face. He'd done his best with the harmony line.

"She always liked that song," she managed on a hard swallow.

Then she'd introduced him to Tall Guy on the way back across the property—the biggest damn dog Devin had ever seen. It was hard to tell if he would have survived the encounter if not for Tiffany's chaperonage. The dog clearly felt that Devin was suspect and kept a careful eye on him as he was introduced to the goats.

If the goat in the grave had looked small, the newborn kid looked microscopic. It weighed only three pounds and was the size of a Chihuahua, a small one. When Devin went to lift it, Tall Guy unleashed a deep, earth-rumbling snarl. Tiffany merely patted the beast on the head and collected the tiny newborn herself. They took it back to her yurt with them as the sun was sliding down to the horizon.

The yurt was a revelation. Funky and remote farm had nothing to do with the way Tiffany Mills lived. A large bank of solar cells covered the south slope beside the structure.

The yurt's outer material was a thick, rubberized cloth, and the windows and doors, as real as any he'd install on a normal house, were well finished with wood trim. Once inside, Devin had to stop and stare as Tiffany carried the goat to a small framed-in pen close beside the propane stove. The floor was polished oak, lustrous and rich in grain. A full kitchen and bath had been installed along one wall and sported the finest fittings: a Five Star gas range and oven, a small fridge, and granite counters on cherrywood cabinets. A large oak dining table stood close by the windows and was covered by a puzzle still mostly in a thousand pieces. The bed was covered with an heirloom quality quilt—at least he assumed it was because he'd never seen one look so sharp.

"I still haven't finished the stitching," she indicated a corner that had simple grid rows of wide stitches rather than the elaborate pattern that covered the rest of the quilt.

A large cat lay on the other corner.

"Fitzinger is indeed orca-colored."

"And blobbish," Tiffany agreed as she pet him. "He's angry because it's past dinnertime." She rushed into the kitchen and quickly set a bowl of food on the floor.

Devin had the distinct impression that the cat scowled at him before deigning to go and eat. He wondered just who was the master of the yurt after all.

Devin brushed the cat hair off the quilt and almost blurted out, "You did this?" Tiffany seemed to always make him want to restate the obvious. Instead he managed, "It's already gorgeous."

"Thanks," Tiffany was making up a baby bottle for the goat. "You first."

"Me first what?"

"Shower. Just shake out your clothes, though. I don't think I have anything that would fit you and my only dryer is the wind."

Devin would actually take that as a good sign. No men here. No men leaving clothes behind. *Cad!* But the appellation didn't stick as he soaped and scrubbed. It went right down the drain with the plaster dust and old sweat. Something inside him was more than just charmed by a woman who sang a country rock song over a goat's grave.

The soap stung his face, but soon he was as clean as he was going to get without fresh clothes. He'd spotted the rainwater catchment tanks outside. Unsure if she also had a well, he finished quickly to save water.

Not wanting to beat his mucky clothes clean in her immaculate bathroom, he wrapped a towel around his hips and carried the dirty clothes out onto the deck. He was thankful that Tiffany was too intent on feeding the little goat to notice that her towels weren't exactly thick enough to hide his body's reaction to wandering mostly naked through her home.

By the time he was dressed and ready to go back inside, the light was failing. The entire horizon was dark with thick clouds, but they looked to be far out to sea. The dome of the sky was a deep blue he'd never seen in Chicago. Mesmerized, he watched the last of the color bleed out of the sky.

He decided that this was a good place to be as he could hear the shower start again. Imagining Tiffany so nearby, naked and covered in soap was a dangerous image. Yet she'd invited him here. And while her thinking might be occasionally straightforward, he'd learned over dinner that a very sharp mind lurked behind that reserved, shy facade that she presented to most people. In fact, Greg had stumbled to a halt as he came up behind Tiffany to serve her while she and Devin were talking about how *To Kill a Mockingbird* could be adapted to modern issues. He'd looked down at the back of Tiffany's head wide-eyed, like staring at a lion's (or rather a lioness') lioness) as the cage door at the zoo as it accidently swung open. He had silently delivered her food and rushed away for the safety of his kitchen.

As the meal progressed, Devin had become fascinated by his dinner companion. She was cloistered only in how she lived. Her comments were sharp, perceptive, and deeply observant of the world around her. Though they had stuck mostly to books and movies, her interpretations of thematic congruencies and dissonances (her words) revealed a deeply thoughtful and caring woman.

"Planet light, planet bright," Tiffany whispered as she stepped up beside him on the darkened yurt deck. "First planet I see tonight." He hadn't even heard the shower turn off.

"Where…oh!" Even as he turned his head toward her he spotted the elusive point of light just emerging from the fading brightness of the day. "Which one is it?"

"Venus. Goddess of love and beauty. The Romans also heaped fertility, sex, prosperity, desire, and victory onto her shoulders, which has always struck me as a little bit excessive. If you're going to go with a pantheon rather than a single god, it feels like you're cutting out a lot of potential good jobs for women by giving so many of them to just one. And can you imagine what her in-basket must have looked like back in the day?"

"Ugly," Devin agreed, growing more aware of Tiffany's closeness by the second. It was as if she radiated warmth enough to push back the cooling evening. Perhaps a goddess power of her own.

"No, beautiful. She's the goddess of beauty after all, so of course her in-basket would be beautiful…just crammed very full."

He laughed because of course she was right. He was beginning to have trouble breathing with Tiffany standing so close beside him on the deck.

"Would you—" "I should—"

"You first." "No, you."

When Tiffany didn't continue, Devin finally spoke. "I should get back. It's getting late." Actually it was getting dark and he wondered what evil beasts lurked in the night forest and how he'd find his way through. "What were you going to say?"

"I was going to ask if you'd like some tea or maybe a hot cocoa."

"I'm not so sure that's smart," Devin turned slowly to face her shadowy outline, "because that would mean keeping my hands off you for even longer than I already have."

There was a long silence. Then he heard a fast flutter of wings overhead.

"What the hell?" He ducked when he saw an outline against the sky like no bird he'd ever seen before.

"It's a little brown. I have a colony of those bats living on the north edge of the property; they like the stream there."

"You have a colony of bats? Are they dangerous?"

"Only to bugs."

"Oh." And the silence returned. He should go. He should do the decent thing and start down the steps in front of him. He should—

Then Tiffany stepped into his arms. As fierce as her final hug had been down in the lighthouse meadow, this time it was as soft as her hair. Her kiss wasn't wild or frantic, instead it was lush. A warm, soft, thorough kiss.

"I'm getting you dirty," though he didn't know why he cared. He could smell her clean freshness and knew that he didn't offer the same, not in his construction clothes.

In answer she tugged at the hem of his t-shirt. Before he could protest, she'd yanked it up far enough that he had no choice but to let her take it off the rest of the way.

A shiver slid over his skin, whether due to the night air or in anticipation of holding her just that much closer, he wasn't sure.

"Well, if one of us is going to be half naked," he began unbuttoning the front of her flannel shirt and she didn't stop him. He wished there was enough light to see. He'd imagined what she would look like: strong yet soft, curved but trim with hard work. She always wore loose clothes that, combined with her long hair, kept her form hidden from view. But when he had opened the last button and could slide his hands about her waist, he decided that his imagination was completely lacking in…imagination.

Her skin was so soft and smooth against his palms that he might be holding water. As he pulled her in by sliding his hands up her back, he could feel the muscles ripple beneath her narrow shoulders. And this time when their chests pressed together there was no mere impression of curves. Tiffany wasn't powerfully curved, but neither was she delicately slender—a man who had the good fortune to hold her knew that a woman's breasts pressed against his chest. He levered the shirt off her shoulders and she put her arms back to let it slip away into the darkness.

Unable to resist, he scooped his hands into her hair and then fluttered it outward in a long billow through his fingers. She wrapped her arms around his neck and giggled as he played with it. It was an utterly ridiculous length for someone who lived and worked on a farm and he loved every last inch of it.

He scooped again, this time flipping it up and over both of them so that they were hidden beneath the sliding tresses. This time when he kissed her, beneath the canopy of her hair, the fierce power was back. The fire reached down and grabbed him hard and he pulled her to him as tightly as he could.

TIFFANY COULD FEEL the crazy need taking her over again, just like the first time she'd kissed Devin. She considered pulling back—shutting it down, or at least tempering her emotions enough that he wouldn't think she was a lunatic. But he made her feel that way and she had promised herself long ago that feelings were not a game; if she felt them, she'd show them.

Her mother manipulated them like weapons until Tiffany doubted that she would know a true feeling unless it introduced itself with an exceptional stock portfolio. And if her ancestors Lillian and Pearl had managed to speak their true feelings so long ago, perhaps all of their lives would have been different.

And Devin made her feel her emotions—and though they were mostly unfamiliar, they were powerfully wonderful ones. His rough hands on her skin made her so aware of being alive. His strong chest pressed against hers was creating a feedback system of hyperawareness. And his obvious joy while playing with her hair kept making her want to laugh. She'd thought a hundred times about hacking it off. There was no longer any need to hide from aggressors, not in Eagle Cove, especially not in the deep woods on a hidden farm. It was also a reminder of her taking control of her past. Now it was a question of taking control of her present.

But Devin's combing fingers brushed all of those memories away except for Lillian's joy at a man brushing her hair through his hands. Lillian's—

No. Not Lillian's.

Tiffany's joy.

She needed.

That became the overriding sensation. She needed Devin. He made her feel; it had been so long since she'd *felt*. Not just physical sensation but also deep in her chest. It was a crazy mix. Today had held grief, near hysteria, joy, and now…need.

When she started to remove his jeans, he laid a hand over hers.

"I brought no protection."

"I did," she owned precisely one box that she replaced on the expiration date each year, but had never opened. Not once, until she'd come out of the shower to see Devin standing barefoot on her deck, silhouetted against the sunset. Then she knew why she'd kept buying them. This time she wouldn't be throwing them out on their expiration date.

He didn't resist as she finished undoing his pants. As she worked them down his legs, she felt the strength that he had. Devin was neither desk jockey nor weekend warrior; he was a man who used his body and used it hard.

Once he'd stepped out of his pants, she quickly shed her own and then moved back against him. Again that dynamic shock as if their bodies recognized each other beyond all possibility.

Unable to wait, unable to delay her need, she pulled him down onto the deck until he was lying atop her.

"I've never made love out of doors," he whispered to her.

Neither had she. Sex was hidden. Dirty deeds in dark corners. In college and grad school, the few times she had allowed it to occur, it had always been in her own bed. She'd never gone to a boy's room; only in a place that was hers, where she felt safe.

She focused past Devin at the now dark sky and could only gasp in wonder. Behind him, like a perfect tapestry, the stars were slowly filling the sky.

"What?" He froze and asked as if he was afraid he'd hurt her.

"Let's trade places and you'll see."

Instead of some awkward maneuvering, he used his strength to roll them over; a strong hand clamped firmly on her butt to help guide them sent a warmth shooting through her from his hand to her toes.

"I don't—Oh!" His gasp of wonder took her by surprise. She hadn't really expected him to understand the magic of the vast openness. It was just the two of them beneath the whole sweep of the sky. But he did. He understood.

"Now," she managed past a tight throat. She flailed around a hand on the deck until she found her pants pocket and shoved the foil packet into Devin's palm. "Now! Hurry! Please hurry!"

He didn't keep her waiting but a moment. Then with his strong hands guiding her hips, she slid down over him, taking him in. Even first contact had sensations shooting through her. Each rocking of her hips blossomed along her nerves. When he pulled himself up enough to find one of her breasts with his tongue, her body bloomed.

Sex had been enjoyable at times, though she'd never really understood the big deal. But with Devin inside her, coaxing, inviting, welcoming, she flew. Flew until she was lost between the stars and the wonderful man who lay beneath her.

When both of their bodies had at long last ceased shuddering and she lay upon his chest, Tiffany decided that she might never move again.

"Your skin is all goosebumps," Devin whispered as he rubbed his hands over her bottom and held her tight against him.

"You're so romantic," she teased him. Then she blinked at herself in surprise. She'd *teased* him. It was a skill she didn't know she possessed. A skill she'd lacked before this moment.

"How about this?" he lifted her off him, despite her whimper of protest. With all of the blood surging through her body, how could she ever be cold again?

But then he swept her up into his arms and carried her into the yurt like some movie heroine, which definitely improved his rating on the romantic scale. The small heat lamp over the sleeping kid in its pen filled the interior of the yurt with a soft red glow. Devin carried her to the bed and together they slid under the covers. He then improved his rating even more by not disturbing Fitz, who lay curled up on his pillow. Instead, Devin shared her pillow and pulled her tightly against him until she had no choice but to rest her head on his shoulder, wrap her arm about his wonderful chest, and throw a leg across his hips.

"I guess I was never the most romantic guy, but I can work on that."

She breathed him in until she was almost dizzy with him. "This works great for me just as we are."

"Me too," he sighed, one hand upon her back and the other hooked over her knee. And between one moment and the next, fell asleep.

"How stereotypical," she whispered but couldn't help smiling. There was a man in her bed, something that hadn't happened in a long time. A man that she wanted there more than any other before. He'd said he had to go back to Chicago at some time, but he was here now and she decided that was all that counted.

DEVIN WOKE to a soft bleating sound and wondered where the hell he was. A strange ceiling of upward-sloping 2x4s arranged like slices of a pie.

Another bleat.

Alone in a large bed with—he slid a hand out—a warm spot close beside him. Somewhere in the night Fitz had relinquished the second pillow to Devin.

A whispered, "Hush you. It's almost warm," brought Devin the rest of the way awake. The newborn kid was on its feet in the little pen with its nose pressed hard against the screen; Fitz was curled up just outside the pen but still in the wash of the heat lamp, revealing exactly where his true loyalties lay.

And then an impossible mirage moved across from the shadowed kitchen, holding a baby bottle.

Tiffany, clothed only in her hair, reached into the pen, lifted out the goat, and then sat on the floor with the kid cradled in her lap as it suckled eagerly on the baby bottle. He could only watch in wonder as she fed, soothed, and coddled the tiny creature. Her fair skin was warmed by the small light, or perhaps it was by the love that shone out of her.

The newborn was falling asleep in her lap by the time Tiffany was done, then she gently returned her to the pen. She rose in a fluid motion, her hair floating behind her as she returned the half-empty bottle to the refrigerator.

There was a lithe strength to her movements and a breathtaking beauty to her form. She didn't have the trainer-toned and balanced perfection that Rebecca Monash had achieved. Instead she had a natural reality that could only come from healthy living and hard work.

"Who are you?" Devin asked in wonder as she slid back between the covers.

"Why? Does it matter?" Tiffany's voice was oddly defensive, a tone he hadn't heard from her before.

"No. I mean. Well it does, but that isn't what I was asking."

"Then what were you asking?" She was keeping her distance beneath the covers and he wondered if she could disappear from her own bed as mysteriously as she could when visiting Eagle Cove.

"I barely know you, yet it's like you've hypnotized me. I don't know if I've ever seen something more beautiful than watching you sit there feeding that goat. Your kindness pours out of you. And this farm. Do you really do all this alone?"

"I hired help to set up here, but that was three years ago. You're the first person ever to trespass on my property."

"Trespass?"

He could see her wince. "That didn't come out right."

"Okay," he'd let that go because he supposed he had been trespassing. "I guess what I'm trying to say is, you're one damned impressive woman."

"Really?"

He laughed at the surprise in her voice. "Really. All this and the best sex of my lifetime, for all of it being over way too fast. I—" but he'd keep those other thoughts to himself. He'd wondered if the joy and the need of sex had been burned out of him by Rebecca's betrayal, but Tiffany had just proven that completely wrong.

"Sex." Her voice was flat when she said it.

Devin could have kicked himself. It had been great sex, or certainly the most powerful ever. But "sex" was what you had when it held no meaning. And impossibly, though he'd known her only a week, this had been so much more.

"This was just—"

Unable to stand the flat tone, Devin cut her off with a frustrated growl. "Let me show you what I meant," and he kissed her. She didn't protest, but it was a long and oddly fear-filled moment for him before she gave in and opened to him.

This time it wasn't over too fast, except that he never wanted it to end. The goat had woken them well before dawn. It was well after before he was done showing Tiffany how he felt about her.

Because it was more than just sex. In fact, he was a little unnerved by how much more.

Tiffany missed Devin even more than she missed Flo, which didn't seem right. Flo had been one of her very first kids, born of Meg. Tiffany had stayed awake for days, sitting in the pen with the goat care books in her lap. She fussed more over the newborn than Meg had, and now Tiffany had buried her.

She could see the other adults looking for their friend, especially Annie who'd been so close to Flo. Her orphaned kid needed such constant care and feeding, that Tiffany slipped her into a sling and carried her through the day. Maybe when Annie finally birthed, she could rub some of the birth matter on the first kid and convince her that she'd delivered two.

But it wasn't to her goats or her garden that her thoughts kept drifting so often.

It was to Devin Robison. The way he'd looked down at her even as the aftermath rippled through her. He might have called it "sex," but she could see in his eyes that it was something more even if he wasn't willing to say it. She wasn't sure that she was either, but had been unable to look away as he searched her face for answers she didn't have.

They'd barely spoken over a breakfast, not out of awkwardness but because there had been no need to chink words into gaps of feeling. The yurt's air had been thick with feeling and it had been enough to keep them trading smiles as they ate scrambled eggs with a sprinkling of reconstituted dried diced ham that she'd put up last year and early asparagus from her garden. His horror that the eggs had arrived chicken-warm and covered in poo had set her to giggling. Again the hysteria had threatened. She was so out of her element. A beautiful man had twice made love to her, had helped her bury her goat, and had left her with such a sweet kiss before heading back down the trail.

How was she *not* supposed to think about him and that confident male stride as he'd headed off across her land? In the distance she'd seen him stop at the very edge of her property. He spent a few minutes there, then she heard the soft banging sound on the breeze as he drove a branch into the ground to mark Flo's grave, using his abandoned crowbar as a hammer.

Or not think about his invitation to go sailing tomorrow morning. The only time she left the farm other than for knitting had been the weddings of Jessica, Becky, and now Natalya and Gina. Going to town on a Sunday felt wild, even a little dangerous, but perhaps in a good way.

That was the most intrusive thought that Devin had left behind. Had she spent too much time alone up on her mountain? Too used to only her own company?

The odd thing was that in Eagle Cove she was a far more social person than she'd ever been in her life. For three years, the women of Eagle Cove had welcomed her, let her sit with them, be with them, all without making any demands upon her.

Devin had intruded on her property, her thoughts, and was now starting to slip his way into her heart. Her heart was hers, it belonged to no one. That was a lesson hard learned.

But Jessica was happy with her Greg, despite her whining complaints about her pregnancy. And Becky's and Natalya's happiness was unmistakable as well. They didn't just stand by their men, they gave their hearts to them.

"I don't know if I can ever do that," she told Tall Guy.

He rolled his eyes at her without even bothering to raise his head off his forepaws.

"Come on, you." She let him out of the goat pen and led him off into the woods to help check the rabbit snares.

"Maybe I'll just skip tomorrow's sailing." Though she'd never been out on a boat despite growing up in San Francisco. It would be a new experience. As if Devin Robison wasn't enough new experience.

And there he was again, back in the center of her thoughts, making her body tingle at just the memory of his touch.

"Or maybe I will go."

Tall Guy didn't look at all surprised as she changed her mind for the hundredth time this morning.

He still didn't look surprised when she petted him the next morning before heading down the trail with little Shprintze riding in a sling under her arm.

DEVIN HAD BEEN at the trailhead by seven-thirty because he was piti-ful. He'd said eight-thirty, but he'd thought that it would be more decent if he hiked up and called for her at her door.

But would that be trespassing? She'd said it that way, *You're the first person to ever* trespass *on my property.* Maybe he shouldn't go without an invitation.

Which had left him cooling his heels in the lighthouse meadow for half an hour and wondering if instead he might have offended her for not returning after work the previous night and now she wouldn't come. Again he stood at the trailhead.

No, he decided again. *Too pushy.*

Then he wondered if he'd been too high pressure by even inviting her out. It sounded suspiciously like a date. To kill time, he couldn't go to work on the cottage; it would just make him all dirty again. Instead he pulled out the half-finished plans and unrolled them on the hood of the truck.

It took him forever to shift his thoughts from the full-body sendoff he'd received yesterday morning to the cottage's redesign, but he finally managed.

He'd add a porch, one big enough to sit under on a warm day and stay dry under while unlocking the door on a wet one. But it also had to be small enough and the right form to fit in without breaking the cottage's exterior charm.

The inside…was still puzzling him. He couldn't yet see what direction he wanted to take the décor yet. The room layout was easy. Because it would be changing from a lighthouse keeper's family into private rooms, he'd have to add several baths. Gina had cleared the idea to make a larger suite out of two of the upstairs rooms, which had saved him finding somewhere for a second staircase. There would be a small kitchenette on the ground floor, but breakfast would still be down at the big Victorian, which simplified that. It would allow him to convert the old dining and kitchen area into an additional cozy room which offset the doubled room upstairs.

A week to finish the teardown and muck out. Two weeks upgrading wiring and plumbing. Another to inspect, insulate, sheetrock. That would leave two months to refloor and do all of the detailed finish and trim work. If everything went according to plan, he could be back in Chicago by September for the tail end of the building season.

Maybe if he…

And there she was. One of her inevitable flowy shirts, this one a russet orange, a light jacket carried loosely in one hand and a tiny goat head peering at him from a sling under her other arm.

"Are you planning to say hello?"

Tiffany was so damned beautiful, the sun shining upon her hair as if she had indeed been manifested anew right at this moment. Star Trek transportered into place. Unable to speak, he circled the truck.

"Your plans!"

He heard them curl back up, roll off the truck's hood, and plop into the dirt. To hell with his plans.

Careful of the tiny goat, but nothing else, he scooped Tiffany against him and kissed her hard. She tasted like heaven. Her soft sigh of pleasure had him considering how she'd feel lying naked beneath him on his truck bed, if he cleared all of the scrap lath out of it.

Something hard fisted him in the ribs. Hard enough to make him break the kiss though Tiffany had tipped her head back and wrapped her arms about his neck.

The baby goat butted him again.

"Hey!" He blocked the third blow with the palm of his hand.

"I don't think that Shprintze likes you much," Tiffany had loosened her arms enough to look down between them without letting go.

"Tevye's fourth daughter?"

"How did you know that?"

"I played Perchik in a high school production back in Chicago." Back in happier, simpler times.

"Do you like acting?"

"No, but Hodel was awfully hot." Then he felt stupid for saying it.

"And did Perchik get his Hodel?" Her smile was forgiving of his own clumsiness.

"He did," he admitted and couldn't stop the smile. They'd ended up going to the junior prom together, a night that had cost them both their virginity. An event they'd commemorated thoroughly and much less awkwardly at their senior prom. "She's now a high-end entertainment attorney in Los Angeles married to one of her superstar clients."

"Is she the one who got away?"

"What? Her? No! I— We— The one—" He sighed. "Crap! No. It wasn't like that. It was a high school thing. Awesome but nothing permanent. How about you? Tell me about the one who slipped away."

And he felt her freeze. Felt her, for just an instant, become as frozen as she'd been when she'd gone fetal on the ground beside her goat's grave.

He did the only thing he knew how to do: he held her tight—as tightly as he could while keeping a protective palm against the kid's forehead.

"Okay. Bad question. Just ignore it. Okay? Just pretend I'm asking about Shprintze. Please?"

She nodded against his shoulder, her face planted in the same spot it had been yesterday. He hoped she didn't start crying again—he didn't know if he could stand to hear the heartrending pain of it again.

"Just know," he told the top of her head. "If I ever meet the bastard who did whatever he did to you, I'm going to kill him. No questions asked."

Tiffany pulled back enough to look at him. Her eyes were swimming, but they weren't spilling over.

Devin met her gaze as it shifted from pain to assessment.

"You would, wouldn't you?"

"In a heartbeat." He'd never so much as punched a man before. But he also didn't doubt that if confronted with the bastard who had so hurt this beautiful woman, he wouldn't hesitate.

"Then you'll be glad…no, wrong word. You'll…want to know that you'll never have to worry about that. Someone else already got to him." She met his gaze levelly despite whatever horror-memory he'd just dug up twice in two days.

"Damn," he barely managed a whisper.

"Sorry you missed your chance?"

"No. Busy wondering what it is about Eagle Cove that makes their women so spectacularly strong."

Her smile went radiant.

But he forgot one thing as he leaned back in to renew their kiss.

The next moment he was on his knees in the dirt. Shprintze the goat had head-butted him squarely in the solar plexus.

TIFFANY DIDN'T NEED to be familiar with the docks on Eagle Bay to know which boat belonged to Hector Jackson because there weren't that many to choose from. The McCall and Baxter fishing boats both had large charter signs on them. And both were busy loading up with whale watch charters as the big grays were busy migrating north along the Pacific Coast.

There were also a half dozen small fishing skiffs and one big sailboat.

She wished she hadn't said anything to Devin about her past, but she had. To make matters worse, she hadn't been able to think of a thing to say on the drive to the marina and had left Devin to fill in the silences. It didn't take him long to understand. Then he quieted and simply reached out to take her hand in his. He held it as he drove one-handed into and through town.

She'd read the literature. Some men were repulsed by knowing a woman had been molested. Other, creepier ones, were attracted by the idea. Not wishing to experience either reaction, she had never told anyone a single word of her past after escaping high school. She'd been re-born at eighteen...until today.

Devin's reaction, she should have known in advance but she hadn't, was completely different. He simply took her hand and held it as if nothing had happened. No, that wasn't right either. He did it as if...it didn't matter. That was quite different. It made all the difference in the world and she held on tighter as he drove.

He's going to leave eventually, she reminded herself. But the inner Tiffany didn't care. She'd seen the truth of his fury and was touched by the simple tenderness with which he held her hand. It was enough.

The sailboat was huge. Devin had said it was a Pearson 42 and she'd spent quite a bit of time online looking up sailboats last night. At first she'd wanted to see what she'd foolishly agreed to, but had soon become fascinated. She had a satellite connection for her Internet and a sat-phone for emergencies...a device she never used except for her twice yearly check-ins that her attorney in California had insisted on. "Want to know you're alive, Ms. Mills. Hear your voice, make sure you're okay." The calls were consistently brief and relatively painless. In retrospect, even appreciated.

Her study had started with the Pearson 42, but she hadn't been able to understand a word of it. That led her into basic sailboat diagrams with all the parts labeled, which had led her into a vast glossary of nautical terms she'd only been able to partly absorb. She'd eventually backtracked to the Pearson 42 and was able to make some sense of it. First of all, 42 meant forty-two feet long.

She also knew that it was often in the top-ten lists for cruising sailboats as distinct from racers and daysailers—the three primary classifications of sailboats. Cruiser meant comfort over long distances and the boat appeared as if it had done a lot of travel. It was neat and appeared to be in good repair, but it looked very…lived in.

At the boat, Hector waved a cheerful greeting.

"Have you sailed before, Tiffany? No? Well, your young man thinks he has. What say we prove him wrong?"

Tiffany stood uncertainly on the dock. Nothing in her research had said how to board a sailboat. The deck rose three feet above the dock, white with a hand-wide red line by the water and a blue one just below the—she couldn't remember the word, perhaps she hadn't found one—the place where deck met hull, built as separate pieces then bonded together. She didn't see a place to crawl between the wires, there was netting attached to the inside of the long safety lines.

Nor had any of her history told her how to respond to Hector's "your young man." She eyed the length of the dock leading toward town, but Devin still held her hand—which she supposed made the "your young man" assumption more valid than she was prepared for.

Using it, Devin led her back—aft—to a short set of stairs at an opening through the boat's lifelines. He helped her up and then stepped up beside her. She almost lost her balance at the unexpected shift in the deck when he boarded. There were some things she couldn't learn online.

"You can put your coats down below, Devin. It's a warm morning, though it may be cooler out on the water."

Devin took hers and headed below. Tiffany set the sling gently down on the knee-high doghouse—no, that was for oversized cabins —cabin roof.

"Is that a goat?" Hector inspected the bundle.

Tiffany opened the sling further for Hector to look inside. "She's newborn and lost her mother. I couldn't leave Shprintze for a whole day. I hope that's okay."

"I don't think that's up to me."

"But it is your boat?"

"No, ma'am. Belongs to the ship's master. Lieutenant Commander Queeg by name, LC Queeg for medium, Q for short."

"Queeg as in *The Caine Mutiny?* The mad commander played by Humphrey Bogart?"

"The same."

At that moment a big, gray-and-black striped cat trotted up on deck using the same door—gangway? companionway? hatch!—that Devin had used to go below. The cat hopped up onto the cabin roof and trotted over to Tiffany.

Hector stood stiffly and snapped a sharp salute that the cat ignored as any egotistical senior officer might. After a sniff and a scratch accepted from Tiffany with a very feline hauteur, LC Queeg inspected the sleeping kid.

Tiffany stood poised to make a grab if the cat didn't approve. LC Queeg was at least twice the size and four times the weight of Shprintze.

After a moment, the cat turned to look up at Hector.

"You tell me, Commander."

The cat then crawled onto the blanket and curled up around the goat. Shprintze woke enough to lift her head and rest it over the cat's belly before going back to sleep. Q began cleaning the baby goat.

"Be damned," Hector said softly. "He's never been a big fan of four-footed strangers on his boat. Nor winged ones. He's been known to face down angry seagulls twice his size if they board without proper orders. Well, let's leave them be." A handrail stuck up along the cabin's roof ensured that they stayed in place, not that the fall from cabin to deck was high enough to cause more than surprise.

He led her forward and she began learning about what had only been pictures and labels last night.

Devin hadn't returned from inside the boat—below. She wondered what he was learning down there.

DEVIN HAD MEANT to drop their jackets on the first level surface and head back up the companionway ladder, but he was stopped by the beauty of the boat's interior. The ones he'd been in before were just daysailers: a fiberglass bunk covered in sailbags and old life vests, a cooler jammed into a corner and filled with beer, maybe a radio.

This was exquisite. There were teak decking and trim, brass fittings, and absolutely no straight lines. Everything was a curve, the joinery work was a thing of beauty. The wood was bright with multiple coats of varnish and smooth as no sander could achieve—it required decades of constant use and patient upkeep to make wood look like this.

He poked though the galley: top-loading fridge, a counter that lifted to reveal a three-burner propane stove, a small but utilitarian two-basin sink. Quaint and impressively efficient. Doing this in the cottage could save half the kitchenette space or more.

Tiffany's and Hector's footsteps, moving about the deck over his head, let him follow their progress. But he continued his inspection—right until it almost ran him head-on into Dragon Winslow. She'd been sitting quietly at a teak table that could seat three—no, it had a drop-leaf, it could seat six, three on either side of the table.

"You *are* a carpenter then," her greeting was abrupt, but no longer struck fear into his heart.

"This is beautiful work," he sat on a bench seat across from her, long enough that it could double as a narrow bunk, and rubbed a hand over the worn trimwork around a tiny propane heater. The heater would probably be enough to keep the whole boat warm on a cold night. The stove itself was burnished steel. "Beautiful."

"I felt that this might provide you with proper perspective for the lightkeeper's cottage."

"It does. It really does." Then he looked at her instead of the beautiful boat. "Thank you."

"Well," she sniffed, "you have some manners."

"I try not to let them get in my way." That earned him her first real smile since he'd met her.

"I hear," she nodded up toward the steps moving back and forth on the deck, "that you managed to coax Tiffany from her lair."

And he remembered their first meeting, when Dragon Winslow had asked questions that Tiffany had done her best to avoid. Then he began to wonder if he was not the purpose of today's invitation, but rather Tiffany was the target. Had the Dragon used him and Hector to isolate Tiffany on the boat where she couldn't avoid questioning? He remembered her hunching response at every question into her past, never mind the full-blown panic he'd caused when he surprised her.

He rose back to his feet. "I brought her as my guest. To sail. No more. I will not have that trust violated. Shall I take her and go?" He'd never spoken this way to anyone. He ran his crews by cheering them along, teaching them quietly what they didn't know. Of all people to take on, he'd chosen the Dragon. He braced for her talons.

She regarded him for a long time.

He held her gaze even as the boat rocked back and forth beneath the motions of Hector and Tiffany above. He could hear her asking questions and Hector instructing. Soon it would be awkward to leave, very soon. Better to face it. Still clutching their jackets, he turned for the ladder.

Then the Dragon laughed. But it was not mean or dangerous as it should be from a dragon. Rather it was amused.

"Well, that will teach me, and with a dose of my own medicine," she shook her head. "You have honor, Devin Robison. And you protect what you care about."

"I do," which was something of a surprise at the moment. Just how much he cared about Tiffany Mills.

"I shall offer you a bargain."

"I'm listening," but Devin didn't turn to fully face her. *I'm still ready to go* he was saying.

"I shall reserve my interest in what she is hiding…"

"If I do what?"

"Bright boy," she rose to stand in front of him. "If you let me know when she is ready to speak with me."

"And if she never is?"

"Then I shall suffer in silence. At least for as long as I can manage. So do not make me wait too long."

"Some bargain."

"It is the best I can offer. That girl has always been a puzzle. I care for her a great deal, which is actually why I will push if I must. I suspect that the puzzle piece she hides may be close to the heart of what troubles her." Then she left him and climbed back up onto the deck.

No, he knew what troubled her, and could feel his hands clench into fists at even the thought. That would not be why she wasn't talking to the Dragon. There was more than that going on...and not just about herself.

Care for her a great deal. Devin sat back down and stared at the fine woodwork, but he couldn't focus on it.

Care for her a great deal? He did.

Devin scrubbed at his face. He was in so far over his head.

TIFFANY HAD ALWAYS AVOIDED invitations to go sailing before. The reason was easy to recall now, though she hadn't thought of it when Devin had invited her.

April 1900

I am so sore of heart as I stand ashore and observe the departure of his ship. My very soul aches that Ernest must leave Eagle Cove, yet he is a foremast hand with a four-year contract.

Our time together was so brief, but I shall be ever thankful that he was led to me. By his word, I shall look for his return in the summer, when I may once more feel the ecstasy that he can evoke from my willing body. In summer then, I may once more wrap my arms and legs about him and again call him "mine."

Tiffany had never wanted to intrude upon the memory of Lillian's departing lover. By always choosing to remain ashore, Tiffany could relive Lillian's moment when Ernest had still been true and the future filled with hope.

But over a century had passed and Tiffany had willing consented to accompany Devin before she could think to refuse. And was gloriously happy that she had. She tried to remember when she had so enjoyed herself. There was something about being out on a sailboat. She could leave the land behind and some part of her natural timidity with it.

For just this once, this lone sunny morning sliding over the water under the pressure of a steady breeze, she could pretend she was someone else. No, she didn't want to be someone else. Didn't want to hide in her ancestor's memories. Perhaps she could pretend that she was her better self…and Devin made that the simplest of all choices. Tiffany lay back against his chest in the cockpit. He had one arm about her waist and they each had a hand on the wheel. This was *her* moment of heaven.

Once the animals were safely out of the way, Hector had given them lessons back and forth across the bay. Finally he'd announced that Tiffany was ready and there was, with a broad wink, at least some hope for Devin. Then he'd headed them out the mouth of the Eagle River and onto the ocean. The forty-two-foot boat made easy work of the six-foot rollers. They were soon sliding south, well off the shore.

She watched the land as they left it behind, curious to see if she could somehow spot herself as they passed. Town gave way to houses. A couple ran along the beach; by his massive stature and her dark hair, she would guess it was Cal Jr. and Natalya freshly returned from their honeymoon. The small dog chasing along at their heels confirmed the identification of the tiny figures.

Soon she saw the two grand Victorians, the one owned by the Slaters that had been Lillian's and the one that had never left the Lamont family. What had been Ernest's thoughts as he sailed this route aboard his lumber schooner? Affection? Love? A belief, at least in that moment, that he would return? Perhaps other, darker thoughts that Tiffany did not want to consider on this beautiful day.

"Look," she pointed out for Devin after they'd passed south of the Orca Head lighthouse. "It appears so small from here."

"Your farm," Devin had followed her direction. "It might look small, but that makes it no less important."

And when he said it, she knew it was true. From out on the water it looked like little more than a cleared patch in the forest. A brilliant reflection of the sun off a solar panel lasted only a moment. But there was her home. There she and Devin had made love. It was enough.

She returned to the sailboat in her thoughts and let Lillian, Ernest, and her farm continue without her for now.

The sounds here seemed so natural. A gull's cry overhead, the shushing of the water along the hull, and the wind as it drove them on. Even the occasional ping of a line against the aluminum mast or the ripple-slap of the three sails felt completely natural. Two "head-sails" (pronounced heads'ls by those in the know, which she now was) rose before the mast, which made this boat a cutter-rigged sloop. The big main stretched along the boom from the mast to well past the cockpit.

She tugged lightly down on the marlinspiked wheel to correct for a wave pushing them off their course.

"Marlinspike—the art of rope weaving and knotwork, often decorative, employed by sailors to pass time on long passages." Hector had confirmed, "Technically that's the name of the tool used, but it is often used to describe the fancier knotwork as well. When everything is going right, which isn't often, a single man has a lot of time when crossing one of the ponds. That's what sailors call the seven seas."

"The Ionian, the Aegean, the Black—"

Hector had laughed. "Okay, little lady. So, you know your history. Ponds are the big oceans. The modern seven seas."

It had been fun to tease him, and that thought had been surprising enough for her to lapse into silence until lunchtime came around. Hector and Mrs. Winslow went below to fix sandwiches, leaving just herself and Devin alone on deck. The cat had gone below in search of treats and the kid had drunk a half-bottle of formula and was asleep again on a blanket in the natural cage of the cockpit's raised sides and benches.

"Devin?"

"Mmm?" he murmured into her hair.

"Can we just stay out here?"

"Sure."

"Forever?"

"Works for me," he agreed lazily, tightening his arm about her waist.

Tiffany hadn't quite meant it the way it sounded in her head. Princess Tiffany seeking a happily ever after. But it was the first time she'd ever been so comfortable around other people. Usually she only achieved this when she was alone. And that meant the farm and there was always something begging to be done there. It was quiet and calm, but in a curious way the State of Tiffany wasn't as peaceful as sailing.

"I'll buy you a boat," Devin continued on the prior topic which she had somehow circled around to in her thoughts. "A beautiful one like this that we'll moor in Eagle Bay. Whenever the wind is up, we'll scoot out onto the sea. I could even host tourist evenings on the sea."

"Perish the thought," Hector said from where he'd stuck his head and shoulders through the hatchway to hand plates and sodas out into the cockpit.

"Why?" Tiffany wouldn't do it because she wouldn't want to speak to all of those people, but Hector had seemed a very gregarious and easygoing man. A good counterpoint to the staunch propriety of the woman that Tiffany couldn't address as any other than Mrs. Winslow.

"Tourists are a cruel thing to do to a perfectly nice boat. I've chartered a bit over the years, passing the time in one port or another."

"But once you've sailed with them, don't they become friends?"

Hector handed her a roast beef sandwich on rye and set the next one on the opposite bench for Mrs. Winslow.

"Well, seems they do sometimes." And Hector's smile said that sometimes they became more than that. Then he glanced below without quite looking. Apparently he was hoping to become more than friends with someone else after taking her sailing.

Tiffany couldn't quite school her expression fast enough and Hector saw that he'd been caught. He offered a sheepish smile and a shrug.

"You don't have to worry about me," Tiffany whispered just loud enough for him to hear. "But I'd be careful around Jessica and Natalya."

"Careful about what?" Devin asked as he took the next pair of sandwiches, having missed everything else that was going on.

"Careful of your heading, Mr. Robison," Hector answered curtly and handed across some cans of soda. Then he ducked back below.

"Careful about what?" Devin asked her.

He really was very cute. Handsome, but cute as well.

"You mean about Hector wanting to date Mrs. Winslow?"

Though not as blind as she'd thought a moment before.

"About *what?*" The Dragon snapped from halfway out the companionway hatch.

Devin winced. "She didn't know yet?" Devin whispered to Tiffany.

She shook her head ever so slightly.

"Oops!" He mouthed to her.

Still cute.

It was well past lunch before the Dragon spoke to Hector again and the poor man had no idea why.

IT WAS midafternoon before they headed back into Eagle Bay. Devin had decided that being in over his head was a good thing, at least when it came to being attracted to Tiffany. They had drifted lazily together all day, whether fighting the wind and bucking the tide or sliding quietly along wing-and-wing, with the sails spread wide to either side to catch the soft tailwind.

Tiffany had unabashedly leaned against him, held hands, and

teased him below with a searing kiss that had fired up both his body and his need for her.

Now they sat on the bow to offer Hector and Mrs. Winslow some privacy. He had followed Tiffany forward as she had followed the goat. She had Shprintze on a thin lead attached to a harness Hector had fashioned. The other end was tied about her wrist, just in case the goat found a way overboard. Hector had no animal-sized life preservers aboard as Commander Q had utterly refused to wear them —a tale Hector had told well this afternoon while the Commander slept in his lap.

Devin contemplated the approaching land. They were far enough out that it was still in miniature—a raised hand could block it from sight, from Greg and the Judge's diner to the Lamont B&B where he had first met and played music with Tiffany. Only the lighthouse and the knowledge of Tiffany's farm over the brow of the hill remained visible, until a shift of the boat blocked those as well.

Today was Sunday.

"A week ago this was a foreign stretch unlike anything I'd ever seen before."

"And now?" Tiffany leaned back against the sloped front of the cabin. The goat had once again wound her lead around a couple of deck fixtures and one of his ankles before curling up in Tiffany's lap.

He leaned back beside her. "It's still a mystery, just for different reasons."

"Tell me."

"There's real community here. It's almost as if the more you try to resist it, the stronger it pulls you in."

Tiffany nodded. "You have no idea."

"I know that there's a circle of women who would gladly castrate me if I were to harm a single lovely hair on your head. And I don't think that's an exaggeration."

"You mean like actually…" she made a snipping motion with her forefingers.

"Natalya promised it in as many words. While I was sitting with you at knitting the other day, Jessica held aloft her knitting scissors to make it clear that she'd do it herself if I wasn't careful."

"And others are ready to make our bridal bower."

"Becky," Devin sighed. If he didn't propose soon, Becky might do it for him. "It's been an interesting week."

At that moment his phone rang. They must be close enough to land to get a signal. He pulled it out and answered without thinking.

"D.R. Builders. Devin here."

"Hi, Dev honey."

Devin almost choked, "Rebecca."

"Hi, honey. It's been a while. I was just chatting with Mama and thinking about you." Her tone was honeyed. He could picture her sitting on the back terrace, a fresh gin and tonic on the table, looking down across the expansive front lawn to Lake Michigan. Sure enough he could hear the wind in the phone's microphone. Her blond hair would be down, swishing gently in the breeze. And her mother sitting close by her side, monitoring every word.

"What do you want?"

"Is that any way to talk to your fiancée? No, sorry. I don't want to fight."

That was a good thing. Her method of fighting was shrill or tear-laden or with her claws out (though always careful not to chip a nail). He'd never been much good at fights and tended to fold to avoid them no matter what form they took.

"I miss you, Dev. I know that you had to have your little pout, but I'm sure you're ready to come back now. We need to pick a date." He could actually hear Rebecca's mother in the background, coaching her softly to say the last line. No surprise there; they thought exactly alike.

Devin pulled the phone away to stare at it for a moment. The screen reported, "Rebecca Monica Monash." She'd insisted that he program her full name into his phone when she'd spotted that it only said, "Rebecca."

This was real, not some nightmare.

Tiffany was trying to get up, but she was all snarled in the goat's lead, and was trying to figure out how to extricate herself without waking Shprintze.

Devin, in turn, attempted to rise, but the goat had somehow wrapped her lead string around both of his ankles. He motioned to Tiffany that it was okay to stay and she subsided back to the deck.

He put the phone back to his ear, "You're kidding, right?"

"Oh Dev. You know Mikal was just payback for that little spat we'd had."

He didn't recall "a little spat." Actually there'd been any number of them, but he had no idea which one she was referring to. Rebecca's relationship tactics included always being on the offensive; something he hadn't understood until this moment. Maybe he could play this game too, for once.

"Mikal moved on, didn't he?"

"No man ever leaves me," her denial was emphatic. Yet he knew Mikal had.

"And you discovered that Dad isn't letting him have any piece of the business."

Her brief silence confirmed that.

Dad might have no morals about what women he bedded, but he protected CMC like the shrewd CEO he was. He and Devin had had frank discussions of Mikal's inabilities in business of any type. He could lose money sitting alone in a quiet room.

"It's not that, Dev. I miss you. I want you back."

"Not going to happen."

"But Dev-vin," she always said it that way when she was frustrated enough to use his full name. "You know what I can do for you."

And he'd expected her to start listing some vacation or—

"Magnuson," she named one of the biggest real estate speculators in Chicago, "has always been sweet on me. You know I could get an exclusive contract for CMC. And that's not all. There are others."

Sure. Others she or her mother had slept with. If they couldn't deliver the contracts with offers of sex, or perhaps more sex, they'd probably blackmail the men by threatening to reveal themselves to the men's families.

"Goodbye, Rebecca."

"Oh come on, Devy. You know that you'll never have a woman half as good as me. I can do things for you. Or…I can do things to you. Is that what you want? A little S&M? I've got this black-leather lingerie and cuffs in my bottom dresser drawer. You can use my riding crop and we could—"

Devin yanked the phone away from his ear. He didn't want to hear it. He could hear that she was still going on.

He couldn't even stand to touch the disconnect button below her name.

At a loss for what else to do, he heaved the phone as high and hard as he could. It arced up into the sky, tumbled in the wind, flashing as it reflected sunlight, then disappeared into the face of a rolling wave without a sound.

Devin could only stare straight ahead and wonder at the narrowness of his escape. He had almost married *that.*

"From the half I could hear," Tiffany said softly, "I'm guessing that didn't go well."

He turned from looking ahead to looking at her. "My wedding was six weeks ago today."

Tiffany flinched.

Devin caught at her arm to keep her in place. "I didn't go through with it."

"You were almost married and then—what? Go bounce the poor girl who lives alone in the woods?" Fury. He'd never expected Tiffany to be capable of fury.

"No. I— Just hang on and—" Then he groaned and told her the whole sordid story. Not about who his family was, but about the wedding, his brother, the social media, and their reactions, all telling him he was wrong. Right down to his father offering to share his secretary with him. He had to look away while telling the story to hide his own shame.

Tiffany calmed and listened and, by the end of it, was even looking sympathetic, once it was clear that she wasn't just some rebound girl.

"I couldn't stand it anymore. And then that," he waved toward where he'd thrown his phone overboard. "She offered to— Let's just say that your goats have more morals than anyone in Chicago."

"Even when they're rutting?" Tiffany teased him.

"Especially then. Rebecca just offered to deliver me anybody needing a building contractor by sleeping with him."

"You were right. Maybe they should meet my mother."

"Part of the reason she's so mad is you'll never guess who my brother bedded next."

"Your father's secretary?"

"Nope, turns out he'd already been there and done that. Rebecca's married sister was next—the two can't stand each other, rivals since they were toddlers. When Rebecca caught them together in the sauna, Mikal started comparing their sexual performances in some detail. 'So that they could learn from each other's shortcomings how to better please a man.' He, of course, had to tell me all about it, smug bastard."

"Eww!"

"I couldn't agree more. That was when I took the job rebuilding the lightkeeper's cottage." Devin slumped low enough to rest his head back against the cabin and stare up at the sky. "And now a week later I've met dozens of people, people who I wouldn't introduce to my family for fear of alienating them."

"Of alienating your family?"

"No. Of scaring off the wonderful people I've met here." Then he turned and looked at her for the first time since he'd started the story. "I especially don't want them scaring you off."

"Ha!" Tiffany practically laughed in his face. "You can't scare me with family. Someday I'll have to tell you about mine. Starting with my stepfather who—"

He could see the shift in her face. "Don't!"

"Don't what?" Tiffany blinked at him caught halfway to inner fury.

"Don't tell me about it."

"Why not?"

"That's past. I don't want you to *have* to remember a single thing from your past. But mostly because I don't want you to feel utterly sullied the way I do right now."

"THAT DID IT," Tiffany whispered.

"Did what?" Devin looked at her, puzzled.

In answer she pulled him to her, pulled him down to kiss her. She could feel how stiff and angry he was, but slowly, ever so slowly, he shifted out of his past and into their present.

Their kiss was different this time. It wasn't about heat, need, passion, or just feeling so incredibly good. It went deeper. It was about meaning, joy, and connection. Had Lillian and Ernest felt this, or had they only had heat and need? If so, for the first time Tiffany pitied her ancestor rather than envying her.

Devin slipped his arms about her, careful not to disturb the sleeping kid still warm in her lap. Devin saw her as a beautiful woman —who wasn't a basket case-recluse-unholy mess—and for him, it became true.

She felt like all of the things he'd called her: beautiful, strong, powerful. Born anew. A woman with no past except what she chose. For Tiffany now understood that she had the power to choose.

When the kiss finally ended by some mutual agreement, he still held her close, tucked under his arm and facing the wind and the future together.

Yes, that absolutely did it.

Tiffany hadn't understood. Not by watching Jessica, Becky, or Natalya fall in love and marry. Nothing that had happened for Peggy or Gina had taught her what to expect. Not even reading Lillian's diary.

Tiffany breathed in deeply as she faced whatever was to come. She no longer felt any fear, because now she knew what love felt like. Really knew.

And whether Devin stayed for just the summer or for a lifetime, he had changed her for the better. Forever.

CHAPTER 6

*O*kay, perhaps not *forever.*

Tiffany sat in the brewery with the rest of the knitters on Tuesday and still couldn't seem to find her voice. There was merry chatter going on about the circle as always, but silence had wrapped around her so tightly over the years that she had as little to say as ever.

Yet when Devin had come to her, walking her home last Sunday night and again returning with the evening light on Monday, she hadn't been able to stop talking.

They spoke of growing up in different parts of the country, of people they'd met, of goats and dogs and farming. It was as if all the silence that had stoppered her for a lifetime now spilled forth. They made love then would talk for hours, after all, they had to keep their priorities straight and she could never tire of Devin's strong hands and gentle touch.

Sleep? She'd never slept so little since she used to cower in the dark, waiting in terror. And she'd never felt so awake. In Devin's presence she had become the manic version of herself and had kept apologizing, but couldn't seem to stop, even after the times that he laughed more at her than with her. She would try to be angry about that, but he laughed at his own shortcomings just as easily, and his laugh inevitably called forth her own.

There were things Devin wasn't saying. Which was only fair; there were things she wasn't either. Deciding she was in love with him didn't mean that she'd gone stupid or incautious. It just meant that she was wallowing in the joy of it the way a newborn goat wallowed in discovery of tall meadow grass bathed in warm sunlight.

But as much as she was transformed in his presence, she was still very much herself around others. Mrs. Winslow couldn't have missed that kiss, the boat wasn't all that big. But then neither had Tiffany missed the rather more than neighborly kiss that Mrs. Winslow left with Hector in thanks for the day's sailing trip.

At Tuesday knitting, she and Mrs. Winslow didn't exchange so much as a word, though they did end up sitting side by side on one of the couches. Dragon Winslow was just as gruff, taciturn, and roughly affectionate to everyone as was her norm.

And Tiffany was as silent as ever, despite the transformation Devin had wrought inside her.

"I can't even see my knitting. My belly pushes it too far away," Jessica was complaining. She was propped in a big armchair, cushioned by pillows and with an empty beer keg pushed close beside her seat. Becky had placed a scrap of plywood on top of it as an impromptu table that was kept stocked with tea, finger sandwiches that May Conklin had made up at the Plover Inn, and cookies that Natalya had swiped from the bakery.

"Can't wait," Becky chimed in.

"Are you…?" Half a dozen of the women spoke at once.

"Not yet," Becky's sigh was splendidly dramatic.

Why couldn't Tiffany be more like that?

"We're not even trying, though we're certainly practicing often enough," she offered one of her cheery laughs that spread among the women. "I promised Harry that he'd get a year of peace and quiet for his first year as a judge. Seven months and counting."

"But you've only been married for three months so far," Natalya pointed out. "Come on, Becky. Basic math. Ten months is not a year."

"What he doesn't know won't hurt him," Becky giggled happily. "I don't know if I can stand to wait even that long. Besides, who says it happens the first time you try?"

"Me," Jessica groaned from her chair. "I thought it might take months, or years. Nope."

"Lucky!" Becky declared. "You were always the lucky one. You got married first."

"And pregnant first," Natalya put in.

"And you had a fine writing career," Mrs. Winslow said approvingly.

"You only say that because she followed in your reporter footsteps," Gina teased her.

"She always was a smart girl," Mrs. Winslow countered. Which nobody could argue with because she'd been class valedictorian and was now excelling as Eagle Cove's marketing manager.

"If I'm so damned smart, how come I can barely count stitches anymore? Every time I get to eight, I think of how long I've been pregnant. Fourteen since Greg first kissed me."

"Now she's just bragging," Natalya reached out a hand to brush it over her friend's hair.

"Show off!" Becky agreed.

"Feed her some orange juice," Tiffany suggested quietly.

Mrs. Winslow actually snorted with laughter and several others joined in.

"Gods no!" Jessica held up her hands in terror. "I can't get within a dozen feet of the stuff without this one breaking into a conga dance around my innards."

A hard-learned lesson from a few months ago that had been fascinating to be a part of. Jessica had drunk deeply from a glass of orange juice at knitting, and her child had awoken with a deep and great vengeance. Tiffany had never felt a life inside another woman. A goat, yes, but that was so different. Jessica had guided Tiffany's hand onto her belly just as a hard kick made her grunt. Even now Tiffany could feel the memory of that tiny footprint upon her palm. It was surreal and miraculous, and had made them both smile at the time.

June 1900

    Ernest, the ship's captain told me, has jumped ship in Eureka, which made little sense to me as it is not a normal port of call for the big lumber schooner. The First Mate, Albert Slater, later told me the truth. Ernest died in a brothel during a knife fight after beating a Chinese whore to death.

    So he has paid the price of his deeds as have I. I had thought that, at forty, I was long past conceiving...I am not.

    My daughter sends word by Albert—a far more trusty man than my Ernest it seems—that she had to miss this ship, but shall return upon the next to sail. It saddens me, for I miss her so.

    I would hate this child growing within me if I could, but such feelings I am unable to discover. I can only feel love for it.

    Though how to tell Pearl of her sibling to be, God alone knows.

Tiffany looked at Jessica as she scowled down at her own bulging belly.

"You will take such joy in this child, Jessica. You will not be able to help yourself and you will guard her as you would no other, not your husband or even yourself." It was a direct quote, but for the name change, of Lillian's instructions to herself.

The only sound in the room was the distant rattle of the bottling machine in the back of the brewery, muffled by the glass-and-wood walls.

"Did you ever..." Jessica asked softly.

Tiffany pulled herself back. "No." She placed a hand on her own belly. "No. Though I have imagined it." So clearly described by Lillian Lamont. Tiffany felt it as if she had lived through an entire pregnancy herself—the joys and the fears.

Had her own mother hated Tiffany as she grew in the womb? Despised her for ruining her mother's figure? Her governess had told Tiffany years ago that she had not been nursed, even once, for fear of misshapen breasts.

Lillian Lamont had loved her children, both of them.

"You are a very strange woman, Tiffany," Jessica regarded her levelly.

Tiffany squirmed in her seat.

"I knew there was a reason I liked you."

Her tease startled Tiffany into looking back up at Jessica. "Takes one to know one, I suppose." And Tiffany could not believe the words that had just come out of her own mouth.

Natalya's laugh sounded first. As others joined in, Natalya winked at her and nodded that she too was a friend.

Tiffany's smile didn't feel tentative on her face as she winked back. Though conversation soon shifted to the next upcoming town festival, just two weeks off, Tiffany could feel the change. For perhaps the first time since her arrival in Eagle Cove, she didn't sit emotionally outside the circle while she physically sat within it. She belonged here. A surprising place where friends cared for her.

There was only one better feeling.

There was also a man waiting for her.

DEVIN SAT on a handy log and Tall Guy sat on the ground beside him, which placed their heads at roughly the same height. The goats milled about nibbling at the flake of hay he had tossed down for them. Beth —at least he thought it was Beth—had, in her patient way, adopted Shprintze along with Chava. The orphaned kid was visibly thriving though she was less than a week old.

The afternoon was fading to evening but Tiffany wasn't here. He'd forgotten it was Tuesday. One of her knitting days. At least he'd showered off the day's work at the B&B before climbing the trail this time.

"A lot of fair ladies here," he told Tall Guy.

The dog studied him silently.

"Wrong species for either of us, I know." Then he felt bad because Tall Guy had no one of his own breed to be waiting *for*, whereas Tiffany would soon return.

Devin watched as one of goats lay down to rest and then one of the kids used her as a platform to leap for the log. A sharp bleat, first from the goat-as-launching-platform, then from the kid as it failed to achieve orbit, scrabbled briefly at the log's bark, then plopped down on the ground.

"I'm losing my mind. Do you know how many goats we have in all of Chicago? About twice as many as you guard, my friend. That's it. And they're all safely in the Lincoln Park petting zoo. You'd hate it there."

Tall Guy snuffled at his pockets again, but he had no dog biscuits. He didn't even know where Tiffany kept them, so he scratched the dog's ear, which was apparently a distant second as far as pleasures went, but was considered better than nothing.

Devin had been here for...he wasn't even sure. The days had already blurred together. And since he'd sent his phone to the bottom of the ocean to "sleep with the fishes" (nothing like a good *Godfather* quote), he'd lost track of time. He didn't miss his phone, not a bit. He'd used the B&B's phone to let his foreman know how to reach him, but he felt no desire to go and replace his electronic connection to the rest of the world. He had a tablet for e-mail, but ignored that as well. The company account messages were auto-copied to his foreman. The rest were all pieces of his past doing their best to yank him back to Chicago, to a life that now disgusted him.

Time moved differently here. Rather than over-scheduled crews and massive project deadlines on a dozen houses being built at once, he had a single project and one worker: himself.

And he had a girl. A woman.

"What am I doing?"

Tall Guy didn't have any idea either.

"You're no help at all."

The dog sighed.

Devin didn't love Tiffany. No exactly. Not so soon. But he...cared for her. The fact that he cared for her more than he'd ever cared for Rebecca—to whom he had been misguided enough to declare his love —was all just one more sad reinforcement regarding his misspent youth. His utterly naive youth of two months ago.

One of the kids sidled over, thinking it was being very sly, and began to nibble on one of Devin's bootlaces.

"Fine. Do your worst."

The baby goat managed to get a good hold of one lace then tried to bolt away while still clamping onto it. In the middle of its first leap, it ran out of bootlace and tumbled to the ground. Then digging in all fours, it tugged and wrestled at it, jerking Devin's boot side to side.

"You'll never get that knot untied."

"I know," he told the dog. "It's like Eagle Cove is tying me up in all sorts of ways."

"It will do that."

Devin looked at Tall Guy. He hadn't said a word.

Then Tiffany held out a biscuit and Tall Guy sighed happily as he took it. He lay down and began crunching on it.

"Hi," was all Devin could manage, now as speechless as the big Kangal. Tiffany was dressed in a pretty blouse of summer-blue that the light wind pressed against her figure. Her jeans were worn soft enough to cling to every curve. There were shapes revealed that he was only starting to learn and definitely to appreciate.

But it wasn't her exceptional body or her amazing hair that stunned him speechless, it was the simple joy of her smile at finding him here. The bright sparkle in her blue-gray eyes.

He pulled her in until she was standing between his knees, where he could wrap his arms about her waist and rest his face between her breasts. She set her knitting bag and her bow on the log beside him and circled her arms about his head.

"The world is so quiet when you hold me," he told her.

"The world is so full for me when I do."

"Full of what?" He placed a kiss on her sternum as an excuse to not raise his head from where it rested in heaven.

"No. It doesn't work that way. It's just...full. As if, when I'm holding you, I don't need anything else. Couldn't need anything more."

Devin could tell that she was looking down at him by how her hair slid about his ears and neck. He was inside the shield, so close to Tiffany that everyone else couldn't help but be outside. He slipped his hands down until he was hugging her about the hips. The hips that welcomed him so deliciously. He locked his arms about her tighter and tighter as if he could find some way to hold on.

"I'm getting lost here, Tiffany."

"I don't see why," she began scratching his head lightly with her short, practical nails. "Tucked in between my breasts would seem like a 'found' place to me rather than a lost one."

He tipped his head up to look at her, her face mere inches above his. He sang the line from "Amazing Grace." "I once was lost, but now I'm found."

Tiffany picked up a sweet harmony that ended in one of her delightful giggles of joy. He'd never met someone so pleased with her life. And it showed on her face all the time.

"This is," he nuzzled back between her breasts, "a *very* found sort of place."

"Told you."

"Chicago isn't."

"Then don't think about it."

"Again that impossible simplicity you have. Your world is so clear. Mine is muddier than a construction site in a Chicago spring. We only have two seasons there, you know: winter and construction."

***

Tiffany laughed dutifully at his little joke, but her thoughts were whirling.

Her life was so clear? What wouldn't she give for that to be true.

"The two-season thing is especially true when you work for a major contractor," Devin continued talking to her breasts.

She'd always felt that men's fixation with breasts was a strange and ridiculous preoccupation. But for Devin, it was a place he changed. Something about resting his head there made him quiet and thoughtful. As close to peace as she ever saw him. He was good at having fun, far better than she was. But he never relaxed—she could feel his mind working ceaselessly.

With his head against her chest, whether after hot, sweaty love-making or as chastely as now, his thoughts went quiet. They moved more slowly. More peacefully.

Maybe her own life *was* clearer, at least when he was with her. The farm kept her busy. Her time occupied, but her thoughts free to lead her where they would. When Devin was with her, life seemed so right. That was it. Just...right.

She freed one hand and began unbuttoning her blouse. When she reached his face, he rolled his head aside onto her breast. When she'd exposed a narrow cleavage down to her waist, she rocked his head back into place using the lightest of pressures.

With one strong arm, he kept her hips pulled hard against his chest. She leaned against him as he began to do more than merely rest his face against her skin. With no sense of shame at all, she rubbed against him, reveling in the slow build of heat. Let him expose her chest to the warmth of the setting sun.

The goats circled about them, like some distant parade. Their play appearing to be but a distant image. Their bleats barely louder than the roar of her own pulse and the gentle wind that cooled and teased.

Tiffany closed her eyes and let the sensations take her as he slowly made love to her.

Devin was right after all. Her life had never been so clear as this moment.

Devin slipped away at first light. He didn't go far, just to the edge of Tiffany's yurt deck. He wanted to see the land, watch it come awake. The night chill was still on the air but he'd grabbed a comforter off the back of the couch and wrapped it around him.

A family of deer slept in the narrow passage between the forest and Tiffany's vegetable garden fence just a few dozen feet away. He'd never seen them so close except in a zoo. They slept lying down, but with their heads up like a submarine periscope, wary of intruders. Only the delicate spotted fawn had lain down its head and given itself up to sleep with total abandon. Safe in the protection of its parents.

"It's cold out here," Tiffany scooted under the comforter with him. A deer ear swiveled to track her, but apparently she wasn't worrisome enough to make them wake all the way up and stand. Though, in sweatpants and a thick cable-knit sweater with a V-neck that revealed she wore nothing beneath it, Tiffany was very worth looking at in Devin's book. She was warm and sleep rumpled. And sex rumpled. He could never tire of the way she gave, with absolute abandon to her own emotions. Nor of the way she inspired him to return the favor. He kissed her briefly, but she pulled away.

"Eww! I have morning breath."

"Don't care. I bet I do too. Still don't care."

"I do. Besides, if I let you kiss me, I'll miss the sunrise." The fact that they faced west, not east, didn't seem to be worth making a point about.

He nodded over toward the family of deer.

"Boris, Natasha, and Nell," she named them.

"*Bullwinkle*," Devin nodded, recognizing the reference. "And if the fawn had been a boy?"

"Dudley, of course."

Devin looked at the deer again. "Seems cruel to rescue poor Nell Fenwick from the evil Snidely Whiplash only to place her into the family of the villains. Though they don't look very evil."

"Neither were Boris and Natasha. They delighted in thinking they were, but they'll make good parents."

Unlike his own, or Tiffany's. He thought about the small bits and pieces she'd dropped. The stepfather who had obviously been the abuser. The mother who had let it happen and who Tiffany mentioned even less than he mentioned his own.

She pointed at a pair of large gray doves with black rings about their necks as they darted about together from one branch to the next and called Who-WHO-who-who.

"What kind of parents will we be?"

"You and I?" Tiffany sounded suddenly breathless.

"Yes. No. I mean—" Devin definitely wasn't awake yet. "I mean I assume…no. *Do* you want to have kids some day? Yourself?"

She smiled tolerantly at his mangling of the question, but nodded. "You?"

"I do. I really do. But I'm afraid that I'll be like my parents."

"Don't worry, you won't be. No more than I'll be like mine," Tiffany replied complacently.

"How can you know? What makes us any different than my parents or yours?"

"Because, like Boris and Natasha, we care. If you need proof, just look at my girls and boys."

Though the goat pen was a couple hundred feet away and still lost in morning shadows, there was no doubting the occupants' physical and mental well-being. They were a very happy family of goats and a dog.

Devin turned to look at Tiffany, huddled so deep into the blanket and so close against him for warmth that he could see little more than her hair and her temple—so he kissed it. She was a woman who cared with all of her generous heart. He pulled her mostly into his lap and she curled up against his chest.

"You, Tiffany Mills, will make an amazing mother." He could see it in her.

She leaned even harder against him for a moment under the blanket in thanks. "I have a great example."

"Your mother doesn't sound like such a great example."

"No," she agreed. "But my several times great-grandmother was an amazing woman. The more I can be like her, the better person I'll be."

Devin knew almost nothing about his great-grandparents, never mind any generations before that except that they had once been Irish Catholics fleeing the Great Famine of the late 1840s.

"There's one thing that Lillian Lamont discovered far too late in life."

"What's that?"

"Come back to bed and I'll show you."

"Maybe," he took advantage of the loose sweater to slide his hand underneath it and cradle a breast. "But maybe I can't wait that long."

"No," Tiffany's delighted giggle only encouraged him.

Her breath caught short and hard as he slid his hand down inside her sweatpants and cupped her.

"I'll freeze."

"I promise to keep you very warm."

She groaned as he began to massage her. The deer startled, quickly rose, and ran away.

Tiffany's reactions also rose quickly but she didn't attempt to run at all. Instead she delighted him as her gasps told him he was capable of doing some things very right.

CHAPTER 7

*T*iffany sat on Mrs. Winslow's porch and watched the McCall's house across Shearwater Lane. Vincent was working in his garage/woodshop, finishing an ornate bedstead. He was the town's leading custom furniture maker.

After half an hour of her sitting and watching him shape and sand, he came over and asked if she needed anything, which was nice of him. He was covered head to toe in sawdust, only the outlines of his safety goggles and dust mask were clean. It reminded her of Devin, coming to her covered in plaster dust. It also reminded her of the first time they had made love, lying beneath the first stars on her front deck. She fought the blush that was rising fast to her cheeks.

"I'm fine. I wanted to speak with Mrs. Winslow."

"She's usually home shortly after my wife and kids. The twins are in her class this year. Shouldn't be long now."

"I'll just wait then. Thank you."

"Sure I can't get you anything? A glass of water or something?"

"Would it be filled with sawdust?"

He laughed as he looked down at himself, "Near enough."

"I'll pass, thank you." She'd meant it seriously, but could now see how it sounded funny. Before Devin she might not have ever noticed.

"Good choice," he offered a cheery wave then re-crossed the street back to his woodworking.

What else was Devin changing about her? Another week had gone by and she was no longer "in love" with him. She had begun to suspect that her ancestor had stopped short of where Tiffany was moving to. A week ago, if Devin had left, she too would have been "sore of heart." If Devin left now, she would be lost.

When they made love, it was like nothing she had experienced or imagined. There was a connection that emerged from somewhere deep within her and it wanted only one thing: him. But that wasn't even the important part of what was happening.

They made each other happy.

Merely being in his presence, even just thinking about him, made her day brighter and happier. And she could see the same in him.

But that had not been enough to save Lillian Lamont.

July 1900

My Pearl has returned to me, a mere shadow of her former self. Her pallor as pale as Chinese silk and she is so gaunt that a corset made her appear heavier of frame rather than lighter. My corset yet hid my condition though it will do so only a little longer.

After I transported her from the dock to our home and sequestered her, I asked after her ailment.

"I could find no trace of him," she wailed. "I stayed an extra month to search, fearing him injured or falsely imprisoned."

When I asked who, she replied, "My true love. My one and only."

I swear that I felt a chill in that moment. Three hundred thousand they say reside in the great city of San Francisco, yet I felt a chill.

"The father of my unborn child is gone. We were to be married. Oh, my beloved." And she wailed upon my breast.

My wonder at the prospect of a grandchild lasted only a moment. With her next words, she cut all the cords that bind my life together. "Tis the messenger you sent to me. My dearest Ernest is nowhere to be found."

The man is dead. Blessedly, none had been so cruel as to speak truth to the young woman seeking him. And the second child, which I had decided was to

*be the joy of my elder years, became sawdust and bitter medicine. My
handsome lover was also my daughter's. And my own child would be sibling
to both Pearl and to her own child.*

A minivan drove up and pulled into the McCall driveway. Seven-
year-old twins climbed out then rushed to their father. Like minia-
tures of their mother, they had matching brunette ponytails and
sparkling blue eyes. It was an easy bet that by high school they would
also have their mother's powerful curves. Or as Tiffany's mother
would have said, "Hussy, bought and paid for." Though there was no
more question that Dawn McCall's shape was authentic than her own
mother's—for she and Tiffany could be twins but for their age and
attitude.

Vincent had shed his dust mask and glasses and was dusting
himself off with whacks of a clean towel. Soon the twins also
had towels and were making a game of thwapping them against
his pant legs, releasing great clouds of sawdust. Once the worst
of it was gone, he hugged them both, then—rather than
returning to his work—he sat down on a sawhorse. By their
animated gestures, they must be retelling the events of their day
though she could hear only the happiness of their tone, not their
words.

When Dawn McCall approached, Vincent moved to one side and
made a show of dusting off the other end of his sawhorse. Dawn sat,
slipped a hand around her husband's waist despite the risk of getting
dirty, and soon the four of them were highly animated.

Tiffany barely noticed the car that pulled into the driveway until
Mrs. Winslow came along the front walk.

"They make a beautiful family, don't they?"

Tiffany could only sigh and nod. So much more than she had
ever had.

"You are still a puzzle to me, Tiffany Mills. Are you here to finally
unravel the mystery?"

She flinched. She'd completely forgotten about her unconsidered
comment at the wedding and Mrs. Winslow's interest in it.

Mrs. Winslow sighed heavily at her response. "Then why the visit, girl?"

Tiffany looked up at her. The irritation was obvious, but Tiffany couldn't think about two things at once, especially not when one of them was so big.

"Ms. Mills?"

"How do you know?" She blurted it out before she could second-guess herself yet again. "Devin? Everything? How do you know when —" She couldn't continue.

Mrs. Winslow regarded her steadily for a long time before speaking. "You have walked all of the way from your farm on a Monday to ask me this."

She didn't make it a question so Tiffany didn't feel obliged to answer.

"Come in now and we'll have some tea." With no further words, she unlocked the front door and led the way in.

———

DEVIN HAD SEEN Tiffany quickly pass by from the second story window of the lightkeeper's cottage. He scraped himself enough to bleed, but was unable to open the window. Too many layers of paint in the track had sealed it shut. He'd had them all replaced except this one because they'd mis-shipped it and the replacement hadn't arrived yet.

By the time he was downstairs, she was gone and he couldn't follow her.

"Well, she's allowed a life as well," he told the main panel as he hooked in the last of the new wiring. He'd pushed hard this week to get it done so that he'd have more time for the extra finish work he was planning. Dragon Winslow had been right—the visit to Hector's boat gave him the interior design style that he'd been missing.

"It's not like we're living together," he mentioned to the plumbing as he set up the pressure test for the inspector, who had agreed to drive out to the coast this afternoon along with the electrical inspector. Of course he hadn't been sleeping at the B&B. Not when Tiffany so welcomed him to her bed. He packed in some groceries and one night won her undying appreciation by delivering a Carrier Pigeon pizza. It had cooled on the hike in, but her oven had reheated it fast enough to not make him feel guilty about propane usage. Unsure what she liked, he'd made it half Hawaiian and half loaded. She'd taken a slice of each and, for New York-style pizza, it hadn't been half bad.

If he stayed here, he'd have to talk to them about offering some Chicago-style as well.

"If I stay here?" There was as unlikely an idea as he'd ever had. He made sure that he had the permits on display. "We're just—"

"Talking to ourselves."

"Oh. Hi, Peggy. What are you doing up here?"

"Thought I'd come see how you're doing. I take it that talking to yourself is a good sign?"

He smiled. "I'm used to working with a large crew. Seems awfully quiet if I don't."

He noticed the way she was looking at his work with more than just a casual eye.

"You know construction?" Then wished he could take it back. She owned a road grader, ran the airport, rebuilt airplanes... "Wait a minute."

She waited him out.

"You're married to Judge Slater."

A nod.

"But Slater isn't your last name."

"It is now. He's still old-fashioned enough to want his wife to take his last name. I didn't see any point in arguing."

"But that was recent."

Again the nod.

"What was your maiden name?"

"Naron."

Devin was standing right next to the permits where he'd nailed them to a stud, but he didn't need look at them; the last name of the contractor who'd arranged the permit for him to work under started with an N. "You're Eagle Cove Contracting."

She shrugged as if it shouldn't be a surprise. "I've done a lot of building in this town."

In Chicago, getting a woman on the crew was such a rarity that she was still often razzed or even harassed until she left. Devin was proud of his D.R. crew because they had two women who insisted they were treated fine whenever he checked in with them.

In Eagle Cove, the main contractor in town was a woman.

"Huh," was all he managed. He made a mental gear shift, hard enough to do some grinding inside his skull. So she was here to make sure that his work was up to whatever standards Eagle Cove Contracting was known for. Because it was Peggy, he now knew that her standards were sky high. And the fact that she hadn't bothered to come by until shortly before the inspectors' planned arrival said something of what she thought of his skills.

"Well," he waved as casually as he could toward the rest of the interior, "let me know if you find anything. Inspectors are due any time."

Without a word, she turned and began walking through the cottage, doing her own pre-inspection inspection. He'd stripped the inside walls down to stud as well, so he could see her moving about. It felt as if someone was silently peeking inside his head to make sure his brain was still operating properly. She took more time than any self-respecting building inspector ever would.

She went upstairs and he resisted the urge to follow though he certainly traced her steps back and forth across the ceiling. When she returned, he realized that he hadn't moved an inch from standing in front of the permits, like some kind of a wind-up doll that someone had cranked full tight and had forgotten to hit the release switch.

"Why not fur out the old two-by-four walls to two-by-six so that you can fit R-21 insulation batts?"

"I'm going to do a closed-cell polyurethane. I didn't want to steal space as the rooms are already small. I'll get the same insulation factor and it doesn't get cold enough here to justify the expense and loss of interior space to push up to R-33. In Chicago, different answer."

"Doing it yourself?"

"Could, except my equipment is in Chicago. Subbing it out."

"To Gregor?"

At his confirmation, she nodded.

"What about sound insulation between rooms?"

"Standoffs and more spray-in foam, open-cell. Guests want their privacy in a romantic getaway but there's no need to waste money on an R-value we don't need."

She never once turned or pointed, demonstrating that she'd absolutely seen every single thing she'd looked at. "Second floor, third stud in the back bath has an age split. You'll need to sister on a new board."

He'd spotted that, but hadn't gotten to it yet.

He had seven items by the time the inspectors' arrival finally rescued him. Was that good, a nice short list? Or bad? He couldn't read Peggy well enough to tell. They were all minor items and not a one would concern an inspector, as none were structural.

Despite their long drive down from Newport, the inspectors completed their inspection in well under half an hour. Devin had the feeling that it had less to do with his workmanship and far more to do with Peggy's presence and her name on the permit.

"See ya', Peg," and they were gone again.

Both permits were signed, "Okay to insulate."

"Wait!" Devin stepped outside but they were gone.

Peggy joined him. "What's the problem?"

"They also signed 'Okay to cover.' I haven't insulated yet and they need to inspect that once it's in."

"John's also a building inspector for remote locales like Eagle Cove. He knows that I'll kick your ass if you don't do a good job. Saves him a trip."

"Oh." Devin blinked at the bright day. The interior of the cottage was relatively dim through the smaller style of windows prevalent a hundred years ago. "Are you going to kick my ass?"

"Nope," Peggy stuck her hands in her pockets. "Nice work."

"Uh, thanks." She'd proven that she expected the same standards of work he did from his own crew and it felt good to find another contractor who truly cared about the quality of work. He handed her a water bottle and took another himself from the cooler he kept in the back of his truck.

"Now what's this about you living up at Tiffany's?"

Devin was glad he hadn't opened his water yet or he'd be choking on it.

———

Tiffany was surprised that Mrs. Winslow understood the peace that making tea deserved. There should be some rituals that are sacrosanct and Tiffany had always enjoyed the process making a pot of tea. Preheating the pot with a swirl of boiling water. Loose tea leaves, then a tea cozy to retain the heat while it steeped.

Mrs. Winslow's cozy was simple, attractive…and tea-colored.

Tiffany's first one had been a nice bit of cable-knit wool, in the purest white. In days it had been stained with brown splashes of tea. It had gotten uglier and uglier until she'd had the idea of doing a tea-leaf dye bath. The white wool cozy had come out nicely tea-toned and she still used it every morning. They carried the tea service out into the backyard.

Mrs. Winslow's back garden was a lush wonder.

Tiffany's gardens were a study in the practical and the robust. Much of her food came from the garden, and it had to be strong enough to thrive despite the massive winds that occasionally slammed into the high ridge. A smaller seventy- or eighty-mile-an-hour wind down in Eagle Cove could easily top a hundred on her anemometer there above the headland. When those big storms arrived, the yurt's fabric flexed and slapped, making it impossible to sleep even by wearing earplugs…one of the only drawbacks to her home.

Mrs. Winslow's garden included a tiny herb bed and not another practical plant in the whole lot. Late tulips and early roses. Snapdragons teased peonies. Freesia borders accented Gerbera daisies.

And it was filled with bird life. Hummingbirds sipped sugar water from floral feeders. Stellar jays, chickadees, and red-winged black-birds abounded at seed and suet feeders.

"Fairyland," Tiffany kept turning about, trying to take it all in. She needed to build a place where she could do this. "It's magical."

"Thank you, Ms. Mills."

"Is it okay if I never leave?"

"I am glad that you appreciate it. You are always welcome in my garden, Ms. Mills."

Mrs. Winslow didn't make it sound like an empty offer and Tiffany retreated into silence.

When the tea was brewed, Tiffany poured while Mrs. Winslow went inside and returned with a plate of cookies. "Scottish short-bread. One of my weaknesses that I indulge in only on special occasions."

"Special occasions?" And Tiffany's nerves shot to life once more. Suddenly she wished she'd never come. She knew that, after Mrs. Winslow's kindness, there was no way that she could avoid revealing Lillian Lamont's story. And when she did, her own life would so pale in comparison. Lillian had founded a town and a matriarchy—two of them actually, here and in San Francisco—Tiffany had founded a farm with six goats. And the truth of her heritage would come out and her connection to—

"Yes," Mrs. Winslow studied her closely. "It is not often you fall in love."

Tiffany attempted to breathe but wasn't having much luck with it. Okay, even scarier than any revelation of her past was that simple, yet ever so true, statement of her present.

<hr>

DEVIN SAT DOWN ABRUPTLY on the lumber he'd stacked up to build the roof over the porch.

"I'm not living with her."

"Oh." Peggy sat opposite him on a large rock he'd nudged into place using the grader. A nice big boulder, it made a statement close beside the front door. "What do they call it these days?"

"You're not helping."

"Wasn't trying to."

"Great. What are you trying to do?"

Peggy kicked at the dirt a bit before answering. "Some people in this town are mighty protective of that girl."

"I'm one of them."

Peggy nodded without looking up. "Thought so. Anyone harasses you about that…"

"Then…" he prompted when she didn't continue.

"Then," she finally looked up at him. Her blue eyes were suddenly hard as steel. "Tell 'em to go fuck themselves. It's between you and her."

He sipped at his water while he considered his next words. "Peggy?"

"Uh-huh."

"If you're ever in Chicago looking for work, I can always use a good crew boss."

"Ha!" It was a single short bark of laughter. Then she stood and pulled her gloves out of her back pocket. "I've got the last replacement window in my truck; just came in."

"I'll do the list and then I'll meet you there."

They finished their water bottles, chucked the empties into his truck bed in unison, and headed back inside to finish the prep work for the insulation.

TIFFANY WISHED SHE COULD ARGUE, but being in love was exactly the problem. Being really in love. She deeply feared that Lillian Lamont had only experienced true lust. And while it had clearly been joyous based upon her entries, it now left Tiffany wholly adrift without any clear guidance of how to be.

"Why come to me? What about your friends?"

"*You* are my first friend in Eagle Cove, Mrs. Wilson."

"Oh damn, child."

Tiffany looked up to see her wiping at her eyes.

"That… Oh dear." She blew her nose into a paper napkin and then reached across the small table to squeeze Tiffany's hand. "Well, if we are such great friends, Ms. Mills, then you had best call me Maggie and I shall call you Tiffany, henceforth."

"Okay, Maggie," Tiffany stumbled a bit over it. Because she'd almost said…well, why not? "Unless Dragon Maggie would be better?"

And Maggie let loose a big laugh that would fit a woman three times her size. "Oh, there's hope for you yet, Tiffany. There's hope for you yet."

Tiffany was surprised. She'd driven Maggie Winslow to contractions—a rare event indeed.

"Seriously though. What about your friends?"

Tiffany considered her teacup, turning it around several times on the saucer. Jessica, Becky, and Natalya. "They're all recently married. I'm not saying that's a bad thing, but I expect that their perspective is that everyone should be as happily married as they are and the sooner the better. I suppose it's a lot like how it must be for you watching Peggy Slater and Gina Lamont's recent weddings."

"Hmm," it sounded distinctly like a dragony growl of dissatisfaction with Tiffany's statement. "And that is not your perspective?"

"I have reasons to be careful. And cautious."

"Which of those are you going to explain first?"

Tiffany half wished she was speaking with someone far less perceptive, but then again, that's why she'd come to Mrs.—to Maggie. She needed a sounding board.

And Maggie waited patiently.

"Cautious," Tiffany decided. "My past relationships have rarely been…pleasant."

"Did you make them pay for what they did to you?" The Dragon was suddenly at the forefront.

Tiffany didn't like to think of it so bluntly, but she had and finally nodded.

"Good! There were events in my life...but those were different times. Or so I thought then.... Now I am less sure. And your present relationship?" She made it sound like a threat to commit mayhem on behalf of all women everywhere.

"He's glorious!" Tiffany assured her. "Devin is the most wonderful man who has—" And she realized that she was effusing. She took a deep breath, which almost turned into an incipient hiccup, but she managed to defeat it by exhaling slowly. She was ridiculous when she got the hiccups; her hair flounced in all directions with each attack.

Maggie was smiling at her.

"He's better than anything I ever dreamed of."

"Thing?" The second-grade schoolteacher tone was unmistakable.

"One. Any*one.*"

"Then what is the problem?"

"How do you *know?*"

"That you are in love?" Maggie shrugged. "I married a good man. We were compatible for over thirty years until he passed. Gave me two sons whom I love very much. But was I ever 'in love' with him? I do not know, which perhaps answers the question itself."

"But Hector?"

And Maggie sighed. "Next you will have *me* asking *you* 'How do you know?' I would much prefer to not consider such eventualities."

"The lady doth protest too much, methinks."

And the two of them shared a laugh as they turned back to watch the birds flit about the lush garden.

Because Tiffany had learned one thing: they were both ladies who already knew.

The rest of the afternoon passed quietly before Mrs. Winslow gave her a ride back up to the lighthouse meadow. Devin's truck was parked there, but there was no sign of him, which told her that he was already up at the farm.

Thankfully, her friend Maggie never asked about the second half: why Tiffany also had to be so careful in addition to being cautious.

CHAPTER 8

"*D*evin!" Gina flagged him down as he drove by the B&B.

He stopped and climbed out of the truck as she swooped down the front stairs. He'd learned, in a small town, there was always time. In Chicago he wouldn't have bothered to exit the truck or even shut down the engine. Here such an action might not be actively rude, but it wasn't exactly sociable either.

"I tried calling you." Gina was a very fine-looking woman, but she was practically glowing this morning.

"You're looking good, Ms. Lamont. Like marriage really agrees with you."

"You have *no* idea. Neither did I. It took me until I was past fifty to find the right man, but oh did I ever," and her smile spoke sufficient volumes for Devin to feel a bit voyeuristic.

"I heaved my phone into the ocean," he told her. "I haven't missed it enough to replace it yet." Which was actually surprising as hell. In Chicago, if he was disconnected for even an hour, he'd worry about what he was missing.

Gina held up a hand and he high-fived it. "Welcome to the coast, Devin."

"Thanks. I think."

"I don't suppose Tiffany has a phone," there was some tease in her voice, but it was friendly rather than judgmental.

"I doubt it. I certainly haven't seen one. She'd have even less use for it than I do."

"Thought as much," Gina leaned back against his truck hood and raised her face into the morning sunlight.

He leaned beside her and did the same. It was late April. Back in Chicago it could be cold-snapping down to the teens, or baking into the eighties. Here it was late morning, so the air was mid-fifties and so fresh he felt better just for breathing it. The sun was different here. He'd never believed that...Monet returning time and time again to Liguria, Italy because the light was so special there. But it was true. The Oregon sun was a kinder, gentler light than the Chicago one. There it was all glare and brightness, hard as a slap. Here it was warm and pleasant, then as often as not, slipping behind cloud or tree branch to leave a cool caress when a breeze slid by.

"Are you busy at the moment?"

He shrugged, "Not really. You probably saw the insulator's truck arrive this morning. Tomorrow I have the sheetrockers in. I've finished the concrete pour for the front porch, but I'd just be in everyone's way if I framed it up now. What do you need?"

"Not me. I'm all set for the festival, but Peggy could use a hand out at the airport."

"Festival?" He'd heard something about a festival as he passed through town on errands, but between the renovation and Tiffany, he didn't slow down often...not even this much. After a month his thoughts might be shifting to Eagle Cove Time, but his body was still clearly on the Chicago clock. Now that he thought about it, that was another thing he should heave overboard...at least for as long as he was here.

"Flameagle Days," Gina didn't look down from the sun. "Jessica's fourth festival. She became the town's marketing manager nine months ago."

"And pregnant eight and a half ago."

"The two are definitely related, but that's a story for another time.

This town wasn't dying, but it was fading. She planned a big festival every three months along with other advertising campaigns. We're financially healthier in the last year than in the prior thirty and it's all that girl's doing. This is her fourth one and no one except her knows what all of the pieces are."

"What in the world is a flameagle? A flaming eagle, like Burning Man in Nevada?"

"Nope. You'll see. Go help Peggy. And I'll expect you and Tiffany to be at the festival, not hiding up in your woods." Gina pushed off the truck and headed back to the B&B. "It's only Tuesday and we're already full. That Jessica is a marketing wizard."

Devin sat there a while longer, watching the sun climb up through the branches.

You and Tiffany.

Your woods.

He didn't know which was stranger. Hearing it stated as simple fact or that it was true. A month ago, the woods had been a strange and creepy place. It now seemed perfectly normal to wander up into the trees after work rather than head down to the B&B. Sometimes Tiffany would walk down to meet him and they'd walk together, holding hands where the trail was wide enough.

They'd greet Tall Guy, check the goats, shower together, cook, and make love. She had no television, so they often talked, read aloud to each other, or sometimes just wrapped up under a comforter on the porch and watched the sun set and the stars come out. He'd brought his guitar up from the B&B and they would often spend the evening serenading Tall Guy and the goats. Occasionally Jake would perch in the nearest fir and look down at them like they were insane, which was a point he wasn't going to argue. Insanely happy.

Devin no longer went out and hit the bar with his crew. No formal dinners at his house or Rebecca's, no social events that, in retrospect, had simply been what he was supposed to do. He'd never thought before about what he *wanted* to do. D.R. Builders was his, but after-hours his lifestyle had been dictated by default, not preference.

The image of strolling through some small-town fair with Tiffany at his side...that wouldn't be default. That would be his and hers.

Your woods.

You and Tiffany.

He knew they were a couple. "An item." He just wasn't sure when it had happened because it had been the most natural thing in the world since that first moment. He'd arrived at a wedding and a nameless woman with amazing hair and an incredible smile had taken his hand to lead him through the crowd.

Devin was smiling himself as he climbed back into his truck and headed for the airport. He didn't know where the future lay, but the present was pretty damned amazing.

"Your mother is looking for you," Tiffany's lawyer said on the satellite phone.

"Tell her no!" She felt sick to her stomach and was glad that Devin wasn't here to see how weak she really was.

"I already did." But there was something in Joel Masterson's voice that told her there was more.

"Why is she looking for me?"

"You recall that she does this every few years."

"Yes," Tiffany did, now that she was getting through the initial panic. "Is there something different about this time?"

"I don't think so..." again that hesitation. Joel was a cutthroat legal shark, one of the reasons she had hired him. It wasn't like him to avoid an issue.

"Joel?"

He sighed. "Ms. Mills. You and I go back well over a decade."

Joel had made his reputation in putting her prominent stepfather behind bars for abusing his teenage stepchild. That one case had led him to be a leading champion of individual women's rights—a very successful one.

"It isn't my place, but have you considered speaking with your mother?"

Tiffany could only manage a strangled sound.

"Hear me out on this. You have escaped her. Run far, and by the sound of it, made good your choices."

Tiffany could only give him silence, but she was listening and he eventually continued.

"I will support whatever decision you make, Ms. Mills. But even your reaction now tells me that you are still running from her. That is not a life, Ms. Mills."

After another stretch of silence, he read off a cell phone number, which she dutifully wrote down.

"I apologize if I have crossed some line, Ms. Mills."

"No," she managed. "I don't think so. I just don't know if I'm brave enough to do this."

"If I may say, Tiffany?" It was the first time she could recall that he'd used her first name in all the years. "Your bravery is not in question here. Neither in confronting your stepfather in court, nor in choosing your own life, nor in building and running a farm yourself. None of those are the actions of the meek. I can only hope that someday you meet a man your age rather than mine who can see and appreciate that."

She thought about that a long time. "Maybe I already have, Joel."

"That, Ms. Mills, is the best news you have ever given me. As always, please call if I may be of any assistance." And he was gone.

"You want me to bale hay?" Devin tried not to feel too surprised. "I've never run a baler before."

"You'll learn," Peggy led him over the mown fields filled with the cut, dried hay neatly piled in long rows. One whole side of the airport had been in hay. They then crossed over a fence heading toward Becky's big, hip roof barn-turned-brewery. It glared blindingly white in the well-risen sun.

"Isn't it early?" Though the cut hay on the ground looked dry and rustled when he stepped on it.

"Wet winter, warm spring, and a drier than normal April. It's mature enough," she kicked at a windrow as they stepped over it. "I'd like to have let it grow another few weeks, but I don't trust Jessica."

"You don't trust her…to do what?" Devin couldn't imagine how not trusting a pregnant woman led to an early haying season.

"Her festival," Peggy raised a big bar on the front of the barn's massive main door.

"Flameagle Days. Gina mentioned that. What about it? What is a flameagle anyway?"

"My part of the festival is a fly-in. Pilots of small planes are always looking for a place to meet up. An event."

"Like a gathering of the Scottish clans. The Highland Games of flying?"

"Right. And Jessica is too good at her job. I expect the airport to get parked out and I'll have to overflow into this field. But I'm not willing to sacrifice the hay to her festival, so we have to take it in early."

Together they dragged the big doors aside and revealed a whole collection of strange machinery.

The barn itself had been partly converted to Becky's immaculate brewery, cordoned off behind wood-and-glass walls on this side just as it had been between her living area and the tasting room on the other side of the building. But part of it was still pure barn, with straw scattered on the packed-dirt floor and some elaborate examples of the steel fabricator's art into forms he couldn't begin to comprehend.

"Hay mower," Peggy rapped one as they passed by. "Hay rake for turning the drying hay and then gathering it into windrows," she pointed to another.

"Uh-huh," he did his best to make it sound as if he knew how these things worked, rather than wondering what medieval dungeon these torture devices had been stolen from.

"Blueberry picker."

That stopped him. "Blueberry picker?"

At a window, she pointed across the airfield that stretched alongside Becky's hay fields. On the far side of the airstrip was a vast field of white blossoms.

"Those are blueberry bushes?"

"Uh-huh."

"And this machine picks them?" It looked more as if it was designed to eat unwary cows, or maybe small elephants.

"Whatever the U-pickers don't harvest."

"Uh-huh." He tried to puzzle out how it could possibly do that when he was distracted by the last machine in the barn. It was bizarre enough for him to stop wondering why Gina had sent him to Peggy, who in turn was having Devin drive Becky's equipment to bale hay. Maybe that was just how small towns worked.

"Here it is."

He'd never driven a farm tractor, but that looked enough like other construction machinery that it didn't worry him.

The John Deere tractor was bright green. He supposed it was a little one, especially compared to the giants he'd seen at work out on the Great Plains as he drove through, but it was still a big machine.

But the contraption attached to the back of the tractor in Becky's barn was alarming. It was a strange, off-center device on two wheels. It had about a thousand, foot-long tines sticking out of a central drum. They must sweep the hay up and then do mysterious things with it inside the rest of the blocky machine.

Peggy led him back, pointing out how to restock bailing twine and where the bales were ejected. Ejected was the right word. The last item in the Rube Goldberg train of equipment was a big cart with wood slat sides. It had definitely been used hard.

"The baler will loft the finished bale into the cart, so don't turn too sharply at the end of the row or it may loft it over the side."

"Don't you have a floor I can sweep instead?"

"I was going to do this myself," Peggy grinned at him. "But that damn Jessica. She may be as big as a hay bale herself, but she knows her marketing. I have a half-dozen flights booked already today and the festival is still four days off. I need this field clear by then." She clapped him hard on the shoulder. "Good luck!"

And she left him. He could tell by her saunter on her way back over the fields to the airport that she was really enjoying leaving him to figure this all out himself. Well, he wasn't scared by the challenge. He was going to take it head-on. After all, he was a Grader Master.

Then he turned to look at the controls and felt much less comfortable with that decision.

"I don't even know how to…" And he stopped himself.

Some forever time ago he'd said those same words to Tiffany back before he earned his Grader Mastership. He'd hated that machine at first, but now it would always have a soft place in his heart. It was the first place he'd ever kissed her—an event that might not be changing his life, but it had certainly changed his summer.

Actually. His life was changing too, he just wasn't sure how.

"Okay," he told the tractor. "You don't scare me," which was only half a lie. On both counts: tractor and mysteriously changing life.

I think, he could almost imagine Tiffany standing beside him, *you should teach me how to use this.*

He'd pretend that she was talking about the tractor and not the life.

And so he did. He went over each control and explained it aloud until he was sure that he understood it. When he was done, he started the tractor and put on his sunglasses before pulling out of the barn.

Then he let out the clutch.

The tractor jolted backward, which shoved against the baler, turning it cockeyed as it jammed against the catcher cart. Then he stalled the engine in his attempt to recover.

He was glad that Tiffany wasn't there to see him; she'd be laughing herself to death in that merry way of hers.

Then Devin turned and saw that someone else was. Inside the brewery, Becky was standing at the window as if she'd been watching him a long time. Though he couldn't hear her, it was easy to see that she was howling with laughter.

Devin turned away, restarted the tractor, and eased forward out of the barn.

TTIFFANY STOOD at the edge of the field and watched Devin baling hay. He looked as if he'd done it forever. He sat just slightly sideways in the seat, often casting an eye back to make sure everything was in order. Every twenty seconds, the baler lofted a fifty-pound cube of hay high into the air where it tumbled into the cart being towed behind. Everything was as it should be, except the madness in her head.

Three years ago she had learned to enjoy the long walks to town as a time of peace and quiet in her day. For the first time, she had been in such a hurry to find Devin that she had come down the back logging road from her property, cutting the four-mile walk to two, and still she was a little breathless from how fast she'd traveled.

But watching Devin, suddenly her world was at peace again. Everything was where it should be.

Almost everything.

He spotted her, though she had stayed in the shade of the trees at the far end of the field. With a wave, he called her to him and her feet were in motion before she had a chance to decide. The tractor was moving so slowly that it was easy to time her steps. She arrived at the end of a windrow at the same moment as the tractor, grabbed a handrail, and stepped up the short ladder without Devin having to even slow the machine.

"Hi!" He kissed her quickly, then turned to check on his progress. "Aren't you early for knitting?"

Tuesday. She'd completely forgotten it was Tuesday. A glance skyward showed that it was still morning, but it would be a long day by the time she walked home to fetch her knitting and walk all the way back.

Then he turned from his baling to look at her once more. His smile faded as he squinted at her face a moment. Without saying anything else, he stopped the tractor and cycled down the machinery. She could hear him talking to himself as he did it. "Once we stop, we shift into neutral. Ease the engine down to idle. Now, disconnect the PTO to stop the baler..."

Just like the road grader. It was charming to think that in a way she had been with him all morning even though they had been in separate places. But it didn't make her feel any better about the phone call.

When finally everything was shut off and the only sounds were soft birdcall and the distant roar of Peggy's Stearman 4 biplane soaring high above, Devin pulled her into his lap.

"What's wrong?"

"Did I—" No. With Devin she didn't need to say when something was wrong. He would simply know. "I—" but she wasn't having any better luck without the "did."

Jake swooped close by the tractor and landed fast in the field less than a dozen feet away. A moment later he was back aloft with a vole or something in his claws. At least she was fairly sure it was Jake, but he'd finished his molt and now looked like any other bald eagle—huge and dangerous.

"Way to go, Jake," Devin whispered. He'd come a long way from diving out of the road grader in panic when an eagle flew by.

"Do you love me?" She blurted it out. "Sorry, that's not at all the question I rehearsed all the way here. That was unfair of me to—"

"Yes."

She stopped and looked at him. "Yes? Just yes?"

"Just yes," he nodded. "Like you just said, not the answer I expected to give at all. But it's the one that came out."

Then he grimaced and she feared he was regretting it already.

"Not exactly the most romantic way to say it. Sorry. I'll have to work on that before we get anywhere near to a proposal," he grimaced again. "And I did not just say that either. I—"

She kissed him and then burst into giggles that were really unbecoming on a woman who had just been told she was loved by someone who meant it.

Once they had both calmed down, she tried again.

"I have to do something awful."

"Why doesn't this sound good?"

"Because I just told you it will be awful."

"Okay," Devin kept his hands tight about her waist. "Would you care to define 'it' or should I start guessing? You have to cut your hair —which I should warn you would make me weep. You have amazing hair." He began toying with an end of it.

She shook her head and then had to dig a handful of it aside so that she could see him. Before she could speak, he continued.

"You have decided to give up the harp in favor of the harpsichord and you will make me follow you about the world carrying it on my back from one concert to the next."

Tiffany laid a hand over his mouth to stop him, but could feel his smile against her palm.

"I think I have to call my mother."

And she could feel the smile go away.

Devin felt as if he'd just stepped onto hot coals. One false move and the Tiffany-who-ran just might reemerge. Then he took some hope in that she'd *come* to him.

"You've been very careful to never mention her."

"You told me not to think about my past, so I haven't. Or very little."

He decided it wasn't simplicity that made her speak this way sometimes, nor was it some complex set of defense mechanisms. Devin thought back to a few nights before when they had been lying together in bed, watching the light of the moon that shone through the yurt's clear dome slowly sweep across the room.

"It's like a celestial searchlight," Tiffany had whispered in awe.

It had reminded him of the searchlights at the party for CMC's latest skyscraper. They had lit up the sky in celebration. Reds, blues, and golds of the CMC logo sweeping over the eighty stories of modernist glass and steel. The D.R. Builders' colors would not translate so well, a pale blue and a—

"Pudding!" Tiffany had exclaimed from beside him.

"What?"

"I just remembered that we have some chocolate pudding. Do you want some?" And already she was up and walking naked through the patch of moonlight, lit up like a magical elf.

"What were you thinking about?" He'd been trying to understand how she got from moon to pudding.

"When?" She opened the refrigerator and the white glow turned her skin from shadowed bronze to blinding alabaster.

"Before the pudding."

"I was thinking about the moonlight."

"What about it?"

"Nothing. I was just watching the light."

And now, sitting on the tractor with Tiffany in his lap, he finally understood. Her mind wasn't simple, it was just a much more peaceful place than his. She had been thinking about the moonlight and then she had thought of pudding.

He'd told her *not* to think about the past, and he'd wager that, for the most part, she hadn't.

Whereas he was *still* replaying Rebecca's phone call in his mind. Which in turn made him wonder how long she'd kept talking after the phone sank. Also how deep the phone had sunk before it shorted out. Or had some component been crushed first by the increasing pressure as it went deeper. And—

"Pudding," he said to her.

"No, mother."

He waited a beat and then she burst out laughing.

"You're still thinking about the pudding?"

"Well, that and how amazing you looked as you walked naked through the moonlight to bring it back to bed."

"Your mind is a very strange place, Devin Robison."

"And yours isn't, Tiffany Mills?"

She closed her eyes for a long moment and when she opened them the earlier sadness had returned.

He kept his hands firmly on her waist in case she tried to flee.

"My name isn't Tiffany Mills."

"Your name could be Lizzie Borden and I wouldn't care. Though I might hide all the axes."

"My name isn't Lizzie either." No tease. Ms. Forthright once again.

"Sooo…" he prompted her.

"Oh. My name is Tiffany Lamont."

"Well at least I had it half right. Tiffany—wait a sec. Lamont? Like Gina Lamont?"

"Yes."

"Is she your mother? She doesn't act like she knows. Are you some long-lost adopted child or—" Devin finally shut up, having learned that Tiffany often needed the room of enough silence to speak.

"No. She's not my mother, my sister, nor my aunt. What matters is *my* mother—who isn't Gina. I think I have to call her."

"Well, Lamont sounds safer than Borden with her axe. Though if that makes you a relative of Natalya, maybe I'll just lay low." He took a hand from her waist and held it out until she finally clasped it tentatively with her own. "Hello, Tiffany Lamont. I'm Devin Robison and I'm still in love with you. Wow! That does feel cool to say. Wait a sec—Tiffany…Lamont?"

She froze, her fingers somehow going cold though he still held onto them.

"San Francisco. You said you were from there. Some banker used to handle some of CMC's investments. He—" And Devin remembered. His father had told him the story one night over a bottle of Scotch about some brat stepkid destroying one of the best bankers ever, who had been put away then stabbed to death by another prisoner.

He was married to some high society bitch who got all his money in the bargain, his father had groaned at the injustice and freshened their Scotch glasses.

"You said your stepfather was killed," Devin was reaching for the rest of the memory.

Tiffany still didn't move. Her head remained bowed and her hair covered her face just as it had that first day when she was playing the harp.

Slowly, carefully, he brushed it back until he could see her face. "The San Francisco Lamonts as in Lamont Construction Supply and Shipping?"

Again no response. There simply weren't that many firms of the scale of CMC and LCSS in the country.

"Wow!"

And finally Tiffany flinched. Then she yanked her hand free of his. When he kept her in place, she began to struggle. He almost let her go, but then he remembered the haunted look on her face each time her family was mentioned—so he held on. It was time they got to the bottom of this.

She made fists, pounded them against his chest, and he wrapped his arms about her until she couldn't move. He'd never held a woman against her will. But this once, he *knew* it was the best choice.

"If you struggle any harder, you'll fall off my lap. It's a long way from a tractor seat to the ground."

"Damn you, let me go!"

So he did.

Caught by surprise, she remained on his lap though he knew it wouldn't last. So he confronted anger with anger.

"Do you think I give a rat's ass about who you were before I met you?"

She squinted at him. The mistrust lay clear upon her features—and it hurt like hell. But he knew that look. That fear. It was the same look he'd seen on his own face when he had realized why Rebecca Monica Monash had come after him. It was why he had never mentioned his father's name or CMC in Eagle Cove. Not in the interview with Gina and Cal, and not with Tiffany.

It all came down to money. And if she was from the LCSS lineage, she had plenty of it, too.

"Okay," Devin closed his eyes for a long moment. You didn't tell a woman you loved her and then keep secrets from her. And he'd done the first, so it was time to fix the second. "Tiffany."

It was strange to address her formally while she sat in his lap but in most ways was being very careful not to touch him. He forged on.

"You already know I'm about as smoothly romantic as a kumquat. So I'll say this straight. Next time you're on the Internet, look up the name of the CEO of Chicago Master Constructors."

TIFFANY WONDERED if this was how the inside of Devin's head felt all the time. Hers felt as if it was going to explode as things shifted so rapidly and emotions slammed about so hard.

Trapped! She'd been so trapped. The feeling had been a slick, greasy shroud of horror.

Then he'd freed her the moment she asked and not struck. Not slapped. Not taken.

He had—kept her from her instinct to flee. No more. It didn't make the awful feeling go away, but he didn't repel her either.

Keeping a careful eye on him, she reached into her small backpack. She'd been out of the yurt and away before she'd discovered the satellite phone was still clenched in her hand. Now she pulled it out and hit last number redial.

"Hello?"

"Hi, Joel. Could you do me a favor and look up the last name of the CEO of CMC in Chicago?"

"Easy, Robison. It has been in the family for generations."

"And the son's name?"

"Heh!" It was the first time she'd ever heard anything close to a laugh from Joel Masterson. "Devin or Mikal? The former posted a nudie of his fiancée doing the latter almost at the altar. It went completely viral on the Internet. If you're talking about Mikal, he's harmless but a waste of time. Devin, though, is the heir apparent to the empire, though I hear he skipped town. He wrote something funny with the picture, but I can't remember what."

" 'I guess the wedding is off.' "

"That was it. Kid became a goddamn meme," Joel laughed aloud this time. "Supposed to be the merger of two empires, which the Monashs needed badly and the Robisons not so much. Are you okay?"

"I think so. I'll call you back and let you know."

"By end of day, Ms. Mills," Joel's voice was suddenly dead serious, "or I'm calling out the police."

"No need to bother him. It's a small town and Martin goes to bed early." And she hung up the phone.

Devin was still waiting for her reaction. Stone-faced, she could no longer see her lover in this careful man she was seated upon. She slipped off his lap but didn't climb down to the hay field.

"Did you say 'Wow!' because of my money?"

"No," Devin bit off the words as he spoke them. "I said that because Mills was so much easier to spell than Lamont. Did you screw me because of mine?"

Tiffany could only blink at him. This was all so messed up.

"Day one," he snapped out as if putting pieces together that didn't belong. "Chicago, contractor, and my name—my real name. Wouldn't have been hard to figure out with a quick search."

"I didn't. I swear, Devin, I didn't." She knew about the paranoia of money—knew how it attracted all the wrong type of attention. False friendship, insincere lovers, and worse. But there was no way that she could ever prove that wasn't her.

Defeated, she climbed down the tractor's ladder.

He jumped down and landed in front of her just as she reached the ground.

"Why did you change your name?" Again that unreadable, neutral voice that felt like a cold San Francisco fog. Or, a better analogy for him, a chilly wind off Lake Michigan.

"Do you know what rich boys do?" She practically shouted it out. She raised her hand to place it on his chest in apology, but instead let it drop. "*Some* rich boys?" She barely managed a whisper.

He waited in careful silence.

"They think they're god's gift," Tiffany explained. "And they think that once you've been abused that you must have wanted it. Then they—"

She could feel the chill of her shattering world as the shards of ice drove into her chest. How she—

And her face was crushed against Devin's chest before she even knew what happened.

"Aw, crap, Tiffany. I didn't know."

How would he? He was a good man.

"I hope to hell you got them all back but good."

"Most of them," she managed. Her nose was once again pressed into the same spot on his shoulder. This time, instead of muddy with plaster, he was going to make her sneeze with hay dust. She didn't care and managed to fight off the sneeze to stay in place. The tears were harder to fight, though she succeeded there as well.

But now what would he say? They both came from rich families, for all the good it had done them. Devin's parents weren't cruel, at least not intentionally like her stepfather. Would he speak first of wealth or of—

"Tell me why *we're* going to have to call your mother," he whispered in her ear.

Her heart was so smart; it had chosen to fall in love with a very good man. She pushed her face harder against his shoulder and breathed him in. Man, honest sweat, and—

Tiffany jerked back and unleashed a monstrous sneeze. Unable to raise her hands because he still held her so tightly, she splattered his shirt.

"Thorry," she managed with a sniffle. "You thmell like hay."

Then Devin laughed, which was the best sound in the world.

CHAPTER 9

Flameagle Days were in full swing and Tiffany was glad they had come, as long as Devin kept holding her hand when the crowds pressed too close. She and Devin had somehow managed to avoid being recruited for the weekend, perhaps because he'd done so much work leading up to the event.

They had tagged along on a bird watching tour, and Devin had made the whole crowd laugh when they'd oohed and aahed over seeing a bald eagle and Devin had called out, "His name is Jake."

Town smelled of strawberries. It seemed that every car had a couple flats of fresh-picked berries. Cal Jr. and Sr.'s Blackbird Bakery was selling strawberry-rhubarb pie and strawberry-custard tarts with a side of fresh-made vanilla ice cream as fast as they could dish it up.

She and Devin washed it down with a shared pint of Becky's Flameagle Stout.

And everywhere about town were the flameagles.

Jessica must have bought out the entire Oregon State supply of plastic flamingos. They had been painted brown, with white heads. The metal sticks of their legs and their beaks had been painted yellow. Every eye was yellow with a black dot for the pupil, even the smallest ones. Some nested in planters of geraniums that decorated the main drag of Beach Way. Some had tiny knitted hats. Other, larger ones, cropped up in the strangest of places: in the trees, out on the beach, and especially out at the airport among the kajillion small planes that had flown in and filled the newly-hayed field.

"What's a flameagle's call?" Devin asked.

"Thock!" Tiffany declared.

"Thock?"

"They started life as plastic flamingos. Drop one on the floor. They go, 'Thock! Thock! Thock!' Each repeated call gets softer as they bounce."

"Okay, Ms. Know-it-all, what kind of eggs do they lay?"

"Very rare. They look just like Ping Pong balls."

He nodded, "That must be why they're endangered. Ping Pong players have been unwittingly harvesting them for years."

"Except in Eagle Cove," Tiffany corrected, for they were every-where. And each had a number, as if they'd been tagged by a wildlife plasticologist. There were scavenger hunts for the most flameagles found, for finding the most that were a prime number, for finding the most that were still molting—identified by their speckled heads. Devin had spooked an enterprising group of teens who were going about with brown paint and a fine brush, speckling flameagle heads as they went.

She and Devin had finally wandered out to the airport, neither minding the long walk—which was good because driving was crazy in the packed small town.

There was an entire plane show going on in the field, like an antique car show. On the runway there were precision landing contests, hitting all wheels between two white lines just fifty feet apart —no bounces allowed.

"Flour-bombing," Devin observed and she followed where he was pointing. "Now that's a noble sport handed down from the times when men were men."

Devin was certainly a man. He was fun and funny, yet so male that she still was having trouble believing he was real.

Pilots flew over the field at five-hundred feet up and dropped tiny bags of flour, trying to "bomb" a giant tractor tire painted bright yellow and lying on the ground. Little splats of flour seemed to be everywhere about the field—except near the tire.

"Looks like fun," Devin was watching the planes avidly. "Care to be my bombardier next year?" It took one person to fly the plane safely and one to drop the flour bomb.

Tiffany was sure he wasn't aware of what he'd just said. He was leaving in three more months, at the end of the summer. His contract would be up when the lightkeeper's cottage was done and he'd be gone.

"Do you know how to fly?"

"I'll take lessons."

He still didn't get it and she did her best to ignore the pain. She couldn't follow him to Chicago. She had her farm, and deep connections to Eagle Cove—ones that she still hadn't told to anybody.

Then something happened. Planes scattered and it didn't take Tiffany long to see why. The ones they'd been watching were all propeller-driven planes. Some faster, some slower, and a few that looked to be plodding they moved so slowly, but they all used propellers.

Now a sleek business jet sliced through the sky, entered something Devin had called "the pattern," and dove for the field. She recognized the LCSS plane even before she saw the sailing ship logo. The Dassault Falcon 7x hit clean between the spot-landing contest stripes and decelerated with a massive roar of its triple jet engines, drowning then silencing all else on the field.

DEVIN COULD FEEL Tiffany's hand trembling in his and he squeezed it tightly.

The phone call had made this moment inevitable though it was still early on Sunday afternoon. The last events of the festival were still on-going and her mother wasn't supposed to arrive until after it was over. But it was too late to be helped.

He led her over to stand by the hangar as the private jet taxied up and stopped on the front apron—the paved area in front of the hangar. He didn't know what to expect when the ladder folded down, but still it was a shock.

An older version of Tiffany walked down the short set of stairs. She wore a designer dress more appropriate for a yachting party than an Eagle Cove fly-in and her hair was an elegant cut of the latest style. At least he imagined it was, because he could easily imagine it on his mother or Rebecca. The face was the same, the body shape, and oddly —the smile.

He'd expected it to be fake or studied or somehow plastic. But she looked actively happy to see her long-lost daughter.

"Oh, Lillian. This place? Really? After five generations you had to come back to Eagle Cove?" But Vivian Lamont's hug looked genuine and she held onto her daughter hard enough that it was clear that her daughter was more important than the neat-pressed lines of her designer sportswear.

Tiffany's face was to his side of her mother and he couldn't resist.

"You're Lillian now?" He whispered the question.

Tiffany sighed and nodded, still trapped in the hug. "I'm Lillian Tiffany Lamont."

"Why, of course you are." Her mother stepped back and did straighten out her dress.

The crowd that had gathered upon the jet's arrival slowly dispersed. Some to admire the jet, others to return their attention to the flour-bombing contest regaining its momentum.

"Of course she is," he agreed amiably. "Lillian," he couldn't resist the tease.

Tiffany started to wince at her name being different *again*, first Mills to Lamont and now...then he could see her catch on to his humor and shake her head ruefully at being caught again.

"Of course I am," she agreed with a smile.

"And who is this?" Tiffany's mother turned a discerning eye on him. He'd dressed in clean jeans and a nondescript button-down denim work shirt, Eagle Cove formal.

"This is Devin, Mother," and he could see Tiffany was trying to protect him by not even including his last name.

He looked at Vivian Lamont. He'd been prepared to hate her. He had reason to. How could she not have known that her husband was abusing her daughter? And wouldn't she have the same alley cat morals of his parents…and Rebecca's? And Rebecca.

But rather than being condescending, or attacking as if he was a gold-digger after Tiffany's money, he could see that she was putting the best face she could on a bundle of nerves.

Her daughter had rejected her a decade before in a desperate grab for self-preservation. But time had passed and now their future was dependent only on these two women—and Vivian *feared* her strong daughter's possible rejection, right down to her designer shoes. The media frenzy was gone, the bastard was dead, and life had moved on. Maybe, with a little help, they had a chance at finding at least friend-ship after all this time.

Devin took a careful breath, reassuring himself that there was no time like the present, and held out a hand.

"Devin Robison, Mrs. Lamont, of the Chicago Master Constructor Robisons. And I'm the one who is going to be marrying your daughter."

"You are?" The two of them said it in unison.

"Oh crap!" Devin turned to Tiffany. "I told you I was going to screw up the proposal."

She stepped forward into his arms and looked up at him. "No. You did it just great." Then she kissed him.

"THANK you all for coming to meet my mother," Tiffany was more than a little overwhelmed that they had.

She'd asked Devin and Maggie Winslow to meet her at Becky's brewery after the end of the Flameagle Days Festival. And that had necessitated asking Becky. Who in turn had invited Natalya and Jessica, who had brought their husbands and parents…so Gina, Cal

Sr., Jessica's parents, and Judge and Peggy Slater were in attendance as well. Even Hector had docked from his last sailing charter to sit close beside Maggie.

Sixteen people—seventeen if she had counted herself but that number was entirely too big so she didn't. She hadn't addressed such a large crowd since mock-trials in law school.

It was a convivial group who had made her mother welcome and she would be forever grateful to them.

And her mother hadn't been merely gracious in return, she'd been…real. The way Tiffany had remembered her when still a child.

"I—" she looked at Devin in a plea for assistance.

He shot her a double thumbs up as if that helped anything.

"I'm not a good public speaker."

"You barely speak at all," Natalya corrected.

"Hush, Natya," Becky nodded to Tiffany. "You're doing great, Tiff. Rock on."

"You couldn't know, but my real name is—"

"Lillian," Maggie Winslow said in wonder.

"What?" Tiffany looked at her in surprise, but Maggie Winslow wasn't looking at her. She was looking up at the big mural above Becky's bar.

"You're the spitting image of Lillian Lamont."

"No way," Natalya protested. "I reproduced that from a historic photo."

Tiffany looked up at the painting. The two women there, dressed as Victorian ladies, didn't look anything alike. But the older one could have been Tiffany's twin. Right down to the long hair. A copy of the same photo had been in Lillian's journal and was the reason Tiffany had grown it out. She'd never noticed because it was a little too much like looking in the mirror.

"How is that possible?" Maggie pointed at the mural but was facing Tiffany.

Tiffany had known this moment was coming and knew she wouldn't have the nerves to tell the story herself. So she'd brought her four-times-great-grandmother's journal. Now she opened it and handed it to Devin who'd agreed to read the marked passage for her.

He rose to stand beside her and cleared his throat. The room went silent.

"This is the journal of Lillian Lamont," Devin began. "Tiffany's direct ancestor."

August 1900

I must leave this town and not return until my child is born. It can never be known to my dearest Pearl that she and I will give birth to half siblings, both sired by a dead man. I sail for San Francisco today. I cannot even bear to speak with her or see her for fear I will not have the strength to hold true to my purpose.

Devin turned to the next page she'd marked.

December 31, 1900

This year opened with a herald of such joy. My Pearl in her own home, preparing for a voyage that may yet cause Eagle Cove to thrive.

Now I am a woman in desperate fear of what has begun. I am old to bear a child, yet I would give anything but this unborn child's life if I could see my Pearl once more. I have prepared for every eventuality. Over my solicitor's protests, I have charged him with the care of my child should I not survive.

If my child lives, it shall have the San Francisco share and my beloved Pearl the Eagle Cove share of all we may achieve. As they are of near equal value, I have instructed him that this is to be done by severing the corporation into two separate entities so that neither child shall know of the other. Ever! However, if my child survives and is a girl, she and her descendants must always retain the Lamont name so that someday the breach may be sealed that lies beyond my power to repair.

"A different hand writes next," Devin's soft tone carried easily through the stilled room.

January 1, 1901

It is with saddened heart that I record the death this date of Lillian Lamont.

Yet with gladdened heart do I record the birth of Tiffany Lamont, so named by her mother from her deathbed.

He closed the journal softly and handed it back to her before sitting once more.

"I am named for both my ancestors, Lillian Tiffany Lamont. This," Tiffany squeezed the book hard, looking for strength, "I found this shelved in the family library when I was twelve and seeking an escape from…"

She saw her mother cower against the coming blow. They had spoken of it earlier, just the two of them, sitting quietly in the jet— Devin insisting that she was strong enough and must face this moment.

Sitting stone-faced in the luxurious leather, her mother had sworn that she didn't know. "Carl was always so charming. But there were certain events that he didn't care for, or so he said. No symphony or ballet for him, nor opera, nor social events with my friends—only with his. I now understand. I didn't then. I didn't even believe you when you charged him and they took away my husband. But I do now. I cannot beg forgiveness, not even from myself for being so blind, but I am so sorry for it."

Tiffany understood now that the stone-faced expression had been her mother's only place of safety in her ever so public life, trying to hide as desperately as Tiffany had in her woods. She nodded to her mother now. Perhaps Vivian could not forgive herself, but perhaps Tiffany could.

"This book helped me when I was seeking an escape from that period of my life," Tiffany explained to the waiting crowd, creating closure. She was now done with that.

Her mother began to silently cry, but they shared a tentative smile.

"This journal was unmarked on the binding and unremembered for most of a century. It has been my keepsake, my strength, for many years."

She looked at Devin, who watched her with the warmest brown eyes and a rapt attention that she'd never dreamed of. He hadn't yet healed the breach between Tiffany and her mother, but he'd made it possible for her to imagine that it might someday be.

"I have found a new source of strength," she told the crowd but she saw only Devin and his confirming nod that he would be just that.

Then she stepped over to Maggie Winslow.

"You declared yourself the keeper of Eagle Cove's history. Here is the founding as told by a woman I have come to love very much." And she handed over the volume. It was like relinquishing herself, but it was also like freeing herself. She was no longer walking in Lillian Lamont's footsteps. From now on, she would walk in her own.

"You," Maggie whispered softly, "are the true keepsake."

Tiffany returned to Devin's side and sat beside him. She was exhausted by the sustained speech and by the emotions of the day. But laying her head on his shoulder, she knew that it didn't matter. As long as there were the two of them, somehow, somewhere together, it didn't matter.

Suddenly there was a commotion behind her and a scattering of the seats Becky had helped her gather together in the brewery.

A curse followed by Jessica crying out, "About time!"

Tiffany jolted up, clipping Devin's nose with the top of her head. She ignored him as he cried out and rushed to help. Jessica's water had broken and the first of her friends was finally having a baby.

CHAPTER 10

*D*evin stood on the yurt's deck and surveyed "their" domain. So much had changed from April to August.

For one, his wedding reception would be held in just a few hours at the two grand Victorian houses of Eagle Cove. They would be coming full circle, celebrating the first weekend of the Second Annual Puffin Days. Jessica's August festival had come around on the calendar once more. And before it truly began, there would a grand town party the likes of which Lillian and later Pearl Lamont had been known for before the Depression had struck. When it did, most of Pearl's fortune had gone into sustaining the town.

Everyone had agreed it was totally appropriate as to make the reception so big because it was also the launch party for the book, *The Life and Loves of Lillian Lamont: an Oregon Pioneer's Journal (unabridged).* The last point had included some hot debate, but Tiffany had been adamant that it was either her whole story or none of the story.

The next debate had been about the addendum co-written by Maggie and Jessica. Tiffany had won most of that one, too. Her own role in the entire history from Lillian's death to the present had been reduced to one small box on the "Genealogy of Lillian Lamont" page —with her name next to Devin's own (and today's ceremony would make that true). Jessica and Natalya were direct descendants of Pearl and, because Becky had married the other Slater brother, they were able to include her as well.

The farm was mentioned nowhere.

The book had been published on the town's behalf and the pre-orders were already several times bigger than the number of people who had ever lived in Eagle Cove—since its founding. Devin liked to think that was his doing, by suggesting that they include Lillian's first-time sexual encounter with Ernest as a teaser in the marketing.

For the big party, the Lamont B&B (which had descended through the direct line from Pearl) would be open. And the Judge had also opened his own neighboring house (that had been Lillian's before First Mate Albert Slater had purchased it after delivering the news of her death).

But the wedding itself was to be a small affair.

Devin had wanted it to be smaller by two people, just the original group that had sat in the brewery that night after the fly-in, but his fiancée had insisted. When he'd extended the final two invitations, he had told his parents that they were not allowed to sleep with anyone except each other for as long as they were both in Eagle Cove. They had eyed each other warily, but reserved only one room and with only one bed, so he had some hope.

The location was the second big change.

They were getting married on Tiffany's farm. It had started small, with a dinner invitation to Maggie and Hector. And once that had happened, Jessica, Natalya, and Becky had initiated an intense round of lobbying for a knitting session to be held at the yurt. And one fine June day, after three days spent in a mad flurry of preparation by the owner, her friends had come and had a wonderful time.

Now, the front deck of the yurt had been converted to an altar with the addition of a few rows of chairs. Both Judge Slaters were officiating, the retired judge as well as his son, Becky's husband Harry, who now served in his father's former seat. It was a dual wedding, but Tiffany and the Dragon had decided to make it a simultaneous cere-mony and he and Hector were allowed no say in the matter.

Natasha, Becky, and Jessica—carrying her newborn Pearl, who looked just like her mother—had decided to stand for the women.

At something of a mutual loss, Hector and Devin had finally chosen Gina and Peggy to stand in the best-person roles to ensure that neither of them screwed up. In a last moment of inspiration, Devin had bribed Tall Guy to stand in as a third for the low price of just three dog biscuits.

Gina and Peggy had maintained the new Eagle Cove tradition and dressed in black for the ceremony. Gina looked as exotic and vivacious as ever, but Peggy was a complete surprise. She might still walk like she was out to conquer the Earth singlehandedly, but freed of her battered jeans and flannel work shirt, she was causing her husband the Judge some severe attention deficit problems.

"You did a damn fine job on that lightkeeper's cottage," Hector told him as they waited for the women to get ready and the ceremony to begin. He could hear the whole lot of them giggling together through the thin yurt walls, though Tiffany's laugh was so distinct that he could pick it out every time.

"Thanks. I took most of the look from your boat."

"It's a wonderful showpiece, Devin," Gina hugged him then brushed at the lapels of his tuxedo to make sure everything was still in order. "I don't know if I can ever thank you enough."

"I think," he nodded toward the latest burst of giggles, "I'm the one who owes you."

Gina kissed him soundly and Devin supposed that meant they were even.

Trying to avoid blushing, he turned to Hector. "I guess you'll be dropping a permanent anchor in Eagle Cove now."

"Thought I might," Hector nodded, "but my Maggie has other ideas. Said something about retiring and sailing up the Inside Passage, for a start."

"The Dragon is retiring?" He, Gina, Peggy, and both of the judges practically shouted in unison. Tall Guy kept his thoughts to himself.

"Seems she has an idea about training up a new teacher this winter to take over."

"Who?" Again the chorus.

"Well, don't want to spill the beans, but it's seven letters, fifth one is an A..." he stretched out the clue. "And you're about to marry her."

"Huh," was all Devin could manage. Tiffany would be spectacularly good with kids, all kinds. "That's actually a great idea."

Hector nodded, then raised a finger to his lips, "Don't tell. She hasn't approached Tiffany yet."

"Dream on, Hector."

"Okay, don't tell that you heard it from me."

"And who besides you has *your* wife-to-be told this idea to?"

"Aw crap! Caught." His easy shrug earned him sympathetic laughs from around the circle.

There was a sudden squeal of delight from inside the yurt. It sounded terribly un-Tiffany-like, yet he'd never mistake her voice. Perhaps the invitation had just been delivered. The noise level through the walls tripled as it seemed everyone inside was talking at once.

"You know," Peggy appeared to be watching the sky as she spoke. "Speaking of retiring, I'm getting busier than I like with flying and so on. Not getting much time to work on that new airframe I'm restoring."

Devin had learned that nothing would change the path of one of Peggy's thoughts, so he just stayed to the side and waited for when she was good and ready to send the train into the station.

"I was gonna start looking for someone to buy Eagle Cove Contracting...if you happen to know anyone who might be interested. Seasonal work sometimes, but it keeps a soul out of trouble."

Devin rocked back on his heels. That had been one problem he and Tiffany hadn't fully resolved. Her farm wasn't big enough to need two hands very often; actually, with two of them, it rarely took even an hour a day. And though she'd offered, there wasn't a chance in hell he was going to let her give it up and follow him back to Chicago.

He *had* let go of D.R. Builders, but that was always the plan. Originally his father had promised to pay Devin ten million as a "nest egg" when he came aboard at CMC. But if he wasn't joining the family business…he'd haggled his dad up to fifteen, still a bargain. His dad, always shrewd, had taken the deal.

"How much you looking to get for ECC? Just in case I hear of anyone who might be interested?" He asked Peggy, joining her in watching the sky.

A pair of eagles were soaring far above. Not too near each other, but still together. He'd have to remember to tell Tiffany that it looked like Jake had a girlfriend.

"Well," Peggy now knew the kind of money Devin had and he hoped that she didn't try to gouge him. He wouldn't like it if his or Tiffany's money changed how Eagle Cove treated them.

"We'd have to make a deal," Peggy drawled out and he hoped she was teasing him. Then she looked straight at him and he stopped watching Jake. "First off, you'd have to keep helping me with the hay and the blueberries. The fields and all of the equipment belongs to Becky, but she leases the fields to me because she doesn't care about the hay and lets me borrow the equipment in the deal as long as I keep it all running. I own the grader, but that's long since paid for. Keep my runway level and I'll throw the grader in."

"Seems fair," Devin nodded, trying not to smile. It wasn't the deal you made with an out-of-town sharpie; it was the kind of deal you made with a friend.

"Got all the money I need between the Judge and me, but I could use a hand now and then restoring the new airplane." Which was most of eighty years old.

"Well," Devin loved living in this town, "now that might cost *you*."

Peggy was grinning back at him. This time *she* waited. He was getting the hang of the slower conversations on the Oregon Coast.

"Flying lessons."

"Deal." Peggy held out her hand and they shook on it.

Gina was chatting with Hector and the two judges. Tall Guy was lying down on the job.

And then gentle music came out of a small boom box.

The crowd quieted.

It was the traditional Bridal Chorus, but played by a solo harp. He'd recognize Tiffany's touch on the strings anywhere.

"Don't screw it up now," Gina whispered to both him and Hector as she positioned them to either side of the altar.

Peggy offered Devin an encouraging slap on the back that was almost hard enough to drive nails—without a hammer.

Jessica, Becky (just starting to bulge at the waist), and Natalya (who hadn't started trying yet, but was "damn well about to") walked out the door and up the short aisle. They were uniformly dressed in little black dresses, like a study in dangerous beauty. Each smiled at him in their own way as they approached. Jessica with the warm hope of a new mother, Becky with a cheery grin, and Natalya still in protective mama bear mode. Once to the front, they sat in the very front row of chairs because Tiffany's deck, *their* deck, wasn't big enough for a large bridal party to be standing.

Then all other thoughts went away.

Tiffany and Maggie Winslow stepped out of the door with Vivian Lamont between them to escort them both down the aisle. Tiffany's mother had also adopted the sexy black dress, but the two brides were dazzling in white. There wasn't a thing schoolmarmish about Maggie Winslow dressed to the hilt.

Devin glanced at his fellow groom, who offered him a happy wink of "Damn but aren't we the lucky ones."

Devin winked back, "No question!"

But if Maggie looked great, Tiffany was dazzling in white satin. Her mother had whisked her away on the jet to some small boutique in Seattle. She'd come back with a wedding dress in an opaque hanging bag labeled "Perrin's Glorious Garb" and a very pleased smile.

It was a simple sheath dress that fit her so perfectly Devin felt as if he was in a dream just looking at her. No longer needing to hide, Tiffany's hair was back in a thick French braid, and that shy smile shown radiant on her lovely face. This was the woman he would happily swear to keep for life. Dragon Winslow—who was looking quite radiant herself—had said it perfectly: Lillian Tiffany Lamont was the true keepsake of Eagle Cove. She would be *his* most precious keepsake forever.

Tall Guy scrambled to his feet and trotted down the aisle to escort his mistress to the altar.

Devin would have to remember to pay him an extra dog biscuit later.

LOST LOVE FOUND IN EAGLE COVE

M.L. BUCHMAN
Lost Love Found
in Eagle Cove
a small town Oregon romance story

CHAPTER 1

*C*ynthia didn't make it down to Eagle Cove's beach very often anymore. It might have even been years. But it spread out before her from her deck perched on the high bluff overlooking the Oregon Coast so she didn't miss much that happened below. She could watch the long waves of the Pacific roll in from far away, stutter on the offshore reef and then break relentlessly on the beach. The drumroll of the waves onto the sand was the backdrop to her life that she missed when traveling even a mile inshore.

The cliff face gave her a true, on-the-edge vista, but behind her the house and the deck would outlast her. Unless of course the big Cascadia quake struck and the whole bluff fell into the ocean, in which case she and the old house would go together. At ninety-four, such possibilities didn't worry her. Though she hoped her granddaughter wouldn't be home if it did happen.

At the moment, Skylar was tucked away in her bedroom nose to the grindstone, or at least to her computer. She was either trying to get a jump on college with her summer courses, or doing that social media thing with all of the boys who were ever hopeful about pretty redheaded girls. Cynthia made use of the opportunity to take her cane instead of the walker that Skylar always insisted on. She hated that damn thing. No matter how her great-granddaughter saw her, she wasn't old…only her body was.

She even had the wherewithal to take the fleece blanket off the back of the couch on the way to the deck. She'd have preferred to take the cable-knit cream-colored afghan that she'd made years ago out of thick Scottish wool. But to move that she'd have needed both Skylar's and the walker's assistance. The light fleece was all she could manage herself anymore.

The house was a blur of memories, though few of their objects remained. Hugh was gone, and he had been most of the memories, as well as their daughter Teresa. Knowing her time was getting short, Cynthia had taken care to give away or sell the things her great-granddaughter wouldn't want. At first it had been hard to let go of each possession due to the memories wrapped around it.

The agate she and Teresa had found on their last walk together down the beach before her daughter, then just Skylar's age, had left for college. And the ever so similar one from the last walk her daughter had managed before the cancer took her.

The model ship that Hugh had spent an entire winter building, and had stood on the bookcase for decades—with broken masts after he'd accidentally dropped a book on it that next summer. Weren't humans curious things. He'd been gone over twenty years, and throwing out that sinking ship had been one of the hardest things Cynthia had done.

It had taken her months, going through these mementos one by one. Each time, after Cynthia had a fresh area cleaned out, she would set a few select items on the well-used maple dining table for Skylar to decide what she wanted. The girl had the good common sense to dispose of most of those as well.

It didn't matter really. This house wasn't about what was inside of it.

It was about the wall of windows that faced the wild Pacific. From here she had watched the soaring seagulls and the mating flights of eagles and ospreys. Ducks often paddled about in the small pond that Hugh had installed off to one side for just that purpose.

Bird feeders attracted all sorts. The upside-down nuthatches contended with the ever so suave goldfinches with their upright posture and gold-and-black jackets. Feisty Rufous hummingbirds faced off the Stellar jays. The flickers were large enough to ignore everyone else while they clung and pecked at the blocks of suet. It was a whole world.

Unlike her younger days, it often took her half an hour or more to tend all of the feeders. Whether it was familiarity or impatience, the birds often fed from one feeder while she tended the next. Though the chickadees, which had always been her favorites, were the only ones brave enough to regularly feed from her hand if she cupped some seed in her palm.

The weather was always fresh here. The air swept ashore as if it had been invented in the mid-Pacific rather than sweeping in from Japan or Hawaii. It arrived in gentle zephyrs like today, or great wintry blasts. During the 1962 Columbus Day Storm, she, Hugh, and dear teenaged Teresa had retreated to the bedroom, peeking out occasionally from the front windows as they bowed under the pressure of the hundred-and-fifty mile-an-hour blasts off the ocean. They had cooked on the woodstove and read by oil lamps for weeks afterward until the electricity was restored, but the house had stood strong atop the cliff.

Every day was different and she loved them all. She'd miss that even more than she missed Hugh when she was gone. Of course she'd had twenty years to grow accustomed to Hugh's loss.

Today she especially wanted to sit out on the deck to watch the beach. Eagle Cove had few events that had survived the decades along with her. The annual kite festival was one of them.

A small breeze almost took the fleece throw out of her hands as she was settling at the small table close against the railing. She would take that as a good sign. Some years the wind didn't come, though that was rare here on the coast. Other years the rain came, and those were hard and sad. Everyone would arrive, but no one could fly.

This year brought warm sun and a growing breeze. Already dozens of kites were in the air and she could see more on the sand, preparing to launch. The excited shouts of children drifted up the cliff. Simple moments of joy.

Cynthia had first fallen in love with the kites of Eagle Cove when she was eighteen and thoughtlessly, deliciously young. Skylar at ten had been more mature than she'd been after finishing high school. The world of today was so different from the world of 1939.

Cynthia had first visited Oregon on a dare.

"We're eighteen," Bea had said pointing at the advertisement in the *San Francisco Chronicle.* "We're single and we may never see each other again."

"That's because you are going to Vassar College. Do you even understand how far away New York is from everything?"

"Farther than Oregon."

Cynthia looked at the advertisement again. It was a small inset on the second to last page of the Daily Statistics section.

Redhead Roundup:
in Eagle Cove, Oregon
Aug. 5-6, 1939
Beauty Contest
Most Freckles Prizes
Cutest Baby and more!
Skate by the Sea
at Hummingbird Roller Rink

It featured a drawing of a woman with long hair and a tight bathing suit diving into the sea. The entire advertisement had been printed in red.

"They put it on the same page as the listings about dead people."

"And newborns," Bea had protested. Her best friend would be gone ten days later. She was bound to meet someone back East. New York City was just a short train ride away from Vassar and Bea made it sound so exciting. Who knew if she ever would return. Cynthia was staying in San Francisco for college. It might truly be their last chance to have an adventure together.

So, Cynthia had climbed aboard a Trailways bus.

"See, it's a sign!" Bea had crowed with delight as she pointed at the red-and-yellow paint design. "Redheads. Red bus. Perfect!" Bea's favorite adjective about everything.

At first Cynthia hadn't noticed. But the farther north they rode on the winding cliff-side Highway 101, the more and more of the passengers had red hair. They had started with a half dozen of them in San Francisco, but two more had boarded in Bodega Bay, another three in Fort Bragg, three in Leggett.

By the time they crossed out of California, the bus was crowded with men and women all traveling to the Oregon Coast. There were women with hair so dark that red was only a bare hint. Others were carrot-orange, so bright that "red" didn't really apply. There was one boy who was certain that he had the Most Freckles contest already won; Cynthia didn't doubt him for a moment, he was more freckle than boy.

She became more and more self-conscious as they went. Her long red hair and fair complexion had earned her attention at the school dances; her proverbial dance card was always full until she had to beg off to preserve her feet from being worn to tatters. But aboard this one bus there was every variety of redhead imaginable. Big men who were Swedish in build, slender women with green eyes and Irish accents, and Bea with her stylishly curly mop who was comfortable in the center of every group.

Dizzy and sore from so many hours on the hard seats of the noisy bus, for they had ridden straight through, she let Bea lead her to a tiny cottage where five of them shared two twin beds and a couch. The couch was too short, but she had it all to herself and that was a relief.

CHAPTER 3

Over the years, Cynthia had loved watching the evolution of the kites that flew above Eagle Cove. What they could now make with nylon fabric and plastic parts was magical. For years she had needed binoculars to make out the hand-painted art on the child-tall paper-diamond kites.

Now, even with her failing eyesight, there was no need. The small triangular wing kites were quick, darting splashes of color and little more. Their wings snapped like angry bees in the growing wind. But the new kites were so large and rather than paint, the fabric itself was the kite-builders' medium.

A brilliant orange octopus was the first big kite aloft. Two stories high with cartoon eyes and eight long legs, it soon flew up until it was staring almost directly at her. She waved at the kite and fancied that the sea creature now floating in the blue sky waved its legs back at her.

A great spinner flew aloft next. It looked like a child's pinwheel built ten feet across with a dozen pointed tips all whirling about.

She could see the next giant kites being rolled out on the beach, but she didn't lean out to peek. Cynthia wanted to be surprised by each one as it lifted.

"Gran! You should have called me!" Skylar hurried out onto the deck. She was a surprise every single time Cynthia saw her. It was like looking in the mirror and seeing her younger self, but dressed in shorts and a tight-fitting tank top with no bra underneath that she'd never have considered wearing herself. Her great-granddaughter was tall, slim, and her shock of red hair tumbled over her shoulders just as Cynthia's had at that age.

Skylar hustled back inside and in moments the cozy afghan was wrapped around her despite the warm day. Her walker now stood close to hand and a cup of herbal tea rested on the table.

"Oh wow!" Skylar's attention finally swung out over the rail.

"Oh my," Cynthia couldn't help but agreeing. "I've always loved the whales."

A gray whale family of two adults and one youngster rose up from the sand. The kites were life-sized and while they'd been coming to Eagle Cove for a decade, they didn't often fly. The wind had to be strong enough to lift them, but not so powerful that they might damage the fifty-foot long works of art. And they were never brought out in the rain, of course. They slowly swam their way into the sky with long ripples down their flanks and lazy flapping of their big tails. The more adventurous half-sized youngster flew almost as high as the octopus that kept a cautious eye on the trio.

Soon there were frogs bigger than the ridiculous Lincoln Continental that Hugh had purchased in 1958. After all, how much car did a family of three need. "But it's beautiful!" Hugh had been enamored. Giant squids rose into the air and creepy spiders with legs a story tall were offset by a car-sized puppy dog and a slender dragon as long as the biggest whale but instead ducked and weaved sinuously about the sky.

"It's magnificent," Skylar whispered out on a soft breath as she sat to enjoy the view. She dropped the fleece throw over her own legs and settled in to watch the show.

CHAPTER 4

Cynthia remembered the Redhead Roundup more like photographic flashes than a continuous memory. It wasn't that her mind was going or the seventy-six years that had intervened; it was the nature of the weekend itself.

The big Saturday-morning, twenty-five cent pancake breakfast in the sparkling new Puffin Diner had to be eaten so quickly because the redheaded line at the tiny seaside café was out the door.

Splashing about in the cold water where the high tide had overridden the mud flats for the "clam-digging" contest. Prizes had been hidden beneath the sand in clam shells, but by the time the tide was down low enough on Sunday, no one could quite remember where the prizes had been buried. Most of the clams that were dug had been real ones which were cooked on the beach that night.

She'd been swept up by "Erik the Red" and the Coos Bay Pirates, much to Bea's frustration as she was left standing on the sand. The pirates' jokes at first seemed quite rude until she found the rhythm of their humor and decided that they were just being campy. They were pirates amidst a field of redheads after all; though she did wish that they pinched her behind a little less often. When she declined to kiss any of the "surly louts," they laughed but finally "set her free to wander the world in lonely solitude to pine after her time on the high seas." Cynthia noted that the next redheads they scooped into their celebrations were not so disinclined to accept the pirates' attentions.

She'd completely lost track of Bea, but did watch the boy from their bus indeed claim honors among the most freckled.

Bea found her again at the crowning festivities for the Queen of the Redhead Roundup. Queen Norlene Haworth's smile was amazing as the dainty sixteen-year-old knelt in her white-satin gown clutching red roses while being crowned by the Secretary to the Governor himself.

"I want to be her," Bea whispered in her ear with a sad sigh.

"There's still the beauty contest tomorrow," Cynthia reminded her.

"You *have* to enter, Cyn. You're sure to win."

After her adventures with the pirates, Cynthia would enjoy less attention rather than more. At the night's big bonfire on the beach that was a problem as well. Ultimately she was the first to retreat back to their room. It was some hours later before the rest of her roommates returned. One of them, a girl named Julie Ann from some place called Wenatchee and who had very willingly joined the pirates' celebrations, never came back at all.

Cynthia was the first out of the room and on the beach the next morning.

CHAPTER 5

"*L*ook at that one, Gran!"

A scantily-clad mermaid fluttered into shape below. Her generous figure dressed in under-sized seashells and the green scales that sheathed her from the hips down left little to the imagination. But her hair was long and flowed as red as Sklyar's did and her own had so long ago.

That was what had captured Jerome's attention.

CHAPTER 6

The sun had only just climbed above the bluff to strike the beach when Cynthia had ventured out into Day Two of the Redhead Roundup. It was still cool, so she'd worn a light shirt and slacks over her two-piece bathing suit for her walk. She hadn't particularly noticed the boy and his kite until she'd heard a soft, "Wow!" after she passed him by.

A glance back revealed that his attention was riveted upon her.

She arched her eyebrows at him, but instead of being cowed, he had smiled.

"Sorry, but your hair is gorgeous."

Cynthia had always tried not to be vain about her hair though she was rather proud of it. The boy's exclamation made her feel better than all of the pirates' gropings.

"And now," she asked, "that you see the face that goes with it?" She didn't know what prompted her to speak so.

"Even better," and again that wonderful smile. He was her age or near enough. He wasn't a big, strapping redhead like Erik the Pirate King. Nor was he some hollow-chested teen. He looked, she decided, nice. His mop of hair was a dark red and a touch unruly. Like it wanted a girl's fingers to comb through it.

705

And then she noticed his kite.

Dozens of kites had been flying over the Roundup yesterday. Simple box kites and diamonds had dominated. There had been a few more elaborate multi-level kites, including a terribly intricate one that looked like the original Wright Brothers craft.

But this one was an unusual design she hadn't seen yesterday. It was as if the box kite and the multi-tiered one had been blended together.

"That's a pretty kite." He'd chosen green paper and painted the balsawood supports brown so that it would look a little like a flying forest. "Does it fly well?"

"We'll find out if you help me launch it." He showed her how to hold it for launching. It felt both strong and fragile. The wind tugged, as if the kite was eager to fly.

Jerome walked hurriedly backwards, spooling out line as he went. He was so intent that when he caught a heel and fell to the sand, he scrambled back up showing no sign of injured dignity.

"Okay!" He shouted and pulled lightly at the now taut line. With barely a rustle it soared aloft.

It was hard to see it straight over her head, so she walked toward Jerome and she wasn't thinking about the kite. He was watching his kite avidly and he didn't look like a dip or a jerk. He simply looked very intent.

"Are you in college?"

"Uh-huh," he kept his eyes upward, so focused that he wasn't looking at her at all and now it was her dignity that felt a little offended. "Just finished my second year at University of Washington. I'm in the brand new aeronautical engineering department."

"That's like designing airplanes?"

He looked down at her in some surprise, "You know what that is?"

"Red hair means smart, not stupid." Cynthia replied, and almost walked away.

"Actually, red hair only means your parents or grandparents had red hair." Then he grimaced, "Sorry. I'm told that I'm a bit of a square about science."

Cynthia wasn't sure about the slang, but maybe she was a bit of a square too. Or else she'd still be in the pirates' clutches. She'd seen them romping up and down the beach followed by clouds of redheads. She would much rather be where she was.

"Smart is certainly nice though. Want to fly her?" He nodded toward the sky.

Before she could protest, he placed the ball of string in her hand. His hand overlapped hers until he was sure of her grip on it. A warm, strong hand that she missed as soon as it was gone.

The kite tugged strongly so she used both hands. It seemed that it was pulling at more than her hands, as if it was tugging at something in her heart.

"I never held something that wanted to fly so badly."

He reached out and she was afraid that he was going to take it back. Instead, he rested his hand over hers again, then pulled it in until he was almost touching her hip. The kite soared higher overhead, pulling harder as it climbed. Then he eased off abruptly and the kite fell and dipped. She almost cried out, before it resettled at the lower altitude and stabilized once more.

"Did you design it?"

"Sure did. I'm going to work for Mr. Boeing's when I graduate; that's what us locals call Boeing Aircraft," he clearly liked that inside bit of belonging. "They took me on as a summer intern this year. He is building the most amazing aircraft of anybody in the world. Why, someday nobody will take a train or a bus anywhere—you'll step on an aircraft and *whoosh!* You'll be there before you know it."

She and Jerome spent much of the day down on the beach flying his kite. He talked about college. She felt a little ashamed about going to the new City College of San Francisco. A two-year program to become a teacher didn't sound very important compared with designing airplanes. But he praised her saying that most girls he knew went to college only trying to find a husband.

When he went and bought them burgers and a Coca-Cola at the diner, he came back with a floppy hat almost the size of a Mexican sombrero.

"You're burning in this sun."

She'd noticed, but hadn't wanted to leave. It was nice that he'd noticed. Though she wasn't sure about wearing the hat. "You are burning as well, Jerome."

He pulled at the hat and she saw that there were two of them nested together. They looked ridiculous, but as they were both wearing them she didn't care much.

Jerome landed the kite while they ate. Afterward he fetched a paint set from a small bag he'd brought with him. He started painting on the kite's upper wing.

When she started to rise to see what he was doing, he shook his head.

"No. Stay right there."

That's when she realized that he was painting her portrait on the wing. Cynthia was dazzled by more than the sun.

She barely heard the call for the bathing beauty contest farther up the beach.

"Hey! You should go. You're a contender, Cyn." She liked his nickname for her, though she'd never liked it before.

"Do you know what the grand prize is?"

He shook his head.

"A trip to the Golden Gate International Exposition. My friends and I are going to it next week anyway. I'm fine staying right here." And she was. Even more as Jerome inspected her over the wing of his kite again and again while he worked.

"Well, maybe this will change your mind." He lifted the kite and almost lost it to the wind sliding along the sand. She grabbed the ball of string to make sure it didn't get away from them.

He tried again more carefully. Then she could see what he'd painted. It was her, but not in floppy sunhat and a loose shirt over her bathing suit.

No, it was her as...

CHAPTER 7

"Gran? Am I crazy or does that mermaid look like me?"

Cynthia shaded her eyes to look at the mermaid kite now climbing into the sky above Eagle Cove. It did look like Skylar. Actually it looked—

She had to hold a hand over her mouth to not scream, but some of it escaped anyway.

In a moment, Skylar was kneeling beside her chair. "Are you okay, Gran? Should I call the doctor? But how am I going to move you? Oh god, I should have gotten that wheelchair. I'm such an idiot—"

Cynthia moved her hand from covering her own mouth to covering her great-granddaughter's.

She managed only a hoarse whisper. "The kite doesn't look like you, sweetheart." She looked at it again in wonder, "It looks like me."

"But—" Skylar mumbled through Cynthia's hand.

"Trust me."

Skylar pulled her hand away, but held onto it tightly between her own.

"But how?"

Cynthia looked up at the mermaid now flying and dancing near the baby whale. She had no idea. But they were going to find out.

CHAPTER 8

The trip down to the beach was an arduous one, but with Skylar's good care, Cynthia managed. There was no parking near the ramp to the beach, but Skylar got her seated out of the sun on the porch of The Puffin Diner then went to park the car.

She'd eaten a breakfast here seventy-six years ago. Now, Judge Slater, who ran the diner in his retirement, was kind enough to come out and offer her some ice tea while she waited. When he asked what had brought her to the beach, she didn't dare speak. There was such hope in the moment that she didn't trust herself. She could only pat his hand in thanks and watch the mermaid now flying high above The Flicker movie house.

Skylar returned with the walker.

In order to use it, she had to give Skylar the thin leather portfolio she'd kept in her bedside table all these years. It was one of the very last personal possessions she had.

"Don't open that, young lady."

"Whatever you say, Gran. Are you sure you're up to this?"

Cynthia looked at the ramp down onto the beach that ran alongside Grouse Hardware and didn't know, but she had to be.

Skylar was patience itself, cheering her along, and helping to move the walker forward through the softer sand. Every time Skylar asked if this was really necessary, Cynthia could only nod, conserving her breath for more effort than she'd expended in five years.

It took a long time and several rest breaks to reach where the kite lines from the mermaid descended into the crowd, but they made it.

The moment the crowd opened so that she could see who was flying the mermaid kite, she knew she'd been right.

A man in his forties and his son were tending the lines together. In the man's face, she could see hints of his grandfather. But in the boy's she could see Jerome reborn. Just like his long ago relative, he had little attention for them—all he cared about was the kite.

The man looked at Skylar for a long moment, the shock of recognition was as clear on his face as the confusion.

Unable to speak, Cynthia reached out a hand and tapped the portfolio that Skylar had carried. When Skylar inspected her cautiously, she tapped it again.

With a shrug, Skylar untied the string.

CHAPTER 9

*J*erome held the kite up for her to see.

Cynthia's face and torso had been painted across the wing. Instead of a bathing suit top, her image wore the scantiest of clam shells. Instead of the bottoms, she wore a long sinuous tail of shining green scales. But most off all, her long red hair billowed across the kite's wing.

Looking up from the beautiful image, made with an engineer's eye, she stepped up to him until they were separated by only the thin paper and balsa of the wing. She pulled his face down to hers and kissed him.

CHAPTER 10

"It was a kiss that I'll never forget. A girl never forgets her first *real* kiss, no matter how old she is," Cynthia said the last to Skylar who only blushed in return. Young girls were kissed and plenty more these days, but by that blush she'd guess that Skylar still hadn't found the right man to make a memory which lasts a lifetime.

Thomas had settled her into a folding lawn chair and sat in another. He held the portfolio as he and his son Simon looked down at the painting within.

"Jerome finished the kite on the beach knowing he had no way to take it home once he had glued it together. It only flew that one day. As the sun set in the waves, right there," Cynthia pointed out to sea, "he cut out the painting and gave it to me."

Simon glanced up at the sky where the mermaid—where *she* still flew. "Dad kept a few things for me when Great-Grandpop died. The design for that kite was one of them. It was dated August 6th, 1939. It also had your first name on it and 'Eagle Cove.' Dad and I decided to try to build it and fly it in his honor. I was kinda named for the kite. Cynthia—Simon," even his shrug was so much like Jerome's that it hurt to watch. "Funny. Guess I was sorta named for you, lady. Now that's kinda cool. Named for Great-Grandpop's old girlfriend. I'm good with that."

And they all shared a laugh, though it took almost all Cynthia had left to join in.

She didn't know how to ask, but being an old lady, she knew she didn't have time to avoid the question either.

"He never came back," she told Thomas after his son had returned his attention to the kite. He was showing Skylar tips on how to manage the big kite and how they'd built it.

Cynthia had come back to the Redhead Roundup from San Francisco in 1940 and 1941, then they had ended with the war. After the war was won she moved to Eagle Cove and taught children for forty years. And every year she had watched the sky during the kite festival hoping to see that unique box kite. Her letters came back marked "Addressee unknown." If he ever wrote, the letters never reached her. Her parents had moved mere weeks after her return from the Redhead Roundup when she moved into the city for college. So many things had been lost.

"He was co-opted into the war effort right out of college," Thomas said softly. "Long before the war. He would have been in England then, helping with their plane designs. Very secret work. I'm so sorry."

"No. No. It's okay. I had a husband and a child. It was a good life. Apparently he did as well." She patted Thomas' hand and wondered which of them she was reassuring. Her life had come full circle. For she had come alive in a man's arms, right here on this same stretch of beach, ever so long ago.

Cynthia sat in the chair and watched Simon and Skylar flying the mermaid that looked like her and her great-granddaughter.

They stood so close in the afternoon sun that the light didn't pass between them.

As close together as she and Jerome had once stood, flying a kite in the sky.

MY APOLOGIES

My small town of Eagle Cove has stolen the twice-yearly Kite Festival from Lincoln City, Oregon, which indeed has a family of life-sized great whales. Eagle Cove has also laid claim to the "Redhead Roundup" from Taft, Oregon which was held as an annual fundraiser for the town on the first weekend of August throughout most of the Great Depression.

WHERE DREAMS ARE BORN
(EXCERPT)

A WHERE DREAMS SEATTLE ROMANCE

Russell locked his studio's door behind the last of the staff, leaned his back against it, and turned off his camera.

He knew it was good. The images were there; he'd really captured them.

But something was missing.

The groove ran so clean when he slid into it. First his Manhattan high-ceilinged loft would fade into the background, then the strobe lights, reflector umbrellas, and blue and green backdrops all became texture and tone.

Image, camera, and man then became one and they were all that mattered—a single flow of light, beginning before time was counted, and ending its journey in the printed image. One ray of primordial light traveling forever to glisten off the BMW roadster still parked in one corner of the rough-planked wood floor worn smooth by generations of use. Another ray lost in the dark blackness of the finest leather bucket seats. A hundred more picking out the supermodel's perfect hand dangling a single shining and golden key—the image shot just slow enough that the key blurred as it spun, but the logo remained clear.

He couldn't quite put his finger on it...

It would be another great ad by Russell Morgan, Inc. The client would be knocked dead—the ad leaving all others standing still as it roared down the passing lane. This one might get him another Clio, or even a second Mobius.

But...

There wasn't usually a "but."

And there definitely wasn't supposed to be one.

The groove had definitely been there, but he hadn't been in it.

That was the problem. It had slid along, sweeping his staff into their own orchestrated perfection, but he'd remained untouched. That ideal, seamless flow hadn't included him at all.

"Be honest, boyo, that session sucked," he told the empty studio. Everything had come together so perfectly for yet another ad for yet another high-end glossy. *Man, the Magazine* would launch spectacularly in a few weeks, a high-profile mid-December launch, and it would include a never before seen twelve-page spread by the great Russell Morgan. The rag would probably never pay off the lavish launch party of hope, ice sculptures, and chilled magnums of champagne before disappearing like a thousand before it.

He stowed the last camera he'd been using with the others piled by his computer. At the breaker box he shut off the umbrellas, spots, scoops, and washes. The studio shifted from a stark landscape in hard-edged relief to a nest of curious shadows and rounded forms. The tang of hot metal and deodorant were the only lasting result of the day's efforts.

"Morose tonight, aren't we?" he asked his reflection in the darkened window, stories above the streetlights of West 10th. His reflection was wise enough to not answer back. There was never a "down" after a shoot; there was always an "up."

Not tonight.

He'd kept everyone late—even though it was Thanksgiving eve—hoping for that smooth slide of image-camera-man. It was only when he saw the power of the images he captured that he knew he wasn't a part of the chain anymore and decided he'd paid enough triple-time expenses.

The next to last two-page spread was the killer—shot with the door open against a background as black as the sports car's finish. The model's single perfect leg wrapped in thigh-high red-leather boots was all that was visible in the driver's seat. The sensual juxtaposition of woman and sleek machine served as an irresistible focus. It was an ad designed to wrap every person with even a hint of a Y-chromosome around its little finger. And those with only X-chromosomes would simply want to be her. He'd shot a perfect combo of sexuality for the guys and power for the women.

Even the final one-page image, a close-up of driver's seat from exactly the same angle, revealing not the model but instead a single rose of precisely the same hue as the leather boot, hadn't moved him despite its perfection.

Without him noticing, Russell had become no more than the observer, merely a technician behind the camera. Now that he faced it, months, maybe even a year had passed since he'd been yanked all the way into the light-image-camera-man slipstream. Tonight was a wakeup call and he didn't like it one bit. Wakeup calls were supposed to happen to others, not him. But tonight he could no longer ignore it, he hadn't even trailed in the churned-up wake.

"You're just a creative cog in the advertising machine." Ouch! That one stung, but it didn't turn aside the relentless steamroller of his thoughts speeding down some empty, godforsaken autobahn.

His career was roaring ahead, his business' growth running fast and smooth, but, now that he considered it, he really couldn't bring himself to care.

His life looked perfect, but—"Don't think it!"—his autobahn mind finished despite the command, *it wasn't.*

Russell left his silent reflection to its own thoughts and went through the back door that led to his apartment—closing it tightly on the perfect BMW, the perfect rose, and somewhere, lost among a hundred other props from dozens of other shoots, the long pair of perfect red-leather Chanel boots that had been wrapped around the most expensive legs in Manhattan. He didn't care if he never walked back through that door again. He'd been doing his art by rote; how pathetic was that?

And just to rub salt in the wound, he shot *commercial* art.

He'd never had the patience to do art for art's sake. Delayed gratification was his idea of no fun at all. He left the apartment dark with only the city's soft glow through the blind-covered windows revealing the vaguest outlines of the framed art on the wall. Even that almost overwhelmed him tonight.

He didn't want to see the huge prints by the *art* artists: autographed Goldsworthy, Liebowitz, and Joseph Francis' photomosaics for the moderns. A hundred and fifty rare, even one-of-a-kind prints adorned his walls—all the way back through Bourke-White to Russell's prize, an original Daguerre. The Museum of Modern Art kept begging to borrow his collection for a show...and at the moment he was half tempted to dump the whole lot in their Dumpster if they didn't want it.

Crossing the one-room loft apartment—as spacious as the studio —he bypassed the circle of avant-garde chairs that were almost as uncomfortable as they looked and avoided the lush black-leather wrap-around sectional sofa of such ludicrous scale that it could be a playpen for two or host a party for twenty. He cracked the fridge in the stainless-steel-and-black corner kitchen searching for something other than his usual beer.

A bottle of Krug.

Maybe he was just being grouchy after a long day's work.

Juice.

No. He'd run his enthusiasm into the ground but good.

Milk even.

Would he miss the camera if he never picked it up again?

No reaction.

Nothing.

Not even a twinge.

That was an emptiness he did not want to face. Especially not alone, in his apartment, in the middle of the world's most vibrant city.

Russell turned away, and just as the door swung closed, the last sliver of light—the relentless chilly blue-white of the refrigerator bulb —shone across his bed. A quick grab snagged the edge of the door and left the narrow beam illuminating a long pale form on his black bedspread.

The Chanel boots weren't in the studio after all. They were still wrapped around those three thousand dollar-an-hour legs: the only clothing on a perfect body, five foot-eleven of intensely toned female anatomy, right down to her exquisitely stair-mastered behind. Her long, white-blond hair lay as a perfect Godiva over her tanned bosom—except for the too-exact symmetry, even the closest inspection didn't reveal the work done there. She lay with one leg raised just ever so slightly to hide what was meant to be revealed later.

Melanie.

By the steady rise and fall of her flat stomach, he knew she'd fallen asleep while waiting for him to finish in the studio.

How long had they been an item? Two months? Three?

She'd made him feel alive…at least when he was actually with her. Melanie was the supermodel in his bed or on his arm at yet another SoHo gallery opening. Together they journeyed to sharp parties and trendy three-star restaurants where she dazzled and wooed yet another gathering of New York's finest with her ever so soft, so sensual, and so studied French accent. Together they were wired into the heart of the in-crowd.

But that wasn't him, was it? It didn't sound like the Russell he once knew.

Perhaps "they" were about how *he* looked on *her* arm?

Did she know tomorrow was the annual Thanksgiving ordeal at his parents? The grand holiday gathering that he'd rather die than attend? Any number of eligible woman would be floating about his parents' house out in Greenwich; anyone able to finagle an invitation would attend in hopes of snaring one of *People Magazine's* "100 Most Eligible." They all wanted to land the heir to a billion or some such; though he was wealthy enough on his own, by his own sweat, to draw anyone's attention. He ranked number twenty-four on the list this year—up from forty-seven the year before despite Tom Cruise being available yet again.

But not Melanie. He knew that it wasn't the money that drew her. Yes, she wanted him. But even more, she wanted the life that came with him—wrapped in the man-package. She wanted The Life. The one that *People Magazine* readers dreamed about between glossy pages.

His fingertips were growing cold where they held the refrigerator door cracked open.

If he woke her they'd have a great time heating up the sheets. Or a great party to go to. Or...

Did he want "Or"? What more did he want from her?

The supermodel in his bed. Companionship. An energy, a vivacity, a thirst he feared that he lacked. Yes.

But where was that smooth synchronicity hiding, like the light-image-camera-man of photography that he'd lost? Where lurked that perfect flow from one person to another? Did she feel it? Could he ever feel it?

"More?" he whispered into the darkness to test the sound.

The refrigerator door slid shut—escaping from his numbed fingers—which plunged the apartment back into darkness, taking Melanie along with it.

His breath echoed in the vast darkness. Proof that he was alive, if nothing more.

It was time to close the studio—time to be done with Russell Incorporated.

Then what?

Maybe Angelo would know what to do. He always claimed that he did. Maybe this time Russell would actually listen to his almost-brother, though he knew from the experience of being himself for the last thirty years that was unlikely.

Seattle.

No! He'd have to go to Seattle, of all ridiculous places, to find his best friend. There was a possible upside to such a trip—maybe there'd be a flight out before tomorrow's mess at his parents'. He slapped his pocket, but once again he'd set his phone down in some unknown corner of the studio and it would take forever to find. He really needed two—one chained down so that he could always find it to call the other.

Russell considered the darkness. He could guarantee that Seattle wouldn't be a big hit with Melanie.

Now if he only knew whether that was a good thing or bad.

Available at fine retailers everywhere:
WHERE DREAMS

ABOUT THE AUTHOR

M.L. Buchman started the first of, what is now over 50 novels and as many short stories, while flying from South Korea to ride his bicycle across the Australian Outback. Part of a solo around the world trip that ultimately launched his writing career.

All three of his military romantic suspense series—The Night Stalkers, Firehawks, and Delta Force—have had a title named "Top 10 Romance of the Year" by the American Library Association's *Booklist*. NPR and Barnes & Noble have named other titles "Top 5 Romance of the Year." In 2016 he was a finalist for Romance Writers of America prestigious RITA award. He also writes: contemporary romance, thrillers, and fantasy.

Past lives include: years as a project manager, rebuilding and single-handing a fifty-foot sailboat, both flying and jumping out of airplanes, and he has designed and built two houses. He is now making his living as a full-time writer on the Oregon Coast with his beloved wife and is constantly amazed at what you can do with a degree in Geophysics. You may keep up with his writing and receive a free starter e-library by subscribing to his newsletter at: www.mlbuchman.com

Join the conversation:
www.mlbuchman.com

Other works by M. L. Buchman: